The Sinbad Novels
Part B

The Collected Novels of P. C. Wren
Volume 2B

Fiction Titles by P. C. Wren

Dew and Mildew. 1912
Father Gregory. 1913
The Snake and Sword. 1914.
Driftwood Spars. 1916
The Wages of Virtue. 1916
The Young Stagers. 1917
Stepsons of France. 1917
Cupid in Africa. 1920
Beau Geste. 1924
Beau Sabreur. 1926
Beau Ideal. 1928
Good Gestes. 1929
Soldiers of Misfortune. 1929
The Mammon of Righteousness. 1930 (U.S. title: Mammon)
Mysterious Waye. 1930
Sowing Glory. 1931
Valiant Dust. 1932
Flawed Blades. 1933
Action and Passion. 1933
Port o' Missing Men. 1934
Beggars' Horses. 1934 (U.S. title: The Dark Woman)
Sinbad the Soldier. 1935
Explosion. 1935
Spanish Maine. 1935 (U.S. title: The Desert Heritage)
Bubble Reputation. 1936 (U.S. title: The Cortenay Treasure)
Fort in the Jungle. 1936
The Man of a Ghost. 1937 (U.S. title: The Spur of Pride)
Worth Wile. 1937 (U.S. title: To the Hilt)
Cardboard Castle. 1938
Rough Shooting. 1938
Paper Prison. 1939 (U.S. Title: The Man the Devil Didn't Want)
The Disappearance of General Jason. 1940
Two Feet From Heaven. 1940
The Uniform of Glory. 1941
Odd—But Even So. 1941

The Sinbad Novels Part B

by

Percival Christopher Wren

FORT IN THE JUNGLE
THE DISAPPEARANCE OF GENERAL
JASON

Edited

by

John L. Espley

Riner Publishing Company
Culpeper Virginia
2016

i

ISBN
978-0692639429

The text of *Fort in the Jungle* will be in the Public Domain as of 1 January 2032 since it was originally published in 1936

The text of *The Disappearance of General Jason* will be in the Public Domain as of 1 January 2036 since it was originally published in 1940

Contents

PREFACE

The Sinbad Novels Part A and *The Sinbad Novels Part B* by Percival Christopher Wren are the second of a multivolume series, *The Collected Novels of P. C. Wren*. The purpose of publishing this series is to make the novels written by P. C. Wren more available to the reading public. His novel, *Beau Geste*, is usually recognized by most of the book dealers I have met over the years, but his other works are not so easily remembered.

I have been collecting P. C. Wren for over fifty years, and have been working on a comprehensive bibliography for almost as long. The text of the twenty-eight novels were easily obtained from copies in my own collection. For that collection, I certainly need to thank the hundreds of used book dealers I have purchased items from, and I need to thank some by name: Steven Temple, David Mason, Walt Barrie and, especially, the late Denis McDonnell for the advice and help they have provided over the years.

Mr. John Venmore and Mr. Philip Fairweather, both descendants of the late Mr. Richard Alan Graham-Smith, Wren's stepson, and the executor of Wren's estate, have both been very helpful in providing information about Wren.

As it has been over seventy years since the death of P. C. Wren (November 21, 1941), Wren's works have passed into the public domain in the United Kingdom. In the United States fourteen of the twenty-eight novels are still under copyright. Thanks to information provided by Messrs. Venmore and Fairweather, the heirs to Wren's literary estate, Mr. Danny Adekoya Campbell and Mr. Christopher Oladipo Graham-Smith, were located and permission has been granted to reprint Wren's works.

I also need to acknowledge the help and guidance of my family members: my daughter and son-in-law, Dawn and Andrew; my son and daughter-in-law, Jared and Claudia; and my long-suffering wife, Cathy. Thank you.

In conclusion, I need to thank Percival Christopher Wren for the many years of great enjoyment that his novels have provided. I know that Wren is not a literary or critical success, but, for me, he is one of the great storytellers of the early twentieth century.

John L. Espley
Culpeper, Virginia
May 31, 2016

INTRODUCTION

Percival Christopher Wren is best known as a novelist, publishing twenty-eight novels from 1912 to 1941, the most famous being *Beau Geste* (1924). Wren also published seven short story collections; *Stepsons of France* (1917), *The Young Stagers* (1917), *Good Gestes* (1929), *Flawed Blades* (1933), *Port o' Missing Men* (1934), *Rough Shooting* (1938), and *Odd—But Even So* (1941), containing a total of 116 stories. There were also two omnibus collections, *Stories of the Foreign Legion* (1947) and *Dead Men's Boots* (1949), containing stories taken from *Stepsons of France*, *Good Gestes*, *Flawed Blades*, and *Port o' Missing Men*. All 116 short stories can be found in the five volume collection, *The Collected Short Stories of Percival Christopher Wren*.[1]

Wren was a man of mystery in that the more popular biographical statements about him seem to be more fiction than fact. A typical biography places his birth in Devon in 1885, educated at Oxford, and having a career of world traveler, hunter, journalist, tramp, British cavalry trooper, legionary in the French Foreign Legion, assistant director of education in Bombay, and a Justice of the Peace. Most of the above biography, however, has not been verified. Wren was born Percy Wren on November 1, 1875 in Deptford, a district of South London on the banks of the Thames. He did attend Oxford University, graduating in 1898 with a 3rd class honours in History leading to a Bachelor of Arts degree. He attained his "M.A." in 1901. In those days, a person acquired a "M.A." after a certain number of years (three in Wren's case) and upon payment of a fee.

After leaving Oxford, he married Alice Lucie Shovelier in December 1899 with whom he had a daughter, Estelle Lenore Wren, born in February 1901, and a son, Percival

---

[1] For further information on *The Collected Short Stories of Percival Christopher Wren* see http://rinerpublishing.wordpress.com

Rupert Christopher Wren, born in February 1904. Percy worked as a teacher at various commercial schools until 1903 when he and his family left England for India. From 1903 to approximately 1919 Wren was employed as an educator by the Indian Educational Service (I.E.S.). During that time he published a number of educational textbooks, some of which are still in use in Indian schools today. It was during this period that he started using the name Percival C. and Percival Christopher on the textbooks. From 1905 to 1915, he also served in the Volunteer Corps (Sind and Poona) in India (see the novel *Driftwood Spars*, which has a description of a Volunteer Corps), and was appointed a Captain in the Indian Army Reserve of Officers, the 101st Grenadiers of the Indian Infantry, in November 1914. He probably saw action in the East African campaign of World War I (see the novel *Cupid in Africa*, which takes place in East Africa), and resigned from the Indian Army Reserve of Officers in November 1915.[2]

Wren's first novel, *Dew and Mildew*, was published by Longmans, Green in 1912. His first novel of the French Foreign Legion, *The Wages of Virtue*, was written in 1913 and published by John Murray in 1916. One of the many questions about Wren is whether he did serve in the French Foreign Legion. Given the chronology of his documented biography it is hard to see where he had time to actually serve in the Legion. Wren himself always maintained that he had served, and his stepson, Richard Alan Graham-Smith, who died in 2006, "strongly maintained that Wren had indeed served in the French Foreign Legion and was always quick to refute those who said otherwise."[3]

The series, *The Collected Novels of P. C. Wren*, is intended to include all twenty-eight novels in seven thematic omnibus volumes. The final number of physical volumes might be as many as fourteen, depending on how large

---

[2] Most of the biographical information about Wren has been obtained through certificates, documents, and original research at the British Library, Bodleian Library, and the India Office papers. Detailed documentation and sources will be cited in the biographical essay to be included in the forthcoming publication, *An Annotated Bibliography of Percival Christopher Wren*.

[3] http://en.wikipedia.org/wiki/P._C._Wren

(number of pages) the later volumes are. The individual volumes will not be in Wren's original publication order, but will instead have a connecting theme such as characters or locale. The seven volumes are:

v. 1 - The Geste Novels
Beau Geste
Beau Sabreur
Beau Ideal
Spanish Maine
v. 2 - The Sinbad Novels
Action and Passion
Sinbad the Soldier
Fort in the Jungle
The Disappearance of General Jason
v. 3 - Foreign Legion Novels
The Wages of Virtue
Sowing Glory
The Uniform of Glory
Paper Prison
v. 4 - Other Novels
Soldiers of Misfortune
Valiant Dust
Cupid in Africa
Mysterious Waye
v. 5 - The Earlier India Novels
Dew and Mildew
Father Gregory
Snake and Sword
Driftwood Spars
v. 6 - The Later India Novels
Beggars' Horses
Explosion
Man of a Ghost
Worth Wile
v. 7 - The English Novels
Bubble Reputation
Cardboard Castle
The Mammon of Righteousness

Two Feet From Heaven

*   *   *   *   *   *   *

Volume Two of *The Collected Novels of P. C. Wren, The Sinbad Novels,* is in two physical volumes and contain the four novels that have the character of Sinclair Noel Brodie Dysart, whose nickname Sinbad derives from the initials **S.N.B.D.** In the first three novels—*Action and Passion* (1933), *Sinbad the Soldier* (1935), and *Fort in the Jungle* (1936)—Sinbad is the narrator of his life story, much like an autobiography. The fourth novel, *The Disappearance of General Jason* was published in 1940, four years and five books after *Fort in the Jungle.* In *The Disappearance of General Jason* Sinbad is a minor, but crucial, character in the story.

*   *   *   *   *   *   *

The Sinbad Novels Part B

The *Sinbad Novels Part B* contains *Fort in the Jungle,* first published in 1936, and *The Disappearance of General Jason*, first published in 1940. *Fort in the Jungle* is the third book (of three) concerning the story of Sinbad (Sinclair Noel Brodie) Dysart, and is the direct sequel to *Sinbad the Soldier. The Disappearance of General Jason* can be a considered a stand-alone novel, as Sinbad is not the major protagonist.

At the end of *Sinbad the Soldier*, our hero, had been captured by French authorities and given the choice of prison or joining the French Foreign Legion.

Fort in the Jungle continues the story of Sinbad from *Sinbad the Soldier*, but instead of being a North African desert Foreign Legion novel, *Fort in the Jungle* is set during the Indo-China colonial wars of the late 1800s with the Black Flag Army.[4] In this novel, Sinbad is sent on a covert

---

[4] http://en.wikipedia.org/wiki/Black_Flag_Army

mission to a secret fort in the jungles of Vietnam. Here he has various adventures and meets the love of his life—the wife of the European advisor to the bandit army.

Part I of the novel is a short introduction to the dangers of jungle warfare during the late 1800s. A fort manned by legionnaires is about to be overwhelmed by the enemy and, on the last night before the final battle, the legionnaires create the "Dirty Dog's Club", where each of the participants tell the others the worst, dirtiest deed they have done in their lives. This scenario is also the setting of the short stories in Part II of *Rough Shooting* (titled "The Dirty Dogs of War"), a short story collection published in 1938. In Part I of *Fort in the Jungle*, none of the stories are actually related, but the legionnaire, Nul Nullepart, is the first storyteller. His story, "A Poisonous Fellow", is the third story in the "Dirty Dogs of War" part of *Rough Shooting*.[5] We learn later that Sinbad is the only survivor of the attack.

In certain parts *Fort in the Jungle* might make anyone who is a veteran of the U.S.-Vietnam war uncomfortable since Wren's description of the jungle and the travel travails in the jungle will probably vividly remind them of their own experiences. For example, there is this description:

> For weeks and weeks we poled along through heavy rain, through light rain, and through thick mist, for a change; until I came to think that there was a kind of rain and a kind of fog peculiar to the Red River and peculiarly wet, depressing, and damping, not only to straw hats and cotton clothes, but to the spirits, yea, the very souls of their occupants.
>
> We made our slow laborious way along water, through water, on water, in water and under water, for, at times, and for very long times, the rain was so heavy that the surface of the river was but a plane

---

[5] All nine stories can be found *The Collected Short Stories of Percival Christopher Wren*, Volume Five, pages 1-82.

dividing a mass of water of normal consistency from a mass of water slightly mixed with air.

The sky, invisible, was one vast mass of leaden grey wool, a cosmic sponge that for days and days on end was in process of steady contraction.

[. . .]

And not only could I hear it as I lay awake shivering in sodden misery, but I could feel it, or rather, feel its damp exhalation penetrating to my mouldy bones and spreading its vile fever throughout my racked and suffering frame.

I would rather do, day after day, the longest of forced desert marches or jungle marches, tortured by thirst, and sore from head to foot with aching pain and unbearable fatigue, than again spend those weeks of crouching in a *sampan* on the Red River of Tonking.

I was always thankful when natural obstacles, the need for provisions, or some imminent danger from nature or from man, drove us ashore and into the jungle.

Here there was hardship enough. Leeches for example—reptiles for which I have an acute natural abhorrence—and the burrowing ticks. After marching through grass, one would emerge with an absolute dado of solid tick all round one's legs, loathsome brutes that fastened on with powerful mandibles and burrowed into one's flesh, swelling as they did so. Each of these foul pests, if not carefully extracted, would leave behind it a sore place, an angry spot, that might develop into a horrible boil. Like the leeches, they were best treated with the glowing end of a cigarette, or with a burning match, when they would fall away without leaving their heads behind them, as they did if pulled out.[6]

The major theme of *Fort in the Jungle* is similar to many of Wren's stories—Duty versus Love. In this novel, Sinbad struggles with his love for Mary, the wife of the European advisor Collins, over his covert mission to infiltrate the bandit army and return with the intelligence that the French army needs. Collins eventually abandons Mary, and Sinbad is left with the choice of returning with the information and abandoning Mary also, or trying to escape into the jungle with Mary. The results are not one which most readers of this type of romantic adventure stories would expect.

Fort in the Jungle was first published by John Murray in 1936, and contains the dedication "To the memory of my comrades of the French Foreign Legion". *Fort in the Jungle* was also published in 1936 by Stokes[7] in the United States, Longmans, Green in Canada, and by John Murray (in their Imperial Library series). The novel was reprinted by Grosset and Dunlap in 1938, and in paperback three times by Murray in 1941, 1943, and 1952. The last English language printing was in 1972 by Tom Stacey.

The second novel in *The Sinbad Novels Part B* is *The Disappearance of General Jason*. As remarked earlier, this story is not a direct sequel to *Fort in the Jungle*, with Sinbad as a supporting character that only appears half way through the novel. The novel is divided into five parts and the plot is concerned with the disappearance of a retired British army general. The first part is not in chronological order with the rest of novel, but it does set up the mystery needing to be solved: what happened to General Jason? The story line and plot elements are quasi-science fiction in that there is a (sort of) lost race that the characters are involved with, aspects of uranium mining, and an H. G.

---

[6] Herein, pages 84-85.
[7] In the United States the title was changed slightly: _The_ *Fort in the Jungle* with a subtitle of *the Extraordinary Adventures of Sinbad Dysart in Tonkin.*

Wells *Island of Dr. Moreau* element to it.

The lost race element is about former Portuguese colonists who were shipwrecked in the 1500s and settled a little known (or very hard to find) island in the Indian Ocean. Only a very few people know about the island and its inhabitants in the 1930s. The rulers of the island, descendants of the shipwrecked colonists, want no (or only very little) contact with modern civilization. The island is a noticeable source of uranium and radium, and General Jason is tricked into thinking he can obtain a concession from the people of the island. But through a comedy of errors (and direct malice from the main villain) General Jason is thought to be a German Nazi, and so, he never leaves the island. The rest of the story is how his wife and his friend try to find him.

The main science fiction element comes from the concept of "Permanent Hypnosis" which when combine with brain surgery can produce permanent changes in human beings. To write anymore about this would be to reveal too much of the plot.

The Disappearance of General Jason was published by John Murray in April 1940, a year and a half before Wren died in November 1941. The novel has the feel of an incomplete story, with elements that are treated only superficially. It is almost as if it was a first draft, and that Wren was not able to come back to it. But even so, there were two novels, *Two Feet From Heaven* and *The Uniform of Glory*, published after *The Disappearance of General Jason* and before Wren's death. Both of those novels do not have the feel of being incomplete or a first draft.

The Disappearance of General Jason contains the dedication "To Davis and Gertrude, Norah, Maureen and Bill: also Mickie and Bonnie and Barkis who will, sometimes." *The Disappearance of General Jason* was also published in 1940 by Longmans, Green in Canada. It was reprinted in 1973 by Tom Stacey. There were no US publications until the 1970s, and even then, the printings were really copies of the Tom Stacey edition with a label over the imprint.

*   *   *   *   *   *   *

The original spelling, punctuation, and grammar, except for obvious errors, have been preserved as found in the latest editions/printings of the stories during Wren's lifetime (1875-1941). The footnotes, in the novels, are also found in the original source material.

FORT IN THE JUNGLE

"I've taken my fun where I've found it,
I've rogued an' I've ranged in my time."
                                    Kipling.

TO

THE MEMORY OF MY COMRADES

OF

THE FRENCH FOREIGN LEGION

"Partout où ils ont passé,
Partout où ils sont tombé,
Ils ont semé de la gloire."
(Song of the Legion)

PART I

I

The jungle fort of Houi-Ninh, its back to the swift and mighty river Meh Song, its front and flanks to the illimitable Annamese jungle, stood like a little rock, almost submerged beneath a deep green sea.

Behind it, a theoretically pacified land of peaceful if resentful villages, set in rice-field, forest, plain and swamp; before it, the unconquerable jungle, its dank and gloomy depths the home and defence of fierce swift jungle-men, predatory, savage, and devilishly cruel.

And beyond that vast uncharted sea of densest forest and impenetrable swamp, a further *terra incognita*; and then China, inimical, enigmatic and sinister.

The little jungle fort was strong, the foundations of its walls great boulders of stone, the walls themselves dried mud and great baulks of mahogany, its vast and heavy iron-wood gate secured by huge steel bars which were lengths of railway-line.

Within the square of walls was the low oblong whitewashed *caserne* containing the *chambrée* in which the men slept, the store-room, the cook-house, the non-commissioned officers' quarters, and the office-bedroom of the Commandant.

The fort was besieged. Hordes of flat-faced, slant-eyed warriors, half brigand, pirate and dacoit, half mandarin's irregular soldier, swarmed about it in the gloom of the jungle just beyond the tiny clearing that surrounded its walls. From lofty iron-wood trees, a galling and decimating fire had been kept up for days, by the Möi, Tho, Muong and Chinese sharp-shooters armed with Sniders, Chassepot and Gras guns, as well as excellent Spencer carbines and Remington repeating rifles, reducing the garrison to half its original inadequate numbers, and inflicting upon it the loss not only of its Commandant, Lieutenant Jacot, but of its half-dozen non-commissioned officers as well.

It was now commanded by an ordinary *soldat première classe*, the *Légionnaire* Paladino, senior man present, and readily-accepted leader.

The last official communication from the outside world had been a suddenly-ended heliograph message, the concluding sentence of which had been ominous.

"Those about to die, salute . . ."

It had come from another fort set upon a hill some twenty-five *li*[8] distant.

§2

A handful of assorted soldiers gathered from the ends of the earth, of very widely varying nationality, creed and breed, of greatly differing education, birth, and social experience, stood in the dark shadow of imminent death; Death ineluctable, inevitable, inexorable; Death now as certain as—death.

These men knew that no power on earth could save them; that no power from Heaven would save them; that this was as certainly the last night of their lives as it would have been had they each been seated alone in the condemned cell, doomed by law to meet, at dawn, the hangman, *Madame la Guillotine*, or the firing-party.

They knew that to-morrow's dawn was the last that they would ever see.

The victorious and triumphant army of the *Pavillons Noirs*, the Black Flags, jungle savages, Möis, river pirates, Tonkinese dacoits and bandits, and Chinese Regulars in disguise, now bearing down upon them to join their besiegers, out-numbered them by a hundred to one. It could, and would, by sheer weight of numbers alone, overwhelm them, obliterate them. Against it, they had precisely as much chance as has a snail against a steam-roller. Should this great force of irregular but magnificent, well-armed fighting men, instead of sweeping over the little jungle fort, trouble to ring it about with fire, the score of defenders'

---

[8] Li = about 600 yards.

rifles would answer a thousand.

And for how long?

Almost with their guns alone could the Tonkinese and Chinese jungle-warriors blast, into its original dust, the mud wall of the wretched little post, already more than half-submerged by the slowly rising tide of the ever-encroaching jungle.

But this they probably would not do. They were very fierce, impetuous and primitive in their swift savagery. Almost certainly they would rush it, destroy it, stamp it flat, and let the jungle in. In a few weeks there would be no sign of where it had stood. It would be sunk full fathom five beneath an emerald sea of leaf and stalk; strangled, choked, drowned beneath the green ocean of leaves.

These men were doomed, for they were abandoned. Not abandoned callously, carelessly or neglectfully, but by necessity, the harsh cruelty of military fate and the adverse fortune of war. To have saved them would have cost ten times their number. To have saved the fort would have cost ten times what it was worth.

And loss of prestige? That would be regained a hundredfold when the General was ready, and reinforcements for his disease-decimated sun-smitten jungle-worn army should reach his headquarters from France.

The only doubt about their certain death lay in the question of the manner of it.

A furious headlong charge of strong swift swordsmen, brown, black-turbaned, Gurkha-like; rush upon rush, and an overwhelming flood which would surge across the stockade as waves break over a child's castle of sand, and then swift sudden death by bullet and blade?

Or, perchance, a long slow day of torture by thirst and heat and wounds as, beneath a hail of bullets from high surrounding trees, they died slowly, man by man, their fire growing slacker and slower until the last wounded man with his last remaining strength and failing sight, reached the last cartridge and fired the last shot of the defence?

According to their Annamese informants, "friendlies" fleeing before the advancing host—this had been the fate of the first of the two forts that the rebel horde had attacked, the only other outposts on that side of the mighty river, deep and swift. It had been enveloped, surrounded during the night, and at dawn had been subjected to so heavy a fire at so short range that by noon the little post had been silenced, the fortunate among its defenders those who had been killed during the battle. The wounded had been crucified, slowly roasted alive, or indescribably tortured with the knife.

On the other hand, the second outpost had been carried by an overwhelming rush, and its defenders had died on their feet, whirling clubbed rifles, stabbing with fixed bayonets in a wild pandemoniac *mêlée*.

But few of the men of this latter fort had lived to suffer torture—fortunately—for these Black Flag pirates, the jungle dacoits of the Far East, are the most ingenious, the most inhuman, the most devilishly cruel and callous torturers on the face of the earth.

And this was the third outpost.

Their last night. How should it be spent?

Had these men been of a homogeneous regiment, whether English, Scottish, Irish, French, German, Italian, Russian, Dutch, Swiss, Greek or Spanish, their general reaction to such a situation might be to some extent predictable.

Condemned to death without the possibility or faintest hope of reprieve, doomed to die at dawn without the slightest chance of escape, the men of one of these nations would have spent the night in grim uneasy jest; of a second in dour resigned solemnity; of a third in hectic nervous gaiety; of another in futile wrath and bitter recriminations against those by whom they had been "betrayed"; of another in a drunken orgy and a brave effort at the consumption of all stores of food and drink; of another in the singing of hymns and of national sentimental songs; and of yet another—in carrying on precisely as usual.

But of these particular men, not more than two were of the same nationality, and they represented most of the countries of Europe.

They were, nevertheless, soldiers of the French Foreign Legion, and as General Négrier had once informed the Legion, they were there to die, they were hired to die.

It was simply their business.

That was what they were for.

And so they sat—a wasteful plethora of tins of "monkey meat" and black issue bread, *bidons* of wine and packets of cigarettes beside them, talked and played *mini-dini*—and ate and drank, and were not merry, in spite of this unwonted luxury.

§3

It was their leader, the suave, cynical Paladino, a baffling enigmatical man, who made the suggestion, as they sat in a circle about the glowing embers of the fire, waiting for death, matter-of-fact, business-like and unperturbed, each man *bon camarade* and *bon légionnaire*.

Although literally a case of eat and drink, for to-morrow we die, they maintained, from force of habit, all correct military procedure, and a sentry paced the cat-walk, the long narrow firing-platform that ran round the inside of the fort four feet below the top of the wall.

"Hell!" yawned Paladino lazily, and stretched himself. "Soon be there, too."

"Wonder whether *le bon Dieu* tries us one by one, or in a bunch," he added, as he lay back against a box of ammunition, settled himself comfortably and lit a cigarette.

"What, us? Us old *légionnaires*? Oh, one by one, of course," asserted Lemoine, "and in camera, too."

"In camera, behind closed doors? Oh, too bad," grinned Borodoff. "We would have liked to hear the worst about one another."

"True," agreed Paladino.

"Well, why not have it now?" he added.

"Afraid we haven't—er—quite enough time," smiled old Bethune. "My own sins alone would take . . ."

"Of course they would, *mon vieux*," agreed Paladino.

"Take a month at least. I wasn't so optimistic as to imagine that we were going to have time to hear it all. Not even just yours. What I suggested was 'the worst'. Let's each confess our worst, blackest, beastliest deed, fully and faithfully, truly and honestly."

"Yes," agreed Lemoine. "And no boasting. Let's form a Dirty Dogs' Club and see who, on his own confession, is the dirtiest dog. He shall be proclaimed President. First and last President of the most short-lived club on earth."

Paladino rose to his feet.

"*Bon!* I declare the Club to be about to be. We are the original and only candidates for membership. I am the founder. Our friends the Black Flags will be the un-founders. Let none of your confessions be un-founded though. . . . You begin, Nul de Nullepart."

Le légionnaire Nul de Nullepart began, and others followed his excellent and stimulating lead . . .

Suddenly a Snider boomed, and Schenko, looking out through a *creneau*, staggered back and fell from the cat-walk down into the *enceinte*.

"*Aux armes!*" bawled Paladino, as every man, grabbing his rifle, sprang to meet the rush of savages that surged over all four walls, like a wave.

The struggle that followed was long and desperate, ending in a wild *mêlée* in which single *légionnaires* with whirling rifle-butts or darting bayonets fought desperately, each against a dozen; dying, man by man, until but one of them was left alive. He, clubbed from behind, had been knocked from the cat-walk down into the *enceinte*, and lay partly buried, and almost concealed, beneath the half-naked corpses of fallen dacoits, brown bodies partly clad in bright *panaungs*.

PART II

CHAPTER I

As I have already told,[9] I was bred to the sea, my father being an Admiral, and my forbears having held rank in the British Navy for centuries.

But my mother, abetted, if not instigated, by my step-father, Lord Fordingstane, decided that she could not afford to send me to the *Britannia* and into the Navy; I was apprenticed to the shipping-firm of Messrs. Dobson, Robson, and Wright, of Glasgow, and made my first voyage, as an Apprentice, in one of their ships, the *Valkyrie* of ill omen.

Sickened, for the time being, of the sea—for this voyage was one of the most tragic and disastrous made by any ship that ever came to port—I decided to be a soldier; and, with my fellow-Apprentice, Dacre Blount, enlisted in the Life Guards, a regiment in which my step-father had been a Cornet.

Having served for a couple of years in the Life Guards, Dacre Blount and I accepted a friend's offer of a chance to go to sea once more, this time on a gun-running expedition to Morocco. Here I was captured by nomad Arabs, sold as a slave, and, later, taken by my master to Mecca.[10]

The pilgrim ship in which we were returning from Jiddah was burnt; and I, escaping from it, was picked up by an Arab *dhow* which, proceeding to Djibouti in French Somaliland, was there seized by the French Naval authorities for the slaver, pearl-poacher, gun-runner and *hashish*-smuggler that she was, and handed over to the civil power. My Arab captors, long wanted by the French, were tried for piracy and murder, and were shot; I, proclaiming myself an Englishman, late in the employ of the Sultan of Bab-el-Djebel, was accused of being a Secret Service agent and spy, left for long in doubt as to my fate, and then, having been tried on an espionage charge, was found

---

[9] *Action and Passion.*
[10] *Sinbad the Soldier.*

probably-guilty and given the choice between enlisting in the French Foreign Legion and suffering indefinite detention.

In point of fact, I was just in the humour to join the French Foreign Legion, being at the moment rebellious against Fate, at a loose end, and somewhat desperate.

Moreover, that way of life undoubtedly promised adventure, and of adventure I was avid.

It seemed to me, too, that I was remarkably well equipped for this new rôle, inasmuch as I was a soldier, spoke and understood Arabic perfectly, had a good ground-work of French, knew the desert and the Arab and the Arab's way of fighting, better than any veteran in the Corps; and, thanks to sea-training, Guards' training, and my extremely active life in the desert, was a remarkably tough, seasoned and active young man.

But Fate will have its little joke; and as I knew Arabic and was an experienced desert fighter, I was sent almost direct to where the only useful language was Annamese; the terrain was swamp and dense jungle; and the mode of fighting was as different as it could possibly be from that of Arab warfare.

§2

Accounts of the routine of joining the Foreign Legion, proceeding to Sidi-bel-Abbès, and undergoing recruit-train-ing are numerous, and their number need not be increased. Suffice it to say that my training as a Guardsman, my size and strength, and my African experience, stood me in very good stead, and enabled me to endure, if not enjoy, recruit days at the depôt at Sidi-bel-Abbès, and to suffer nothing worse than boredom.

It was at just about the time when I was dismissed recruits' drill that a notice appeared in *rapport* that a draft would shortly be going as re-inforcement to the Legion battalion in Tonking on active service against the rebellious or, rather, unsubdued, followers of the Emperor of Annam, who had recently been defeated by the French and exiled from Indo-China.

These mountaineers, Annamese of the Dalat plateau and other highland parts of Tonking, aided by vast hordes of dacoits, brigands, and pirates, known as Black Flags, and secretly subsidized and supported by the Chinese Government, who reinforced them with bodies of irregulars and regiments of Chinese regular troops, were a powerful and dangerous enemy who had inflicted more than one definite defeat upon French Generals.

Promptly I put in my name for the draft and, presumably on the strength of my previous military training and experience, my physique, and the white crime-sheet of a blameless life, I was accepted, our Commanding Officer, *Chef de Bataillon* Wattringue doing me the honour of speaking a few words to me as he inspected the special parade of applicants for foreign service.

"What's your name, *mon enfant?*"

"Dysart, *mon Colonel.*"

"Previous service in the British Army, I'm told. Regiment?"

"Life Guards, *mon Colonel.*"

"Your father an officer?"

"Admiral, *mon Colonel.*"

"Why did you come to the Legion?"

"For adventure; active service, *mon Colonel,*" I replied, telling him the truth and nothing but the truth—if not the whole truth.

"Is he a good shot, a good marcher and a good soldier?" he enquired, turning to Captain Dubosque, commanding my Depôt Company.

"Excellent," replied that worthy man.

"And you wish to proceed forthwith to Tonking, eh?" he asked, turning again to me.

I assured him that I did.

"Well, perhaps you will. And equally—perhaps you won't," he replied, and passed on.

A fortnight later my name was published in Orders among those, my seniors and betters, who, having had six months' service and not having suffered imprisonment during that time, were to be formed into a separate section, receive flannel uniforms and a white helmet, and parade with the troops under orders for Tonking.

Of the men who entrained at Sidi-bel-Abbès for Oran to embark in the troop-ship *Général Boulanger* from Marseilles, already full to capacity with troops of the *Infanterie de la Marine*, few returned, most of them leaving their bones in the swamps, jungles, and military cemeteries of Indo-China.

Not a few died of heat-stroke, disease, and wounds before the troopship reached Pingeh, the port of Saigon in Cambodia.

Of those who died of wounds, two were shot attempting to desert in the Suez Canal where the ship tied up for the night; three at Singapore where we stopped to coal; while one man, who had succeeded in swimming from the ship at that port, was taken by a shark.

These deaths led to others, as, the deserting *légionnaires* having been shot by sentries of the Marine Infantry, there was, for the rest of the voyage, a very strong Legion feeling against the men of that Corps, a reciprocated bitterness of spirit that was expressed in more than one desperate and murderous conflict.

After calling at Saigon in Cochin China, the troopship proceeded to the mouth of the Red River, where the Legion draft was transferred to a couple of river gun-boats, the *Lily* and the *Lotus*, and taken some six hours' journey up the river and disembarked at the town of Haiphong.

From the wharf, our draft marched by way of a fine *boulevard*, the *Avenue Paul Bert*, to the Négrier Barracks, whence, a day or two later, we were taken on gun-boats another day's journey up the Red River to the base camp at a place called Hai Duong.

Thence, after rest, re-organization and re-fitting, we marched to a spot we called Seven Pagodas, and thence to the camp of the Second Battalion of the First Regiment at Houi-Bap—the seat of war.

I was on regular active service at last.

CHAPTER II

We soon learned that the Annamese army, known as the Black Flags, and by profession river-pirates and jungle dacoits—together with their allies, a large force of Chinese irregulars, also bandits in time of peace, reinforced, according to our scouts, by regiments of regular soldiers of the Chinese army who were led by white officers—held a strongly fortified position at a place called Quang-Ton. Already one considerable battle had been fought near this place, and, whoever claimed the victory, the enemy undeniably held the ground.

Our camp at Houi-Bap was the nearest French base to this strong enemy position; and with us, besides details, lay a battalion of *Tirailleurs Tonkinois*, native Annamese troops of the Delta, led by French officers and drilled by French non-commissioned officers.

Our battalion of the Legion had been divided into three companies, one of which occupied the base with its stores of food and munitions, while the other two marched out and operated, for several weeks at a stretch, as flying columns in the enemy country.

In my time at Houi-Bap I played many parts, having been, on different occasions and for varying periods, a cook, for the first and last time in my life; an exterior decorator, with whitewash only; a wood-cutter; a water-carrier; a stone-dresser; a carpenter; a road-navvy and a brick-maker.

A kilometre or so from our fortified barracks, within the stockade of which was quite a strong *réduit*, a clay-pit and brick-yard had been constructed, and here, under the guidance of a Sergeant who knew nothing about it, a dozen of us were employed in modelling bricks in clay, and stacking them in the kilns in which they were to be baked.

Nor did we make bricks without straw. While we worked, a section of native soldiers, *Tirailleurs Tonkinois*, chopped rice-straw for our use, while others carried buckets of water from the brick-yard well, and another section fed the kiln fires with wood.

These Annamese were under the command of a *Doi* or native Sergeant, who struck me as a remarkably intelligent man, very active, forceful and competent, as well as a good disciplinarian.

Later, I encountered *Doi* Linh Nghi in a different capacity, came to know him better, to like him very much, and to rank him among my real friends.

I cannot say that I found this aspect of life in the Foreign Legion thrilling or even attractive, for the work was extremely hard and dirty, the climate exceedingly hot and humid. So it was without regret that I learned, one day, that, enough bricks having been made, my Section was to join the Company that was going out on patrol, and was to be left by it at a distant outpost beyond the River Meh-Song at a place called Houi-Ninh.

We fell in, that morning, in full marching order, khaki uniform of cotton drill; rifles and bayonets; a hundred and twenty rounds of ammunition; filled water-bottles; ground-sheets rolled up, tied in a loop like a horse-collar, and worn over the left shoulder; laden knapsacks and haversacks; and a very heavy *mâchète* in a wooden sheath. The *mâchète* was both tool and weapon, like a broad thick straight-bladed sword, very sharp, and extremely useful for hacking one's way through the jungle where there was no path, or the track was so overgrown with creepers, bamboo, bushes, high grass and undergrowth that it was invisible. Incidentally, I once saw a powerful Yunnanese take a man's head right off with a *mâchète*, severing the neck as cleanly and neatly as though it had been a cucumber.

On our flank fell in a company of *Tirailleurs Tonkinois*, their uniform, of the same material as ours, consisting of a kind of vest, shorts, and their own native Muong puttees. They were bare-footed, and they wore round flat bamboo hats like plates, held in place by red cotton bonnet-strings.

These men were armed with carbines which took the same cartridges and bayonets as our own rifles, but were lighter and shorter weapons.

Out, through the great gates of the palisade—which ran right round our barracks, fort, store-sheds and various quarters and buildings, quite a village in itself—out, along the river bank between the rice-fields, and away into the jungle, we marched; far away out into the open country.

And through that open country of the Delta we continued to march, generally over a well-cultivated plain, with here and there villages nestling in clumps of fine trees and surrounded by growths of graceful bamboos. Between the villages, the country was covered with thick and luxuriant vegetation of brightest green, with very tall grass, and with patches of dense jungle and forest. Here and there, small hills broke the usual flatness of the terrain.

In this country, within a few days' march of Houi-Bap, the villages that were occupied were also, in theory, pacified, and the headman and elders would usually come out, kow-tow, and produce fruit, betel-nut, sugar-cane, milk or tea as peace-offerings to the soldiery.

Those that failed to come out were promptly brought out. For had they not accepted the protection of *Madame la République*, and had they not now the privilege of paying their taxes into her treasury at Phulang-Thuong?

Occasionally we came upon a village which was merely a charred heap of smoking ruins, this being the work of the exiled Emperor of Annam's Viceroy, the Annamese General De-Nam, and showed that they had refused to pay taxes to him likewise.

As my friend *Doi* Linh Nghi pointed out to me, when we talked in camp at night or on the march, it really was a little hard on the unfortunate villagers of this "pacified" zone, that, if they wished to keep the roof over their heads and the crops on their fields, they had to pay taxes twice, a toll of rice and money to their late Emperor in the person of General De-Nam, and also the taxes levied by the French authorities.

As we got further from our base, the spirit of the villagers changed, either their courage being greater or their wisdom less. The gates of the stockades with which the villages were invariably surrounded, would be barred and the place would show no signs of life. The Commander of the column would order the leading section to pull down the great iron-wood beams which, placed one above the other, their ends resting in slots cut in the huge and heavy door-posts, secured the stout resistant iron-wood doors.

The first of such places that we visited caused us some annoyance, for, having entered with bayonets fixed, rifles at the ready, mouths grim, and eyes glaring watchfully, we found—nothing. The place was absolutely empty. The villagers had all departed through some postern in the stockade at the other side of the village and escaped into the dense jungle beyond, where their cattle and other worldly goods were already hidden.

Day after day, week after week, we marched; and now, when approaching villages, were frequently met with a shower of bullets. In such cases the Commander would practise the column in attack drill, skirmishing up to the place and finally carrying it with the bayonet—quite unopposed. The training was good and the assault bloodless, the villages invariably being found to be empty.

It must have been policy rather than cowardice or doubt of the issue that made the Annamese peasants behave so, for each one of these villages was a strong post in itself, quite a jungle fort, surrounded as it frequently was by a deep moat, an embankment, and either a double or triple stockade of very stout bamboo.

In addition to such obstacles, entry into these jungle villages must be made by way of a passage through the embankment and stockades, only sufficiently wide for the domestic buffalo to make his way when he went forth to graze in the morning and returned at eventide.

It seemed to me that when we did have to attack one of these villages, occupied by a well-armed and determined garrison, we should only capture it at considerable cost, the narrow entrances being commanded by loop-holes through which a hot fire could be poured at close range upon the attacking force.

And, in due course, and not before we were extremely glad to see it, we reached the distant outpost of Houi-Ninh, beyond the Meh-Song River which we crossed, one at a time, by a swinging "bridge" of rattan and bamboo.

At Houi-Ninh my section, under Lieutenant Jacot, relieved the garrison; was left behind by the departing column; and remained in occupation until those who had not died of fever were ready to die of boredom.

CHAPTER III

While I and my Section were forgotten here in Houi-Ninh, things went rather badly with the French. The enemy, reinforced it was supposed, from China, became extremely active, over-ran great areas of the Pacified Zone, re-conquering and occupying the whole country up to and beyond the River Meh-Song, on the banks of which our little outpost stood.

The three outposts, on the further side of this river, of which ours was one, were attacked. Two of them fell at once, and their garrisons were put to the sword.

Ours was then besieged, was assaulted, and, after a desperate fight, was overwhelmed. I, thanks to a blow on the head from a rifle-butt, was stunned and left for dead.

Coming to my senses, I found myself the sole survivor of the garrison, alone in the silent post, now tenanted but by the dead.

§2

It was a shocking situation, one calculated to unhinge the mind of any person not inured to horrors. Fortunately for me, I was not without experience of such. The fort was a grave, strewn—I had almost said filled—with the hacked and mutilated bodies of my comrades and the corpses of those whom they had slain in the fierce barter of lives.

All that was wrong with me, physically, was an appalling headache, and a wound which, although it had at first seemed to me to be a depressed fracture of the skull, was merely a scalp wound. My thick *képi* had saved me from the worst injury, and doubtless the confined space in which we had been struggling on the cat-walk had prevented my assailant from doing himself justice. . . .

Never shall I forget the first awful minutes of recovering

consciousness, when I found myself pinned down, half-crushed, almost smothered, by the bodies of the dead.

At first I thought I was myself dead; and then, when convinced that I was alive, was sure that I was dying, for I was in hideous pain, and could move neither hand nor foot.

When, however, I fully recovered consciousness, I found, after a few mighty heaves and struggles, that I could sit up . . . stand up . . . and walk about.

What amazed me was the fact that the fort should be deserted, almost intact; and I concluded that there must be some more attractive object to which the pirate and rebel force had passed on, as soon as our post of Houi-Ninh had fallen and its garrison been exterminated.

As I staggered round the *enceinte*, averting my eyes from the bodies of my comrades—some of which had been deliberately mutilated—and entered the barrack-room, store-room and other quarters, I saw that the place had been looted and wantonly damaged; but there had been no attempt to set the buildings on fire. Nor had all the tinned provisions been removed.

I wondered whether policy or haste was the reason for this only partial destruction; whether the *T'uh Muh*, the leader of this horde, had decided that it would be foolish to destroy a captured fort that might later be extremely useful to himself; or whether he had been in too great a hurry to pass on to join General De-Nam and be in at the death.

I decided that haste was the reason; and that it accounted for the fact that only a few of the dead had been mutilated.

Possibly these had fallen, wounded, unable to defend themselves longer, and had been tortured to death. Possibly the mutilation was merely a wanton and savage hacking of the dead by the actual slayers of the fallen *légionnaires* whose desperate resistance had enraged them.

There lay Paladino, his khaki uniform dark-stained with blood from head to foot, his face in death still wearing its cynical expression, still looking as baffling and enigmatic as in life.

Near him, lay his friend Lemoine who evidently, back to back with him, had sold his life as dearly; for about them was a heaped circle of dacoits, shot, bayoneted, clubbed, in the last struggle of two against a score.

Old Schenko, veteran of a hundred fights, lay where he had fallen from the cat-walk, a bullet through his head.

Near him, savagely slashed and hacked, was the man I had known as Nul de Nullepart, a hitherto attractive man.

There they lay—my comrades; Paladino, Nul de Nullepart, Schenko, Pancezys, Gusbert, Richeburg, Van Diemen, the men who so shortly before had been confessing each his worst sin (some of which had been pretty awful); the men with whom I had lived and marched; eaten and drunk; worked and sung and talked—stiff and grim and gory in death.

And I felt that the least I could do was to give them decent burial.

Having stripped, washed, and bathed my head in a bucket of water, I made coffee, had a meal of cold boiled rice, tinned meat and biscuit; and then walked round the cat-walk staring over the wall into the surrounding jungle, thick, dark and dank, that seemed about to advance across the little clearing, some forty yards in width—studded with thousands of little bamboo stakes, hardened by boiling in castor-oil, and sharpened to a knife-like point—that lay about three walls of the fort.

Not a sign of a human being.

I thought of the heliograph. It was just possible that I could get a reply if I flashed it long enough.

Climbing, by way of the inside staircase, to the heliograph platform on the roof of the high watch-tower, I found that it had been smashed. What surprised me was the fact that the tricolour had been left flying, or rather, drooping, from its mast.

Uncoiling the halyard from the cleat at the mast-foot, I raised and lowered the flag many times. Should any far-distant telescope trained upon it, see this movement of the flag, it would be known that something was wrong at the fort of Houi-Ninh.

I could do nothing more in that way, and I must get to work.

For the next hour or two I laboured like a horse between shafts, seizing the feet of each dead dacoit and dragging him behind me, through the gate, and out across the clearing into the jungle.

This work was not as difficult as it was horrible; and, before long, I had cleared the fort of the bodies of its invaders.

This done, I shut the big iron-wood gates and dropped the steel bar into place. I had had some compunction about opening these, but as the enemy had completely departed, it seemed safe to do so; and, in any case, if there were another attack upon the place, it would be completely impossible for me to hope to defend it alone. In these days of machine-guns, rifle-grenades, and "pineapple" bombs thrown by hand, one *légionnaire* might do a good deal from a fort wall, against such an enemy. But, at that time, it would have been merely a case of a man with a rifle and bayonet against hundreds, perhaps thousands, equally well-armed. So it really mattered little whether the gates were open or shut.

I then, wearing only my boots and a pair of cotton shorts, began to dig. Fortunately the ground inside the fort was soft; and, by swinging mightily with a pick, and then putting my back into it with the long-handled French army shovel, I made good progress.

Had I had unlimited time, I would have dug a grave for each of my comrades. As it was, I should have to be content to dig one big grave six feet wide and long enough to take them all—in three or four tiers.

With intervals for rest and food, I worked all day, in spite of the heat and a splitting headache; for I had a great feeling of urgency, apart from the fact that, in that climate, the sooner burial follows death, the better. Unless I did this I could not possibly stay in the fort, and I could not drag my comrades out to be devoured by vultures and wild beasts.

I must undoubtedly have had a pretty savage clout on the head, for I distinctly remember that, at one time, when throwing heavy spadefuls of earth up out of the deepening grave, I thought I was on the slag-laden lighter in Valparaiso harbour; that lighter in which I had done the hardest and heaviest labour that I ever did in my life, shovelling the slag, heavy as lead, into great baskets for the ballasting of the ship *Valkyrie*. I also remember thinking that the vultures that settled on the walls of the fort, and eyed me, were the men of my Watch who, instead of helping with the cruel, heavy work, took a spell and loafed—watching.

It was well for me that I was strong beyond the ordinary and inured to the hardest of labour.

That evening I rested for a couple of hours, and then began work again, closing my ears, as I did so, to the sounds that came across the clearing, from where leopards and other wild beasts disputed over the bodies of the slain dacoits.

By moonlight I buried my comrades, carrying each to the edge of the grave, lifting him down into it, and disposing him as well as I could.

It is not a night that I willingly look back upon; but I am glad that I did what I did, my only regret being that I had to place them all in the one grave, row upon row, like sardines in a box.

When I had finished, and filled the grave in, I carried stones and laid them in an oblong upon the tamped earth. In the midst of the stones I planted a rough cross, formed by nailing a length of packing-case to a wooden post; and on the short arm of the cross I printed, as neatly as I could, with indelible pencil, the usual

Morts sur le Champ d'Honneur.

And on the upright of the cross I wrote their names.

Well, I had done my best, and if France cared to do better, she would have the opportunity.

§3

My work finished, I threw myself down on my string-and-frame bed and instantly fell asleep. I had intended to think out the problem of my line of conduct, and decide what should be my next step; but I must have been asleep by the time my head touched the bag of straw that was my pillow.

When I awoke it was evening. I had slept all day. Going out into the court-yard and walking round the fort, I realized that nothing had happened.

There was the tidy grave as I had left it. There were the little heaps of kerosene-soaked torches lying on the cat-walk beneath each embrasure of the wall, just as they had been left, all ready for use at night. The bamboo ladders were in place, and so far as I could see, neither man, beast nor bird had crossed the wall.

Having climbed the cat-walk and slowly circumambulated the fort, carefully studying the green wall of the jungle as I did so, I returned to the *chambrée* for a meal.

As I boiled the water for my coffee, I realized that I must come to a decision and stick to it.

Once I had made up my mind, there must be no shilly-shallying; and I must make it up soon.

I must decide whether to go or to stay.

My earliest inclination had been towards the former course.

Certainly I must stay, otherwise what should I be doing but deserting my post?

That, at first, seemed obvious. Just as the garrison of yesterday would have remained where they were and defended the fort to the last, so must I. The principle was the same, whether the garrison consisted of a hundred men or of one.

But would Lieutenant Jacot, had he known what was happening, have remained here, in view of the fact that all three outposts on the far side of the Meh-Song River must be cut off, and were of necessity abandoned to their fate, by reason of the fact that big rebel armies were between them and their base?

Since the little outposts must inevitably go, need their tiny garrisons perish with them?

I came to the conclusion that, had it been possible to withdraw and retire, he would have done so.

Once we were surrounded by a hundred times our number, he had no choice but to remain.

My position was different. The siege was raised; the enemy gone; and I, a single individual, might very well be able to make my way back along the route by which the *compagnie de marche* had come from Houi-Bap, should I decide to do so.

And what good could I do by remaining? Obviously I couldn't defend the place. And though fine phrases about Keeping the Flag Flying and Defending the Place to the Last sounded very well, the flag would fly by itself all-right, and I couldn't defend the place for five seconds if the returning hordes attacked it.

Nor would anything be gained by giving the impression that the place was once more fully garrisoned. Even if the ruse were successful, it would not impress the Black Flags in the least. They knew perfectly well that they could take the place, as they had done before, by sheer weight of numbers; and the question of the strength of the defending force would not interest them in the least.

No; one man could do nothing at all in Fort Houi-Ninh. He would be absolutely useless.

If I stayed, I should be completely idle and worthless if the place were not attacked, and promptly killed if it were.

And there was another consideration. If I stayed there alone in that haunted place, I should go mad.

Summing up the pros and cons, I came to the conclusion that the sensible thing to do was to go where both I and my information would be of some value, and not to remain where both would be perfectly useless.

The decision made, I started to put it into execution.

I would rest until my head felt better, eat and drink plentifully of what provisions the looters had not taken or destroyed, and regain strength for the long march that I was going to undertake to rejoin my Company at Houi-Bap, if I might do so.

I could there give an account of what had happened on the far side of the Meh-Song River, and resume my place in my Company. . . .

Having rested, I would tidy the place thoroughly, leave it all ship-shape, lock up and fasten the gates, let myself down over the wall, and march off.

Unfortunately I could not do so with the honours of war, carrying arms, drums beating, and flags flying. I had no arms to carry, the dacoits having, of course, taken every rifle and bayonet with them. There was no one to beat the drum; the honours were doubtful, as my side had been defeated; and the only comfort was that the flag still flew over the fort.

And, curiously enough, it was a real comfort. It seemed to promise that we should return, and that my comrades, advance-guard in the Army of Civilization, would not have died in vain.

Apart from the fact of being unarmed in enemy country, and passing through a jungle swarming with dangerous beasts and more dangerous savages, it was extraordinary how lost I felt without my rifle. I really think I could have marched better with my right hand occupied and encumbered with its familiar weight.

On the other hand, I was for the first time in my marching experience, glad of heavy extra weight—that of food—as, before lowering myself and dropping from the fort wall, I had thrown over as many tins of meat and sardines, and as much biscuit as I thought I could carry in addition to the mass of cold boiled rice with which I had stuffed a haversack to bursting.

I had also filled a couple of *bidons* with half a gallon of wine. Of water there would be no lack.

It was a nightmare march. Time after time I was terrified almost to death, especially in the hours of darkness when unseen forms moved about me in the jungle; when I heard the sound of following feet; when twigs cracked under the weight of approaching man or animal; when I saw the gleam of twin orbs and momentarily expected to be smashed to the ground by a springing leopard.

By day things were not so bad. Time after time I dived from the track into dense jungle, and lay hidden, as parties of men who might have been villagers, pirates, wayfaring pedlars, dacoits, scouts, brigands or wandering Chinese soldiers, came in sight.

Over the greatest fright of all, I still smile.

One morning I awoke, stiff, aching, foot-sore and miserable, from a short dawn sleep among the roots of a great tree.

Rising to my feet, I was about to force my way through the undergrowth on to the path, when I was alarmed by a most terrific crashing clatter. It was so near, so loud and so intimidating that my heart stood still. It was a strange noise too, for I had heard nothing quite like it, and could assign it to no known and reasonable cause. It was almost as though all the slates were falling off a house on to the stones of a court-yard—which was a quite impossible phenomenon in that uninhabited green hell. It was as though coolies on a ship were slinging stacks of crockery down on to a quay, which was equally absurd. It was as though a thousand small boys were shattering cakes of toffee with hammers, an improbable event in the heart of the Annamese jungle. And the sound seemed to come from all round.

Hastening to escape, I came upon the cause of it. Two gigantic tortoises were fighting on the path.

Really, a dozen men armed with swords and shields could hardly have made more noise. With the anger of fright I cursed the beasts from the bottom of my heart. They were not noticeably affected thereby.

And one day I heard distant rifle-fire. Not only the sustained din, rising and falling, of independent firing, but the regular crashes of the *tir de salve* or volleys; and knew that I was within a short distance of French troops.

Scouting forward with the utmost care, I found, to my unspeakable joy, that a *compagnie de marche* of *Tirailleurs Tonkinois* was skirmishing with a band of Black Flags into whom they had bumped on patrol.

Luckily for me, I was on the flank of the Black Flag force, and could make my way past them to within shouting-distance of the opposite flank of the French firing line.

Luckily also, I was in full Legion uniform, otherwise I should have run an excellent chance of being shot by my own side.

A French non-commissioned officer of *Tirailleurs Tonkinois* having briefly questioned me, took me to his officer who, having heard my story, offered me his congratulations on my escape, it having been assumed at Houi-Bap that there were no survivors of the three forts on the far side of the Meh-Song River.

To my great pleasure, my friend *Doi* Linh Nghi was on this patrol, his task being the gathering of information from the villagers. These could be divided into two classes, those who feared the French more than they did the Annamese General, De-Nam; and those who feared the Annamese General De-Nam more than they did the French authorities.

Of the former but few were left alive in this area; and of those who were, the majority were homeless fugitives. It was from these that the *Doi* got his information concerning the movements of the rebel parties.

Those whose terror of General De-Nam was greater than their fear of us, had saved their lives and their villages, by giving the rebels every assistance in their power; rightly arguing that, whatever punishment the French might inflict upon them for this, it would not be wholesale slaughter after hideous torture.

Some of the sights I saw in the villages that had not been amenable to the dacoit leader were horrible beyond telling. I did not imagine that human beings could be such bestial brutish devils as those must have been who had so tortured and mutilated the victims they were about to murder.

The principal leader of the band operating in this particular part of the country was a former *ly-truong*, or sub-prefect, named De-Nha of whom much more anon.

With the patrol I returned to Houi-Bap, reported to Captain Bonnier of my Company, and was taken before the Officer Commanding the garrison, now a small Brigade consisting of a battalion of the Legion; a battalion of *Tirailleurs Tonkinois*; a mixed battalion of the Biff, as we called the French regular troops of the line; a company of *Infanterie de Marine*; and a battery of mountain artillery.

Somewhat to my relief, this officer took the view that I had done a sensible thing in endeavouring to rejoin my Company, and that it would have been merely foolish to sit down and do nothing in an empty and abandoned fort until I starved to death, went mad, or died of fever.

In point of fact, he said, orders had been sent to the officers commanding all three posts, to blow them up and retire, but the orders had never reached them. So swift and sudden had been the incursion of the Chinese bands, the assembling of General De-Nam's pirates and dacoits, and the universal uprising of the "pacified" districts, that all patrols, pickets, and outposts had been cut off and destroyed.

Being an emaciated fever-stricken wreck, a poor pitiable object, looking far worse than I felt, I was sent to hospital and then put on light duty.

CHAPTER IV

It was at about this time that I had the good or bad fortune to come in contact with the famous Captain Dele-uze, *doyen* of the Military Intelligence Service in Indo-China.

. . .

One day I was talking to my Annamese friend, the *Doi* Linh Nghi, at the door of his hut, in the street of the village of Houi-Bap, that had grown up in the vicinity of the Fort of the same name. The *Doi* was seated cross-legged on the ground.

Suddenly he sprang to his feet and saluted, as a shadow passed across us. Looking round, I saw that an officer, in Legion khaki, somewhat stained, was standing, apparently listening to our conversation.

He was a small, dark, rather sallow-faced man, about whom there was nothing remarkable—with the exception of his eyes. These were extraordinarily bright, clear, and pierc-ing; save when, deliberately, he made them appear dull and lifeless, a thing that, apparently, he could do at will.

What it was about his eyes that gave this impression and expression of alertness, watchfulness and penetration, I do not know; but it was probably partly due to the fact that the iris was curiously pale, varying from a kind of Cambridge blue to an indescribable light hue that was scarcely any colour at all.

When he spoke, one noticed another peculiarity, his voice being extraordinarily soft, low, and quiet, but at the same time perfectly audible. I believe that I never failed to hear what he said to me, and yet it seemed that he always whispered.

Save for these two slight peculiarities, he was in appear-ance most ordinary and insignificant, a man to whom one would not give a second glance or second thought, unless it were to wonder how so completely commonplace a person, one so lacking in presence, distinction and soldierly appear-

34

ance and carriage, should have been an officer at all.

But not only was Captain Deleuze an officer, he was a very fine one indeed, one of the best in the French army of his day, and worth almost a Brigade to the General commanding the army of Indo-China.

I sprang to attention and saluted him.

"Ah!" he whispered in French with a quiet smile, "plotting great things with a Sergeant of Annamese *Tirailleurs*, are you? What language were you talking?"

"His, *mon Capitaine*."

"So I thought; and that is as it should be. Why shouldn't every soldier of France, serving in Tonking, learn the language and talk it to *les indigènes* instead of letting them grunt horrible 'pidgin' French at them? I suppose you never allow the Sergeant to talk French to you, do you?"

"*Oui, mon Capitaine*, I do. It is part of the bargain. He teaches me Annamese, and I'm teaching him French."

"Ah! There's some sense in that. Teaching him proper, grammatical, French, are you? And he is teaching you proper, grammatical, Annamese?"

"*Oui, mon Capitaine*. That is how it goes. He wishes to qualify as an Interpreter."

Captain Deleuze smiled.

"Oh. He does, does he?"

I did not then know that the *Doi* was a very valuable agent, assistant and spy in the service of Captain Deleuze.

"And are you learning to use the honorific as well as the ordinary? Can you handle the *tao* and *toi* properly?" he asked.

"I am learning, *mon Capitaine*, though it's a difficult language, as, apparently, there is no grammar, not to mention an alphabet."

Captain Deleuze smiled again.

"I know," he said.

So did I, for, until recently, I had been very dissatisfied with my progress, finding the Annamese language infinitely more difficult than Arabic. This is not remarkable, inasmuch as it is, like Chinese, made up of an enormous number of small noises, groups of which contain sounds so like each other that it takes not only training, but very careful attention, to distinguish any difference between them.

Time after time, for example, *Doi* Linh Nghi would say to me,

"No, I didn't say *binh*. Listen; I said *binh*," apparently making precisely the same sound. Or,

"No, you are saying *adhow di*, whereas you mean *adhow di*," or,

"If you mean 'peasant', 'countryman', the word is *nhaque* not *nhaque*. Understand?"

No, I didn't understand. I simply could not hear any difference, and at times I despaired of ever speaking Annamse correctly.

This very day, just before Captain Deleuze had spoken to me, *Doi* Linh Nghi had just insisted that if I thought I was using the word 'home,' I had better say *phteah*, and not make the barbarous noise, something like *phteah*, which I had just uttered. . . .

"Tell me. Of what nationality are you?" asked Captain Deleuze, addressing me in Annamese, and properly referring to himself as *tao*, the form appropriate to a superior addressing an inferior.

"Give me some account of your life up to the time you joined the Legion," he continued in Annamese.

I replied to the best of my ability in the same language, and using the *toi* self-reference which is correct when an inferior addresses a superior.

"Why, that's pretty good. That marches," he said, when I had finished. "Positively fluent. Are you a student of languages?"

"No, *mon Capitaine*," I replied. "I can pass for an Arab, and have done so in the sacred city of Mecca; and I can speak French quite fluently. I know no other languages."

"Well, you are on the high road to knowing Annamese, *mon enfant*; and with English, French, Arabic and Annamese to your credit, I think we could do something with you. Yes. Positively I almost think we could nearly do something with you. . . . Meet me here at this time to-morrow evening."

And turning on his heel as I saluted, he passed along on

his way to the Fort.

On the following evening, being off duty, I strolled down to *Doi* Linh Nghi's reed-thatched *caigna* for my usual hour's Annamese conversation-lesson, sitting and chatting while an aged hag (who was not his wife), perhaps his girl-friend and perhaps his mother, cooked his rice, which, with dried fish and green local vegetables, she would bring him on a brass platter, with perhaps a handful of fresh-water prawns on a banana leaf.

This *Doi* Linh Nghi would eat while we talked, a thing that at first surprised me, as I was under the impression that no "native", be his religion what it might, cared to sit and eat in the presence of a person of some other race and creed.

Nevertheless, this he would do without the slightest embarrassment, ceasing not to talk as he shovelled the food into his somewhat capacious mouth, a feature whose natural ugliness was not improved by its interior decoration of black-lacquered teeth.

Of all things in the Annamese Heaven above, on the Annamese earth beneath, and in the waters under the earth, we talked, not forgetting local politics, military information and mis-information, and the state of the country.

Fast as we talked, and interested in our subject as we might be, *Doi* Linh Nghi never forgot to pull me up and correct me when I made a mistake in pronunciation.

When he had finished dinner, the flat-faced, slant-eyed, good-hearted and evil-looking little chap would say,

"*Et maintenant nous parlerons Français, Monsieur le Légionnaire Dhysaht.* You belong teach me speakee all the same Frenchman. But what good I suppose you do that, when you belong different *Nais*?"

Thus he would relapse into the horrible broken French which is to that language what the Gold Coast 'pidgin' English of Sidi boys and the traders' house-servants is to the English language.

And his heart was really in his linguistic studies, just in the way that mine was, for he had a great desire to learn the

French language thoroughly and to rise in the world. Before long he would, nevertheless, bid his lady-friend, mother or maiden aunt to bring out his *sahat*, his rice-straw mat, and on this he would stretch himself at full length.

An idea would then occur to him—the same idea at the same moment, every night of his life—and he would ask the aged lady if she could see anything of a wooden tray inside there in the *phteah*; a tray on which was a lamp, a bowl, a silver skewer, a little box and, in point of fact, what you might call something like an opium pipe. Yes, and probably she might find his pillow knocking around somewhere near the tray.

And always she would find these things exactly as he described them, the pillow being nothing more nor less than a shaped block of blue china-ware—solid, hard, shiny blue china—ornamented, believe me or believe me not, with a neat linen frill tied about it. Later, I saw many of these amazing china pillows, thus enclosed in a frilled pillow-case, their angularities and asperities proclaiming themselves at the corners.

"I think I'll have a puff or two of the black smoke," observed *Doi* Linh Nghi as usual, this evening.

"I'm sure you will," said I.

And he picked up the opium pipe, a thing some twenty to thirty inches long and a couple of inches thick, one end covered by a silver cap, the other having a jade mouthpiece far too large to go into the mouth, and in the middle of it, a small hole through which the smoke was drawn. A quarter of the way up the stem was the pipe bowl, a large silver receptacle completely covered in, save for a hole, in diameter no bigger than that of a large needle. On top of this hole, the burning pill of opium rested, and through the hole, the smoke was sucked down into the bowl, along the stem, and through the mouthpiece into the mouth and lungs of the consumer.

First, *Doi* Linh Nghi lit the lamp, opened the silver box, and, taking the little silver skewer, collected on the point of it a small lump of the thick heavy opium, semi-liquid in consistency, and dark brown in colour.

This he passed through the little flame of the lamp so that it bubbled and thickened, when he dipped it again into the box and collected more opium upon it.

Having done this, half a dozen times, he had got enough opium for a pipe-smoke. He then put the pipe into his mouth, warmed the upper surface of the pipe-bowl in the flame, placed the opium over the hole in the bowl-cover and held it above the flame. The opium sizzled and burned, and *Doi* Linh Nghi sucked strongly at the mouthpiece, inhaling the whole of the smoke so that none escaped even from the bowl, into the circumambient air.

When he could inflate his chest no longer, and must cease to draw, he puffed for a brief space as does an ordinary tobacco-smoker, smoking quickly.

The opium being all consumed, he laid the pipe down upon his mat and gently and slowly exhaled the black smoke from his lungs.

Watching it float upwards, dark, heavy and opaque, he heaved a tremendous sigh of utter content and grunted,

"*Biet! Meh! Biet!* . . . Ah, that is good."

And a great peace and silence fell upon him.

The silence was broken by the sound of a foot-step, and looking up, I saw a dirty little Annamese *nhaque* approaching, wearing on his *chignon* a little turban surmounted by a lacquered *sakalo*, a round flat hat made of bamboo, and shaped somewhat like an inverted plate, but coming to a point in the centre. He also wore a dirty cotton vest and short trousers or long knickerbockers, such as are worn by the Muong tribesmen.

This strange little man, shuffling near, stood and stared at the opium-drugged *Doi* Linh Nghi with lacklustre eyes, his half-open mouth exposing teeth apparently carved from polished ebony.

"*Kamm môk phdâl!*" he murmured, and subconsciously I repeated his observation in the common Arabic phrase *Mektoub rebib*—It is written and will come to pass. "He must follow his Fate and act according to his Karma."

"Opium!" he added. "Smoking opium. Now he's happy. But he will die of smoking opium."

"*Sday er chéat mûy*," I observed sapiently. "One can only die once."

"*Kamm môk phdâl*," countered the coolie, who seemed to have no other conversational gambit; and the *Doi* snubbing him and showing off, repeated this in unexpectedly accurate French.

"*Le Karma se réalise.*"

"He's wandering in his mind already," observed the coolie censoriously.

"And who might you be, fellow, that you speak to a white soldier and to a Sergeant of *Tirailleurs Tonkinois*?" I said, speaking *de haut en bas*, further to practise my Annamese.

The *nhaque* grinned foolishly.

"Me?" he said. "Me? I am a plainsman."

"Well, I can see that, you black-toothed yokel," I replied politely. "And hear it too, for your voice is as ugly as that of the rain-bird—or of a horn-bill, for that matter. Do you suppose I take you for a *tho*?"

Again the man grinned foolishly.

"I am a plainsman," said he.

"You don't say!" said I.

"Oh yes I am, and the Lu Thuong of Phulang-Nguyen sent me here to see if the *linhtap lanxa* had gone away yet."

"Oh, the Headman of Phulang-Nguyen sent you to see whether the French soldiers had gone away, did he? Why does he want to know?"

"Fruit and vegetables," was the reply. "He's not going to send us down here with them if the *Ong-quang-Ba*,[11] the Lord of Three Stripes, has taken the *linhtap lanxa* away."

"I see. And has he distilled any *choum-choum* to sell to the *linhtap lanxa*?"

"Oh no," grinned the yokel. "He'd never do that, or the Lord of Three Stripes would give him more than three stripes. He! he!"

And thus we discoursed on high important matters; I discovering that I could understand all the coolie said, and, what was more pleasing, that he obviously understood all I

---

[11] Captain.

said to him.

By and by, *Doi* Linh Nghi bestirred himself and prepared another pipe.

Watching him with idle stupid eyes, his face vacant, his mouth hanging open, the peasant was deeply interested and apparently envious.

Again we talked.

Again *Doi* Linh Nghi prepared a pipe and smoked it.

And several times again.

Whereafter, remarking in perfect English,

"Well, if that lad has another, I'll say he's doing himself too well, in the opium line," the coolie rose to his feet.

"Not at all bad, Dysart," he continued. "Not at all bad—for both of us. You didn't spot me, did you?"

"No, Sir, I certainly didn't," I replied, nearly as open-mouthed as the late coolie, now Captain Deleuze, had himself but recently been. It was a wonderful piece of acting and a marvellous make-up, for not only had it deceived me, but had completely taken in the experienced and oft-deceived Sergeant Linh Nghi of the *Tirailleurs Tonkinois*—himself a *tho* mountaineer from the Tam-Dao highlands of Thai-Nguyen in the west.

This was the beginning of my connection with Captain Deleuze, for, from this day, started my long and absorbingly interesting service under this remarkable man.

Among his other great abilities, gifts and accomplishments was a very high degree of skill In the art of military topography, for every form of sketching, surveying and map-making was as easy to him as the writing of a report. And not only had he a wonderful eye and artistic gift, but his draughtsmanship was that of a professional, being as accurate as it was neat.

In this extremely useful art, he later trained me with great care, taking me out on reconnoitring expeditions, and each time showing me how to make a *topo*, both of the journey and of its objective.

But here I am running ahead too fast, as it was some time before I was seconded, nominally as his batman, and lent to him for Intelligence work.

§2

I do not know whether it was because I was an English-man that Captain Deleuze first took to me. Of the British he was a great admirer, and he had a very high opinion of our Secret Service and of the efficiency of our army generally.

Having questioned me and discovered that I had served in the Life Guards, he was interested at once; and more so when he knew that I had not only been a sailor, but had lived as an Arab among Arabs in Morocco and Arabia, and had actually made the Pilgrimage to Mecca. He seemed to think that the fact that I could, in such surroundings and circumstances, pass as an Arab, showed that I had a great natural aptitude for native languages, and for disguising myself as a native, too.

Having got me put on special duty under him for study of Annamese; of military surveying, map-drawing and map-reading, he made something of a friend of me, treated me in private as an equal, and talked very freely of his ambi-tion, both for himself and his country, in Tonking; of the his-tory and geography of Indo-China; of its ethnology; and par-ticularly of the French connection with the country since 1585 when a Jesuit Father, Georges de la Mothe, estab-lished missions, churches and schools throughout the Delta of the Mekong River; of the French campaign which began in 1867; and which, flaring up from time to time, had been active again ever since 1886—so active that, as recently as 1892, Hanoi, the capital itself, had been captured, sacked, and partly burned by an army of Annamese aided by Chi-nese irregulars.

He also told me a thing which surprised me—and he was in possession of the most accurate information—that in 1883, 1884 and 1885 alone, over fifteen thousand of the best troops of France had died in Tonking.

One evening, when I reported as usual at Captain Dele-uze's office room, I found him seated at his desk with an array of saucers of paint, brushes, wigs, crêpe-hair and spirit-gum—in fact a complete actor's make-up outfit. Beside him on the floor lay a small and varied heap of native clothing and weapons, *panaungs*, *pasinns*,[12] *sakalos*, sashes, turbans and such.

"Well, my lad, I'm going to turn you into a damn great ugly Chinese thug. We'll start by painting you yellow. Then touch up your eyebrows with a razor and black paint, doctor your eyelids with gelatine, and fake the corners with some glue. . . . I'll show you. . . . Give you a long straggling moustache, I think . . . and a pig-tailed wig, of course. . . . Or I wonder if you'd look better as a *poogni* in canary-yellow robes, with a begging-bowl. . . . How would you like to have your head shaven? Nice and cool, anyway. . . ."

§3

Both in my study of Annamese, and my practice in disguise and the pursuance of correct behaviour appropriate to that disguise, I contrived to make progress which satisfied Captain Deleuze.

On several occasions he permitted me to accompany him when he made excursions to neighbouring towns and villages or up the Red River, himself disguised as an Annamese lowlander, a pedlar, a priest, a dacoit, a coolie, a camp-follower, a shop-keeper, a railway contractor, a cafe servant; as a seller of carved wooden models and toys and figures modelled in clay and split bamboo; as whatever was useful in the attainment of his purpose—observation, verification, personal communication with his spies, and the collection of information.

On the occasions when I accompanied him, I myself, owing to my height and bulk, always went in the rôle of a Chinese tough, a truculent ruffian who earned his living as a "strong-arm man", personal bodyguard and bully; a rôle for which Captain Deleuze unkindly informed me I was admirably fitted by my appearance, if not actually so intended by

---

[12] Lengths of coloured cloth draped about the body.

Nature.

Certainly I could use my fists, and, upon more than one occasion, had to do so, to the utter amazement as well as discomfiture of aggressive and truculent persons who were either over-inquisitive or disposed to be arbitrary, high-handed and interfering.

With us went the admirable *Doi* Linh Nghi and the half-dozen members of his Section whom we called his family, they being, in point of fact, brothers or near kinsmen of his, from the same Highland village of the district whence came the admirable *thois* who are to the French what the Gurkhas are to the British.

Our most ambitious effort in the guise of wandering *budmashes*, rag-tag-and-bobtail jungle-ruffians, was a visit to the camp of the famous Luu-Ky himself, a Chinese brigand-leader who was harrying the railway under construction from Phulang-Thuong to Lang-son; swooping down and slaughtering working-parties; actually carrying off French engineers for ransom or torture; ambushing convoys going by road to Lang-son; and generally making himself a thorough nuisance. During the week before our visit to his camp, he had suddenly rushed the escort of an ammunition-column, captured twenty-five cases of Lebel rifles, and ten thousand rounds of ammunition, killed Commandant Bonneau of the *Infanterie de Marine*, and after mutilation, had crucified, upside-down on trees, all who fell into his hands.

He had also captured a prominent railway engineer named Gautrin, and notified General Voyron that, unless a ransom of one hundred thousand silver dollars was paid for him within a week, his ears would be forwarded; within a fortnight, his hands; within three weeks, his feet; and at the end of the month, his head. . . .

Our visit was a great success, for we learned that, in the attack on the convoy, Luu-Ky had been wounded, that the wound was doing very badly, and that he was unlikely to recover. On the strength of Captain Deleuze's report, Luu-Ky's hitherto amazingly mobile force was surrounded, attacked, and handled so severely that it practically ceased to exist.

§4

Captain Deleuze next turned his attention to a dacoit leader who was making himself extremely active in the vicinity of Houi-Bap, collecting revenue for General De-Nam from villages not more than a few days' march from our Brigade Headquarters.

This was that previously-mentioned brute, De-Nha, concerning whom *Doi* Linh Nghi had already gathered information, a former sub-prefect under the Emperor Ham Nghi, and now an officer in General De-Nam's rebel army.

According to information, he was prominent in, if not at the head of, General De-Nam's intelligence department, and was a man of great ability, considerable activity, and most devilish ingenuity in obtaining both information and subsidies from the wretched villagers in what was officially termed the Pacified Zone.

Concerning this man and his movements, Captain Deleuze gave me all the information he had; and then, himself being unable to leave Headquarters, offered me no less an opportunity and task than the capture of this redoubtable villain.

"Since he has had the courage to venture so near to the jaws of the apparently sleeping tiger, we'll let them take a snap at him, eh, my son? Show him whether the French tiger is alive or dead, asleep or awake. . . . What about it?"

CHAPTER V

"Well there you are, S.N.B.D., *mon enfant*; Sin-bad, *le grand pêcheur*. Let's see what sort of a mess you can make of it. Don't bungle it wholly, as it's rather important. Your orders are to *get* him. Alive or dead. Preferably very much alive. Far preferably. Use what brains you've got; make your own arrangements; and tell me afterwards exactly what you did and why—and how your plans mis-carried. Take that Annamese, *Doi* Linh Nghi, and let him take whom else he wants. Leave that to him—so long as he understands it is rather a kidnapping than a raid. I should think half a dozen of you would be ample. Any questions?"

"No, Sir. I think not. . . . Alive or dead. Preferably alive. If I am successful, well and good. If I fail . . ."

"If you fail, I know nothing about you. You are absolutely repudiated," smiled Deleuze.

"By the way," he continued, "don't get caught there. And if you do, don't squeal. But you won't do that, I know. Nor would the *Doi* Linh Nghi. There is absolutely no torture on earth that would get anything out of those chaps, once they have decided that they won't utter. . . . And the men he takes with him won't know anything, and wouldn't talk if they did."

That evening I slipped out from Deleuze's quarters, looking, I flattered myself, an extremely convincing brigand. Just the type of burly ruffian that might have been a man-darin's kept bully, or leader of a gang of jungle banditti.

Making my way as unobtrusively as possible to *Doi* Linh Nghi's hut, I found him awaiting me, the only outward and physical signs of his military profession being his rifle, belt and cartridge pouch. At his left side hung a naked *mâchète*. For the rest, he looked the part he was about to play, and a regular jungle dacoit.

With a low laugh and a quiet greeting he led the way to where, in the dark shadows of the trees at the end of the row of thatched *caignas*, lounged a small group of men.

As we approached, these instinctively straightened up; and when we joined them, fell into line, ordered arms, came to attention and stood as rigid as though on parade.

Doi Linh Nghi swore, and I made a mental note to learn the oath, for it sounded good to me.

"Look at them," he said. "Why, the buffaloes, the crocodiles, the coolies, the women! And I chose them for intelligence and because they are relations of mine. Look at the mud-fish. They look more like policemen than dacoits, don't they? Dragons tear their entrails!"

"Stand at ease, you worms. Stand easy, you maggots. Stand anyhow, you ticks."

And in low but definitely persuasive voice, the *Doi* Linh Nghi bade them forget that they were soldiers—not that they really were what he would call soldiers—and to remember that they were *yak*, pirates, Black Flags, jungle devils—and act accordingly.

Grinning cheerily, the Gurkha-like *tirailleurs* endeavoured to obey as we set off, *Doi* Linh Nghi leading, I behind him, and the rest following, silent as shadows, in single file.

At first, our road lay across miles of narrow ridges, those difficult and heart-breaking paths that run between the endless flooded paddy-fields.

Marching by way of these paddy-bunds is trying enough by daylight, especially if one is not at, or near, the head of the file. For the little low dams are of soft earth, and by the time a few feet have trodden this, it has become softer and softer and quickly turns to mud, and the causeway deteriorates and degenerates into semi-liquid slush. It is almost impossible for a number of men to follow each other quickly along one of these crumbling bunds, as those at the end of the line, endeavouring to keep up, are soon slipping and sliding, when not actually floundering in the water that covers the rice. At night, it is of course ten times as difficult to keep on the narrow ridges serving as paths.

It was both fortunate and unfortunate that the night was pitch dark, for, while it aided concealment, it made progress extremely slow, and increased not only the danger of our losing our way, but of losing each other.

This last danger, however, I obviated by ordering each man to "catch hold of the tail of the monkey in front", a most feeble jest extremely well received.

Thus, groping blindly through the darkness, we must have covered about a couple of miles every hour.

Personally, I was glad when we reached the jungle, because pitch-black as the night was, it was really no darker than it had been out in the paddy-fields; for there had been no sign whatever of moon or stars, our only help being the occasional flash of lightning which showed *Doi* Linh Nghi where we were.

Though in no wise, and in no slightest degree, braver than other average people, I am, nevertheless, not what you would call a nervous person; but I freely confess to detesting the jungle at night, particularly on a pitch-black one. Whenever it has been my misfortune to make a night march alone through the jungle, I have always found my imagination far too active, doing its best to persuade me that I am being followed by a silent-footed savage whose knife or sword, spear or arrow, I may, at any moment, receive between my shoulder-blades; that at the next step I shall plunge headlong into the hole dug in the jungle path as a trap for big game; that a tiger or a panther is keeping pace with me close by, stopping when I stop, going on when I go on, and awaiting an inviting opportunity to spring. . . . That sort of thing.

So that on this occasion, in spite of the slight extra noise inseparable from the company of seven other people, I was very glad that these born jungle men were with me.

As we made better progress, owing to the improvement in the quality of the path, I wondered whether it could be true that *Doi* Linh Nghi could, as he professed, see in the dark, or, at any rate, see very much better than a European can. It certainly seemed so, for although our pace improved, we never left the path or ran into any obstacle. Before long, the question that had been exercising my mind—as to whether such little noise as we made might be heard by the rebel scouts, pickets or patrols—ceased to trouble me, for the occasional flashes of lightning gave way to a really tremendous thunderstorm.

Suddenly the black veil of night was rent by a most brilliant flash of lightning, which seemed to pass across our immediate front—illuminating the jungle and imprinting upon my mind an unforgettable picture of mighty tree and enormous creeper, lofty palm and graceful bamboo—immediately followed by a crashing earth-shaking peal of thunder that was literally deafening. All to the good, until the torrential rain that followed turned the jungle path to a ditch, and our hot perspiring selves to shivering teeth-chattering miseries.

For at least three hours more we splashed along, our way lit by lightning, our approach unseen, unheard, and unknown.

One thing was certain—no warrior of the rebel army would consider it right or reasonable of his Commanding Officer to expect him to operate on a night like this. It was no part of his military duty to face the fiends and devils, the ghosts and *peis* which, as anybody knows, arise and disport themselves on occasions of nocturnal thunderstorms, roaring up and down the jungle, seeking whom they may devour, and looking particularly for poor harmless banditti, pirates, and dacoits who have a few odd dozen murders, robberies and torturings to their account.

Yes, this terrific storm, unpleasant as it was, and this torrential rain, chill and fever-inducing as it might be, were all to the good. I only hoped it would last until we were into Yen-Trang and out again, our object accomplished.

Suddenly *Doi* Linh Nghi halted so abruptly that I bumped into him. By the light of a flash of lightning he had seen something.

"The village," he whispered, waiting for another lightning flash, and began again to move forward slowly along the path.

After a while, he halted again, turned aside and forced his way into the undergrowth. In a clearer patch of long grass, brushwood, cactus, saplings, and hibiscus shrubs, he stopped.

"We'll camp here till dawn," he whispered.

'Camping' was a simple process and consisted of squatting, or lying down, in the mud.

With my back against a tree, drenched to the skin, and shivering with cold, I sat; and, in spite of extreme discomfort, in fact, sheer physical misery, I dozed off.

From this doze I suddenly awoke, wondered for a moment where I was, and then realized that I was sitting in the middle of a steaming dripping Annamese jungle, surrounded by half a dozen men as alien to me as human beings could be, about to embark upon a somewhat desperate undertaking, and incidentally serving a foreign power in the Far East; I, who had thought, at one time, to lead a peaceful life as a British sailor; and at another, as an officer in the army of a Moroccan potentate. Seaman, trooper, slave, cavalry instructor, pilgrim to Mecca, French political prisoner. And now a ha'penny-a-day *légionnaire*. *Vogue la galère*. What was I doing in this galley? Nodding, for one thing.

In the jungle something stirred. And the *Doi* Linh Nghi seated himself beside me.

"It's all right," he whispered. "He's there. I've been into the village. Had a talk with a well-beaten *nhaque* whom they've 'taxed' of all he possessed. He doesn't like them much. He won't hinder—if he hasn't the pluck to help. I've left the gate unfastened. No risk. No danger. Not the slightest. All drunk on *choum-choum*, or disgracefully drugged with opium."

"Shameful," I observed, and *Doi* Linh Nghi, opium addict, chuckled.

This was excellent news, and the remarkably fortunate state of affairs would greatly facilitate operations. Not only had Deleuze impressed upon me that this important De-Nha would be much more valuable to him alive than dead, but I had most definite scruples about killing him or encompassing his death. I think I should have felt the same had he been an enemy of England instead of rebel against France, in spite of his horrible record for fiendish cruelty, torture, and murder.

Nor, most definitely, did I want to be killed, much less to

fall into the hands of these people.

I shuddered as I thought of some of the revolting soul-shocking sights that I had seen when we had recovered the bodies of our wounded, victims of these fiends.

Doubtless, there again, the tremendous thunderstorm which had lasted with unabated vigour for most of the night, had befriended us, for it was the custom among the *yak*, Black Flags, river pirates and jungle dacoits, to carouse, drown fear, and give themselves Dutch courage on the occasion of a big storm at night coinciding with some war-like undertaking or predatory excursion.

While probably they would stoutly deny that they were either religious or superstitious, they would be willing to admit that one never knew; that the gods or devils who hurled the thunder-bolts and shook the world with their rumblings and grumblings, their ravings and roarings, might well be inimical, jealous of the prowess of warriors like themselves and of the fame of their leaders.

Anyhow, draughts of potent rice-alcohol and pipes of opium produced not only a joyous and care-free spirit, but a succeeding peace and, eventually, oblivion to din, devildom and danger.

Again I nodded and dozed, and was awakened by *Doi Linh Nghi* shaking me gently.

"Eat and drink, *Nai*," he whispered and, nothing loth, I took my hard-boiled eggs and bread from my haversack, ate them with relish, and took a pull at the cold coffee in my water-bottle. Not a particularly elegant or hearty meal, but how many a time would I not have given all I possessed for such a feast when I was a starving Apprentice in the *Valkyrie*.

By the time I had finished, there was a suggestion of dawn in the sky, and I rose to my feet.

"Hear and heed me," whispered I to my followers. "Load rifles," and each man put a cartridge into the breach of his Gras rifle, carefully licking the bullet with his tongue as he did so—whether for luck or with the idea of facilitating its passage through the barrel and the air, I don't know, though I have frequently seen *légionnaires* do the same thing with each cartridge that they used.

"Rifles in the left hand," I ordered. "Draw *mâchètes*. No man is to fire unless I do. Understand, if any man fires his rifle before I fire mine, I will kill him—and fine him too. We are going into this village and out again, as quickly and quietly as we can; and we are going to bring a man with us. Don't forget. We are dacoits and this is a raid, a *dah*. But without robbery or bloodshed, if we can help it."

I then bade *Doi* Linh Nghi repeat my instructions and give them any further details, orders, and information.

"Listen, Yellow-bellies," he said. "The dogs of brigands are opium-drunk. And if the villagers had the guts of lice they'd cut their throats, for last night the dacoits looted them of everything they couldn't hide. The *lu thuong* doesn't love them any more than he does us. The *nhaques* won't interfere. If anyone tries to do so, flick his nose off with a *mâchète*. No need to be rough, though. But if the people in Yen Trang all wake up, and do want a fight, they can have it. With *mâchètes*. No shooting, though, until the *linhtap lanxa* here gives the word. Remember and obey, or the bellies of pythons be your graves. Very suitable too. . . . Follow me."

"Yes—and you follow me, *Doi*," I added, damping the spreading fires of his importance; and, taking the lead, I crept in the direction of the village, now dimly visible in the growing light.

Moving slowly and silently, we made our way along the path that we had left during the night, and followed it to where it ended at the gate in the stockade surrounding Yen Trang.

As we approached I saw that this stockade was itself surrounded by a quite considerable moat, covered with lily pads or lotus plants. Across it, the path was carried by a bank of earth. Creeping along this, I found that, as *Doi* Linh Nghi had said, the great ironwood gate was unfastened.

Slowly and gently as I could, I pushed it inward; though, careful as I was, there was a hideous groaning when the clumsily-constructed door moved.

As soon as it was possible, I slipped through the aperture, my heart in my mouth, while I wondered whether I should get a big Snider bullet or a spear in my chest as I did so.

But again the *Doi's* information was accurate. The villagers were not astir, and whatever rebel sentries had been posted had evidently taken refuge from the storm and solace from care.

Save for the yelping of pariah curs and the crowing of a rooster, the place was like a village of the dead.

Before me was an inner wall or barricade of bamboo, thick hedge, and earth-backed wattle. In this, opposite the main gate, was a door of the kind that does not open and shut, but is raised and lowered. It was raised. The knocking-away of a bamboo pole that supported this would cause the heavy door to fall, like a portcullis, and close the second entrance to the village.

Glancing through this, I found I was looking down the main street of Yen Trang, the houses appearing well-built of sun-dried mud, and thatched with reeds, some actually having green chicks or blinds of split bamboo hanging down across their doorways.

"Which *caigna*?" I whispered to the *Doi*, and he answered my question by again taking the lead.

Swiftly, in single file, we went up the street, glancing anxiously from left to right and—speaking for myself, at any rate—with swiftly beating hearts.

Turning a corner, *Doi* Linh Nghi glanced back at me, grinned cheerfully, and pointed to where, a few metres further on, was a chick-covered doorway in a high wall.

As, unconcernedly, he raised this for me to enter, I wondered precisely how far this expedition would have penetrated into the village of Yen Trang, but for the great thunderstorm and the consequent orgy of its present garrison. It would have been a very different and more gory story—had any of us lived to tell it.

Stepping under the raised chick, I found myself in a tiled *patio* or garden court-yard, in the centre of which was a well, over-hung by a blossoming guava tree.

Round three sides of the courtyard were huts and

stables. On the other was a superior house whose neat thatch and split bamboo blinds gave it a curiously smug and urban air. To me it was a most unexpected villa to find inside that savage stockade, planted in the heart of the Cambodian jungle.

Even as I glanced round the court-yard and up at the house, a door opened, and a small fat man came, or rather staggered, forth; a shifty-looking person with a weak chinless face from which depended the longest and thinnest moustache and most stringy straggly beard I have ever beheld.

"*Toi!* Stop!" cried *Doi* Linh Nghi in a harsh stage whisper. "*Adhow di?* Where are you off to?"

The sight of seven desperate-looking ruffians, each with a rifle in one hand and a *mâchète* in the other, appeared to afford this man no surprise whatever.

It was he who afforded the surprise, for, staggering toward me in a drunken fashion, he emitted a piteous groan, collapsed at my feet, grinned amiably, joined his hands, and extended them toward me as though in prayer.

It was not until I observed that one of the extended hands held a cord, which the *Doi* promptly seized and wound about the man's wrists, that I realized that this was the *lu thuong*, the headman, and that the simple villager was acting according to arrangement, playing his artless part in the drama of De-Nha's capture.

With his *mâchète* the *Doi* cut a superfluous end from the cord, and tied together the man's feet. I then witnessed a small example of the curious matter-of-fact cold-bloodedness with which these people are wont to behave, upon occasion; for, pinching up a considerable portion of the *lu thuong*'s plump cheek, the *Doi* drew the edge of his *mâchète* across it, making quite a nasty cut, which was promptly followed by the considerable effusion of blood.

Upon this gash the *Doi* pressed his palm and then dabbed it about the man's face until he was a most sanguinary spectacle. Not content with this, he then pulled up the man's cotton sleeve and treated his arm in like manner.

Nor did the *lu thuong* flinch, much less object, when the sharp *mâchète* was drawn across the flesh of his biceps.

The whole affair had not occupied more than a minute, but by the time the *Doi* again picked up his rifle, the *lu thuong* was a mess.

Obviously he was a brave man who had put up a strong resistance and suffered severe wounds in the defence, not only of hearth and home but of the rebel officer and spy, De-Nha, for whose safety he was, for the time being, responsible.

With a surprisingly occidental wink, the *lu thuong* groaned as the *Doi*, having admired his handiwork, kicked him in the ribs.

"*De-oh! De-oh!*" moaned the *lu thuong*.

"Is he still in the inner room?" hissed the *Doi*.

"Yes, on the bed, under the mosquito curtain," whispered the *lu thuong* between groans.

"*De-oh! De-oh!*" he wailed. "I am undone."

"Without doubt," replied the *Doi*, adding for his victim's further comfort, "and I'll flick your head off as we come back, if anything goes wrong."

"Hurry up, *Doi*!" I urged nervously. "Come on. . . ."

Leading the way, again, with my heart in my mouth, I raised the bamboo chick, opened the door through which the *lu thuong* had come out, and found myself in a big screened verandah.

Opposite was another door. This proved to open into a passage, on the left side of which was a room.

Glancing in, I saw that this was evidently the inner room to which the *lu thuong* had referred.

Leaving two *tirailleurs* in the court-yard, two in the verandah, and one in the passage, with orders to give warning of danger and to use only their *mâchètes* if attacked, I entered the room, followed by the *Doi* and the other *tirailleurs*.

On the floor lay a brawny and burly Chinese, dressed in felt-soled boots, black trousers and a thin white linen coat. Beside him was a rifle and cartridge pouch, and in his belt a big knife.

Judging from his size and obvious strength, and the fact that he was sleeping across the doorway, I decided that he was De-Nha's personal bodyguard, and probably a very useful one, when sober.

On a large wooden couch, under a mosquito curtain, lay the man who must be De-Nha, dressed in a black silk *sarong* and white silk singlet.

His yellow-ivory face was not one that, in any circumstances, would have inspired me with admiration, affection, or confidence.

Beside him lay an opium pipe, and on a little table, close to the bed, the usual lamp, skewer, and silver box.

"De-Nha, the *ly-truong*," grunted the *Doi* . . . "Shall I cut this fellow's head off?" he added, staring contemptuously at the insensible Chinese.

"What were your orders?" I asked coldly. "Are you sure that the man on the bed is De-Nha?"

"Look at his green silk turban. Look how his hair is rolled. Look at his little finger-nail."

And indeed the nail of the little finger of his left hand was some six inches in length; a revolting sight.

Beside him lay a Winchester repeater and a revolver of the latest American pattern.

"Looks as though we have got to carry him," I said.

The *Doi* snorted.

"Let him carry himself."

"How are you going to wake him?"

"Light a cigarette and stick the red-hot end up his nose. Or I'll shove the point of a knife under his fingernail."

"Nothing of the sort. Try hauling him off the bed."

And, *con amore*, the *Doi* seized De-Nha by one foot, put his own against the side of the couch and hauled.

A moment later the rebel officer was lying beside his faithless bodyguard.

"Up, you dog," growled the *Doi* and planted a most useful kick in the prostrate man's ribs.

On the window-sill stood a porous earthenware water-*chatti* in a state of perspiration.

Seizing this, I inverted it above De-Nha's head, and a

stream of cold water splashed down upon him, to the detriment of his white silk vest, as the earth of the floor turned to mud.

With a deep shuddering sigh De-Nha opened his eyes.

"Kill me," he said, and closed them again. Obviously there was no need to fear that this drunk would raise an alarm. He was opium-drugged to the point of insensibility.

And again the *Doi* kicked him heavily in the ribs.

"I wish you wouldn't do that, *Doi* Linh Nghi," said I.

"What did he do to a dozen of our men after the fight at Cao-Lang?" growled the *Doi*. "Fed them—on each other's eyeballs."

"He did, eh? Well, tell him I'll feed you on his, unless he gets up and comes quietly."

This the *Doi* did. Then, going beyond these instructions, and adding performance to promise, he spat a stream of red betel-nut juice on the man's throat, laid down his rifle, drew a line with his fore-finger across the bare neck and raised his *mâchète*.

"Yes, kill me," smiled De-Nha, and closed his eyes.

This was definitely annoying. The minutes were passing, and I was extremely anxious to go. Also determined to take De-Nha with me, alive.

"We'll drag him," said I.

Promptly the *Doi* seized one of De-Nha's bare feet and signalled to the *tirailleur* to take the other.

"Gag him, tie his hands together behind his back, and then drag him."

The *Doi* snatched the green turban from the man's head, turned him over, wrenched his hands behind him, bound his arms tightly together with the long silk turban, cut off a foot from the end of it, forced the man's mouth open, and stuffed as much of the silk as possible, and apparently more, into his mouth.

A moment later De-Nha was travelling rapidly out of the room, out of the house, and across the court-yard, face downward, and emitting strange muffled sounds.

Across the *patio* we hurried, down the village street, pursued only by yelping dogs, out through the gates, across the bridge and into the jungle.

Here, panting with haste and exertion, the four men in charge of De-Nha, at a signal from the *Doi*, flung him down.

"Going to walk?" asked the *Doi* and was answered by a vigorous nodding of the long-haired head.

"Untie him and take the gag out," I ordered.

"Let two men go in front as point; one man as connecting file; and you and three men will be in charge of the prisoner. I'll march ten metres behind you. Drop a man for rear-guard, a hundred metres behind me. If we are followed, he is to shoot. Tie one end of the turban to the prisoner's right hand and the other end to a *tirailleur's* left hand. If he attempts to escape, knock him out with a rifle-butt. But tell him he'll be cut down with *mâchètes* and that I'll shoot him too. Tell your men I'll shoot them also, if he gets away. Shoot everybody. Shoot you. Shoot myself. Shoot the moon. Come on. We'll hurry along before it gets hot."

Definitely I was elated, joyful; and probably nervous and chatty by reason of a rising temperature.

And on, at a jog-trot, we made our way back through the jungle, to the obvious indignation of flocks of white-breasted jays which followed us along, squawking their protests and ribald comments.

Soon the sun came up, a great ball of fire, and in spite of the dense shadow of huge iron-wood trees, areca and macaw palms, bamboo and wild plantain, it grew quickly hotter, so that our soaking clothing dried, and, sweat as we might, dry it remained.

Hours later, we emerged from the jungle and began our weary crossing of the long paddy-bunds, until at long last we reached the Fort, where, on a chair in the shadow of the gateway, sat Captain Deleuze watching and waiting.

He rose to his feet and came to meet us, as our ruffianly mud-bespattered party approached.

"Got him, eh? Well done, *mon enfant*. Let the *Doi* and his men dismiss, but tell him to parade here at Retreat. I'd like him to be present when I question De-Nha. He's bound to have some bright ideas, especially if De-Nha won't utter. You'll come too, and take down question and answer, *verbatim*, in French. Can do? Good. Dismiss."

CHAPTER VI

That evening I was accordingly present at the extremely interesting interview between Captain Deleuze, wonderful Intelligence Officer, and De-Nha, Black Flag pirate, dacoit, rebel officer and confidant of the great De-Nam who was Chief Mandarin and principal fighting General of the exiled Emperor Ham-Nghi, and himself uncrowned king of all Yen-The, and northern Indo-China.

It was a remarkable contest of wills; Deleuze, cold, relentless, determined, and with unlimited power over the fate of his prisoner; De-Nha, diabolically clever, subtle, elusive, supple, but equally determined, and with complete power over Deleuze's power, inasmuch as he valued his life at nothing, and feared pain not at all.

Deleuze sat at his table, note-book and pencil before him. I was at a smaller one, to one side, with paper, pen and ink. *Doi* Linh Nghi, in undress mufti, squatted on the ground at Deleuze's left hand; the prisoner, a cord about his neck held by an Annamese Corporal, stood between two *tirailleurs* with loaded rifles and fixed bayonets, his feet fastened together by a short chain, and a large and heavy log of ironwood attached to his right ankle.

Deleuze was taking no chances with so slippery a customer as De-Nha. The man, while a prisoner, would be well fed and reasonably well housed and treated, receiving no brutality, injury or insult; but he was, from the French point of view, a traitor taken in armed rebellion rather than an ordinary prisoner of war, as well as a man with a shocking record of fiendish barbarity to such wounded and prisoners as came into his hands.

Searching question and evasive answer followed more quickly than I could translate and record; and, from time to time, I had to beg for respite while I caught up.

"All-right. Plenty of time," said Captain Deleuze. "I want you to get everything down. What are you writing there for his last answer?"

" '*I have never seen any European at General De-Nam's headquarters. Nor have I ever heard of any European officer being at General De-Nam's headquarters. Nor have I ever heard of the Chinese Generals Ba-Ky and Luong-Tam-Ky.*' "

"That's right. Quite right. Ready?"

And question and answer proceeded.

"Of what nationality is the European who is well known to be helping General Luu-Ky."

"I have never heard of Luu-Ky."

"When were you last in the Quang-Yen province?"

"I have never been there."

"When were you last in Lang-Son?"

"I have never been there."

"In Lam?"

"I have never been there."

"In Cao-Bang?"

"I have never been there."

"In Ha-Giang?"

"I have never been there."

"In fact, you know nothing, and you know that wrong, eh?"

"I know nothing of these matters."

"And you are going to tell nothing but lies, eh?"

"I cannot tell what I don't know."

"And you know nothing and know that wrong, as we have just said? Ah. . . . Exactly. . . . Now my friend. You have given me no information whatever. Suppose I give you no food whatever?"

"Then I shall die of starvation, and you will still know nothing."

"And suppose I allow you no sleep whatever?"

"Then I shall go mad and die from want of sleep, and you will still know nothing."

"And suppose I allow you no drink whatever."

De-Nha gave Captain Deleuze a quick look, and his eyes fell. He licked dry lips.

"I shall tell you nothing," he said.

"We shall see," replied Deleuze, eyeing his captive thoughtfully as he tapped his note-book with his pencil.

"Take him outside and wait in the verandah," he ordered the Corporal of Annamese *Tirailleurs*.

Deleuze sat in silent thought for a minute.

"Well, *Doi* Linh Nghi," he said. "What steps would you take to get information out of this man?"

"Just what you had better do, *Ong-Quang-Ba*," grinned the *Doi*. "This jungle dog is fool enough to be an opium addict, and by the look of him has got to the point where he cannot live without it; where he'll do anything for it. Keep him without any, until he's going mad, and then allow him one pipe of *sai*. Just one pipe. That will make the craving far worse, and before long he'll reach the stage at which he'll do anything, *anything*, for more opium. Do anything on this earth—even tell the truth. Then save his life with half a dozen pipes of good *chandu* while you find out whether he has told the truth or not. Then cut off his opium again until he's ready to tell you some more."

"Better than torture, eh?" smiled Deleuze.

"Better than torture? It *is* torture. The very worst that could be devised. And the only one that will make him talk. You couldn't get a word out of him with a knife or with fire. No—not if you crucified him upside-down on a sunny wall. I'll say that for the dog. But no man who is as accustomed to opium as he is, could stand its being suddenly cut off. It isn't possible. Even I couldn't do it."

"But you don't use opium, *Doi*, surely?"

"Oh, no, *Ong-Quang-Ba*. Not to say use it. Just occasionally, perhaps I . . ."

"But never more than once a day. And never more than ten pipes, eh?"

Doi Linh Nghi grinned sheepishly.

"Smoking opium is a very bad thing," he said.

"Well, if smoking opium is a bad thing, we'll see how bad not-smoking it is—for our friend De-Nha," decided Deleuze.

§2

It proved an immeasurably bad thing for De-Nha, and broke him completely, mind, body and soul.

Had I not witnessed the results of this sudden deprivation of opium, I should never have believed that they could have been so drastic and comprehensive—in fact, fatal; for had he not received a pipe of opium when he did, undoubtedly he would have died.

That there might be no possibility of bribery and corruption, Captain Deleuze placed De-Nha in my charge, with the *Doi* to assist me, he selecting a couple of other *Tirailleurs Tonkinois*, relatives of his, who, in the first place, could be trusted to obey his orders absolutely, and who, in the second place, would have no opportunity of disobeying them.

Ordinary guards and sentries, about the hut in which he was confined, would prevent De-Nha's escape; my particular business was to prevent his purchasing opium from anybody, a thing he would certainly endeavour to do, and be in a position to do, if not watched and prevented.

Subtle and cunning as he was, the *Doi* was a match for him; and, as De-Nha's condition soon proved, our arrangements were efficacious.

His prison was a room provided with one barred window, some eight feet from the ground, and a strong door, in which there was a grill, opening into an outer room.

Beneath the window was not only the sentry on duty, but one of the *Doi's* followers; while I myself—or, in my absence, the *Doi*—always occupied the outer room into which De-Nha's cell opened.

In the verandah of this outer room squatted another of the *Doi's* Annamese, and very frequently, at irregular intervals, I would bid him go and change places with the colleague who was on duty with the sentry beneath the window.

My strict instructions to the *Doi* and his men were to the effect that, whenever De-Nha begged for a pipe of opium, the reply should invariably be,

"Certainly. As much as you like of the finest *chandu*—provided you answer the *Ong-Quang-Ba*'s questions truthfully."

I doubt whether anybody who has had no experience of the amazingly strong hold that opium-smoking gets upon its addicts, can visualize or imagine the horrible sufferings that deprivation causes these poor wretches.

De-Nha, at certain times in the day, suffered real torture; acute agony so obviously terrible that I would certainly have alleviated it, had it not been my duty to do otherwise. Badly as he suffered throughout the day, the torture reached its climax at the times at which he was wont to indulge in his horrible vice. It was quite clear that midday and sunset were the hours when he "drank the black smoke".

Toward noon he would begin to yawn, the yawning increasing in length and strength until it became prodigious. This phase would be followed by one of a jerking of the limbs, a spasmodic and violent starting and jumping, a sudden rictus of nervous twitching. This would only cease when he burst into the most profuse perspiration that I had ever seen. The man did not sweat. It was as though he were a great sponge suddenly wrung by a giant hand. He spurted water from every pore.

And he wept like a child and,

> Albeit unused to the melting mood
> Dropped tears as fast as the Arabian trees
> Their medicinal gum.

And then, even by the second day, he would literally pray to be given a pipe of opium, one tiny pellet; and he would swear by everything he held sacred, and with obvious sincerity, that he would pay for the opium with a diamond bigger than the pellet itself.

I was present, both at noon and evening, on the second day; and found it very painful to witness this man's sufferings, and to hear his desperate prayers. I was glad when the praying gave place to swearing.

There was nothing pathetic, pitiful or pitiable about this phase, this truly amazing stream of violent malediction and filthy invective. It was really remarkable, something new even to me, who had heard the worst efforts of drunken sailors; of stevedores and wharf rats; of blue-nose Captains and bucko Mates who were artists; of angry Life-Guardsmen; of enraged Arabs, who are no mean performers, and—of comrades in the Legion.

Never before, and never since, have I heard anything to equal De-Nha's range, violence and fluency.

The next stage was collapse. Words would fail him, and then, quite literally foaming at the mouth, he would fall back on his frame-and-string couch and into a shuddering rigor distressing to witness, his sunken eyes staring blindly from their darkened sockets, his face a yellow death-mask.

And there he would lie and gasp, fighting for breath and, apparently, for life.

At the end of about an hour from the beginning of the attack, he would be still and, seemingly, dead. From this state of coma, he would, later, emerge, weak, miserable, and ill.

I was surprised that such a seizure, occuring twice a day, did not have fatal consequences; but Captain Deleuze, a man of wide experience in this and all other matters pertaining to Indo-China, concerning which he was even then writing his famous book, *Notes Cambodgiennes*, was quite certain that nothing of the sort would occur.

"He'll suffer all right, poor devil; but he won't die," he said. "What remains to be seen is whether his opium-smoking has left him with enough guts to withstand deprivation for long. Personally I doubt it."

He was right. The attacks grew worse and, after bearing his agony for a week, De-Nha gave in, offered to answer any one question Captain Deleuze liked to ask, return for one pipe of opium; and to give him all the information that lay in his power, if he would give him the daily allowance to which he was accustomed.

Accordingly, just before noon, the yawning and trembling De-Nha was again brought before the Captain as on the previous occasion.

"I'm going to ask you a question, and you are going to answer it. I shall then give you one pipe of opium," pronounced Captain Deleuze.

His shaking hands clasped, his black eyes almost starting from his head, De-Nha profusely thanked his captor, swore to tell the truth, and begged him to ask quickly and give him the pipe.

"I shall do that at midday and evening, until I find out whether you have told me the truth. If you have, you will get a pipe for each question, until I know all I want to know; and, thereafter, the daily allowance to which you are accustomed. If I find you have not told me the truth, you will get no more opium from that moment. Also you will be brought to trial for armed rebellion in a pacified zone, making war on the French Republic, and for murder—for the brutal torture and murder of French subjects."

"The question! The question! . . . and the pipe," begged De-Nha.

"*Bien!* The question. Now then, speak the truth. What is the name of the European whom the Chinese Government has sent to help General De-Nam's *Pavilions Noirs*?"

"Kar-Ling."

"Say that again," said Captain Deleuze, putting his hand to his ear and listening with the utmost care.

"Kar-Ling," repeated De-Nha.

"Again."

"Kar-Ling."

"Now," said Deleuze, turning to me. "Think of an English name that sounds like Kar-Ling."

"Well, there's Carling. I've never actually met the name, but it sounds English."

"Yes, now shorten the 'a' which they always lengthen."

"Kolling," I said. "That might be English, but I don't know the name. Oh, there's Colin, though; but that's a Christian name in my country."

"Yes, now put on the 's' which these people always drop."

"Oh, Collins! Yes, Collins. That's quite a common English

and Irish name. Or, possibly, an Irish name that is quite common in England. I don't know which . . ."

"That's it," said Deleuze, a note of triumph in his voice. "Collins. An English and Irish name. That there *is* such a man, and that his name is Collins, accords with my previous information. . . . De-Nha, I think you are speaking the truth. You shall have one opium-pipe, and I will see you again at sunset."

And at Retreat, De-Nha was again brought before Captain Deleuze and questioned.

"Are the Chinese Generals who are helping General De-Nam and the Black Flags, named Ba-Ky and Luong-Tam-Ky?"

"Yes, they are," was the prompt reply.

And again De-Nha was given a pipe of opium.

Day after day, the broken man was questioned, and on each occasion he gave a piece of information in return for a pipe.

But one pipe, to a man accustomed to a score, was the merest palliative, and only served partially to tide him over the worst of his awful nerve storms.

Before long, he was only too willing to tell everything he knew, in return for five pipes of opium at midday and five at sunset.

It occurred to Captain Deleuze, that, by raising the opium reward from five pipes to seven, De-Nha might be induced not only to tell everything he knew, but to suggest everything helpful to the French that he could; and the *Doi* accordingly received instructions to change his attitude, or, rather, his manner, toward the rebel.

He and his followers were to do their utmost to cultivate his friendship. So far was this to be carried, that the *Doi* was, on his own account, to give De-Nha an extra pipe of opium. This was to be done in pure kindliness and *bon-homie*, though if De-Nha chose to reward the *Doi*, there would be no harm in that.

To me, Deleuze explained that he really saw no reason why De-Nha should not be won over to the French side, especially if he had some experience of the benefits that had undeniably accrued to those leading Annamese who had accepted French protection and friendship, and who had remained loyal to their new allies.

If he contrasted this with the fate of those who proved disloyal, he might draw a moral and learn a lesson, an object lesson sufficiently striking to impress the said moral deeply upon his mind.

And apart from this, there was the question as to whether he might not consider life, in the rôle of a well-rewarded and faithful friend of the French, as being vastly superior to that of a hunted jungle-dacoit, whose ultimate end must, at very best, be exile from Cambodia to China or elsewhere.

"Anyway," decided Deleuze, "it's worth trying."

And there again opium was to play its part.

This does not mean that it was to be suggested to De-Nha that he would get more or better opium by joining the French; but that Deleuze the Psychologist was going to use De-Nha's opium craving, first to introduce to his mind, and then make it something of an *idée fixe* therein, that his welfare and his life depended on fidelity to the French.

"Now then, Sinbad the Bad Sinner," said Deleuze to me, one day, as I reported at his room, which was the Intelligence Bureau of the garrison. "I've got absolutely everything out of De-Nha, both in the way of information and advice. From information to sound advice was a short step under the opium urge. Let's see how long a step it will be from good advice to active assistance; and from that to the turning of the coat.

"Yes, that turning of the coat, which the conqueror calls loyalty—to him," he added cynically. "Now look. Cut down his pipes by two a day, one in the morning and one in the evening, until he begins to get desperate again. Then let *Doi* Linh Nghi be a friend in need, the true friend in sore need. Let him give him one, unknown to you, and say to him, as he does so, the first time,

" '*Why don't you join us—and have plenty?*' And again in the evening, the second time,

" '*What a fool is the man who lives like a beast in the jungle, when he can live like a mandarin in a town, protected by the French flag.*'

"To-morrow when he has got De-Nha begging on his knees for the extra one, let him say,

" '*Why don't you join us? Look at me—wife, house, rations, pay, pension. Nothing would induce me to go back and be a jungle dog.*'

"Then in the evening,

" '*I wish I were you, De-Nha. The French would make you an officer, a civil official, a judge, a rich man, a mandarin.*' That sort of thing. Understand?"

I assured Captain Deleuze that I quite understood.

"Then, at the end of about a week, take a hand yourself—along the same lines, until you think the time is ripe for making him a fair offer—and we'll see how he reacts to it."

"But could you trust him, Sir?" I asked. "He strikes me as being a most awful scoundrel."

"It is because he's a most awful scoundrel that I trust him," smiled Captain Deleuze.

And, doubtless noting my look of puzzled bewilderment, added,

"It is only because he's a most awful scoundrel that I can get him to betray his side—in return for a handful of opium. It is only because he's a most awful scoundrel that I can appeal to a scoundrel's self-interest—that being his only ideal. . . . When the time comes, I shall promise him that, if he joins us, his past sins will be forgiven him. He shall have rank and pay as an agent—in the Intelligence Service. And, after the war, a civil job proportionate to his ability and usefulness. All this, provided he proves his good faith by undertaking a certain job I have in mind.

"And you'll be in on that, my lad," he added, giving me one of his straight, piercing glances.

"And, meanwhile, I think we'll stage an execution for his benefit; or, at any rate, let him witness one, at a moment when he's not feeling too good—somewhere about midday or sunset, eh?"

That struck me as definitely cruel; but I reflected that

inasmuch as De-Nha was a notorious past-master in the art of cruelty, there would be a certain amount of poetic justice about it.

CHAPTER VII

Definitely it was a cruel business, though I imagine De-Nha would not have suffered nearly as much, had he not been on the edge of one of his terrible nervous breakdowns.

At midday on the following Saturday, seven brigands, taken in the act of dacoity and murder in a little village within the pacified zone of French influence, expiated their crimes of robbery, torture, and wanton murder.

De-Nha, almost yawning his head off, jerking and twitching like the victim of an acute attack of St. Vitus's Dance, was led from his cell and, his hands tied behind his back, taken to join them.

These seven dacoits, captured in the administered zone, had been sent for trial before the Annamese mandarins whom the French had appointed as judges—it being part of the excellent French system that, as soon as a province is declared pacified, the administration of justice is handed over to the sort of people who would have been performing the function had the French not come there.

Thus, these pirates had probably been tried by the identical functionaries who would have tried them had they been taken in dacoity in the days of Ham-Nghi, the exiled Emperor of Indo-China.

They had been tried according to Cambodian law, by Cambodian mandarin judges, sentenced, and condemned to death.

By whose direction I don't know, the Judges, as well as the condemned men, were brought from the scene of the trial in Bac-Ninh to the appointed place of execution here at Nha-Nam.

The execution was a most impressive and unpleasant business; and it made at least one of its witnesses very definitely sick.

A square having been formed by the European and Native troops stationed at Nha-Nam, the Bench of Judges— and these mandarins looked truly magnificent in their cere- monial robes of rich embroidered silk of red and gold, with handsome silk turbans of similar colour upon their heads— marched in state, at the head of a retinue of retainers, to the shaded seats provided for them.

Behind their judicial thrones stood the bearers of their huge umbrellas, each mandarin being provided with two of these, so that no ray of sunlight might strike upon his sa- cred person; their banner-men, bearing aloft the triangular flags appropriate to their rank and station; their sword- bearers; their pipe-bearers; the bearers of the silver boxes in which were their betel-leaf and areca-nut (the *pan-supari* of India) and a motley horde of retainers, in somewhat dirty red uniforms, a shabby riff-raff crew, of duties unspecified.

I don't know whether their journey from Bac-Ninh and the present pleasant spectacle provided for them a sort of Bank Holiday, but this herd of retainers certainly seemed remarkably happy, behaving like children at a Sunday School treat, laughing, singing, jabbering and pushing each other about, while indulging in futile and infantile horse- play. Anything less like the sober and serious retinue of Judges of a High Court of Justice could scarcely be con- ceived.

Nor did the mandarin Judges seem in the least surprised or annoyed by the conduct of their henchmen, refraining from rebuke or remonstrance, even when the Officer Commanding the garrison took his place in the seat of honour in front of their grand-stand.

All being ready, and the troops being called to attention, the prisoners were escorted from the *canha-phâ*[13] into the hollow square formed by the ranks of soldiery, French Line and Infanterie de la Marine, Annamese, and Foreign Le- gion.

The guard surrounding the dacoits were *linh-le*—manda- rin bodyguard men—in ill-fitting ill-kempt green uniforms,

---

[13] Condemned cell of native prison.

shouldering rusty rifles and wearing side-arms of which the only uniformity was their unpolished dirtiness.

Following the prisoners and guard, marched the executioner, a huge powerful Chinese wearing a red singlet on which was embroidered, in gold, a Court of Justice crest or other device; black silk trousers and felt-soled boots. His bare arms and shoulders were enormous, and in his right hand he carried a great curved sword of which the blade was over a yard long; a sword of unusual shape, in that the great gleaming blade, instead of tapering from hilt to point, grew broader as it grew longer.

I decided that doubtless this curious shape added weight to a blow so struck that only the lower part of the blade came in contact with the object to be cut.

The seven rebel dacoits and the unfortunate De-Nha walked in single file, their hands bound behind them; and I must say that they displayed the utmost courage and *sang-froid*.

It is all very well to say that Chinese, or other people, don't fear death, and do not regard it as we do. But I think that is rather begging the question (of courage) and refusing to give credit where credit is due. For the fact remains that all of them, with the exception of the first man executed, were to witness the infliction of a particularly hideous form of death that was about to be similarly meted out to themselves.

Anyhow, I was impressed by their coolness and courage, and only hoped that if I were in such circumstances, I could bear myself as bravely and stoically as these robbers did. Certainly nothing in their lives became them like the leaving of it.

When the prisoners and escort were halted in front of the Commanding Officer and the Judges' grand-stand, they talked, laughed, and chatted as though they were about to witness a race-meeting, instead of the slaughter of each other; turned about and took a lively interest in their surroundings; and, from time to time, with great nonchalance, yawned, scratched themselves, and ejected the red betel-nut juice with which their mouths were, as usual, filled.

The executioner, being ready, made them extend to the left at four paces interval, De-Nha being at the end of the line of eight men, and some thirty yards from the first one.

The prisoners being in their appointed places, the executioner's assistant visited each one, unbuttoned and turned down the collar of his cotton coat, and bade him kneel.

It interested me to note that this young gentleman—evidently an executioner's apprentice hoping to rise by industry, zeal, and the closest attention to duty, to the lofty rank of executioner himself—was concerned to see that there were no stones, lumps, or other undesirable irregularities which might cause discomfort to his patients when they knelt. Obviously he bade them take such ease as might be possible to those who kneel with their hands bound behind them, their heads bent and necks offered ready for the edge of the sword.

Of De-Nha I took particular note, and saw that he was as cool, unconcerned and courageous as the other seven. As he looked about him, between his terrific yawns, and glanced at the Commanding Officer, at the Judges, at Captain Deleuze and at me standing behind that officer, there was not the slightest suggestion of appeal in the look he gave us, nor were his tremendous jerks and twitchings in any way to be confused with the ordinary trembling and shivering of a frightened man.

Had he at that moment made any appeal, whether to man or to the gods he worshipped, it would have been for opium, and not for his life. . . .

The eight prisoners being on their knees and, by the standards of the assistant executioner, comfortable, the sentence of the Mandarins' Court was read aloud, that all the Annamese natives assembled might know of the offences of these men, and bear witness to the righteousness of the punishment that they so richly deserved.

This having been done, the executioner looked toward the Commanding Officer, who raised his hand. The executioner then thrust the index finger of his left hand into his mouth, advanced to the first of the condemned men and traced a wet line of red betel-juice, almost like red paint, across the back of his bare neck, just where the spinal column joins the skull.

He then took the long hilt of his great sword in both hands, stepped back a pace, swung it aloft, remained motionless for a second while he took aim, and then brought it down like a thunder-bolt or a flash of lightning upon the outstretched neck of his victim. One heard the *swish* of the sword through the air, and the dull *thud* with which it encountered the neck; and one saw the head straightway fall to the ground and roll.

An absolutely clean cut, removing the head as neatly as a flower is struck from its stalk by a cane.

I noted that the body did not fall immediately. For quite a perceptible time it remained kneeling, while blood spurted to a distance of at least six feet. It moved to and fro once, while yet erect; and then slowly collapsed.

Personally I did not feel at all well. I glanced from the decapitated man to the others. All had their heads turned to the right and were watching with deep interest. On the face of not one of them was there any look of fear, horror or disgust. Definitely they took a sporting interest in the executioner's technique and degree of skill.

The executioner, I noticed, stooped, touched the blood with his finger, and then smeared his own lips; this being, as I learned later, a specific charm against any retaliation, by evil influence, on the part of the spirit of the dead man.

He then approached the second captive, and as he did so the man spoke.

Looking up into the executioner's face, he uttered his last words.

"A damn' good swipe!" said he—that being an exact translation of his remark in Annamese.

The executioner nodded his appreciation of the compliment.

Again he wetted with betel-juice the neck now well outstretched for his convenience.

Personally I had seen enough, and closed my eyes.

I could not close my ears, however; and seven times I

heard that dreadful swish and thud, *swish* and *thud*, *swish* and *thud*, at intervals of about two minutes.

And then Captain Deleuze, as doubtless had been arranged between him and the Commanding Officer, walked over to where De-Nha knelt.

Having talked with him for a while, Captain Deleuze bade him get to his feet and return to his hut, to which place I, *Doi* Linh-Nghi and his corporal's-guard, escorted him.

Captain Deleuze afterwards told me that at the psychological moment when De-Nha had seen the heads of his seven fellow-captives fall, he had offered him his life and all the opium he wanted, if he would forthwith abandon the utterly lost cause of the exiled Emperor Ham Nghi; leave the service of General De-Nam; and accept the authority of the French Republic that had supplanted the late rulers, and that would, henceforth and for ever more, rule Indo-China.

De-Nha, observing that opium was essential to his happiness, and life essential to the proper enjoyment of his opium, agreed to make his submission to the French, and to take service under them in return for opium, life, freedom —and for reward and promotion in accordance with his deserts.

After having smoked a dozen pipes and slept for a few hours, De-Nha was accordingly allowed to leave his cell, and to walk abroad in the excellent, if not desired, company of myself and the *Doi*.

As we passed the entrance to the Fort, we beheld seven long bamboo poles, on the top of each of which was a head, recently the property of one of the murderers executed at midday.

"They'll never smoke again," grinned the *Doi*, jerking a thumb in the direction of the heads.

"Just what I was thinking," replied De-Nha.

Our instructions, and De-Nha's condition, were now changed. His cell became his bedroom; the outer, or guard-room, his sitting-room; and the verandah, the abiding-place of his servant, the said servant being one of *Doi* Linh-Nghi's *tirailleurs* who had orders to do anything in reason that De-Nha desired, but never to let him out of his sight.

My duty, for the time being, was to cultivate the man; and, if not to grapple him to my soul with hoops of steel, to attach him thus to the French cause, appealing alike to his cupidity and his ambition.

It was a somewhat distasteful, but extremely interesting, task to make a study of this dacoit, ex-officer of Mandarins' Irregulars, whose outlook on life, experiences, philosophy and standards differed so widely from my own. He was, of course, infinitely cleverer than I, as well as being equipped with weapons that were not in my armoury at all— such as a complete lack of scruple and truthfulness, and all that Europeans regard as necessary to common honesty and the preservation of self-respect. In saying this, I do not lose sight of the fact that it was a game of wits, and that it was my duty to pit the man's cupidity and self-interest against any loyalty that he might cherish towards his exiled Emperor and his former employers. What I mean is, that, in small matters and in great, he would lie in the most circumstantial manner, while asseverating the truth of what he said with every binding oath of which he could think; and that therein I was handicapped.

Every day I indulged freely in the pleasures of his society and conversation, and carried out Captain Deleuze's instructions that I should see a great deal of him, endeavour to win his confidence, and form an accurate conclusion as to his real sentiments and intentions, particularly the latter.

Nor did I have to play any Judas part of false friendship, attempting to delude and deceive him. Incidentally, that would have been a rather funny sight and a foolish undertaking; unless, as is indeed possible, my blunt and straightforward simplicity were even more baffling and deceptive to him than were his subtleties, lies, and cunning wiles to me.

Anyhow, we got along together famously, De-Nha's approval of me being enhanced by the fact that Captain Deleuze was allowing him a fair ration of opium, while instructing me to increase this allowance surreptitiously when De-Nha piteously implored and entreated me to do so.

Our *Mèdecin Majeur* Baillot, himself an opium-smoker and student of the pathological effects and values of the drug, had been very interested in De-Nha's violent reaction to deprivation; and, on one occasion of his paying a visit to De-Nha, I asked him whether it would be possible to break the man of his vice by very gradual diminution of the allowance. He was of the opinion that it would not, and that when a man had gone as far along the opium-addict's path as had De-Nha, the best thing for him was—opium.

He further expressed the view that, provided De-Nha did not increase his present allowance, he would live longer with its use than he would if it were curtailed even very gradually, with a view to final elimination.

"Anyway," said *Mèdecin Majeur* Baillot, "the man is incurable, and if you were to put him on a desert island where opium was unprocurable, he would soon die, even if he were 'cured'."

I believe that Captain Deleuze had asked him for a pronouncement on the subject, with the object of keeping De-Nha alive and well—so long as he was ready, willing and able to use his undeniable talents and knowledge in the service of the French Military Intelligence Department.

CHAPTER VIII

And one day, some weeks later, Captain Deleuze took me into his confidence, paid me a great compliment, and proposed to give me the opportunity of showing what I was made of, as he expressed it in his excellent English.

When we were alone, he always talked to me in my own language, partly, doubtless, for practice in idiom, pronunciation and accent, though that was not in the least necessary, and partly for secrecy and safety, as there was not a soul, so far as we knew, European or Annamese, who could speak or understand English.

"Well, now, Sinbad the Sailor and Fishmonger, what do you make of your catch? Can he be trusted?" he asked.

"A difficult question to answer, Sir," I replied. "But I quite believe he can be trusted to be absolutely true and faithful —to his own interests."

"Quite so," smiled Deleuze, who had held long conversations with De-Nha. "Quite so. I think he has seen the light. The light of his own advantage. Seen the light and tasted the flesh-pots. The flesh-pots of French rewards. Yes, I think he has seen the light and tasted the flesh-pots and heard the sweet reasonable sounds of the chink of French gold-pieces—the wages of virtue. And he certainly realizes that the wages of sin is death. Yes, I think it is time he touched some wages, and smelt the incense of praise in high quarters. Then we shall have appealed to all his senses."

Captain Deleuze gnawed the tip of his right forefinger, a trick he had when thinking deeply toward a conclusion, while as yet undecided as to the issue.

"Think the bonds of his senses will hold him?" he asked, shooting one of his penetrating glances into my eyes.

"While he's here, Sir, with sufficient opium on the one hand and sudden death on the other."

"Think he'd run away if he had the chance?"

"Not unless he could run with a stock of opium," I opined.

"And suppose he could?"

"I don't know. Sir. He's so deep, so cunning, and such a liar, that it is very difficult to say whether he firmly intends to stick to the French connection for ever, or whether he means to bolt at the first opportunity, and tell General De-Nam all that he has learned here."

"Well, we'll come back to that in a moment, Sinbad the Fisherman. Listen. Suppose I give you a little longer for the casting of your nets about the soul of your queer fish, and I give him every possible inducement to remain within those nets, will you stake your life on your skill as a fisher of men?"

"Bet my life on his complete conversion—or perversion?" I asked.

"Wager it. Literally. Look; suppose you feel that you've won his confidence, so far as a creature of that type trusts anybody; and suppose I feel I've made a sufficient appeal to his cupidity and ambition; and supposing he agrees to what I'm going to propose—will you take a risk on his fidelity? His fidelity, partly to you personally, and partly to his own interests? It will be a case of greed and ambition being up against heredity, breed, blood, instincts, old loyalties, and such faith and honour as an Annamese dacoit possesses."

"Take a risk, Sir? I will if you will, of course."

"How do you mean?"

"I mean if you like to entrust me with the job, I'll do my utmost to—er—bring it off."

"I'm sure you will. Take the risk, I mean, and it will be some risk. I'm going to bank on De-Nha seeing his profit in sticking to us. I'm going to send you where only he could take you. To the Annamese Headquarters."

"General De-Nam's headquarters, Sir?" I asked, astounded.

"No. Worse than that. I've got two or three native spies there, pedlars, camp followers and such. . . . No, I'm going to send you to the real Headquarters. To the fountain-head whence flows the stream of subsidy. The place where the sinews of war are strengthened and renewed, exercised and developed. Yes, the Headquarters whence General De-Nam gets his help.

"I am quite certain that regular reinforcements and supplies of arms, ammunition and food, reach De-Nam's headquarters from a superior one, a base that is either somewhere far away on the other side of this Province, or on the actual Chinese border. Or, possibly, in China itself.

"And I want to find out all about it.

"I want to know where the base is. Of what it consists. Who commands it. And, most particularly, whether there are any European military advisers there. And if so, who they are.

"I believe that, under the influence of the opium-deprivation torture, De-Nha spoke the truth in saying that the Emperor of China has got three of his best Generals there, helping De-Nam, the former Viceroy in Yen-Thé of the now exiled Emperor of Indo-China.

"Also that they have a European adviser, the man whom he called Kar-Ling.

"Now, if Kar-Ling is the man I think he is, and of whom I have heard from other sources, he is an English adventurer and swashbuckler and soldier-of-fortune named Collins.

"And that's where you come in, my son.

"I want you to get to the real base of operations with the help of De-Nha, and there introduce yourself to your compatriot—as a fellow soldier-of-fortune. I want you to find out everything there is to be found out, not only present facts, but future plans—I'll give you details later—and make your way back here again as soon as you can. I must know what the plan of campaign for next season is, and what China is going to do about it. . . . What do you say? Can do?"

"I can try, Sir. But it seems that it will all depend on De-Nha. If he turns traitor to us . . ."

"Exactly. It will all depend on De-Nha—and on the courage and ability of Sinbad the Sailor turned Soldier, eh?"

"Now then—Committee of Ways and Means. De-Nha will have to show you the way and I shall have to find the means —of keeping him faithful . . . to us."

§2

Again Captain Deleuze told me all that he knew—and it was a good deal—about the position of affairs on the Chinese border beyond Lao Kai.

He spoke about the political situation as between the Imperial Government of China and the French Republic: about the French suspicions concerning the surreptitious assistance given, in spite of former solemn treaties, to the rebel Annamese by the Chinese, who looked with fear and suspicion upon the foreigner's encroachment not only upon the coastal lands of Eastern Asia to the south of the Flowery Kingdom, but actually in the direction of their South Eastern border (where the longer there was an active enemy of the French between the Yunnan-Kwangsi borders and Annam, the better): about the probable existence of the camp of a large force of Chinese regulars on the border beyond Lao Kai: about the probability of there being a concentration of bands of Chinese irregulars under the leadership of Chinese ex-Generals operating on this side of the border, and, from time to time stiffening the armies of the Viceroy, De-Nam, with invaluable reinforcements of well-armed, well-trained fighting men: about the frequently-confirmed suspicion that there were European adventurers, quite possibly secret and unacknowledged emissaries from European Governments, advising and assisting these forces.

He also advised me as to the dangers and difficulties of the journey right across Tonking from Houi-Bap to the Chinese border, and as to the best means of surmounting them.

Once I had crossed the border near Lao Kai, and located the camp of the Chinese Generals, I must act according to circumstances, fend for myself, gather what information I could, and return with it as quickly as possible.

"I shall send *Doi* Linh Nghi and his gang with you, Sinbad, and on them you can, of course, rely absolutely. They'll do the Faithful Unto Death business all-right.

"De-Nha himself, your guide, will be your great danger; and we'll make it quite clear to him that, whatever happens to you and the rest of the party, one of them will see to it that De-Nha is disembowelled if there is any treachery. It is just possible, in fact I think we may say it is reasonably probable, that, with big rewards on the one part and the likelihood of a dirty death on the other, he may keep his oath of fidelity to us.

"On the other hand, he may not.

"Anyhow, there it is; and you must take it or leave it, on that understanding. I'll fit you out with a good-sized *sampan* and crew; and you'll go up the Red River as far as possible.

"You can start off as a party of pedlars, and turn into pirates as soon as you are well away from Houi-Bap. The boatmen will quite understand that. They've been seeing simple villagers turn into dacoits, and river-pedlars into river-pirates, all their innocent lives.

"You yourself had better be extremely terse and taciturn —if not generally dumb. When anyone seems to think your Annamese is faulty, you are a Chinaman whose appropriate language is the To-jen of Nanningfu Kwangsi, or the Pu Tai of Yunnan; and you are not very much at home with the barbarous Tai Dam of Tonking; and if you run into a gentleman who speaks the purest To-jen of Nanningfu Kwangsi, or the Pu Tai of Yunnan, then your real tongue is the Chin Tai of the Yangtze; or, if you prefer it, Laos Yun; Kun Lu; Shan, or Ngio; Tai Nua of Muang Baw—or any other damn thing you fancy. See?

"Which language *do* you prefer?" he asked, in reply to my sickly smile.

"Deaf and dumb language, I think, Sir," I admitted.

"And a very good one too. . . . When in doubt, pull out a big knife, and stare at your questioner's stomach. . . ."

CHAPTER IX

Among the things that I shall not forget, is that journey up the Red River from a spot near Houi-Bap right across Tonking to Lao-Kai, and beyond into China.

Not that we went the whole way by water, of course; but before I finally escaped from that dreadful river, it seemed to me that I had been born on it, had lived on it, and would certainly die on it, a positive Styx, hundreds of miles in length, with De-Nha my enigmatic Charon.

By the time I had done with it, I also knew something about gorges, rapids and waterfalls; something about rain; and something about the gentle art of crouching.

For we lived in a sailing *sampan*, a craft in which one can neither stand upright nor comfortably lie down; a kind of floating one-roomed house, the room being, as I have indicated, of insufficient length and insufficient height to afford comfortable accommodation for anything bigger than a monkey or a small Chinese.

In the thatched hut of plaited straw, we squatted to cook our miserable stew; we squatted about the pot to eat the mess, our fingers sufficient for our simple needs and simpler manners; in the hut we squatted all day and all night; and shivered, wrapt in melancholy and clothed in misery as in a garment.

For weeks and weeks we poled along through heavy rain, through light rain, and through thick mist, for a change; until I came to think that there was a kind of rain and a kind of fog peculiar to the Red River and peculiarly wet, depressing, and damping, not only to straw hats and cotton clothes, but to the spirits, yea, the very souls of their occupants.

We made our slow laborious way along water, through water, on water, in water and under water, for, at times, and for very long times, the rain was so heavy that the surface of the river was but a plane dividing a mass of water of normal consistency from a mass of water slightly mixed with air.

The sky, invisible, was one vast mass of leaden grey wool, a cosmic sponge that for days and days on end was in process of steady contraction.

If the river voyage had lasted much longer, I think I should have gone mad, for I found that I had come to endow the Red River with life, with personality; a detestable devilish water-fiend of dark and muddy complexion; swift, silent, hateful, and hating, determined to sweep everything before it, on, down to the sea; everything from ant to tiger; from castor-oil plant to mighty tree.

And when, at night, I was disposed to feel grateful that I could no longer see it, I heard it; for ever sucking at its banks; for ever bringing down small avalanches of earth and clay and mud.

And not only could I hear it as I lay awake shivering in sodden misery, but I could feel it, or rather, feel its damp exhalation penetrating to my mouldy bones and spreading its vile fever throughout my racked and suffering frame.

I would rather do, day after day, the longest of forced desert marches or jungle marches, tortured by thirst, and sore from head to foot with aching pain and unbearable fatigue, than again spend those weeks of crouching in a *sampan* on the Red River of Tonking.

I was always thankful when natural obstacles, the need for provisions, or some imminent danger from nature or from man, drove us ashore and into the jungle.

Here there was hardship enough. Leeches for example—reptiles for which I have an acute natural abhorrence—and the burrowing ticks. After marching through grass, one would emerge with an absolute dado of solid tick all round one's legs, loathsome brutes that fastened on with powerful mandibles and burrowed into one's flesh, swelling as they did so. Each of these foul pests, if not carefully extracted, would leave behind it a sore place, an angry spot, that might develop into a horrible boil. Like the leeches, they were best treated with the glowing end of a cigarette, or with a burning match, when they would fall away without leaving their heads behind them, as they did if pulled out.

I think it amused my companions that I was far more concerned with ticks and leeches than I was with such trifles as tigers, black panthers, mighty pythons or poisonous snakes.

And, now and again, stretches of the jungle near the river would be delightful, especially on sunny days; and, to me, the lofty bamboos, so huge and thick, yet fragile-looking; so straight and aspiring; so pliant and supple, and yet so strong, were a delight to the eye and a constant joy.

In places the bamboos gave way to bananas, the glossy sheen of their great waving leaves of a deep and delightful green, with which the great red flower contrasted so strikingly. Often about this huge deep crimson flower, apparently lavishly cut in velvet, fluttered lovely little birds so small that, at first, I had thought they were big insects. What always surprised me was that a stem so soft as is this of the banana, so spongy that one could thrust one's thumb into it and watch the wound bleed clear crystal blood, colourless as water, should have the strength to uphold such a wealth of heavy foliage.

For miles we would march in silence over the rich black soil, probably pure leaf-mould, judging from the strong odour of decay that arose from it. Frequently we traversed a narrow path on the edge of a ravine, a wooded cliff rising precipitously on one side, the *khud* or *huey* sloping sharply on the other. It was here that I realized, glancing down into such a canyon, how truly enormous is a big tree. One could see the trunk of some mighty monarch of the forest rising out of the sea of evergreen that formed the bed of the *huey*, a tree whose roots must be many yards down out of sight, among the shrubs and younger trees, and looking upward, one could see its branches spreading aloft incredibly high above one.

Plodding along in a kind of waking dream, I would note new insects, creatures I had never seen before; flowers of which I knew nothing; and mighty trees, the names of which I could not tell. Most things were unfamiliar to me in this wild and beautiful primæval jungle.

And, from time to time, we would emerge from park-like

glade, upon open savannah, and thence enter dense dark forest, bamboo thicket, and typical jungle; and so back to the banks of the accursed Red River where it swept fiercely along, wide as the Thames at London, red with the clay it scavenged from its own crumbling banks, and toothed with jagged rock.

In spite of the apparent speed of the river current, great patient Chinese junks, their huge sails of plaited straw, trimmed to the breeze, would progress, inch by inch, under the propulsion of tough tireless men, strong yet agile who, indefatigable, ran to and fro, from stem to stern, poling incessantly, literally pushing the heavy junk along with the great iron-bound bamboo poles. Some time they would reach China; and what was time to them?

And, occasionally, De-Nha saved our lives, as we encountered suspicious hostile villagers, sullen and unsociable; or worse still, wandering bands of dacoits and river pirates, men who, whatever their professions of military attachment to this or that insurgent mandarin, were plain marauding thieves and murderers.

With the river pirate, the Black Flag, the dacoit and the jungle robber, as well as with the surly and unfriendly villager, inimical both to predatory dacoit and to encroaching foreigner, no-one was more competent to deal than De-Nha.

By robber and villager alike he was accepted as the genuine article—because he was the genuine article. Although now—professedly—ally and agent of the French, he had spent much of his life in the jungle; and up to the day whereon I captured him, had been precisely what he was pretending to be now, leader of a gang of dacoits, masquerading as soldiers of General De-Nam. . . .

Thanks to De-Nha, this journey across Tonking was no more dangerous to me than to any other humble traveller exposed to the ordinary risks of drowning in the Red River; of starving in the jungle, through losing the way; of suffering mishap from savage man, beast or reptile; and of death from fever and disease. Without De-Nha's guidance, help and protection, I should probably have had my throat cut, or met with other fatal mishap, before I had covered a quarter of the journey.

No, the expedition might be arduous, but, thanks to De-Nha, it wasn't dangerous. The real danger would come when I reached my destination. Even if he did not turn traitor, I should probably die a very sticky death; and if he did turn traitor, I should certainly do so.

I looked forward with more interest than enthusiasm to our arrival at the Chinese border and thereafter at the Headquarters of Generals Ba-Ky and Luong-Tam-Ky.

In spite of my anxiety I enjoyed the overland part of the journey, ever avid as I am of new sights, smells, and sounds; ever seeking a new thing; loving new scenes, and contact with strange peoples.

It was on one of the upland paths of the highlands of Tonking that I first saw, or perhaps noticed, the ubiquitous walnut-men, strange people who apparently make a living out of a few walnuts, and travel hundreds and hundreds of miles to do so. From time to time, we encountered tiny caravans of the most minute ponies that I have ever seen, laden with walnuts, travelling from China southward, and visiting the various native markets on the route.

The walnut-merchant will set forth from his village, leading his string of ponies or perhaps mules, on a journey often occupying several months, and taking him through the Shan States, Burma, Northern Siam, or through the Lao country down to Cambodia.

It was always a delight to me to meet one of those little caravans, the foremost ponies jingling with silver bells attached to their brightly-coloured halters, two *hahps* strapped pannier-fashion across their backs, steadily walking, walking, in single file, along the narrow tracks and jungle paths.

Doi Linh Nghi informed me that, on the return journey, they were generally laden with coloured blankets which the merchants buy in the bazaars of the South. These are in great demand in their own country, especially the bright red ones.

Now and again, the larger caravan of a more ambitious merchant would carry betel-nut and potatoes as well; and, occasionally, the ponies and mules would be followed by the cheaper and even more sure-footed coolies, each laden with a precious burden of brick-tea.

One night we made our frugal camp near that of such a merchant—obviously to his great anxiety and discomfort— and I instructed *Doi* Linh Nghi to buy a brick. This I discovered to be a solid block of compressed tea, weighing at least seven pounds. Personally I had never used brick-tea, and did not know how it compared with the more familiar kind, in the matter of strength and quantity per cup; though I had heard that it was, for some reason, the finest tea procurable.

I asked *Doi* Linh Nghi whether he were familiar with its use; whereunto he replied by enquiring whether I thought he was a savage. What did I take him for? Of course he knew how to make tea from the block.

I bade him go to it, and watched the process.

First he knocked a lump off with his *mâchète* precisely in the manner in which a bricklayer knocks a lump off an ordinary brick which he is trimming to shape. This he put in an iron pot which he set on the camp fire to boil. As the water boiled, the lump disintegrated, and the water turned to stew. After a time, and to me it seemed a terribly long time, the *Doi* produced a very dirty cotton rag and a short length of hollow bamboo, one end of which was closed by the natural joint.

Into this bamboo receptacle he slowly poured the brew through the filthy rag strainer. Into the tea he then dropped a small handful of salt and a lump of butter—cadged, purchased, or stolen from the merchant's cook. That none of the precious butter might be lost through adhering to his fingers, he washed these useful members in the tea. And, even while my soul, not to mention my stomach, was filled with wonder, he produced a third ingredient, held it above the wide mouth of the bamboo vessel—which, incidentally, was about nine inches in diameter and held quite a quart— before dropping it in.

"What's that?" I asked; for obviously it was neither salt nor sugar.

"Washing soda," replied the *Doi*; and let go.

Then placing his hand and the dirty rag over the top of the bamboo, to prevent loss, he agitated the receptacle violently, somewhat in the manner of the modern shaker of cocktails.

This rite performed, he drew his *mâchète* and stirred the brew, even as one's maiden aunt was wont to stir the tea with a silver spoon, in the vicarage drawing-room.

Anon he poured me forth a generous measure of this 'tea' into one of the wooden bowls we now used instead of army *gamelles*.

Dubiously I tasted it, and found it—extremely good.

Nor were the tea-leaves wasted, for under the close superintendence of the *Doi*, his brother, who masqueraded as a cook and was a villainous impostor, made a dough of barley flour, mixed the tea-leaves with it, broke the mass up into lumps, rolled it into dirty balls, baked them by the fire, and invited me to enjoy myself.

Having eaten our evening meal of rice, walnuts, dried fish, and soaked apricots, we paid a ceremonial visit to the unhappy merchant, with the view to learning anything that he might be in a position to tell us.

Doi Linh Nghi of course took the lead, and I attended in the capacity of his faithful but stupid follower, retainer, and bodyguard.

By the merchant's, perhaps unwillingly, hospitable fire-side we had a sort of second supper of *tsamba*-cakes of barley flour, moistened with excellent *chang*, grain beer, which I thoroughly enjoyed. Thereafter this good man pro-duced a bundle of *biddis* or *birris*, native cigarettes, and, foul as they were, I doubt if I ever enjoyed a smoke more.

Expressing to the *Doi* my surprise at finding tobacco of any kind here, I was told that the man was not only a vendor of walnuts, betel-nut, potatoes, tea, and salt, but was also a tobacco-merchant.

A tobacco-merchant? Had he got any cigarettes or cigars such as the French officers smoked down in Hanoi and Haiphong?

No, grinned the *Doi*. Of course not. He had only got these *biddi* things and water-pipe tobacco.

What was that like?

Not the sort of thing that I should care about, intimated the *Doi*, and bade the merchant show us a sample of his pipe-tobacco.

Whereupon the good man produced a fat bamboo cylinder from a package, pulled a wad from the end of it, and gouged out some of the alleged tobacco.

It bore a faint resemblance to tobacco as I had known it at sea, in one of its less refined manifestations, but only a very faint one. To me, it looked like a compound of dead leaves—some of which might have been tobacco leaves—treacle, water, rum-soaked navy-plug tobacco, mud, rice-husks, and the floor-sweepings of a small tobacconist's shop situated in a busy and dirty thoroughfare; and, so far as it smelt at all, it smelt of opium and stale tobacco-juice.

I forbore to lay in a stock of it.

I suppose the most dangerous part of our overland journey was through the country infested by the Möi, who are real savages, some being mountaineers, others nomadic jungle dwellers, while others again are arboreal, living somewhat after the fashion of the Sakai of the Malay Peninsula.

Being fierce and predatory, they are easily formed into bands of brigands—by such people as De-Nha, who seemed to understand them and to get on with them quite well.

When we approached one of their villages, De-Nha would beat a *réveil* on the village drum which is always hung up outside the village, and upon which every visitor is expected to "knock." To enter the village without banging the village drum is rather like entering an Englishman's house without knocking or ringing at his front door.

I was always glad when we had got away with whole skins from one of the Möi encampments or villages. With their forbidding, ugly faces, unpleasant manners and truculent bearing, they filled me with alarm.

In one Möi stronghold in which De-Nha advised us to show no undue anxiety to depart, lest it be supposed we were afraid, I was privileged to see a beauty-specialist at work.

Sitting on the chest of a prone candidate for loveliness, he was busy banging his customer's teeth with a hammer and primitive chisel, the idea being to break off every tooth at the level of the gums.

This work being completed, so that there were no signs of teeth in the upper jaw, he would set to work with a file and bring each tooth of the lower jaw to a sharp point.

"Well, well," reflected I. "*Chacun à son goût* and *de gustibus non est disputandum.*"

Yes, it was an interesting journey, and village life not the least interesting part of it.

I have seen many devices for the patient irrigation of plots of land, varying from pot-bearing wheels, bullock-dragged bags of water, and tread-mills worked throughout the day by innocent men, to the carrying of water in goat-skins, that it may be sprinkled drop by drop upon the thirsty ground. But it was in this strange country that I first saw water *shovelled*—with long-handled coal-scoops. By the patient shovelling and shooing of water along little runnels it was made, contrary to natural law, to flow upward to a level above its source.

Another difficulty with which the peasants have to contend in the cultivation of their rice, is the choking growth of the Japanese lily, a small mauve flower, clusters of which over-run their rice-fields and obstruct their water-courses. Originally, it was planted here and there by the Annamese in commemoration of a forgotten Khmer Queen. It does indeed keep her memory green (or mauve) and has become a perfect pest to the peasants, who have the utmost difficulty in keeping their rice-fields free of this prolific and quite useless weed.

I have also seen many forms of threshing and husking, but it was on this journey that I first saw the strange pounding system whereby rice is separated from its husk, leaping women being the motivating power.

Into a kind of vast wooden bowl, the heap of rice is shovelled. On the rice rests a great ball of wood, stone or iron; and, attached to the ball, is the end of a see-saw.

On the far end of the see-saw plank leaps a lady. Down goes her end of the plank and up goes the ball attached to the other end. Off steps the lady. Down goes the other end, *bump*, and with it the ball which drops with a heavy thud upon the rice.

She then repeats the process—and continues to repeat it all day long.

Fine exercise, and, in that climate, tiring even to watch. I had heard the curious distinctive thudding noise thus made, many times, and had not accepted the explanation offered me by *Doi* Linh Nghi—that it was doubtless the sounds made by the *lu thuong* beating his wife.

As we approached one village—Fo-lu, if I remember rightly—on the road to Lao Kai, we met a curious pair who provided the *Doi* with an opportunity to deliver himself of a parable, an exercise to which he was addicted.

An amazing lame man was leading a blind one; and, stopping for a chat, in search of information as usual, we learned that the two men, who were probably Laos, had received their injuries at the same time and place, when pursuing their innocent and peaceful avocation of honey-seekers.

The man who had been blinded, proceeding along a jungle path, found his way barred by the trunk of a great tree that had been felled by teak-cutters. Thinking that there might be a deserted bees' nest among the branches, he went to climb on to the trunk. At the same moment, as he explained, a small, equally innocent and peaceful honey-bear, also thinking that there might be a deserted bees' nest in the branches, reared up from the other side. They met face to face, and it was the face of the Lao that suffered; for, with one blow of his paw the "quite harmless" honey-bear removed it, including the eyes. The man was still an unpleasant sight, and must have been a worse one at that awful moment.

The other honey-gatherer, while looking up into a tree in

search of bees' nests, received a tap on the back of the head. Turning about, he too found himself face to face with a denizen of the jungle. This was a python, dangling by its tail from the branch of a tree. Promptly seizing him and enveloping him in a cold embrace, it proceeded to crush him to death.

Most luckily (or not, according to the point of view) his right arm was free from the coils of the great snake, and in his right hand was the *mâchète* without which he never ventured into the jungle. He had time to strike one mighty blow with the razor-edged blade of the heavy *mâchète*, and it almost took the python's head off.

The coils relaxed and the huge serpent fell to the ground, the man collapsing with it, and being found later 'almost unhurt' as he said, there being no other damage done than the fracturing of his thigh bones, the dislocation of his ankles, knees and hips, the smashing of his left arm and collar-bone, and the breaking of an unspecified number of ribs. And yet, after a time, miraculously he walked again; and here he was, cheerfully leading his cheerful companion in misfortune, over the face of Asia.

'I should grouse and grumble!' thought I, as I saw that pair set off again, each riotously happy with the *biddis* or *birris* (whichever it may be) that I had given him to smoke.

In Fo-lu, if that were the place, I saw a fire; and watched with interest the proceedings of the local Fire Brigade. Amateur, I imagine.

As we turned the corner and came on the scene, a house was burning merrily, its bamboo woodwork and attap-leaf thatch lending themselves to conflagration.

Happily the house was situated within a hundred yards of the river. Less happily, its proprietor and other would-be saviours possessed but one bucket, and that not a large one.

As we approached, a fat and furious man dashed past us with the bucket, panting and wheezing stertorously. A minute or two later—for he did not do the hundred yards in the level ten seconds—he returned, yet more furious, puffing and panting even more stertorously, and spilling water at every step.

Arrived at the burning house, he whirled the bucket about his head, liberally sprinkled the interested bystanders, and sent at least a half-pint of the 'precious fluid' against the cold and solid wall of stone.

Loud cheers rose above the frenzied shrieks of the Fire Brigade.

But a long lean man, thinking he could better this performance, gave the fat runner a cruel push, snatched the bucket from his willing hand, and showed him really how to run. It was good running too, until, tripping, he fell, rolled headlong, and decided not to rise. The whole Fire Brigade rushed for the bucket. Two stalwarts seized it by the handle and, side by side but not in step, ran to the river. Here they fought for its possession, the victor returning at a steady jog trot with the bucket on his head. A coolie who had risen from the ranks, he now reverted to type.

With the bucket of water still balanced upon his head, this intrepid fireman entered the house and was lost to sight.

He emerged some minutes later without the bucket, but carrying a very small and very pink pup which seemed to resent being taken from home so young.

"*Meh! Lombâk!* . . . The *samrap sy nam*, the bucket, where is it? Where's the bucket?" wailed the fat man who, I think, owned it and the house.

With the air of one who soothes and propitiates, the coolie placed the pink dog in its master's arms, and smiled brightly. Though he spoke not with his mouth, his whole bearing said,

"There, there! Hush now! What of buckets and houses? Here is the pink dog."

The pink dog bit the fat man and the crowd cheered. But not, as I thought at the moment, in approval of the dog's conduct.

It was cheering a peculiar monkey which now appeared on the roof. Aloft he bore the bucket. First he tried the bucket as head-gear. Then finding that it acted rather as an extinguisher than as a hat, he used it otherwise.

It was an amazing monkey, called, I think, a gibbon; tall but not large; and the arms which were attached to its narrow shoulders were of such an incredible length that rather it was a small monkey attached to long arms than a pair of long arms attached to a small monkey.

Be that as it may, it had the bucket, and fire-fighting operations were at a standstill.

The Brigade was nonplussed.

And then the fireman who had been a coolie had a brilliant idea, though I admit that the same idea had also occurred to me.

Dashing off, he later re-appeared carrying a long light bamboo ladder.

Meanwhile the monkey too had an idea. It occurred to him that he personally might help by filling the bucket—and without going to the river. This he proceeded to do forthwith.

"*Wah!*" exclaimed the Fo-lu Fire Brigade.

The coolie, then arriving, placed the ladder against the wall of the house on the side that was not burning, mounted it quickly, and climbed to the roof.

The monkey equally quickly descended on the other side.

"Well, that's done it," the coolie seemed to say as he returned.

And then *Doi* Linh Nghi, standing beside me, in turn had an idea; one which, I admit, had not occurred to me.

"What about getting another bucket? Why not borrow another bucket?" he asked.

He went and offered this idea, for what it was worth, to the fat man.

"Good Joss!" said the fat man, or words to that effect. "That's an idea. Now that *is* a notion."

And rushing up to a tall cadaverous melancholy man whose moustache was not quite as long as his beard, that being at least three feet in length, he shook him violently and begged for the loan of his bucket; for the love of Heaven to lend him a *samrap sy nam*, in short, a bucket.

"Bucket?" quavered the ancient. "Bucket? What do you want my bucket for?"

"To put my fire out."

"Why?" was the reply.

"Why not?" countered the fat man.

"Yes, but *why*? Why should *my* bucket put out *your* fire?"

"Oh, Hell!" or words to that effect, moaned the fat man, "I'll *hire* your bucket."

"Well, that's a funny thing to do! I never heard of hiring buckets before. However, I'll certainly hire you my bucket. Or, rather, I would do so if I had one. I haven't got a bucket. What should I do with a bucket? I'm not a milkmaid, am I?"

"No, you are a . . ."

But I'll not put down at my leisure what the anguished householder said in his haste.

Suddenly a bucket fell, as from Heaven. In point of fact, it fell from a high tree, either of the *neem* or mango variety, whence the monkey had taken it. Having, for the time being, exhausted its possibilities as a plaything, he had dropped it.

At once the Fire Brigade got to work with that promptitude and dispatch, that vigour and indeed abandon, for which Fire Brigades are noted.

As one man they rushed to the river, the empty bucket borne in their midst.

As one man, they rushed back from the river, the bucket borne in their midst, empty. *Trop de zèle*—in their struggles they had lost the lot.

They were not discouraged.

Realizing that it is useless to cry over spilt water, they again dashed back to the river.

What they did not dash, was any water upon the fire; for again none survived that violent passage.

It was my turn to have an idea.

"Why not form a chain?" I mildly suggested to the fat man.

"Chain? Chain? Chain of what?" he enquired testily.

"Chain of men," I replied. "They should stand in a line, and pass the bucket from hand to hand. Thus all would be helping. There would be no confusion. The bucket would arrive and return with speed—and with water."

"Oh, go away!" replied the fat man. "Can't you see I'm busy. . . ."

It was at about this time that a small Chinese boy emitted a shrill yell and fled from the scene.

I wondered what had bitten him, and learned later.

A hitherto somewhat lethargic fireman, so broad in the shoulders and bowed in the legs as almost to be deformed, suddenly realized that this method of fire-fighting was all nonsense, and himself started to fight. He fought for an idea and for the bucket.

He won it.

To the river he fled. With the bucket almost full, he returned; dashed up the ladder that the coolie had left standing against the wall; climbed the roof; walked along it; poured the water down a hole which I presumed was some sort of a chimney aperture; came back with the bucket; and retired from active life as one who has not only set a good example but done his good deed for the day. And sufficient unto the day.

Again the bucket went to the river.

But this time, one who had grasped the idea of the broad squat man, and wished to emulate him, met the returning party half-way; fought desperately for the bucket; won it; did precisely as his exemplar had done; and also retired. Beside the broad man he sat upon the ground and fanned himself.

The breeze fanned the flames.

Merrily they roared; soon they seized the entire house in their embrace, and swiftly devoured it.

As the roof fell in and the walls started to join them, a procession approached, headed by the small Chinese boy who had so suddenly fled from our midst.

Behind him came a vastly quivering huge Chinese; and behind him a string of coolies bearing each upon his head a zinc pail. A dozen coolies, and to every man a pail.

"Saved!" I murmured dramatically.

"At a price," I added, seeing the light of battle and the

lust of barter in that shining Chinese eye.

But alas, too late, too late. That bitter cry.

And I bethought me,

> "*The saddest words of tongue or pen*
> *Are those sad words—'It might have be'n.*"

The fat man shook his head.

Even the Chinese merchant realized that he was a day after the fair; or, at least, some hours after the fire had grown beyond reasonable proportions.

Having cuffed the small boy, he led the procession away again.

The fat man kicked the pink dog and walked off the scene—whither I know not.

I never enjoyed a free public entertainment more.

§2

I have said little about the conduct of the man De-Nha on this journey, because there is little to say. Although he was, in a sense, our leader, he was with us but not of us. Brooding, aloof, unfriendly, he walked apart, and held no communication with us beyond what was necessary.

On the other hand he played his part and did what he was there to do, inasmuch as he explained us away when explanation was necessary, and led us away when departure from camp or village was advisable. Without him we could not have got along; but, on the other hand, there were undoubtedly times when he was extremely glad of our company, times when he was recognized, and accused of being precisely who and what he was. It was then that I and the *Doi* and his merry men ceased to be merry, looked extremely truculent, drew ugly weapons and showed our teeth.

Studying the man, I came to the conclusion that it would be foolish to come to any definite conclusion at all, inasmuch as he himself did not know what he was going to do. If ever the silly phrase 'a prey to conflicting emotions' were justifiable, it was here; for, undoubtedly, his emotions preyed upon his mind and undeniably they were conflicting.

He hated us. He hated the French; and I am sure that he would a thousand times rather have been a *ly truong* under the Emperor of Annam than a petty official of the French. What would keep him faithful to us if anything would, was the knowledge that the Emperor's cause was lost; and that if De-Nha rejoined General De-Nam in the jungle, a jungle life would be his to the end of his days. And he was a man who could, and did, hope for better things than a rough and barbarous existence, living from hand to mouth, and certain, sooner or later to be deprived of those luxuries, such as opium, that had become necessities.

What I did feel pretty certain about, was that he would very promptly succumb to any offer that was a real temptation, and take any chance of exchanging the French connection for something that promised at least as well. I was equally sure that he was devoid of what is known as honour, entirely unhampered by any scruples of common honesty, and that if he remained faithful to us it would be because we represented his best material interests.

Looking back on that time, De-Nha is curiously shadowy; as distrustful as he was distrusted; despising *Doi* Linh Nghi and the other *thois* as much as they despised him; a grudging and unpleasant companion who was no companion at all.

And so, at length, we reached Lao Kai, a little town of definitely Chinese appearance, with its tiled roofs, up-curled and dragon-adorned eaves, its superior pagoda-like *wat*, and its long paper-banner bedecked bazaar, shaded by rain-trees.

Led by De-Nha, who had evidently been this way before, we passed through Lao Kai, and, a few days later either close to, immediately upon, or actually over the Yunnanese border, came upon a vast fortified perimeter camp.

CHAPTER X

This great camp of Phu-Son, each entrenched and stockaded side of which must have been a mile in length, was built about an already fortified village, beside which was a really fine fort of mediæval pattern. It was clear, even to me, when I had time to study the place, that it had been built either by a pupil of Marshal Vauban, the great military engineer of the days of Louis XIV, or at least by a most competent European engineer working to the plans of a Vauban fort.

It was extremely interesting, and in some curious way heartening, to find, in a place like this, a building so obviously European, one that might have come straight from Strasbourg, Landau, or Clermont, or any such French place fortified by Vauban himself.

In point of fact, it was similar to, and nearly as strong as, the citadel at Bac-Ninh, built about 1715 by French military engineers borrowed by the then Emperor of Annam from Louis XIV.

This fort inside the great perimeter camp was octagonal in shape, each side having a frontage of about a furlong's length, and strengthened with regular old-fashioned bastions and demi-lunes.

Inside it, as I came to know later, were the excellent houses of the two Generals commanding the Brigade of troops encamped here; as well as very good officers' quarters; staff-offices; and barracks for a battalion. I imagined that it had originally been built as a Chinese border fortress for the defence of Yunnan against invasion by the Annamese.

Within its precincts was a great old pagoda, now used as a sort of *yamen*, military court-house, and general headquarters, by the two Generals who were in joint command of the garrison, or perhaps respectively in command of the two forces composing it, of which more anon.

Although the perimeter fortifications of the place were modern, and indeed recent, there was an air of strength, solidity and permanence about this camp that surprised me.

§2

I now, for the time being, entirely resigned leadership and initiative to De-Nha and *Doi* Linh Nghi. It was up to them to get our party accepted and enrolled in the heterogeneous dacoit army of which this was the headquarters. This was, in point of fact, a simple matter, as all able-bodied men, accustomed to the use of arms, and willing to accept the discipline and terms of service, were welcome, be they Yunnanese, Annamese, Black Flags, Laos, Möis, or other.

De-Nha, of course, had no difficulty whatever in presenting himself as an ex-dacoit seeking better service than that of the nomadic jungle bands of General De-Nam. Nor were *Doi* Linh Nghi and his men suspected of being anything but Delta Annamese patriots who preferred exile to servitude—in other words, easy robbery to hard work.

And when the *Doi* and his relatives were accused of being deserters from some regiment of *Tirailleurs Ton-kinois*, they grinned coyly and, with bashful mien, forbore to refuse the blushing honours thrust upon them.

And, inasmuch as both De-Nha and *Doi* Linh Nghi vouched for me, I too was accepted as a good fellow likely to succeed by my honesty, industry, and close attention to all branches of dacoit duty.

True, they admitted, I was only a Mongol lout of sorts, and intensely stupid, but see how strong and (as they would observe later) what a marvellous marksman with a rifle; firing it as I did from the shoulder, using the sights as the *Farangs* do, and able to put a bullet not merely within a given area, such as a town, but on a given spot, such as a house, or even a window of a house in that town.

These things were later tested and found to be true. I also, by request, gave an exhibition of strength and skill with a sword. This was so successful that a brilliant career was prophesied for me—as an executioner.

Little did I think when learning sword-drill from my Troop Corporal-Major, and the art of sabre-fighting from the Corporal-Instructor of the Life Guards, that I should ever exhibit my skill to such an audience or earn such encomiums. It never occurred to me that a man who could divide the leaden bar, sever the hanging sheep into two halves, or cut the dangling handkerchief, was qualifying for the post of executioner.

With my companions, I was enrolled with this dacoit army, mainly Chinese, encamped near the Annamese border, and commanded by the Generals Ba-Ky and Luong-Tam-Ky.

As a brigand-recruit I walked warily; taciturn, truculent—and in considerable danger. Without the help of De-Nha and *Doi* Linh Nghi, I should have been in infinitely greater danger, and my career as a dacoit considerably shorter. With them, I occupied a hut in the camp lines outside the fort; was given a crude yellowish uniform, consisting of a long vest buttoned up to the throat and slit up the sides, worn over what were either short trousers or long breeches, a broad conical hat, a fairly good rifle of Russian make, and a belt and cartridge-case containing thirteen rounds—an unlucky number—of cartridges which, still more unluckily, did not fit the rifle.

Thus accoutred and equipped, I attended drills and parades which would have charmed Mr. Frederick Karno, appealed to his peculiar sense of humour, and enlarged his horizon.

Squad-drill and Company-drill were rendered easier than are these exercises in the West, by reason of the fact that unanimity of movement was not exacted—only a general unanimity of spirit, an acceptance of the fact that something else was to be done now, and by practically everybody. Thus *"Quick march"* meant "Go forward, more or less in a body"; *"Halt"* meant "Now you can stop and either stand up or lie down"; *"About turn"* meant "Shuffle back here again"; and *Right* or *Left Turn* meant "Go more or less

East or West or somewhere".....

The rifle-range I did not attend, being excused this particular parade by reason of the admitted fact that my rifle, like those of many of my new comrades, could not be fired. I did, however, attend daily instructional classes in aiming-drill and the use of the rifle. These exercises differed materially from those prevailing in European armies.

At the word of command, we removed our rifles, from all the varying and different positions they might happen to occupy at the moment, and took the butts firmly beneath our right arms. Or the left, if preferred. The Squad was then directed to look more or less in the direction of the object to be aimed at; such an object, say, as the fort itself, the distant village of Pac-ho, or a mountain in China.

The recruit having looked in this direction, could then either close his eyes or keep them open, whichever he liked; or indeed, could do both—in other words, blink them repeatedly should he prefer that method of sighting. But what he must do, without option, was to point the muzzle of the rifle—especially, particularly, and notably the muzzle—in the direction in which he was, or had been, looking. Then, grasping the rifle about the waist, middle, point of balance, or anywhere else, with the right hand, he must bring his left hand smartly or slowly across his chest, insert it beneath the right arm and the rifle, give the trigger a good shove with his thumb, index-finger, coat-sleeve, button, or anything else, until, happily, the thing went off, *bang*.

The rifle having been fired, the recruit must then, without further word of command, re-load the rifle and repeat the process until his ammunition was expended or his *Ong-Tu-phian*[14] clouted him over the head and told him to do something else.

The great thing, it was explained to us, was to make a noise.

That was the real aim and object of rifle-fire.

And the noise, we must note, served a double purpose. It intimidated foes and enheartened friends.

---

[14] Sergeant.

Therefore the good rifleman, the marksman, the sharp-shooter, must bang off frequent and free; high, wide, and handsome; and the more often he fired, the better man was he. And there is nothing better than rifles for the purpose of noise, except artillery. That, by reason of its greater noise, was the more important arm.

And therein the *Farangi* were our superiors; but only to the extent that they could make more noise. . . .

One of our Instructors, a superior man, who had un-doubtedly held similar rank in the regular Chinese army, pointed out to us that, in point of fact, there was often more to it than that. He told us, what was perfectly true, that if we lined a stockade, looked toward the enemy and kept on firing, they would, as they advanced toward us, sooner or later come literally under our fire. As even such silly buffaloes as we must know, bullets fall, and the enemy approaching must enter the zone in which they are falling. He estimated that, provided we held our rifles reasonably level, there would be in front of them a danger zone of anything from three hundred to six hundred yards wide, a zone beginning about a furlong away from our rifles.

Once the enemy had come within a third part of a *li* of us, a couple of hundred yards, *rifles were of no further use*, as they would only send bullets over the heads of the approaching foe.

And it was then that the rifles should be discarded—when the foreign devils were a couple of hundred yards distant.

Yes, that was the time to throw them down and take to the sword, *mâchète, mīt, lâp, pīa*; spear, *mai-tau, chawk*; halberd, axe, *khwan, khio*; and indeed, if anyone cared about such new-fangled foreign things, the bayonet.

Anyway, what was true was that, once the enemy had got to within a furlong of the position, it was no use to try any longer to frighten him with loud bangs. Having got so far, he was evidently coming right on; and that was the time when good drill, good discipline and good soldiering told; the time to take to the sword and be willing to die by the sword.

A good stout lad, that Sergeant-Instructor, who knew his job. . . .

Some of his drill-orders, though not, I believe, to be found, then or now, in any drill-book, remain with me still:—

"*Squad!* Take those rifles off your shoulders, off the ground, off your backs and wherever else they are. Under the arm-pits; place *rifles*.

"Look at the pagoda on the hill.

"No—that squint-eyed fool near the middle of the back row—I'm not a pagoda. Don't look at me. Oh, you're looking at the pagoda and not at me? Right. Try and look at it with both eyes at once, then.

"Now, fire *rifles*. Go on.

"Good!

"Now go on doing it till I wave my arms about in the air."

I enjoyed my drill-lessons with the Chinese-Annamese Dacoit Pirate Brigand Patriot Army at the Phu-Son Barracks more than I did those I received in the British Army at the Knightsbridge Barracks.

§3

I soon discovered that these Chinese dacoits were really good material.

Given a year in the hands of British officers and British drill-sergeants they would, in battle, led by these same Britons, have given a good account of themselves against any troops in the world, for they had the root of the matter and all the essential makings of a soldier.

The first military quality they possessed in abundance— courage. Led by men who had at least as much courage as themselves, they would go anywhere, attack anything and stand up to the attack of anybody.

The second qualification was theirs also, for they were physically strong. Mostly Yunnanese, they were definitely sturdy, tough and most enduring.

And thirdly, they were definitely amenable to proper reasonable discipline, understanding the necessity for it, and accepting its restrictions without a murmur; and in point of fact, these troops would have had but little respect for an officer whom they did not regard as somewhat ruthless, even cruel, in his punishments.

They were, moreover, of extremely cheerful spirit, given to easy laughter, appreciative of a joke, and though devilishly grim when about the business of warfare, ordinarily merry and light-hearted.

Moreover, they could travel light, light as any troops in the world, and subsist indefinitely on a handful of rice a day. Their health was good, their needs small, and if properly handled and looked after, their morale always high.

Excellent troops, in fact, and in their native jungle a desperate and dangerous foe, capable of dealing with an equal number of trained European troops on equal terms. Against white soldiers their crying need was of course officers, men of character and education superior to their own, trained in the science and art of war.

To set against their military virtues, they were severely handicapped by two military vices. They would not fire their rifles from the shoulder and they would not march in step. This was, of course, because they had never been trained to do so; and it was to remedy these two grave faults that I was supposed to set to work.

Had I been going to train these men to fight on my own side, turn them from the dacoits and pirates that they were, into Tirailleurs Tonkinois, I should have enjoyed the work, and with such material could have made a good job of it.

I could have made them into far better soldiers than the Chinese regulars whom later I saw.

And even as it was, in spite of their horrible habit of firing the rifle with the butt stuck under the arm-pit or planted against the hip, and in spite of the fact that at drill not two men in a Company were in step, they were formidable fighters.

Had they ever been taught to use the rifle properly and been given sufficient ammunition wherewith to practise shooting and improve their marksmanship, the conquest of Annam would have been an even slower and more costly business than it was.

§4

And here I lived in a strange waking dream, a dacoit among dacoits, as in the Sahara and Arabia, I had lived as an Arab among Arabs.

It was fantastic—and the most fantastic thing about it all was the fact that it did not seem so. Before very long, incredible as it may appear, the weird nightmare life took on the hues of reality, of normality; and I ceased to wonder at it and at myself.

And, meanwhile, I learned a very great deal concerning the local situation, local politics, plans and people.

People! One day it appeared in orders—in other words, it was bawled out by the Chinese Sergeant-Instructor, after one of our drill-*divertissements*, that on the morrow we should be inspected by the Generals and the Colonel Kar-Linh, Commandant of the horde, herd, force, mob or Brigade.

This pleased and interested me greatly, for I was most anxious to see the famous General Ba-Ky, the possibly more famous General Luong-Tam-Ky, and the mysterious Colonel Kar-Linh or Kar-Ling.

"*Attention!*" bawled the Sergeant-Instructor. . . . "Here! Come back, you! I didn't say '*Rice*', I said, '*Attention*' . . . Stand up, those three at the end of the row. You can't stand at 'attention' if you are sitting down. . . . Put out those *biddis* there. European troops don't smoke at 'attention'. Not openly, like that. . . . Stop that laughing and listen to me, damn you, or I'll come and disembowel a few of you, and you can laugh at that. . . . I'm going to have you as smart as *Farangi* General Gardan's army before I've done with you. You may have broken your mothers' hearts but you won't break mine. . . ."

Sergeant-Instructors are very much alike, all the world over.

"Now then, stop shoving and shuffling, and listen. Parade to-morrow at sunrise. There will be a General

Inspection—and I will give any mud-fish a week's *cangue* who parades without his hat, without a coat of some sort, without a belt or a cord or something round his belly, or with his rifle bunged up with mud. . . . No rifles to be loaded before coming on parade. No man to smoke, spit, scratch, talk, laugh or sit down while the Generals are passing along the line. See? . . . Right. Now you can all push off. . . ."

Along the ragged line, next morning, after we had been standing at complete inattention for at least a couple of hours, rode three men on short-necked sturdy Chinese ponies, followed by a miscellaneous crowd of officers, aides-de-camp, banner-men, pipe-bearers, executioners, halberdiers and orderlies.

Two of the mounted three were obviously Chinese. The third was as obviously European; and I think my heart beat a little faster at the sight of him—a fellow-European, very possibly a brother Englishman, here in this amazing assembly of "drilled" and uniformed Chinese and assorted robbers, dacoits, brigands and what-nots.

The Generals rode in front of this man, one of them a huge savage-looking desperado, the sort of creature one might see in a pantomime, or, nowadays in a film, without any amazement. He was so like one's conception of a ferocious Chinese bandit-chief or pirate as to be almost incredible; almost too bad to be true, too realistic to be real.

The other General was of a very different type, half the size of the first one; and, whereas the latter's face expressed cruelty, rapacity, villainy and brutality, this one's face expressed precisely nothing at all.

Beside his horse walked—or rather, stalked—a very dreadful-looking man, who must have been at least seven feet in height, and who, in spite of that fact, looked disproportionately broad to the point of deformity. Such arms have I never seen, in point of length and size; nor more enormous thighs and calf-muscles. This monstrous person —who was clad in nothing but a tightly-folded loin-cloth— bore over his right shoulder a great and gleaming sword. He had the most sinister face I have ever seen in my life, a curious and freakish malformation of his lips and teeth adding to its bizarre hideousness; for the lower canine teeth were as abnormally long as were the arms and was the creature himself. These fangs protruded and lay flat against the upper lip—and outside it. Thus even in complete repose the expression of the horrible face was a ferocious tooth-baring snarl. . . .

The third man might have been a well-fed weather-beaten, tough British field-officer masquerading in some outlandish Oriental uniform at a Tattoo or Military Tournament spectacle. For he, like the Generals, was dressed in a yellow cotton tunic and trousers; high felt-soled riding-boots; a curious mediæval-looking velvet hat, typically Chinese in style; assorted belts and cross-belts; and odds-and-ends of decorative braiding, aiguillettes and shoulder-straps. He wore a European sword and a revolver which looked to me to be of British Army service-pattern. As he rode slowly past me, I summed him up for a stout soldier of fortune, and learned later that I was not far wrong. . . .

The Inspection followed.

We marched forward in line; the line became two ranks as the taller and more enthusiastic forged ahead; the two ranks became two parties, as the left of the line edged off to its left and the right of the line bore away to its right.

We were ordered to turn about and many of us did so.

We were requested to form line again and open fire upon the Fort.

This we did, most of us looking earnestly toward it while tucking the butt of the rifle under the right arm-pit and fumbling for the trigger either with the left hand or the right. Many of us looked for the trigger instead of the Fort.

One man, a happy warrior who was not quite all the perfect man-at-arms should be, discovered, on jerking the trigger, that there was a cartridge in his rifle after all. It was unfortunate—for him at any rate—that the bullet narrowly missed General Ba-Ky who was, somewhat recklessly, rather to the front than the flank of the firing-line.

Pour encourager les autres not to be wasteful of ammunition, the General ordered the man to be reprimanded by being suspended from the Fort wall (on a piece of telegraph wire bound about his united big toes) until he dropped off or otherwise showed improvement.

I wondered whether he would have been more severely admonished if he had missed General Luong-Tam-Ky in like manner—or Colonel Kar-Linh.

§5

My next pre-occupation was the problem of the best method of establishing contact with the European officer, Colonel Kar-Linh, in such a manner that I should not be immediately arrested as a spy and shot out of hand.

Life was cheap at this interesting place, and the question as to whether a man should die seemed subordinate and indeed subsequent to that as to how he should die.

For the authorities—the Generals Ba-Ky and Luong-Tam-Ky—were specialists, artists and scientists in the art and science of painful slaying, and were ever on the lookout for subjects for experiment. I never heard that the Colonel or any other subordinate presented the Generals with the case of a man worthy to die, without discovering that the Generals fully agreed with the justice of the sentence. Or, at any rate, with the sentence.

If Colonel Kar-Linh took one look at me when addressed hlm in French or English, said,

"You are a spy and you'll die to-morrow," I should certainly die to-morrow—or to-day.

I decided to walk warily, bide my time, and exercise the excellent Scottish virtue of caution. Too often in my few short years had I been impulsive and "glaiksome." On this occasion, glaiksome I would not be.

Meanwhile *Doi* Linh Nghi, in conversation with his new comrades, learnt a great deal, and, among other valuable items of information, that the Viceroy De-Nam was constructing a vast and impregnable fortress in the jungle, a place that, when completed, would be citadel, arsenal, treasure-house, base and General Headquarters of the insurgent army of Annam.

From *Doi* Linh Nghi's description of the description given by those who had seen it, the Great Fortress was quite evidently modelled upon the plan of this comparatively small one, itself a copy of the Vauban fort at Bac Ninh.

According to eye-witnesses' accounts, it had three tiers of fire from the great outer stockade; a vast surrounding moat, dry and deep, filled with sharply-pointed poisoned bamboo stakes; two inner stockades both similarly defended; high flanking towers, and a most cunningly devised and constructed fort within.

Entrance to this latter could not be obtained except through passages that turned at right-angles and were so narrow that only in single file could invaders pass through them—and only under a blasting and withering rifle-fire. Evidently this was a place with which nothing but artillery could deal; and, apparently, was so sited that artillery could neither approach nor see it.

What was needed, I decided, was not only an accurate plan of the place and its surrounding defences, but an even more accurate contour-map of the adjacent country.

I would not leave here until I had made these or had concluded that such a thing was really impossible. . . .

In time, the Company, gang, band, or troupe to which I belonged was moved from the camp lines into the Fort, for guard purposes.

Here we were quartered in a foul and filthy barrack-building that had the loveliest old grey stone-tiled roof with up-curling super-imposed eaves.

We were now taught the whole art and mystery of guard-mounting and the performance of all the duties of a sentry in a smart and soldier-like manner.

Before long, we could do things, if not in the Buckingham Palace sentry style, at least quite as well as these things were done anywhere in Annam, if not in all China.

Guard would be mounted and sentries posted at the great gates; over the arsenal; at the main-guard; over the houses of the high officers; over the arms and ammunition stores, and around the walls.

One, having business or having no business, would approach a sentry, and a listener—or indeed anyone within ear-shot, whether listening or not—would hear,

"Halt! Who goes there?"

"Hullo, Ah Fat! What about a flutter at fan-tan. I've got the makings and twenty-five *sabuks.*"

"Show us your money. Right. Wait till I get these belts off. . . ."

Or, perchance, visiting-rounds, their approach wholly unchallenged, would halt and patiently await the smart and soldierly voice of the watchful keeper of the midnight vigil. Having waited in vain it would, still patiently, but a shade reproachfully, ask to be challenged, whereupon would follow a prolonged loud yawn, and a sleepy voice from the darkness of a doorway would enquire whether anybody had got a match.

At first *Doi* Linh Nghi was livid with rage at such a slovenly travesty of the military ceremonial and smartness that he loved; soon he became merely contemptuous; and, finally, much amused.

Being a man whose humour was apt to express itself unconventionally, he played a practical joke upon the Sergeant of the Guard, one night, a jest which I could not approve. Standing in the complete darkness of a recessed gateway, he awaited the dawdling slouching approach of the visiting-rounds in motionless silence, allowed the Sergeant to ask three times that he be challenged, and then suddenly fired his rifle.

Visiting-rounds fled; the guard and most of the Company, if not the entire population of the Fort as well as of the camp, turned out; sentries left their posts and came running, and chaos and darkness reigned. When lights had been procured and an angry officer, followed by a score or two of armed warriors, came to investigate, there was nothing to investigate, *Doi* Linh Nghi having relieved himself of his duties at this post and taken up those of another.

I professed to be very angry with him; and had he been caught he would certainly have been punished in some manner calculated to render him no longer useful to himself or anyone else.

Thereafter a certain liveliness reigned at night, and the business of sentry-visiting was taken quite seriously.

One evening, as I squatted with my back against a wall at a spot I often occupied because, from it, I had a good view of the door of the excellent little house occupied by Colonel Kar-Linh, that officer came to the window.

Behind him I saw the figure of a woman, apparently wearing European dress. She seemed to be looking out, over his shoulder, as might a captive permitted to take a glimpse of the outside world from his prison door.

Softly I began to whistle *Rule Britannia*. Colonel Kar-Linh heard, started and stared.

I changed my tune to *The British Grenadiers*. The Colonel came to the door of the house, and placing his hands upon his hips, his arms akimbo, planted himself four-square in the porch, the expression of his face, of his whole body in fact, one of "What the Devil!"

I next favoured him with a few bars of *Ye Banks and Braes*, and, as I did so, the scene seemed to change and his house in the Fort of Phu-Son to be the house of the Nawab of Aundhara at Mecca in Arabia.

When I had finished, the Colonel whistled the first two bars of *God Save the King* and I obliged with the next two.

For the best part of a minute he then stood perfectly still, staring hard at me.

My heart beat fast, for I had now burnt my boats, and my fate lay in the hands of this soldier of fortune whose reputation, even in this robber stronghold, was not too savoury.

Suddenly he raised his hand and beckoned to me to approach. Rising to my feet, I slouched over to where he stood, and gave the best representation that I could achieve of a stupid and bashful coolie, sullen and uncomfortable in the presence of his superior. With hanging head and dangling arms, I stared foolishly at the dust wherein I scrabbled with the big toe of my left foot. I then rubbed my left calf with my right foot and mechanically scratched my ribs.

"Well?" growled the Colonel in English. "What's the game?"

He was certainly English, I decided.

I grinned sheepishly and grunted the Annamese noise of interrogation.

"Who are you?" he then enquired in French, adding,

"And where did you study—music shall we call it? And why English music?"

I grunted again, and the Colonel tried me in German, whereat I shook my head. He then spoke in Russian and Chinese, and I continued to gape and grunt.

Just as he was about to get angry and do something regrettable (from my point of view) I waxed eloquent and confidential.

"I'm an Englishman, Sir," I said. "British, rather. A Scot. Served in a British Regiment. Gentleman-adventurer, like yourself, and a soldier of fortune."

"You're British all-right," agreed the Colonel, and I think there was a look of satisfaction, if not a smile of pleasure, on his face at hearing his native language. "Don't know about gentleman, though you must be a bit of an adventurer to come here. As for soldier of fortune, you've been a soldier all-right and the fortune may follow—and be damn' bad fortune too."

"I'll risk it, Sir," I grinned.

"You're certainly taking a risk," he replied, and the tone of his voice was not altogether reassuring. "I've had my eye on you, or somebody else's eye, ever since I heard there was a man here who fired from the shoulder and could hit a target every time at five hundred. At first I thought you might be one of Gordon's former men from Kwang-si, but you are too young. Afterwards I guessed you might be a deserter from the French Foreign Legion, and then I guessed you might not—because you'd never have got here through the jungle, even if you'd known where to come. . . . Now I've heard you talk, I'll tell you who you are, if you'd like to know. You're a deserter from the 90th, and you've made your way here from Burma. Isn't that it?"

I looked as sheepish, confused, and guilty as I could, and forebore to contradict my superior.

"And a hell of a long time you must have been wandering," he decided, "judging by the look of you and the way you behave and sling the pidgin. . . . Gone completely native, haven't you?"

I admitted, not entirely without complacency that I had pretty much 'gone native'.

"You didn't take *me* in, you know," said the Colonel.

"No, Sir," I agreed, knowing perfectly well that I had taken him in completely; although, no doubt, he had been puzzled as to how and where I had come to learn musketry.

For a minute or so he studied me, summing me up, and suddenly seemed to come to a decision.

"I suppose you want a job?" he said. "Promotion and all that. . . . Well, come here just after sunset, and I'll talk to you. If you can keep off drink, opium, or whatever your trouble is, I can use you. You teach these swine a bit of drill and discipline, musketry and fire-control, and turn them into something like soldiers, and you'll be worth your corn to me. Good corn too and plenty of it. . . . What's your name, rank and regiment?"

"Sinclair Noel Brodie Dysart," I replied, "formerly Trooper in the Tins—I mean Her Majesty's Life Guards; and sometime Inspector-General of Cavalry in the army of His Highness the Sultan Mahommed el Kebir of Bab-el-Djebel."

The Colonel smiled wryly.

"I'm sure you were," he said, "and at about the time I was Standard-Bearer to the Devil in the Holy War in Heaven. . . . Well, whether you were that or Sergeant Jock Gordon of the 90th Highlanders, late of Mandalay, doesn't matter, so long as you can do Sergeant-Instructor here, with the rank of—Captain shall we say? I'll give you a trial, anyway.

"And give you Christian burial," he growled with an ugly scowl, "if there's any trouble. See?"

I saw.

That evening I had a long talk with Colonel Collins, Military Adviser and Chief of Staff to the Generals Ba-Ky and

Luong-Tam-Ky, joint Commanders-in-Chief of the Independent, and mainly Chinese, army of Phu-Son. Having listened to my account of myself, without comment or evidence of credulity, Colonel Collins offered me the post of Sergeant-Instructor with the rank and pay of Staff Captain and the additional duties of personal aide-de-camp to himself.

He made it clear to me that if I succeeded in satisfying and pleasing him I should never regret having found my way to Phu-Son, and that if I failed to satisfy and please him I should regret it very bitterly for the remainder of my life, which would be brief.

To the Generals Ba-Ky and Luong-Tam-Ky he formally presented me, at a sort of durbar in the *Yamen* building, describing me as a young friend and protégé of his who had, at great risk and with extreme courage, made the difficult journey all the way from Burma to join his famous examplar, Colonel Collins, and to take service with him under the flag of the illustrious Generals Ba-Ky and Luong-Tam-Ky whose fame had penetrated even to those distant and barbarous parts.

The illustrious Generals grunted with one accord.

General Ba-Ky, huge and forbidding, smiled ogre-like and hoped, for my own sake, that I should give satisfaction.

General Luong-Tam-Ky, small and most enigmatic, smiled not nor spoke any word at all. . . .

By order of Colonel Collins I was given a one-roomed house In the Fort garden, a small building that had been a store of some sort, but which, furnished with a table, chair, and heavy teak-wood bed, made a sufficiently comfortable dwelling.

Doi Linh Nghi I appointed my orderly, and two of his relations my batman and body-servant, while a third was selected by the *Doi* as cook for the five of us. Certainly the worthy *tirailleur* knew enough to boil water in an iron pot and throw rice into it.

An excellent Chinese regimental-tailor devised me a noble uniform of brilliant yellow; and, in this, with a sort of mandarin hat, belt and cross-belts, high felt-soled boots and a big sword, I must have cut an imposing if unconvincing figure.

And so, without great amazement, I found myself a commissioned officer in the highly-irregular forces of the auxiliaries of His Majesty the (exiled) Emperor of Annam and in a position to see and hear most of what was going on, and to learn what I had come to discover.

So far I had succeeded beyond all expectation or hope—thanks to my splendid *Doi* Linh Nghi and the less splendid De-Nha.

CHAPTER XI

The Generals Ba-Ky and Luong-Tam-Ky fascinated me, both independently and in their amazing contrast. No two men in this world were ever more unlike in character and physique, in characteristics and technique.

And yet, in spite of their utter and complete difference one from another, I don't know which of them terrified me the more. One was the prototype of Chu Chin Chow himself, a huge powerful and villainous semi-savage; and the other was a tiny, gentle, and mild little man who might have been Private Secretary to Confucius.

And I don't, I repeat, know which of these twain terrified me the more.

General Ba-Ky (Chu Chin Chow) almost frightened me to death: General Luong-Tam-Ky (the Private Secretary) almost frightened me to death; the one by what he threatened to do, and did do, to many and many a victim of his wrath or suspicion; the other by not threatening to do anything at all, and by what one imagined he had done to the victims of his wrath or suspicion—who disappeared and were seen no more.

General Ba-Ky's slogan and signature-tune might well have been,

"*We are the Robbers of the Woods*", for that is precisely what he was; a powerful robber-chief of the most truculent type; a ruffian who stuck at nothing whatsoever; a swash-buckler whose simple creed was "What a man dares he may do"; a brute devoid of mercy, kindness, magnanimity or compassion.

General Luong-Tam-Ky would have acknowledged nothing so blatant as a slogan nor so individualistic as a signature-tune, if such things had been known in his day. Had he been a Christian, his favourite text would have been,

"*Blessed are the meek, for they shall inherit the earth,*"

119

for a more apparently meek person I never encountered—nor one with a firmer intention to inherit all the earth he wanted.

Another text which would have appealed to him, competing for his preference, almost successfully, with the above, would have been,

"*Blessed are the poor in spirit, for their's is the Kingdom of Heaven,*" inasmuch as he was so apparently poor in spirit and desirous of a Kingdom in Heaven—after he had enjoyed one on earth.

And doubtless, without a smile, he would have murmured quite frequently,

"*Blessed are the peacemakers, for they shall be called the children of God,*" because he loved to make a solitude and call it peace, and to walk before men as a humble child of God. And I am quite certain that before, during, and after, an execution, especially if accompanied with examination by the torturer, he would have murmured,

"*Blessed are the merciful, for they shall obtain mercy,*" his own mercy, *bien entendu*, which was like that of the great Amir:

> "*But three days hence, if God be good, and*
>   *if thy strength remain*
> *Thou shalt demand one boon of me and*
>   *bless me in thy pain.*
> *For I am merciful to all, and most of all to*
>   *thee. . . .*"

Nor to this day am I certain as to whether the man was a colossal hypocrite.

Somehow I don't think he was.

I got the impression, rather, that his idea of good form and good style, was meekness, humility and poorness of spirit; and that he considered his colleague, General Ba-Ky as vulgar, blatant, and, on the whole, rather a Bad Man. Certainly not a Good Egg.

Over an execution, General Ba-Ky would smack his lips, laugh hugely, and gloat.

Very bad form indeed.

For General Luong-Tam-Ky, watching the ugly business just as carefully, would, with completely expressionless face, murmur the equivalent of

"Sad! Sad! Sad!"

Very gentlemanly.

When some wretch was to be put to the question with indescribably hideous torture, General Ba-Ky would openly enjoy the show, occasionally suggesting ideas that would win the admiring approval of the executioner himself.

But when General Luong-Tam-Ky questioned a man, albeit his methods were even more excruciatingly agonizing than those of General Ba-Ky, he would permit no sign of approval, much less of pleasure and enjoyment, to appear upon his inscrutable face.

And when he suggested another and improved method of persuasion, it would be regretfully, deprecatingly, and with a remark to the effect that though bitter constraint and sad occasion dear drove him to suggest this now, it must not be regarded as a precedent.

A melancholy duty performed in the very best manner. Most gentleman-like again.

I don't think that General Luong-Tam-Ky could have thought very much of General Ba-Ky's Old School, and I am sure he would have been the first to black-ball him had anyone put him up for the exclusive Service Club to which, in Peking, General Luong-Tam-Ky doubtless belonged.

No, I'm not sure; but on the whole, I think perhaps I would rather have been condemned to death by General Ba-Ky, or even put to the torture by him, than have suffered at the hands of the gentle and pious General Luong-Tam-Ky.

It would perhaps have been a quicker business, but, nevertheless . . .

In person, General Ba-Ky was as tall as I—and I am over six feet—heavily built, and very powerful; a robustious noisy person who ate Gargantuan meals, drank very freely of *chang*, *choum-choum* and what he called indifferently *nam-fai* and *ram-fai* and *lam-fai*, and which appeared to me to be a kind of brandy; shook with Homeric laughter; bawled unseemly jests; roared savagely at trembling servants; was given to the wearing of fierce raiment; and generally behaved as though he knew himself to be the spiritual ancestor of our Chu Chin Chow.

In person, General Luong-Tam-Ky was tiny, small-boned, fragile, frail, and delicate; a dainty cat-like person who went softly, ate sparingly, drank only scented mandarin tea, very very rarely smiled and never never laughed; neither made nor noticed jokes of any kind; spoke gently and kindly to servants and inferiors; never threatened, scolded, nor uttered abuse; never showed anger, annoyance, interest, desire nor any other emotion whatsoever; was of pleasant and learned discourse; and generally behaved as though he knew himself to be the spiritual descendant of the immortal sage, saint, savant and philosopher, K'ung Fu-tze known to the West as Confucius.

One could not say that at feasts and communal meals General Luong-Tam-Ky regarded General Ba-Ky and his manners with disgust or disapproval, for signs neither of those sentiments nor of any other ever showed upon his completely impassive and utterly inscrutable countenance.

No stolid Chinese face carved from a block of ivory ever showed less, told less, or changed less, than did that of General Luong-Tam-Ky; the surface of no lake ever revealed less of what was hidden in the depths beneath it; the face of no statue of Buddha was ever more changeless, more secret, more unreadable.

And as I have said, these two Chinese Generals terrified me, the gentle polite and humble "Private Secretary" as much as the roaring ruffianly Chu Chin Chow. Both were to me so alien, so strange, as to be entirely beyond my comprehension.

CHAPTER XII

And what of the man whom both these mediæval War-Lords, these Robber-Barons, these Chinese *tuchuns*, trusted?

Being a fellow-Englishman, I thought I could understand him in a way in which I could never understand the Chinese.

But what at first I could not understand was how a man of his race and up-bringing, education and training, could possibly behave as he did.

Later I learned the reason.

Had you seen this man, bearing, rightfully or otherwise, the widely-known, highly-respected, and indeed welcome, name of John Collins, you would have said that he was apparently a typical Englishman, or rather representative of a very well-known type of Englishman—somewhat John Bullish; of full and ruddy countenance; four-square, thick-set, bluff and hearty.

Clean-shaven and properly dressed, he would have been well in the picture in the cattle-market of any English country town, as a prosperous farmer about the business of the buying and selling of beasts. He would have walked around, a straw in the corner of his mouth, a considering look in his eye, a bucolic stick in his hand; and, from time to time, he would have prodded specimens of fat stock.

Or again, strange as it may seem, in cassock and surplice, academic hood and stole, he would have been well in the picture in a pulpit, the pulpit of an ancient village church; a sporting parson who rode to hounds (and why not), who liked his glass of port after dinner (and where's the harm), who was hail-fellow-well-met with all men, be they County gentry or humble villagers; be they bluff cheery squires or furtive poachers; a fine crusted Tory who stood for Church and State and the good Old Order of things that had made Merrie England what it was—or used to be.

Not that there was anything whatsoever of the

sanctimonious or parsonical about John Collins. I allude merely to his appearance, and say that, according as you dressed him, he would have looked a typical British farmer, squire or fresh-faced parson, open-airy, breezy, jolly and debonair.

And in this he was, in a way, even more deceptive than the two Chinese Generals, his colleagues, or rather his employers and masters; for Chu Chin Chow looked the ruffian he was, and Luong-Tam-Ky, the Private Secretary to Confucius, looked the quiet scholar, the austere ascetic that he was; whereas John Collins looked the open-hearted, open-handed, bluff and honest John Bull that he was not.

Most definitely he was a crook, a rogue and a rascal, a fact that relieved me of any sense of treachery when considering my own conduct toward him. Inasmuch as the man was utterly dishonest and faithless, I felt no compunction whatsoever in deluding him, in playing my part as spy and secret agent, to the utmost of my power and ability.

Of his history it was extremely difficult to learn anything at all, as he was a congenital liar. When he was pretending to have nothing to conceal, to be quite proud of his past, and to be telling one all about it, his statements were probably then the furthest from the truth. It was only from other sources and by unguarded remarks of his own, that I could get anywhere near the facts of his undeniably remarkable history—until I learned all about him from an accurate biographer.

According to his own account, he had been a British Officer—whether naval or military unspecified—and had been lent by the British Government to China.

His agreement with the Chinese having terminated, he had returned to England, sent in his papers, and thereafter gone back to China and resumed service with the Imperial Government privately. According to his own story, he had been not only an officer of high rank, but had reorganized the Chinese Consular Service; put life, efficiency and honesty into the Chinese Customs Service; and had generally played the sort of part in China that such men as General Gordon and Sir Robert Hart actually did.

At first he took me in, with his plausible story but, although somewhat simple-minded and naturally prone to believe what I am told, I am not really gullible, and am protected by a very valuable gift of character-reading and an intuitiveness concerning people with whom I come in contact—more especially people of my own speech and nationality.

So that, even to me, it was fairly clear that a man who was, as he described himself, a sort of cross between Gordon and Hart, would not now be here as a kind of military dry-nurse and adviser to a pair of Chinese Generals, on a surreptitious and somewhat disreputable bush-whacking expedition into neighbouring territory and against the forces of a nation with whom their government maintained diplomatic relations, and was outwardly at peace. The Chinese Government might order such filibustering and might give every support, in secret, to the enemies of France; but no such man as Collins professed to be, would have lent his countenance, much less his sword and military skill, to its support.

Moreover, the man himself did not fit in with the account that he gave, for although he was very well veneered, the veneer was thin; and it was early quite evident to me that he had never been a British Officer nor moved in the military, naval, diplomatic, or consular circles that he described.

When he drank too much, as frequently he did, quite definitely he went to pieces, spoke In the manner that was natural to him, and behaved according to his kind. And this was very revealing.

No, I set Colonel John Collins down as a bold, brave and resolute soldier of fortune; a very competent and courageous fighter and leader; and the type of man who, at an earlier date and in the right place—say the India of Clive or Wellington—might have risen with the help of his sword, his ability, his pluck, and his lack of all hampering scruple, to a very high position.

John Collins having told me the wonderful story of his

life, or rather a wonderful story about his life, I told him the simple truth concerning mine.

I gathered the impression that he rather 'handed it to me' as possibly the bigger, better, and brighter liar of us twain.

CHAPTER XIII

"Come and pick a bone with us to-night," suggested Colonel John Collins to me, one evening, as he passed the door of my hut on his way from the parade-ground to his own house.

I gathered from this form of words that he was inviting me to dinner.

I accepted with alacrity, as I was definitely interested in his wife, or rather, to discover what manner of woman had the honour and distinction to be Mrs. John Collins.

Was she a Frenchwoman who had drifted out to the East in the wake of an officer—or an Officers' Mess? Was she one of those smart, active, tight-corseted, beady-eyed Frenchwomen of whom there were so many at Saigon, ably officiating in shops and hotels?

Was she an American from one of the wonderful night-clubs or houses of Shanghai?

Was she one of those inevitably golden-haired women who, poor souls, are left stranded by illness in the trail of a travelling theatrical troupe?

Was she one of those European boarding-house keepers to be found in every port from Bombay to Hong-Kong *via* Colombo, Calcutta, Rangoon and Singapore?

I somehow fancied that she would be some sort of European, though I didn't know why I should think so. It was just as likely that she'd be a fascinatingly pretty Chinese girl, a golden-skinned Southern Siamese lass, or a dainty, yet capable, Japanese wench.

John Collins was much more of the type that instals a *congai*—what the *Doi* termed a *teasphiryéa*—than of that which marries a European according to his own law and custom, and remains faithful to her.

Besides, if he had married a European woman, it was hardly likely that she would have accompanied him on such an expedition, and to such a place, as this.

No, it would be a girl of the country, who went well with the wine of the country, of which John Collins was so fond.

Nevertheless I made myself as presentable as possible in the yellow uniform that Colonel Collins's extremely clever Chinese military-tailor had made for me.

As I approached John Collins's house, an hour later, the *conyam* rose to his feet, opened the door, bowed low, and ushered me into the presence of his master, who, in a sort of ante-room, part office, part den, was mixing himself a sun-downer.

"Have a drink, Dysart," said he with a smile which showed all his teeth but did not extend to his eyes, the hard, cold, penetrating eyes that watched so warily.

"May I have a . . ."

"What you are going to have, young feller, is a real whisky and soda, whisky from Scotland and soda from—God knows where. Probably cost more than the whisky by the time it got here."

"Thanks," said I; and, lacking something to say, asked *à propos* of nothing in particular.

"Does Mrs. Collins speak English?"

I don't know what made me ask this foolish question; but possibly I had been wondering subconsciously whether she talked Annamese or French, because if she spoke nothing but Chinese, she and I would not get much forrarder.

Why should we get any forrarder? I didn't know; but again, subconsciously I imagine, I must have been wondering whether I could learn, in conversation with her, anything about Colonel John Collins and his present undertakings.

John Collins swallowed his drink at a draught—more like a thirsty soldier, drinking water to save his life after a desert march, than a man taking an *aperitif*, or what should have been a mere *aperitif*, before dinner.

"Does she speak English?" he said with a laugh, as he looked into his empty glass and promptly replenished it; but made no further reply to my question.

"Have another?"

"No thanks."

"Not much of a performer on the bottle, are you?"

"No; very poor."

"Well, you'll excuse me if I . . ."

And John Collins opened another bottle of soda-water and poured himself a third drink.

The bottles were of the kind closed with a glass marble fitting against a rubber ring, and I noticed that Collins needed no bottle-opener. His right hand must have been pretty strong, for, holding the bottle in it, he pressed the marble down with the fore-finger without apparent effort.

"Come along then," he said, having swallowed the third drink as hastily as the others, and pushed open swing-doors that only partly filled a wide doorway, inasmuch as they began about two feet from the ground and only extended to within three feet of the top—thus admitting air from above and below and giving some privacy, as one could not see over them.

The room into which he ushered me was furnished as a sitting-room, and I could see at a glance that a woman had made pitiful efforts to make it look like a Western drawing-room. There were flowers in what appeared to be vases but were really silk-swathed or even paper-draped, tins, jars and bottles. Over crude teak and blackwood chairs were thrown lengths of silk; and across what had once been a settee was an undeniably Spanish shawl, a beautifully embroidered thing of heavy silk with long trailing fringe.

As I looked round, the door on the other side of the room opened and a woman entered the room.

"Mr. Dysart, Poppy," said Collins. "My wife."

I stared open-eyed, if not open-mouthed, at a picture by Goya; a typical Spanish woman with black hair, arching black eye-brows, brown eyes, long black lashes, a small red mouth and a lovely complexion, very white save where a healthy and delightful glow coloured the cheeks to rose-pink.

She smiled, and her teeth were small, regular, and perfect.

She was beautiful.

And what surprised me even more than her beauty and the fact that she was European, was the expression of her face. It was essentially kindly, sweet, and gentle. At the same time, it was grave, serious, and had about it an air of, what shall I say? Resignation is perhaps the best word.

This was no French camp-follower from Marseilles; no manageress of shop, stores, or hotel, from Saigon; no flotsam of a travelling theatrical company from Paris; no escapee from a Shanghai brothel.

This was a gentlewoman, and there is little wonder that I stared, glanced from her to Collins, and back again.

What language did she speak?

Not Spanish, I hoped, for I knew not a word of it. It would have surprised me, too, had she done so, as I didn't think that Collins knew that language.

French?

Probably . . . Well, I could get along quite comfortably in that language.

"How do you do, Mr. Dysart," she said, extending a tiny, shapely, and well-kept hand.

She was English!

"How do you do, Mrs. Collins. This is a truly delightful surprise for me."

"And for me too," she smiled. "I'm so glad you are English."

"Well, British," replied I, for the sake of something to say, and to keep the ball of conversation rolling. "I'm a Scot, as a matter of fact."

"Ah, of course. Dysart. But when we English say 'English' we mean 'British', naturally. Just a little boastful pride and self-esteem—our including the Scots," and she smiled again, delightfully.

I liked her voice tremendously, and voices mean a lot to me. I think there is nothing more revealing, both as to social origins, education, and background, on the one hand, and as to character and personality on the other.

It was the voice of an educated person of good-breeding, and it was a gentle, pleasant, and sweet voice that accorded well with the mouth from which it issued. Her voice was like herself; like her face; like, as later I learned, her character and nature.

Is there such a thing as love at first sight?

I don't know.

But I do know that this woman made a deep and indelible impression upon me at first sight.

But, good God! What was she doing here in China, here at this Chinese headquarters; here in the camp of two such men as Chu Chin Chow and the Private Secretary of Confucius?

And for that matter, how came such a woman to be the wife of John Collins, cold-hearted callous crook; rascally swashbuckler, and tough soldier of fortune?

I could have understood it had he been deserving of the honourable title of gentleman-adventurer—for though adventurer surely he was, gentleman definitely he was not. And when in this sense and connection I use the word 'gentleman', I have no thought whatsoever of birth, breeding, and social origin. I have myself been a sailor (on nine pounds a year), a private soldier in two armies, and a bought-and-sold slave standing daily on a sale-block, but I try to keep a decent standard of morals and manners.

And she was this man's wife!

How she was dressed, I do not know; but it was somehow in the European fashion of the day, and it was somehow evening-dress. Probably the regimental tailor had copied some copy of a copy of a *dhirzie*'s or rather a *konnyip-pah*'s copy of an evening dress that she had brought from Home, or that had been sent out from Home.

I suppose that, had she been in that uncharted wilderness before war broke out, it would have been possible for her to get clothes up from Haiphong by way of the Red River, though I doubt it.

Part of my surprise at seeing her looking so *soignée* must have been due to the fact that, according to John Collins, his wife had always accompanied him wherever he went; and that he had not been anywhere near civilization for years, not even to Peking, much less Shanghai, Hong-Kong or any town boasting a European shop. . . .

A Chinese servant, presumably the Number One Boy, announced that dinner was ready, and we went in to dine in the adjoining room.

Here again it struck me as pathetic that this English-woman should have attempted to reproduce, in this god-forsaken spot on the Tonking-Chinese border, a British dinner-table with white napery, polished silver and cutlery, glass and flowers.

In the centre of the table was a floral ornament, a bouquet of beautiful jungle flowers in what I felt sure was a most unworthy bowl, judging by the fact that it was swathed around with silk.

About the dinner there was no doubt, however. An excellent meal, admirably cooked; and though I doubt not that the *fons et origo boni* was goat and jungle fowl, the meal was worthy of a first-class hotel.

Conversation was difficult.

Collins, as usual, talked shop when not pumping me, as he was wont to do, with questions suddenly shot at me in the midst of his campaigning disquisitions; whereas Mrs. Collins most obviously, and very naturally, wished to talk of Home and to learn the latest news from England.

Unfortunately my own personal knowledge of English affairs was some three or four years old; but we could talk of London which she knew and loved, and of which I had seen a good deal in my Guardsman days.

It gave her pleasure even to hear such names as Hyde Park, Kensington Gardens, Drury Lane and Covent Garden; Bond Street, Regent Street, and Piccadilly; and I made a mental note of the fact that Collins himself seemed to know scarcely anything of the London of my day, and but very little of England. This fact I pondered even as he talked, switching off my conversation with his wife as frequently as he could, and sometimes with gross rudeness, to matters of local and personal interest.

From the first I had not liked Colonel Collins very much, and during this dinner I found myself heartily disliking him, for his manner toward his wife.

This was most boorish and ungentlemanly, and whenever he directed a remark to her, it was either of a sneering or a snubbing nature. I gained the impression that it annoyed him when some witty remark of hers caused me to laugh; that he disliked her to monopolize the conversation even for a minute; that he felt that women, or at any rate this woman, should be seen and not heard, and only seen when he wanted to look at her.

Throughout the dinner, he made me feel uncomfortable, and at times made my blood boil by his insufferable rudeness. Whatever I had thought him before, I now thought him an oaf and a churl; for, undeniably, in relation to the person for whom, surely, his best manner and manners should have been reserved, he was boorish, churlish, and mannerless in the extreme.

Had he only been mannerless it would have been bad enough; but he was intentionally rude; so rude that, at times, she flushed; and at such times I relapsed to schoolboy and half-deck crudity, and frankly admitted to myself that I would have liked to punch him on the jaw—obviously one of those sad examples of evil communications corrupting good manners.

After dinner, Collins proposed taking our drinks into the drawing-room, and to that room we all three went, the Number One Boy appearing and placing the whisky and bottles of soda-water on a low table beside the silk-draped deck-chair in which Collins reclined—evidently a regular part of the evening ritual.

Mrs. Collins having resumed her place on the sofa, motioned to me to sit beside her; and, watched by Collins, who sat and smoked and steadily drank, we talked of Home.

As he drank, Collins grew more silent and morose, eyeing me, I thought, and indeed his wife also, with increasing disfavour, though he interrupted our conversation less and less, and finally ceased to speak at all.

Opposite to us he sat and glared, favouring her with a long, considering, and unfriendly look, as she spoke, and turning the same baleful regard upon me when I replied.

I felt thoroughly uncomfortable; and so, I thought, did

Mrs. Collins. I began to understand whence came that look of quiet resignation, that air she had as of a grave wise child, a child that is too thoughtful and not too happy. Not that there was anything in the least degree childish, in the derogatory sense of the word, about her; but there was a simple sweetness, an unaffected naturalness, a kind of fundamental innocence that reminded one of a child; of, as I have said, a grave wise child that loved to smile but had almost forgotten how to laugh. . . .

In a brief silence that fell between us, I heard a sound that made me look up sharply. It was, as I had thought, a snore. The excellent Colonel Collins was sound asleep, his face presenting a much less prepossessing sight than when, full of animation and hearty false good-fellowship, it smiled and smiled and could not possibly belong to a villain.

Mrs. Collins eyed him long and thoughtfully.

"Your husband is asleep," I said fatuously.

"Yes. Pray don't speak loudly enough to wake him," she replied.

For the first time that evening there was a faint edge to her voice; and I gathered—though I did not for one moment think she intended me to do so—that she greatly preferred the Colonel asleep to the Colonel awake.

Accordingly I lowered my voice to the soft level of hers and, talking almost in whispers, we conversed for the better part of an hour.

Better part, indeed, for I doubt whether I ever more enjoyed an hour, or had ever been happier, in all my life.

I realized this, and it amazed me.

At the time, I put it down to the fact that this delightful person, so friendly, simple, kind and sweet, was the first white woman to whom I had talked for years, the first one with whom I had held real conversation since I left home to join the Life Guards.

For during those days in London, I had scarcely spoken to any of the women of the class with which most of my comrades associated, as they did not interest me in the very slightest degree. I had met none whatsoever in Africa or Arabia, and had never encountered a native girl to whom

I could talk at all, or with whom I had any desire to talk.

As I thought the matter over, I realized that Mrs. Collins was the very first woman with whom I had had any real conversation since I had last seen Elizabeth at Wellingbury, and Celia on the *Valkyrie*, just before.

Elizabeth I had loved as a boy loves a very young girl, but she had grown up, grown away from me, and married a young cavalry officer whom she had met out hunting; and Celia I had never greatly liked, much less loved.

I suppose it was because Mrs. Collins was the first woman of my own class and kind whom I had met in all these years—coupled with the fact that I was so emotionally starved, having led not only a completely celibate life but a practically womanless one for several years—that now made her conversation, her presence, her self, so irresistible, delightful, charming, so fascinating alike to my senses and my soul.

Not that she made the faintest attempt to be fascinating or had any intention of charming me. Of that I am as certain as I am of anything in this world. She was just completely natural; just her real self; and that was, as I say, charming, fascinating, and delightful.

What we said I scarcely remember, though it was of Home, of herself, and of myself. Without inquisitiveness or anything in the nature of idle curiosity, she asked me about my past life because I interested her; and, like everybody else, I was only too pleased to talk about myself. And as she interested me, I asked her about herself, while endeavouring to refrain from being indiscreet or seeming to pry.

And the more we talked, the more I marvelled that she was what she was, and that she looked as she did look; that she showed so little trace, indeed no trace whatever, of what she had been through.

Although there was nothing of complaint in what she told me, it was obvious that her life had been one long frustration, suppression, disappointment; that she had had none of the things that make life endurable, if not happy, for women of her sort.

It was obvious, in short, that her life must have been a

most unhappy one, and a very hard one.

And yet she did not look unhappy. There was nothing whatsoever to suggest that she had had such a life, except what I have termed a slight air of mild resignation, the air of one who expects nothing good from life, and gets precisely that.

Nor was her face lined, her eyes anxious or hunted, her mouth bitter, her look disillusioned, her speech cynical or plaintive. . . .

With a sudden loud snort, Colonel John Collins sat upright, opened his eyes, and glared at us.

"About time for another drink, what?" he said, grinning, "and then if you'll forgive me, Dysart . . ."

I took the hint and rose to my feet.

"If you'll excuse me, Mrs. Collins. . . . Thank you so much for a most delightful evening. I can honestly say I have not enjoyed myself so greatly for years, and . . ."

"And all that," jeered Collins, in a harsh, sneering and unpleasant voice, using what I felt was his normal domestic tone.

For the sake of peace I took another unwanted drink, said good-bye at once, and made my way back to my hut, feeling that, somehow, to-night was epochal and marked a turning-point in my life.

CHAPTER XIV

Thereafter I cultivated Colonel Collins assiduously; at first, I believe, with a view to learning more and more about the plans of the two Generals for the coming season's campaign, and, before long, I am certain, in the hope of seeing Mrs. Collins again.

More than anything in the world, I thought, I wanted to find out what the Imperial Chinese Government was doing, and was going to do, to help the cause of the Emperor of Annam.

More than anything in the world, I soon realized, I wanted to see Mrs. Collins again, to hear the sound of her voice, to talk to her about myself and induce her to talk to me about herself.

I was undoubtedly starving for the least crumb of affection, acutely suffering the pangs of hunger for self-expression.

I was yearning to free myself from the iron repressions clamped upon my soul by my mother, who, hating my father and loving another man, had always denied me her affection and prohibited the demonstration on my part of the love that I, as a child, undoubtedly felt for her and yearned to express.

I am not seeking to make an excuse, only an explanation—an explanation of the fact that soon I found myself seeking and seizing every opportunity of going to Collins's house, and looking forward throughout the whole day to the minute when at sunset I could go to his door and ask the *conyam* whether his master were at home and would speak to me for a minute.

I occasionally saw her by this means, and I felt certain that she was always glad when this happened.

Naturally I rightly attributed it to the fact that the sight of a British face and the sound of a British voice would inevitably be most welcome to any woman situated as she was;

an oasis in that dreary desert of alien environment and wearisome ennui of exile.

Few people who were not prisoners were ever such a prisoner as she was in that house in a fort in a camp in the occupation of that great horde of semi-savage bandits.

It may have begun in pity but it ended in love—for before long I realized that it was not anticipation of seeing the cunning and cruel face of Colonel Collins, hearing his growling and minatory voice, that made my heart beat painfully fast as I approached his house, made me sing merrily within myself as I did so, and caused me to rise in the morning happy in the thought that at evening I should have excuse to walk in that direction.

One day the *conyam* informed me that Colonel Kar-Linh had left the camp and would not return until dinner-time. I was just about to turn away from the door when Mrs. Collins appeared at the entrance to the Colonel's room which opened into her drawing-room.

"Good-evening, Mr. Dysart," she said, smiling her adorable slow sweet smile, the expression of the very essence of gentle friendliness and kindness, "you have just missed my husband, I'm afraid. Can I give him a message for you?"

"No, thank you, Mrs. Collins," I stammered in great confusion. "I really came to see . . ."

This was unlike me, for I am not usually quite so gauche, diffident and stupid as all that—and I had actually been about to blurt out "I really came to see you", which was the plain truth.

Perhaps there was something about her that constrained one to tell her the plain truth—her candour, grave simplicity and unaffected naturalness.

Suddenly she smiled and asked me when I had last had an English afternoon tea—with a tablecloth and thin bread-and-butter.

I laughed.

Certainly I had not had an English afternoon tea in Annam, nor on board the transport *Général Boulanger*, nor in Sidi-bel-Abbes, nor in prison in Djibouti, nor on the Mecca pilgrimage, nor in Bab-el-Djebel, nor perhaps precisely a typical English afternoon-tea when I was a trooper in the Life Guards.

No, the last time must have been during my brief visit to my home, on my return from the voyage in the *Valkyrie*.

"Not for years," I replied.

"Then come and have tea with me now," she said, and again my heart beat almost painfully fast as she led the way to the drawing-room.

Here her Number One Boy brought a very dainty tea indeed, and in that room I seemed to have stepped from the sixteenth century into the nineteenth, and from barbarism and brutality into beauty and brightness.

It was really quite wonderful to be sitting in a drawing-room and taking tea with a gentlewoman, and unspeakably wonderful to be sitting thus and talking with Mrs. Collins.

I forget most of what was said.

I was too intent on listening to the sound of her voice, to pay much attention to her words, too occupied in watching her lips, her eyes, her grave sweet face, to notice what she was saying.

I did however realize that she was asking me all about myself, though never about my business, and it delighted me that she should be interested, and should ask me to tell her more concerning my adventures and experiences.

When I said that I would rather talk about her, she replied that possibly she might tell me about herself some day, but not now.

I think I was on trial, and I think she longed to find me to be the sort of person to whom she could really talk and of whom she could make a friend.

How she must have longed for the society of another woman.

For a while we sat silent, and I stared at her as she poured out tea.

Yes, she was lovely by any standards, and though at least as old as I, had somehow the fresh and innocent face of a child—of a grave wise child, as I have said, one to whom Life has been a very serious business, devoid of laughter.

While there was nothing in the slightest degree miserable, peevish, bitter, or discontented about her expression, there was that elusive look of resignation, of patience, of suffering controlled and indeed denied, that I found pitiful and pathetic. I put it down to the fact that through being what she was, she was where she was, and I was conscious of a surge of futile anger at the selfishness of a man who could condemn an Englishwoman, especially one of obviously educated, refined and cultured (one has to use these words) antecedents, to live in such a way in such a place.

Not the most overwhelming love could excuse such monstrous selfishness, unless it were returned in equal measure—and then, of course, the wilderness were paradise enow. But, somehow, I could not imagine Colonel Collins inspiring such a love and devotion. Rather he struck me as the sort of hoggish man in whose society any delicately nurtured woman would find Paradise itself to be wilderness enow.

As I sat and looked at Mary Collins and listened to her voice, I fell deeper and deeper in love with her, headlong, desperately in love, and life became a joyous thing because she was in the same world with me.

I loved everybody and everything because I loved her.

I loved the moon that looked down upon us both and beautified the house in which she dwelt.

I loved the stars because that night she came to the door with me, and looking up, remarked upon their apparent extra brilliance. Never again would I look up at the stars without thinking of her and of the night when I dared to wonder, in my folly and presumption, whether they appeared the brighter to her, as they did to me, because her heart was singing too—as the stars of the evening sang.

I loved Life and Man and God and . . . In short—I was in love: and madly in love with lovely Love, as well as with lovely Mary Collins.

§2

And so my sufficiently amazing life in the robber-stronghold of Phu-Son became yet more amazing, for that grim and blood-stained place, scene of torture, savage punishments and sudden death, was made my brief Paradise on earth, because in it dwelt the woman who turned existence to a thing of beauty, joy, ecstasy and gratitude.

I was never so happy in all my life as I was there; never so miserable; never so filled with delight, hope, misery, fear, doubt and anxiety.

For soon I must go, and the sooner the better for the success of my mission. I must go—probably never to see her again; go, leaving her not only in the place most unfit of all places in the world to be the habitation of such a woman, but leaving her in the gravest and greatest danger.

For what was to become of her if anything happened to Colonel Collins—and undoubtedly anything might happen to him at any time, whether because he gave offence to one or other of the *tuchuns*, the War-Lords, or through any of the other manifold dangers of battle, murder and sudden death to which his life in the fever-stricken jungle and as a fighting soldier in the frequent battles, skirmishes and forays constantly exposed him.

What would be the fate of lovely Mary Collins if the man who had so callously brought her there were killed?

Every possible opportunity of seeing her that occurred, I seized; and, before long, I was making opportunities when none fortuitously befell; planning, plotting, scheming and watching for the least chance of seeing her for however brief a space.

Nor had many days passed, many such occasions been seized or made, before I, however humble and modest Love may have made me, could not fail to be aware that Mary Collins welcomed them, was glad to see me, looked forward to our next meeting, found in me something that so long she had lacked and desperately needed—someone reliable and trustworthy, someone kind and understanding, someone who cared what became of her and would strain every nerve to prevent any evil from befalling her, would protect, cherish and befriend her.

For, as I then guessed, and later I came to know, she

suffered that most dreadful of all miseries—loneliness; had that most terrible of all knowledge, that she had not a friend in the world, not a soul to whom she could turn for sympathy and support.

§3

One day when she was again alone, suffering her usual solitary confinement in the house that was her prison, she invited me to tea with her and told me the story of her life.

CHAPTER XV

Mrs. Collins told me her story—which was of course part of that of Colonel John Collins, about which I was more than anxious to hear—very much as follows.

"I was born in Kent. Our house was in the Elham Valley—in the *Ingoldsby* country.

Do you know Canterbury? Oh, good! Don't you love it? I simply adore the place. The Cathedral, the Precincts, St. Augustine's, the Dane John, St. Martin's Church, Harbledown. I love every inch of it. I used to sit for hours in the Precincts, just looking at the Cathedral; and for hours in the Cathedral itself, especially when there was no service in progress.

My father was a Canon. I don't remember my mother. When he died, he left no money, and a maiden aunt of mine adopted me. I believe she was very poor, and even prouder than she was poor.

As a child, I thought of her as old; but, as a matter of fact, when she took me she must have been in her twenties, and a most attractive woman, well-educated and with a great fund of humour and commonsense. And she was so good to me that I really don't know that I lost a great deal in not having a mother. I don't see how any mother could have been more loving, kind and understanding than she was. And, considering how really hard-up she must have been, she was generous beyond praise. She must have worked like a slave too, because the house was quite big, and very frequently she was without any maid at all.

A neighbour of ours was a Sir Stanbury Macke Collins, a retired *taipan*. He had made quite a big fortune in China, lost a good deal of it when he invested it in England, and settled down in Kent to grow fruit. He was one of those apple-growing experts, quite fanatical on the subject.

I liked him very well. So did Aunt Phoebe, and I think Sir Stanbury liked her more than very well.

Unfortunately, as I realized when I was older, poor Aunt Phoebe was hopelessly in love with a doctor in Canterbury, a splendid man, very clever indeed, and yet without sufficient sense to see what he was missing.

Oh, how dull life was in the Elham Valley. Canterbury Cricket Week was the high spot of the year, when we would go over and watch the cricket and see the play given by the famous Canterbury Amateur Theatrical Society, the 'Old Stagers'. One looked forward to it from one August to the next.

We had practically no social life; and almost our only visitor was Sir Stanbury, who must have been twice as old as Aunt Phoebe.

Then, one day, things looked like brightening up, for Sir Stanbury announced that his son, of whom he was always telling us, was coming home from China for a holiday.

He came; and, the next day, Sir Stanbury brought him over to see us.

I rather liked him at first. He was something entirely new in my experience. And after I had got used to his face, I got used to him, too. I found him amusing and full of most interesting information. He talked extremely well, and he talked the whole time. I say 'when I got used to his face', because, at first, it struck me as the most extraordinary face I had ever seen. It was so curiously round and smooth then; and there was something very strange about the eyes and hair.

One doesn't notice it here in China, but there, in Kent, in the peaceful backwater of the sweet Elham Valley (one can call it that—or a beastly dead-and-alive hole) John Collins was somehow—shall I say—exotic.

I was eighteen then, and a fool, apart from being about as ignorant and innocent as only a girl of that age, brought up in a Canon's house in the Cathedral precincts and then in a maiden aunt's house in a village, could be. Because Sir Stanbury had been so kind to us and such a friend to us, almost our only friend in fact, I was prepared to like his son, anxious to like him, in fact; and when a girl is determined to like a man, she generally succeeds. Nevertheless, there were times when John Collins jarred; times when he puzzled me very much; times when I felt that definitely I did not like him.

I have only myself to blame, of course, for I saw a great deal of him, as both he and his father used to come over to our house almost daily, besides entertaining us to tennis and tea, and inviting us to dinner.

One day, when Aunt Phoebe and I were sitting under the cedar on our lawn, she suddenly said,

'Well, Mary, how do you like John?'

'John Collins? Oh, I don't know . . .'

'He likes you well enough, my dear. What are you going to say when he asks you to marry him?'

I never pretended with Aunt Phoebe.

'What do you advise?' I asked.

'Well, I can only tell you what I should do. I should marry him. I should want to get away from here—not just vegetate, grow old, and die, in the Elham Valley. It isn't as though I could take you about—so that you'd meet . . . people.'

'Perhaps he won't ask me.'

'He will. I'll tell you something. Don't tell anybody else. Sir Stanbury asked me yesterday if I would marry him.'

'Marry John?'

'No him, himself.'

'Why he's old enough to be . . .'

'Anyway, he asked me to marry him; and when I told him I was awfully sorry but it was impossible, he said he hoped John would have better luck.'

'Perhaps he meant that John was going to ask you too.'

'Perhaps. However, the question is what are you going to say when he asks you? Do you like him?'

'Sometimes I do—very much. Sometimes I don't?'

'Well, I imagine there are times when most women like their husbands very much, and times when they don't. . . . I wish you were in love with him. Still, I think every woman ought to marry, if she can. . . . And eligible men don't grow on every bush round here, do they?'

Aunt Phoebe sighed.

'I believe he's quite well off. And he's going back to

China. You'd like to travel, wouldn't you?'

'Love to.'

'And to see China and probably Japan?'

'Love to.'

'Well then . . .'

And the more I thought about it, the more the idea of getting away from the village and the terribly narrow dull life that we led, appealed to me. The more I thought about it, the better I liked the idea of travelling—a sea-voyage; foreign parts; strange peoples. . . . And, of course, the idea of the fuss and importance of being a bride also appealed to me.

And one day something Aunt Phoebe said—though I'm sure she did not mean it to have that effect—brought it home to me that she was really terribly poor, and that I was an expense and a burden to her. I knew perfectly well that she never would have admitted that she felt the burden, or that she would not have been only too delighted to have shared her last penny with me.

Well then, thought I to myself, didn't that make it all the more up to me to relieve her of the burden; to be an expense to her no longer, since this opportunity offered.

And that is how I came to marry John Collins.

He brought me out to China directly, without other honeymoon; and, after spending a little while at Hong-Kong and Shanghai, we went to Peking.

At Peking he took me to see his mother.

His mother is a Chinese woman who cannot speak a word of English.

When I learned this, and knew that my husband was a half-caste, son of Stanbury Macke Collins and this Chinese woman, I realized what it was about him that had puzzled me, and the reason for the curious shape of his smooth round face, his unusual eyes, and stiff black hair.

Many other things too, mental and moral, as well as physical.

Quite evidently he loved his Chinese mother, and

certainly treated her far better than her husband had done.

She had refused to leave China when Sir Stanbury retired and left the country for good; and, apparently, he had not been very particular to see that she was comfortably provided for, and well looked after.

In Peking, my husband 'went native', as they say; became entirely Chinese, and, whereas many English merchants, officials, traders and adventurers had dealings with the Chinese, as foreigners retaining their own traits, manners, customs and nationality, my husband had dealings with Europeans as a Chinese, which I believe a great many of them supposed him to be.

Naturally he speaks the language perfectly; and, in Chinese dress and surroundings, no-one would imagine that he was a half-caste, much less suppose him to be a European.

The Chinese authorities apparently thought a great deal of his father, Stanbury Macke Collins, but less of his son who was so like one of themselves.

What exactly his position was, and what exactly he did, I cannot tell you, but he was *persona grata* with all the important people, from mandarins of the lowest rank up to the Empress herself.

We used to go away from our Peking house for long periods at a time, and on these occasions visited the Treaty ports, Japan, Russia, and Annam and French Cochin China; always, I believe, on Government business of some kind.

As a young man he was certainly a soldier, but whether he had an officer's training and went to Sandhurst or Woolwich I don't know.

For some reason that I can never understand, he always took me with him wherever he went; and yet contrived to keep me in almost complete ignorance of what his business was, though from time to time I met various Europeans, sometimes French, sometimes German, sometimes Russian, but never English. These foreigners were nearly always soldiers.

Why did he always take me with him—and yet always keep me in complete ignorance of his affairs?

It wasn't as though he was so in love with me that he couldn't bear me out of his sight, or that he was anxious for my safety if he left me behind in Peking. There was nothing of that sort. Why he married me I don't know, for he tired of me very quickly; and, from his manner, one would imagine that, on the whole, he rather disliked me, and at times positively hated me.

There again I don't know why, for, being young and, as I have said, a fool, I took the line of least resistance, did everything I could to keep the peace and to make life bearable. I hate quarrelling, squabbling, bickering. It is so wearing, tiring; so degrading, disgusting. And, to me, there was one thing worse than being weak and meek and sub-missive—flabby and spineless, if you will—and the one thing worse was a chronic state of quarrelling; constant rows.

I simply couldn't have it.

You see I had married him to get away from home, and to relieve my aunt of a burden; and I felt that I must do my part, that I must pay what I owed.

I paid.

I have paid ever since.

I have paid all the while.

He strikes me—with his fist—quite frequently . . .

And he's strong, forceful, ruthless; a far stronger charac-ter than I. I don't suppose I was very remarkable for lack of firmness of character and strength of will; but he domi-nated me completely, broke my will and made me what I am —his obedient servant, his slave.

When I realized—and he made it impossible for me to do otherwise—that he had quite ceased to love me, I begged him to let me go back to England. I told him he need not support me. I'd find work of some sort. But no, he wouldn't hear of it. In fact, he flew into a rage, struck me in the face, and told me if I ever talked like that again I'd—regret it.

Why on earth did he marry me? Was it that he wanted an English wife in his business? Wanted to keep up his English? Wanted to be, and to seem, as English as possible, should occasion arise? I have often wondered."

CHAPTER XVI

I didn't wonder. It was clear enough to me. His love had been desire, passion. Not the desire of the moth for the star, but of the half-caste for the Englishwoman to whom he must needs look up. The dislike that followed the attainment of his desire was the expression of his inferiority complex.

He hated her because he had loved her, because he had been unable to help loving her; because she was so infinitely his superior in everything but strength and cunning.

I could see it all, or I thought I could, and probably I was right.

§2

If such a thing were possible I loved Mary even more, after she had told me the pitiable story of her spoilt, wasted and tragic life, than I did before. Certainly thoughts of her filled my mind more constantly and completely than they had done hitherto, and it was with conscious effort that I switched them from love to duty.

I think I rendered this difficult feat more easy and acceptable by vaguely combining the two incompatibles and promising myself that, somehow, I would rescue her from her extremely dangerous situation—one that was a shameful disgrace to her husband—when I left Phu-Son and returned to my headquarters. I told myself that somehow, by discovering all I could about the position, strength and garrison of the great New Fort, the arrival of reinforcements of regular troops from China, and the time, route, and nature of the big convoy of munitions, money, uniforms, and food, I should be helping her by shortening my stay and hastening the date of her departure.

For though I neither would nor could formulate actual plans for taking her away from her husband and from Phu-

Son, the feeling was growing, strengthening and hardening in my heart, that it would be quite impossible for me to go without her.

This feeling was almost subconscious, for until the situation changed and events forced my hand, I shied away from the thought of what I felt.

My mind did not frankly admit, so to speak, that any such feeling really existed. I am no psychologist in that sense, but I imagine that it was a case of Reason and Emotion acting independently, Thought and Feeling going about their separate affairs without reference the one to the other.

In fact, at this time I felt that I should most probably interfere and take Mary away from this vile dangerous environment—and I thought that I should do nothing of the sort.

What right had I to endeavour to combine abduction with Secret Service work; and what hope had I of being able to take a European woman through those ghastly jungles? A fine thing if I—falsely pretending that what I desired to do was what I ought to do—took her from the comparative, if temporary, safety of the armed camp and exposed her to infinitely greater hardships and dangers, dangers to which she succumbed.

I had asked myself, times without number, what was to become of her in this den of thieves, if anything happened to her husband.

I now asked myself what was to become of her in the most pestilential and dangerous jungle in the world if anything happened to me.

Suppose I and my tiny band of followers were killed and she fell into the hands of the Black Flags, the river pirates and jungle dacoits, notoriously the cruellest devils in the world.

No; Intelligence and Reason boggled at the idea.

But Feeling and Emotion clung to it, hugged it closely, and refused to let it go.

The horns of a dilemma indeed.

I could not go away, leaving the woman I loved in such a situation.

I could not go away taking her with me into a situation far more hazardous.

And I could not much longer remain where I was.

Meanwhile, De-Nha had most urgent instructions to find out all about the New Fort; and, for a beginning, most important of all, where it was. If I could return to Captain Deleuze with really definite detailed and reliable information on that subject, I should have earned my corn—and his gratitude.

What I could now tell him about the camp and fort of Phu-Son, about the Generals Ba-Ky and Luong-Tam-Ky, about Colonel Collins, about the Chinese bandit army, and about the help in money, materials, and regular troops from China, would be interesting and valuable; but the real facts about General De-Nam's great citadel, arsenal, and treasury, the New Fort, would be priceless.

That I must learn and then I must go.

And Mary Collins must go with me.

Of course Mary Collins must not, could not possibly, go with me.

§3

One day it dawned upon my somewhat dull mind that General Luong-Tam-Ky was interested in me.

In other words, I consciously realized a fact of which I had been subconsciously, if increasingly, aware, that General Luong-Tam-Ky came and watched me at work rather more often than he did the native officers of the force of which he was joint Commander-in-Chief, sent for me and questioned me on points of European drill, musketry, commissariat and tactics, and generally took notice of me.

Frankly I found this disturbing, and, as his questioning proceeded from general military and European matters to private and personal ones, I found it rather more than merely disturbing.

The man was so wily, so enigmatic, so inscrutable and unfathomable, that I grew increasingly uncomfortable.

Time after time, he tried to trap me into betrayal of the

fact that I understood French; and repeatedly he endeavoured to prove that I knew the Annamese Delta country and places like Hanoi, Haiphong, Bac-Ninh, Phulang Thuong and other towns in the occupation of the French.

Either he was suspicious that I was a French spy, or else, thanks to the treachery or carelessness of De-Nha he knew that I was.

Probably the fact that I loved Mary so utterly and desperately saved me from worrying unduly over what was undeniably a dangerous situation.

Nevertheless, there were times when I could not refrain from speculating on what would be my fate if this cold, infinitely cruel and relentless man decided that I was a spy, and that he would deal with me accordingly.

I should be as helpless as a kitten in the hands of a brutal lout, or as a very small fly in the web of a very large spider; and not only would General Luong-Tam-Ky be on his mettle to learn me to be a spy, but to do something calculated to discourage others from visiting him in that capacity, when the news of my fate was bruited abroad. For doubtless he would forward some portion of my anatomy to French headquarters with a detailed description of what had happened to the rest of me.

I tried, at first, to persuade myself that I was fanciful, that the situation was getting on my nerves; that his interest in me was only the natural interest of a keen General in the valuable work of a foreign expert; and, at times, in my higher flights of optimism, that he liked me personally, and took an interest in me for my own sake. "For my *beaux yeux* in fact," thought I, and laughed aloud at my own foolishness.

When the matter became obvious beyond all doubt, and beyond the possibility of ignoring it as a fear-bred fancy, I consulted Colonel Collins on the subject.

His re-action was peculiar, interesting, and again, in its way, disturbing. For he too, both by reason of his Chinese blood and his long residence in China, could be extremely Oriental himself, as incomprehensible and devious, as inscrutable and enigmatic, as any of them.

At first, he pursed his lips, frowned, and eyed me searchingly. Having questioned me as to what made me think General Luong-Tam-Ky was specially interested in me and becoming increasingly so, he smiled slyly and nodded his head several times.

As I gave him instance after instance of the General's exhibition of attention to my humble self, my past life and present activities, Colonel Collins appeared to grow impatient, to be annoyed, and to exhibit feelings of anger. Studying him carefully and then thinking the matter over very carefully at my leisure, I came to the conclusion that, at first, he was afraid that the General was growing suspicious, and that he, Colonel Collins, was about to lose the services of a valued, if not esteemed, colleague; that, secondly, he began to wonder whether, perhaps, that was not the real situation, but that I was "making up" to the General and pretending that it was the General who was cultivating me; and that, thirdly, and finally, he decided that both these theories were wrong, and that the General was about to remove him and put me in his place.

I decided, in fact, that Colonel Collins was jealous and angry, and that the savage stare with which he favoured me indicated a suddenly aroused suspicion that I was playing the part of the cuckoo in the nest. And as there was a distinct and definite sneer in his words, tone, and manner, at the end of this interview, I felt quite sure that, should the fledgling prove to be a bird of the cuckoo variety, his place in the nest would soon be vacant.

Deeply I regretted taking my troubles to this man, a self-centred schemer, an ego-centric and unscrupulous careerist, devoid of kindliness, friendliness, or the faintest desire or intention of doing anything for anybody except himself, and imbued with both the desire and intention of removing from his path anybody who in any way obstructed it.

Life thereafter became more of a strain than ever, as I made my anxious way between pit-falls and death-traps, fearing the brutal General Ba-Ky; very greatly fearing the more dangerous and more watchful Luong-Tam-Ky; and now fearing, almost as much, the suspicious and treacherous Colonel Collins.

And there was another man whom I think I feared, in a way, more than any of them, because I hated and despised him; regarded him as a loathsome worm; and yet knew that at any moment the grovelling and humble worm could turn into a serpent of the deadliest kind. This was the traitor De-Nha, who had sold his cause for a handful of opium.

I could not rid myself of the suspicion that he would prove a double traitor, would find familiar lures stronger than foreign temptations, decide to bargain with the Generals and throw in his lot with theirs, if it seemed likely that they would make it worth his while to do so.

It seemed to me that he could make a fine story of how he, having been captured by the French, had tricked and fooled them, and succeeded in bringing the star-turn of their Military Intelligence Secret Service straight to the feet —or rather the hands—of the ever-victorious Generals.

And when I tried to persuade myself that he had left it too long and too late, and that the Generals would say, "Why didn't you denounce him at once?" my better judgment replied that doubtless he had done so at once, had betrayed me as soon as we arrived.

It would be just like these marvellous Chinese to fool me to the top of my bent; to indulge themselves to the top of their own; to employ me in their service, make the utmost use of me, let me teach their troops everything I could—and then torture me to death.

Yes, life was something of a strain.

Possibly the strain would have been too great, and I should have broken down through anxiety, fear, and insomnia but for my great and glorious love.

Perfect love casteth out fear—to some extent. Mine was very perfect, and it must have cast out much of my fear.

And yet there remained, ever present and chief of my problems, unanswerable and insoluble, the question,

"How can I remain much longer—and live? How can I go —and leave Mary here?"

§4

And, as a cat watches a mouse, *Doi* Linh Nghi watched De-Nha. By night and by day that evil and cruel Annamese was under the incessant and unwavering observation of the *Doi* or one of his men. Never was he permitted to walk alone, to sleep alone and to be alone, for, in his comings-in and his goings-out, his risings-up and his lyings-down, one of them accompanied him as did his shadow—as did indeed The Shadow watch and accompany his admired master the General Luong-Tam-Ky.

CHAPTER XVII

My next social function was a dinner party, or rather a *dîner tête-à-tête* with General Luong-Tam-Ky; an extremely interesting, indeed, painfully interesting, function; for I felt as though I were an insect pinned firmly down beneath the microscope, although the lenses of that extremely powerful microscope were but the aged-looking and myopic-seeming eyes of the man to whom I mentally referred as the Private Secretary to Confucius.

Never before in my life had I been treated with such extremely contemptuous courtesy, or should I say with such extremely courteous contempt.

I was made to feel that, in the presence of the meek, the humble, the pure-hearted, the poor-spirited, the peace-making General Luong-Tam-Ky, I was a low and vulgar savage, an ignorant thing that had crawled in from the outer darkness of foreign parts, and up from the primæval slime of Western barbarism.

I was also made to feel slightly uncomfortable. For behind the General stood this man whom I had seen at the General's inspection and who was known throughout the camp as The Shadow. Something of a misnomer, for The Shadow was one of the most substantial people I have ever seen. I personally am tall, broad and thick beyond the ordinary, but beside—or rather in front of—The Shadow I felt, and doubtless looked, small.

He was, as I have said, a truly enormous Chinese or other Mongol, with colossal muscles and one of the most sub-humanly savage faces I have ever seen.

What made me uncomfortable was the fact that never once during that long meal did he take his eyes off me.

I should greatly have enjoyed telling him that it was rude to stare, but doubtless that was what he was there for. And undoubtedly I made no motion, particularly with my hands, that he did not follow with the utmost attentiveness. I felt that The Shadow was the last man whom many a poor wretch had seen on this earth. In another sense, he was the last man whom I wanted to see—again. . . .

My first shock was suddenly to discover that General Luong-Tam-Ky was an English scholar; and when I say scholar I don't mean merely that he could make himself understood in English.

Not only did he speak the language perfectly—and, apart from his thin piping voice, almost without accent, save an occasional weak 'r' that tended to turn into a liquid consonant—but the English that he spoke was admirable in matter as well as manner.

He must, of course, have lived for years in England; and he had studied English literature to some purpose. Had I closed my eyes, I could have imagined that I was in the study of some aged don or vicar, listening to high discourse uttered in the thin piping voice of age. Not that he was by any means old.

Incidentally General Luong-Tam-Ky did not talk as so many English-speaking Chinese do, as though he had a plum in his mouth.

But unfortunately Shakespeare, and the greatest of all the European poets, play-wrights, authors, philosophers, scientists and divines were as nothing in his sight, which could see but a little way beyond the great Confucius.

I, of course, was ignorant on the subject that most interested and informed the acute, highly-developed, and well-stocked mind of my host.

And though, at this dinner we were not amused, I was almost amused at the thought that I should have dubbed him the Private Secretary of Confucius, when I discovered him to be not so much a student, a follower, a disciple, as a fanatical worshipper of the god-like sage.

To my shame I did not even know the Saint's date; and, like most Englishmen, knew practically nothing at all about him, save that he was the Wise Man of China, and that Confucianism was a philosophy that was practically a religion.

I was surprised and interested to learn that

Confucianism was much older than Christianity, the Sage having been born some half a century before Christ.

As, between courses—of shredded pork with chilli sauce, stewed shoots of young bamboo, rotten eggs with mercifully strong onions, chicken curry, pickled turnips, fishes' eyes and other such dainties—we drank our ceremonial mandarin tea from saucerless and handleless cups, General Luong-Tam-Ky would quote the Master and I imagine his translation was admirable.

"But, ah," observed he, "Greatness. Strength. Wisdom . . . What says he of these things?

> " 'The greatest hills themselves must
>   crumble,
> The strongest beams must break,
> And the wisest of men must wither and
>   die like a flower.'

As he himself did," he commented with a sigh.

And suddenly from the midst of his abstraction, he shot at me quick look and sudden question,

"*Quelle heure est-il, Monsieur?*". . . and he very nearly had me. Almost my hand moved instinctively toward my pocket, as though I were about to consult a watch.

"I beg your pardon, General?" I said; and no flicker of smile or look of interest disturbed the calm serenity of his face.

"I merely asked, in Chinese, whether you would take more tea," he said.

And after we had, in silence, consumed the anonymous contents of the next bowls that were placed before us— something that tasted as one's hands smell after taking a fish off the hook—he asked,

"And have you, from your studies of the Christian religion, educed a Golden Rule?"

"Yes, General, I have. But I don't profess to follow it— always."

"And what is it, may I ask?"

"To prefer the Good; and to treat my neighbour as I would myself."

"Ah, yes, yes. I must teach you the Golden Rule of Confucius. It is more comprehensive than that. In fact, it is a Golden Fasces of Golden Rods or Rules, the least of which is like your only one concerning your neighbour. On this subject Confucius says,

" '*What you don't like to be done to yourself, don't do to others.*' "

"The same precept," I murmured.

"And again," continued the General,

" '*What the superior man is seeking is always within himself, but what the small man seeks is always in others.*' "

And, with supreme insolence, he added,

"Is there anything *I* can do for *you*, young man?"

I smiled wryly.

"At the moment, General, I seek nothing in you," I replied; and again received the quick look from the expressionless eyes which were the only things alive in the inscrutable face.

"Ah, '*The supreme man is dignified and does not argue*'," he quoted.

This I received in silence.

" '*He is social but is not a partisan.*' "

"It is my pleasure at the moment to be . . . social," commented the General on this Confucianism, and promptly shot a question at me.

"Are you a partisan, young man?"

"At the moment, a partisan of yours—and your cause, General," I bowed.

The General vouchsafed no comment upon this, but daintily drank a cup of tea, savouring it as does a port-drinker his wine, and admiring the delicate egg-shell china which I thought an incongruous item of Military Headquarter furniture.

"And what says Confucius with regard to Man and Words?

" '*He promotes not a man because of his words, but*

neither puts he good words aside because of the man.'

"*Qu'est-ce que c'est que vous tenez dans la main?*"

In point of fact I had my chop-sticks in my right hand and nothing whatsoever in the other, and I don't think that I glanced at the empty hand, or that it moved at all. If the old devil were bent on making me confess to a knowledge of French, I thought I could defeat him.

"I beg your pardon, General?" I said again.

"I merely said in Chinese, 'Don't you agree that the superior person would not favour a man on account of what he said; but, on the other hand, would take note of anything, worth hearing, that was said by the most despicable of men?'

"Have *you* anything of interest to tell *me*?" he added with the suavest insolence.

"Nothing whatever, General, despicable though I am," I replied coldly.

In point of fact I could have told him something of the greatest interest, and I could have done something that would have interested him still more, but this was neither the time nor the place to betray the fact.

" '*The cautious rarely err,*' saith Confucius," observed the General sententiously, but whether in praise of my own caution I did not know.

"Propriety is a virtue," he further observed, *à propos* of nothing, unless it were of the propriety of my present conduct.

" '*A poor man who never flatters, and a rich man who is not proud, are good characters; but they are not equal to the poor who are cheerful and the rich who love the rules of propriety!*' . . . How wonderful, how beautiful, how truly exquisite and exquisitely true are the words of The Sage," he said, and metaphorically smacked his lips over the flavour of these words of wisdom.

"And, like that of Confucius, has your Christian ethic, your Excellent Way—borrowed from the East, of course—anything on the subject of . . . insubordination?" he asked, as with parallel chop-sticks he delicately pursued fragments of meat floating in a thin clear soup.

And while hastily I reviewed my somewhat scanty array of remembered texts, he continued,

"Insubordination, disobedience . . . Terrible sins, especially in the soldier. What saith Confucius?

" *'Extravagance leads to insubordination, and parsimony leads to meanness; but far better it is to be mean than to be insubordinate.'*

"How do you punish the insubordinate soldier in your army? It is with *crapaudine*, is it not?"

For a moment he almost had me there, for I was on the point of saying,

"No, not in the English army," but, remembering in time that the word *crapaudine* should convey nothing to the simple English soldier and adventurer that I professed to be, I replied,

"*Crapaudine*? What is that, General?"

"Ah," he lied, "in Chinese, we call it the Death of a Thousand Cuts. Have you ever seen that punishment?"

"No, General."

"You shall. I mean, you must. It is interesting. We bind and compress the culprit, naked, in a net of thin wire. So tight is the wire-netting that his vulgar flesh, bulging, protrudes slightly through every mesh. The executioner, with a knife of razor edge, removes every bulge."

"Ingenious," I said.

The cold eyes held mine with a long look.

" *'All that is required for true style in conversation is that it conveys the meaning'*, saith Confucius," he observed, and again looked me in the eyes.

It was a meaning look, and I grasped the meaning; and, immediately, as though reading my thought—and it would not in the least have surprised me to learn that this Intelligence Incarnate, calling itself General Luong-Tam-Ky, read every thought of mine as it entered my mind—he again quoted his confounded Confucius.

"*Speech must reveal, and not conceal, thought.*"

This seemed to me an unexceptionable, if platitudinous statement; and, further to point his moral and adorn the tale of Confucius, he added,

"Yes. The Death of a Thousand Cuts . . . Life and Death . . . On this subject what saith Confucius?

And I forbore to remark, "Oh damn Confucius," as looking at me and through me, he favoured me with the Confucian *obiter dicta* on the subject.

" *'While we know so little of life what can we know of death?'* saith the Sage."

"Still, to a man of principle," he went on, "what are Life and Death but interchangeable terms? Life is the gateway inevitable to death; death the gateway inevitable to Life. Yes; what are Life and Death to a man of principle? And on the subject of principles, what do we find in the Golden Rule?"

I didn't know. I hadn't looked. But I promptly learned.

" *'A man can command his principles; but principles do not always command the man. . . .'* Do your principles command you, young man?" he asked.

"I hope so, General," I replied; not a little bored, and more than a little uncomfortable.

"Then I hope they are high principles," countered General Luong-Tam-Ky, and made me a neat little harangue in French, wherein he pointed out to me that by the sacrifice of my principles and my wise refusal to allow them to command me, I might do for myself a very neat stroke of business indeed! There and then!

With blank uncomprehending stare, I listened to his excellent French and when he had finished, murmured,

"I don't understand Chinese."

"No, but you understood every word of what I have just said," replied General Luong-Tam-Ky.

Whereat I could but smile and shake my head.

"Pardon me for contradicting," I said.

"Oh, I'll pardon you for contradicting," replied General Luong-Tam-Ky, "but I shan't pardon you for any—er—indiscretion; and I would recommend strict caution. Yes, *'The cautious rarely err'* saith Confucius—and they never have to die the Death of a Thousand Cuts."

CHAPTER XVIII

That same evening, as though sufficient unto the day had not been the evils thereof, *Doi* Linh Nghi came to my hut, bringing with him not only the impedimenta of his vice, but two opium pipes where one had come before.

"What's this?" I asked him. "Do you think you are going to pervert and demoralize me?"

The *Doi* grinned somewhat uneasily, displaying his ebony teeth.

"No," he whispered in Annamese, "but we are going to pretend that I've done so. We are going to spread our mats side by side, lie face to face, and look as though we are drinking the black smoke together. Then if any yellow-bellied devil spies through the key-hole or the torn paper of the window, he can but report that we indulge together, as good opium-smokers should. And if any burst in, let them find us senseless, drugged. I've something to tell you. Try a pipe, *Nai*."

"No thank you," I replied, "especially if you've got something important to say, and I need my wits about me."

"Oh, it's important enough."

And the *Doi* spread our mats, and then set about the cooking of the first opium pill.

Having inhaled, held on, puffed repeatedly, and finished the first pipe, he laid it down, and, with his face a foot from mine, began to whisper—in Annamese, of course.

"It's De-Nha," he began. "I am quite certain that he's going to cook his rice in a Chinese pot."

Ah! Feathering his own nest, was he? Exactly what I had subconsciously been expecting to hear, though I had really had nothing to go upon; nothing palpable. But I had had an instinctive feeling that such a man as he must be weighing profits, must be at any rate endeavouring to find out whether he could find a better market here than at French Headquarters.

And, in addition to an intuitive feeling that this was the obvious course for him to take, there was also the rational conclusion that, granted he'd do much better for himself on the winning French side than on the losing one of General De-Nam and his exiled Emperor, he might decide that he could do better still with the Chinese than with either of them.

Trying to put myself in De-Nha's place, I imagined his preference for a Chinese *milieu* rather than a French one; and the probability that he would see not only his immediate profit, but his future gain, in selling his secret concerning me to Collins and the Chinese Generals. Added to this was the certainty that the man was an utter rascal to whom the crooked path would inevitably be more attractive than the straight one, for its sweet crooked sake alone.

"What do you actually know, *Doi*?" I asked.

"That he visited General Ba-Ky late, the night before last, and stayed with him while a man could march four miles. Late last night he visited General Luong-Tam-Ky, and with him also he stayed for long. And now, at this present moment, he's in the house of the foreign devil, the Colonel Car-Ling."

"And you had no possible chance of hearing what he said to the Generals, and couldn't have got into Colonel Collins's house to-night?"

"Ask yourself," replied the *Doi* in his somewhat independent and off-hand manner, as he prepared another pipe. "Is it likely that General Luong-Tam-Ky or General Ba-Ky would talk with De-Nha where they could be overheard?"

"No, it isn't likely at all," I agreed, "but what about the house of Colonel Car-Ling? People come and go there in a way that is not possible at the house of either of the Generals."

"I know they do," grinned the *Doi*. "I come and go quite a lot, myself."

"Oh? On what business?"

"The business of giving my good opium to his chief slave."

So the *Doi* was in touch with Collins's Number One Boy

was he? This was interesting.

"Good. Well done. Any results?"

"No. There has been little reason for any until to-night."

"Would money help?"

"No. The best *chandu* is far above money, here."

"You can give me money to buy some more, though, if you wish to," added the *Doi*, with his ingratiating grin.

"Right . . . Have you learned anything at all?" I asked.

"Nothing of any interest or importance. The *tuchun* drinks the black smoke and the fire-water of the *Farangs*."

So Colonel John Collins was an opium-addict, was he?

No. I doubted it. Hadn't I heard somewhere that the opium-addict is never a dipsomaniac, the drunkard never an opium-addict? On the other hand, perhaps a man could use both alcohol and opium to excess, without being either an actual drunkard or an advanced opium-addict. This would account for Collins's "nerves", his uncertain temper, surliness, and general sullen and smouldering liverishness.

"He is an angry man of uncontrolled wrath, who beats his servants. He also beats his *batham-phiryéa*."

"*What?*"

"He beats his wife, which I believe is not the custom of the French, is it?"

I felt sick; literally and physically sick. That even the servants should know this awful and incredible thing. . . . And then I found myself seeing red, flying into such a passion of rage that I clenched my fists and dug my nails into my palms. Had my hands been about John Collins's neck at that moment . . .

"He takes bribes," continued the *Doi*, "and, as he has the commissariat contract for one of the Chinese regiments, he makes a lot of *ngurn*. If he only got ten *sabuks* a week for each soldier, he'd make a lot, wouldn't he? A very good squeeze indeed."

"Oh, this gossip is of no value," said I, when I could control my rage sufficiently to be able to speak calmly.

"It shows the character of the man, doesn't it?" objected the *Doi*. "He's a man of bad character, and therefore not to be trusted. On the other hand, he is a man of bad character and therefore to be trusted to be not honest. Therefore it is probable that the Chinese do not trust him much, and would readily believe evil of him. He is a taker of bribes, and is avaricious. Therefore he might take bribes—from the French."

"Yes, he might do all sorts of things. Let's get down to bamboo pegs. Is it likely that his Number One Boy, I mean his chief slave, as you call him, will over-hear anything of what De-Nha says to him to-night?"

"It won't be his fault if he doesn't."

"You've told him to try, eh?"

"Yes. With enough *chandu* for ten pipes, as a reward."

"How did you know De-Nha was going to Colonel Car-Ling's house?"

"I didn't know. I followed him there."

"And then?"

"Went round to the back, to the servants' quarters, and asked the chief servant if he wanted some opium," grinned the *Doi*.

"And he did, eh? And you showed him how to earn it? How do you know he'll tell you the truth?"

"I don't. But why should he tell me lies?"

"He'll make up something or other, to get his opium."

"Well, that's where you come in. You can decide wheth-er it sounds like the truth."

"Yes, there's something in that. It isn't likely that Colonel Collins's servant could make up a story, about what De-Nha said to his master, and deceive us with it. If he heard nothing, he wouldn't have the least idea as to what De-Nha and his master were likely to talk about, and couldn't make up a tale that would lead us astray."

"That's just what I thought," said the *Doi*. "If he made up a lot of lies, it wouldn't take us in. There'd be no harm done."

"Except a waste of good opium," he added.

"By the way," said I, "in what language would De-Nha talk to Colonel Collins?"

"Chinese," replied the *Doi*. "The Tai Yoi of Kwangnan Yun-nan, or perhaps the Kon Yai of Kwangnan Yun-nan, or again, it might be the Pu Tai of Yun-nan."

"Oh, De-Nha speaks that Chinese, does he?"

"Oh, yes."

"Well then, in what language does the Number One Boy talk to you?"

"The Tai Dam of Tonking," was the reply. "He has been a servant in Saigon, Haiphong and Hanoi."

"A travelled gentleman," I mused. "Does he speak French?"

"Sure to, a little. He was in French service down there."

"And he is not faithful to his present master."

"Yes, he is," contradicted the *Doi*, cynically. "Opium is his present master."

"I wonder whether Colonel Collins knows that his Number One Boy understands French, Annamese and Yunnanese."

Personally I thought this over-hearing eavesdropping scheme a pretty forlorn hope. In the first place, it would surprise me a great deal to learn that a servant had been allowed to overhear so important a conversation as that which De-Nha was likely to hold with Colonel Collins, late at night; and, in the second place, it seemed to me that there was far too great a babel of tongues for any accurate information to emerge, even if all that was said was clearly overheard.

I was also aware of the fact that two pure-bred educated Chinese, each talking Chinese, could be utterly incomprehensible to each other; that a Chinese from one part of China was as foreign in language and everything else, to a Chinese from another part of China, as a Turk to a Laplander or a Spaniard to a Pole.

This being so, I didn't think there was much chance of the production of an accurate French version of the gist of an Annamese conversation with a Peking half-caste Chinese overheard by a Yunnanese, and reported by him to a Tonkinese highlander whose account of it was again to be translated by a Scot into French!

And I was right. Once again the *Doi*'s optimism had not been justified. But far better an unjustified optimism than a fully justified pessimism.

Nevertheless, something quite useful did materialize, and the idea originated in my own un-subtle blundering Western mind.

§2

For when, on the following night, the *Doi* again came to drink the black smoke with me, and we lay down side by side upon our mats, and he unfolded for my consideration his tale of the Number One Boy's tale of De-Nha's tale to John Collins, I rejected it utterly.

And then a small brain-wave further agitated the disturbed surface of my troubled mind.

"*M-e-h-h! Ma-chai!*" I jeered in Annamese. "Rubbish! Bosh! I hope you didn't give the rascal opium for that pack of lies."

"Not I," declared the *Doi*. "Only just enough to make him want some more."

"Well now. Here's an idea," said I. "It can't do any harm, and might do a lot of good. Get hold of the Number One Boy again, and promise him a whole *bât* of opium, a regular *khong-hõ* of it, if he does what you tell him to do."

"And what shall I tell him, *Nai*?"

"To come and have a talk with us here."

"Yes, and then?"

"Bribe him to go to De-Nha with a false message from Colonel Collins, and then to come and tell us what De-Nha said."

"What sort of message?"

"That if De-Nha would meet Colonel Collins at a certain place and time, he'd pay him what he asked for the information he had got—about me."

The *Doi* considered the matter with pursed lips.

"Might lead to something," he said at length.

"Yes, we might get at him, and bribe him to tackle De-Nha himself," I said, for I hadn't really much hope of his overhearing anything.

"Look, *Nai*; suppose De-Nha has already given us away,

and we are as birds with strings tied about their legs, but don't know it until they go to fly?" asked the *Doi*.

"Well?"

"Then what about telling the servant the truth, and promising him not only a lot of opium but a lot of money, if he can discover that from De-Nha?"

"How?"

"Why, we'd tell the servant the truth, and then send him to De-Nha to sell him the *truth*. Then he comes back and tells us what De-Nha said—whether De-Nha just laughed at him for his pains and said he knew all about it. . . . And then see whether De-Nha comes to us and warns us that John Collins's Number One Boy has discovered us to be spies!"

"Yes," I replied, "that improves on my idea of trying to get the Number One Boy to make De-Nha give him money in return for not spoiling De-Nha's market by exposing the same goods for sale. See what I mean?"

"Surely, *Nai*."

"Yes. It would have annoyed De-Nha very much to have found that the Number One Boy had as good a secret as he had," I continued, musing aloud, "but what you suggest is better. If the servant tells De-Nha that he knows we are French spies, and De-Nha doesn't warn us, that's clear proof of his treachery. If he is being quite straight, being quite honest, he will come to us immediately, in a great fright, tell us all about it, and warn us that our secret is discovered and that we had better vanish."

"True," replied the *Doi*, "but look, *Nai*. Suppose De-Nha hasn't said a word about us, and we go and tell this servant who we are! What then?"

"Very awkward indeed . . . But you feel pretty certain yourself, don't you, that De-Nha has betrayed us, or is going to?"

"Yes, undoubtedly. Why else should he visit both the Generals and Colonel Collins, separately, late at night . . . Who's De-Nha? What is De-Nha to them that they should give him interviews, in secrecy, like that? He must have gone behind our backs and told them something. He must have convinced them that he has got something to say, and something to sell. Otherwise, for all they know, he's just an ordinary jungle dacoit who follows me as I follow you."

"Quite so. I think it's perfectly safe, or as safe as anything could be, in this place."

"Yes, he has either told them or he's going to tell them—or going to tell it to that one of them who offers most and promises best. . . . We couldn't be much more unsafe than we are, whatever we tell Colonel Car-Ling's servant. Besides—he's an ignorant fool and opium-addict who couldn't make good use of valuable information if he had it."

"We needn't tell him much, either."

"No. You leave it to me, *Nai*. I'll tell him a tale that won't do any harm if he takes it straight to his master, but that will serve our purpose if he takes it to De-Nha—as I think he will. . . . Anyhow, I'll go on getting more and more friendly with him. Perhaps it might be a good thing, after all, to mix a little money with the opium. Those Chinese are avaricious rascals."

"Yes, so different from the Annamese," I agreed gravely.

"Have you any French gold pieces, *Nai*? Any twenty-franc pieces?"

"Yes, I have some of the small and some of the big, in the belt next my skin."

"Well, I'll give him one of the small ones and promise—what? Two of the big? If he finds out all we want to know. You leave it to me."

I felt quite certain I could leave it to the *Doi*, so far as honesty went, and fairly sure, as far as intelligence and diplomacy were concerned.

I accordingly gave him a gold ten-franc piece and authorized the promise of a twenty-franc piece if the man succeeded in proving to our satisfaction that De-Nha was behaving treacherously.

"Ten thousand fire-breathing dragons!" exclaimed the *Doi*. "I'd like to roll De-Nha down the side of a mountain bristling with knives. I'd like to sit him beside a pond and feed his entrails, foot by foot, to mud-fish."

"Quite so; but that wouldn't help us, would it, *Doi*?"

"No. We shall have to help ourselves."

"It's about time we went back to Houi-Bap," he added, looking up from his pellet-cooking.

"Yes, we'd have gone long ago if I could have found out where the Big Fort is, and when the money, ammunition and reinforcements are coming from China, and by which route."

CHAPTER XIX

The next day was an important one for me—in some ways one of the most important of my life; for I learned two pieces of invaluable information, the first concerning my official business, and the other my most intimate personal affairs.

A spy who was in the private pay and very private service of Colonel John Collins had come, post haste, with most important news, bringing with him an Annamese dacoit to bear witness of the truth of his story, and to provide further evidence.

In my capacity as adjutant and aide-de-camp to Colonel Collins, I was present in the old pagoda orderly-room of the *Yamen* at the examination of the spy and his witness, who were questioned—though not in the locally sinister use of that word—in the presence of Generals Luong-Tam-Ky and Ba-Ky.

The great news—and it was of the utmost importance to the French—was that General De-Nam, the great leader of the Annamese revolt, and formerly Viceroy of the vast province of Yen Thé, was dead.

"Dead? Dead? Killed in battle?" asked General Ba-Ky. "One of the French ninety-millimetre shells, or what? We ought to have got him some of those mountain-artillery guns. He could have beaten the French then—or kept them busy for years longer."

The spy smiled and shook his head slowly.

"No; oh, Lord," he said, "the great Viceroy of the Emperor did not fall in battle. Nor was he assassinated by enemies. He was merely poisoned by friends."

"And who were these kind friends?" silkily enquired General Luong-Tam-Ky.

"Chinese, oh Lord," replied the spy.

"*What?* . . . . Do you want to ornament a tree-trunk, upside down, with nails through your feet?" whispered

Luong-Tam-Ky.

The spy spread deprecating hands.

"I do but speak the truth. The truth gushes from my mouth as water from a hole in a rock. Is the rock to blame?"

"Speak on," commanded General Ba-Ky, sitting with his sword across his lap, and looking more like Chu Chin Chow than ever.

"Gun-runners," replied the spy, "vendors of rifles, arms and ammunition."

"And why should they kill the Lord General De-Nam?" enquired General Ba-Ky with ominous calm.

"Wouldn't he pay them for the arms and ammunition?" enquired General Luong-Tam-Ky.

"Yes, Lord, he paid in full," was the reply.

"Well?" asked Colonel John Collins.

"He won back every *sabuk* of the money at *bacquang*.[15] Not only that, but every *piastre* they brought with them."

General Ba-Ky roared with laughter.

"Cleaned them out, did he?" he chuckled.

"And then bade them go," smiled the spy. "But ere they went, they poisoned the rice cooked for his morning meal. And so he died. He died in great pain. But as he was about to die, he smiled and said,

" '*The Chinese win. As usual.*'

"Then suddenly he sat upright, looked around him and, in a great voice, cried aloud,

" '*Srok Khmer mün dèl sun*'—'the Khmer Country shall never die' and straightway fell back—and died."

Whereupon General Ba-Ky shook with great guffaws of hearty laughter.

"And who rules in his stead?" asked General Luong-Tam-Ky.

"Lieutenant-General De-Tam," replied the spy.

"Yes, that's probable," agreed General Luong-Tam-Ky. "He was his Second in Command, and completely in his confidence. So General De-Tam now commands the armies of the Emperor of Annam? We must send him a military

---

[15] Fan-tan.

mission."

"Recognizing him at once?" enquired General Ba-Ky.

"We will ponder a while; talk of it; sleep on it," replied General Luong-Tam-Ky. "To-morrow morning, having decided, we will act."

"Is it known throughout the Annamese forces that General Lord De-Nam, is dead?" he asked the spy.

"Yes, Lord, they made no secret of it," was the answer. "They made him a grand funeral, a mighty *tamboun*. It was a big *tamasha*, with much grief and feasting."

"And where is he buried?" asked General Luong-Tam-Ky.

"Inside the great New Fort at . . ."

The man glanced at me.

"At you-know-where," he concluded.

I would have liked to present him with half a dozen of the best on his own you-know-where.

"Oh, buried him inside the Fort, have they?" said Luong-Tam-Ky. "They'll defend that to the last. . . . Yes, that'll be the main Headquarters and the Citadel too. And they'll fight for that so long as there is a loyal Annamese on his feet."

"H'm. So much for the good De-Nam," he added, nodding his head.

"And what of his son?" he asked the spy.

"He had no son," growled General Ba-Ky.

"And what of his son?" repeated General Luong-Tam-Ky, who was evidently better informed than General Ba-Ky, and had refrained from sharing the information with him.

"What of the son of De-Nam? Is he born yet?"

The spy shrugged desponding shoulders and again spread deprecating hands.

"Born; lived; and dead; oh, Lord," he replied.

"H'm. How do you come to know so much?" enquired General Ba-Ky.

"The time being so near, I waited that my information might be complete; and General De-Tam had given orders that the woman's bodyguard should retreat northward, which was the direction in which I must come."

"Why did General De-Tam give such orders?" asked

General Luong-Tam-Ky.

"Because the French were advancing and firing with guns at the stockade line held by General De-Tam."

"Well?"

"I followed the bodyguard of the chief wife of the late General Lord De-Nam as they retreated in advance of General De-Tam and his two Lieutenant-Generals, De-Truat and De-Hué; and we came into the mighty forest of Quinh-low where the trees are bigger than any in the world, and where there are the ancient iron-mines worked by the Khmer people a thousand years ago. Here they had to halt for a night, that the son of De-Nam might be born. And on the second day of the fifth month of the year, his first son was at last born to our late Lord the Viceroy De-Nam."

And here the man broke into a sort of threnody,

> "Alas, that he lived not to see that day!
> Alas that his child should be born
>   fatherless!
> Alas that the great Lord De-Nam should
>   die childless!"

"I'll give you an 'alas' on your own account in half a second," promised General Ba-Ky. "Who asked you to sing a funeral song?"

The spy, who seemed to be genuinely moved, glared for a moment at General Ba-Ky and then, somewhat sulkily, indicated the dacoit whom he had brought with him.

"This man knows the facts. Saw everything himself. Let him speak."

And, as a matter of practice and accurate recording, and to take back a document that would surely interest Captain Deleuze, I wrote down in a field pocket-book that I had obtained from Colonel Collins, exactly what he said. It was as follows.

"The beloved favourite wife of our great and honoured chief the Lord De-Nam was approaching her time, when, suddenly, great fire burst forth from the big guns of the

Farangs and the scouts came in with the news that great numbers of infantry soldiers were advancing into the jungle, not only Annamese in *sakalos* but *Farangs* in white helmets.

"Then, in spite of the fact that her hour was very near, the Lord De-Tam bade her arise and journey far into the Quinh-Low jungle; and he bade the Commanders De-Truat and De-Hué to follow with their bands, while he himself with his main army fought a rear-guard action.

"And as we journeyed into the jungle of Quinh-Low, we heard the sound of the battle far behind us.

"And after marching for a day and a night, the lady, the wife of our great Lord De-Nam said,

" 'I can go no further'. And straightway her child was born, the son of our Lord De-Nam.

"And the leader of the bodyguard sent word quickly back by me, to the Lord De-Tam, saying,

" '*A son is born unto our late Lord and Viceroy De-Nam. Come then and protect him, lest harm come to him. For Generals De-Truat and De-Hué have marched on.*'

"And when I, the messenger, reached De-Tam and gave him the message, De-Tam said,

" '*This news comes at an ill moment, for behold I have bidden my troops to disperse, and now they are scattered like rice-husks before the wind, and they cover the face of the country, hiding in their villages until the French retire. And when the French have retired, my troops will assemble again in the great Fort where De-Nam is buried and which the French will never find.*'

"And even while I, the messenger, spoke with the Lord De-Tam, scouts arrived saying,

" '*Fly, oh Lord, for the foreign soldiers are here, led by a traitor.*'

"And De-Tam said to me, the messenger,

" '*I will join the bodyguard with the fifty men who are with me.*'

"And it was so: I, the messenger, leading General De-Tam and his fifty men back to where the bodyguard waited, protecting the woman and the new-born babe.

"So now the Lord De-Nam's son was guarded by General De-Tam and seventy-five men.

"And in a day or two, when the woman could again march, General De-Tam and the men advanced further into the jungle of Quinh-Low, taking the woman and the child with them.

"And they marched from one secret food-store to the next, there being rice in plenty in these hiding-places, where the great Lord and Viceroy De-Nam had, in his wisdom, concealed it, that his troops might not starve when retreating.

"But the traitor who was leading the *linh-lanxa* followed, and day by day, the white soldiers fired upon General De-Tam's force, and the retreat became a rear-guard action, with night attacks and dawn attacks, daily.

"And so hard did the white soldiers press upon General De-Tam, that of rest there was but little, of sleep there was none, and scarce was there time to cook our rice.

"And one day a man of the bodyguard said that near-by there was a hiding-place beneath the earth, for he knew of the entrance to a cave from which was a passage leading underground.

"And we found the entrance to the cave behind rocks and bushes, but the passage leading from it into the bowels of the earth had fallen in, for it was an ancient place of iron-workings long abandoned to the jungle. And there, in the cave, De-Tam and all his party abode, protecting the woman and the young child, until our food was almost gone, and there was but little water.

"And one day, I, the man whom De-Tam sent out to bring water, was seen and followed by an Annamese soldier of the French. But discovering this in time, I led the soldier astray and came secretly to the entrance, after darkness had fallen, and told General De-Tam of this thing.

"Nevertheless, in spite of my cunning, the *tirailleur* who had seen me brought other soldiers to the spot where he had last beheld me, and there they made constant search throughout a morning; and at midday they sat down to rest and eat food, and they were close to the entrance to our cave.

"And suddenly the child began to cry and to scream.

"The mother lay sick and ill and scarcely conscious.

"The child, whom she could not feed, ceased not to cry and to scream, doubtless because it was hungry and in pain. Bananas it would not eat.

"And De-Tam, fearing lest its cries and screams be heard by the searching soldiers, ordered me to dig a little hole quietly in the soft earth.

"This I did. And in the hole, De-Tam laid General De-Nam's son, and covered it carefully with a piece of silk, as was fitting, the child being a young prince.

"He then bade me fill the hole up, tread the earth flat, and place stones upon it. This I did.

"So, without dying or being slain, the child went to join its ancestors.

"And presently after, the mother's soul came up from the depths, her mind came back from its wandering, and she asked for the child.

"And when De-Tam told her that it had gone to join its father in the way that was fitting, she was so stricken with grief that she became as one who is mad.

" 'Where is it? Where is it?' she cried.

" 'Out in the jungle,' replied De-Tam, wishing to be rid of her.

"And out into the forest she fled.

"Next day, De-Tam sent me out to scout, and I found that the soldiers had gone. So we left the cave and continued on our way.

"And in the path we found the body of the woman, with a knife driven to the handle in her body, the blade being through her heart and protruding behind her. This she had done herself, for her right hand still held the handle of the knife, showing that she had died fittingly, as became the daughter of a great man who was the wife of a great man and the mother of his son."

"And I have come here with this man," added the dacoit, "on promise of great reward."

"And what of De-Tam?" asked General Ba-Ky of Colonel Collins's spy.

"He, making a wide circle, returned to the great New Fort at—you-know-where. It is his intention there to reassemble his troops and hide until a big French army, passing on far into the jungle, in ignorance, leaves the great Fort behind them. Then when the French go to attack the strong stockaded place of which they shall receive full information, General De-Tam, having cut their lines of communication, will take them in the rear, leaving a strong force to prevent reinforcements from reaching them."

Invaluable information indeed, and the sooner I could get it back to Captain Deleuze, the better.

But first I must know where the Fort of "You-know-where" was situated. On the strength of this information the French General would doubtless be able to ambush the ambushers; and I imagined him playing De-Tam's game as far as it suited himself—sending a force to attack the "strong stockaded place" that was to be betrayed to him; another one to deal with De-Tam's main army that issued forth from the Fort of "You-know-where"; while yet a third French force entered and occupied that great New Fort, sacred burying place, treasure house, arsenal, and last citadel of the rebels of Annam.

CHAPTER XX

And so the great General De-Nam was dead. . . .
What would be the effect upon the situation here?

§2

Late that evening, after I had eaten my frugal dinner of rice, *tsamba*-cake and dried pears, and was drinking cup after cup of brick-tea sweetened with *mauri*, I received the other information that so concerned me privately.

As I sat in my hut, after a hot and hard three hours on the parade-ground and a route-march, one of our *tirailleurs* brought the *Doi* a note for me.

It was from Mrs. Collins.

With my heart beating faster than usual, I read as follows:

"*MY DEAR,*

J. went off at sunset with a party on some expedition or other, and will not be returning in less than a week at earliest. I must speak to you. Will you come over in about an hour's time, when the servants, except my amah, will have gone to their quarters? I believe she is trustworthy, though of course I don't know. I don't really trust anybody but you.
M. C."

I knew that something serious must have occurred, or she would not have written to me like this, would not have taken the risk of writing a letter at all—still less of asking me to go to her house late at night.

I thought it better to tell the *Doi* where I was going; and I bade him remain in my hut till I returned.

Keeping to what shadow I could find, I made my way to Collins's house. As I approached the door, it was opened by a Chinese woman in a black silk coat and trousers, her hair like a black lacquer casque, her yellow face expressionless.

Fastening the door behind me, she led the way to the drawing-room where Mrs. Collins was sitting on the black-wood couch. The room was dimly lit by one lamp turned low.

As soon as we were alone, I took Mary's hands in mine and kissed them, and she drew me down beside her on the sofa.

"Oh, my dear," she said. "I'm so glad you've come. What a day! I don't know where to begin. Forgive me if I am a little incoherent. You will agree there is some reason. My husband went at sunset, and said he would only be gone for a couple of days or so; but I gather from General Luong-Tam-Ky that he won't be back for ten days at least, as he has gone to the great Fort at Thay-Taong. . . ."

I instantly noted the name. *Thay-Taong*. So that was where the great rebel Citadel was! She had given me a piece of information indeed; though, I was perfectly certain, unintentionally and quite unconsciously.

"General Luong-Tam-Ky told you?" I said.

For this also was an interesting and, indeed, amazing piece of news, although valueless. How and why should General Luong-Tam-Ky be in communication with the wife of Colonel John Collins?

"Yes, General Luong-Tam-Ky," she repeated. "He honoured me with a state visit this evening."

I repeated the name *Thay-Taong* to myself that, in my surprise at this information, I should not forget it.

"Paid you a visit here!"

"Yes, and as I say, in state. Carried in his chair. With a bodyguard. Flags and all complete. I wonder he didn't have a band."

"What did he want?" I asked.

"Me."

"Wanted to see you? What about?"

"He wanted *me*. He came to inform me that it was entirely unnecessary that my husband should ever return from the journey on which he had been sent by General Ba-Ky and himself."

"Not return?"

"No. Do you remember the little story of Uriah the Hittite?" she asked.

And then I saw a great light. Saw in a flash. And 'flash' is appropriate, for I felt as though a thunder-bolt had fallen at my feet; and almost as though I had been struck by lightning.

She had been speaking so calmly, so quietly—as was her wont—that I had not suspected how great her fear and trouble were; how terrible her danger.

"He told you that your husband . . . ?"

I stared incredulous.

"He did me the honour formally to propose that I should become his . . . his *pu-ying*, his *kon-ying* . . . presumably his *prapon thom*."

"But, God bless my soul! You already have one husband, and he . . ."

"And he 'need not return from his journey' according to General Luong-Tam-Ky—as I have just said," replied Mary.

"You mean that General Luong-Tam-Ky would simply have him murdered?"

"It wasn't put as bluntly and coarsely as that. Nothing more was actually said than that there 'was no reason why he should ever return'. But the meaning was perfectly clear."

"Yes, I have had some experience of Luong-Tam-Ky's ability to make himself perfectly clear."

And I thought of the great patriot and warrior De-Nam, poisoned by a gang of filthy gun-runners because they wanted their money back after he had won it at *fan-tan*. And this man, John Collins, was also to be poisoned, or shot or stabbed in the back, because Luong-Tam-Ky wanted his wife.

"Has he ever shown any signs of this sort of—madness—before?"

"No. It came as an utter surprise to me. Had it been the other one, Ba-Ky, it would not have been such a shock. Ba-Ky leers at me horribly every time I see him."

I could imagine Chu Chin Chow's leer at a woman. But, so far, it had been another case of the dog whose bark was worse than his bite, or of the Chinese proverb that the barking dog does not bite.

"What did you say?" I asked.

"Used the very word you did just now.

"Madness.

"Without stopping to think, I asked him if he had gone mad.

"He said Yes, he had. He had been driven mad by Beautiful Quiet Fairy . . . I gathered that I am the 'Beautiful Quiet Fairy' in question. . . .

"Then I talked to gain time, wondering which would be safest for my husband; whether I should put him in more danger by telling Luong-Tam-Ky that Colonel John Collins would thrash him within an inch of his life and then hang him to a tree; or whether it would be even more dangerous to pretend to appear to be somewhat pleased and honoured and friendly, and that I would—consider the matter."

"And what did you say?"

"I hardly know what I did say. I tried not to make the beast savage, and I tried to show him that it was absurd, impossible . . . lunacy. It was simply terrible. Heaven knows I have little reason to wish John well, seeing how he has treated me all these years; but he is my husband, and I have got to save him. . . . And myself too. Just think what a position I should be in if . . . if . . . Alone here among these Chinese—and with that man Luong-Tam-Ky . . ."

"You aren't alone, Mary," I said, "and you are not going to be."

"Oh, my dear. . . . Thank you . . . It was to you I turned . . ."

"Of course. How did you get rid of him?"

"It is like remembering a dream. A nightmare, rather. I said,

" *'You don't mean to say you'd commit a murder? Murder my husband?'*

"And he smiled and repeated that same phrase. *'There's really no reason why he should come back. Accidents happen in the best regulated little expeditions, you know.'*

"So, for want of something more effective to say, I told him that I should certainly die if my husband did. That seemed to amuse him, and he observed that 'Beautiful Quiet Fairy' was much too lovely to die.

"I told him that was where he was wrong; as in point of fact, I shouldn't have the slightest objection to dying."

She stared before her with tragic eyes.

"At first my mind seemed numb, and I couldn't think. Then I had an idea. I made a shot in the dark. But whether what I said also amused him, or whether it gave him something to think about too, I don't know. I said,

" *'You ought to know my husband pretty well by now, General Luong-Tam-Ky. He's a very clever man, or he wouldn't be what he is, an officer of high rank under the Chinese Government. He's not a fool, you know, and he knows how to take care of himself.'*

" *'Oh no, he's not a fool,'* Luong-Tam-Ky agreed, *'and I am quite sure he knows how to take care of himself.'*

" *'Well, then, do you think that if you had him murdered, you'd survive him long?'*

" *'What do you mean?'* he asked.

" *'What I say. Colonel John Collins isn't a very trusting person, you know. He wouldn't be alive to-day if he were. Don't you think that he has arranged that if anything happens to him, something will happen to you too? . . . And that he counts on your having enough common sense to realize it.'*

" *'Why should anything happen to me?'*

" *'Because he knows perfectly well that if anything happened to him, it would be through you.'*

"And I tried to read his face, his eyes, to see how he took it. I might as well have tried to read a closed book. Better. There would be something on the cover of a closed book. . . . But I think he turned the idea over in his mind, for he was silent for a minute or two."

"Yes, Mary. He'd certainly think it over," I observed. "Sort of idea that would appeal to him. Just about what he'd do himself. What did he say next?"

"That my husband wasn't the only man who could take care of himself. . . . By then I had decided what would be my best line," continued Mary Collins.

" *'Suppose anything happened to my husband and he didn't return here, I should certainly die. Whether you would or not, I don't know; but I do know that I should.'*

" *'Because you love him so much?'* sneered Luong-Tam-Ky.

" *'No, because I love life so little,'* I replied.

"He thought this over for a while, his face absolutely inscrutable.

" *'And suppose your husband unfortunately did not return from this expedition, you really think that something would happen to me, do you?'*

" *'I know it would.'*

" *'My food would disagree with me; or I should meet with an accident?'*

" *'I don't know in the least what would happen to you, except that you wouldn't survive him long.'*

" *'Ah! And who is there in this camp so faithful to Colonel John Collins that he would carry out his instructions —after he was dead?'*

" *'I don't know,'* I replied.

" *'You think there is such a person?'*

" *'I am certain there is.'*

"And then I thought I could see that he was reflecting, turning over in his mind the names of the people who might be as obedient and faithful as that. For he shifted his eyes and stared at the floor.

"Suddenly he looked into my eyes again and said,

" *'How long has your Number One Boy been with you?'*

"Well, I thought I'd follow that up.

" *'Oh, ever so long,'* I lied. *'I couldn't tell you. He has been with my husband longer than I have been married to him.'*

"Then the thought crossed my mind that he might think of you, Sinbad, and that this might be dangerous for you."

"Well, he knows that I am not an old friend or faithful servant of Colonel Collins, Mary," I said.

185

"Yes, but he also knows that you are a compatriot," replied Mary, "and might very well think that my husband had left me in your charge, and that you had promised to look after me if anything happened to him—and to see to it that something also happened to General Luong-Tam-Ky. . . . How can one tell what such Chinese as Luong-Tam-Ky think? We can't enter into their minds at all."

"No," I agreed. "I think about the safest guide is to consider what we would do in any given circumstances, and then decide that they would do just the opposite. . . . What was the end of it?"

"Well, he went away, with my firm assurance that if my husband died I should die."

"Do you think he believed you?"

"My dear, who's to say? I certainly did my utmost to make him believe me. And if you weren't here, that is of course what would happen. I have no intention of becoming the property of a Chinese—after having been that of a Chinese half-caste, all these years."

"I'll send word to your husband," I said. "I'll send a messenger, or go myself—to Thay-Taong."

"No, you mustn't go. Please. Please don't leave me here alone."

"All-right. I'll send a couple of my *tirailleurs*."

"You trust them?"

"Absolutely. I think there's no-one I trust more, except yourself. I'll send them off at once."

"Look here, Mary," I added, not stopping to wonder what she would reply to such a proposal. "Would you like me to stay here to-night? I could sleep on this couch or on a mat in the verandah."

She met my gaze for a moment.

"I'm not frightened," she said. "Nothing will happen to me—yet awhile. Good-night, and thank you, oh so much. Take care of yourself, Sinbad."

I put my arms about her, and she clung to me while our lips met in a long kiss of love.

And then I hurried away, my mind in turmoil and in torment.

CHAPTER XXI

Next day *Doi* Linh Nghi hung about the compound of Colonel Collins's bungalow until the Number One Boy left the house and retired to his own quarters at the bottom of the garden, for his afternoon opium-smoke and *siesta*.

To him the *Doi* made overtures, opening up bright vistas adown which the servant might glimpse a gleam of gold and eddying volumes of the ineffably desirable 'black smoke.'

If he desired the gold piece which the *Doi* showed him, and a couple more of twice that size, with enough opium to give him a score of pipes a day, he was to hold converse with my other follower, De-Nha. He was to tell De-Nha that he had learned something about me, the *Farang* who was now a *Nai-tha'han*, a Lieutenant, and had joined Colonel Car-Ling. Did he understand?

Oh yes; he understood.

Well, that *Farang* was not a white officer from *Muang Angrit*[16] at all, he was really a *linh lanxa* of the French army. He was a French spy. Did the Number One Boy understand?

Yes; he understood all-right. He was to go to De-Nha and say that he knew that this European was not an English officer but a French soldier and a spy.

Right. He was to say that to De-Nha.

Well, what then?

Then he was to say to De-Nha,

"I am going to sell this information to General Ba-Ky or to General Luong-Tam-Ky or to Colonel Collins himself, whichever seems likely to pay most."

Right. He was to say that to De-Nha.

Well, what then?

Then the Number One Boy was to note very carefully what De-Nha said to that. And if De-Nha told him he mustn't do such a thing, he was to ask De-Nha how much he would

---

[16] England.

give him to keep the secret.

Did he understand?

Yes, he understood quite clearly.

Then—and this was very important—he was to tell *Doi* Linh Nghi exactly what De-Nha said. Exactly. And if he was very clever, and did all this very nicely, and reported accurately, he was to get the two big gold pieces as well as the small one which he would have in advance. And opium.

Now he must repeat what he had to say to De-Nha, to make sure he had got it all right.

Yes. . . . He, the Number One Boy, was to go to De-Nha; tell him that the new white man was a French spy; and see how De-Nha took the information. He was then to say that he was going to sell this secret to the highest bidder; and then note carefully how De-Nha took that piece of information.

Good. Quite right, agreed the *Doi*; and particularly he was to report whether De-Nha seemed surprised and horrified; seemed strongly to object to his selling the secret to the Chinese; and report whether De-Nha tried to bribe the Number One Boy to do nothing in the matter at all.

In fact, the *Doi* clearly explained to the Number One Boy that what he really wanted to know was whether De-Nha had already learned the interesting secret, and was in the market for its sale before ever the Number One Boy knew there was any secret to sell.

And indeed, by the time the *Doi* left the Number One Boy, the mind of that admirable servant must have been most abundantly clear on the subject of finding out whether De-Nha was behaving, or about to behave, treacherously toward those whom he professed to follow and to serve.

It seemed all-right; but the same question gave me pause again, for a moment. When I had heard all that the *Doi* had to tell me about his interview with the Number One Boy, I asked once more,

"And what about the Number One Boy himself? Did he seem at all interested in the question of whether we are what we pretend to be; or really are, French spies?"

"No," replied the *Doi*. "Why should he be? As we said

before—he's only a servant and not particularly interested in anything beyond opium—and money."

"He didn't even ask whether it is true that we are French spies?"

"Well, he did say, when I was leaving the compound,

" *'And is the white Nai-tha'han really a linh lanxa, a French soldier and spy?'* "

"Oh, he did, did he?" I mused. "What did you say?"

"Oh, I just said,

" *'No, of course he isn't! But I believe that dirty dog De-Nha is going to tell the Chinese that he is. Going to get an innocent man tortured and put to death, just for the sake of what he himself may get out of it. That's what we want to find out about him.'* "

"And what did the Number One Boy say to that?"

"Just grinned like the vacant-minded *khon khi ya,* the silly opium-addict, that he is, and said,

" *'Oh, what a dirty dog. What a yellow-belly,'* " replied the *Doi.*

And it seemed to me that if the *Doi* were entirely satisfied, there should be no reason why I should worry as to the cogitations of the Number One Boy.

If De-Nha were a traitor we were for it.

If he were not, the Number One Boy really did not matter.

Suppose he did go with a cock-and-bull story to his master or to the General, who'd believe him?

Who was he, and how should he know, any more than they did, who I was or where I came from?

No, the vapourings of Colonel Collins's opium-sodden servant would interest nobody; and might be a considerable danger to himself, if they came to my ears—or so he would argue.

CHAPTER XXII

And the next night I received another piece of information; another shock, one which made that of the previous night seem comparatively gentle.

Again Colonel Collins's *conyam* gave one of my *tirailleurs* a note for me, from Mary. It ran,

"*MY DEAR*,

More trouble—and worse in some ways! Thank God you are here—and are what you are. Will you come over again to-night, fairly late?

M."

In a state of fuming impatience and great anxiety, I waited until I thought that the servants would have left the bungalow and gone to their houses at the bottom of the compound, and she would be alone save for the trusted *amah*.

Again this woman, with her boot-button eyes, lacquer-like hair, and expressionless face of old ivory, admitted me, fastened the door behind me, and showed me into the drawing-room.

As soon as we were alone, Mary came to me, and as we kissed, my arms about her, I felt she was trembling.

"What is it, Mary?"

"Sinbad, what isn't it?"

"The General again?"

"No, not yet. . . . Another—admirer!"

I had those sensations known as 'blood running cold' and goose-flesh.

Not General Ba-Ky? Good Heaven, where were we, if these two all-powerful Chinese, here in the world's wildest back-of-beyond, were going to fight—for the woman whom I loved far better than I loved my life?

"Ba-Ky?" I asked.

"No," replied Mary. "Not Ba-Ky, thank God. And you'd never guess from whom my second proposal of—protection —has come. Two in two days. Who am I? What am I?"

I took her hands and tried to soothe her.

"Tell me, Mary."

And to my utter astonishment, amazement so great that I did not really understand, the first time she said it,

"The Number One Boy," she replied.

This was beyond common comprehension.

The Number One Boy?

What was this? What did she mean? The head servant; the butler; the Number One Boy as Europeans call them, in the Far East? That he had attacked her? That he . . . ?

"The Number One Boy," she said again.

I sprang to my feet, and if ever a man had murder in his heart, or rather righteous homicidal rage . . .

"Where is he?"

I had certainly never in my life wanted a servant as badly as I wanted the Number One Boy at that moment.

Mary caught at my hand.

"Sit down, my dear, and listen. He's not a servant at all."

"Your head servant, your Number One Boy—is not a servant? What do you mean?"

"He's not a servant at all. He's an officer of the regular Chinese army—rank of Major—and prominent Secret Service Agent."

And once again, what on earth was this?

What were we talking about? Colonel Collins's head servant, butler, Number One Boy—a Chinese officer, a Secret Service agent? . . .

Well, why not? Anything was possible to these people. Nothing more possible than that such a man as Colonel John Collins should be watched, spied upon, reported about; particularly on such a mission as his present one, when it would be a simple enough matter for him to set up as a *tuchun*, a War Lord, on his own account if he thought he would.

Yes, it was quite possible.

And suddenly, to Mary's very great surprise, I laughed

aloud.

"It's not really very amusing," she said.

"No, it isn't," I said, shocked and ashamed of myself. "Do forgive me, Mary! But I've just remembered something. I've been using your Number One Boy—your Chinese Major and Secret Service Agent—to find out whether my guide and spy De-Nha is betraying me—denouncing me for a French spy! We have just told the man that we *are* French spies!"

"My dear! What will happen?"

"God knows."

"It's no laughing matter, surely."

"No. And I'm not laughing. I'm making funny noises with my mouth, Mary. I could kick myself from here back to Houi-Bap."

And indeed I felt that I could go and tell Captain Deleuze that I had declared myself as a French spy—to a Chinese Secret Service officer . . . and that I could then go and blow out my brains. . . . *Brains!*

I felt that I must laugh; and I never felt less like laughter in my life. I could have hanged myself.

And then I realized my colossal selfishness. Here was I, thinking of myself and my own affairs when Mary was not only in terrible trouble but in the greatest danger.

"I'm so sorry," I said. "I beg your pardon, Mary. It took me rather aback—to hear that the servant was an officer—and to realize that I have been giving him money and opium and telling him all there is to know about myself and my mission. . . . I'm so sorry. Tell me what happened."

"When he had cleared away dinner and finished his work, he came into the room and stood in front of me, bowed, and said in excellent English,

" '*Will the Nai Mem please excuse me? Yesterday Luong-Tam-Ky said that the Nai Colonel need not return from his expedition to the new Fort.*'

" '*Well?*' I said.

" '*He will not return,*' was the reply.

"And I got that horrible pain deep down inside, again; and I seemed to be growing very cold, almost as if my heart were turning over and going to stop. It's a horrible feeling."

I took her hand in mine, and she continued.

" 'What do you mean?' I asked. 'That something will happen to the Colonel?'

" 'No, I mean that he will not return. He doesn't intend to return. He has gone.'

"I stared at him absolutely incredulous, and he said it again.

" 'Colonel Collins has left the Nai Mem for ever. He will never come back. He has left her alone in this camp of soldiers. He has abandoned her.'

"And again I could only think as I had done about Luong-Tam-Ky, that the man had taken leave of his senses.

" 'Are you mad?' I asked. 'How dare you come and say such things to me?'

" 'Because it is true,' he said. 'I have been watching him for a long time. Ever since he came here. It was to watch him that I entered his service. I am on special duty, seconded by the head of the Military Intelligence Branch of the Chinese Secret Service. . . . I have read everything that he has written, and everything that has been written to him. There is nothing about him that I don't know, and that I have not reported to my superiors. And he is now carrying out a scheme that he has contemplated for some time. . . .'

"He talked just like that, Sinbad, and I knew that the man was speaking the truth—about himself, I mean. His English was practically perfect. There was nothing of the servant about him. When I said,

" 'Who are you?' he replied,

" 'Your very humble servant, Major Li Hsian Chang of the Imperial Army and Chinese Secret Service—at your orders, Madam.'

"I had to believe him. As regards what he said about himself, at any rate. He was so convincing; and though he was, of course, dressed as a servant, it was plain enough then that he was not one. He held himself differently, spoke differently, was different.

"A different man altogether.

"It was extraordinary how he turned from a menial into a masterful and cultured person of consequence, a person of quality. He's what he says he is, Sinbad. Whether he's speaking the truth about my husband is another matter."

"And what did he propose?"

"To take me away."

"What, to . . ."

"To take me away—to a place of safety. To get me out of this camp. 'Rescue' me, in fact. Then it appeared that he had heard everything that General Luong-Tam-Ky said yesterday. He showed him in here, you know, just as though it was the visit of an ordinary afternoon caller. And then he listened, and heard every word that was said. He made no secret of that. Part of his job, I suppose."

"What, just listened at the key-hole?"

"I don't know. Probably he has a proper 'listening-place' as they call it. It is likely that there is nothing but a sheet of wall-paper between this room and the next, in some spot. One's heard of that sort of thing in China. Anyhow, the fact remains that he knows exactly what was said. And he asked me what I supposed was going to happen to me when Luong-Tam-Ky realized that there was no need to prevent my husband from returning from Thay-Taong—as my husband had no intention of going there. In fact, he had simply run away and abandoned me here. He then hinted that I should be lucky if Luong-Tam-Ky did get hold of me and not Ba-Ky—or something worse happen to me."

"What did you say, Mary?" I asked.

"I said,

" *'If you are what you tell me you are; and if there's a word of truth in what you have told me about my husband; I can look after myself.'* "

"And then?"

"Well, he practically told me not to talk nonsense; asked me how on earth I could look after myself, here in a camp with a couple of thousand soldiers—and Luong-Tam-Ky, not to mention Ba-Ky.

"I told him what I told Luong-Tam-Ky—that I had no wish to live.

"But, I must say, he frightened me. I don't know whether I am at all lacking in imagination; but by the time he had finished, I was far more frightened than ever I have been when I have tried to visualize exactly what I should do here, if anything happened to my husband.

"And having succeeded in completely terrifying me, he begged me to escape while there was time, and before anyone knew—what at present only he knew—that my husband had left the Chinese camp and the local Chinese service for good, and had abandoned me here in the middle of it.

"Then I asked him why, supposing for one moment all he had said was true, he was so interested in my fate. I said I should have thought he'd have been more concerned to send the information about my husband as quickly as possible to his superiors at Peking.

"He replied that it was what he was going to do; that he was going to leave the camp at once, and hurry to the nearest point whence he could send the message, and that he wanted to take me with him.

"I asked him why, once more, and remarked that surely he'd travel faster alone . . . Then he told me why . . ."

"Yes?"

"Luong-Tam-Ky's story over again. . . . He said that he was in love with me, had been in love with me since the first time he saw me, and had been longing for a chance to save me from a life in which I was unhappy and from a position in which I was not appreciated . . . He made love to me . . ."

Again I sprang to my feet, uncontrollably enraged.

"The impudent hound! The damned insolent Chinese dog. I . . ."

"That's how I felt, my dear, but I must say he was very careful not to be offensive."

"So will I, when I get hold of him," I swore.

"Don't imagine there was anything in the nature of—an attack . . . or a threat . . . or anything of that sort. In point of fact he merely begged me to escape while I could. Implored me to let him save me. And it was only when I asked him why he should wish to help me, that he told me the reason—because he loved me."

"And what was to happen when he had saved you?" I asked.

"He didn't go into that. He was going to get me safely to Peking."

"Yes. Perhaps!" said I. "Is he in the house now?"

"No. There's only the *amah*, and the doors at the back and front are bolted inside, as well as locked."

"Was he in the house when you told me about Luong-Tam-Ky?"

"No. No, he couldn't have been."

"And what was the end of it?"

"Well, I pretended that I didn't believe a word he said, and that I was not in the least frightened—only angry beyond words, and that he himself had better escape from the camp, before my husband came back.

"Then he repeated that my husband never would come back, and begged me to believe it. I said I didn't believe it, didn't believe a word he had said, and that even if it were all true, I should not attempt to escape—with him, at any rate. . . . That I should, of course, wait for my husband. . . . And that, supposing he did not return here, Peking was the last place I should go to. Then he asked me where on earth I supposed I could go, and who on earth would take me there.

"I had half a mind to reply that, if I had to leave here, you would take me. But I thought I had better not say that, especially as you are supposed to have come from China yourself."

I pondered this for a moment.

"Just as well, perhaps," I agreed. "Though I really do not think it would have made any difference. He knows who I am and where I came from, thanks to my own idiotic folly. But who on this earth would ever have dreamed that that dull plate-licking servant was a Chinese officer and agent?"

"Well, I didn't mention you. What I thought at the moment," continued Mary, "was that it might make him jealous of you and bring you into still greater danger."

"Yes," I agreed, "if what he says is true, and he were really jealous of me, it would probably complicate things. What line he might take with regard to me as a French spy I don't know; but one can imagine what it would be if he thought that I was your . . . your . . ."

"Lover," said Mary.

"Yes; and if he thought I were going to help you to get away, and try to get you safely down to Hanoi."

"I wonder if he's speaking the truth," I added.

"About himself or about my husband?"

"Either. Both."

"Well, I believe he's speaking the truth about himself, for as I said before, he's certainly no servant. I have met Chinese 'officers and gentlemen' in Peking, and he's of that class."

"And about your husband?"

"That I don't know. It would be quite like him to abandon me here, if it were to his interest to do so. If there were the slightest reason to do so. He doesn't love me in the very least; and he has shown me nothing but unkindness, un-friendliness, neglect, rudeness, and at times, actual cruelty. Blows. And it has been like that for years. Time and again I have wondered why on earth he didn't get rid of me. And it is quite likely that he has done so now."

"Suppose he has gone off for good. Gone right away. How would this fellow, this Number One Boy know?"

"Well, as he said, he has read everything that my husband has written, and every letter that he has received. Then, of course, he did his packing. He may know that my husband took everything of value that he had; and may have seen him destroy papers and that sort of thing, as though he were never coming back. He may have overheard him in conversation with some messenger or spy. That man who brought him the news about De-Nam's death has been coming here every day. I've no doubt the Number One Boy . . . or 'Major Li Hsian Chang' . . . has heard every word of their conversation—exactly as he heard my conversation with Luong-Tam-Ky."

"Yes, he overheard, no doubt, and he probably knows all about Colonel Collins—as servants do in the East. . . . I say, do you think that perhaps Luong-Tam-Ky knows too, and that is why he came to you with his . . . foulness . . . the moment your husband had gone?"

"I wonder," replied Mary. "The Number One Boy declared that he himself was the only person who knew."

"Well, clever as he may be, he can't really say what Luong-Tam-Ky knows and doesn't know. No-one can. It's entirely possible that, whatever your husband has done, he has done with the complete knowledge of Luong-Tam-Ky; possibly not only with his knowledge, but with his approval and assistance."

"Yes, it is possible. Particularly in the light of what the Number One Boy told me about these two Generals."

"What was that?" I asked.

"According to him, Luong-Tam-Ky and Ba-Ky are not Annamese by birth and nationality, and not regular Chinese Generals either," replied Mary. "They are Chinese, and they are Generals here, all-right; but they are not on the Chinese Army List, and they take no orders whatsoever from the Chinese War Office or Imperial Court."

This was intriguing and would interest Major Deleuze if ever I got the news to him.

"What are they, then, according to the Number One Boy, *alias* Major Li Hsian Chang?"

"Chinese masquerading as Annamese. He called them powerful Barons; the commanders and leaders of the independent Chinese forces in North and West Tonking. He said that these Chinese bands are trained, disciplined armies of brigands; and Luong-Tam-Ky and Ba-Ky are really Robber Chiefs, Brigand Chiefs, each one king of an enormous province north of the Yen Thé. According to him, both these great Chinese brigand chieftains had established their kingdoms, south of the Chinese border, long before the present French armies ever came to Tonking."

"And the Chinese Government supports them?"

"Yes; and this man, Major Li Hsian Chang, is liaison officer between the Chinese Government and these two *tuchuns*, War Lords, Generals of armies of—banditti."

"And part of his job was to watch Colonel Collins?"

"Yes; so he says. It seems that my husband really left the regular Chinese Army and took service in the joint army of these two Robber Chiefs."

"Let's suppose he told you the truth. Did he say what his excuse or reason would be for leaving his job here and going to Peking?"

"Yes, he did—to make a personal report on the general situation; on my husband's activities; on the results in Tonking of the death of General De-Nam; on the strength of the French forces; and to bring back powerful Chinese reinforcements."

"That seems likely enough. Plausible, anyhow . . ."

What a mess! What a sudden development of affairs. And where did I stand now?

Either this Chinese was, or was not, Major Li Hsian Chang of the regular Chinese army, accredited liaison officer and secretly a spy of the Chinese Military Intelligence Service.

And he was now in possession of the fact that I also was a spy.

Luong-Tam-Ky and Ba-Ky either were, or were not, Chinese Generals; and were probably merely powerful Robber Barons subsidized and helped by the Chinese Government, and—of the uttermost importance if what he had told Mary was true—Chinese regular forces, secretly sent to aid the late De-Nam against the French, were likely soon to arrive at this camp. Not only reinforcements, but most probably the great convoy of provisions, munitions, and bullion for the payment of troops.

If I could only discover the truth—and relevant details— what a piece of work I should have done for my chief. . . .

"Sinbad, my dear, what are we to do?"

And again I realized my selfishness.

Duty was one thing—and I would do my duty to the utmost—but self-centred egoism, a desire to distinguish Sinclair Noel Brodie Dysart, was a different matter.

And surely I had a duty to my own countrywoman as well as to the foreign country that I served.

And, provided I did not attempt to escape from this place before I had learned all there was to know, it was, for once, a case of love and duty marching hand-in-hand. Herein I was more fortunate than the hero of fiction who inevitably, in such circumstances, stands between love and duty.

As soon as I knew a little more, as soon as I could confirm the truth of what this alleged Chinese officer and spy had told Mary, I could escape. Go while the going was good, and take her with me.

But take her with me through the jungle? Down the Red River?

Practically impossible.

And wholly impossible to leave her here if, indeed, Colonel John Collins had deserted her.

"What am I to do, Sinbad? You tell me, and I'll do it."

"Wait," I replied. "Wait a little while. My messenger will return from Thay-Taong where your husband is supposed to have gone. . . . And we'll see whether your husband returns. If he does, it's a pack of lies; and he'll know what to do with Mr. Number One Boy and with Luong-Tam-Ky, too, I should think. If he doesn't return, it will look as though the Number One Boy is Major Li Hsian Chang, and has told you the truth."

"And suppose General Luong-Tam-Ky or, for that matter, Major Li Hsian Chang, if that is his name, becomes . . . dangerous? Suppose one of them or Ba-Ky threatens me . . . ?"

"Then we shall have to escape. Leave it to me. I'll keep the closest possible watch on the alleged Major Li Hsian Chang, as well as on Luong-Tam-Ky and Ba-Ky; and I'll have one of my men always near this house, by night now, as well as day, so that you could send me a message at any moment. Your *amah* could give it to him, or come to me herself if necessary. I wonder if she is really faithful?"

"God knows. I believe she is. I think she is truly attached to me. I've always treated her most kindly and have never had any fault to find with her. As a race, the Chinese are honest; and these *amahs* have a very good name for trust-worthiness and faithfulness."

"You keep her in the house with you?"

"Oh, yes. She sleeps outside my room, and only goes down to her hut for meals."

"Shall I come here myself to-morrow night, in any case; whether you send for me or not?"

"Oh, Sinbad, I should so like to see you. You are like a rock . . . and I am so lonely . . . have been for years. Yes. Come and talk to me. After the servants have gone for the night."

"Including the Number One Boy," I said. "I suppose he will . . . go for the night?"

"I'll send for you if he shows any signs of doing otherwise."

"Well, then, unless I hear from you before, I will come over at this time to-morrow night."

But I did not do so.

CHAPTER XXIII

As I returned to my hut that night, keeping as far as possible in the shadows of the trees, bushes, and bamboo clumps, I was suddenly aware that I had company—quite a number of companions—who, ghost-like and silent, surrounded me; a most eerie and unpleasant sensation.

As I passed from black shadow into patches of lesser darkness, I saw vague outlines of two or three men in front of me, two or three to left and right, and, glancing behind, saw that I was followed.

What was this? Luong-Tam-Ky's bodyguard, his—assassins?

What had I better do?

I was unarmed and, so far as I could make out, the odds were at least ten to one; the men big and brawny. Suppose I made a dash for it, whither should I run, supposing I escaped?

The moon came out from behind a cloud as suddenly something was pressed hard into the small of my back and a quiet but compelling voice said,

"*Halte-là! Levez les mains! Vite!*"

And I partly saw, partly heard, and partly felt, that the circle of men closed round me. Discretion seemed the better part of valour.

I put up my hands.

"*Bien! Vous êtes discret. Avez-vous un pistolet? Tenez-vous tranquille. Je vais vous fouiller. Et écoutez, Monsieur l'Anglais—tenez les mains au-dessus la tête. Eh bien! Vous comprenez la langue Française!*"

The speaker then gave orders for me to be seized and bound, and on the spur of the moment, I decided that again discretion would be the better part of valour, there being a good dozen of them. In any case they had got me, and I should be of more use to myself, and to Mary, whole than damaged; more likely to escape whatever threatened if I were uninjured, than if my skull were split or I was stabbed, shot, or otherwise wounded.

My hands being firmly secured behind my back, and my arms bound to my sides, a halter was put somewhat tightly about my neck, the end of it held by the leader of my captors, and I was bidden to march.

"*A votre maison, s'il vous plaît,*" indicated the man in command.

And to my hut I was taken, and the end of the halter was tied to my frame bedstead of heavy teak-wood. The leader then bade me sit on the ground, and gave orders for my feet to be tied together. This having been done to his satisfaction, he peremptorily motioned to his followers to go outside.

This they did, closing the door behind them and leaving me alone with their commander.

This individual proceeded to light the hurricane lamp that dangled from the roof; and, by its light I saw—what did not surprise me—that he was Mary's Number One Boy, *alias* Major Li Hsian Chang.

He had changed his house clothes for a yellow tunic and trousers of somewhat military cut, and this change of dress seemed to alter his whole appearance, manner, and bearing.

He now looked taller, more slender and wiry. His complexion was fair for a Chinese, more like that of a sallow European than of a Mongol; his cheek-bones were prominent and high, and he had the forceful jutting chin associated rather with the West than with the East. His eyes were curious too, being much larger and handsomer than is usual with Chinese, and were now, at any rate, very bright, keen and intelligent.

His look had completely changed, and was of a commanding and compelling quality, in marked contrast to his former humility and apparent respect, if not servility. There was nothing whatsoever of the usual Chinese blank noncommittal evasive quality about it. When he looked me in the eyes, I realized that I was up against a man of character; not only of character and of brains, but of action.

"Shall we talk French or English?" he asked, seating himself in my chair and eyeing me coldly.

"All one to me," I replied in Annamese. "I am an Englishman; but, like yourself, I know a few words of French."

The Chinese smiled.

"I know in what language Colonel Collins will talk to you when he returns," I added. "A language you'll understand— and probably the last you'll ever hear."

"Colonel Collins will not return," he replied. "And if he did, he would not find me here. Nor you."

"No?"

"No. Now, as Mrs. Collins has already told you, I am a Chinese officer. And as your *Tirailleur Tonkinois* has already told me, you are a French spy. It wasn't, perhaps, very clever of you to send him to tell me all about yourself so that I could help you to trap your faithless follower De-Nha. But we will take it that it is perhaps a greater tribute to my own cleverness than to your stupidity. You can hardly be blamed for not realizing that I was anything but what I appeared, a domestic servant addicted to opium."

"I don't give a damn whether you are a domestic servant addicted to opium or a Chinese spy," I replied. "But whatever you are, you don't surely suppose that you were told the truth, do you—when you were told I was a French spy? Ask yourself, man! Is it likely that if I were a French spy—I should tell anybody?"

"I shouldn't have thought it likely," the Chinese replied.

And I writhed internally with shame and self-reproach.

"But the worthy De-Nha was able to confirm your story concerning yourself," he added.

I laughed.

"De-Nha! Good man. He seems to have carried, out my instructions well."

Again the Chinese smiled.

I grew to dislike that smile.

"So my renegade Annamese Linh Nghi, who was once a *Doi* of *Tirailleurs Tonkinois*, and my renegade Annamese dacoit, De-Nha, who was once in the service of De-Nam, have succeeded in persuading you that I am a French spy, as I bade them, have they?"

"They have," replied the Chinese. "Completely. And you are a French spy. When you so clumsily sent the *Doi* Linh Nghi with your ten-franc piece and instructions for me to sound your suspected follower De-Nha, I followed those instructions promptly. Most willingly. Eagerly, in fact. I didn't quite see what the game was, and didn't suspect that it was as simple as it turned out to be. . . .

"My good fool, your De-Nha is an invaluable person—to me. About as clever as ten of you. Nearly as clever as I am, in fact. It didn't take me long to turn him inside out, and to get his whole story, from the time you captured him at Yen Trang to the time your Captain Deleuze (of whom I begin to think less than I did) sent him up here with you. . . .

"Oh yes, the whole story in detail, and the details checked. I know all about the opium torture and the witnessing of the executions ordered by the mandarins of Bac-Linh. I have personal knowledge of the truth of that part of the story, as I was there myself—in the crowd. . . .

"Oh, that interests you, does it? That makes you look up sharply! . . . No, of course I wasn't there, in the crowd or anywhere else. But a spy of mine was. Oh yes, De-Nha 'came across' all-right, as they say in America. 'Came clean.' And I'd have cleaned him inside and out—if he hadn't done so. He knew that—and preferred opium to my—cleansing process."

"What a long story, Mr. Servant," I yawned. "For a Number One Boy in good service, you . . ."

"Don't be silly. And don't let's waste any more time. Now look here. I have a proposal to make. You are a soldier of the French Foreign Legion, attached to the mis-named 'Intelligence' Bureau, run by Captain Deleuze. You are a French spy, and came up the Red River and through the jungle, guided by the dacoit De-Nha and followed by a *Doi* and half a dozen *tirailleurs* of the French so-called 'Secret' Service, and Military 'Intelligence' Branch.

"What you wanted to find out, was whether there were any regular Chinese forces here; and, if so, whether they had any European advisers and instructors—any French

Foreign Legion deserters, or other renegade Europeans, helping them. Well—you have discovered that there are. And that more are coming. But you are most certainly not going back with that information."

"No, Mr. Servant?"

"No, Mr. Englishman-in-French-pay."

"What am I going to do then?"

"One of two things. You are either going to die—slowly and in some discomfort—or else you are going to . . . join me."

"Join you? As a fellow house-servant in good service, and . . ."

"Yes. The Imperial Chinese Service."

"That would be nice. But suppose I prefer my present service with Colonel John Collins and the Generals Luong-Tam-Ky and Ba-Ky?"

"In that case you can choose between Heaven and serving—the Son of Heaven, my Imperial master."

"But surely anybody who is in the service of the Generals Luong-Tam-Ky and Ba-Ky is in the service of the Son of Heaven, your Imperial master?" said I, partly to gain time, partly to gain information, and partly—for the sake of something to say.

"By no means. The thread that joins these two 'Generals' to Peking is extremely tenuous. They are nothing more nor less than brigands. They have their uses politically, and maintain a buffer State between China and the French invaders of Annam. But they are no more subjects, servants, or agents, of the Son of Heaven than is the Ruler of Afghanistan the servant or agent either of Britain or of Russia . . .

"Regular Chinese Generals! Why, they are little better than the 'ear-men' who live by kidnapping and ransom, and send to recalcitrant slow-paying relatives an ear of their captive as a hint and a warning.

"Luong-Tam-Ky and Ba-Ky and their three thousand soldiers live entirely on the country and the wretched peasants, by levying toll on all trade-routes, markets and roads; and on the river traffic too; by raiding; by robbing towns; and by what they call taxation; and by loot of every description.

"We merely permit them to exist as long as they operate on the other side of our border, and as long as they are useful to us in keeping the French occupied. Your 'Colonel' Collins merely plays the honourable rôle of Third Robber. And if you were what you pretend to be, you'd merely be the Third Robbers' parasite, a glorified drill-sergeant, making robber-bands more efficient, and turning Chinese dacoits into hireling soldiers."

A loquacious gentleman, this Chinese; and telling me quite a lot. But the reason and excuse for his communicativeness was not far to seek. He was talking with what he regarded as either a dead man or a recruit to his following.

"Yes, that's the situation, Mr. English-Frenchman, but you are not going back to French headquarters to describe it."

"Why should I? Who wants to go to French headquarters —to describe the uninteresting situation here or anywhere else?"

Again the Chinese smiled.

"Why waste time?" he asked persuasively. "You haven't very much, you know. Unless you join me, that is . . . Now, if you like to give me your word, your solemn promise—to join me and be loyal to me, I'll accept your promise and I will trust you absolutely."

"Why should you accept my bare word and trust?"

"Because I have lived in England, and know your type. Also I am a physiognomist and can read faces. What are they but indexes? Indexes to the book within. The book of character. Yes, I can read such indexes. If you give me your word, I will accept it."

This was interesting.

"The Chinese should always trust the English, and the English trust the Chinese—instead of the Japanese. That's where they make a mistake, and what you call back the wrong horse. Will you join me?"

"In what?"

"In my work. Will you, an Englishman, drop the French

connection altogether, and take service with the Chinese? There can never be a real Anglo-French alliance, you know. Whereas a firm Anglo-Chinese alliance would be a very great thing indeed, both for England and China; both for Europe and Asia. Think how a man like you could rise in the Chinese service, and what you could do for your great country. Look at Sir Robert Hart, who rose from student-interpreter to British Minister Plenipotentiary at Peking. Look at Charles George Gordon and his influence with Li Hung Chang and the Emperor. Why, the Emperor gave him the rank of *Titu* and the Order of the Yellow Jacket, the highest rank and the highest decoration in China, when he was no older than you. You too could go very far."

"You seem to know a lot about me. What makes you think I should be useful?" I enquired.

"Because Captain Deleuze thinks you are useful; and, in spite of what I said just now, I know him to be a very clever man. Very clever indeed. Besides, the sort of man who can make his way here from French Headquarters and deceive Colonel Collins and the Chinese *tuchuns*, is a man not only of ability but of—guts. . . . That's a vulgar word, isn't it? . . . Will you join me and work with me?"

"What would the work be?" I temporized.

"First of all, to get Mrs. Collins safely away from here and into China. I am short-handed for a job like that. Secondly, to tell me absolutely everything you know about the French plans. Thirdly, to take service permanently, honourably, and loyally, in the Imperial Chinese army; and teach and train certain units, in European warfare.

"Efficient discipline and modernity are what we lack. The Chinese army isn't up to date, either in equipment or methods. What we want is a nucleus of troops trained on the European model, and made equal in every way to a corresponding unit of the best European troops. Mind you, the material is good. None better. What we want is officers and training. Once we had the nucleus, properly trained and properly officered, it would become a New Model for the Chinese armies. We could have such a New Model in every State, like Li Hung Chang had, thanks to General Gordon, when he was Governor in Kiang-Su. You've heard of his Ever-Victorious Army, of course, in Sungkiang, and how it captured Chansu, Suchow, Chanchufu and every other place it attacked?"

"Well, I'm an obscure and humble soldier of fortune. I'm afraid I am not a Sir Robert Hart, and I'm not a General Gordon," I replied.

"No, but the one was a clerk and the other a subaltern of Royal Engineers—before they entered Chinese service and had their chance of greatness. Will you join me?"

"No. And since you are so sure my man De-Nha told you the truth, what's the good of asking me? If you know I am a French soldier, a French Military Intelligence spy, what's the good of asking me to join you? If I'd betray my service, I'd betray yours."

The Chinese smiled again.

"Life is dear, especially to Europeans—for some reason," he said.

"Well, supposing I were in French service and would leave it to save my life, and join you, would you expect me to be very trustworthy?"

"I am willing to risk it. If you give me your word, and promise that, if I spare your life, you will join the Chinese Imperial Service and be loyal and faithful, I will take your word and keep mine."

"I believe you would," I said.

"And I am quite sure that you would. I know the type."

Subtle flattery.

What would be the best thing to do? If I flatly refused his offer, I should most probably never see Mary again; never see the base at Houi-Bap again; never take back to Captain Deleuze such information as I had gleaned. If I cheated this man and he found me out, as he would do, I should get even more short and painful shrift than if I flatly and finally refused his offer now.

Should I save my life, and do what seemed the best thing for Mary, by leaving the French service and joining the Chinese?

Undoubtedly there was far more scope and opportunity

in such service than there was in the French.

The utmost I could hope for in the way of promotion in the French Foreign Legion was to rise to the rank of sergeant-major, and possibly *adjudant*, the highest rank of non-commissioned officer. There was practically no chance at all of a Commission; and, if there were, and I got one, I should probably end my days as a grey-haired lieutenant, or possibly captain, in the French service; and retire, if lucky, on a pound a week or so. Much more probably I should leave my bones in some nameless hole-and-corner place in a Tonkinese, Madagascan, or West African swamp, if not in the sands of the Sahara.

No, there were certainly no prospects in the French service; and I had no intention of sticking to it beyond the five years for which I had contracted to serve.

On the other hand, in the Chinese service there was un-limited scope; and a man of ability and integrity—and I could provide the latter requisite—could rise to almost any height. Certainly to rank, fame, honour, and wealth.

And there was the little matter of one's life; and what, honestly, was far more important to me then, the matter of Mary's safety.

A career, life, Mary . . .

The alternative, death by torture.

It seemed foolish to hesitate.

And yet—those curious inhibitions.

Somehow I felt I could not do it, much as I might want to.

True, I was in an alien service, and had been more or less pitch-forked into it as a way of escape from a Djibouti gaol; and yet I *was* in that service; I had joined it by my own choice; I had signed a contract, however one-sided; and I had taken service under a flag which bore in letters of gold, the motto 'Honneur et Fidélité'.

I was a soldier of fortune, a mercenary. I had joined a mercenary army, and the foundation of such a force is the fidelity and loyalty of the men who join it.

And in a way, in my immeasurably humble capacity, I represented England in that polyglot heterogeneous army.

And Colonel Wattringue, Captain Dubosque, Lieutenant

Jacot, had all noticed me, referred to me as "the Englishman".

And Captain Deleuze. . . . Yes, that was the chief part of the trouble. Somehow, I could not let him down. Captain Deleuze had trusted me; chosen me for this job; believed not only in my ability, but, of course, in my faithfulness and loyalty.

On the other hand, he would probably never know what had become of me.

No—but I should.

All my life I should know that I had ratted under pressure; under threats—and promises.

Life would not be worth living if one had that constant regret; that constant shame at the back of one's mind, the knowledge that one had betrayed the flag under which one had taken service, gone over to another one, an Oriental one, an enemy's flag, really.

No, I felt I couldn't do it. And I honestly felt, in my bones, that Mary wouldn't wish me to do it.

But hadn't I a debt to her, quite as real and strong as my duty to Captain Deleuze and to my present employer *Madame la République*. Since I loved Mary and she loved me, hadn't she the first claim on me? It seemed like it. I wanted it to seem like it. The wish was father to the thought.

But no, it wouldn't do. I knew that all argument was specious. I was a soldier of France; and in furthering the interests of France my duty lay. The first claim on me was that of my military superiors. . . .

All very portentous.

But I was still fairly young, and, though rapidly growing older and lapsing from grace, I still took myself seriously.

"Well?" asked Major Li Hsian Chang.

"The answer is in the negative," I said. "And final."

"Which, of course, goes to prove, though further proof is entirely superfluous, that you are a French spy."

"Well, whatever I am, I remain."

"Then I'm afraid you will have to die."

"Well, look here, Major Li Hsian Chang, or whatever you are—can't we be a little more comfortable about it? We have had a very pleasant and friendly conversation, and you have tried to improve my mind and prospects. What about cutting this cord and letting me have a stretch? I've got cramp most damnably."

"Cramp! My dear Mr. French-Englishman. . . . Cramp, did you say. . . . You'll be tied in knots of utmost agony shortly, raving mad with unbearable pain. Have you ever seen any Chinese torture? I don't mean jungle stuff, I mean really artistic performance by a master?"

"But look here, Major, I thought you were civilized, and all that."

"Yes, we were civilized beyond the rest of humanity when you were naked savages daubed with woad."

"Well, why talk about torture? Civilized people don't go in for that."

"You mean Western people don't. We do. Custom of the country. I'll show you."

"But with what object?"

"Oh, primarily to make you change your mind."

"Well, I shouldn't be much good to you after being tortured, should I?"

"Oh, there are some tortures that make the strongest men shriek and scream like young girls, without doing them the least harm. Permanent bodily harm, I mean. It cows them mentally and spiritually, though, for quite a while."

"And suppose I didn't change my mind, in spite of having to shriek and scream like—a Chinese, did you say?"

"Well, since you insist on being so French, it will teach you not to be a Frenchman, won't it? You'll wish you had stuck to your own country."

"Hardly be worth all that trouble for so small a result, would it?"

"Oh, no trouble, I assure you. Besides, there's the deterrent aspect of it. When news gets back to your Headquarters of how you died, there won't be any more volunteers for this sort of job, will there?"

"Any number," I replied. "Captain Deleuze will probably come himself."

"And, finally, you know too much. You are not going back

to French Headquarters with the information you've gathered here about the *tuchuns* and Chinese assistance. Why, it might precipitate a Franco-Chinese war—the last thing we want."

"Well, there's no need for torture to prevent my going back, is there?"

"No actual need; but you are going to die—and that's the way you'll die. Custom of the country. *Autre pays, autre mœurs*, as you say in your present service, Mr. Renegade."

"Well, I admit that you surprise me, after your talk about civilization. Why the most filthy degraded savages in the Cannibal Islands don't . . ."

"No hope along those lines, Mr. Renegade. You don't suppose you could 'shame' me into adopting your Western standards, do you? Do you know what Confucius says on the subject of the Problem of Pain?"

What, another of them? Damn Confucius!

"But of course you don't. The Problem of Human Pain is one of the most interesting and intriguing conundrums propounded for the consideration of the philosopher. Pain. That strange two-edged gift of the gods. Some there are who think that the whole solution of the right treading of the Excellent Way lies in the understanding of the infliction and bearing of pain."

"Couldn't we study it, the other way round?" I asked. "I'll take the infliction side, and you study bearing it."

Again the Chinese smiled, this time quite pleasantly.

"By inflicting pain on you, I shall suffer it," he said, with apparent sincerity, "for I like you. Among the barbarians of England, of America and of France, in all of which countries I have studied engineering and the other military arts and sciences, I have occasionally encountered such as you, men whom I have liked. It will give me great pain . . ."

"Well, why not spare yourself?"

"Duty," sighed Li Hsian Chang, and the smile that followed the sigh did not strike me as at all sincere.

He rose to his feet.

"Think it over. I'll ask you once again, and then put you to the question, the torture. If you withstand that, I'll have you shot or, perhaps, since you are doubtless a good Christian, crucified."

He turned to go.

"Look here, Major Li Hsian Chang," I said. "Don't behave like a Möi dacoit—since you are so highly civilized. At least undo my hands and feet. You've got your gang of ruffians round the house. Aren't a dozen of them enough to keep me here?"

"I am awfully sorry," was the reply. "I'm afraid I must leave you tied up. The worse the cramp gets, the more clearly you will think, or perhaps, the more wisely."

"Can't you take my word for it that the answer is No. And if you feel you've got to shoot me as a captured spy if I don't change my mind, shoot me and have done with it—as an officer of any decent army would do to a prisoner, even if he were a spy. If you've been a military *attaché*, and mixed with the officers of the British, American, and French armies, surely you've learned . . ."

"My good Mr. Renegade, when I was attached to units of the armies you mention, I made no effort to change their military customs. I didn't urge upon them my views on capital or other punishment. Since you've been good enough to come to the East and to meddle in Oriental matters, suppose you accept the customs of the East as I did of the West.

"You find them 'barbarous'. So did I yours. Horribly barbarous. Here we torture spies, to make them talk; to make them change their minds, or their side; and if they don't do it, we shoot them. I'm awfully sorry, as I say, for I like you very much. Nevertheless, I don't propose to modify our excellent national customs on that account, and if I decide that you are not amenable to the torture that doesn't permanently damage, we'll use the other, and you will be most incurably damaged, maimed, deformed, deprived, for the rest of your life, which will be about one hour. Depilation and total flaying for a beginning of this second process; and going on to the bow-string; a red-hot iron nut or bolt under the arm-pit, or inside the bound-up hand; the foot in a pot of boiling oil; the hand-crusher.

"Do you know the Beauty's Bar and The Parrot's Beak? It was one of our Judges who invented The Beauty's Bar for the benefit of his wife—a naughty woman. A very ingenious man.

"I expect you know the burning splinter one. We fill you with inch-long splinters until you bristle like a porcupine. Then we set light to them, and they burn and fizzle right down to the buried point, half an inch deep in the flesh. But I may not be able to get the proper wood for that. . . . Still, we'll do our best.

"And I have a few that I am sure you've never heard of. Nobody has, for I invented them myself, and have found them most efficacious for the extraction of information.

"One of them I have never known to fail. It will be interesting to see how you stand up to it, or rather lie down to it. It is done in the horizontal position. As I say, it will spoil you for good . . . how do you put it—ah, yes . . . for keeps. But we needn't regret that unduly, as you won't outlive to-morrow in any case, unless you join me."

I tried another line.

"Look here, Major What's-your-name. Give me time to think it over. Cut this damned cord and set me free for twenty-four hours. I undertake not to leave the camp and . . ."

"Not to shoot me in the back or take any other steps against me, eh? I believe you'd do it too. Keep your word, I mean. But I don't think I'll risk it, much as I'd like to try the experiment, and see whether you kept faith. But business first and pleasure afterwards, as you say in the West. Yes, duty first."

"But if I give you my promise . . ."

"Now look here, if you say another word, I'll have you gagged very painfully—and put a *cangue* round your neck too. And unless you are looking for really solid trouble, don't shout and call for help. If you do, my man will come in and knock you on the head. Not fatally, of course, but sufficient to soothe you for a few hours. Then you will have a head-ache as well as cramp."

"*You*'ll have something, when my turn comes," I replied,

eyeing this solemn slight man, whom I could have broken across my knee, and yet from whom power, resolution and forcefulness seemed to emanate.

"Well now, think it over. I'll come back later when I have made my arrangements. Make no mistake. You are either going to die very painfully, or join me."

And opening the door, he spoke to a big Chinese who, having glanced at me, nodded his head with an expression of willing and cheerful obedience.

I cannot say that he actually licked his chops.

CHAPTER XXIV

I suppose the hours that followed were among the worst of my life, although, thanks to the fact that I have adventured in many places and sought sorrow far and wide, I have had some unpleasant ones.

"I have taken my fun where I've found it", and it has been very varied, and some of it not so very funny.

I felt utterly dejected, miserable, frightened, and most thoroughly wretched.

When I thought of Mary, I felt sick and faint with horror, fear and anxiety.

Had I not also been face to face with death and the probabilities of horrible torture, I should still have had sufficient to account for that frame of mind, inasmuch as I was weak with hunger, suffering the pangs of thirst, horribly cramped and in great distress of mind.

What had this accursed Chinese meant by 'other arrangements'? The kidnapping of Mary? For that was what it amounted to, whether he called it rescue or not.

The one faint gleam of light in that particular darkness was the thought that she would probably be better off in his hands than in those of Luong-Tam-Ky, and but little worse off than she had been in those of her husband, the surly and ruffianly Chinese half-caste, calling himself Colonel John Collins, whom I now knew to be but a swashbuckling free-booter in the pay of the two Robber Barons and Bandit Chiefs, Luong-Tam-Ky and Ba-Ky.

I hope and I believe that my anxiety for the woman I loved was greater than that for my own miserable fate of being tortured to death or, at best, killed in a hut in a robber camp.

And how I regretted having sent my faithful follower and friend *Doi* Linh Nghi and his remaining *tirailleurs* scouting and spying to Men-tsz, Fo-lu and Thay Taong respectively, for news of Collins, that very day. It had occurred to me that he might not have gone to the New Fort at Thay Taong at all.

Had the *Doi* been here, either this would never have happened or he would now be doing something to rescue me. I could imagine him and his men dealing most faithfully with the Chinese who were guarding the hut. The Annamese would move as softly and silently as cats in the darkness, and would account for them one by one. The Chinese would never know what killed them.

As it was, the *Doi* probably would not return to this place for several days.

What a miserable fool I had been to land myself in such a position as this!

Thinking back, where had I been a fool, apart from attempting to undertake so difficult and hazardous a task as spying on this camp of the brigand allies of the Annamese rebels?

I could hardly blame myself for not discovering that Collins's Number One Boy was a Chinese officer.

I could hardly blame myself for obeying Mary's request to go to her house that night.

I could hardly blame myself for coming back in the darkness unarmed. Had I shown fight I should probably have been killed, then and there, when the Chinese surrounded me, and Major Li Hsian Chang put his pistol against my spine.

Could I blame myself for having fallen in love with Mary? Was that where I had gone off the rails, and was it the cause of my present plight?

Anyway, I couldn't help it. Collins had invited me to the house. I had seen her and I had fallen in love with her as unconsciously and inevitably as I fell asleep at night. To me it seemed as natural and inevitable a phenomenon as the rising and setting of the sun.

No, I could not blame myself for having fallen in love with her.

Could I blame myself for having admitted the fact and acted upon it?

No. It would have been an act of prudence and virtue bordering on the mean and the cowardly.

In spite of the fact that I am a Highland Scot, member of a race supposed to be noted for caution, I am not cautious. I have little respect for excessive prudence, and I am afraid that the contemplation of virtue, as virtue in the abstract, does not attract me. Certain virtues I do admire and love, such as courage, loyalty, honesty and kindliness, but I cannot remember ever yearning to be The Virtuous Man.

No, I had fallen in love with Mary; desperately in love; and I had had the honesty to admit it and accept its implications and *sequelæ* without conscious casuistry or self-deception.

I felt that I should have been something of a coward and a cad to deny it, and to refuse her, in the circumstances in which she was placed, such comfort and help as that admission gave her. In spite of my Scottish conscience, I could not blame myself for loving Mary; for being Mary's lover.

In point of fact, I gloried in it. And, little as I like the type of person who makes bad luck the excuse for every failure, disaster, fault and sin, it seemed to me that I had been unlucky in the fact that this damnably clever Secret Service agent should have been at his headquarters when I arrived, and particularly that he should have been a member of John Collins's household.

What an exceedingly clever man he must be, to have played such a rôle as that of a servant in that *ménage*, so successfully. I recognized fully and freely that it could only be through amazing cleverness, astuteness, resolution, and ability, that he had done what he had.

And I touched the depths that night, possibly the lowest depths, as I half-crouched, half-lay, there in an agony of cramp, unable to rise to my feet, unable to do anything but roll from side to side, tethered by my slip-knot halter to the heavy native bed.

In the story-books, I should doubtless have burst my bonds—a thing that, had I been the strongest man alive, I could not have done, as I had no purchase or lever for my strength. Or I should have been able to slide my hands out from the cord which I should have loosened.

In point of fact, the more I struggled, the tighter they became, and the more I twisted them, the more my hands swelled.

It was an extremely efficient piece of work, and the idea of tethering me by the noose about my neck, an admirable one, for the least attempt to increase the distance between myself and the short thick bed-post, immediately suggested strangulation. One effort was quite sufficient, for the halter, already uncomfortably close-fitting, was yet further tightened, a condition of affairs that I had no means of improving.

No, in the absence of the *Doi* there was no hope of rescue from without, and none of self-help within. I could do nothing but wait. Await my fate like a sacrificial ox—or ass.

I toyed with the thought of calling to the Chinese sentry at the door, and endeavouring to bribe him, but remembered Major Li Hsian Chang's parting remark, and the face of the said sentry. He'd probably come straight in and crack my skull with a rifle-butt if I made a sound, without waiting to hear what I had got to say.

Nor was it likely that he'd be open to bribery and corruption. Obviously he and the rest of the squad, band, or gang, that had captured me, must be Major Li Hsian Chang's men, and devoted either to his person or his interests, or both. Doubtless they were picked soldiers of the Chinese Imperial army, or more probably, Chinese Imperial Secret Service spies and agents.

No, I should get nothing but a frightful welt on the head if I attempted to call the sentry.

Oh, for my faithful *Doi*! Oh, for one of those sharp projections against which I could patiently rub my bound wrists, as the hero, thus unfortunately situated, invariably does in the story-books.

When was it that I had previously been in just such another fix, my hands bound behind me, tied up like a chained dog? It must have been the time the nomad Arabs captured me on the Moroccan coast when my shipmate, Halling, and I had rowed ashore from the gun-running ship for a stroll on the beach.

Yes, in a way, I had been worse off then than I was now, for I was pretty badly knocked about, and in the hands of ruffianly savages, one of whom was more than anxious to hack my head off, and with difficulty restrained by others whose cupidity exceeded their brutality.

On the other hand, those people, murderous as they were, had not resorted to actual torture, other than that of blows and kicks, and dragging me along behind a horse. Anyway, I had been in a most parlous condition and position —and the point was that I had come through all-right.

Never say die. While there's life there's hope.

And what about Mary and her life and her hope?

How long I lay brooding, shivering with fear and fever, at times almost in a state of torpor in spite of the agonizing cramp, the pain of which was driving me mad, I don't know.

Suddenly I raised my head and glanced toward the door. I had heard a sound from that direction, a sound of movement and of voices.

The door was flung open. Now for it.

Give way? . . . Give in? . . . For Mary's sake and to save my life? Or stick it out like the British Soldier of whom Lord Elgin wrote, who died under devilish torture rather than give information, or kow-tow to his Chinese enemies.

I would try not to give way; try to stick it out. . . .

But, oh, for an intimate minute with Major Li Hsian Chang, my hands unbound, and he and I unarmed.

I stared in amazement as someone entered.

It was not Major Li Hsian Chang.

CHAPTER XXV

It was that amazing disciple and student of Confucius, the Robber-Baron, the *soi-disant* 'General' Luong-Tam-Ky.

What now? Had he come to see the fun? And while deprecating the shocking cruelty of his Chinese friend and colleague, to suggest other and greater refinement of fiendish cruelty?

Were General Luong-Tam-Ky and Major Li Hsian Chang about to give a competitive exhibition of their skill in the arts of torture, myself providing the *vile corpus* of experiment and demonstration; literally butchered to make a Chinese holiday?

But no, he was alone.

And when I came to think of it, so far as I could think at all, how did Major Li Hsian Chang, *alias* Number One Boy of the Collins's *ménage*, stand in relation to Luong-Tam-Ky?

Or didn't he stand at all?

Had Luong-Tam-Ky any idea whatsoever as to who Collins's Number One Boy really was?

That I should soon discover, and if Luong-Tam-Ky did not know, I would promptly enlighten him. Quite conceivably he might object to Collins's Number One Boy proving to be a Chinese officer, Military Intelligence agent, and spy—upon the comings and goings, the doings and undoings of the Robber Chiefs, Luong-Tam-Ky and Ba-Ky.

As this thought flashed through my mind, Luong-Tam-Ky stood and stared at me, the surprise he certainly felt in no way reflected on the unchanging mask that was his face.

I thought it politic to wait for him to begin, and to see what line he was going to take, for from it I might learn something.

"Well, well," he said, and continued to stare at me.

Evidently it had also occurred to the excellent Luong-Tam-Ky that it might be politic for him to wait for me to begin, and to see what line I was going to take.

"Good evening, your Excellency," I observed, non-committally.

"Or morning," he corrected, contributing but little to my own conversational offering.

"And not very good either, is it?" he added.

"Not very."

"What has been happening?"

"Violence," replied I.

" '*And how deplorable is violence*', as Confucius says."

I agreed.

"And who has been acting thus violently?"

"Not Colonel Collins," he suddenly added, shooting a probing look deep into my eyes.

"No, he has gone away."

And for some reason or for no reason, perhaps because I was a little depolarized, if not demented, by fright, fever, anxiety about Mary, and the untoward happenings of the night, I added,

"Gone to the New Fort at Thay-Taong."

Once again Luong-Tam-Ky did not look surprised, but he looked at me with obviously increased interest.

"Ah, the New Fort at Thay-Taong. Yes, that rather bears out what I thought."

"What did Your Excellency think?"

"Oh, a lot of things. In point of fact, I came to have quite a little talk with you about them. But I find . . . somebody else has been before me—also to have a little talk. Who was it?"

"I wonder if you'd know him under his right name?" I replied.

"I wonder," observed His Excellency.

"It is someone whom you know, but don't know that you know. And don't know, although you think that . . . I am getting muddled . . ."

Definitely my temperature was rising high and fast.

"Parables, parables," murmured Luong-Tam-Ky "Meanwhile, wouldn't you be more comfortable . . . if I were to have that cord cut?"

I stared in amazement. Somehow, I hadn't looked upon

this cold cruel villain as a possible friend in need. Surely he could have come for no other purpose than to add to my trouble, and to make my plight possibly worse.

And doubtless he was only playing with me as a cat with a mouse. He must have found out how things were between me and Mary, and come to eliminate a miserable rival, to take a jealous revenge on . . .

Luong-Tam-Ky went to the door and spoke to someone without.

To my further bewilderment, the moon-faced sentry whom Major Li Hsian Chang had left on guard, entered, and at Luong-Tam-Ky's bidding, drew his bayonet. It was dull and it was dirty, but quite obviously it had been very recently and very thoroughly sharpened.

So this was the end?

I closed my eyes—and the man cut the thong close beside the knot, cut the thong that bound my ankles together, unwound about a *wah* of cord, and then cut the cord about my wrists.

Luong-Tam-Ky then, with kindly and gentle solicitude, loosed the tight halter from about my neck, and helped me to rise to my feet.

Thankfully I sat down upon the pallet of my bed.

With his own hands he poured out water from an earthenware *chattie* into a tin mug, and gave me one of the best drinks I have ever had.

As the soldier went to leave the hut, Luong-Tam-Ky, with a sharp word, bade him mount guard inside.

I wondered whether this were for his own personal safety or to keep the man in sight, and handy for further questioning.

Apparently the fellow realized that, whatever orders Major Li Hsian Chang had given him, those of 'General' Luong-Tam-Ky had to be obeyed—and promptly. Whatever he might be in the sight of God and Peking, Luong-Tam-Ky was a General here, all-right.

"Now then, tell me what happened," said Luong-Tam-Ky in English. "It was not done by a dacoit, a common robber, because such things don't happen inside a camp that I command; and moreover, I found that Chinese on guard outside your door, mounted as a sentry. It appears that he has forgotten who stationed him there. We'll stimulate his memory later! . . . Now, my young friend, tell me all about it."

So kindly and sympathetic was his voice, that I almost wondered that he did not say 'Tell Papa all about it'.

What should I tell him—the truth, the whole truth, and nothing but the truth; or the truth with reservations?

How much did he already know; and for what reason had he come; and exactly what would happen if Major Li Hsian Chang came back and found him here?

And where were the rest of the gang who had captured me? And if they had faded away into the darkness, at the approach of General Luong-Tam-Ky, would they not go straight off and warn Major Li Hsian Chang of what had happened?

"Might I first ask what auspicious event has brought your Excellency so opportunely to my help?" I temporized.

Luong-Tam-Ky's thin lips parted in what was perhaps intended for a smile.

"The desire to enjoy your delightful company," he said.

"How honoured is this miserable and unworthy one," I bowed. "I can scarcely believe it."

"I'm sure you can," replied Luong-Tam-Ky dryly.

"Listen," he added in quiet tones. "I came to make you a proposal. Or rather, to discuss with you a most important matter out of which might arise a proposal—one that I am sure will be most welcome to you. Also to make you an offer of the most advantageous kind."

I murmured my chastened delight.

"Yes," he added, leaning back in my chair, folding his arms beneath his sleeves and eyeing the lamp pensively, reflectively.

"Yes, I have been having a little conversation, indeed a long conversation, with a friend and follower of yours—one De-Nha, late a subordinate leader in the service of the lamented General De-Nam."

Oh, so De-Nha was a traitor, as I had supposed, and Doi Linh Nghi had known.

And he had been to Luong-Tam-Ky and betrayed me.

And Luong-Tam-Ky had come straight to me.

Yes, the cat playing with the mouse, as I had supposed, or rather the fierce fanged tiger with the bleating foolish calf.

And yet, granted that the kindliness, sympathy and friendliness were savage mockery, why the cutting of my bonds? Why had he set me free and given me water? For the pleasure of having me trussed up again twice as painfully as before?

I had heard that one of the cruellest Spanish tortures of mediæval times was to allow the prisoner to escape from his cell, to escape from the prison building, to escape from the court-yard and precincts, to get out through the last great gates, clear of the gaol—and then to gather him in again. . . .

Should I spring on this devil as soon as the cramp had completely left my limbs, and circulation had returned to normal; spring on him and break his neck across my knee—and take my chance with the sentry there by the door?

And then what? Doubtless Major Li Hsian Chang's men were still about the hut, and if by chance I evaded them, where could I go? Certainly not to Mary's house.

"Yes," continued the soft and silky voice. "I have been having a most interesting conversation with De-Nha, an unreliable person, but doubtless, in this instance, a speaker of the truth. It was, as I said, for the pleasure of paying you a social visit and enjoying the charm of your conversation that I came, but I thought one subject of conversation might be—the interesting information that he gave me.

"And now"—the voice altered completely, and its silky quality changed to one of steel—"what happened here to-night?"

Well, he had given me something to think about, and now I'd give him something to think about—and something perhaps equally important and unpleasant.

"Has your Excellency ever visited the house of Colonel Collins?"

It cannot be said that Luong-Tam-Ky frowned or that the probing concentration of his stare increased, but it seemed to do so. The expression of his face did not change, but behind his eyes it was as though something crouched, ready to spring.

"The house of Colonel Collins," he murmured. "Let me see. Yes, yes. I distinctly remember returning his formal visit of honour. We drank tea together with due ceremony."

"Did your Excellency happen to notice Colonel Collins's butler, major-domo, chief servant—what Europeans in China call 'Number One Boy', I believe?"

"No," replied his Excellency. "I cannot honestly say that I did. I don't notice servants much. One ant is very like another."

"Well, this ant isn't," said I.

"No? . . . He is more . . . ant-like?"

"Much. Colonel Collins's Number One Boy is Major Li Hsian Chang of the Imperial Chinese Army, Military Intelligence branch. He's a Secret Service agent, here to spy on you and General Ba-Ky, and to report on everything that happens."

I think Luong-Tam-Ky's expression did, for once, change. Certainly he rose to his feet.

"If you are speaking the truth—just repeat it, will you?" he said quietly. "If not, don't—for your own sake. I hate violence, but if you are telling me a pack of lies . . ."

I don't think I ever heard anything more sinister than Luong-Tam-Ky's quiet voice.

"I am telling you the absolute truth," I replied.

Yes, I had given the Brigand Chief something to think about—and he was thinking hard.

"Tell me again," he whispered and wiped his lips.

"Colonel Collins's Number One Boy is Major Li Hsian Chang of the Imperial Chinese Army, and an agent of the Secret Service Military Intelligence Department. He's a spy—and reports to Peking everything that happens here, everything that you and General Ba-Ky say, and do, and propose to do."

"How do you know?" whispered Luong-Tam-Ky; and had

I been lying, the black eyes would have been difficult to meet.

"He has told me so himself."

"Why?"

"He had me seized . . ."

"Where?"

"Just outside my house."

"When?"

"About midnight."

"Where were you going?"

"I wasn't going. I was coming. Coming back from visiting the sentries."

"Yes?"

"And he had me bound—as you found me."

"How many men?"

"About a dozen."

"And he told you this tale. . . . Why?"

"Because our little friend De-Nha had been talking to him also."

Slowly Luong-Tam-Ky nodded his head, reminding me of a china mandarin, in my mother's drawing-room at home, which interminably nodded its head in just that fashion when set in motion.

"And De-Nha told him—what he told me, eh?"

"I don't know what he told your Excellency."

"I think you do. *He told me that you are a French spy* sent by the Intelligence Bureau at Houi-Bap, to spy on this camp, to find out whether we were Chinese regulars, whether we had any European advisers and instructors, whether we were receiving regular assistance from the Imperial Chinese Government, where the late General De-Nam's new headquarters and citadel are, and anything else you could discover."

"Yes, that appears to be the tale he told Major Li Hsian Chang," I agreed. "Major Li Hsian Chang believed it and had me seized, as you see—which seems to prove that the Number One Boy of Collins's domestic staff is—what he says he is. He proposes to torture me to death unless I confess everything and also join him."

"Join him? In what?"

"In his Intelligence work."

"Leave your service, or rather the French service," murmured Luong-Tam-Ky pleasantly . . .

". . . and enter the Imperial Chinese service. In other words, enter his own employment; spy for him instead of . . . Serve him instead of you," I corrected.

"And tell him everything you can about the present French dispositions and future plans, eh," whispered Luong-Tam-Ky.

I stared blankly, open-mouthed, and trying to look more foolish than usual.

"Do you still deny that you are a French spy and came here direct from French Headquarters?"

"But of course."

"Then most certainly you die. This 'Number One Boy', or spy, or whatever you call him, can get on with the good work. He can deal with you as he likes—and *I* will deal with *him* afterwards."

And he turned to the slant-eyed slab-faced lout guarding the door.

No, I didn't want that thong back again cutting into my lacerated wrists and swollen hands, and I certainly didn't want to encounter further trouble from Major Li Hsian Chang, in whom definitely I recognized the man of action, the man of his promise—who performs even more than he promises.

Compared with Ba-Ky and, perhaps, even with this Luong-Tam-Ky, Major Li Hsian Chang was the biting dog that did not bark much. In his hands I had no hope but through treachery to my employers, falsity to my adopted flag.

Obviously in Luong-Tam-Ky there was hope, otherwise why was he here in the small hours of the morning?

"Die if I am *not* a spy?" I said.

Luong-Tam-Ky turned to me, hopefully I thought.

"Yes, die—if you are *not* a French spy."

"Why?"

"Because if you are a French spy, I can make use of

you."

"How?"

"You shall see. If you are a French spy I can help you, serve you, save you, in fact. For you can help me; serve me."

"And save you?" I asked, wondering what on earth the man was talking about.

Luong-Tam-Ky smiled unpleasantly, or rather, showed yellow teeth through thin lips.

"A humorist," he murmured. "Well, are you French?"

Was it a trap?

"No, I am English," I replied, playing for time.

"I know you are," replied Luong-Tam-Ky patiently. "According to De-Nha, an English member of the French Foreign Legion; and I may add that De-Nha has quite convinced me of the truth of his story.

"As, obviously," he added, "he convinced this spy of yours, this Major Perhaps, possibly of the Imperial Chinese Army . . . Yes, De-Nha convinced him all-right; and he convinced me also."

"He almost convinces me!" I admitted, with what I intended to be a quizzical smile.

"Yes, I'm sure he does; let us decide that he is right, shall we?"

"And if so, your Excellency?"

"And if so—you are a free man. You return to your head-quarters at Houi-Bap . . . and to your—Captain Deleuze, isn't it?—full of information and advice; and you receive reward, promotion and decoration."

"All that, your Excellency?"

"Yes. I will stipulate that you do. You will . . ."

Suddenly a great light dawned upon my somewhat low mind, and my heart beat faster.

I was conscious for the moment of a feeling of over-whelming relief, thankfulness, joy almost.

His excellent Excellency, the self-styled General Luong-Tam-Ky of the small, compact and independent army of Chinese brigands, was going to—do a deal.

Unless this were an improbable refinement of cruelty,

he was going to save, rescue, befriend, me and set me on my way back to Houi-Bap.

And not only should I be the bearer thither of the information for which I had been sent by Deleuze, but the wearer of a very fine feather in my cap. I should bring back proposals that would be most warmly welcomed by the French authorities—nothing less than a treaty with one of the most valuable of the enemy's allies.

Too good to be true? A trick? A trap? A grim jest?

No, he hadn't come to me at three o'clock in the morning to crack a joke. He meant it.

The death of General De-Nam had decided the rascally schemer that it was time for the rats to leave the sinking ship, and he was going to be the first rat.

Luong-Tam-Ky, Robber Baron and Bandit Chief, had decided to go while the going was good. To go over to the French.

He would turn his coat while it had some value.

He would join the French while there were rewards for doing so; become their friend and ally instead of remaining their enemy and becoming their captive.

That was it.

General De-Nam was dead, leaving no heir, and his mantle had fallen upon De-Tam, who was not of a stature to wear it.

I had guessed rightly and I must think quickly.

Doubtless the news that I had given him concerning Major Li Hsian Chang would strengthen him in his decision to open negotiations with the French.

Why with the French, and not with the Chinese?

Because the Imperial Chinese Government would never permit him to operate on their side of the border; whereas doubtless the French would be entirely willing for him to do precisely as he pleased in the wild jungles and mountain fastnesses of the border country along the frontiers of Yunnan, Kwangsi, and Kwangtung, throughout the then unadministered and probably unadministrable districts of Ha-Giang and Cao-Bang, and throughout the upper reaches of the Red River.

Yes, I could quite imagine the French, without a smile upon their faces, without a tongue in an official cheek, declaring the excellent General Luong-Tam-Ky to be the new Governor, Mandarin Judge, and tributary ruler of undefined Northern Tonking—until such time as they were ready to make other arrangements.

Yes, that would suit the French; and most admirably it would suit Luong-Tam-Ky in the new circumstances; and doubtless he would get in on the ground floor and get in first—the rest, nowhere.

Luong-Tam-Ky the winner; General Ba-Ky and Colonel Collins literally nowhere—on this earth.

Luong-Tam-Ky first, the rest also-ran, though I didn't somehow think that General Ba-Ky and Colonel Collins would run far.

And as for a moment I sat silent, and stared, deep in thought, at Luong-Tam-Ky, so did that astute man sit in silence and stare, deep in thought, at me.

How had Major Li Hsian Chang's intervention affected the matter? Speeded things up, probably.

I didn't know, though probably Luong-Tam-Ky knew, how near the promised Chinese reinforcements were.

Regiments of regular soldiers from the Imperial Army were to be placed at the disposal of the Robber Chiefs, to be used against the advancing French; used, but not acknowledged, turning, as they shed their uniforms, from drilled and disciplined troops, into border dacoits indistinguishable from the General's own followers.

If those troops—and doubtless they would be specially selected units—were not only on their way, but near at hand, the matter was urgent for Luong-Tam-Ky.

If the disguised and secret liaison officer, or rather, agent, Major Li Hsian Chang of the Imperial Chinese Army, knew, should come to know, or should even suspect, Luong-Tam-Ky's intentions, the situation would become difficult, dangerous and critical, for the latter gentleman.

Doubtless Major Li Hsian Chang's influence with the General Commanding these reinforcements would be paramount; for almost certainly he would be, though not the ranking officer, at least in a position to give definite instructions and orders to the Commandant of the Chinese reinforcements.

As the man on the spot, Major Li Hsian Chang would have instructions to use his own discretion and initiative, according to the demands of the local situation. So that anything that had to be done about Major Li Hsian Chang had better be done soon and quickly.

Yes, the effect of Major Li Hsian Chang's intervention would be to speed things up.

What was Luong-Tam-Ky saying?

"I will stipulate that you receive reward, promotion, and decoration. You will return to your Headquarters the bearer of proposals for an alliance, offensive and defensive, between General Luong-Tam-Ky and General Voyron commanding the French forces in Tonking."

Here was a turn of Fortune's wheel; a *volte-face* on the part of an apparently unkindly Fate. One minute, a helpless prisoner with a choice between horrible death and treachery; the next minute a free man, successful beyond his wildest dreams.

It was all too good to be true, and I must walk warily for there must be a snag somewhere.

Why? If Luong-Tam-Ky were going to make me his messenger, he'd see to it that I had every chance to arrive safely at my journey's end.

Was it possible that such good fortune could be mine? I knew this man to be not only fiendishly cruel, but cruel with a clever refinement far beyond that of Ba-Ky, himself no mean practitioner of the art of torture.

Was he paying me the compliment of inflicting mental torture before proceeding to physical, his opportunities for the use of the higher form being somewhat restricted in such a place as Phu-Son? But Ba-Ky . . .

An idea . . .

"And what of General Ba-Ky, your Excellency?" I asked, still unbelieving, hanging in doubt, and wondering whether this and other questions might lead to elucidation; perhaps to the confirmation of my hopes.

"Ah! . . . And suppose I could lead General Ba-Ky along the same Excellent Way in the direction of a French alliance, how great would be the gratitude of those noble people."

"And suppose he declined to be led?"

"Then how equally great, no doubt, would be the gratitude of my noble new friends if General Ba-Ky—met with an accident."

"And General Ba-Ky's troops?"

"Would find me an even kinder and better leader than General Ba-Ky was."

"And the Chinese reinforcements?"

"Well now; if the leader of the Chinese reinforcements, and this excellent young man who has hitherto been Colonel Collins's servant—what did you say his name was? . . ."

"Major Li Hsian Chang . . ."

"If they both knew nothing of the change of circumstances here, of the new political and military situation, why —the Chinese troops might go astray, mightn't they?"

It looked to me as though they certainly might.

"Yes, they might be led into quite a strange situation, might they not? A situation in which they would have a choice of laying down their arms and being captured to a man, or being massacred to a man."

"By the French forces, do you mean?"

"Well, well, why trouble the French forces?"

And I saw the point, quite clearly. Why trouble the French forces when, no doubt, the admirable troops of General Luong-Tam-Ky could quite easily, in the rôle of allies, lead the Chinese regulars into some hopeless *impasse*, disarm them, and give them a probably not unwelcome opportunity of changing their status; changing from service as regular soldiers to that of highly irregular dacoits. The Chinese regular, ill-paid, ill-treated and badly-led would have little compunction about joining a force that was really a huge dacoit band wherein discipline would be easier, conditions far pleasanter, and loot plentiful.

Here again their change of flag, from that of Imperial China to the Black Flag of Piracy, would now bring a considerable force to the assistance of the French cause, doubly valuable in view of the fact that not only was it added to their own side, but taken from that of their opponents.

Once again I was hoping even more than I was doubting.

And then, suddenly, what had loomed at the back of my mind, casting a dark shadow upon nascent hope, advanced and became clear.

Once again I was amazed at my selfishness and egocentric pre-occupation with my own affairs.

Mary . . . What would become of her if I, with Luong-Tam-Ky's assistance and protection, set forth on my return journey, leaving her in this robber camp.

And what was the truth about Colonel John Collins? Had he abandoned her to her fate, or had this man decided to put him out of the way?

And Major Li Hsian Chang? Would he have acted as he had, if the Chinese reinforcements were not close at hand, giving him adequate power to implement all threats?

How much of what he had told me had been the truth?

Somehow I felt that he was an infinitely more forthright, direct, and truthful person than Luong-Tam-Ky; though at the same time, I realized that a Secret Service agent rarely benefits his country, or attains his object, by simple ingenuousness.

"And Colonel Collins?" I asked suddenly. "How will he be affected by your change of—er—attitude?"

"There soon will be no Colonel Collins," was the quiet reply; and the boot-button eyes staring at mine looked, I thought, defiant, or were they completely without expression?

They reminded me of those of a crab. Or a snake.

"How is that?"

"He will not return from—the place to which he has gone."

"The New Fort at Thay-Taong?" I said.

Luong-Tam-Ky showed no surprise.

"Yes, you know where the New Fort is, don't you?" he smiled. "Clever. You shall take an excellent map and a plan of it, back with you. . . . No, Colonel Collins will not return from Thay Taong."

"Major Li Hsian Chang says he has no intention of returning."

"No intention of returning?"

"No. He says he has gone. Run away. Left your service altogether."

"What?"

And then I thought I would play what might prove a trump card.

"Yes, he says he has gone for ever—and deserted his wife."

Luong-Tam-Ky inhaled deeply and slowly, making a hissing noise between his teeth. A curious sound and unpleasant.

"This house-servant, calling himself a Major and a Secret Service Agent, told you that Colonel Collins has fled from this camp, leaving his wife and everything else, and is not going to return?"

"Yes."

"Where has he gone? To China?"

"He didn't tell me."

"Why did he tell you at all?"

"Because when I asked him what he wanted me to do, since he gave me the choice of joining him and working with him or being tortured to death, he replied that the first part of the work was to help him to get Mrs. Collins safely away from here and into China."

And again Luong-Tam-Ky drew a long whistling breath.

Gently, softly, he rubbed his hands together, one over the other, as though washing them.

"We will talk with him," he whispered. "We will talk with him. We will ask him questions."

"Are you sure he hasn't run away too?" I asked.

"Why should he? Wasn't he coming back here to talk with you, to ask *you*—questions?"

"Yes. But won't his men have warned him that you've come here?"

"Of what should they warn him? Do I not command here? Being challenged by the Chinese sentry at your door, I praised him for his watchfulness, and brought him inside here with me, as you saw."

"But the others? There must have been a dozen of them."

"Well, if still on duty, they saw me brought in here by the sentry, didn't they? And if one of them mentions that to Li Hsian Chang, he'll promptly come in to see what's happening, won't he?"

"I suppose he will."

"And what about this sentry?" I asked.

"And what about The Shadow?" smiled Luong-Tam-Ky.

And I remembered the great grim silent man whose presence at my dinner-party with Luong-Tam-Ky had made me a little uncomfortable.

"Oh, he's handy, is he?"

"As always," was the reply. "With his men. Why do you suppose he's called 'The Shadow'?"

"Your Excellency has a shadow, even at night?"

"Especially at night," smiled Luong-Tam-Ky.

"Now listen. Let us know how we stand before this— servant—comes. You admit that you are a French spy. I admit that I wish to enter into negotiations with the French. I will send you back with a letter to the French General pro- posing a meeting between myself and an officer of suitable rank, who will be empowered to make terms with me. Meanwhile, I take no steps against the French. And I keep them informed as to any steps about to be taken by De-Tam and his Chinese allies—regular Imperial troops, I mean. I will send a personal letter by you, and you will bring back an answer. Yes, you will return with it yourself."

I thought not.

No, I somehow felt I had had enough of this camp and of the neighbourhood of Luong-Tam-Ky. Once I had got safely away and back to my base, someone else could bring the answer.

And I would not go alone. By some means or other I would take Mary with me.

The door opened and Major Li Hsian Chang stepped into

the hut.

Behind him loomed the gigantic figure of The Shadow.

I had never expected to be really pleased to see this individual.

CHAPTER XXVI

As the door opened and Major Li Hsian Chang stepped into the room, so close behind him was The Shadow that I gathered the impression that The Shadow was shepherding and impelling, not to say hustling him, through the doorway.

Things happened very rapidly. There was a swift brief exchange of Chinese words, somewhat like the hissing and spitting of angry cats; the moon-faced sentry grunted or hiccupped and sank to his knees, and one great hand of The Shadow seized Major Li Hsian Chang by the neck, while the other closed upon the revolver that he attempted to draw from its holster.

Definitely the clever Secret Service officer had been surprised, caught napping, and was trapped.

General Luong-Tam-Ky did not rise from his chair, moved not a limb, remained entirely passive of countenance, and only issued his orders in a sibilant whisper.

Like a small boy handled by a big man, Major Li Hsian Chang was thrown to the floor by The Shadow, turned upon his face, and bound hand and foot. At first he struggled violently and fiercely, but a short-arm punch below the ribs so winded and distressed him that he could only lie gasping like a fish.

With celerity and dispatch The Shadow fastened his wrists together behind him, united his ankles, his knees, and his elbows, in bonds and thongs of leather, and then placed about his neck the halter that had so recently adorned my own, and tied the end of the cord to the bed-frame.

In fact, and in the space of about five minutes, Major Li Hsian Chang was occupying the position and situation that had so recently been mine.

Time's whirligig and the turn of the wheel of Fate, indeed.

He took it well, and I felt that I was about to see how a

Chinese of birth and breeding, of honour and tradition, could die.

General Luong-Tam-Ky almost smiled as he turned to me. At any rate, his teeth showed between his lips as he spoke, which was unusual.

"Would you like to kick him in the face?" he asked.

"No thank you," I replied.

"Why not? You can kick him as much as you like and anywhere you like. There are places where it is even more painful to be kicked than in the face. Or will you beat him with a bamboo?"

"I don't wish to kick him or beat him," I said. "When I was his prisoner he showed me how Chinese treat captives, and explained why. I should like to show him how the British treat prisoners."

"What would you like to do?"

"Untie him and let him get up. Take his parole and treat him decently. He'll keep his word if he gives it."

"Childish," whispered General Luong-Tam-Ky. "You Western barbarians are illogical silly children. What would this dog do to me or to you if the positions were reversed? What *did* he do to you?"

"Well, I'd like to show him the better way, the way of civilized people."

General Luong-Tam-Ky spat and turned to serious matters.

"So you are a spy, are you?" he said in English, and I wondered whether he spoke in this language for my benefit or because he and Major Li Hsian Chang came from different parts of China, spoke a different dialect, and might not completely understand each other.

Major Li Hsian Chang made no reply, but watched Luong-Tam-Ky warily with his hard bright eyes, so deep and so shallow, expressionless and unreadable. If he were frightened, as surely he must have been, he gave no slightest sign of it.

"Will you talk—and save yourself?" asked Luong-Tam-Ky.

Major Li Hsian Chang answered nothing; merely sat and

stared unflinching at the face of his questioner and judge.

"Will you join me, tell me everything, give me all documents you may have in your possession, and save your . . . reason?" Luong-Tam-Ky slowly enquired.

Major Li Hsian Chang made no reply, and the expression of his face remained blank.

"No? Well, I think I can promise you one thing, and honourably keep my word. No dying man ever took so long to die as you will."

For all notice that Major Li Hsian Chang took of this sinister promise, he might have been stone deaf.

"As your information might be of some use to me—and to the French," continued Luong-Tam-Ky, "I will give you one more chance to save yourself from a really memorable death. Listen.

"I am going to join the French. General De-Nam is dead, and De-Tam neither wields the same influence and power nor has the same ability. The cause of Ham-Nghi the Emperor of Annam is lost, and only fools will continue to support it. I am going to negotiate with General Voyron for the hire of my army and, satisfactory terms having been arranged, I shall transfer my services from the Emperor of Annam to the President of the French Republic.

"Incidentally I shall be appointed Governor of Yen Thé with a great salary, great subsidiary emoluments and no—interference.

"Yes—taxation will be heavy in Yen Thé. Incidentally, General Ba-Ky will meet with an accident, and the joint command of the Army of Phu-Son will be unified. There are objections to dual control, really. And decidedly there are objections to General Ba-Ky."

Major Li Hsian Chang yawned.

"Well, I was about to observe," continued Luong-Tam-Ky in his silky whisper, "that if you chose to join me *and* bring with you the reinforcement of Chinese regulars now on their way here, we could make an arrangement mutually and entirely agreeable.

"The soldiers would sooner fight the Black Flags and dacoits of the Annamese army than fight the French—with their loud artillery and their superior discipline, weapons and tactics; there would be far more loot for them; they would have an easier and better time altogether—and no one in China need know.

"You and I could come to an arrangement—also mutually and entirely agreeable—about the consignments of money, and so forth, for their support, and we could use the troops as we saw fit. Should their Commanding Officer prove—difficult—which is improbable, he too could meet with an accident.

"Should some garbled tale reach Peking concerning the situation here and the employment of the Chinese regulars, we could temporize as long as possible, and then when Peking got obnoxious and the situation became acute, we could sever the connection altogether. The Imperial authorities couldn't do much, as we should then have the French behind us; and if they sent a force against us, it couldn't cross the border for fear of provoking war with France. . . ."

There was a minute's silence in the hut while Luong-Tam-Ky and I watched Major Li Hsian Chang's face.

"Well?" continued Luong-Tam-Ky, "will you join me and bring over the Chinese regulars—or shall The Shadow and I devise something new and really great in tortures, something to which we will give your name—and make it famous for all time?"

Again Major Li Hsian Chang yawned, and did it extremely well.

"Ah," whispered Luong-Tam-Ky and turned to The Shadow.

"Collect his ears and his eyes," he said, "and put them in a bottle. I'll send them to his family. Stab his ear-drums. Cut off his nose and cut out his tongue—and put them in the bottle too."

What orders he had given The Shadow I did not know as he spoke to him in a dialect of Chinese.

I glanced at the moon-faced sentry who had never moved since he had hiccupped and collapsed. I saw that he was lying face downward in a pool of blood that had oozed from beneath him. Presumably there had been something in The Shadow's hand when he struck the man. As the giant, grinning amiably, now advanced upon Major Li Hsian Chang, his razor-edged knife drawn, I asked Luong-Tam-Ky what he was going to do. His reply told me what the order had been.

This was too much for me. Major Li Hsian Chang had undoubtedly intended to kill me, and probably to torture me too, but I couldn't stand by and see a fellow-creature's eyes gouged out and his ears sliced off, however good cause I had to dislike him.

"No, your Excellency," I objected, "don't do that. What does Confucius say?"

I hadn't the vaguest idea as to 'What Confucius said in 'eighty-four,' or whenever it was, but I felt certain that he must have said something apposite.

"And what does he say?" enquired Luong-Tam-Ky blandly.

" 'Ne'er let your angry passions rise' and also 'To err is human, to forgive divine', and 'A merciful man is merciful to a beast'—which this fellow certainly is. And besides, think of what Confucius says about the Problem of Pain."

"True," replied Luong-Tam-Ky. "He says, 'Pain is the strangest and the most valuable of all the Gifts of Heaven.' We will give this spy the most valuable of gifts in full measure—and the strangest too."

"If you blind and deafen him now, he won't be able to see and hear," I pointed out somewhat unnecessarily, "and you may want him to see—to sign something; and to hear what else you may have to say to him. Besides, if you make him dumb, he obviously won't be able to answer any questions, if he changes his mind about it."

"He won't answer any questions," replied Luong-Tam-Ky. "He's not a European," and the robber-chief sat considering me for a while, in silence.

Obviously he was wondering what axe I had to grind that I should thus intercede to save the life of the man who had himself been about to kill me. That it should be mere humanitarianism was beyond his comprehension and did not enter into his calculations in the least. No, I must obviously have some excellent ulterior reason for this peculiar line of conduct, and Luong-Tam-Ky was trying to fathom it and the depths of my cunning.

I think he came to the conclusion that I wished to keep Major Li Hsian Chang as a kind of second string to my bow, with a view to having a friend in him should the Chinese reinforcements arrive suddenly, unexpectedly, and in great strength.

Whatever his conclusion may have been, I think that my well-meant intervention sealed the Secret Service agent's fate—or rather expedited it.

Turning to The Shadow, Luong-Tam-Ky hissed an order, and the giant strode forward again, his gleaming sword raised above his head. I sprang to my feet, and received a blow from The Shadow's left hand that dashed me against the wall, knocking the breath out of my body and stunning me almost. It was as though I had been kicked by a horse or struck down by an elephant.

I don't wish to set down gory details and blood-curdling descriptions of horrors, so I will merely state that when I pulled myself together and rose to my feet, Luong-Tam-Ky had, as he said, 'taken precautions to prevent the spy from escaping'.

I had heard, as I lay partially stunned, four sounds—such as I had often heard when passing a butcher's shop—and when I looked, I saw that the unfortunate man had neither hands nor feet.

No, he would not run away.

Nor would he die of loss of blood, for The Shadow was binding the cords about his wrists and ankles as string is bound about the handle of a cricket-bat.

Having finished his task, he went to the door, looked out, and then, turning, picked his victim up and flung him across his shoulder.

(I afterwards learned that, before returning, he carried the poor fellow to the prison beneath the *Yamen* building, where, later, under the direction and supervision of Luong-Tam-Ky, he tortured him to death.)

My anger boiled over as I glanced from the mess of blood, and the horrible débris, to the calm face of Luong-Tam-Ky, and I foolishly endeavoured to scald him with the vituperation that flowed forth from the seething cauldron that was my mind.

The torrent of my words might have been a gentle zephyr wafted across sweet flowers for all the effect it had. He merely murmured, when I had finished, that the sight of a Western barbarian blundering blindly in the Red Mist of Wrath was an interesting and amusing one. And now to business once again, after the annoying hindrance caused by the unseemly irruption of the fool who called himself Colonel Collins's Number One Boy and Major Li Hsian Chang of the Imperial Chinese Secret Service, and perhaps was neither.

"Look here, General Luong-Tam-Ky," objected I, "if you want to talk, we must go somewhere else. I feel sick. I can't sit here and listen to you . . . with a dead body in the room, and that poor devil's hands and feet lying about, and this filthy mess of blood all over the place. I am not a—Chinese."

General Luong-Tam-Ky almost smiled.

"What are hands and feet but things?" he jeered. "And what is blood but a fluid? What is a dead soldier, but a man asleep? . . . I do not want it to be known, yet, to Ba-Ky, that I have been in conference with you. We will talk here, and if you *must* notice trifles of débris, be thankful that you have not—yet—contributed to them. Now then, is there any reason why you should not start at once for your head-quarters, taking my letter and my verbal message?"

"Yes. Several. For one thing, I am not going back to Houi-Bap until I have seen De-Nam's great New Fort at Thay-Taong, been all over it, sketched it, and mapped the country round it."

"No necessity," replied Luong-Tam-Ky, "I have a most admirable scale plan and elevation, an excellent sketch and an accurate map of the country."

"I should want to compare them with the original," I replied.

"Well, you can visit Thay-Taong on your way back

without making any very great detour."

"Is it true," I asked, "that De-Nam's treasury is there?"

"It is," replied Luong-Tam-Ky, "but it won't be there much longer. As soon as I hear from General Voyron that my proposals—and terms—are accepted, I shall seize the New Fort. That will be simple enough, as I shall offer to strengthen the garrison, and march a battalion of my troops into it—as allies of De-Tam."

"And you will hold it for the French?" I observed, rather as an obvious statement than as a question.

"I shall hold it for myself. I, the new ally of the French, will occupy the New Fort of Thay-Taong as my permanent headquarters, my base, and the impregnable outpost which will render the invasion of Annam by Chinese troops quite impossible. I shall in fact, be the local French representative, Commander-in-Chief, and Governor of the border province."

This seemed good enough, seemed to be, in fact, precisely what the French military authorities would desire and warmly welcome. If anyone could keep the wild northern marches of Annam quiet and peaceful, it would be this powerful robber-chief. If there were any trouble from the local Annamese insurgents, he would promptly 'make a solitude and call it peace,' and peace was the one thing desired by the harassed French Government against whom murmurs concerning the cost and futility of the Indo-China campaign were turning to shouts—a growing tumult that in Paris was causing the insecure foundations of its popularity to tremble.

Yes, this little arrangement would be an admirable one; a powerful enemy turned into a friend; a source of weakness and danger turned into a means of strength and safety; and the cost—ever the first and last word in Cochin China—defrayed entirely by others, those other people without a voice or a vote, the hapless Annamese villagers, the amount of whose taxes Luong-Tam-Ky would fix, and which he would himself collect.

Little or nothing as I personally had had to do with bringing about this incalculably valuable detachment of

Luong-Tam-Ky from the Annamese and Chinese connections, I had made the journey and the highly dangerous contact successfully, and it would be a splendid thing for me to be able to return with the wonderful news; with Luong-Tam-Ky's own letter and message to General Voyron; with the ability to give an absolutely accurate estimate, and indeed description, of the position of affairs at Phu-Son; and with the plans, sketches, and maps of the New Fort and the Thay-Taong country. . . .

I had indeed been lucky, fortunate beyond all hope, expectation and desert. And if I had done nothing more, I had deserved well of my officer and justified his belief and trust in me.

And then I remembered Mary Collins.

How could I possibly go and leave her here?

I could not. Certainly not until I knew the truth concerning the fate, movements and whereabouts of her husband. If he had been murdered by order of Luong-Tam-Ky, or had departed finally from Phu-Son, I must rescue her from the hideous danger in which she was.

If the statements of Luong-Tam-Ky and Major Li Hsian Chang were both false, as was quite probable, and Colonel Collins might return at any moment, presumably I must leave her here, though it seemed a terrible thing to do, and I should be leaving my heart and my happiness behind.

But what could I do, if Collins came back here? After all, he was her husband, and while he was alive she was as safe as ever she had been in the wilder parts of China. And what could I, a private soldier on a half-penny a day, do to support her, even if I got her safely down to Hanoi?

That, however, would be a secondary consideration if Collins were dead or had deserted her. First things first, and the very first thing would be to get her away before Luong-Tam-Ky seized her and she disappeared, probably for ever, into his house and the guardianship of The Shadow and his squad of other shadows.

"Yes," mused Luong-Tam-Ky aloud, "I shall be French *préfet* of the Province, and General in the French Colonial Army . . ."

"What about Colonel Collins?" I suddenly interrupted.

"He has outlived his usefulness here, I think," replied Luong-Tam-Ky silkily. "And in point of fact, he seems to have realized it. . . . Though I realized it first, I believe."

"It would be as well if your Excellency told me everything," I said. "I shall be very fully and carefully questioned when I return to Houi-Bap; and the Intelligence Department won't make recommendations to the General until they know all the facts. . . . Suppose Colonel Collins also thought that the death of General De-Nam had so changed the situation that . . ."

"I have supposed it," was the quiet reply. "And I took steps. Colonel Collins was to have gone to the New Fort, to decide whether the field of fire from the outer walls really needed widening; and I made arrangements that he should not return. He was to have met with an accident. But—you know how it is—people are so suspicious. And some are so untrustworthy. Really there's quite a lot of deception and unreliability here. Flagrant dishonesty . . ."

"*No?*" said I.

"Yes," re-affirmed the good General. "You'd hardly credit it. . . . And either Colonel Collins decided for himself that the wind had changed a little, and that he'd better be going, or else the scoundrel whom I entrusted with the business went to Collins and sold him the story and his life. Positively that amounts to fraud-when-in-a-position-of-trust. Flagrant fraud. And the man must be punished. Of course he'll say that Colonel Collins never went to the New Fort at all, and that he waited there for the Colonel in vain. . . . Anyway, Colonel Collins has left us. He has got away all-right, safe and sound, and just in time. A very clever man, our Colonel Collins."

"Yes," observed I, "Major Li Hsian Chang told me that he had gone—for good."

"*What?* . . . How did he know?" asked Luong-Tam-Ky quickly.

"Why, he was his Number One Boy. He packed his kit and noted that he spent some time in destroying papers and documents. And he took away with him things that he had never taken on expeditions before, when going from Phu-Son out into the jungle—things he would not have taken had he been intending to return."

"Yes, of course," whispered Luong-Tam-Ky, "the spy was his house-servant. . . . Well, the spy shall talk, if human ingenuity can make him talk. Though I doubt it."

So did I. I very much doubted whether the will-power of Luong-Tam-Ky, backed with the power to inflict incredible agony, would defeat the will-power of Major Li Hsian Chang, backed by nothing but his cold courage.

"He also said that he had read every word of every letter received or written by Colonel Collins," I added, "and I have reason to believe that he was speaking the truth when he said that the Colonel had gone, and gone for good. I believe, too, that he knows where he has gone—and why he has gone there."

Luong-Tam-Ky shot me a suspicious glance.

"He did not tell you that?" he asked.

"No," I replied, and forbore to admit that he had told me nothing, and I only knew these things because he had told Mrs. Collins—and had told them to her for his own private and personal reasons, because he wished to persuade her to let him rescue her from Luong-Tam-Ky and the perils of Phu-Son.

"Yes, a very wily man, Colonel Collins," mused Luong-Tam-Ky aloud. "He has always gone while the going is good, as he puts it, and known enough to stand from under, and come in out of the rain. But not really straightforward. Not ingenuous . . ."

He murmured on, soliloquizing apparently, and then suddenly shot a question at me.

"*Where has he gone?* Peking? Yes?" he hissed, and the look that accompanied the words was sufficiently daunting.

"I don't know," I replied. "How should I? I am not in his confidence."

"If I thought you knew—I'd have it out of you," he whispered, and at his tone The Shadow handled his sword and seemed to calculate the thickness of my neck.

"Well, don't think it, General," I replied, "if you want me

to negotiate for you at Houi-Bap. I'm the only person who can give them a verbal message from you and assure them that it is genuine, and that the situation is as you describe it."

"I was only joking," the General assured me, and I felt that if that were so, I should prefer him to remain serious.

"Well, we will see what the spy thinks when I hang him up for a day or two on a meat-hook—to think . . . Anyhow—I'll soon get news of the good Colonel Collins—and if he is on his way back to Peking—he won't get there. And if he has gone to meet General Wun Kai Shek and the Chinese reinforcements, he'll meet his death too. . . . He can't escape me. . . . There isn't a village in a circle of a hundred miles where they'd dare to tell me a lie. I'll soon find out where our Colonel Collins has gone. . . . Yes, that'll be it—he has gone to meet General Wun Kai Shek to tell him to hurry up. No doubt, that'll be it. He couldn't actually know, I think; but he made a pretty good guess. Thought he'd go where it would be healthier for him—and where he could curry favour with Peking. Foresaw the end of his job here."

"I wonder he didn't take his wife," I drew a bow at a venture, thinking that the remark could do no harm, and might produce an enlightening reply.

"Do you?" replied Luong-Tam-Ky drily. "And advertise the fact that he was—escaping?"

"I hadn't thought of that," I said.

"No?" sneered Luong-Tam-Ky. "He was only supposed to be going to the New Fort at Thay-Taong, and to be returning in a few days."

"Then he has deserted her?" I said.

"Absolutely. He knows he can never return here, having disobeyed my instructions to go to Thay-Taong, and gone to meet the Chinese army instead—if he hasn't actually gone to Peking."

"That's very terrible for Mrs. Collins, my compatriot," I remarked.

"Oh, she'll be cared for; she'll be cared for," replied Luong-Tam-Ky airily. "Don't worry on her account . . ."

"A hostage," he added, eyeing me inscrutably, and

almost smiling.

"To ensure the eventual return of Colonel Collins?" I asked feigning stupidity.

"Nothing could ensure the return of Colonel Collins," was the reply. "We shall never see him here again—unless it is with his hands tied behind him, and a rope round his neck. He may perhaps come in that style, of course. I think he will, if he has gone to meet General Wun Kai Shek with a tale about me, and proposals that Wun Kai Shek takes my place—and my army. . . . Yes, I think I have made General Wun Kai Shek a rather better offer than Colonel Collins can. . . . It will be amusing if Wun Kai Shek does bring him here."

And I think it is no exaggeration to say that General Luong-Tam-Ky smiled.

"What will happen if he does?" I asked.

"I shall hang them both, after giving them a little salutary pain," was the prompt reply.

"Hang the Chinese General?" I exclaimed.

"Yes. He's not trustworthy. He's the sort of man who'd march in here, in pretended innocence and ignorance, and who'd agree to join me and go over to the French, and then double-cross me. Curry favour with the Imperial authorities by betraying me. . . . And then blackening my memory," sighed General Luong-Tam-Ky.

"But it's more likely that General Wun Kai Shek will hear all that Colonel Collins has to say, and then strangle him—so as to keep for himself the credit of having found me out. Then he'll arrive pretending to know nothing, and intending to assassinate me, take over command, and march the whole army to the New Fort and General De-Tam. . . . A cunning and deceitful fellow, this General Wun Kai Shek."

"Quite a dirty dog," I opined.

"A dirty dog," agreed General Luong-Tam-Ky.

§2

And by the time he had finished talking to me, I felt that I had a pretty clear understanding and good grasp of the actual situation—and knew that I was utterly undecided as to what I was going to do.

I accepted, as definite facts, that General Luong-Tam-Ky really wished to desert the Annamese cause, dispose of General Ba-Ky, and join the French with his bandit army; that he intended to deal, as circumstances indicated, with the Chinese General, Wun Kai Shek, and his force of Imperial regular troops; that Colonel Collins had deserted his post and his wife, fled finally from Phu-Son, and either gone to meet General Wun Kai Shek or returned to Peking; that, in either case, he would be seen no more, as, on the one hand, General Wun Kai Shek would seize him, on Luong-Tam-Ky's information that he was a traitor; or, on the other, the military authorities at Peking would do so on General Wun Kai Shek's accusation.

That, I was sure, was an accurate estimate of the position of affairs; and I could not deny that it was now my business to go as soon as I possibly could; to return with all dispatch to Houi Bap and Captain Deleuze with the information I had gathered; and, infinitely more important, with the letter and verbal proposals of General Luong-Tam-Ky.

I could not deny it, but I tried to do so.

I argued that it would be a much better plan to wait and see what happened to the Chinese reinforcements, and find out whether General Luong-Tam-Ky succeeded in incorporating that force with his own.

If he did, with or without the co-operation of their General Officer Commanding, General Wun Kai Shek, he would be a much more valuable ally to the French, as the regular Chinese troops, though neither trained nor disciplined to the European standard, were good material, stout fighters, and quite able to meet De-Tam's dacoit army on equal terms and their own ground, be it swamp, jungle or hill.

Yes, I really ought to postpone departure until I could tell Captain Deleuze exactly what happened to the reinforcements from China, and the big convoy of provisions, munitions and money that it was escorting.

And, in any case, I could not go until *Doi* Linh Nghi returned from his spying expedition to the New Fort at Thay-

Taong.

I must see the place for myself, of course, as well; but I couldn't go without the *Doi* who, other considerations apart, would be absolutely necessary to the success of my return journey.

And when I had thought of every specious argument for delay, I produced the real one.

I could not go and leave Mary here, now that I felt certain that her husband had deserted her.

That he had done so was incredible.

And that he had done so was certain—in the light of what Major Li Hsian Chang had said about the preparations he had made for departure, and what General Luong-Tam-Ky had said about the excellent reasons there were for that departure.

He had gone; and he had failed to take his wife with him, as that would have betrayed the fact that he was going for good, and probably because she would have been a hindrance to his movements. Also, doubtless, he thought that the fact of his leaving her and his household there in Phu-Son would for some time postpone any suspicion that he had deserted, thrown up his job and fled; thought that it would delay pursuit, and give him time to get sufficiently far away from General Luong-Tam-Ky's sphere of influence to be safe.

How could I emulate the scoundrelly hound—desert her, too, because she would be a hindrance to my movements; because by taking her with me, I should bring down upon me the wrath and vengeance of General Luong-Tam-Ky?

But of course, reason as I might, I knew that the whole argument was specious.

It was my duty to go, and to go without her; because, by taking her, I might jeopardize the whole situation, now so favourable to France. For that might well be a result of Luong-Tam-Ky's anger if he discovered what I had done. It might be a result of my delay if he did not; for, naturally, I should not be able to travel as fast with her as I should with only my hardy *tirailleurs*, born jungle-men.

And indeed it was a hideous position in which I found

myself, and the horns of the dilemma cruelly sharp.

How could I possibly leave the woman I loved, the woman whose image was never out of my thoughts, in such terrible danger? It would have been heart-rendingly painful to leave her at all, a sickening agony of spirit, but to leave her to the unthinkable fate that was inevitable, to leave her to what amounted to torture—how could I do it?

And how could I possibly fail in my duty, ruin the whole undertaking, spoil the, hitherto, incredible success of the expedition and throw away the chance of greatly shortening, if not actually ending, the whole war—for my own private reasons, in consideration of my own inclinations . . . because, in short, I had fallen in love! It will be believed that I did not sleep very well that night.

CHAPTER XXVII

Next day *Doi* Linh Nghi returned.

I have seen few uglier faces than his, and fewer still of which the sight has given me more pleasure than it did on this occasion. And, judging by the grin that raised his ears and exposed thirty-two teeth lacquered like black china, *Doi* Linh Nghi was glad to see me.

His news was interesting.

"It's a wonderful Fort they've built there, *Nai*," he said. "A regular castle. You might call it three forts really, the second inside the first, far stronger; and the third inside the second, strongest of all. And a town inside the third. All General De-Nam's treasure is there too, buried with his body, right in the centre. They'll never surrender, if it comes to a siege. Never. You must come and make a picture of it, and of the country round. It's wonderfully sited—a deep river round two sides, a deeper swamp round the third; and the fourth, the only one that can be approached on dry land, is nearly as bad with moats and deep staked pits, each big enough to catch a herd of wild elephants. It's wonderfully hidden in the jungle too, but the jungle has been felled and cleared for a thousand metres from this only dry-land side. . . . And now about Colonel Collins. He never went there at all . . ."

"No, I didn't think he went there. I have been hearing things," said I. "Have you any idea where he did go?"

The *Doi* grinned. Evidently he had a tale to tell, and was going to tell it in his own way.

"He never went there at all," he repeated. "But somebody else did. Went there to meet him. And who do you think that was?"

"How should I know? Out with it, you chattering old woman."

"De-Nha! . . . Went to Thay-Taong New Fort to meet Colonel Collins."

Here was news indeed.

"What—by arrangement with him? To talk quietly about —something?"

"No. By arrangement with General Luong-Tam-Ky. . . . To kill him quietly about—something."

"Did he do it?" I gasped.

"No. I've just told you Colonel Collins never went to Thay-Taong at all."

"No, of course not. . . . Well, now tell me all about it."

And over the preparation of a pipe of the 'black smoke', *Doi* Linh Nghi did so.

He and his brothers made their way to Thay Taong and, in the rôle of good dacoits anxious to join De-Tam's army, hung about the Fort, saw everything, heard all the news, and suddenly ran into De-Nha.

The embarrassment was mutual, for if De-Nha was in a position to denounce them as French *tirailleurs*, they were in a position to make things equally uncomfortable for him, the renegade who had led them to the Phu-Son camp and vouched for them as good honest bandits. Nevertheless, they took care that he should never be out of sight of at least one of them; they talked unkindly at him; sharpened knives in his presence, and considered his throat and his paunch.

Also they made him drunk with rice-spirit, and induced him to talk.

Yes, he assured them, he was, of course, a staunch stout friend of the French, and entirely loyal to me. What he was really doing at Thay-Taong Fort was spying out the land in the interests of his dear French allies, and to assist me. . . . Also to catch Colonel Collins off his guard, either approaching the Fort or leaving it! Somewhere in the jungle where he camped for the night.

"To *catch* him?" asked *Doi* Linh Nghi. "But why?"

"To slash him across the back of the neck with a mâchète," was the reply.

"But why, once again?"

"Oh, because he is a very bad man, and to oblige General Luong-Tam-Ky"—who was going to advance De-Nha to very high preferment if he contrived the neat and quiet assassination of Colonel Collins.

And why did General Luong-Tam-Ky particularly desire the assassination of Colonel Collins.

Because he was intriguing against General Luong-Tam-Ky and had something up his sleeve.

"Yes," thought I to myself, as *Doi* Linh Nghi paused to inhale a deep draught of the black smoke, "and because he has a beautiful wife upon whom General Luong-Tam-Ky has cast a covetous eye."

"And why did General Luong-Tam-Ky choose you for the job?" enquired *Doi* Linh Nghi of De-Nha.

"Choose me?" replied De-Nha, grinning drunkenly. "Well, you see, he has rather got me by the tail, since I gave myself away to him, trying to drive a bargain; and now he knows who I am. If I didn't do what he asked, he'd have me tortured. He'd tell General Ba-Ky all about me, and have a torturing match with him. See which of them could do the funniest things to me. Also I was a good man for this job because no-one would suppose that General Luong-Tam-Ky was behind it. If he had had it done by The Shadow at Phu-Son, people would have suspected him, and General Ba-Ky might have got nasty, and the Chinese General who is coming with the reinforcements would certainly have got nasty. . . . Yes, I'm going to slash him as he sleeps, one night—or more likely, put some of this arsenic in his cooking-pot when he camps."

And then, without deep and lasting regret, I learned of the end of the matter—and of De-Nha.

Having too little opium, thanks to the machinations of *Doi* Linh Nghi, and too much rice-spirit, De-Nha went to pieces and, in a state of combined nervous break-down and drunkenness—what must in point of fact have been a condition bordering on *delirium tremens*—said too much, told his deeply interested hearers all that was in his very evil mind.

Also he told them of a torture of his very own, his private patented invention, a lovely inspiration that had come to him one night when he was tax-collecting in the "pacified zone", for General De-Nam; and which he had practised on innumerable villagers, particularly women.

And in their little jungle-camp, on the track between Phu-Son and the New Fort, the *Doi* and his brothers pirated the patent, plagiarized the brilliant idea, and tried it on De-Nha, its author.

As he himself had said, it was wonderful—and death, though certain, was very slow. . . .

And Colonel Collins had, as General Luong-Tam-Ky said, fled, without going near Thay-Taong, and the only question was whether he had gone to meet General Wun Kai Shek and the convoy, or gone to Peking to tell the military authorities what was happening at Phu-Son, and how De-Nam's death had affected the position of affairs in Annam. Anyhow, the sooner General Luong-Tam-Ky made his little arrangement, the better; the sooner he was an accepted and officially recognized ally of the French, the sooner could he deal effectively with whatever local situation might follow upon Colonel Collins's action or the attitude of General Ba-Ky.

Having thanked and praised the *Doi* for his good work at the New Fort, I bade him see that his men continued to keep a close watch on Colonel Collins's house, and inform me instantly if anything happened there.

Sending for me to his house, that night, Luong-Tam-Ky told me that I must be prepared to depart at short notice; that his letter to General Voyron would be ready in a day or two; that he would provide me with a guide whom I could trust; and that he would do everything to facilitate my overland journey to the Red River and my passage down it to Houi-Bap.

I gave General Luong-Tam-Ky my solemn promise to do all that he desired (but forbore to add that I should do more than he desired) and to make my way when he gave the word, straight to Houi-Bap and give a full and true account of the situation at Phu-Son.

But I must, I stipulated, go by way of Thay-Taong so that

I myself could sketch the New Fort and map the country; and must take back with me the men who had accompanied me on my journey to Phu-Son.

"Especially De-Nha," said I maliciously, and carefully watched for any change of expression on the inscrutable face before me. "He is a man who can be particularly useful to the French, knowing the southern country so well, and so much about the methods and affairs of the late General De-Nam."

"Of course," agreed General Luong-Tam-Ky, "take him back with you. An excellent honest fellow. I'll tell him he must be your guide again. You won't need mine. I was talking to De-Nha about you, only this morning. . . ."

Which was curious in view of the fact that *Doi* Linh Nghi and his brothers had killed him in the jungle a week ago.

§2

So I was to be prepared to depart at short notice, was I? Thank God for that.

The one thing I wanted was to be gone from this fantastically treacherous atmosphere, this haunt and home of lies and cruelty and violence. For I had made up my mind that I would do both the things that I so desired to do.

I would keep faith with Captain Deleuze who trusted me; and I would keep faith with the woman who trusted me.

I would take Mary Collins with me.

Obviously her husband had gone. Obviously he would not, and could not, return—for if he did so, he would be murdered by General Luong-Tam-Ky.

So to leave her here would be to act almost as villainously as her husband had done.

CHAPTER XXVIII

But it was one thing to make the decision, and quite another thing to carry it out.

The first obstacle was Mary herself.

On leaving Luong-Tam-Ky's house, I went to hers, learning from my watchful *tirailleurs*, as I approached, that no-one had visited the place since yesterday, when I myself had been there.

She looked ill, haggard, and unhappy, as, in the circumstances, was very natural; but her face brightened, her eyes lit up, and she looked a different woman as I came into her drawing-room, and told her that she must come with me, must make what preparations were possible, and be ready to leave at any moment.

"Darling," she said, "I shall not do it. I won't come with you."

"Why not? You don't think he'll ever return here? You don't think he deserves to find you here, if he did return? . . . He simply can't come back. He'd be coming to his death, and he knows it, after disobeying Luong-Tam-Ky, who has made one attempt to kill him already. . . . I think Luong-Tam-Ky knows something about him and . . ."

"It's not that," replied Mary. "I'll never speak to him nor see him again, if I can possibly help it. I'd sooner die than go back to him as his wife. I'd almost sooner that Luong-Tam-Ky. . . . No, I am not coming with you; because I should be a drag and a hindrance and a danger. You'd travel twice as fast without me and . . ."

"Nonsense, Mary," I interrupted. "Your being in the sampan won't make it go down the Red River more slowly, will it?"

She smiled sadly, and kissed me.

"No, dear—but what about the jungle-marches from here to the river? Can you pretend I shan't be a burden and an anxiety? And there's another thing. Luong-Tam-Ky would guess that you had taken me with you, directly he found that I had gone. He'd send his soldiers after us. And instead of just marching, which would be wearisome enough, you'd have to fight as well."

"Then we'd fight."

"My dear, he'd send a hundred, two hundred, five hundred men, rather than let you escape him. . . . *And they'd have orders to take you alive.* . . . No—I'm not coming with you—but oh, how I wish I had words to thank you for . . ."

"Mary," I said solemnly, "do you trust my word—believe me when I assure you that I am speaking the truth?"

"Yes, absolutely," she smiled, her sweet face glowing with the sort of look that, as a child, I would have given anything to see on my mother's.

"You are truth and reliability and honesty itself," she added. "I did not know there were men like you, dear. . . . Of course I believe you."

"Very well, then. Listen. I give you my word that I will not leave Phu-Son without you. . . . I mean it. . . . If you will not come willingly, I will carry you off."

"Darling, I cannot let you run the risk of . . ."

"Well," I interrupted again, "I have given you my word. Directly I get permission from Luong-Tam-Ky to go, I shall do so—and I shall not go without you. Nothing on earth will induce me to do so."

"And it will be a thousand times more difficult if you resist abduction," I smiled.

Mary broke down, sobbed quietly, and gave in.

"Suppose I cause your death," she wept.

"Suppose you don't talk nonsense," I replied.

"Well, I could die too," she said, "and how willingly, if you were dead."

"But I shan't be," I assured her. "I am going to get you safely down to Hanoi, and you'll never in all your life set eyes on John Collins again."

"Oh, if I could only think so!" she whispered, and I seemed to get a glimpse of what the horror of life with that Chinese half-caste had been.

And then we tried to make our plans; and she agreed with me that it would be best for her to disguise herself either as a Chinese woman of the coolie class, or as a young dacoit. That, it seemed best to leave to her. She could try both disguises, and see whether, in the tunic and trousers of a Chinese woman, or in the cotton coat and *panaung* of an Annamese, she made the more convincing figure.

It would not matter greatly. We should be a well-armed and truculent party; we should avoid villages as far as possible; our guide, provided by Luong-Tam-Ky, would be only too anxious to deliver us safely, and would easily and convincingly explain us; and he would be able to use the dread name of Luong-Tam-Ky, should that be necessary, between Phu-Son and the Red River.

No, what I feared was not the dangers of the journey, great as those undoubtedly were, but those of pursuit and capture by Luong-Tam-Ky.

What would happen in that case, was a nightmare thought, something from which the mind shied away like a terrified horse.

For, after all, apt and useful tool to his hand though Fate had made me, I was not indispensable.

There were others whom he could send to General Voyron with his letter proposing an alliance. Naturally I was by far the best messenger in the circumstances, but I was not essential. He could send a regular diplomatic mission under a flag of truce.

And, if I had read the man rightly, vengeance on anyone who thwarted, deceived, defied or robbed him, would be very sweet, very dear. Probably even sweeter and dearer than gratified ambition.

And, as I have said, I realized that I was not absolutely necessary to the gratification of his ambition.

If I read him rightly, my capture and punishment would be the prime and primary desire and consideration of his cruel soul. . . . Punishment! He would surpass himself.

And what of Mary, if pursuit and capture were success-ful. Her punishment would be different from mine, and it would be lifelong—mine a matter of days, perhaps hours; hers a matter of years, perhaps decades.

And yet I could not leave her.

No, of course I could not; for if I went off in peace with honour and his blessing, abandoning her there, her fate would be almost as bad as if I took her and she were recaptured.

If I seem to labour the point of my terrible anxiety and indecision, my arguing back and forth, I may be conveying some faint impression of the labour of my soul, the fear, the agony of mind, that I endured while awaiting Luong-Tam-Ky's orders, and making preparations for the journey.

And if that journey had seemed a pretty hopeless undertaking when I was contemplating getting into Phu-Son as a spy, what did it seem now, when I was proposing to make it accompanied by the woman I loved more than anything in the world, and pursued by the man I feared more than anything in the world.

Three days later, Luong-Tam-Ky sent for me, said that he had learnt that Colonel Collins had joined General Wun Kai Shek, that Luong-Tam-Ky's own emissaries had reached General Wun Kai Shek first, and that he himself had come to a most satisfactory understanding with the Chinese General. They understood each other perfectly— both on the subject of the unpleasant fate of Colonel Collins and of the future employment of General Wun Kai Shek's troops and General Wun Kai Shek himself.

"But was Colonel Collins proposing to return here with General Wun Kai Shek?" I asked.

"He was not," replied Luong-Tam-Ky. "He was on his way to Peking with a tale about myself. And now he is on his way to Heaven, with a tale about himself; doubtless plausible— but unconvincing, I fear."

"Start to-night," he concluded, "and make all dispatch by the shortest route. There is no point whatever in your visiting the New Fort at Thay-Taong for, as I have informed General Voyron in this letter, I march in a few days to take it over, garrison it with my men, and hold it henceforth as my own Headquarters—the seat of government of the Northern Province of Yen Thé of which I shall be *Préfet* and Commander-in-Chief."

And, the wish being father to the thought, I endeavoured to persuade myself that, since the French would jump at the chance of this alliance, the New Fort would never be besieged by them, would indeed become their own fort, as its Commandant would be their ally, tenant and nominee.

This would shorten my journey greatly, and lessen the number of days to be spent in the jungle, on the way to the Red River.

But it would not do, argue with myself as I might.

It was entirely possible that Luong-Tam-Ky's scheme might go wrong; that the Chinese General Wun Kai Shek might remain loyal to his Emperor, bluff Luong-Tam-Ky, double-cross him, and put a spoke in his wheel—or remove the wheel altogether; that, having disposed of Luong-Tam-Ky, he might seize the New Fort himself, or, at least, strengthen its garrison (of De-Tam's men) and defend it stoutly against the French.

No, I must explore the place, learn all about it, make a plan of its fortifications and defences, and map the surrounding country.

Of course I must. How could I possibly go back to Deleuze, having achieved what I had, and confess that I had left undone the most important thing of all, failed to seize one of the most golden opportunities ever vouchsafed to a spy?

The immediate question was as to whether I should tell Luong-Tam-Ky that I must see the New Fort before I returned to my Headquarters; make it a stipulation that he should allow me to do this if he wanted me to be his ambassador to the French, or at least his completely informed messenger and plenipotentiary.

And, even while Luong-Tam-Ky stared at me, his hard bright boot-button eyes expressionless, I decided that I would say nothing. He was giving me the chance to leave Phu-Son, and I would take it without suggestion, argument, or cavil. If I said I must go to the New Fort and he said I must not, he would probably see that I didn't.

If I said nothing at all, he would assume that I acquiesced in what he said about there now being no need for me to go there.

No, I would say nothing. Let me get away from this place, taking Mary with me, before the situation changed and something worse befell.

Upon this I decided.

Would the whole of my life thenceforward have been different if I had decided otherwise?

"Very well, your Excellency," I replied. "I will start to-night."

"Come here toward midnight, and you shall repeat to me exactly what you are going to say to your Intelligence people. I will hand over this letter to you, and give you your orders. You may go."

§2

Thankfully I went from the *Yamen*.

As I passed Colonel Collins's house I hastily glanced round.

No-one in sight.

Unceremoniously opening the door, I slipped inside. Mary, her heart in her mouth, had been watching from behind the partly-closed shutters.

She came to me, and I threw my arms about her. Taking my face between her hands she drew it down to hers; and among the things that I shall not forget is that kiss. Not only our lips but our hearts, our very souls, met and mingled and became one.

"To-night, Mary," I whispered as soon as I could speak. "Have you decided on the disguise?"

"Yes, I'm going to be a hill-man. I can make myself look just like a villager from the Northern Shan States or a Karen or a Kamu jungle man. They are about my build and the dress lends itself splendidly. Dirty baggy trousers and loose coat and my hair scraped up on top and tied up in a *muäk* or *kän*, a sort of little turban. I could look the part to perfection, and nobody would dream that I was a woman."

"And you really dare make the venture, Mary?" I asked.

"My darling, nothing on earth would induce me to remain here—alive—after you had gone. Would you have me do so?"

"No . . . Luong-Tam-Ky says that your husband is dead. Wun Kai Shek killed him—at Luong-Tam-Ky's request—as a traitor. I should think it's true. He *must* speak the truth sometimes."

And of course I would not leave her, in any case. It was unthinkable. Collins having left her to her fate (and whether he were still alive or not), there was nothing else for it but to take this desperate chance of saving her from it.

And there, in the very shadow of Death, we had our hour of love.

And when I rose to go,

"My darling," she whispered, "whatever happens, we have had this."

CHAPTER XXIX

That night there assembled at my hut, a band of cut-throat ruffians; the biggest ruffian, in every sense, of them all, myself; my faithful *Doi* and his brethren as choice a gang of jungle dacoits as ever terrorized a peaceful village or raided and robbed the caravan of a harmless trader.

Armed to the teeth, we were arrayed in motley garments, partly correct jungle wear of *panaung* and short cotton coat, partly a travesty of Chinese military uniform. But there was nothing burlesque about our Lebel rifles and ammunition, our razor-edged *mâchètes*, and the heavy revolver that dangled from my belt.

To the *Doi* I explained the situation as it concerned the wife of Colonel Collins—that she was a compatriot of mine whom I was going to rescue from the robber camp because her husband had deserted her there; and made it abundantly clear to him that, whoever did or did not arrive safe and sound at Houi-Bap, the *Nai-Mem* Collins must do so. And that, like myself, he and his brothers must be prepared to lay down their lives in her defence.

Then and there I bade him harangue the other *tirailleurs* to that effect, and to make it clear to them that the present sole reason for their existence was to get the white *Nai-Mem* in safety down the Red River.

This he did with most obvious earnestness and sincerity, and I could see that the others received and accepted his instructions as a sacred charge.

I was cheered and enheartened by their patent willingness, loyalty, and fidelity, and promised myself that, if all went well, when we reached our destination, they should not find me lacking in gratitude and the expression thereof.

I was touched and grateful, and was, somewhat dumbly, moved to give expression to my feelings. To their amazement, I solemnly shook hands with each one of them, a gesture which gave me pleasure and some relief for pent-up emotion, and gave them a sense of the importance and solemnity of the occasion.

The *Doi* was delighted, and explained to his brethren that this was not only a signal mark of honour, but an expression of my utmost confidence, and an unbreakable seal upon our verbal compact to carry the matter through and to be faithful unto death.

I then bade the *Doi* go to Colonel Collins's house, give three double knocks and three single knocks upon the shutters nearest to the door, and wait till someone dressed as a Shan, a Karen or a Kamu man came out. That would be a smallish person, in very baggy trousers, a very loose baggy coat, and hair scraped up under a small turban-like head-binding.

This small hill-man was to be taken to the gate where the party would await me. None of them would speak to, or know anything about, this individual except that "he" was my personal servant or boy. If anyone at the camp gates was in any way inquisitive on any subject whatsoever, they were to be extremely truculent, pull out their *mâchètes* and ask whether the inquisitor hadn't got an ear too many.

In point of fact, it was extremely improbable that any notice would be taken of them. General Luong-Tam-Ky would have seen to that.

I felt quite sure that, unless he were playing some incredibly devious cat-and-mouse game, our departure would be facilitated in every way. Nor was it likely that one so immersed in affairs of state and matters of high policy, including his own immediate future, would be likely to interest himself in the slightest degree concerning my domestic arrangements, and whether I did or did not travel with a personal servant.

No, in point of fact, I had little or no anxiety in the matter of getting Mary safely away from Phu-Son.

It was the dangers of the journey that appalled me, and, greatest of all, the danger of pursuit and capture by Luong-Tam-Ky as soon as he discovered that she had vanished, and guessed, as immediately he would do, that she had escaped with me.

"Carry on, *Doi*," said I, saw my faithful band creep away into the darkness, took a last look round the hut in which I seemed to have lived for years, and made my way to Luong-Tam-Ky's house in the *Yamen*.

With a grim smile, The Shadow met me at the door and conducted me to the well-furnished silk-hung room where Luong-Tam-Ky spent his leisure hours in the study and contemplation of the teachings of Confucius.

From beneath a cushion of the wide low dais-like bed on which he sat, the General produced a sort of small scroll which was, in point of fact, a letter written on a long narrow strip of paper, rolled about a small cylinder of wood and tied round with thin silk cord, and sealed with wax.

"Here is my message to your General," he said. "See that he gets it safely," and proceeded to wrap it in a piece of oiled silk. "Should you lose it—and I recommend that you do not lose it—give General Voyron my verbal message.

"Tell him that by the time you reach him, I shall be sole and supreme Commander-in-Chief of the Chinese irregular army hitherto commanded by myself and General Ba-Ky, and of a strong force of Chinese regulars (at present) commanded by General Wun Kai Shek; that my headquarters will be the Citadel of the New Fort of Thay-Taong; and that, in return for my assistance in suppressing the Annamese rebellion and guarding the Yunnan frontier against invasion from China, I shall expect to be appointed *Préfet* of the Northern Province of Tonking; receive a subsidy to be mutually agreed upon hereafter, and such munitions of war as I may consider necessary for the proper pacification of Northern Tonking and the protection of the Yunnan-Kwangsi Marches.

"In point of fact, the sooner your General agrees to my terms and comes to a satisfactory arrangement with me, the better it will be for the French, inasmuch as this long and wearisome war will be the sooner ended."

And much more to the same effect—all very interesting, and not the least interesting feature of it being the fact that this devious-minded villain in whose hands Machiavelli himself would have been but a babe, obviously trusted me completely. I suppose that was one of the secrets of his power and success—knowing that there were people whom he could trust, and trusting them. A lesser man than he, Ba-Ky for example, would have trusted nobody, and been the loser thereby.

And, having received his last instructions, I took my leave of General Luong-Tam-Ky, and never in my life did I with greater pleasure bid anyone farewell.

Escorted by The Shadow, who, I felt, regretted our parting inasmuch as I was still whole and hale, and sound in wind and limb, I made my way to the southern gate of the camp, and found my little company awaiting me.

At The Shadow's bidding, the gates were opened, and we filed out on to the track that led to the jungle, our numbers the same as on our arrival, but how incredible a change—Mary Collins in the place of the detestable De-Nha.

And in my heart I prayed that the same number might in safety reach Houi-Bap.

CHAPTER XXX

I will not set forth wearisome details of our jungle march, one day of which was so like another; nor of my visit to General De-Tam's wonderful Citadel, called by the Annamese the New Fort, at Thay-Taong.

Suffice it to say that, even to me, no expert, it was obviously a marvel of military engineering skill, a place of such strength that no force unequipped with artillery could hope to take it by assault. Quite evidently it was a stronghold that would yield only to long and patient siege, or to intensive pounding with shrapnel and high-explosive shells, and it seemed to me a most particularly fortunate thing, from the French point of view, that Luong-Tam-Ky was proposing to hold it as an ally and confederate of the French.

It solved an almost insoluble problem, for how a brigade, with artillery, was ever to reach and invest this distant jungle place, I could not see.

And while I spied, measured, and mapped, Mary remained hidden in our little secret jungle camp, a kilometre or so from the Fort, in the care and guardianship of the *Doi*. Always he or I was with her, and I felt that with him she was as safe as with me, probably safer, for he had a trained jungle sense that I lacked.

In the course of a long and somewhat varied life, I have met few men whom I trusted as I did this semi-civilized Annamese ex-dacoit. He was a man, and in the essentials he was a gentleman, for all his yellow hide, blackened teeth, and deplorable attitude to the acquisition of loot, the smoking of opium, the slitting of throats, and the torture of deserving enemies.

And to my overwhelming love for the woman who had put her life in my hands were added respect immeasurable and the highest admiration for her courage.

Battle bravery is cheap enough; the expression of

271

physical courage, in hot blood, easy; but how many men possess the dogged and enduring cold courage of women in the matter of bearing pain, hardship, and suffering, and that acute and cruel discomfort which combines mental misery and physical wretchedness.

It made my heart ache to see her suffering, to see her reduced to living like a savage; marching mile after mile, hour after hour, until she was ready to drop with fatigue; to see her sleeping on the ground like an animal, with no covering or protection above or beneath her; to see her eating the horrible, ill-cooked food on which we had to subsist, mainly dirty rice, stinking dried fish, garlic, unripe unpalatable jungle fruit and berries.

Occasionally, when camping, or rather halting, for the night near a village, the *Doi* would be able to scrounge a pot of stew, the chief ingredient of which might or might not have been dog, sometimes was undoubtedly snake—for eels are not found in the heart of the jungle—or a curry of bamboo-shoots, sweet-potatoes, brinjals and other strange vegetables.

One memorable feast remains in my mind, provided by a headman who gathered from the *Doi* that we were the advance-guard of a large Black Flag force, a feast of which the *pièce de résistance* was stewed iguana, and which Mary, in the firm belief that it was veal, thoroughly enjoyed.

But when night found us on our jungle track, far from any village, rice and tightened belts comprised the dinner menu, though breakfast was sometimes better than dinner by reason of our companions' cleverness in setting snares for "small deer" on the jungle run-ways. Skinned, cleaned, dissected and cooked, these forest fauna could, and did, pass as rabbits, hares, jungle fowl, and similar acceptable articles of diet. In point of fact, they were nothing more than rats and other little beasts of that kind. I am no naturalist, but fancy that some of them may have been creatures of the *genus* ichneumon and civet-cat.

The method of cooking these was simple. The meat was cut into small pieces. Each morsel was then impaled on a small wooden skewer and held over the camp fire, being constantly turned about until cooked on all sides. It was then eaten off the skewer, and another piece took its place to be cooked in turn.

One disappointment Mary suffered owing to the *Doi*'s unfounded enthusiasm as to the acceptability of a novel item for the bill of fare. For, one day, we entered a tract of jungle which was suddenly alive with the sound of a loud and incessant whirring and hissing and a curious chirping noise.

"Good!" grinned the *Doi*, "we shall feast to-night!"

Abruptly halting and grounding their rifles, he and his brethren promptly started the hunt. And, unlike men who hunt by sight, and dogs who hunt by scent, they hunted by ear, each man selecting a noise and pursuing it to its source. The source might be half-way up a tree, in the heart of a bush, under a pile of boulders, or a foot deep in the ground, but with dogged and untiring zeal they tracked it down and secured it.

"It" proved to be a large insect of the beetle or grasshopper variety, presumably some local brand of cicada. These roasted, the *Doi* informed me, would provide a noble feast that night.

They did, a feast in which Mary and I did not join. To the wonderment of our Annamese friends, we ate a handful of rice, while they, with smacking of lips, grunts of joy, and rubbings of happy stomachs, fed fatly on their roasted beetles.

I think, on the whole, they decided that our religion forbade the eating of insects, and they respected us for our self-denial and strict observance of our law.

And so we fared along, over the hills and through the jungle, our return journey being very similar to the upward one, in its daily experiences and adventures. . . . But oh, how different for me!

On the outward journey I had been full of doubt, anxiety and fear. Now I was happy. In spite of my anxiety for Mary, I was filled with joy. My heart sang with happiness, and daily, hourly, my love for Mary seemed to do that which was surely

273

impossible—to increase. Undoubtedly my admiration did, as I marvelled at the cheerful courage with which she faced the hardships of this forced march that was no mean feat of endurance for a man as strong as I, no light undertaking for those born jungle men, my *tirailleurs*. Foot-sore, half-starved, weary to death, she never uttered one word of complaint, one syllable of self-pity. On the contrary, her sole concern was lest she should be a drag, a hindrance, a brake upon the wheel of our progress. Never would she allow us to show consideration for her in the matter of wayside halts, earlier camp-making at evening, or later camp-breaking in the morning.

I use such expressions from military habit, as though we pitched *tents d'abri* and formed a real camp, whereas in point of fact, our sole bivouac gesture was the lighting of a fire when this was possible. Where we halted we sat and ate, and where we ate we lay down and slept, save whomsoever of our party was on sentry duty.

And actually Mary proposed that she should take her turn at this, alleging that we were just as tired and as much in need of sleep as she was.

Here, however, I drew the line, of course.

But in this one particular alone did her daily routine on this journey differ from ours. As we rough and hardy men lived and ate and marched, so did this delicately-nurtured woman, and when I endeavoured to commiserate and offer the comfort of hope, she assured me that she was happier than ever she had been in all her life.

"Dear," she said, "what is a little physical weariness, a little hunger? Don't you realize that I am marching out of a prison in which I have lived in misery of mind, body and soul; in which I have suffered for years that have seemed like centuries? . . . Sinbad, I am with you. What more do I want? I would sooner live like this, in this jungle, for the rest of my life than be separated from you. . . ."

§2

One night, at a spot where the *Doi* calculated that we

were some three marches from the river, he woke me up. I was sleeping beside Mary, beneath a great thick spreading tree. On the other side of it, three *tirailleurs* slept with their feet toward the ashes of the camp fire, over which they had cooked joints of rat on little skewers. Each man was swathed from head to foot in a dirty cotton sheet which, by day, must have functioned as a turban, a loin-cloth, a sash or a shawl. There, beside the jungle path, the *Doi* had stretched himself, while, in a circle about us, patrolled the sentry with shouldered rifle. This man, the *Doi*'s brother, had wakened him because, as he expressed it, he felt unhappy, uneasy in his mind.

This, to me, sounded a somewhat inadequate reason for disturbing the camp, but obviously not so to the *Doi*. He could quite understand a sixth sense telling a man that something was wrong and that some danger threatened, something unspecified and unknown, but nevertheless both real and imminent.

"Has Ai Pow seen or heard anything?" I asked.

"Nothing, *Nai*, but he feels, smells, and tastes something."

"What in the name of the Great Grandfather of all Devils and Dragons do you mean?"

"What I say, *Nai*. He feels that we are surrounded. He smells something in the breeze. And he has a taste in his mouth, a sort of Chinese flavour."

I knew enough to realize that it was quite pointless to argue about the matter, or to ridicule the *Doi*'s statement.

"Tell him to wake the others and stand-to," I ordered. "What do you think we had better do, *Doi*? Break camp and move on?"

I had sufficient sense, sufficient faith, wisdom and understanding, to put myself in the *Doi*'s hands when in the jungle and in the presence of some jungle danger.

"No, *Nai*," he replied. "If we are surrounded as Ai Pow thinks, and as I believe we are, it would be far better to wait for dawn, so that we can see where we are going and what we are doing. If we go blundering along in the dark, we may get shot or slashed by friends."

"Have we any friends?" I asked.

"Who knows? If it is some dacoit *tha'han*, we can soon persuade them we are friends."

I spent the rest of that night in the greatest mental discomfort and anxiety, for the *tirailleur*'s suspicions and apprehension had infected me with the fatal microbes of doubt and fear.

Truly he who loves gives a hostage to fortune. Had this happened on the way up, I should have been merely excited. Now I was frightened.

Slowly the night wore away, and it seemed many long hours ere "morning in the bowl of night had flung the stone that put the stars to flight."

As soon as it was light enough to see the tree-trunks and make out the track, I gave orders for departure. No fire was to be lighted, and we must move off unenheartened by food or so much as a drink of hot tea.

Poor Mary. Her preparations for leaving her resting-place and starting on a day's march consisted merely in rising from the rough ground on which she had lain in uneasy slumber.

Ai Pow and another *tirailleur* I ordered to march a hundred paces ahead; then *Doi* Linh Nghi; Mary just behind him; I just behind Mary; and the other two *tirailleurs* a hundred paces in the rear, so that we had our point and rear-guard and our main body of three.

And just as I gave the order to march, a Snider banged.

"That wasn't half a kilometre away," whispered the *Doi*, and I myself had estimated the distance at about three or four hundred yards.

"It wasn't fired toward us," he added.

And, scarcely had he spoken, when heavy firing broke out, increased in volume and spread in extent, until we seemed to be almost ringed by skirmishing troops.

What on earth could this mean?

Was it possible that a French force had made its way as far north as this, and been attacked at dawn by a force of Black Flags?

No. That was absurd. Quite impossible. And if there had

been a small French *groupe mobile* or a big patrol, in this part of the world, which of course there was not, it would not be distributed in a wide circle—as evidently these opposing forces were.

"What's happening, *Doi*?" I asked.

"*Mai rü!*" ejaculated the *Doi*, and spat. "The gods alone know. There are no French or auxiliaries for hundreds of miles, and the Black Flags don't fight among themselves."

"Could the Chinese regulars be fighting the Phu-Son force?" I asked, realizing, as I did so, that the question was a foolish one.

"Not down here," shrugged the *Doi*. "If they fought at all—and why should they?—it would be north of Phu-Son, away up on the border. But the Emperor of China sent them to help De-Tam, not to fight him."

"What had we better do?" I asked.

"Hide. Get off the track, and hide," was the reply which accorded entirely with my own views.

It seemed to me that the best thing to do, indeed the only thing to do, was to lie down and see what happened. Whoever the opposing forces were, both could not be our friends, and probably neither was. It was the most puzzling affair I had ever encountered, and the only conclusion at which I could arrive was entirely unsatisfactory—that a large force of Black Flags was practising military manœuvres, staging a sham fight, in short—which was absurd.

Gathering my little force together again, I got them off the jungle path; and, in a tiny grassy basin in the heart of a bamboo thicket, itself completely surrounded by saplings, shrubs, undergrowth and thick scrub, we settled down to wait.

"Quite a *ka'n rop phung*—a regular battle," observed the *Doi*, as the volume of musketry increased.

Evidently Ai Pow had been right, amazingly right. We had been surrounded during the night; and, at dawn, the force that, intentionally or unintentionally, surrounded us, had been attacked.

"The attackers are the stronger," observed the *Doi* later.

"How do you know?"

"There are far more rifles being fired toward us than are being fired away from us," he said; and, as usual, he was right.

The sound of a rifle fired toward the listener is quite different from the sound of one fired in the opposite direction; and I noticed, the *Doi* having mentioned it, that the whip-like cracks of the attacking rifles were much more numerous and frequent than the duller reports of the defending rifles.

"Hark!" said Mary suddenly, a somewhat curious-sounding remark to make in the circumstances, until she added,

"I can hear voices," and, a moment later, shouts were distinctly audible and sounds of battle other than those of rifle-fire.

"Chinese," observed the *Doi*, as a loud screaming, yelling and shrieking—the noise that in the case of European troops would have been the cheering and hurrahs heralding and following a successful charge—suddenly broke out.

The distant hubbub subsided, a few shrieks and screams, horrible and suggestive, rent the air, and then silence fell.

"That's over," observed the *Doi*. "Nothing to do now but kill the wounded," he added.

"But who on earth are they?" I asked again. "What's happening?"

"We shall know before long," replied the *Doi* grimly. "We are in the middle of the ring."

At the moment I rather wished that I knew the Annamese for 'Job's comforter', for undoubtedly the *Doi* was a good specimen of the breed.

All very well for him to be enjoying life; but although he would undoubtedly die in Mary's defence, he wasn't dying a dozen deaths hourly, as I was, listening to these sounds of savage battle and realizing the terrible danger in which she was, a new danger somewhat unnecessarily added to the thousand which I had realized, allowed for, and expected.

"What about trying to creep away now?" I suggested to

the *Doi*, all sounds of conflict having died away.

"What about staying where we are?" he replied, in his usual blunt but not disrespectful manner. "We don't want to run into them, do we?"

"No, my good fool," I replied irritably. "We want to make our way through them and do a forced march to the river."

"You stay where you are, *Nai*," he replied. "Half of them will be hunting the fugitives down every jungle track there is; and the other half will keep a complete circle to catch those who are still inside it. While we are hidden here, we are safe. . . ."

But we were not.

Even as he spoke, there came crashing through the bushes a large party of dacoits.

Seizing our rifles, we sprang to our feet and faced them—and with as much hope and chance as a litter of blind puppies would have against a mob of hobnail-booted cudgel-wielding louts.

The *Doi* stared, swore and laughed.

"Luong-Tam-Ky's men!" he said. "What a fuss about nothing. . . ."

And as he spoke, I recognized the Sergeant who, in my first days at Phu-Son, had instructed me in the use of the rifle and the mysteries of military evolution.

How had they found us? Evidently they had seen signs of our having left the track and made our way to the bamboo thicket. Good jungle tracking. What did it mean? Whom could General Luong-Tam-Ky have been fighting?

Before I could ask the question, another band bore down the jungle path, turned aside in the direction of the Sergeant's mob and joined them.

Friends or enemies? Were we captured only to be dragged back whence we had come? Or would these people speed us on our way to the river?

And again, before I could ask a question, there was another irruption of men clad in the yellow cotton cloth uniform of the Phu-Son army; and, for some reason—instinct, intuition or subconscious horror of these men, my heart sank as I realized that their leader was The Shadow himself, and his followers Luong-Tam-Ky's own bodyguard.

As one having authority, The Shadow thrust his way through the mob that clustered clamouring around us, clapped his huge hand heavily down upon my shoulder and smiled in a manner that even at that moment reminded me of the smile on the face of the tiger who carried the young lady of Riga.

"Good," he grunted. "Come along. The General wants you."

"He's been looking for you," he grinned, as I hung back. "Come along."

And there was nothing for it but to 'come along', though my knees were ready to knock together with terror as I realized that this pursuit and capture of my party by General Luong-Tam-Ky was the pursuit and capture of Mary. He had discovered her flight, immediately guessed that I had taken her, and had set out in pursuit. And the fact that he himself had led the hunt in person, showed the importance that he attached to her capture.

I felt physically sick with fear and horror.

What would he do to her? At best, force her to be his *congai* or *téasphiréa* or whatever they called it. At worst, punish her for daring to insult him by escaping.

And I had some idea of what Luong-Tam-Ky's punishments were apt to be.

And what would he do to my faithful *Doi* and his brethren, for helping her to escape?

The glimmerings of a faint hope dawned on the blackness of my despair as it occurred to me that, possibly, I might be able to use the political situation to help her. Conceivably it might be possible for me to persuade him that my assistance was so important as to be almost essential to the success of his plan for entering into alliance with the French.

But then again, what reason had I to suppose that I was the only messenger whom he could use?

On the other hand, I was undoubtedly the best and most appropriate envoy, ambassador plenipotentiary, for his purpose, inasmuch as I was not only in the confidence of the

Military Intelligence authorities, but their own agent. There was a hope, a chance, it seemed to me as I stumbled along, humiliated to the uttermost depths, impotent and ashamed, and feeling more like a whipped cur than ever I had felt in my life.

I, the clever fellow, the big brave strong man—who had been going to save Mary and take her to a place of safety—outwitted and captured by the Chinese bandit, seized and brought back when he wanted me, like a broken-winged crow on the end of a string.

I glanced back at Mary following close behind me, the *Doi* and his *tirailleurs* in single file behind her. Not by word or movement had she betrayed the fact that she was anything but what she purported to be, my Kamu jungle-servant. She was still brave, stout-hearted and enduring. She returned my look, and forebore even to whisper a word in English; and her courage gave me strength, for I realized —or did I?—what it must mean to her to be going back into the power of Luong-Tam-Ky; and moreover, to be going back into the power of that sub-human fiend straight from the arms of the man whom she loved.

And I think I put it coldly when I merely say 'whom she loved', for she had made it clear to me that she worshipped and adored me with the pent-up thwarted passion of a life-time of repression.

And suddenly I realized that there still swung at my right hip the heavy revolver loaded in six chambers with big soft leaden bullets.

Had I the strength and courage, the unselfishness and nerve to shoot her dead; to shoot Luong-Tam-Ky; to use three other cartridges in ridding the world of The Shadow and a couple of his assistant torturers, and then to shoot myself?

And if I had, was it likely that Luong-Tam-Ky would give me the opportunity? . . . But what an amazing thing that I had not been disarmed!

And glancing around me, I realized that the *Doi* and his men still carried their rifles and wore their *mâchètes*. Was this an oversight for which someone would pay dearly when it was noticed, or was it sheer contempt of our paltry half-dozen surrounded by hundreds of equally well-armed dacoits?

And suddenly the jungle path debouched into a savannah-like glade in which was a considerable camp. In its centre was a big tent, its front rolled up.

Inside the tent, surrounded by his officers, scribes and attendants, sat Luong-Tam-Ky, sipping tea.

As we approached the marquee, the dacoit mob dispersed about the camp; the bodyguard, headed by The Shadow, closing in about us.

Entering the tent, The Shadow kow-towed, spoke in some swift hissing dialect of China, and drawing his great sword, took his stand in his accustomed place, behind his master.

A hundred curious eyes gazed at us from faces expressionless.

In desperate anxiety I stared at the inscrutable visage of Luong-Tam-Ky, foolishly and vainly hoping to gather something from its expression, whether of anger, triumph, hate, or contempt.

Again it was as though I tried to read the contents of a closed book.

I did my best to maintain an unrevealing poker-face; and, anyhow, I could match his silence and let him speak first.

He did.

"Good morning, my young friend," quoth General Luong-Tam-Ky. "I am very thankful to find you are safe. I was quite anxious about you."

Now, what was this?

Some hideous mockery, no doubt.

Thankful to find I was safe, was he!

Safe and sound and hale and whole—for torture? He had been anxious, had he!

Anxious lest I should get to the river and escape before he overtook me?

I made no reply.

"Yes, I was very much afraid that that evil man Ba-Ky

had caught you."

Ba-Ky? What was he talking about?

"It was what you call a near thing—isn't that the expression?—touch and go. He'd have got you at dawn to-day, if I hadn't got him first. My one regret is that the rascal escaped. But we shall catch him, we shall catch him. And meanwhile I must see you safe to the river. Yes, I shall not enjoy that tranquillity, which is the wise man's *summum bonum* in life, until I have seen you safely embarked in a good sampan on the Red River.

"Yes, and with two or three escorting sampans, I think, with some of my best troops in them. Not that that really would be necessary, for I will take good care that Ba-Ky never interferes with you—or with me and my plans—again."

"Ba-Ky?" I stammered. "You were fighting General Ba-Ky this morning?"

So that was it, was it?

"Yes. A treacherous fellow. Disingenuous. Distinctly dishonest, in fact, and a fool. He actually thought that he could make overtures to the Chinese General Wun Kai Shek, join forces with him and eliminate me! . . . Yes, 'eliminate' is the *mot juste*. . . . And then, no doubt, he'd have turned upon General Wun Kai Shek and made himself Commander-in-Chief of the Phu-Son army and the Chinese reinforcements too. . . . Why, I shouldn't be surprised to learn that he actually contemplated going over to the French, entering into an alliance with them in return for being made *Préfet* of Northern Tonking with headquarters at the New Fort of Thay-Taong! That's the sort of man General Ba-Ky is."

And all this Luong-Tam-Ky said without a smile, without the flicker of an eyelid.

And without a smile or the flicker of an eyelid, I agreed with him that that was indeed the sort of man that General Ba-Ky was.

But what had this to do with me and my capture?

Luong-Tam-Ky enlightened me.

"And, of course," he continued, "his one idea was to catch you and prevent your reaching French Headquarters with my message. And now you are wondering how he knew about that."

And here I fancied, doubtless wrongly, that the unsmiling Luong-Tam-Ky smiled reminiscently.

"Yes, that was Major Li Hsian Chang's last effort; his attempt at revenge," he explained.

For a few moments Luong-Tam-Ky fell silent, evidently in contemplation of a pleasant memory.

"Yes, he died well, that one. Suffered pain like a true Confucian. And I assure you, my young friend, it really was pain. For I gave him of my best. But not a word did I get out of him. Not a syllable. Not a sound. It was an almost perfect performance on his part. Practically perfect, for it was marred only by one faint sound of an indrawn breath. So, on the whole, I think I may say that I won, for I did wring just that expression of suffering from him. Faint and slight, I admit, but undeniable.

"Yes, he drew in his breath when I . . ."

But I cannot set down here in cold print what Luong-Tam-Ky then said.

"On the other hand, perhaps he died thinking that he won, for he admitted nothing, confessed nothing," he continued. "And he did have just that small satisfaction —that when Ba-Ky went to have a look at him, in my absence, to see how he was getting on, to see how certain little ideas of mine had worked, and to try a few of his own—the good Major Li Hsian Chang did have the slight satisfaction of telling General Ba-Ky what I was going to do.

"How did he know? Why, since he was *in articulo mortis*, on the very point of death, I had amused myself by showing him how far his own plans had gone astray, and how nicely mine were prospering. I had told him how I was going to delude and eliminate General Wun Kai Shek, take over his troops, eliminate Ba-Ky, seize the New Fort at Thay-Taong, and then, really powerful, with my large new army and fine Citadel, propose myself as ally to the French and enemy of the Chinese.

"And I told him how I had sent off you, his late captive, as my ambassador.

"Well, there he scored a point, for as I say, when I went away to dine, Ba-Ky came into the torture chamber to enjoy an hour's sport with the Major, and, in a nasty vindictive spirit of vengefulness, he told Ba-Ky everything. . . . And promptly the beastly Ba-Ky, impetuous as a bull and clumsy as a crocodile, himself started off in pursuit of you with a company of his best Chinese!

"Luckily for you, your visit to the New Fort put him off the scent, and he actually got ahead of you, reached the Red River and turned back.

"On the return journey he got news of you at Phu-lu, turned back once more, made an encircling drive and had got you in the middle of it, when I fell upon him this morning, just in the nick of time. . . . I, of course, was far better informed as to your movements than Ba-Ky was, and knew that you must be pretty close to the point at which he was making his drive."

I was beginning to breathe more freely. Not a word had he said about Mary. Could it be that in the sudden upheaval, the *coup d'état* at Phu-Son, he had been too occupied to think of her; too busy plotting and planning and taking steps for his own advance and his rival's downfall, even to realize that she had disappeared?

And, as though by telepathy, by an act of thought-reading, he straightway spoke of what was in my mind.

"Yes, I could calculate your progress pretty accurately—apart from reports that my spies brought back from time to time—as your speed must be that of the slowest member of your party. Though I must say that Beautiful Quiet Fairy has kept up wonderfully. Yes, a remarkably fine performance. And I must compliment her on the disguise. . . ."

And here he bowed gracefully to the dirty, sullen-looking, loutish coolie—who was Mary Collins.

Instinctively she shrank against me as that dreadful, though expressionless, mask of a face was turned toward herself, those cruel eyes probing her own.

"Yes, Beautiful Quiet Fairy has been wonderful," he whispered.

Luong-Tam-Ky turned the stare of his cold eyes from

Mary's face to mine.

"I am very glad you took her away from Phu-Son," he said. "Very glad. Good! . . . See that you get her safely to Houi-Bap. It gives me great pleasure to know of your forest idyll, of how happily she went away with you, of your joyous honeymoon in these sylvan glades."

And, once again, what was this? Could I believe my ears? Was this devil mocking me, dispelling my fears and raising my hopes, the better to torture me thereafter?

"But I thought . . ." I blurted out.

"Yes, I know you did," soothed Luong-Tam-Ky. "No doubt Beautiful Quiet Fairy has told you of the talk I had with her when I visited her at her house. Only a little subterfuge, a trick. Hardly that; more of a jest, really. What I really wanted to discover was the exact relationship—mental and spiritual relationship, I mean—between Beautiful Quiet Fairy and the man Collins. To find out how far she was in his confidence, and what she really knew of his movements and actual intentions. I very quickly came to the conclusion that she knew nothing at all; that she was not in his confidence in the slightest degree; and that she was of no use to me whatsoever."

"But you . . ." I blunderingly began in my bewilderment.

"Made love to her? Proposed to take her into my household? . . . Do you really suppose that I, I of all people, could love a European woman; could really interest myself in, could actually desire, anything so—undesirable? A person so ugly, unattractive, unpleasant? I suppose you Europeans will never realize that, to Chinese of culture and refinement, you are most repulsive, with your horrible pointed noses, your ghastly red or pink-and-white colouring, your hideous hair, your dreadful eyes, set at such an unnatural angle. And I suppose, too, you will never realize how extremely objectionable you smell.

"Make love to a woman—and to a *European* woman? *Pah!* The thought makes me feel sick."

As this sub-human or super-human devil talked, my feelings were a curious mixture of rage and relief; of anger that the impudent little yellow beast should speak thus of

Mary; relief that he was not in love with her (to call it love); relief that he did not desire her, had no interest in her whatever. A tremendous load was being lifted from my mind as, slowly, I realized that we had not been pursued and captured that Luong-Tam-Ky might seize Mary, but that, on the contrary, we might be saved from Ba-Ky.

Then the thought crossed my mind—why should Ba-Ky be so anxious to prevent my reaching French head-quarters?

And I decided that what he really wanted, of course, was documentary evidence of Luong-Tam-Ky's treachery to the Emperors of Annam and China.

He would conclude that I must be the bearer of a letter to the French General, and would be prepared to make any effort to obtain this letter for the undoing of his rival; or if he were able to kill him, to use it as evidence, reason, and excuse for the murder of his colleague.

And yet an insoluble sediment of doubt still lay at the bottom of my cup of happiness, beneath the joy and relief that was so quickly taking the place of the terror, horror, and despair with which our capture had filled my mind.

Did this man ever speak the truth?

Were things in this horrible *milieu* ever what they seemed?

Could it really be possible that he was entirely indifferent to Mary and her fate, and that he in no way resented my rescuing her from Phu-Son?

Well, that I should soon know, and could put it to the test at once.

"Then if your ever-victorious troops have defeated those of General Ba-Ky and driven them off, we can continue our march to the river?" I asked.

"But certainly. Immediately. The sooner the better. As I have said, I shall not feel easy in my mind until I have seen your sampan on its way. If you and Beautiful Quiet Fairy will honour my poor table with your presence at what I fear will be but a rough camp meal, I shall be charmed—and then you can resume your march at once. And since General Ba-Ky is still alive and presumably dangerous, you shall be preceded by a strong advance-guard, followed by an even stronger rear-guard, and accompanied by an escort. I myself will, meantime, take the field in search of the treacherous and detestable Ba-Ky himself."

And that excellent breakfast to which we—in the shadow of The Shadow—sat down in General Luong-Tam-Ky's luxurious tent, was, I suppose, the very strangest social function in which I have ever taken part.

I have no doubt that the General enjoyed himself.

Mary and I did not.

Luong-Tam-Ky took a malicious pleasure in making Mary uncomfortable, in addressing her ironically as Beautiful Quiet Fairy as he glanced at her torn, soiled and ragged clothing, her dirty hands, her stained disfigured face and tousled head.

Had the scoundrel had a trace of the hospitable intention that he repeatedly professed, he would have given her an opportunity to take a bath, and would, at any rate, have provided her with a change of clothing.

From time to time he professed to wonder how she would enjoy life at Houi-Bap as a camp-follower, a temporary protégée of a private soldier living in barracks when not on active service. . . .

Following my lead, Mary wisely and patiently refused to be angered; pretended not to understand the point of many of his observations, to be oblivious to the venom of his shafts of malicious wit, and impervious to the wounding stabs of his malignant tongue.

Inwardly I seethed and boiled. Outwardly I remained cool, telling myself how utterly harmless was this annoyance in comparison with what I had feared when first we were brought into his presence.

Still, we got a thoroughly good meal of well-cooked food, however little we enjoyed it; and, unpleasant as the present might be, the future was roseate.

Nevertheless, I was thankful that I carried his letter and message; thankful that he had a use for me, or I should have eaten that excellent curry, stew, shredded pork with chilli sauce, pickled turnips and fishes' eyes with unpleasant thoughts of poison.

For I felt intuitively—and, as I have said before, I am extremely intuitive, with a perception at times amounting almost to second sight—that, for some reason, this man hated me, hated Mary, hated us both so bitterly that nothing would have given him greater pleasure than to wreak some horrible vengeance upon us, though vengeance for what, I knew not.

Toward the conclusion of this fantastic nightmare meal, Luong-Tam-Ky bade The Shadow call an officer whom he named.

To this man, the General gave instructions to send off a *Nai Roi Tri* at once, with twenty-five men, along the track to the nearest landing-place on the river; to order another *Nai Roi Tri* with twenty-five men, to parade at once and accompany me on my march; and to instruct a *Nai Roi Ek* to be ready to march, with fifty men, half an hour after I had started.

Evidently the worthy General most certainly intended that we should reach the Red River and our sampan in safety, if an escort of a Captain, two Lieutenants and a hundred men could ensure it, while he and his army not only covered our retreat, but scoured the countryside for the remaining forces of our would-be captor, Ba-Ky.

An hour later we resumed our march and, in spite of our advance-guard, rear-guard and escort, I maintained our former order; a couple of *tirailleurs*, then *Doi* Linh Nghi, Mary just behind him, I just behind Mary, and a couple of *tirailleurs* behind me.

The Chinese soldiers of our immediate escort under their *Nai Roi Tri* straggled along the path, some preceding us and some following.

In point of fact, I should have been much happier without their company, and should have felt safer lacking their protection.

On asking him, I found that the *Doi*, like myself, was unable to make up his mind as to whether we ran more danger from our escort, from parties of Ba-Ky's searching forces, or from wandering bands of dacoits, whether nominally in De-Tam's service or not. . . .

That night, we camped in greater luxury, the *Nai Roi Tri* producing two tiny tents, *sahats* for ground-sheets, and clean *thi*'s or *nons* (a kind of thin mattress or *resai*); as well as hot cooked food—stew, curry and rice. Undoubtedly the officer had received instructions to care for our comfort as well as our safety.

But even then, so suspicious had I become, that to myself I murmured,

"*Timeo Danaos et dona ferentes*", as I eyed our plentiful and appetizing supper and the two tents complete with bedding. Positive luxury.

Feelings almost approximating to gratitude filled my mind as I realized that Mary would not be sleeping on the hard damp ground, exposed to dew or rain, to irritating or poisonous insects, or whatever might befall.

I woke in the morning almost happy. Sumptuously we breakfasted, and soon after sunrise, broke camp and resumed our march.

The second day of this phase of our journey was a repetition of the first, and at nightfall on the third we reached the Red River at the tiny three-hovel village of Bahn Cao, and made camp for the night, between the bivouac of the advance guard who had arrived some hours previously and that of our escort.

An hour later, the rear-guard under the *Nai Roi Ek* arrived and camped between us and the river.

Again we had an excellent supper and comfortable beds in our respective tents.

After supper, the three officers joined us for the ceremonial drinking of tea, and although it was mandarin tea of admirable flavour, it undoubtedly contained some narcotic.

For in the morning I did not wake as usual, before dawn, but was awakened later by the *Doi*. . . .

Slowly I came to full consciousness to find him shaking me violently. This fact alone warned me that something was wrong, for only the utmost urgency could excuse so gross a breach of Annamese manners as this laying-on of hands by a social inferior.

"Wake up, *Nai*, wake up!" he shouted, as with both hands he shook my shoulders. "Pull yourself together, quickly. *Wake up!* They have gone. *Pai lao! Pai lao!* They've all gone. . . . Listen. . . . *They've gone, and taken the Nai Mem with them.*"

They had gone—and taken Mary with them.

CHAPTER XXXI

It is curious how little we remember of the details of the happenings before and after the greatest crises of our lives, even though the facts of the crisis itself may be indelibly seared upon the consciousness, deeply branded upon the memory.

I suppose I cannot have run the whole way from Bahn Cao to the spot at which Luong-Tam-Ky had been encamped. And yet it seems to me that I did—that I ran night and day without stopping. But that is absurd, for no man, no European at any rate, can run for two days and two nights—even with the incentives which were mine—without rest, food or sleep.

One reason, of course, why that return journey seems a featureless nightmare, an unbroken period of superhuman attempt continuously to run and to walk and to stagger on, is because I was still under the influence of the narcotic drug which had been administered to us.

Whatever the drug was, its action was peculiar, for when the *Doi* shook me into wakefulness, I am quite sure that I grasped what he was shouting with the utmost urgency, in his frenzy of anger, of apprehension.

They had gone and taken Mary with them.

I grasped it.

I went to spring to my feet and was immediately crushed and buried beneath a land-slide of cool yet molten lead. I could not lift a finger, move an eyelid or utter a sound. I was conscious of this—and then lost consciousness completely.

Again I recovered sufficient consciousness to be aware that I was enclosed in a tightly-fitting coat of lead, a leaden shell moulded exactly to my body and placed in a coffin. . . . And then, that the *Doi* was tearing this thick leaden wrapping from about me; tearing it with his voice, a sharp-edged weapon that pierced and penetrated my brain, a

292

white-hot instrument of agony that, torturing me, burned its way into my consciousness, my soul, my inmost being.

They had gone and taken Mary with them.

I knew it was he. I knew his voice. I grasped what he was saying. With horror I understood it, and again went to leap to my feet—and was again overwhelmed, embedded, as a toad enclosed in a pocket of limestone a hundred feet beneath the surface of the earth; in Stygian darkness; in a silence that could be felt; in an immobility terrifying, annihilating.

And again I would recover consciousness of the fact that I was alive; that I had an identity; that someone was shaking me violently and shouting in my ear; that it was the *Doi*, and that they had all gone and taken Mary with them.

They had gone and taken Mary with them.

And at last the phenomenon had changed.

Instead of being overwhelmed in the black annihilating sea of molten lead, I managed to struggle free of it—to reach, as it were, dry land; to sit up; to look around; and then, with swimming senses, with a feeling of deadly nausea, a sensation that I was about to faint, and that if my head did not cease to spin round I should die, to seize the *Doi* with feeble hands for my support, and to understand what he had so long been trying to tell me—that we had all been drugged.

We had all been drugged.

Either I had been drugged more heavily than the others, or, being a European, had suffered more severely, had been less able to tolerate the drug.

According to the villagers—when the *Doi*, returning to consciousness, pulling himself together and shaking off the effects of the narcotic, had questioned them as to what had happened—the Chinese force had departed twenty-four hours before, the three officers taking my "servant" with them.

They had noticed this because the servant had struggled, fought and screamed.

Some of them, hanging about the camp on business of supplies and futile endeavour to get payment for them, had noticed the little scene, mainly because it struck them as curious that leaders of a dacoit band should take the trouble to drag away a servant thus, particularly an unwilling one; and curious that a flick with a *mâchète* had not ended the noisy and obstreperous coolie's protests.

And then—what helped to bring me to my senses even more than the cold water that was being dashed upon my head—was the *Doi* telling me that I had been unconscious for a day longer than he had.

With a supreme effort I got to my feet.

"They've been gone for two days?" I cried. "The *Nai Mem* was taken away two days ago?"

"Yes," replied the *Doi*. "The *lu thuong* here said I had been '*dead for a day*,' and I have been working for a day trying to get you back to life."

"You fool," I shouted. "Why didn't you start off after her at once? You cowardly, brainless . . ."

Reaching up, the *Doi* patted my shoulder soothingly.

"I sent the others, *Nai*," he said kindly, as a father to a distraught child. "As soon as they could crawl, I sent them. I thought I had better stay by you, and get you back to life."

"And they are a day behind them?" I said.

"Yes, *Nai*. The dacoits had twenty-four hours' start, and my men were very sick. But they'll hang on."

And it was then that I, reeling, staggering, and falling to the ground; rising and lurching on, scarcely stopping to be sick, began my two days' forced march back over the jungle track along which I had come so happily but two days ago.

As I have said, I remember no details of that journey, nor of my setting out. But the *Doi* must have flung haversack and water-bottle over my shoulders, and seen that I belted on *mâchète* and revolver ere I started. Also, either he or I had put my boots upon my feet and my turban on my head.

What I do know is that I out-distanced the *Doi* himself, that stout enduring hillman, half of whose life had been spent on jungle tracks.

Heaven alone knows how far and fast I ran before I fell and rested, but I left *Doi* Linh Nghi behind, and reeled into the camp of Luong-Tam-Ky alone.

§2

I was expected.

Quite evidently, Luong-Tam-Ky had counted on my doing precisely what I had done.

As I burst forth from the jungle track into the wide savannah in which Luong-Tam-Ky's camp was pitched, an officer in charge of a picket, the *Nai Roi Tri* who had been with my escort, sent a man running in the direction of Luong-Tam-Ky's headquarter tent.

As I reached this, Luong-Tam-Ky himself, The Shadow as usual at his elbow, appeared in the opening.

"You've come back?" he said, his voice, though not his face, expressing surprise.

"Where is she?" I gasped, as soon as I could speak. "If you have harmed her, I . . . ."

"But I thought you were four days' journey down the Red River by now!" expostulated Luong-Tam-Ky. "I thought you were the bearer of dispatches—of the utmost importance to your General and to me! I thought you were on special duty! And I thought I had entrusted you with . . . ."

"Where is she, you dog?" I growled, and my flexed clutching hands must have risen toward his throat, for The Shadow raised the great naked sword that rested on his right shoulder.

"What turmoil of mind! What lack of self-control! What perturbation. . . ! You Europeans who think so highly of yourselves. . . ! Will you tell me why you have turned aside from your duty; oh, man of the nation that prates so much of *Duty*?"

I took a grip upon myself. Useless to have my skull split by The Shadow while I strangled his master. Useless to shoot them both, if I hoped to rescue Mary from this . . . this . . .

"You know why I have turned aside," I answered. "You know why I have turned back. What have you done with her? Where is she?"

"Of whom are you talking? Of Beautiful Quiet Fairy?"

"I am talking of Mrs. Collins."

"But what is she to you?"

"You know what she is to me. My compatriot. An English-woman, abandoned by her husband in a camp of Chinese . . ."

"Soldiers," supplied Luong-Tam-Ky. "Well? Did I send you from Phu-Son to take your . . . your—compatriot—to Houi-Bap, or to take my letter and message to your General? What are you, a Secret Service Agent or a woman's 'bearer', a male nurse, a 'Boy'? Or are you, perchance, a pimp or *procureur*?"

I think I must have raised my clenched fist. Certainly The Shadow raised his sword again.

"Or just a lover . . . of one who is another man's wife? And if I offered no objection to your taking a woman with you for your delight, is that any reason why you should lose a week on the journey? And then you have the insolence . . ."

"Listen," I interrupted. "I was taking Mrs. Collins down to Houi-Bap. You raised no objection. On the contrary, you went out of your way to be insulting about her appearance and person. You said you had no interest in her, whatso-ever. . . . Why have you drugged me and my men, and kid-napped her? Did you think I'd go on, leaving her here in your hands? Where is she? Do you think I will go without her? If you want your message and letter taken to the French General and . . .

"You said 'listen'," interrupted Luong-Tam-Ky, his voice still as silky, soft, and low as ever. "Suppose you listen while you have ears with which to hear. Are you, or are you not, a Secret Service Agent on a mission from your General? Have you, or have you not, a message of the utmost importance for him? Is there, or is there not, the greatest need for haste, the greatest urgency? Do you suppose I can stave off Ba-Ky and General Wun Kai Shek and De-Tam indefinitely? Not only must I know where I stand with the French, but they must know too. And here you waste days and days chasing a woman, while . . ."

"Waste days?" I shouted, almost foaming at the mouth with impotent rage, as this smooth liar tortured me. "Waste days? Waste time? By whose orders was I drugged so that I was forty-eight hours unconscious?"

"I was not aware that you had been drugged," was the soft quiet reply. "If you mean you were intoxicated, blind and senseless, on *choum-choum*, could you not have been carried down the Red River in a sampan, drunk as a hog? Couldn't your men have taken their sottish leader on to the boat and let him sleep off the effects of his swinish debauch?"

"My men were drugged too, by your orders."

"Indeed? This is interesting news. Pray whence did you gather it? And, since you insist on wasting my time—suppose that, for some incredible reason unspecified, I had had you and your men drugged. Just supposing such rubbish, what was to prevent your getting on board your boat instead of coming rushing back here? Is that your European idea of trustworthiness, fidelity, duty?"

"Europeans do not abandon their friends," I replied. "My duty was to find out what had happened to Mrs. Collins. . . . Now then, I've had enough. Tell me where she is. I am going to see her; and, what is more, I'm not going on without her. If you want me to take your message and letter to Houi Bap, you can see me safe on board a sampan at Bahn Cao with Mrs. Collins—for I will not go without her."

"So! . . . You will not go on without her, eh? . . . Now why? . . . Sense of duty? I love and admire this wonderful 'sense of duty'—of which Europeans have the monopoly, of course. Your 'sense of duty'—to this woman—brought you back. . . . But, do you know, I should have thought your sense of duty to your military superiors, your sense of duty to your bond and promise to me, would have carried you on. I should have thought you would have said to yourself,

'*I have General Luong-Tam-Ky's message to repeat; I have his letter to deliver. The whole issue of this long and terrible war depends upon it. The fate of nations. My duty is to go on, even if I leave a thousand weeping, wailing women behind me.*' . . . A curious thing, this European sense of duty."

Will it be believed that such was the power of this man's personality, the hypnotic stare of his compelling eyes—or else the absolute truth of what he said, that I was confounded, convicted, ashamed?

He was right, of course. I had no duty but to Captain Deleuze and my military superiors. I had done absolutely wrong in turning back.

And then I remembered this devil's treachery, his poisoning of myself and my followers, with some foul drug. How could he prate of urgency when he had delayed me thus?

But did two wrongs make a right? Did his villainy provide any excuse for me? If he could afford to cause a couple of days' delay, that didn't prove that Captain Deleuze and the French authorities could. And if Luong-Tam-Ky, for his own ends, and to the danger of his own plans, had delayed me for two days, had I any right to add five or six more days' delay—to the danger of the French General's plans? Of course I had done wrong in turning back.

And as these thoughts flashed through my mind, my blood boiled again.

Let it *be* wrong! To Hell with their plans. What were they beside Mary's happiness, safety and life?

"Well?" continued the voice that was rapidly driving me mad. "What of this devotion to duty? Or was it devotion to the woman? . . . Now, tell me the truth—and you shall see her. Was it devotion to the woman?"

"What is that to you?" I growled as I fought to restrain myself from springing on him.

"Nothing. But it may be something to you—if you wish to see her again. . . . Do you love this woman? Was it because you loved this woman that you have failed in your duty to your superiors, broken your oath to me?"

"What is that to you?" I growled again. "Mind your own business. Why should I answer your question?"

"Because unless you do, you will never see her again. If you don't love her, presumably you don't want to see her. If you do love her, you shall not see her—unless you admit it."

"And if I do admit it, shall I see her?"

"Immediately."

"And shall I be free to take her away with me?"

"Absolutely. Perfectly free to do anything you like with her."

"Very well then, I do admit it. I do love her."

"*Ah-h-h-h-h!*" breathed Luong-Tam-Ky.

My confession seemed to give him the utmost satisfaction; for though his face showed nothing of his feelings, the sound that he uttered was definitely an expression of the greatest gratification.

"Come," he said. "She is in here."

And rising, he led the way to where a heavy curtain, consisting of a ceremonial *panaung* of thickest silk, richly worked in gold thread, hung over a doorway in the side of the tent.

Pulling this to one side, Luong-Tam-Ky passed through into another smaller tent forming a kind of annexe to the main marquee.

Impatient, excited, my heart beating fast, I followed close behind him, The Shadow treading on my heels.

He had spoken the truth.

Mary was there.

On a kind of bed or couch, and covered, all but her head, with a purple silken sheet, she lay.

Her eyes were closed, her face waxen white.

She was dead.

Even as I threw myself down beside the camp bed, now her bier, I knew that she was dead. Even before my lips found that hers were as cold and unresponsive as marble, I knew that she was dead.

Mary was dead.

So, for the time, were my heart, my brain, my mind.

My heart indeed was broken.

My spirit was broken.

And I was numbed, mind, body and soul.

So numb, so cold, that there was not even any warmth of anger in me, not a glow or spark of rage and wrath, as I turned to Luong-Tam-Ky and asked stupidly, as might a stricken child of a cruel elder,

"*Why did you do it?*"

I think nothing can so convey the utterly crushing weight of this blow, as the fact that I, Sinclair Noel Brodie Dysart, huge and powerful, should turn, still kneeling, and piteously ask of the slight small General Luong-Tam-Ky, who had murdered Mary, murdered my love, my life, my soul, my hope,

"*Why did you do it?*"

And as, dazed, numb, half-comprehending, and but semi-conscious, I knelt and seemed to feel my heart dying within me, Luong-Tam-Ky answered me.

"Why did I kill Beautiful Quiet Fairy?" he whispered. "Because she slighted and insulted me. Because she replied with harsh and evil words when I came to her house and told her that I loved her. Because she fled from Phu-Son and from me. . . . And incidentally, this is your punishment for helping her to do so. . . . Yes, Beautiful Quiet Fairy was foolish, and had she done nothing worse than I have said, I might have spared her life—that, for the rest of her days, she might make atonement. But, alas, she herself made it impossible for me to show forth my clemency, my forbearance, my great and earnest desire to be merciful.

"Do you know what she did—only last night?

"She struck me in the face.

"To you dogs of Western barbarians that is but as—a kick to a dog. To me it was a matter for life-long remembrance. Not a cause for fierce red anger and deep black shame. I do not permit such intrusions upon the calm of my spirit. No—merely a matter of life-long remembrance for me, and punishment and death for her.

"I wonder if you've ever heard of the great Judge whose wife misconducted herself and then struck him in the face, and for whose sake he invented the marvellous torture thenceforth famous under the name of The Beauty's Bar . . . ? Beautiful Quiet Fairy misconducted herself with you and struck me in the face, and she too suffered the wonderful punishment of The Beauty's Bar.

"And thereafter she died."

His words beat upon my brain, penetrated to my understanding.

He had tortured, as well as killed, Mary.

This brought me trembling to my feet, but still so crushed and so broken with grief that I was not a man.

"And you," continued Luong-Tam-Ky, "are suitably punished too, I think, by your own act and deed. You loved this woman. You dared to love her, knowing that I proposed to raise her up and take her into my own house. Treacherously you used the privilege and position to which I had appointed you as my ambassador, to take her from me . . .

"Fool! Did you think you could escape from my country, having thwarted, insulted and injured me?

"And when I had re-captured you and her, I did you the unmerited honour of devoting a whole hour to thought of you and your fate; and I decided that though I punished you, yet you should serve me. But though you should serve me to the full, yet would I punish you with a torture that should tear and rend and burn your mind and soul—instead of your worthless body. And I fooled you and re-assured you and soothed your trembling doubts; told you I had no use for her, and sent you on your way to where I wanted you, on the banks of the Red River, to the spot where your sampan awaited you; your sampan, on board which your followers would carry you when they recovered from the smaller dose of my drug.

"And there was your punishment—had you been faithful to the trust I reposed in you. You would have lost your woman, knowing only that I had re-captured her. But, were you faithless, as you were, and did you return in the hope of recovering her, as you did, then was your punishment to be two-fold, as was your offence. For, to your crime of taking

301

the woman from me, you added the crime of neglecting the duty with which I had entrusted you.

"You committed the second crime—and you have your punishment. You have lost your woman and you have gained some knowledge that will remain with you for the rest of your life, the knowledge that she was tortured to death through fault of yours. . . ."

So it was my fault, was it, that Mary lay there dead, that Mary had suffered the incredible agonies of the most devilish torture that this . . .

And the realization—that there, actually before me, prating and babbling and accusing her and me, was the man who had done this unspeakable, unbelievable thing—brought me to life.

At the same moment, I was sub-consciously aware of a din without, and of wondering that Luong-Tam-Ky seemed unaware of it.

"Yes," he said, "Beautiful Quiet Fairy offended me, and now she is dead."

"*And so are you*, you mad dog," cried I, and pulled my heavy revolver from its holster.

As I did so, I felt a sudden sharp pain in my back . . . The Shadow! . . . Behind me . . . The point of his sword was between my shoulder-blades.

"I?" smiled Luong-Tam-Ky. "Dead? Far from it. And far from it are you."

And, without moving a muscle of his face, without the flicker of an eyelid, he stood and calmly gazed at me as I raised my revolver.

"Of course you cannot kill me," he said. "That high sense of duty—of which Westerners have the complete monopoly—forbids . . . What a blow to the French if their new ally were killed! What a sad thing for the French if this deplorable war began again, and dragged on interminably, because the only man who could stop it had been killed. Killed by their own agent, too! And all over a woman—and a dead woman at that.

"Yes, Captain Deleuze's chosen spy, envoy and agent,

while about the business of the French Republic, runs off with a woman and, on her account, prevents a Treaty of Peace, prevents the stopping of the war, prevents the quiet and peaceful annexation of Indo-China."

For a second his fate hung in doubt . . . His fate and mine . . . The fate of thousands of men; tens of thousands, perhaps; the fate of villagers, men, women and children; the fate of Annamese and Chinese soldiers; of dacoits and French troops, hung in the balance.

For a second that seemed interminable, the madness of righteous rage, burning boiling indignation, love, pity and despair, fought with—conscience, sense of duty, realization of right and wrong.

I had but to pull the trigger and he was dead.

And I should die on the sword of The Shadow.

And I should be at peace.

And I should find Mary.

And I should have failed utterly, sinned most grievously, and, in my selfish vengeance, prolonged a war.

Like an arrow striking through my brain went the question,

"What was this devil saying?" And the answer,

"*The truth.*"

And to the shame of my manhood or the credit of my conscience, I momentarily lowered the revolver.

And, mandarin-like, Luong-Tam-Ky nodded his head.

"And that is the other portion of your punishment," he said. "That you cannot kill me. '*That you can do nothing but further my interests.* . . . You may go now. Proceed with all dispatch to Houi-Bap and—further my interests. You can help me. You can show your gratitude, and reward my merciful forbearance. . . . You can *assist* me, my young friend, but—you cannot kill me."

Bang! . . .

For once in his life, the face of Luong-Tam-Ky showed what he felt, shock, surprise, agony, as his knees gave way beneath him, he swayed, collapsed, and fell to the ground.

Had I killed him?

Had I, unconsciously, beside myself with rage, knowing not what I did, raised the revolver and shot him dead?

Stupidly I gazed at the weapon in my hand. No.

And, as I glanced from it to the quivering body of Luong-Tam-Ky, I was aware of a horrible face that glowered grinning between the curtain and the tent wall, and of a great figure that, thrusting the curtain aside, strode into the tent with a roar of Homeric laughter.

Ba-Ky!

With the snarl of a tiger, The Shadow sprang at him.

And Ba-Ky fired a second time. And again

And The Shadow, reeling back, fell across the body of his master.

With another roar of triumphant mirth, Ba-Ky strode forward, seized a wrist of each of his victims and dragged them thence into the pavilion, to show them to the swarming soldiery.

And I was left alone with Mary.

EPILOGUE

For the benefit of those who may be interested in this phase of my Odyssey:—

General Ba-Ky assumed precisely the political attitude taken up by the late General Luong-Tam-Ky, and sent me on my way with the same message and a letter identical save for the change of name!

Perhaps because I did not in the slightest degree care what happened to me, I reached Houi-Bap safely and was there commended, rewarded, decorated and promoted to the rank of Sergeant.

It would have been all the same to me if they had shot me.

My heart, my happiness, and for the time being, my only interest in life, were buried with Mary in the heart of the Annamese jungle, a hundred miles away.

And when the time came for me to leave Indo-China and return to Sidi-bel-Abbes to take my discharge at the end of my service, my sole regret was parting with my dear and faithful friend *Doi* Linh Nghi.

May we meet again—in this life or the next—for he was that rare phenomenon, a true, loyal, and faithful friend.

THE DISAPPEARANCE OF GENERAL JASON

To DAVIS AND GERTRUDE,
NORAH, MAUREEN AND BILL:
ALSO MICKIE AND BONNIE
AND BARKIS WHO *WILL*,
SOMETIMES.

PART I

Lady Jason's butler summed up her visitor, Mr. Samuel Palsover, at a glance. Bowler hat, wrong shape; big face, on the sloppy-chops side, with big heavy moustache, wrong shape; stiff white collar, wrong shape; tie brilliant and deplorable, wrong in every way; thick brown suit, wrong for the country; thick blue overcoat, wrong for the time of year; thick-soled heavy boots, wrong for anyone who wished to pretend he was not a country policeman in plain clothes.

Yes, that's what he would be, detective or rural policeman in mufti. Come about this queer business of the General's disappearance.

"Name of Jones. Davie Jones," observed Mr. Samuel Palsover in answer to the butler's correct if cold look of enquiry. "To see Lady Jason. Got an appointment for three o'clock."

Yes, Her Ladyship had said that a person would call that afternoon, and that he was to be shown into the library.

"Come this way, please," said the butler, and forthwith conducted Mr. Samuel Palsover to the room that had been General Sir Reginald Jason's study.

Seating himself on the edge of a small chair, Mr. Samuel Palsover gazed round the handsome room, book-lined and spacious, much used, slightly shabby, and very comfortable.

So this was where the old bird used to put in his time, read his books and smoke his cigars. Well, he wouldn't smoke any more. Not here, anyway, and very doubtful whether he would where he was now. No Smoking in Heaven, or wherever he might be. Hope for the best about that, anyway. A good sort, if on the hard short-and-sharp side, and a bit of a martinet. A proper gent, though, and the handsomest fine figure of a man that Mr. Samuel Palsover had ever clapped eyes on. Not his fault that he hadn't brought home the bacon, but someone else would do that all right, and for Mr. Palsover too. Meanwhile, there was this five hundred quid for the picking up, or Mr. Palsover's name wasn't Samuel or his nickname Soapy Sam.

A pity he didn't know more about Her Ladyship, but there, women were all alike, and Sam was the man to handle them, Judy O'Grady or the General's lady. Used to be a lovely fine piece, but that was about all he knew of her, hundreds of times as he had seen her and dozens of times as he had heard her talk. There shouldn't be any trouble about it really. She had made the offer, fair and square, in the newspapers, and if there was anyone who could fill the bill, it was Samuel Palsover. She wouldn't wrangle or show a mean suspicious mind. She'd be too thankful for the news. Full of gratitude she'd be, not only because the General was her own lawful wedded husband—and so far as he had ever heard there had never been a word of any disagreement between them—but because it must be a rotten position, not knowing whether you were married or single, a wife or a widow.

For example, she couldn't marry again, not if it was ever so, until she knew one way or the other. There would be money trouble too. She couldn't do business properly, sign cheques on his bank-account and such, or sell anything, until she knew whether he was dead, good and proper, or still wandering about somewheres.

Yes, she'd be easy enough to handle, and if . . .

The door opened and a tall stately woman entered, dignified, aristocratic and still beautiful. Obviously she had been very lovely, with her almost perfect features, statuesque figure and easy graceful carriage.

Mr. Samuel Palsover sprang to his feet and stood at attention.

"Mr. Jones?" said Lady Jason.

"Yes, Your Ladyship. Name of Davie Jones," replied Mr. Palsover.

Cor! What a lovely piece she still was. Hardly looked a day older than when he had last seen her in India. She had never seen him, though. Not to notice. Not the sort that takes much interest in the dirt beneath its feet.

In that assumption Mr. Palsover was entirely correct, for never to her knowledge had Lady Jason seen this man before. Was he just another impostor, or might there be something in it, this time? As her butler had done, and with equal inaccuracy, she summed Mr. Palsover up, at a glance.

That large face, with the yearning trustful eyes, humble and steady, like those of a faithful hound; that general expression of benevolence, kindness and simplicity belonged to an honest man, or she was no judge of physiognomy and character. He looked like one of those nice big policemen who are so obliging, kindly and helpful. He reminded her of those splendid sergeants whom her husband had always admitted were the backbone of the regiment. This was the sort of man who would love children, be adored by his wife and be the generous prop and stay of his aged parents. A pity his face was so—well—puddingy, and that his huge moustache, like a buffalo's horns, completely hid his mouth. Anyhow, he was a very different type of person from some of those greasy ingratiating creatures, rat-like and cunning, who had tried to swindle her before. Nothing of the tricky rogue about this fine specimen of the plain British man. Besides, he professed to have documentary evidence, which none of the others had done; and that would very soon settle the matter. She would be able to tell at once whether it were genuine or not.

"Yes," she said. "I have your letter here," and from her hand-bag she took the curious and intriguing document which she had received two days ago.

"Do sit down Mr. . . . . Davy-Jones . . . did you say?"

"Yes, Ma'am. Davie Jones." And sinking gracefully into an arm-chair, Lady Jason read the letter through once again.

White Hart Inn,
Crossford.

LADY JASON.

Your Ladyship, dear Madam,
I am writing this in answer to your par in the Papers, and

313

am very glad to be able to do my Duty. I don't do this because of the £500 Reward you offer for anyone giving you information as to the fate of your husband General Sir Reginald.

I can do this and give you proofs. In writing. Which no-one else can do, as I am the sole witness except the One Concerned in it.

Your Ladyship, it will be a melancolly occasion, and for me as well as for you. I'll say no more at present, except that unless I hear from you to the contrairy at the above, I shall do myself the pleasure of waiting on your Ladyship at your house at three p.m. on Thursday afternoon.

Ever your most respectful
DAVIE JONES.

Yes, the letter tallied with the man; straight-forward and respectful; and it offered documentary proof. Could it be possible that this person really was an eye-witness of . . . Could it be possible that she was going to learn, here and now, the real truth for which she had waited for years? Those dreadful years through which she had watched and worried and wondered in an ever-increasing state of cruel uncertainty and suspense, a most wearing, agitating time of anxiety and trouble. Terrible.

"Well, Mr. Jones, first of all—tell me. . . . And then produce proof of the truth of what you say."

"Well, Ma'am," replied Mr. Palsover, as he took a fat amorphous wallet from some capacious inner pocket, "did you ever hear of the Irish Sergeant-Major who undertook to break to Mrs. Brown the news of the death of her husband, Sergeant Brown, accidentally killed by the discharge of a rifle? Announce it in the married quarters, to the poor wife of the deceased. They let him do it because, besides having an Irish tongue, he had *tact*. . . . He pushed open the front door of the quarters, and hearing deceased's missus singing about her work, he called out in a loud voice, '*Is the Widow Brown at home?*' "

Mr. Palsover paused, fixed his hearer with a large and liquid eye, soulful, yearning and benevolent, and with solemn mien added the words,

"Ma'am, you are a widow."

Tact.

Lady Jason suddenly sat upright.

"My husband is dead?" she whispered.

"Dead, Ma'am. *And* buried," replied Mr. Palsover, and seemed to brush away a tear. Certainly he produced a colourful handkerchief and with its aid blew two or three notes which offered to a sensitive mind quite a strong suggestion of the Last Post.

Lady Jason undoubtedly displayed great self-control.

"You are absolutely *sure*?" she asked quietly. "You positively *know*?"

"I had ought to, Ma'am. I saw it done."

"Saw what done?"

"His death, Ma'am."

"Done? What do you mean? Tell me! . . ."

Mr. Palsover thrust finger and thumb, both extremely thick and stubby, into one of the compartments of the bulging wallet.

"One moment, your Ladyship, before we go any further. Now it's like this. You are a Lady, a perfect Lady, and I trust your word without scrape o' pen or sign o' signature. But I'm a poor man, and I couldn't afford for there to be any mis-understanding. What I want to ask you, straight and simple, and get your answer fair and square, is whether I am eligible for the reward mentioned here in plain print. Five Hundred Pound. It says '*For information as to the where-abouts of General Sir Reginald Jason or, otherwise, as to his fate.*' Well, Ma'am, if I can satisfy you that I have full and complete information as to both whereabouts and fate, do I get the said reward and receive same?"

"Certainly," replied Lady Jason. "Of course you do, provided you can assure me as to your *bona fides*, and convince me that what you tell me is true."

"*Bone a fidees!* Ma'am, do you know where the General went when he left here? Did he write to you from any place, giving name and address of same? Did he tell you the name of any place to write to?"

"No, he didn't. He was extremely secretive about both his object and his destination; but he did write to me once from what he called the jumping-off place for—wherever he was going. The letter was deliberately vague, since secrecy, he said, was most essential; and he said that if at any time I thought he was overdue, as he called it, there would be no point in my writing to the British Consul, as there wasn't one there. This jumping-off place was . . ."

"Stop, Ma'am. Stop, I beg Your Ladyship. Let it come from me as partly showing the truth of my—what you said. Might the name of that place be Santa Cruz?"

"Yes. It was Santa Cruz. How did you know?"

"Well, Ma'am, just an accident. Strange how these things turn out. I happened to be on the ship in which the General went to Santa Cruz. And I had the good fortune, Ma'am, to do him a service, a good turn, as you might say. Very oppreciative, the General was. And very pleasant and friendly. Well, to make a long story short, I went ashore at Santa Cruz."

"And stayed there, with Sir Reginald?" asked Lady Jason, as Mr. Palsover paused and appeared to ruminate.

"Well, in a manner of speaking, Your Ladyship. Yes and no. With him, as it were, and then again, not with him, so to say."

"And you know where he went from Santa Cruz? And why he went and what happened to him?"

"All of it, Your Ladyship."

"Well, where did he go?"

Mr. Palsover looked up from the wallet in which he was still rummaging, gave Lady Jason a swift searching glance, and looked down again.

He thought quickly. How much did she really know? Things were going nicely, and he mustn't get himself in wrong with her. He wasn't going to give anything away, but if he told her a lie now she might have him shown out, and there would go five hundred quid. On the other hand, if she contradicted him, he could take it back and say he was only being a bit careful and secretive, like the General himself.

With a scarcely noticeable pause,

"Up-country," he said. "What they call the hinterland. Inland, you know, Ma'am. A bit back o' beyond."

"And what was the name of this place?"

"Well, that I couldn't hardly tell Your Ladyship. You see it hadn't hardly got any name. It was just country. The *mofussil*."

"Oh, you've been in India?"

"Er, yes, Your Ladyship. I've bin in India."

"Is this place Santa Cruz in India?"

"Oh, no, Your Ladyship. No."

"South America, I suppose."

"Well, that way. In a manner of speaking. Or Africa. More or less."

"And did my husband tell you why he was going to this place? And what he was after?"

"Well, no. I want to be strickly truthful with Your Ladyship, in act, word an' deed. He didn't. Very close about it all, 'e was. But it was money. *Big* money."

"A concession of some sort?"

"Ar! And you can lay to that, Ma'am. Worth millions."

"Diamonds? Gold? That sort of thing?"

"Ar! That's right. That sort of thing. Only more valuable."

"Oh? Is there anything more valuable than gold and diamonds?"

"Yes, Ma'am. Lots of things. Platinum is more valuable than gold, I believe; and there's sumpthink more valuable than diamonds. Ten times more!"

"And did the General get this concession?"

"He did not, Your Ladyship. He got sumpthink else, and he got it in the neck."

"What . . . ?"

"He got *his*."

"D'you mean he was killed? . . . By natives. . . . Savages?"

"No, Ma'am. He was killed by another gentleman."

"Why?"

"The concession."

And as Lady Jason stared aghast, Mr. Samuel Palsover bowed his head, shook it sadly to and fro, and lowering his voice, added in a portentous whisper,

"And somethink else."

"What?"

"A woman."

"You mean to tell me, Mr. Jones, that General Sir Reginald Jason quarrelled with another white man over this amazing concession and a woman, and that the other man killed him? . . . I don't believe a word of it! It's fantastic! Absurd!"

"Yes—and it's true, Ma'am," murmured Mr. Palsover, the deep diapason of his muted voice rich with tragedy. Obviously he spoke in great sorrow, sadness and regret.

"You mean they . . . fought?"

"No, Your Ladyship. That would have been bad enough but . . ."

Mr. Palsover appeared to swallow a lump ere he added,

"He was murdered, Ma'am."

"Shot?"

Oh, why was she asking these foolish futile questions? What did such stupid details matter? She wanted the truth. The truth. To know the worst and get it over. What were the right questions to ask him? Why should her brain fail her now; now that she was, as she felt, really on the track of the actual truth?

"No, Ma'am. Worse than that, I'm sorry to say. He was . . . poisoned. Poisoned by one as he thought to be his friend."

And at this point Mr. Palsover again produced the handkerchief and the mournful musical tribute.

"How do you know?"

"Because I were there, Ma'am, present and corr . . . I mean, present at the end."

"And who was the man with whom he quarrelled? Some foreign prospector? Some half-caste Dago person as in a novel, Spanish or Italian or . . ."

How she was babbling on. She of all people. She must control herself.

"No, Your Ladyship. Believe it or not, it was an officer and a gentleman, a British officer, as done it."

"*What?* Nonsense! This is really too much. Utterly ridiculous."

Mr. Samuel Palsover raised his large face, sad and sympathetic; his earnest, yearning eyes, all but tearful.

"Name of *Carthew*, Ma'am," he whispered.

Lady Jason sprang to her feet.

"*Bosh!* . . . *Nonsense!* You must be mad. I won't hear any more of such . . . I was going to say lies. Rubbish! Lunacy!"

Mr. Palsover sighed as again he gently shook his head.

"Yes. I was afraid Your Ladyship would look at it like that. I expected it. It's natural. But fac's is fac's, Ma'am. An' fac's is stubborn things."

"But it's incredible. It is . . . I have no words for it. To come here and tell me a tale like that, and with no sort of proof or evidence of any kind. Why, I wonder you *dare* to . . ."

Mr. Palsover picked up the wallet from where he had laid it on the floor beside him, and again fumbled in it.

What huge powerful hands he had, and how curiously he used them when talking. Cupped, beseeching. He was like some great animal with enormous flippers. He was like the Mock Turtle, what with his great calf's eyes, huge bulk and enormous flapping flippers. . . . He was like a great bear with mighty paws. . . . Beseeching. . . . How idiotically her mind was behaving, but they were amazing hands, and he really did use them in the most astonishing way. It was as though the subject of conversation were a baby which he dandled, holding it out before you, beseeching, begging, imploring you to look upon it reasonably, kindly, if not with an actually loving eye. He metaphorically handed things to you all the time.

Terrible great hands. Strangler's hands.

Oh, come! This really would not do. He was an honest man and he was telling her the truth.

But no, it was lunacy; sheer midsummer madness. Henry Carthew quarrelling with Reginald over a concession and a woman, and killing him. *Poisoning* him! It was just about the silliest absurdest utter idiocy that she had ever heard. It was nightmare stuff.

Mr. Palsover produced a sheet of paper. Rising and offering it to her, he said in his persuasive sympathetic voice,

"There, Ma'am. You will recognize that as the General's handwriting, I believe, though it might differ slightly from such as he would write at that desk, sitting up to do it and in full health. He was far from it when he wrote that. Lying on a camp-bed, he was. Shaken with fever—and worse—and writing with the pocket-book in his left hand as he lay on his back."

Yes, it was a leaf from the sort of field-service pocket-book that Reginald used; and the writing was undoubtedly his. Not, as the man said, exactly like his usual writing; but, allowing for the fact that it was written in pencil while on a sick bed, she was sure that it was really his.

Yes, every 's' was as he always wrote it, like a small capital; and each 'r' was of the shape that he always made; and that was his 'g,' looking almost like a 'q.' And the initials, which he always wrote as signature, were undeniably his. The R and the J with the down-stroke in common, the curl of the J at the bottom to the left, and the back of the R to the right, and with that little flourish.

This was genuine. It was a note written by her husband in his pocket-book. The only curious thing about it was that it began "*My dear wife*" which was unusual. She would have expected him to write "*My dear Tony.*" But then Reginald had really written her very few letters, and had not by any means always begun in the same way. It had sometimes been "*My dear Antoinette*" and occasionally "*Toinette.*"

But that was nothing. Being lonely and sick and neglected, he might have felt more affectionate than usual, and put "*My dear wife*" as looking more loving. Well, obviously he had, for there it was,

MY DEAR WIFE,

You can trust this man. What he tells you will be the truth. I don't want to write it here. But he knows all about it and can tell you everything. I am very ill and have had a lot

of fever and dysentry and I feel as though I have been poisoned. I should think it was dysentry except for the horrible pain. In fact, I know it, though I couldn't prove it. I don't want to say too much, but the only food or medecine I have had has been given me by Carthew. I will write more if I can. I would write plainer if I could post the letter some-where safe. I'll write again later if I can, but I doubt it.

And then the initials in the curious way in which he always wrote them, like a monogram.

But no, this wouldn't do. Reginald, the purist, was absolutely incapable of saying "*I would write plainer,*" or of mis-spelling a word, and surely there were two 'e's' in "dysentery." But perhaps she was wrong about that. And weren't there only two 'e's' in "medicine"? She'd look the words up by-and-bye.

But how absurd of her to quibble over the style and spelling of a letter written by a man incoherent, almost delirious, with fever. As well expect him to talk with the utmost accuracy and lucidity when unconscious under an anæsthetic, or when in a complete state of delirium at the height of a bout of malarial fever. She was being absurd. What further proof did she want than Reginald's own writing and signature? She would have been suspicious at once if it had been signed 'R. Jason,' a form which he never used. He might have done so on official documents, but he never did so in private correspondence, and how would this man know that?

No. The letter was genuine and this man was genuine.

But Henry Carthew!

It was unthinkable.

On the other hand, what wouldn't men do when they were poor, and the prize was, as this man put it, millions. Gold, diamonds and something more valuable still—what-ever that might be.

And a woman!

Surely neither Reginald nor Henry Carthew was the kind of man who did that sort of thing? But there again, you never knew. Thousands of miles in space, and years in time, away from home; no feminine companionship; no restraining public opinion; and some more-or-less-coloured Venus.

Well, men were like that, she supposed, but . . . No. Nonsense.

"And has Colonel Carthew got this marvellous concession?" she asked.

"Not yet, Ma'am. Not as I knows of. But now the poor General's gone, there's nothing between him and it, in a manner of speakin'.

"Except me," he added; and there was a faint note, as of a growl, in his voice.

"Except you? How do you mean?"

Again the enormous powerful hands fumbled clumsily with the wallet, and Mr. Palsover withdrew another folded paper from its recesses.

"Will you read that, please, Your Ladyship?"

Reginald's handwriting again. Undoubtedly his—though different.

What was this?

"I hereby give and bequeath all my rights in the concession of which Major Carthew and Mr. Davie Jones know, to the said Mr. Davie Jones, as is his right. Nobody whatsoever, especially Colonel Carthew, has any rights in it whatsoever. I hereby request and direct my wife not to give the said Colonel Carthew any document that may be in my safe or desk bearing on the same. Any such document is the rightful property of the bearer of this paper, Mr. Davie Jones. Please see without fail that such document does not fall into the wrong hands, but only those of the said Mr. Davie Jones. Beware of Colonel Henry Carthew who I firmly believe is poisoning me, that he may get what belongs to me and the said Mr. Davie Jones—to whom I leave ALL *my rights in the concession."*

And then again the unmistakable monographic initials.

Somewhat vague, not to say incoherent. But then again Reginald was ill, of course. Dying, according to Mr. Jones.

Dying of fever and of *poison*.

Henry Carthew. To think of it!

And then again, common sense rebelled, and she refused to think of it, refused to entertain such an idea for another moment.

Henry Carthew of all people!

"This certainly appears to have been written by my husband," she said, "but I know nothing of any document referring to any concession. There is none in my possession."

"Well, Ma'am, I would not press that, for I would be very sorry indeed to give you any trouble. Never mind about the concession, except . . ."

And here again, Mr. Palsover, looking up, shot a quick glance at her face.

". . . *except* that, as the General says there, no such document should ever be given to Colonel Carthew. Never! On no account whatsoever.

"Not that he'd ever have the face to come here and ask for it, surely, the wicked murderer!" he added.

"But, my good man, I cannot *possibly* believe such a thing. Why, Colonel Carthew was my husband's oldest and best friend. Do you know that he went out to Santa Cruz especially to look for him? After he had been missing for over two years."

"Ho! He did, did he!"

"Yes, he went to Santa Cruz with the sole object of trying to find out what place it was for which the General used Santa Cruz as a starting-point, a jumping-off place, as he called it. I wrote to him myself. To Colonel Carthew, I mean, and begged him to try to find my husband, as I was getting desperate about him. . . . At least a couple of years, without a word. . . . The papers were talking about it. Full of it. I never picked one up without expecting to see the heading cropping up again—'The Disappearance of General Jason' or 'Where is Sir Reginald Jason?' or 'Strange Disappearance of famous British General' or 'Is General Jason lost?' That sort of thing. Colonel Carthew had just retired and was free; and when I asked him, he said at once he'd be only too delighted to go and look for him."

"Well, he found him all right," sneered Mr. Samuel Pals-over, if the word sneer could be used with regard to the vocal and facial expression of so kindly and benevolent-looking a person.

"Yes," he continued, "he found him all right. And he stayed with him too, when he found something else—that he was on to a concession that meant a thundering big fortune! Not to mention the woman. A kind of princess, she was. What they'd call a princess in such Gawd-forsaken 'oles at the back o' beyond. . . . Found him, stayed with him, and done him in."

"Bosh! I don't believe it," snapped Lady Jason who was not given to snapping. "I can't believe it. Have you any other sort of proof?"

"Well, Your Ladyship. I have proved to you that I knew that Sir Reginald went to Santa Cruz. I've proved to you that I knew him there. I've proved that I knew all about Colonel Carthew going to find him. I've brought you letters written by the General himself. . . . And there's this, Ma'am."

Fumbling at the massive silver chain which adorned his waistcoat, Mr. Palsover hauled a large silver watch from his pocket, detached the watch from the chain, and released a ring through which the chain had passed.

"There, Your Ladyship!" said he, with an air of modest triumph, as he gave her the ring. "What's that?"

Even before she took it she recognized it as her husband's signet-ring, ancient and worn, bearing the Jason crest, a ring that had belonged not only to him but to a dozen Jasons before him. There was the half-obliterated crest, suggesting the wilted carcase of a sheep, but intended to represent the Golden Fleece.

Yes, this was most undeniably her husband's ring. About that there could be no possible shadow of doubt.

Lady Jason never wept, and had a profound contempt for women who did—save with some excellent purpose in view—but there was a faint suspicion of tears in her eyes and of a break in her voice as she asked,

"Where did you get this?"

"He gave it to me, Your Ladyship.

" *'Take that, my dear friend,'* he said in his dyin' voice; and almost his very last words they were, *'and give it to her Ladyship, with my love, so that if she has any doubts about you whatsoever, or of the truth of your story, this will prove it.'* And as he took the ring from his little finger of his left 'and, he said, *'This is the first and last time this ring leaves the 'and that has worn it all me life.'* "

Mr. Palsover did not break down, but he ceased speaking, in the manner of one who can speak no more, his heart too full for words.

With another searching glance at Lady Jason's face, as she regarded the ring lying on the palm of her hand, he decided that the moment was ripe. Obviously she was deeply affected, and surely would be in no mood for unseemly bargaining. He rose to his feet.

"You 'ave my proofs, Your Ladyship," he said, with a quiet dignity, "and, as a poor man who has travelled all the way from South—er—all the way from Santa Cruz to set your mind at rest, I respectfully claim the Five Hundred Pounds Reward offered to him as should give you 'evidence as to the whereabouts of General Sir Reginald Jason or, otherwise, as to his fate.' I have proved to you that I knew his whereabouts; and I have proved to you that he is dead, by bringing you the ring which never left his hand until dying. Also letters from him begging you to trust me and do as I says."

Lady Jason also rose to her feet, her mind a tumult, her notable poise, aloofness, and *sang froid* disturbed.

Her woman's intuition told her that this nice man, so kindly and sympathetic, so patently honest, simple and straightforward, had told her the truth, the whole truth and nothing but the truth.

Her common sense, likewise notable, told her that it was also perfectly impossible that Henry Carthew should have done such a thing as this. It would be a dreadful deed even to believe so appalling an accusation, brought against him by a stranger, and completely unsupported. Although this Davie Jones had provided satisfactory credentials and what really amounted to proof of her husband's death—for how otherwise would the man have been in possession of this ring—she had only his bare word as to the means, manner and cause of his death.

That Reginald was dead she did not for one moment doubt.

That Henry Carthew had killed him she did not for one moment believe.

But that had no bearing on the right or wrong of this claim for the offered reward. She glanced at the letters, her husband's handwriting, his ring, and felt that to demand more in the way of proof would be absurd, unjust, and something like a mean and despicable piece of evasion. The man had brought the desired information and proofs of the truth of his story. . . . If only he had not mentioned Henry Carthew! But that again was a form of proof. What should any impostor know about Henry Carthew going to Santa Cruz?

Yes, she must accept this man's evidence, give him his reward, and henceforth regard herself as a widow. But wait a moment, would a Court of Law allow her to presume her husband's death? It was, after all, only circumstantial evidence—convincing, and bearing the stamp of truth—but was it proof, legal proof? Would not the Court require something more than this?

"Where is the General buried?" she asked, looking up and seeming to see the large face that loomed above her, distorted with avarice, cupidity, avid hunger for . . .

But how absurd! She was getting positively distraught. It was a benevolent face. The eyes that for a second had seemed hard as marble, fierce and terrible as those of a hungry tiger, were gentle, smiling and friendly. Hard? They were limpid, soft and child-like.

"In the jungle, Ma'am. Up-country, behind Santa Cruz. I buried him meself with me own 'ands."

He held them out to her as though tenderly supporting the body.

"Yes, Your Ladyship, though there was only me, the poor General had Christian Burial. I knew the drill and . . . done everything correct. All as laid down in the book. . . . That must be a relief to Your Ladyship's mind."

"And where was Colonel Carthew then?"

"Gone, Ma'am. Gone. D'rectly he knew that the General had passed over, he hurried on. The concession . . .

"And the woman," he murmured, with obvious distaste.

Lady Jason was a realist. Business and sentiment are bad partners. Incompatibles. Poor Reginald was gone, and that was that. The story about Henry Carthew she rejected. Mr. Davie Jones she accepted—but there was something wrong somewhere. What poor Reginald used to call "fishy." She must pull herself together and be business-like.

"Listen, Mr. Jones," she said. "Up to a point I don't doubt your story. I don't question that my husband is dead. But I cannot, and do not, believe that Colonel Carthew had anything to do with his death."

More in sorrow than in anger, Mr. Palsover made with his hands a wide and sweeping gesture more eloquent than words.

"No. Listen," interrupted Lady Jason, as his mouth opened, while the great hands offered her, as it were, the solid concrete truth. "I shall not pay you the reward—not the whole of it, at any rate—at once. I shall try to get into communication with Colonel Carthew."

"But Your Ladyship," expostulated Mr. Palsover, and the voice was now possibly a shade less deferential, sympathetic and benevolent. "I have brought you proofs, and it ain't likely that Colonel Carthew is goin' to say anythink that will get himself into trouble, is it?"

"I shall try to get into touch with Colonel Carthew," continued Lady Jason, ignoring the outburst, "and if he confirms your statement that my husband is dead, I shall at once accept it, and pay you the balance of the reward."

"And suppose you can't get into communication with him?" asked Mr. Palsover.

"Well, we will fix a time limit. I will give you . . . a hundred pounds . . . now, and the balance when I get confirmation of my husband's death."

Mr. Palsover smiled tolerantly and with a touch of

amusement, the kindly smile of one humouring a child.

"Come, come, Your Ladyship! As I said before, you are a perfect Lady, and would never squibble with a poor man when it came to the payment of a promised and well-earned reward. You say there, plain and clear, in the paper, that you will pay Five Hundred Pounds Reward 'for information as to the whereabouts of General Sir Reginald Jason or, otherwise, as to his fate.' I've give you that information, and I've brought proofs, and all I ask of Your Ladyship is that you will now fulfil your promise and keep your word.

"But of course you will," added Mr. Palsover with a sort of chuckle, as at one who will have her little joke.

"I will do exactly as I say, Mr. Jones," replied Lady Jason. "I will write you a cheque for a hundred pounds now; and I'll pay you the balance, another four hundred, six months from to-day, or directly I hear from Colonel Carthew—whichever may be the sooner."

Mr. Palsover's hands expressed resignation but not defeat. An excellent judge of character and no mean judge of women, he knew when to wear the velvet glove, when to bully and when to wheedle. This was a thoroughbred with a snaffle mouth. No good trying curb or spurs and whip here.

"Very good, Your Ladyship," he sighed. "I admit I had expected to have pleased you more than I seem to have. 'Owever, I done me best. I can wait six months, for I doubt if you'll ever get 'old of Colonel Carthew. If you do, he'll have to admit that the General is dead. Prob'ly say he died of malaria, or pitch some other yarn. Any'ow, he can't and won't pretend that General Sir Reginald Jason is still alive."

It was perhaps fortunate for him that Lady Jason was unable to see Mr. Samuel Palsover's face as she sat at the desk and wrote the cheque.

"There you are," she said, handing it to him. "An open cheque which the Bank will cash across the counter. Where shall I send the other cheque? To the address on your letter?"

"Thankin' you kindly, Ma'am, the same. It will be forwarded to me quite safe, if I am not there. But I hope I shan't have to wait that long. Not after all the trouble I've taken and the expense I've been at."

"I hope not, Mr. Jones," agreed Lady Jason coldly. "I shall naturally do my best to get a cable from Colonel Carthew. What I do not understand is why I haven't had one from him before."

"*I* understand it all right, Ma'am! So'd you, if you'd seen what I've seen," was the grim reply.

What was it that had been at the back of her mind as she wrote the cheque? What was it she had been going to say to this man? . . . Yes.

"Look here, Mr. Jones. If what you say were true, and Colonel Carthew actually did murder my husband, are you prepared to give evidence against him in a Court of Law: to stand up and be cross-examined by defending Counsel?"

Mr. Palsover's large features settled in a firmer mould as a look of righteous indignation hardened his ingenuous countenance.

"Ma'am, I'd give anything for the oppertunity. Yes, anything. But where's me proofs? Just my word against his. Me, a poor ordinary common man; him a British officer and gentleman. Who'd believe me? Where's me witnesses?

"Even if you cared to run 'im in, Ma'am," he added.

And, indeed, Lady Jason entirely failed to visualize herself bringing an action concerning the murder of her husband against his life-long friend and brother officer, Colonel Henry Carthew, on the unsupported testimony of Mr. Davie Jones.

Crossing the room she touched a bell.

"I must thank you very much indeed for what you have done, Mr. Jones," she said formally, "and you must not think me suspicious or over-cautious about the paying of the reward. Five hundred pounds is a large sum of money, and I am quite sure that my lawyer and man of business will approve of what I have done."

Privately Mr. Palsover doubted that Her Ladyship's man of business would approve anything about the whole affair —save the withholding of the four hundred pounds.

"Well, Your Ladyship, I shall hope to hear from you soon. Thanking you, and my best respects, yours most sincerely,

Ma'am," he said as he backed away, bowing.

As the butler opened the door, he turned and bowed again in Lady Jason's direction.

"Most sincerely, Ma'am," he repeated.

And indeed he looked the very essence of sincerity.

PART II

I

On a day some years previous to that of his visit to Lady Jason, Mess-Sergeant Palsover superintended with special care the work of his subordinates, the servants of the Officers' Mess of the Royal Wessex Fusiliers—then stationed at Sitapur in India. For this evening was a special occasion and what he himself would term a melancholy occasion, the last appearance at dinner in that Mess of Lieutenant-Colonel Jason, up to that day commanding the Regiment.

So, not only was it Guest-night, but a kind of farewell dinner to the Colonel, to-night almost a guest in his own Mess.

Mess-Sergeant Samuel Palsover, a little distrait, ran an experienced professional eye over the set dining-table, with its snow-white crest-enwoven Regimental linen; its wonderful array of silver trophies, some of them over two hundred years old; its beautiful glass, tankards and cutlery; looked upon the handiwork of his staff of mess-servants, and found it good. Nevertheless, he sighed, for not only would the departure of the Colonel mean the going of the man whom he admired and approved, but the stepping into his place, temporarily, if not permanently, of a man whom Sergeant Palsover could neither admire nor approve.

That Major Carthew . . . !

He'd have it in for Sergeant Palsover. . . . There'd be no pleasing him . . . Nothink wouldn't go right no more. . . . Why, almost from the day Samuel Palsover joined the Royal Wessex, Carthew had had it in for him, whether as Private, Lance-Corporal, Corporal or Sergeant.

Fact was, Major Carthew didn't like him, and made no secret of the fact.

On the other hand, Sergeant Palsover didn't like Major Carthew, though he was constrained to make something of a secret of the fact. At any rate, as far as the Major was concerned.

Picked on him, the Major had. Always picked on him, from the time Palsover had been a young recruit and Carthew a subaltern. Always trying to catch him out and crime him. . . . As though it weren't a good thing for the men to have a quiet gamble, a bit on a horse, a flutter at the Crown and Anchor game, and such. Kept 'em happy, 'specially in the hot weather when there was nothing to do, and all day to do it in. And wasn't it a good thing for a man who had run short, or who was in difficulties, to be able to know where he could borrow a bit to tide him over? . . . Calling him a shark and a sharper, a corrupt influence, and a—what was it —u-su-ry-ous Shylark. All right for him to go to a bloomin' bazaar *sowcar*, *chetti*, *bunnia*, *shroff*, or whatever you like to call 'em, and borrow a hundred pounds at twenty per cent, as no doubt he had done many a time and oft, when he was a subaltern. That was all right; but for poor old Palsover, the soldier's friend, to lend 'em a bob and charge a penny for the accommodation, oh, no, that was all wrong and wouldn't do at all. The Officer could have his native money-lender and borrow till he was broke, but Other Ranks couldn't even have a kindly Sergeant they could go to and ask to help 'em along. What was it the old devil had called him, only the other day? A bloated blood-sucker. And said that a penny a week on a bob was interest at the rate of *four hundred and thirty-three and a third per cent per annum*! What a silly way to talk. "Other ranks" didn't want no per cents nor per annums. They wanted a bob, and were glad to pay a penny for the accommodation, when they were thirsty—and broke.

Interfering old devil! What had it got to do with him? Wasn't it better to keep the boys at home, instead of letting 'em go borrowing from some greedy native rascal who'd skin 'em alive. . . . Too fond of pickin' on people.

And now he was going to command the Regiment.

Well, there wasn't so long to go now, and Mess-Sergeant Palsover hadn't done so bad. Far from it. Be a damned sight better off than the Major himself when they retired; for, from the time he had joined, the silly beggar had only just kept his head above water. There wasn't much Mess-Sergeant Palsover didn't know about the Officers' financial affairs, and while the Colonel wasn't rich, Major Carthew was definitely poor. His man Jackson knew it too. Practically no pickin's at all. Jackson himself had to borrow from Sergeant Palsover more weeks than not.

Well, well, when he commanded the Regiment, Carthew would have plenty to keep him busy. Keep him out of mischief; picking on people and poking his nose into their private affairs.

Huh! What would the new Colonel say if he knew that Mess-Sergeant Palsover held the careers of at least two of his promising young Subalterns in the 'oller of his 'and. . . . Thinking of which, they'd have to pay up, in the course of the next two or three years. Pay up or be sold up, when Sergeant Palsover retired. Pity, too, for the way the interest on them nice little debts mounted up was surprisin'. Go off the deep end proper, Carthew would, if he knew. But there again, where was the 'arm? Young Officer wants a polo pony—well, he's got to play polo, hasn't he? Young Officer has a bad day at the Races—well, he's got to pay his bookie, hasn't he? Better a young Officer should go to a good honest Briton than to some rascally ol' vulture of a native *bunnia*. Those bazaar money-lenders were just robbers and thieves. Why, Mess-Sergeant Palsover had been a boon and a blessing to many, saving them from the clutches of them merciless vampires.

Have a lot to say about discipline, Carthew would, too. . . . Oh, an 'orrible thing for discipline, that a Subaltern should let a Mess-Sergeant get him out of dangerous trouble. . . . Tripe! As if Mess-Sergeant Palsover didn't know his place, or would ever presume on having lent half a dozen fivers, or five hundred rupees, to young gentlemen in difficulties. Never. Treat 'em more respectful than ever. Friendly. More like a kind father, so to speak, than one of those stony-'earted grasping money-lenders. . . . P'raps he'd rather a young Officer went borrowing from the Parsi mess-contractor or the Hindu bazaar furniture-wallah?

There went the massed bugles playing the Regimental

Call. . . . Now the Officers' Mess Call. He'd better go and 'nounce dinner ready.

Then they'd be comin' out of the ante-room in good time. Ol' Carthew'd be fancying himself to-night, now 'e was going to command the Regiment.

Well, Mess-Sergeant Palsover would have to watch his step. But the man who had been clever enough to keep on the right side of Colonel Jason was clever enough to diddle half a dozen Colonel Carthews, provided he was careful. And if the worst came to the worst, Mess-Sergeant Palsover had made his pile, and when he got into civvies, would be Mr. Samuel Palsover, Esquire, with such a comfortable bank account that the interest from his investments would make his nice little pension look like chicken-feed.

Ar! And they'd be *some* investments too, when he got back to Blighty, and had nothing else to do but addle his brass.

Well! Here they came. Time to tip off the Band Master to pipe up *The Roast Beef of Old England*.

§2

"Splendid-looking chap, isn't he?" said the Senior Subaltern's guest, Mr. Croombe of the 9th Bengal Lancers, eyeing Colonel Jason far away on the other side of the table. "You must be devilish sorry to lose him."

"Yes. Best Colonel the Regiment ever had. Best Colonel any Regiment ever had," replied the Senior Subaltern. "There's not a man in the Regiment that doesn't admire and respect him, and who isn't sorry he's going."

"Popular, eh?"

"No. No, I wouldn't say that. Admired and respected is what I said. But not exactly beloved. Just a trifle on the in-human side. The Kitchener touch. I've been in this Battalion now, man and boy, for ten years, and haven't had a kind word from him once, the whole time. Nor an unjust one. I've never seen him lose his temper nor heard him bawl a man out, but I'd sooner walk twenty miles in bare feet than walk on to the mat and get a telling-off from him, for all his quietness. Quiet, cool and—deadly."

"Not like our Old Man," smiled Mr. Croombe. "Raging like a lion. Blow your head off, curse himself blue in the face, swear he'll have your scalp and your blood, and forget all about it by the evening. Never lets the sun go down upon his wrath."

The Senior Subaltern smiled.

"Same here. Sun never goes down upon his wrath because there isn't any. Don't go in for wrath here. Cold. But I'm not sure I don't prefer a hot hell to a cold one, especially a hot hell that is soon over. But don't you think for one moment that I'm crabbing him. Truly magnificent chap. Just what a Colonel ought to be."

"I think he's one of the handsomest men I ever saw," replied Mr. Croombe. "So austere. So superior, in the best sense of the word. Wonderfully dignified too."

"Yes, dignity incarnate, isn't he?" agreed the Senior Subaltern. "Not exactly overflowing with the milk of human kindness; but although you might call him hard . . . curt . . . clipped . . . and perhaps proud and haughty, he has got something to be proud about."

"Yes, the type of British Colonel that our knowledgeable penny humorists caricature and laugh at, and whom the foreigner is apt to understand a bit better than some sections of the British Public do."

"Yes, rigidly correct, imperturbable. Why, do you know, I've heard fools wonder whether he had much brain, and whether he wasn't dead from the neck up. Rather amusing to anyone who knows he's as clever as a fox. He may look like a bronze bust, but the bronze is still molten hot in the middle. . . . And a more honourable and upright man never lived."

"Spot of hero-worship?" smiled Mr. Croombe.

"Well, no. You can't get sufficiently fond of him for that. Can't make any sort of human contact with him. There's always that sense of a thick glass wall in between. But that doesn't prevent one from appreciating his outstanding soldierly qualities, and admiring him unreservedly. Perhaps, if one could get to know him . . . But you feel that, after ten years, he doesn't remember either you or your name; and that when you say 'Good-morning,' he might at any time reply 'Good-morning. And who the devil might you be?' "

"I see. Icy isolation, what?" smiled Mr. Croombe.

"I should say there is only one man in the Regiment that really knows him; and he was at school and Sandhurst with him, as well as in the Regiment all their service."

"What, Major Carthew?"

"Yes. Now there you might talk about hero-worship. I should say that old Cart-horse believes in God, King and Jason. Don't know which he puts first. I'd say loves Jason, honours the King and fears God, in that order—and that he loves Jason more than anyone or anything on earth. Real case of hero-worship, if you like."

"What sort of a chap is Carthew?"

"Oh, he's got his points. One of the best, really, but not in the same street with Jason. Kind-hearted a chap as you'd meet in a day's march. An incredible linguist too. Interpreter-rank in all the Latin languages from French to Portuguese, and takes the Higher Standard in a new Oriental language every year, out here . . . Persian . . . Arabic . . . and what not. Keen as mustard. And absolutely married to the Regiment, but he'll find it a difficult matter, stepping into Jason's shoes."

"Certainly a great contrast to him in appearance," observed Mr. Croombe, as he glanced at Major Carthew.

"Yes. No beauty, is he? I believe he has always been a sore trial to Jason. Going on parade with his helmet backside foremost or his most important buttons undone. Never looks right, somehow. Still, he's a damn fine fighting soldier, though no great Mess ornament. Wonderful gift for upsetting inspecting Generals. Been a good thing for him, once or twice, that Jason is really fond of him. About the only thing Jason is fond of. Don't believe he has ever owned a dog in his life, and I've never seen him pat a horse, let alone a deserving human back. Such as mine, for example. . . . I shouldn't think that his Mrs. . . . H'm!"

The Senior Subaltern stopped abruptly, somewhat shocked to realize that he had been about to mention a lady's name, a thing which is not done in British Messes.

"Why, God sweeten my soul! Hasn't young Bickersteth got a coloured handkerchief up his sleeve? I'll have him undressed later on, and if he has, he shall eat it. Foul little hound! The sort of thing he would do! Handkerchief up his sleeve, and a coloured one at that! What's the Army coming to?"

§3

"Well, Reginald," said Major Carthew to Colonel Jason, "it doesn't seem *possible* that this is the last time you and I will sit at this table. I simply cannot believe it."

"No. Hardly believe it myself. Almost sorry, in a way," replied Colonel Jason. "A great change. Probably find being a General quite a lonely sort of job, at first."

"Yes. But you won't be as lonely as I shall. I can't tell you how much I shall miss you. Probably don't know myself yet. Don't realize it, quite. No one's more pleased than I am that you've got your Brigade, Reginald, but . . . I feel like sending in my papers. You and Antoinette gone! It doesn't bear thinking of."

"Oh, don't talk nonsense, Henry. . . . Make me cry in a minute. Twelve o'clock to-night you'll be our Colonel Carthew. Now you've got the Battalion you'll have something else to do than think of old times and old friends."

Did Reginald really think that he'd ever have anything better to do than think of old times and his old friend? Didn't *he* feel it at all? Probably not, and a good thing too. He wouldn't like to think that Reginald was hating it as much as he was. Really suffering. It was awful. And he hadn't quite realized it yet, himself. He'd do that to-morrow morning when he saw him and Antoinette off. It was like a bad dream. How he wished he could only wake from it.

Mess-Sergeant Palsover approached, bent over and whispered in Colonel Jason's ear, was answered with a curt nod, and departed.

"I shall positively miss that old scoundrel," smiled Colonel Jason.

"I should like to have the opportunity," replied Major Carthew.

"You do hate him, don't you, Henry? I don't know why. I'm rather fond of Palsover."

"Well, you gave him his right name just now."

"Scoundrel? A term of endearment," smiled Colonel Jason.

"Never endeared himself to *me*, although he has done his best. He is a scoundrel. A damned scoundrel. Biggest scoundrel unhung," growled Major Carthew.

"Oh, come, come! He's not as bad as all that. It's not like you to talk like this, Henry. No doubt he has his little tricks. Possibly heard of watered beer and wonderfully-blended whiskey, and what are called 'illegal gratifications,' I believe. But . . ."

"Oh, I suppose most Mess-Sergeants have their little ways," interrupted Carthew, "but Palsover's an out-and-out wrong 'un. I don't mind telling you now"—he had been going to say *"now that you are going,"* but found it difficult, painful, to put the plain and simple fact into so many words —"that I believe he was wholly and solely responsible for the death of young James."

"But Private James committed suicide. There was never the slightest shadow of doubt about that," objected Colonel Jason.

"Yes, he committed suicide. Shot himself with his own rifle; but it's my firm conviction that part of the pressure on the trigger came from Palsover's finger."

"You don't mean literally?"

"No. I don't mean that Palsover was there when it happened, or had the least idea that it was going to happen. He'd have prevented it if he had, for fear the wretched lad left a letter. But I am absolutely certain, in my own mind, that Palsover drove him to . . ."

"But how?"

"Dunning him. Putting the screw on him persistently. He had kept on lending him small sums of money until the total was, from James's point of view, a very big one; and then he not only put the screw on, and made the wretched lad's life a burden to him, but used his power over him in various ways, till James couldn't stand it any longer."

"But none of this ever came out at the time. There was no evidence that . . ."

"No, I know there wasn't, unfortunately. It was all hearsay. But everybody knew. And nobody knew—when it came to saying what they knew—in evidence at the inquest. I had it all from my man. Long afterwards, of course. Knowing my Palsover and his little ways, I made it my business to learn all I could. Of course, Jackson tied my hands by speaking in strictest confidence—whenever he would speak at all. But . . . well, there was no doubt about it, I knew he was the regimental bookie and that *sub rosa* he ran various games of chance—or no chance—and that he lent everybody money at about five hundred per cent per annum, though it was all very difficult to prove. And I know that—although it was the last thing he wanted to happen, if only because he lost his money—he was the cause of James's death."

"I wish I had known before," said Colonel Jason.

"You could have done nothing. No evidence whatever. Neither Jackson nor anyone else would have said a word—officially."

He emptied his glass.

"But I'll catch him out, if it's the last thing I ever do," he said. "And then . . . !"

Mess-Sergeant Palsover, his hands looking fantastically colossal in their white gloves, placed a decanter of port and one of madeira before the Mess President at one end of the table, and a similar pair before the Vice-President at the other. These officers, each with his left hand, sent them on their way.

A few minutes later the Mess President at the head of the table rose to his feet.

"Mr. Vice, the King!" he called.

The Vice-President at the other end of the table also rose.

"Gentlemen, the King Emperor!" and chairs were pushed back as all present stood up, and raised their glasses.

Mess-Sergeant Palsover at the central door of the Mess waved a vast white hand to the Band Master without, the band struck up *God Save the King*, and the Officers of the Royal Wessex Fusiliers drank the loyal toast.

II

"Well, good-bye, Henry," said Mrs. Jason, as it came to the new Colonel Carthew's turn to say the last farewell. "We shall be off in a minute or two now, I suppose. Hope so, anyway. One feels so extraordinarily silly, saying good-bye at a railway-station, doesn't one? '*Good-bye, good-bye. Now we're off,*' and then we're not, for another half an hour."

Why couldn't the poor man utter, instead of holding her hand and gazing at her like a nice dumb animal that has got so much to say and cannot say it.

Poor dear Henry, she'd really miss him. She would only realize how useful he had been, now that he wouldn't be there to—be useful. Yes, she would really miss him. After all these years. What a pity he couldn't come too. Perhaps Reginald would be able to wangle it? Surely Henry would rather have got a job on Reginald's staff and come with them, than stay here and command the Regiment? Brigade-Major or something. She must talk to Reginald about it.

"Good-bye, Antoinette," said Colonel Carthew, making a kind of convulsive grab at her hand and raising it to his lips. "Good-bye. I . . ." and stood staring, still holding her hand in a grip that was beginning to hurt.

"I really don't know what I'm . . . It will be simply awful. . . . I don't know how . . . It doesn't bear thinking of."

"You must come and see us, Henry."

"Oh, *rather!* Yes, *rather!*" But how often would he be able to get over to the other side of India, especially now that he commanded the Regiment?

It couldn't be possible that she was going; that this train would start in a minute, take her out of this station, out of his sight, out of his life. . . . He hadn't felt quite like this since the day when, as a small boy, he had said good-bye to his mother, as she went off leaving him stranded to face his first term at school. A dreadful sense of loss, desertion, loneliness. He'd be glad when the parting was over. Had Antoinette the faintest idea as to what he was feeling, how her going affected him, what it meant to him? She looked, as usual, perfectly calm and cool; apparently absolutely untouched, unaffected, her magnificent beauty unruffled; unflushed, not a hair out of place, not a sentence hurried, not a movement uncertain, much less a tear in her eye or voice. Perhaps she felt more than she showed? She could hardly feel less.

Did he himself look as composed, as indifferent, as that —after sitting up all night wrestling with his misery, wretchedness and pain? Certainly Reginald did. Dignified and aloof, of course, but if anything, a little more human than usual; a pleasant smile for everybody, he who so rarely smiled. But as for grief or even regret, not the faintest sign of it. One would think he was going off for a month's shooting-leave instead of parting for ever from the Regiment with which, in which, and for which, he had lived for quarter of a century. If he felt nothing at leaving the friend who had been with him at school, at Sandhurst and in the Regiment, from the time they were small boys in their earliest teens, to this day when they were grizzled veterans, surely he must feel something at leaving the Regiment? Well, perhaps he did. Of course he did. But no one would think so, for he showed devilish little sign of it.

What a magnificent General he would make, and what a picture of a magnificent General too. The most truly dignified man he had ever seen in his life. He'd be positively stately by the time he was a Field-Marshal and Commander-in-Chief, as he certainly would be. There was scarcely a King in the whole world who might not envy his bearing, his appearance, carriage and unassumed and unassuming— well—*dignity*. That was the word.

He had followed Reginald all these years; followed him, admired him, slaved for him, loved him. Now he was going to lose him, and the flavour of life henceforth, though he had, at last, got the command, would be as dust and ashes in his mouth.

Well, he'd probably do as he said. Send in his papers.

Damn the Regiment! He'd clear out and go where he wouldn't be reminded every day of the friends he had lost, the man and the woman who were his greatest friends, his best friends, his *only* friends.

That was the worst of being such a one-man dog as he was. Splendid to have a man friend and a woman friend, to concentrate on them, to grapple them to your soul with hoops of steel and to dull not the palm with entertainment of each unfledged comrade, and all that. Wonderful—until they went and left you stranded high and dry; and life was more dry than high; dry as a damned desert.

"Well, good-bye, Henry," said General Jason cheerily. "Don't look so down in the mouth. The best of friends must part, as the song says. Send us a line now and again. I shall never be able to hear enough about the Regiment. . . . All the gossip—and how you get on. . . . Don't break old Palsover! . . . You're going to have the time of your young life. So's the Regiment! . . . Good-bye! . . . Good-bye, all. Good-bye, Mowbray. Good-bye, Weston. Good-bye, Fontwell. Good-bye, Carey. Good-bye, Wray. Good-bye, Blacker. Good-bye, Henry. Good-bye, everybody. Good-bye. . . . Don't forget to write. Specially if I can help you at any time. . . . And come and see us. . . . Good-bye, good-bye! . . ."

Yes, Henry Carthew was just one of the crowd. Still, he was the only one whom Reginald had called by his Christian name, and Antoinette had looked at him last.

They'd soon forget him. . . .

Turning abruptly away as the train rounded the curve, Colonel Carthew walked quickly off in the direction of his bungalow, oblivious of the heat, the dust and everything else, save the fact that the Indian scene looked different, empty. Life looked empty, null and void.

Reginald had gone and Antoinette had gone, and there was nothing whatever left here—save a score or so of officers and about eight hundred men.

§2

"Well, that's that," observed the newly-promoted General Jason, as he turned from the carriage window and seated himself on the long leather-cushioned bed-settee opposite to that occupied by his wife.

"Phew! . . . Gad, how I hate these tearful ceremonies."

"I didn't notice you wiping your eyes—General!" replied Mrs. Jason.

"Didn't you? No. Your handkerchief's fairly dry too."

"Yes. Though I could have wept with—not exactly boredom, but . . . the state of being bored."

"Yes, I know. Very trying. However . . ."

"Quite so, Reginald. Is Flagstaff House pretty good at Allahpur?"

"From my point of view, yes. I think you'll find it all right. Nice change."

"Yes, and the climate is better than at Sitapur, isn't it?"

"Much. Jolly good hill-station quite near too. You won't have a bad time up there in the hot weather, Tony. Quite a young Simla, in its way."

General Jason removed his helmet, placed it on the rack, sat down upon the broad seat, some seven feet in length, a couch by day and a bed by night, and leant back upon the rolled bedding and cushions arranged for that purpose by his servant.

Antoinette Jason regarded her husband, as she was wont to do, with coolly appraising speculative eye, a faintly mocking smile upon her lips. How like him to keep his coat on, hot as the morning was, and complete as was their privacy. Reginald must never relax, must never be caught unbuttoned—in mind, body or soul. If present, then correct. What a wonderful sight it would be to catch a glimpse of Reginald in an undignified posture or situation. It would be almost a pleasure, certainly a relief, to see or hear him being undignified. Not that there was any pose about it, or that he ever stood on his dignity. He was born dignified, had lived dignified and would die with the utmost dignity, be the circumstances what they might. Had he never been drunk or excited in all his life? Of course he hadn't, any more than he had ever been called anything other than Reginald. . . . What would he say if, for once, she addressed him as Reggie, or, worse still, as Reg? He wouldn't say anything at all. He wouldn't hear. He wouldn't imagine that it was he who was being addressed by so familiar and foul a term. It would be like addressing a reigning monarch as Bert, Perce, Herb or Alf. No, it was just real natural dignity, as genuine as his imperturbable coolness and calmness, his inflexible honesty and untarnished honour, his flawless courage, and his perfect courtesy.

Damned old icicle!

Her eyes twinkled and her mouth smiled, faintly sardonic.

"Happy, Reginald?"

"Why?"

"Brigade, staff and flag-staff, galloper, sentries on the doorstep—and all that. Burra-sahib."

"Happy? Well, if to be glad is to be happy, I'm glad I have got my Brigade."

"In a way, you'll enjoy life at Allahpur, won't you?"

"Plenty of work. And I like work."

"Like work! You love work, Reginald."

"I suppose I do."

"It's the only thing you do love, isn't it?"

"Oh, I don't know. . . ."

"I do. Would you mind if I went to England?"

"Why, no, my dear, certainly not. If you feel you'd like to go Home this hot weather instead of . . ."

"Think you'd get on better at Allahpur without a wife?"

"Why, no, not at all. I didn't mean that. But if you'd like to go Home for the hot weather, or for a year or so, there's nothing on earth to . . ."

"No, I'm sure there isn't, my dear."

"Well, you asked, didn't you, Tony?"

"I did. I'm a silly woman. A poor thing, but thine own. Not that anyone would notice it. I'm not really your wife, you know."

General Jason looked up from the paper on which,

between the lurches of the carriage, he was endeavouring to jot memoranda.

"What *do* you mean? Have I ever, in all our married life, done anything to suggest that you were not my wife?"

"No, my dear, never. . . . Nor anything much that ever indicated that I was."

General Jason got on with his work.

§3

Mrs. Jason was awakened in the morning by the stopping of the train at a wayside station. She glanced at her watch, fastidiously dusted a light deposit of sand from her sheet and pillow, and glanced across at her husband.

Reginald. . . . Twenty-four hours a General. . . . Lying like a warrior taking his rest with his martial dignity around him. As dignified in sleep as when riding at the head of his Regiment. As dignified in pyjamas as in full war-paint, his hair as tidy, his lips as tightly closed. No man, and presumably no woman, had ever heard Reginald snore.

The perfect soldier, the perfect man, the perfect husband. Yes, the model was perfect. Pity it wasn't a working model. Or did she mean a playing model?

Perfect model of a husband! But models are so apt to be hard, rigid, mechanical. Models have no emotions. If she had been blessed with a son or a daughter, she would have been inclined to advise neither of them to marry a model. Not a model of a husband or wife, that is to say. Of course, a model soldier was different. Kitchener was her idea, her ideal, of a model soldier, and Reginald was like unto him. Very. But in mercy to some fortunate woman Kitchener had remained a bachelor. A pity Reginald hadn't. From her point of view, that was.

She certainly hadn't done him and his career any harm, the career that was a beautiful blossoming tree which was just beginning to bear fruit. Brigadier to-day, Major-General to-morrow, Lieutenant-General and K.C.B. the next day, and then Field-Marshal and Commander-in-Chief in India next week, metaphorically speaking.

No, she had done him no harm. Always present and correct when required for social purposes. Never un-present or incorrect when put back in the box.

That damned box of a bungalow!

No, never incorrect. Never tempted to be, either. Caesar's wife. Was Mrs. Caesar also one of those unfortunate females who inspired terrific respect and nothing more—or less?

Poor dear old Henry. How she'd miss him. Dear old Henry! Literally everything that Reginald was not. Loving, warm-hearted, simple, clumsy, *gauche*, unkempt and untidy. Positively unsoldierly. Always present and never correct, except in his attitude to her.

Too correct for words, there! He thought himself a perfect devil, kissing her hand in farewell, yesterday. Absolute Don Juan, going about kissing women's hands once every quarter of a century, without fail.

What would life have been like if he had done what he had wanted to do, any time in the said quarter of a century, and kissed her on the lips until it hurt?

She'd have loved to have been hurt like that, just once or twice in her life.

Poor dear old Henry. Followed her about like a dog and worshipped the ground she trod on, all that time. Loved her desperately, passionately, for twenty years and—kissed her hand at the end of it!

Why couldn't Reginald have loved her like that? What a time they could have had together; and what a joy it would have been now that the grand steady river of his life, unsullied, unbroken, unhurried, was broadening out into an almost boundless sea of pride, ambition and reward.

But in point of fact, he didn't give a damn whether she went Home or not; whether she went Home and stayed at Home.

And there, back in Sitapur, was Henry eating his heart out for her. Henry, almost literally broken-hearted.

Ah, well! Life was like that, and it was time that Tulsiram brought tea. Not that he could do that until the train stopped at another station.

Well, so perfect a servant of so perfect a master should be able to produce a station.

Would Henry have been more on-coming if she had encouraged him? An idle if interesting speculation, since she'd probably never see him again. Not for years, anyway. Two wasted and frustrated lives, hers and Henry's. Nonsense. She had never really loved him. Not been in love with him, anyhow. How could a woman of her type and temperament ever be in love with a man whose back hair would stand up in duck-tails, whose tie would wriggle round, who never could look as though he had shaved that morning, although of course he had. A man who trod on your toes when he danced with you; trod on the train of your gown if he got a chance; dropped things if you spoke to him suddenly; and always blushed. No wicked sinner ever blushed as the virtuous Henry did. . . . What little things have colossal effects—influencing our whole lives. Things like that. Why, if Henry's nose had not been a bit of a blob, rather round and shiny and inclined to be red, she might not be lying here gazing upon the really rather beautiful face of her immaculate and impeccable lord and master, General Reginald Jason, Field-Marshal-in-the-sight-of-God Sir Reginald Jason, K.C.B., C.M.G., etc.

Well, he was a lovely creature and she'd certainly be Lady Jason some day. She'd be Lady Jason in Wildflower Hall, the Commander-in-Chief's house at Simla.

Better than being Mrs. Henry Carthew in lodgings at Exeter or somewhere.

Still . . . *Love!* Real mutual unquenchable love. . . . Passion. . . .

The train slowed down again and General Jason sat up. No, not a hair out of place. Perfect.

"Good morning, Antoinette," said he.

"And to you, my Reginald," she said, suppressing behind her faintly mocking smile, "my passionate lover."

"Do you know what day it is?" she asked.

"Thursday."

"It is even more than Thursday."

"How?"

"It is the bright anniversary of our wedding-day."

"Really? How time flies. . . ."

"D'you think it does?"

"Well. Look at us. . . . How old are you to-day, Tony?"

"Thirty-five, my dear. Thirty-five years and seven days. I had a birthday last week."

"They do come round, don't they?"

"Yes. Mine do. But no one notices the little things. So what matter they, my Reginald?"

"Why should they matter? Thank God I'm only forty-seven and . . ."

"In time to be the youngest Commander-in-Chief in India. Splendid, my dear. . . . How I wish I were only forty-seven in spirit—and that Tulsiram would bring tea in a brown pot. . . ."

PART III

Mr. Samuel Palsover, better known on the little coasting cargo-passenger ship *St. Paul de Loanda* as Fritz Schultz, bedroom-and-table steward, knocked at the door of Senhor Pereira's cabin and entered simultaneously with the knock.

Mr. Palsover believed not so much in the knock-and-enter system as in the enter-while-you-knock; and, even more firmly, in the watch-while-you-wait. Particularly in the case of this silly beggar of a Senior Pereira. He'd bear a lot of watching while Mr. Palsover waited on him.

That biggish flat steel box with a tray! Like a cash-box. Mr. Palsover had caught a glimpse of it once when it was open and the Senior was putting papers into it. When a gent carries a little key on his watch-chain and uses it to open a box of that sort, there's generally more than moths in it.

"Good morning, Sir. Your coffee," he said, as he closed the door behind him, and observed that Senhor Pereira hastily pushed something under his pillow.

"And will you be getting up this morning, Sir?"

Senhor Pereira regarded his cabin-steward thoughtfully. According to the name-card in the slot on the bulkhead, the man was named Schultz; and he professed and called himself German. Fritz Schultz, a citizen of Hamburg. And yet he spoke what to Senhor Pereira seemed fluent, easy and fairly idiomatic English, but at the same time he stubbornly and unaccountably refused to understand German!

That this might, to some extent, be due to his own ignorance of the language and faulty pronunciation of the few words and sentences that he did know, Senhor Pereira was prepared to admit. Yet it was curious that the fellow never responded to, or even appeared to understand, such simple orders as

"Kommen Sie hier!" or *"Weggehen Sie!"* or *"Konnen Sie mir sagen, wieviel Uhr es ist?"* or *"Geben Sie mir das Buch!"*

A citizen of Hamburg, possessed of a German name,

and calling himself a German, who understood nothing of the German language, seemed to Senhor Pereira to be something of a curiosity; and concerning all curiosities he was himself curious when approaching Santa Cruz. And apart from idle curiosity, he felt he really must get to the bottom of the mystery, for it intrigued him.

Could he actually have done this, he would have discovered it to have a very simple explanation, not unconnected with the sudden and probably quite painless death, in a queer house in one of the queer streets of La Boca, of an authentic German steward, and the annexation of his passport and papers by a cosmopolitan sort of gentleman who later sold them in Shanghai to Mr. Palsover, at that time interested in such curios.

"*Guten Morgen*, Herr Schultz," smiled Senhor Pereira playfully; and then, in what he believed, to be German, observed that he was free from fever this morning and would be getting up for *Mittags-essen*.

Silly old cove! Why couldn't he talk plain English, since he could talk plain English as good as anybody? The ship was enough of a bloomin' floatin' Noah's Ark and Tower of Babel already, without this old blighter—whose own lingo was Portuguese and who not only talked proper English but had been heard to jabber like a maniac to boatmen, in what must have been Arabic—wanting to talk German and make Mr. Palsover talk German as well!

He had told the silly geezer once that, personally, he had forgot all his German, having been kidnapped as a child and brought up as an orphan, speaking only English and Hindustani.

"You understood what I said then, didn't you?" smiled Senhor Pereira.

"Ar! That's right, Sir. Every word of it. What was it all about? Your bath? I'll go and turn it on for you immediate."

"Now, now, Schultz! You know I didn't say anything about my bath. You know perfectly well what I said. I believe you are a bad man, Schultz," and Senhor Pereira shook his finger reprovingly.

Mr. Palsover smiled in a manner that might be

described as the waggish non-committal, thereby increasing Senhor Pereira's doubt and suspicion the more.

Curiously enough, he, on his side, decided that Fritz Schultz would bear watching.

As soon as the door closed behind his steward, Senhor Manöel Pereira rose from his bed, went to his medicine-chest and busied himself about prophylactic measures against the return of the malarial fever to which he was something of a martyr, in spite of the fact that he was an amateur of medicine, who considered himself almost as good as a doctor, and who was deeply interested in the etiology, course and cure of tropical diseases. Intravenous injection of quinine. The Saints grant that he steered clear of black-water fever, and that he was not sickening for another bout of tropical jaundice.

Having doctored himself, he took from the shelf above his berth a well-worn copy of his beloved Camöens, and lay down again to read. After a while, having reached for note-book and pencil, he settled down to his current hobby and relaxation, the making of a metrical translation into English of the beautiful and sonorous lines of what he considered the poet's finest work. . . . Put it into Arabic verse later, perhaps.

But soon he tired, frowned, lay back and closed his eyes. He could not concentrate.

That confounded steward.

A most likeable man, a really perfect servant, capable, skilful, attentive; positively fatherly. There was something benevolent about him, almost affectionate. One was tempted to regard him rather as a friend than as a servant—and the paid servant of someone else at that; a servant of the Anglo-Portuguese Equatorial Steam Navigation and Trading Company.

Why, those terrible great hands of his were gentle as a woman's, though powerful as a giant's. The Senhor had been as a baby in his hands, when the good fellow had changed his wringing wet pyjamas after the breaking of the bouts of malaria when the life-saving sweat had streamed from every pore of his body. As good as a nurse. In fact, he was a first-rate male nurse. What an invaluable chap to have about one always, as a general factotum, handyman, valet and nurse when one was ill.

This damned fever. . . . It wasn't doing his heart any good either. He'd really give the matter a second thought, if it weren't for the fact of the fellow being so obviously a German, while pretending that he knew no German. Why, the very first time the man had come into the cabin, he had shot the question at him, quite suddenly:

"Are you a German?" and he had replied,

"Why, yes, Sir. Name of Fritz Schultz. I'm German all right. Got me papers to prove it."

And privately, Mr. Palsover had wondered what the silly old geezer was driving at. What did it matter to him, anyway?

And now, as he went along to his glory-hole for dust-pan and brush, Mr. Palsover again wondered what was biting the Portuguese gent. Why couldn't he mind his own silly business? He didn't look like one of those blasted Nosey Parkers that go out of their way to get an innocent man into trouble. He had got his papers proving he was Fritz Schultz all right, hadn't he? And he had oiled the right palms to get his job, hadn't he, all good and proper? And he was paying the Head Steward what he asked, wasn't he? Well then, couldn't he be an English-speaking German on an old tub of a Portuguese black-beetle barge without being beggared about and badgered by every silly old geezer who wanted him to sling the German *bāt* because he had got a German name? He'd have to get hold of a few German words.

Ja! Ja! Schnitzelheimer! Schlossenboschen poop! and Mr. Palsover broke into a soft and blithesome whistle.

Cor! What a World it was. What a thing was Life. Fancy him, late Mess-Sergeant in the Royal Wessex, stewarding on a ship! Nice and warm and cosy again—after the 'orrible English winter. More like good old India. And piling up the dollars, not to mention the francs, pounds, pesos, pesetas, rupees, escudos, lire and what not. But wait till he was

Head Waiter or Chief Steward—Purser, even—on one of these old cockroach-coffins. Be in the big money then. Nice pickings as well as tips. Even better than being a money-lending Mess-Sergeant in a British Regiment. And no earthly reason why a downy bird who had been a first-class Mess-Sergeant shouldn't rise to any rank in the stewarding line of business, if he kept his eyes open and squared the right people. That's the way the money comes—and pop goes the beetle, every time you put your hoof down in one of these dark corners here.

Dirty foreigners. . . .

What had that funny old Portuguese got in the big cash-box that he was always diving into? One thing he had got, and that was what looked uncommon like a fine fat wad of nice clean new paper money. Big denomination, probably. British one-pound notes too. . . . And some foreign-looking ones, out-size, with photos of Presidents and things on 'em.

The old boy seemed to have plenty of dough, and to be free with it.

There was no doubt about it that the old Portuguese duck was getting pretty bad. Mr. Palsover had seen tropical illness and sudden death in India. Cholera camp, once. And any amount of nasty tummy troubles—dysentery and such—that the R.A.M.C. poultice-lancers said was microbes caused by eating bazaar melons and mangoes, not to mention drinking out of irrigation ditches on manœuvres, or out for a bit of sport. Malaria too. That could knock a strong man end-wise, as quick as anything. Yes, fever, bowels and sudden death; here to-day and here again to-morrow, if you was lucky.

What the ole geezer wanted was a bit of barrack-room treatment-and-cure; a quart of beer, boiling hot, with a tumbler of gin in it, a fistful of quinine tablets and then all the blankets, dhurries, horse-rugs and what not that could be piled on to the bed. Sweat it out of him. Still, since he thought he could do more by jabbing that little squirt in his arm, let him. It wasn't for Mr. Palsover to interfere uninvited, especially with that little key on the gold chain dangling from the watch hanging from the hook on the bulkhead beside the old boy's pillow.

Time Mr. Palsover shoved that little key into the lock of that very interesting-looking steel box. Always had an enquiring mind, he had, right from a boy. Full of curiosity. Made it worth while sitting up with the old bird, even if it was all night. Nothing Mr. Palsover wouldn't do to oblige. Stooard? Reg'lar sick-bay stooard he was, nowadays. Well, well, perhaps the funny old bloke would leave him something in his Will. Might leave him something without any Will. Leave him something without knowing it, if he popped off, one night. Seemed to feel the heat even more than Mr. Palsover did himself, although he was some sort of a Dago and ought to be used to heat. This wasn't nothing much, not compared with a real hot night in Umbala, say, about the middle of June. Be hot enough when they coaled, though, and shut every port-hole and door in the whole ship. Then it would get nice and warm. Pop off then, as like as not. Heat apperplexy. Good job, from Mr. Palsover's point of view, that there wasn't any doctor on this old floating bug-walk.

Did the silly blighter know what he was saying, or was he just talking through his hat, delirious like, the way the lads with malaria and what-not used to do when they went one over the hundred and reached the winning-post on the thermometer.

Sounded as though he was talking barmy whenever he talked his own lingo—whatever that was. Portuguese presumably. But it sounded all right when he talked English. Just as though he wanted Mr. Palsover to get what he was saying. Wasn't likely though, because he wouldn't gabble such silly nonsense if he wanted to talk sense. Stood to reason, didn't it?

Uncommon fond of him the old boy was getting. What about hanging on to him for what he was worth? Pickings. Worth thinking about. Might take on the job as his nurse, valet, confidential man, and so on, and then leave his service all of a sudden, one day, in a great hurry, with something useful in his ditty-box. Something like that couple-of-inch-thick wad of pound notes—if that's what they was—that he'd caught a glimpse of in that box.

§2

Senhor Pereira raised his head, stared round and let it fall back again upon his sodden pillow. Stretching out a hot and shaking hand, he seized Mr. Palsover's wrist.

"It's *wrong*, really, you know! It's *wrong*!" he said in the quick, almost toneless, staccato accents of the delirious.

"Ar! That's right," agreed Mr. Palsover.

"It should be used instead of lying there, benefiting nobody. Enough of it to bring the price down to that of—silver. To that of any common drug. Bring it within the reach of every hospital, every doctor. Why, in a year, cancer could be stamped out. Mankind could be for ever freed from that terrible scourge. For ever, throughout the whole world. It could be made a thing of the past, conquered more effectually than consumption has been. Other diseases too. All microbic diseases—typhoid, cholera, anthrax. . . . Think of the results of merely having radio-active water, for example, available in every centre of civilization, in every city, town and village in the world. Think of the radium-application discoveries that might be made, that certainly would be made, if every research-institute, every research worker, had unlimited radium with which to experiment. There are no bounds to the good that might be done."

"Ar! That's right," agreed Mr. Palsover, as the clutch of the burning hand tightened on his arm.

"And They need not fear publicity . . . exploitation . . . invasion. Of course it would be worse than any Alaskan or South African gold-rush, worse than any diamond-rush, if the news leaked out, and it were known generally. The sort of secret that would spread like wild-fire. Encircle the globe in a day. Compared with that, the Klondyke rush would be child's play—two crippled men and a blind boy. Do you know that to-day the price of radium is twenty thousand São Thomé moidores a gram! Fifteen thousand pounds a gram! Do you realize that the man who owned a pound of it would be the richest multi-millionaire in the whole world?"

"Ar! That's right," agreed Mr. Palsover, yawning cavernously.

"Eh? What?" he said, suddenly sitting upright and turning toward Senhor Pereira. "What you talkin' about?"

"Why, the other day a great philanthropist gave fifty thousand pounds' worth of it to a London hospital. A princely gift, and all in a little glass bottle in a little lead case that you could carry in your trousers-pocket without inconvenience."

There was nothing somnolent about Mr. Palsover now. Late as was the hour, there was no hint of weariness in his manner or expression.

"Have you got some with you, Senior?" he asked in an urgent whisper, putting his large bland benevolent face down toward that of the sick man.

"And They've got what is probably the only example of free barium-radium in the world. Nature has done in São Thomé what Madame Curie did in her laboratory. . . . Great underground heat . . . alkalis . . . acids. . . . Crystallization under boiling water . . . terrific pressure. . . . I don't understand it—but Norhona does. And They've got the biggest pure uranium deposit in the world. Certainly by far and away the biggest known one. Norhona says there's actually almost unlimited radium there just for the refining, as well as the uranium. And none of it's your one-gram-in-a-hundred-tons stuff. There's more uranium in that mountain in São Thomé than in all the Belgian Congo, Czechoslovakia, Colorado, Utah and Australia put together. Norhona says the richest ore in the world only contains one gram to five tons, and this ore is pure uranium. And They refuse to let a grain of radium go out of the island. It's wrong. It's the biggest crime against Humanity. I've told Them again and again. Mind, They are right, a thousand times right, in preferring Peace to Prosperity, the 'prosperity' of wealth, commercialism, finance and the rest of the devilish damnable lures to destruction. A thousand times right. They have all They need. São Thomé is self-supporting, self-contained. Why should They deliberately introduce the filthy poison of what passes for Progress and is called Civilization? Why should They turn that Garden of Eden, that Eden on the sea, into a Hell upon earth?"

"Ar! That's right!" agreed Mr. Palsover, again nodding his sagacious head.

What was the old bird talking about? Rayjum? Rayjum? Fifteen thousand quid a gram? Off his onion. Clean off his poor old rocker.

"But there's not the slightest need to run the risk of anything of the sort. They don't suppose that I would ever disclose Their secret, do They? They don't think I'd ever bring evil to São Thomé, do They? I would rather die."

" 'S right," agreed Mr. Palsover. "So'd I, any day."

"They need not fear that I should be traced to São Thomé, and the Island become known as the source of my huge stocks of radium. I could take away a big supply in proper lead and glass containers, in a strong steel case, just nailed up in a crate marked . . ."

"Tinned salmon," suggested Mr. Palsover.

"I could distribute it from Stockholm, Vienna, San Francisco, New Zealand, anywhere. Why should it ever be supposed that I got my supplies from São Thomé? But They wouldn't hear of it. They won't listen to me."

"Dirty dogs," yawned Mr. Palsover.

The old bird wasn't talking sense, and if he didn't soon wilt, pass out unconscious, or go to sleep, he'd give it up for to-night. And Mr. Palsover eyed the curious-looking key as he licked thirsty lips.

"They could trust me. They do trust me. What They fear is Chance, Fate. That some accident might let the secret out. Yes, They trust me absolutely—otherwise how should They let me come and go. Few come and still fewer go. Almost none. I; because I am a son of São Thomé. The Hadji; because he is trustworthy, though They only trust him because They must, since he is essential. I, the Hadji, the future Archbishop, the future Commander-in-Chief, and a few others of the Blood. Yes, They trust me, but They would destroy me as readily as They would trust me, if it were for the country's good. And if They suspected me of wrong-doing? They would not kill me then. No. . . ."

And Senhor Pereira shuddered.

"I almost fear to ask again. What do They care about the good of Humanity? And why should They? The good of São Thomé is enough for Them. The only humanity of which They know is São Thoméan. . . . Narrow. . . . Hide-bound. . . . Insular. . . . But how should it be otherwise?"

The high metallic voice fell suddenly silent. Bending over again, Mr. Palsover studied the dark handsome face, lined, yellowish, the skin now drawn and of a parchment-like quality.

Asleep? Fainted? Passed out? Proper ill, he looked. Better wait a while.

"And that amazing quicksand. God alone knows what wealth that contains in rare metals and elements. . . .

Helium, Strontium, Cerium, Polonium, Canadium, Barium, Pitchblende, Thorium, Carnotite, Autunite, Inonium, Rutile, Uranium and compounds of which as yet we know nothing. Priceless, invaluable. And all They use it for is—as a grave. A bottomless pit for the disposal of the bodies of those whose disappearance is considered desirable. And as a moat and a defence. I tell you that quicksand at the entrance to the Great Ravine is an eighth wonder of the world. It is an inexhaustible mine. No, not a mine, a store-house. Of the things that mankind values most, and some of which are of the utmost value to mankind, whether he knows it or not. . . . Rarity value; utility value; curative value. . . . And the radium with its highest of all values, a combination of all values. . . . Well, there it is, and there it will remain, unknown to anyone outside São Thomé, and to very few within. Properly understood, in its true value, to only one within. To one, the greatest of them all—and who is as rigid and hide-bound a patriot, as narrow and fanatical a reactionary as the worst of them. Yet the greatest brain in all the world, in its own line; greater than Freud; greater than Mesmer, Braid, Liebault, Bernheim, Janet, Charcot— greater than Einstein. The greatest scientist; the greatest psychologist and neurologist in the world; one of the greatest physicians, and perhaps the greatest surgeon.

"And all he cares about is to be the greatest São Thoméan.

"It is incredible, even to me, the wandering São Thoméan, the ever-seeking dove of that ever sea-girt Ark. To think that he, doctor, surgeon, alienist, scientist to his finger-tips, the world's greatest hypnotist, who can play upon human heart-strings and do what he will with the human brain, should support Them and refuse me, refuse Humanity!

"Refuse to release one gram of those tons of radium for fear São Thomé should be opened to the world; be invaded. And that not even by troops, by greedy country-grabbing annexationists—but merely by an alien civilization; merely by strangers; by commercialists, industrialists; by the foreign flag that precedes the foreign trade. . . .

"How could he? Such foolishness with such immeasurable cleverness; such ignorance with such stupendous knowledge; such foolish fear with such immeasurable courage; so little faith and trust in me who am so trustworthy; such terrifying narrowness in one whose mind is as broad as the Universe. For him to think that the secret should ever be betrayed through me!

"Why, without one soul in all the world dreaming that the supply came from São Thomé, I could reduce the price from fifteen thousand pounds a gram to . . . to . . . a shilling."

Mr. Palsover stretched, yawned and rose to his feet.

"And *that*'d be a damn silly thing to do, that would!" he said.

Cor! About enough for one night. . . .

III

Next morning, Senhor Pereira was undoubtedly better. Weak, but perfectly clear-headed. Clear-headed and light-hearted, until a word let fall by Mr. Palsover, as he tidied the cabin, reduced him to something more than his normal gravity, not to say depression or anything like a pessimistic condition of mind.

"Well, Governor, you don't look so much like the Wreck o' the 'Esperus this morning. Fair worried me, you did. Light-'eaded a bit, at times, you was," observed Mr. Palsover as he stood and beamed at the Senhor.

"What about a nice glass o' salts before your coffee?" he asked. "No?

"That was a rare ol' tale you told me last night, Senior," he remarked with friendly and benevolent geniality, as he placed shaving apparatus and hot water beside the basin which he had just cleaned.

"Tale? What about?" asked Senhor Pereira, sitting up with a sudden movement that almost spilled his coffee.

"St. Tommy. And some stuff called rayjum. Millions of pounds' worth of it," smiled Mr. Palsover.

"*São Thomé? Radium?*" whispered Senhor Pereira. "Did I . . . ? Well, well! What extraordinary matters to talk about! And did I speak in English?"

"Ar! That's right," replied Mr. Palsover. "Some of the time. And some of the time in that funny lingo you slings to your Portugeese friends. Unless it was the Arab *bāt*."

Senhor Pereira lay silent, staring at his steward in obvious perturbation, the expression of his face reminding Mr. Palsover of a well-known army phrase—"calculated to cause consternation and alarm." He was consterned and alarmed all right. Not 'alf he wasn't.

He had shut his eyes—like as if he had fainted clean off. What was biting the funny little blighter, now?

Suddenly Senhor Pereira looked up and shot a cunning

367

glance at him.

"And some German, I suppose?" he asked quickly.

"Now, now, Senior!" soothed Mr. Palsover. " 'Aven't I told you, time after time, I don't know any German. I don't understand it and I don't talk it."

"Yes, you certainly *told* me," was the reply. "And you say I talked to you about a place called . . . What did you say it was?"

"St. Tommy. Fair old yarn about it."

"São Thomé. Strange. I never heard of the place."

"Well, I heard about it. Hower after hower."

"And what else, did you say?"

"Rayjum, I said. So did you. A lot."

"And what did I say about radium?"

"Any amount. . . . That it was worth fifteen thousand pounds a gram, and that St. Tommy was stiff with it, and that you could bring out enough in your trousers' pocket to make you as rich as Jesus."

"Rich as Crœsus!" Senhor Pereira said something in his own language, something that even to Mr. Palsover sounded like a prayer to God, His Son, the Virgin Mary and all the Saints, if that was what '*Todos los Santos*' might mean, in the Dago's silly lingo.

Didn't look so well now. Seemed to think he had given himself away—bad. (Something *in* this.)

Yes, this undoubtedly was interesting. Very. The Senior might have been barmy and talking through his hat, but he had said something. And now he wished he hadn't said it. Therefore there must have been something in what he said. Stood to reason.

"Yerss. You got a lot off your chest last night, Senior. All about millions of pounds' worth of rayjum, and how there'd be a fair old rush that would make the Klondyke scrimmage look like a kids' Punch and Judy Show, and how you'd plant the stuff in 'Frisco and Bombay and Chamschatker and Berlin and sell it artful-like, in small packets—so as to keep the price up."

"What else? What else? Tell me."

"Oh, lots. All about your pal in St. Tommy. Him that's the

greatest doctor in the world."

"What was his name?"

"Same as the Goanese bloke that keeps a sort of little dry canteen in the Sudder Bazaar at Sitapur. What's his name—Machado? Fernandez? Gonsalvez? . . . No, Norhona! That's it."

Senhor Pereira's eyes appeared to be starting from his head in terror.

"Wonderful what nonsense people talk in delirium, isn't it?" he said, smiling mechanically with his lips. "Amazing nonsense. And you know, they can actually talk of things of which they know nothing. Sometimes in a language which they have never heard."

"Ar! That's right," agreed Mr. Palsover. "I do meself. I've 'eard soldiers too. . . . 'Orrible, sometimes. Shocking. Language that you'd hope they'd never heard."

"There's the famous case of the servant-girl who, in an induced hypnotic trance, talked Greek," said Senhor Pereira.

"Just as well, perhaps," opined Mr. Palsover.

More and more interesting! The silly old geezer—trying to put him off with this sort of stuff!

"Well, you talked good English and plenty of it, last night, Senior," he said.

"Yes. Talked in what is to me a foreign language, though I know it perfectly; and talked of places of which I have never heard and of things of which I know nothing."

"Never heard of this St. Tommy, eh?"

"Never. I know no place called São Thomé."

"And never heard of rayjum, eh?"

"Of course I've heard of radium. But I know nothing whatever about it. Not any more than you do, that is to say."

"Not even its price, eh—fifteen thousand quid for a gram? Well, well, now! Will you be gettin' up for lunch to-day, Senior?"

"Yes, yes. No. I don't know. I'll ring."

What had he done? He who would give his right hand rather than give one word of information on matters that were *tabu*.

What had he said, he who had always been a model of discretion, silent as the grave on all subjects that should not be discussed? Discreet, secretive, trusted by Them for those very qualities.

But who could control the subconscious mind? Who curb its follies and babblings when itself was not controlled? It was hard that he who had never in his life touched alcohol—because of its power to weaken inhibitions, to loosen the tongue, and to dethrone the conscious mind from its empire over the unconscious—should be defeated by a wretched microbe, should be turned, by this infernal fever, from a respected and proved repository of secrets into a babbling fool, a wretch that shouted aloud the things that he would willingly give his life to keep concealed.

He had talked of São Thomé! He had talked of the radium-producing deposits that would make the place a magnet for every gold-seeking ruffian, syndicate, mining company and financial corporation in the world. Their prospectors would come down upon the place by the ship-load. They would settle down upon it like a cloud of flies upon a carcase. Yes, and before long, São Thomé would be a carcase, stinking, rotten and corrupt. What had he done? Sooner would he have cut out his tongue.

He, Manöel Pereira of São Thomé, had talked? And to this man! Almost certainly one of the Nation-that-Breaks-Faith, one of the people whose Rulers' bond is as worthless as their word! Fritz Schultz, clumsily pretending that he knew no German, that he understood no German! They were the clumsiest people in the world in their international psychology, in their attempted diplomacy. But apart from his name, one would never have suspected him. Why didn't he take a French, Italian or Spanish name; or, since he spoke English quite well, why not an English name? Passport difficulty, presumably. Of course Fritz Schultz was a German. A Nazi German agent and spy.

But what if he were a German? There was no reason to suspect the worst of him. No reason to imagine that he was on this boat because it touched at Santa Cruz, the one and only place whence there was regular communication with São Thomé, and that only through the Hadji.

There was no doubt that They had rather got Germans on the brain. She, especially. Norhona too. It might have been the merest accident that the last intruder in São Thomé was a German. He might have known nothing whatever of the radium, nor of the quicksands. He knew all about them in the end, anyway, poor devil. But his coming might have been purest accident. Or he might, perhaps, somewhere, somehow, have heard something, and just come, not as a prospector, but in a purely exploratory spirit without any special knowledge and without any ulterior motive.

Well, as They say in the Citadel, 'Few come and fewer go.'

In point of fact, none at all ever went. Scarcely one, in the memory of living man.

What would be the best thing to do? The fellow might be innocent enough, but—there it was. He had got what were to Senhor Pereira the two most important words in the whole world: São Thomé and Radium. And he had got them in juxtaposition. Or rather, had got them in union, in close connection; had got them linked in his mind. São Thomé—Radium. São Thomé *for* radium. Radium at fifteen thousand pounds a gram.

Even if he were the most innocent and ignorant of Germans, even if he were not a Nazi German at all, the fact remained that he was a human being with human passions, almost the strongest of which would of course be greed of gain. And he was free now to go up and down the Coast talking of São Thomé and radium—at fifteen thousand pounds a gram; free to sail the Seven Seas talking of São Thomé and radium—at fifteen thousand pounds a gram! In every port and every pot-house in which sailors congregate, he would talk of São Thomé and radium—at fifteen thousand pounds a gram. Free, too, to go home, to go to the great commercial and financial centre of his country, Berlin, London, New York, whichever it might be, and get in touch with one of those ruthless men whose life-work it was to discover and exploit to the utmost such secrets. Financiers they called themselves. Company promoters. In São Thomé it was by other names They called them—vultures . . . thieves . . . destroyers . . . *vermin!*

And what a secret for such a man. São Thomé and unlimited radium. Radium at fifteen thousand pounds—seventy-five thousand dollars, three hundred thousand marks—a gram.

What had he done? And what would They do to him, if They knew? Mercifully put him to death, in consideration of his past services to the State? Or hand him over to Norhona with orders that he be hypnotized and . . .

Again Senhor Pereira shuddered.

Norhona! A pity he was not here now. Whatever might be the ultimate fate of Pereira, there would be no question as to this steward fellow, Schultz, ever becoming a danger to São Thomé. Why, in ten minutes Norhona would . . .

It might have been a recrudescence of his fever that caused Senhor Pereira, at this point, to shiver slightly.

What to do? How to undo? Can mischief ever be undone?

It can be arrested. It can be stopped. It can be prevented from going further.

This steward must be prevented from going further; prevented from going where he could talk of São Thomé, radium and untold gold, all in one hideous relationship.

How could he be prevented from going further?

What about endeavouring to attach the man to his own person? Keeping him under his own eye? Strange that he should already have dallied with the thought of making him his valet, body-servant, nurse. But even so, he could talk. Where could he get him, place him, keep him, so that he could not talk?

Senhor Pereira was well aware that dead men tell no tales, but although that may be a fine-sounding and, in certain circumstances, comforting proverb, it is not always either safe or easy to turn live men into dead men. No—apart from the fact that, to a sound Catholic in good standing and satisfactory state of conscience, there are objections to the turning of live men into dead ones. But better the death of ten thousand potential tale-bearers than that one of them should live to lift the veil that guarded the secret of São Thomé.

And without wasting any time in considering nine thousand nine hundred and ninety-nine potential spies, what about this one—the one who had actually cried aloud in this very cabin the words, "São Thomé. Radium. Fifteen thousand pounds a gram"?

Might he not be already uttering them in the steward's pantry, telling the tale to a crony, whispering it in the ear of the Purser?

No, he'd have more sense than that. Either he was too dull a clod to give the matter another thought, or he had just sufficient intelligence to consider his own interests, to keep the matter secret until he could divulge it to someone with whom he could do real business, either by selling his secret outright, or going shares in the fabulous profits of exploitation.

No, assuming that he were a man of intelligence, the real danger to São Thomé would arise when he got back to Europe.

Then he must not go back to Europe.

And since it would be almost as impossible as it was distasteful to kill him here and now, on this ship, he must be inveigled ashore, when Senhor Pereira landed.

Inveigled! A better idea. Far, far better. At first sight, anyhow. He must 'inveigle' the fellow into São Thomé itself. Once he set foot ashore there, he'd be absolutely harmless, a serpent sterilized of poison. Perfectly harmless. He'd be at liberty to talk of radium and its value all day long, especially as he could only do so in German, English and Hindustani, none of which languages was of much value on an island where the aborigines spoke some strange Polynesian tongue; the middle classes an impure and debased Arabic, somewhat akin to Malayan; and the aristocracy a Latin-Arabic language which, though recognizable as Portuguese, was not that spoken in Lisbon.

That was a splendid idea. Offer him much better wages than he was getting on the ship, take him ashore at Santa Cruz, keep him there until the Hadji arrived, take him to São Thomé—and then leave it to Them to dispose of him.

Splendid. . . . Excellent. . . . Very good. . . . Good. . . . No! . . .

No—not so good.

Senhor Pereira's ingenuous countenance fell. No. Not good at all. For what would They say, even to their privileged Senhor Manöel Pereira, when he confessed that he had uttered words that were completely *tabu*, words the pronunciation of one of which was a death sentence for the pronouncer.

How could he go to Them and say, "I have brought you a man who knows the secret of São Thomé, a secret that he learned from me. From me, who am myself a living secret. From me, who exist only to know that there is no such place as São Thomé whenever You let me leave her shores"?

Of course he could plead that it was done in delirium. But the most lenient view that They could take would be that a man who indulges in the luxury of delirium is not the sort of person to be entrusted with even the least important of São Thoméan affairs. The most lenient punishment They could give him would be to prevent and prohibit his ever leaving São Thomé again; and, much as he loved his native land, he loved this freedom even more, this precious privilege of being allowed to travel far and wide, to visit the capitals of Europe, to be the emissary, the agent, the eyes and ears, though never the mouth-piece, of the Council.

But more likely—almost certainly, in fact—They would say to Norhona, "Apparently a case for a little of your wonderful hypnotism, Doctor. Obviously our good Pereira needs mental treatment, a little suggestion. You will know what to suggest to him."

And They might order Permanency. They might . . . they might . . . they might even make him . . .

And Senhor Pereira raised thin yellowish hands to his face and placed them across his eyes, as though to shut out some vision too painful, indeed too terrible, to contemplate.

IV

Senhor Pereira, lying awake that night, worried, anxious, very ill indeed, and giving much thought to the problem of what would be the best thing to do, long halted between two opinions.

It might be catastrophic to take Schultz to São Thomé and confess the truth; and on the other hand, it might be extremely dangerous to leave him to go his way and do his worst, whether intentionally or unintentionally. That was to say, whether by organizing an attempt upon the fabulously valuable resources of São Thomé, or by merely talking about them until, inevitably, other persons made the attempt.

Senhor Pereira could not but feel that to let Schultz go whither he would, to talk as he pleased, was for himself almost as dangerous a course as taking Schultz to São Thomé. When it was known to Them that the secret had leaked out, it would be Senhor Pereira whom They would suspect either of carelessness or of treachery. The thought that They would scarcely be likely to accuse him of the latter, was of little comfort. A trusted emissary and agent who could be careless was just as dangerous as a traitor, and his suppression just as desirable. Nor, for suspected carelessness, would They punish him with death, torture or imprisonment, but They would completely end all possibility of his being careless again.

Alive, free, not halt nor lame nor blind, not deaf nor dumb, not suffering in any way—but rendered quite incapable of further carelessness or treachery for as long as he lived, and that might be to a great age. . . . He must not think of it.

It did not bear thinking about.

He must do something. He must save himself.

He was not a cruel man. Of that he was certain. He was not violent. His hands were clean. He had never shed, or caused the shedding of, blood. But how excellent a thing it would be if this Schultz should die. In no spirit of cruelty, punishment, hate or vindictiveness would he think of Schultz—but how desirable it was that he should die.

Murder? . . . No, no! No! But what They would do to him, Pereira, would be far, far worse than murder. And They would do it in no spirit of cruelty, punishment, hate or vindictiveness.

Kill Schultz? No, he could not possibly kill the man in cold blood. And if he would, how could he? The great powerful fellow, with his enormous hands, huge and strong as those of a gorilla. He could shoot him, of course, and especially if he had a pistol, and knew how to use it.

He had never shot anything in his life. Of course he could not kill him. Not on this ship.

He dare not take him to São Thomé.

He must not leave him to wander and to talk; to go to some financier, some Company-promoter, with the words *São Thomé* and *Radium* on his lips. He might be what he appeared, a mere ignorant menial—which was extremely doubtful—but a shout can stir an avalanche, a whisper can start a legend which may go round the world, till everybody knows it and somebody looks into it.

Anyhow, one thing was certain, Fritz Schultz must come ashore and stay with him at Santa Cruz, until he had made up his mind as to what was the best thing to do. He must not lose sight of the German. Perhaps at Santa Cruz he could . . .

No, he could not kill him. But he might get him killed.

Mr. Pereira's mind recoiled from the horrible thought and what he realized to be a strong and swiftly-growing temptation.

§2

Curiously enough, though for somewhat different reasons, a similar intention with regard to Santa Cruz and Senhor Pereira was forming in the mind of Mr. Palsover.

It would be easy enough to jump ship at Santa Cruz. He

could get a couple of hours' shore leave and get left behind; or, for fear of leave being refused, he could get the Senior to ask that the services of his steward be granted him, to help him get safely ashore and up to his hotel, he being ill and very weak.

The old geezer would jump at the chance; and even if the two of them did not fix it up beforehand, he could go to him after the ship had sailed and suggest that, now that he was out of a job, no doubt the Senior would like to take him on as valet and what not.

Yes, he had a sort of a feeling, a hunch, that it would be a more paying proposition than this stewarding. Stewarding wasn't much, even with a view to something better later, a job with rake-off attachments and frills. The graft would be good when he had the catering contract and such, but it would take a long time to get to it, and it could cost a good part of what it was worth.

There might be something to this rayjum talk (fifteen thousand quid a gram!) or there might not, but it was the sort of thing that ought to be looked into, and that was how millionaires made their piles. All bunk and bilge about millionaires getting rich by always leading pious lives; being virtuous apprentices; staying in the office and working after the others had gone home; leading old ladies across the street; getting in good with Chaplains and the Y.M.C.A., and saving your pence till you could take care of somebody else's pounds. Chicken feed!

Why, you c'd do it quicker on the race-course, with a bit of luck. Think of the bloke who had the stable-tip and put his shirt—ar! and his employer's shirt too—on the hundred-to-one outsider belonging to the Agger Kann, and sat back next day with a hundred thousand quid in his pants pocket. Get that out at five per cent, and you'd got five thousand a year. Take the virtuous apprentice a bit of a long while to do that, working overtime after the clock-watchers had cleared out of the office, and goin' to church on Sundays.

The way to get into the big money was to get hold of a good tip and have the sense to know it was a good tip, whether it was a horse, stocks and shares, diamonds kicking about round a native kraal, or nuggets of gold up the Amazon. Some of them savages didn't know it from brass, if half the tales were true. Why, gold cooking-pots they 'ad. Gold jerries too, like as not. But you had to get the tip where to go. And better still, you had to know how to get away with a boatload of the boodle.

There was Buried Treasure too. Those pirates all round Jamaica way. Lots of the lucky lads had had tips about buried treasures, written on bits of old parchment. Maps. Treasure Islands.

Ar! And what about old Kroojer! Buried all the sovereigns in the Johannesburg Bank before he hopped it. Stood to reason, there must have been others in it too. That'd be a tip worth getting.

And the whole lot put together didn't amount to much alongside of this rayjum at fifteen thousand quid a gram.

That was a tip, if you like. And that was the way tips came to the people who had the savvy to pick 'em up. Why, it was just like they wrote in books. Old geezer dying. Can't die with a secret on his chest. Tells his faithful servant or what-not all about it and how to get it. Like that yarn old Dinty O'Donnell was always reading at Sitapur. King Solomon's Gold Mines. Old Dinty reckoned he was going to go and have a dig in 'em some day. All rubbish, got up to make a book of! Only fit for kids or barmy Irishmen like Dinty O'Donnell.

But this was something different. What really opened his eyes to it was the way the old Senior tried to take it back next morning. No such place as St. Tommy, eh? And no rayjum on it neither? Tell that to the Marines! When he was talkin' through his hat owing to delirium trimmings, he kept on about St. Tommy, and he kept on about rayjum too. And he only said it because he didn't know he was sayin' it. Stands to reason that when a man keeps on talking about a place, there is such a place; and talkin' about stuff worth fifteen thousand quid an ounce, whatever it was, there must be such stuff. Anything couldn't come out of his mind that wasn't in it.

And then to deny it. He must listen in, good and plenty,

next time the Senior's malaria came round.

Yes, just how it happened in real life. The dyin' man tellin' the faithful servant. Only the silly beggar didn't die. Bobbed up again next morning and took it all back. That wasn't playing the game. Having said it all, he had ought to die. . . . Perhaps he would, next time. Would, if he had a little help. . . . Snuff out like a candle, the old Senior would. Mustn't do it till he'd told it all, though.

Suppose he told it all, and gave what they call clues. That'd be the time for him to die!

And if it turned out there was nothing in the story, there was something in that box! And he'd got a lot of stuff in the baggage-hold.

Mr. Palsover decided, then and there, that he would not desert the Senior sick and lonely, when the ship reached Santa Cruz.

V

There may be less desirable spots on the surface of the earth than Santa Cruz de Loango; and it is, though with difficulty, conceivable that there are less hotel-like places, calling themselves hotels, than the *Casa Real*—though Senhor Pereira in his wide experience did not think so.

The town of Santa Cruz de Loango consists of a few streets, and these are not paved with gold but only with sand. Nor is the sand gold-bearing. It is, however, deep and dirty, with a top-dressing of fine flour-like dust. There are no pavements or boarded side-walks. Nothing but sand.

This makes Santa Cruz a curiously quiet town; and, for some reason or other, the quiet is of a sinister quality. Almost the only sounds are those of human voices; not as a rule pleasing voices, nor raised in laughter, good-fellowship and merriment.

Senhor Pereira had a theory that the inhabitants lived by taking in each other's washing and selling it, as new, when washed. Anything in Santa Cruz could look almost new, if washed. As rain but rarely fell upon this City of the Holy Cross of Loango, its cleanliness was about on a level with its godliness.

When he had once remarked to the Hadji that Santa Cruz was the last place God ever made, that widely-travelled man had demurred,

"No, Senhor, the first place. A somewhat amateurish effort. As for the people . . . !"

And now to wait for him. God send him soon, or he might be too late. For what with malaria, jaundice and abdominal unhappiness that suggested typhoid, he was not feeling too well, especially as the repeated and increasing dose of quinine wherewith he endeavoured to combat the malaria, seemed to promise an addition to his little troubles in the shape of black-water fever. And his heart was getting very troublesome.

Meanwhile . . . Camöens.

And lying on a very dreadful bed, in an oven-like filthy room of the adobe-and-corrugated-iron two-storeyed shed that called itself the *Casa Real* and leading hotel of the salubrious city of Santa Cruz, Senhor Pereira endeavoured to merge the present with the past, to raise the threshold of his consciousness, and rise superior to himself and his surroundings.

What a joy, what a triumph, if he could live to make Portugal's great epic writer, greatest lyric poet, Luis de Camöens, better known to the English-speaking world; worthily translate him and make an English metrical version that would be real poetry, great poetry, like that of the original.

It seemed impossible that it had not been done before; that *Os Lusiads* was not as familiar to the educated British public as were the Greek *Odyssey* and the Latin *Aeneid*. Were not both the story and the verse of the *Lusiads* as noble as the Greek and the Italian? Was not Camöens as true an epic poet as Homer or Virgil? In his mother tongue he was. He who denied it was unfit to hold an opinion. The *Lusiads* was, to any cultured mind, as delightful as the *Odyssey*, as magnificent as the *Aeneid*. Oh, that he could render it into such English as would deserve an enlarge-ment of the phrase "the glory that was Greece and the grandeur that was Rome," and include 'the wonder that was Portugal' in the days of Vasco da Gama! He would like to do that. And when he had done it, why should not he, Manöel Pereira, do for the founders of São Thomé what Camöens had done for Vasco da Gama and his super-men of the Golden Age when those heroes first rounded the Cape of Good Hope and made their way to India's mythical strand, whence they ventured and conquered far and wide till they held the golden East in fee.

That would be a worthy ambition.

And if he were an artist, what a picture he would paint of Luis de Camöens swimming ashore when his ship was wrecked off the coast of Cambodia, by the mouth of the river Mekong; swimming ashore, holding something above his head. His money-belt? The jewels that represented his fortune? His commission as *Provedor* at Macao? No, his manuscript, the manuscript of the *Lusiads*! Holding it high above the hungry water, holding it from the grasp of envious Neptune, as he swam, saving his life that he might save his manuscript, his gift to the ages to come. Why, oh why, had Fate not willed that Camöens himself should write the glorious history of the founding of São Thomé by just such men as those who built the Portuguese Empire, and made Portugal the foremost nation of the world? Had not Camöens himself landed at São Thomé, on his way from Goa to Mozambique, where he was stranded and lay sick and wretched, even as Senhor Pereira himself lay sick and wretched, stranded in this dreadful Santa Cruz? Why could he not have remained in São Thomé and written one of the world's great epics about that semi-Eden set in the tropic sea?

But no. Fate was wiser than Manöel Pereira. That would have meant the end of São Thomé—as a Garden of Eden. An unveiling. Inevitable exploitation. The curse and barbarity of Civilization. Strange to think in this present year of grace and dreadful twentieth century, that Camöens, nearly four hundred years ago, had written a fine ode "*To the Discontents of the World*"!

Well, well. Now first to make a good prose translation of the lovely *canzone* beginning "*Van as serenas arguas*," and then to try his hand at some *redondilhas*, Portugal's native octosyllabic verse at which, if he might say so, he was not too bad; or perhaps some *quintilhas*, the five-lined octosyllabic stanzas on which Norhona, no mean judge, had been good enough to congratulate him.

Well, he couldn't do everything at once; and, so far, he had done nothing, for his head ached most terribly. But when he got better he really would translate the *Lusiads* worthily and write exactly seventy-three *quintilhas*, as Camöens had done.

But oh, what an inspiration it would be if only it were

permissible for him to take São Thomé as his subject.

An inspiration! He would be to São Thomé what Camöens had been to Portugal, Shakespeare to England, Molière to France, Cervantes to Spain, Homer to Greece, Tolstoi to Russia, Dante to Italy. . . .

Pereira . . . to São Thomé. . . .

Pereira . . . to sleep. . . .

VI

Treading softly as a mouse, looming bulky as an elephant, Mr. Palsover slowly, gently, opened the door.

Gawd! What an 'ole. Worse than the native *chawls* and *gurs* in the slums of an Indian town. Ceiling-cloth sagging down a yard, dirty as the Duke of Hell's ducks; walls oozing bugs, and covered thick with the marks where they and bloated mosquitoes had been squashed; floor covered in plaited palm-leaf with a top-dressing of dust and dirt that came up in clouds if you dropped anything on it; furniture—a rusty iron bed, legs leaning all ways, with a stained straw-stuffed mattress that just stank; remaining junk—two chairs that anybody would be a fool to sit on, and a rickety table with a rusty jug and basin.

Poor old Senior! And him a perfect gent and used to the best.

And he had got it. The best room in the best hotel in Santa Cruz.

Well, well! . . . No doubt he'd be glad to leave it. . . . And he had better leave it, glad to or not, before this Arab bloke came. What a rum game it was, the Senior a real toff, with wads of money, hanging about in a God-forsaken Hell-blistered dog-hole like this, to meet a bloke who only turned up in these parts twice a year, according to the story. Poor old Senior. Not dead, was he? He did look bad.

Moving almost soundlessly across the room, Mr. Palsover bent over the apparently lifeless body of his patron and employer. Hardly breathing. Now where was that watch and chain with the key on it? Under the pillow?

Senhor Pereira opened his eyes.

Where was he? In Hell? The dark frightened eyes focused on the considerable target of Mr. Palsover's benevolent face. Ah! Thank God! The splendid fellow! The noble fellow! The mere sight of him made one feel better at once.

"You wouldn't leave me!" he gasped. "You'd never leave

me here alone to die!"

"Naow, naow, Senior, don't talk silly. Of course I wouldn't. I'd never leave you, Senior," replied Mr. Palsover.

"Not while you got a shilling," he added in a pleasant aside.

"No news of the Hadji? You've watched? You've looked out for him? You've done your best? . . . You couldn't mistake him."

"No. He hasn't come yet."

"But of course he'd come here to the hotel, wouldn't he? The first thing that he would do, would be to come and enquire whether I was here. A man like the Hadji would be sure to do that."

"Ar! That's right," agreed Mr. Palsover.

Very annoying if the perisher walked in on them too soon, though. Might be a difficult bloke to talk to, and an expensive one to square. Might be too much of a Nosey Parker. Might be a bit of a nark too.

"Yes, yes," babbled Senhor Pereira, "he would. He'd never go on to São Thomé. I mean he'd never sail away without having made sure as to whether I was here or not. He only comes twice a year, and he'd be expecting me last time, this time, or next, and he'd make sure . . . Schultz, it would be a terrible thing if we missed him. Think of waiting here for six months till he came again."

"Think of somethink better than that, Senior. Think of a number and double it."

And Mr. Palsover thought of the number of English pounds there might be in the steel box, and of how he could double it.

"No," he continued, "if he doesn't come within a month we'd take the next Anglo-Portuguese that put in here."

"What? To São Thomé? God in Heaven, no! You can't go to São Thomé by a ship of the Anglo-Portuguese Steam Navigation and Trading Company, my good Schultz. In the first place, they don't know where it is, and in the second . . . No, no, what nonsense! There's only one way to São Thomé from here, and no one but the Hadji has the chart, the sailing-directions. . . . Do you know, there is only one harbour in all that vast island; and that nothing bigger than a *dhow* can get into that harbour."

"Reely?" observed Mr. Palsover, suppressing a yawn. The old Senior was working himself up. He'd be talking barmy in a minute.

Senhor Pereira grasped his wrist.

Cripes! How hot the old bird's hand was! Fair burnt you.

"Don't leave me! Don't go! Stay here till I'm asleep. Get me the medicine-chest and then sit by me till I go off."

"Ah! That's better. This cursed fever again. I feel terrible. Thank God you came with me, Schultz. You are a tower of strength and comfort. Schultz, I trust you absolutely. You must stay with me always. You must come with me to São Thomé. They will accept you for my sake; accept you when I tell them how you stood by me and saved my life—and the reports for Norhona. . . . So you must watch for the Hadji.

"Swear you'll keep a constant look-out for the Hadji. Watch every *dhow* that comes in, and the men who come ashore from it.

"Swear you'll get me on to the Hadji's *dhow*, whatever happens, at any cost. Swear, Schultz, that. . . . But no, there is no need for you to swear. If you are a bad man, your oath is worth nothing; if you are a good man, your word is worth everything. And you are a good man, Schultz. You shall have your reward. Get me on to the Hadji's *dhow*, and you will never regret it. You will bless the fate that made you my servant . . . that impelled you to help me.

"I believe in Fate, you know, for Fate is only another name for God. It was Fate that sent you and me on to that dreadful ship; Fate made you my steward, and now my servant . . . and friend.

"All you have to do is to whisper *São Thomé* in the Hadji's ear.

"You can't mistake the Hadji. He stands head and shoulders above the rest of them, the tallest Arab that ever lived. A great broad-shouldered powerful man, such a man as I should have loved to be. And his face, like yours, Schultz, is good. Strong and firm. Hard, perhaps, but a good face, and his eyes steady and straight and true. Slow of speech and economical of gesture, he is a fine man. He is a man whom those, who know him, do not ask to take his oath upon the Koran, for his Yea and his Nay are reliable and are accepted. A model to all merchants, an ornament to his Race and his Religion. You cannot mistake him, Schultz. There is no such other man on all this coast. No, nor in the Red Sea or the Persian Gulf. Not such another in all Arabia or Africa.

"You'll know him by his stature. You'll know him by his face and by his bearing. And you'll know him by his green turban of a Hadji."

"In fact, I'll know him, eh?" observed Mr. Palsover.

VII

Three o'clock in the morning. . . .

Yes, the poor old Senior was sleeping like an innocent child. And that was just about what he was too.

One of Mr. Palsover's great hands slowly, softly moving, scarce perceptibly, extended flat, explored beneath the pillow.

Ah, the chain. . . .

With the utmost gentleness, hardly seeming to move, the hand withdrew, drawing the watch, chain and key after it.

Now for the box, the box packed round with underclothing in the cabin-trunk.

Nice of the Senior to have given him charge of his keys—except this little one, of course. It showed a good trusting spirit, a right and proper spirit between a man and his confidential servant, valet and nurse.

From his pocket Mr. Palsover drew a bunch of keys, unlocked the trunk, very gently raised the lid which was apt to creak, removed a layer of silken underclothing and unlocked the box.

Yes, they were English one-pound notes, brand-new, and the packet a couple of inches thick. And the other wad? That must be Portuguese money. Nice-looking stuff, but you could never tell with these foreigners.

Reis? Escudos? And what might they be? Anyway, it was money, and money's—money. Interesting, to think each of those might be worth a five-pound note. From time to time Mr. Palsover glanced toward the bed.

Sleeping like an 'og.

Well, there was a nice bit of stuff, if anything happened to the poor old Senior.

And these papers in the big envelope? That was

important-looking stuff and it would be too, locked up in such a box as this. Pity it was all in some silly foreign lingo. He'd hang on to it, nevertheless, when the time came. Might be all about this rayjum concession. Something of that sort.

Senhor Pereira opened his eyes and glanced across at Palsover. Quickly he closed them again.

Ah-h-h-h-h! As he had thought. As he had feared. It had been too much to hope. Of course the fellow was a Nazi German. It had been foolish of him to hope, on the strength of his always talking English, that he might, after all, have been an Englishman calling himself a German. It was the other way about, of course. Not a Briton pretending to be a German for some reason, but actually a German, as indeed he professed to be, who always talked English—for some reason.

The British, ancient allies of Portugal, did not behave like this. Not for people of this man's kind had that honourable phrase been coined: "Word of an Englishman."

And this dog had given his word; had solemnly sworn that he would serve him with the utmost fidelity and truth and honesty.

A liar, a thief, a snake. . . .

Well, well. Life was like that, unfortunately. Very disappointing. He had come quite to like the man, almost to regard him as an Englishman, as he spoke nothing but English, and had almost decided to let him live, in spite of his having learnt too much. Almost decided to take him to São Thomé and—keep him there as his servant.

But now! Now he should certainly go to São Thomé—but he should not live.

Or if he did live . . . he would scarcely . . .

No—it would not be as the big powerful Fritz Schultz that he would live, nor as any other kind of Schultz.

He looked again. Yes, he was not mistaken. The cur had got the box open and was rummaging in it.

Turning his head away, he closed his eyes and groaned aloud. In a few seconds, without a sound of closing of boxes or moving feet, Palsover was beside him.

"Not so good to-night, Senior? Mustn't give way, now. Nice drop o' medicine, eh? Have a taste of something good out of the medicine-chest, eh? What would you like?"

"What I really want," whispered Senhor Pereira, "is paper and pen. I'm a little worried, my friend; a little anxious, in addition to not feeling too well. I am troubled in mind—as to your getting safely to São Thomé . . . if anything happened to me before the Hadji comes."

"Naow, naow, don't you worry about that, Senior. I'll get there all right. The Hadji'll take me when I tell him all about it."

"No, that's just what he won't do. No one is taken to São Thomé. But I'll write you a pass. I'll write the Hadji's name on an envelope, and a short letter that will explain matters to him. Then he'll take you. And the other letter which I will write you must give to Them."

"Who's 'Them'?" enquired Mr. Palsover.

"Well, show it to the Port Officer and the Officer who stops you at the Ravine bridge. Show it to anyone who asks you who you are and where you are going; and at the Capital you'll have to give it up. You will be taken to Doña Guiomar, or to de Braganza, or to my friend Perez de Norhona, or the Marquis Sebastien da Barettero or to Dom Xavier da Silva, or one of the other *cavaleiros fidalgos* of the Council. You know, there are two da Gamas among them to this day; brothers, Simão and João. Yes, same family. Not direct descendants of Vasco but descendants of the great Estevão da Gama—Count of Vidigueira really, in Portugal.

"Yes, the letter will receive every attention—and so will *you*, my good Schultz.

"And what'll the letter say?" enquired Mr. Palsover, the wary man.

"Why, that you have befriended me. That, as my fate overtook me here in Santa Cruz de Loango, I have sent on the information, notes, papers, documents, all that sort of thing, that my friend and patron, Dom Perez de Norhona, required. . . . That you have heard about the marvellous deposits of all the most valuable minerals in the world;

about the uranium wealth—and especially about the radio-active quicksands, and that you want to know more about those. (And you will, Schultz. You'll know more about them, all right.) And that you are fully deserving of reward. Don't doubt that They will reward you fully, my good Schultz.

"Now, a pen, a couple of stout envelopes, and some sheets of paper. You'll find everything in my attaché-case. I don't think the ink in the fountain-pen will be dry yet, even in this heat.

"Ah! Good! That's better. Now prop me up, and give me something flat to rest the paper on. Yes, the attaché-case will do. Thank you."

And painfully Senhor Pereira wrote, in plain round hand, but in a curious language. The person who read it accurately would require a knowledge of medieval Portuguese; of Arabic; of a Polynesian tongue akin to that spoken by the natives of certain of the South Sea Islands, as well as of a number of code-words known only to the members of the Council that governed São Thomé during the minority of its hereditary ruler, and to the few who were their emissaries and messengers.

The gist of the letter was to the effect that the writer, at the point of death, was making the best arrangements he could for the despatch to São Thomé of—that for which he had been sent to Europe. The paragraph relevant to the bearer, Herr Fritz Schultz, stated that he was, as his name implied, a German, and that if he changed his name he would still be a German; that he was obviously a commercial agent; the prospecting representative either of a financial and commercial group, or of the Foreign Commerce Department or Board of Trade of the Nazi Government; an investigator of mining and other concessional interests; an exploiter spy, and one of the vanguard of the vultures of Civilization.

He was, moreover, apart from his commercial position and interests, a rogue, a liar, a thief and a swindler. And, worst of all—he knew something; he knew too much. He knew about the radium-bearing deposits.

Senhor Pereira therefore commended and committed him to the especial notice and care of Dom Perez de Norhona who might, with clear conscience and easy mind, make good use of him—experimental use.

"There," said Senhor Pereira, as he folded the letter and placed it in an envelope, "it may never be needed. I sincerely hope that it will not. But if it is, you may rest absolutely assured, my good Schultz, that, if only you get that safely to São Thomé, the result will surprise you. They won't be able to do enough for you. . . . But They'll try. They'll do their best. . . .

"And now to make sure that the Hadji will take you—in the melancholy event of his arriving too late to take us both."

Mr. Palsover spoke soothing and reassuring words while Senhor Pereira made curious hieroglyphics that ran from right to left across a sheet of paper, and then more on an envelope.

"There," said he, "that's Arabic—of a sort. Show it to any *dhow*-master, to any Arab, in fact, who looks as though he might be the Hadji, a huge great man, probably wearing a green turban. And when you feel sure that you have found the right man, whisper 'São Thomé' in his ear. He'll know you are authorized when he hears that and reads this.

"Can't he talk English?" enquired Mr. Palsover, with a faint note of contempt in his voice.

"I should think not. Why should he? He trades north from here to the Persian Gulf—Bahrein way—for pearls, I believe. To Cairo, Alexandria, Haifa, the Holy Land and Turkey. And to Bombay, where I understand he meets other pearl-merchants from the South—Ceylon and the pearl-bearing lagoons of the Southern Islands. He might have learned a little English in Bombay."

"Hindustani, perhaps?" hazarded Mr. Palsover.

"Quite possibly. I don't know."

"How do you talk to him then—you and the other Seniors of St. Tommy?"

"Arabic. A kind of Arabic, anyway. More like Malayan;

but we understand each other quite clearly. Anyhow, his name is on this envelope, and this note says that if he finds that I have died here, he is to take you to São Thomé without fail, and to see that you get safely up to the Capital."

"He'll go there, then?"

"To the Capital? Oh, yes. He'll probably have a consignment of pearls for Doña Guiomar, the Regent, as well as crates and boxes of various articles of luxury that São Thomé does not produce. Quite a little cargo. Sacramental wine for Father Xavier; his special cigars for Senhor João da Gama; clothing and haberdashery from Cairo perhaps, for Dom Miguel de Braganza; silks and finery for their ladies—that sort of thing. He executes all sorts of commissions, every round. And in fact, he's our chief—what d'you call it? Pedlar? Purveyor? Yes. All sorts of little foreign luxuries.

"And he'll take the trunks and cases that came ashore with me from the ship. Give him the list and papers attached. There's a case of drugs and apparatus for Norhona and a box of books. Very special and important. And I'm afraid the cases marked 'Sewing-machines' contain something even more impetuous. For the Chief of Police. So do those marked 'Typewriters' For the Commandant. The list is all right, written out in Arabic, in the despatch-case here. This is it. You'll want that. . . .

"You'll help him in every way, won't you? And when you get to São Thomé you will receive your worthy reward.

"But there! I expect I shall be up and about before the Hadji comes, and be able to see to everything myself."

Mr. Palsover privately doubted this.

VIII

Mr. Palsover doubted it very much indeed.

In fact, it would not do at all; and he must see that nothing of the sort occurred.

As he figured things out, it would be quite a mistake for the Senior to see to everything himself, or to see the Hadji either.

Mr. Palsover—who was fond of a quiet bit of fishing off the end of a nice pier, with a nice pub handy, for preference —thinking in piscatorial terms, decided that there was certainly a sprat, probably a mackerel, and possibly a whale, all to be fished up out of this queer business, if he were skilful and lucky—as, of course, a fisherman needs to be.

If this perishin' Arab turned up all of a sudden, Mr. Palsover might lose the lot. Almost certainly he would lose the lot, and all he would have left would be the melancholy pleasure of telling himself—as he could scarcely tell any-body else—of the size of the sprat, of the bigness of the mackerel, and the thundering enormousness of the whale, all of which had got away—just the usual melancholy conso-lation of the unsuccessful fisherman.

And he wasn't an unsuccessful fisherman, nor did he intend to start being one now. Especially now; now when everything was cut and dried and all ready to his hand, including the introduction to the Hadji, which would be his ticket to St. Tommy in the *dhow*, and the letter that would be his safe-conduct to this Capital place, and his intro-duction to the Nobs there.

Not that he intended to go that far with it, not by any manner of means. He hadn't the education nor the experi-ence for that sort of game. Ask him to run a catering job, now, and he'd undertake anything, from a Sunday School Treat to a Buckingham Palace Ball. Anything. He'd cater for a Battleship Dance or a Brigade Dinner; quantity or quality or both; superintend everything himself, and give entire satisfaction to all concerned. Ar! And pocket a pretty rake-off for Samuel Palsover.

And there were plenty of other nice things he could handle, outside his own line of business. But this, he realized, was altogether too big a do. Too strange, too difficult, too awkward for him.

This wanted not only the brains that he himself had got, and the experience that he hadn't, but special knowledge that wasn't so common. It would want financial experts and mining experts, both of 'em; and working together. And it would want big Capital.

What was more, it would want somebody who could find all three, and play fair by the man who was behind it all, who started it, found it, and could lead 'em to it.

That was the worst of Big Business. You couldn't trust nobody, and if you could, they did you down.

The moment he had given the secret away, where would he be? Mug Street.

What he wanted was a gent, somebody like a Bishop or a Judge or an Officer. Colonel of a British Regiment. That sort.

But what did they know about business? Nothing or less. Mugs from Mug Street, when it came to that. Gave their money to somebody else to invest for 'em. (And he'd have a shot at that game himself by and by; investing other people's money.) If he went back to London and walked into one of those City Offices, whether it was the Bank of England or McIsaacstein's On-note-of-hand-alone, or any sort or kind of Financial Corporation, how could he sell them what he had got in his head? They wouldn't pay until they knew, and when they knew they wouldn't pay.

And perhaps it was all moonshine, after all?

No! Not it! The old Senior here was the goods. Straight as an arrow, honest as the day, and simple as an Army Chaplain. Half-witted, almost.

Of course it was all right. Otherwise why all these precautions? Nobody mustn't go to St. Tommy except in this Hadji's *dhow*. Nobody couldn't go ashore without a pass.

Few as there were got into the island, still fewer got out. What about all that?

Anyway, he had a hunch he was on to a good thing. He'd got a grand nose for money, there was a strong smell of money about, and he was going to get to the bottom of this. Follow it up for all it was worth. But they weren't going to give Samuel Palsover the muddy end of the stick. He wasn't going to burn his own fingers, and he wasn't going to dive ack over tock, head foremost into this St. Tommy—like a fool who couldn't swim, walking up to his neck in a swift river and that full of muggers.[17]

No, he'd go about this in the right way.

Suddenly Mr. Palsover sat bolt upright, and though his eyes gazed upon the face of Senhor Pereira, he saw that of the man whom above all others he admired.

That proper gent; that fine figure of a man; that downiest of wise birds; that best of Commanding Officers, his old Colonel, now retired, General Sir Reginald Jason, K.C.B., C.M.G.!

Raising a mighty hand, Mr. Palsover soundlessly smote his thigh. The very man! Honest and truthful as a perishin' Archangel; with the brains of a bookie, the guts of a prize-fighter, and the style and gentlemanliness of two kings and a dook. Retired, at a loose end and—unless he had come into money—about as hard up as any gentleman could wish to be. Young too.

Lord love us, thought Mr. Palsover, what a brain I got, and what a bit of luck. The very man. He'd know exactly how to go about it; how to form a Company, raise Capital, get hold of the right kind of mining-expert fellers and engineers, and start getting a Concession.

And if, for any reason, he wouldn't go into it himself, there'd be nothing lost, for he'd keep his head shut. General Jason was a gent, and not the sort who'd get the secret and then, if he didn't want to use it, sell it to somebody who did, and leave the rightful original owner, the Old Firm, out in the cold.

---

[17] Crocodiles (Hindustani).

No, he'd take it or leave it, and say nothing to nobody.

Or better still, if he didn't want to come in on it himself, he'd tell his old friend and Mess-Sergeant how to go about it. Give him good advice, so that he shouldn't be cheated out of his lawful dues.

But he'd come into it. He would come into it all right, bald-headed. He was that sort. Just the very man to be Chairman of a big Company, a wealthy Corporation. Fine figure-head, too, for a prospectus.

The St. Tommy Radium and Precious Minerals Corporation. Capital One Million Pounds. Chairman, General Sir Reginald Jason, K.C.B., C.M.G.

That's the stuff to give the troops.

Fine. And all Samuel Palsover would have to do would be to sit back and take his share of the money that the Company earned.

What would that be? Halves? Well, he'd talk it over with the General, and leave it to him. But he'd start with asking for halves. Halves for him because it was his own property, and without him they couldn't make a Company; half for them because they'd find the capital and do the work.

Anyway, he'd leave it to the General.

Mr. Palsover sat staring with unseeing eyes at the sweat-bedewed pale yellow face of Senhor Pereira who lay with closed eyes, his quick and shallow breathing audible above the trumpeting of the justly-famous mosquitoes of Santa Cruz de Loango.

Yes, that was the way to do things, and there was the scheme cut and dried. He'd get the sprat, use it for the catching of the mackerel—for it would cost a bit to go home and do the thing properly—and then see what sort of whale-bait the mackerel might make.

Right!

And Mr. Palsover, a man of quick decision and prompt action, stood up. That perishin' Arab might walk in at any minute and queer the whole pitch!

Senhor Pereira opened his eyes and raised his hand to his left breast.

"My heart," he whispered, ". . . I have these heart

attacks. . . . Medicine-chest."

"Yes, yes, in a minute, Senior. What you want first of all is your pyjammers changed. All of a muck sweat, you are. And a pair of nice clean sheets and a clean pillow-slip. All comfortable."

"Medicine-chest," whispered Senhor Pereira again.

"Half a mo', Senior, now. Don't you take on. You're goin' to be all right. Fair all right you'll look soon as I've fixed you decent an' proper."

Crossing the room noiselessly, Mr. Palsover went out and descended the rickety stairs to the floor below. Pushing open a door that led into the bar, he ignored the gigantic coloured barman who snored in a corner, lifted up his voice and called for the landlord.

"*Boy!* Diego! Hi, you pink-eyed Dago. Where are you?"

The tiny wizened Goanese who owned the *Casa Real* scuttled into the bar.

"Sah?" he said. "You calling?"

Mr. Palsover had had considerable experience of Goanese mess-boys, servants, and bazaar shop-keepers in India and, holding them in low regard, was toward them rarely kind. His benevolence ended at the line that marks off the lesser breeds without the Law and the Palsover pale.

"Calling? No. I was whistling like a perishin' canary to show I didn't want you. Strike me pink if you and your seven-foot bar-keep don't look like the dwarf pimp and the giant pander. Fact. . . . No, I was 'ollering, not calling." Silly beggar.

"Sah?" And Mr. Felice Diego automatically turned about for bottle and glass.

"Yes, that's all right, Boy. Quite a sound idea. But what I also wants is a couple of clean sheets and a pillow-case for the gent upstairs. And jump to it."

"Very good, Sah. But the sheets and pillow-case in Number One were clean only . . ."

"Yerss. Clean only once—and that was when they was made. Go and get me two clean sheets and a clean pillow-case, or I'll . . . *Jalditum!*" he bawled, bitterly insulting Mr. Felice Diego who, though bred and born in Goa, educated in

Bombay, and widely experienced in domestic employment in every part of India, affected to understand no word of Hindustani. Nowadays he was a Portuguese. Portuguese was his mother-tongue, though as a man of education and travel, he spoke serviceable English. Mr. Felice Diego was, however, accustomed not only to insults, but to loud-voiced Europeans and especially to Britons of the Sergeant-Major type, urgent and impetuous people who always got what they wanted—if they didn't always want what they got.

"Si, si, Senhor. All right, Sahib. I getting."

And a couple of minutes later Mr. Palsover ascended the creaking stairs with sheets and pillow-case that, by the standards of Santa Cruz, were practically clean.

Senhor Pereira still lay breathing quickly and audibly, and looking, to Mr. Palsover's experienced eye, definitely 'queer.'

From an unlocked cabin-trunk he took a clean pair of pyjamas and then, with the tenderness of a mother dealing with a month-old baby, removed Senhor Pereira's wet things. Placing the rusty water-jug and basin beside the bed, he took the Senhor in his arms, gently and skilfully sponged him from head to foot, and dried him with a towel and the top sheet. Folding these latter on the floor, he then carefully laid the sick man down, removed the other sheet from the mattress, changed the pillow-case and re-made the bed.

Again handling Senhor Pereira as though he were an infant, he clothed him in the clean pyjamas, laid him on the bed and covered him with the top sheet.

"There, Senior. All ship-shape and army-fashion. . . . Your 'air could do with a brush though. And for two pins I'd shave you. If I only knew how much longer that Wandering B . . . that Wandering Boy of an Arab, I mean . . . was going to be, I'd do it. . . . Lumme! I'll take the risk. You've been a perfect gent to me and I'll do the same by you."

Again descending to the bar room and bawling "*Boy!*" Mr. Palsover demanded "*Gurrm pani*[18]!" and bade Mr.

---

[18] Hot water.

Diego to look slippy.

"Bring it up to Senior Pereira's room," he directed. "And in less than two shakes of a duck's fanny.

"Bring it yourself," he added. "I want you to cast an eye on how Senior Pereira looks this mornin', seeing there isn't so much as a horse-doctor in this Gawd-forsaken 'ole. Santy Crews! Out of bounds for the Devil's Own troops in 'Ell I sh'd reckon," he grumbled.

When, a few minutes later, the proprietor of the *Casa Real* knocked and entered the best bedroom of his hotel, he was constrained to agree with Mr. Palsover that Senhor Pereira didn't look none too good.

"*Sahib bemar hai,*[19]" said Mr. Palsover.

"Without doubt," agreed Mr. Diego in good if queerly-accentuated English. "The poor gentlyman! Looking not so good. No doubt he has perhaps got fever probably."

"Ar! 'S right," agreed Mr. Palsover, "and you can lay to that. Fever! Not 'arf. His chubes too. Hark at 'em. And his heart. Poor gent's heart don't hardly tick over. I took his temperature and his pulse just now. Bad. Very bad."

"How much fever?" enquired Mr. Diego.

"Hundred and ten," Mr. Palsover assured him, "and still risin'."

Mr. Diego clacked a sympathetic tongue and shook a foreboding head.

"And his pulse beatings?" he asked.

"Fifteen to the minute. Exactly nine hundred to the hower," admitted Mr. Palsover.

"Thatt nott so good?" enquired the Goanese, who was a little vague on the subject.

"Bad as can be. Farenheit too. . . . 'Not so good?' It's absoberlutely rotten," sighed Mr. Palsover. "You haven't got a bottle of champagne wine, I suppose," he asked. "There's nothing I wouldn't do for him."

Mr. Diego smiled sadly.

"Whiskey. Brandy. Gin," he said. "Best Bombay Spirits."

"We don't drink even the best o' the methylated class of

---

[19] The gentleman is ill.

liquor," snubbed Mr. Palsover.

"Anyt'ing I can do?" enquired the proprietor.

"Bung off," requested Mr. Palsover as he started to strop a razor.

With the care and skill of a first-class valet, Mr. Palsover lathered and shaved his apparently-unconscious employer, carefully unfastening the neck of the pyjamas, and so arranging the towel that they should not be soiled.

Having sponged the waxen face, he powdered it as he had seen Senhor Pereira do, brushed the silky moustache and combed and arranged the greying hair to his satisfaction.

"There! Proper picture he looks, don't he?" he murmured aloud, with a pardonable self-satisfaction.

Senhor Pereira opened his eyes.

"Schultz," he whispered, "don't leave me. You won't leave me, Schultz? There's something I want to say to you. I want to apologize, Schultz. I'm sorry. So sorry I misjudged you. I know you were doing it for the best. You were anxious and concerned about me, and, naturally, about yourself and your future. . . . Our future. Now listen. I'm weak and confused—but listen carefully.

"If anything happens to me, *don't* fail to meet the Hadji, whisper '*São Thomé*' to him, and give him the letter, I implore you. The envelope with the Arabic writing on it. And whatever you do, *don't* fail to take the other letter with you to São Thomé. It's absolutely essential. For your own sake, I mean. I want to make you a rich man. It's the least I can do for you in return for your care and kindness. And see that Norhona gets the steel box that is in that trunk. It's full of manuscript. Notes, information, opinions, all sorts of writings—things that are not of the slightest value to anybody but him. He'll be *most* grateful to you and he will reward you well, apart from . . . apart from . . . "

The voice died away.

"Yes? Apart from what, Senior? Speak up! Go on. Apart from that Rayjum Concession, was you going to say?"

Senhor Pereira smiled weakly, deprecatingly.

"Well . . . well. . . . No good trying to deceive you, Schultz, is it?"

"Not a bit," Mr. Palsover assured him. "Not a bit, Senior."

Senhor Pereira smiled again. God bless and help São Thomé. God forgive him for endangering her sacred privacy and peace. God guide this dangerous German reptile safely there—and the Council would draw his sting, once and for all.

Would the Hadji never come . . . ?

Painfully raising himself a few inches from the bed,

"*God save São Thomé!*" he crowed feebly, and collapsed, gasping for breath.

IX

Well, thought Mr. Palsover as he gazed mournfully at the sick man, he had probably said it all; and if he hadn't said it all, he wasn't likely to say the remainder.

So the time seemed to have come. Nothing much to learn, nothing more to do, and the poor old Senior just about ripe for it.

No need for any unpleasantness.

Nothing of the sort of rough stuff the Police call "with a blunt instrument." Nothing of the kind of evidence that looks ugly in a Police Court . . . "Signs of a struggle" . . . "Pools of blood." Nasty expressions, those were. 'Orrible. Vulgar. Mr. Palsover didn't like them. Bad as "Disgraceful frackass." "Great force had been used." "Signs of terrific violence." "Clear evidence of manual strangulation."

Leave all that to criminals.

Not, of course, that the Police of Santa Cruz took much interest in that sort of thing. Too busy earning their livings, as they couldn't get their salaries. Get away with anything here, if you paid for—transport.

But these were morbid thoughts.

Looked quite nice, the poor old Senior did, now he had shaved him and done his hair. . . . Might as well have that watch and chain beforehand. Wouldn't want to go disturbing him afterwards. Disrespectful, for one thing.

Once again the great hand explored beneath the pillow.

Ar! Yes, there it was.

As Mr. Palsover drew out the watch and chain, with the key of the steel box attached, Senhor Pereira opened his eyes, almost automatically it seemed. It was as though his mind, his soul, his conscience watched even though he himself fainted or slept.

"Now is there anything more you want to tell me, Senior?" enquired Mr. Palsover. "If so, now's your time. . . . Never mind about the watch. I'm only going to wind it up. . . .

You're sure you've told me everything?"

With his eyes on the watch that Palsover was winding, Senhor Pereira smiled, raised his eyes to those of his faithful servant and whispered,

"Wait for the Hadji. Whisper the words 'São Thomé' to him. He'll take you to São Thomé. Give the letter to Norhona."

"Yerss, yerss! *That's* all right, Senior. Don't you worry. What I meant was, anything *more*. Anything you kept back, like. Anything about getting the rayjum out of the country? You know—Sufferin' Humanity. Getting out a hundredweight or so at Fifteen thousand pounds a gram, and bringing it within the reach of all, at a bob a time. Sell it in small packets in Timbuctoo and Strathpeffer, Singapore and Skibbareen, like you said. . . . Think of all them hospitals, doctors and Sufferin' Poor, and tell me how I can help."

"Norhona will tell you everything," whispered Senhor Pereira, and closed his eyes.

"Well, that's that, then," sighed Mr. Palsover, and softly crossing the room, locked the door.

Returning to the bed, he long and regretfully regarded Senhor Pereira with moist pale eye, and then gently, and with great care, seated himself on that gentleman's narrow chest, placed his right hand over his mouth and nose, and began to sing lustily and not untunefully. His mother had been quite musical and a confirmed admirer of the operas of Messrs. Gilbert and Sullivan. This may have been the sub-conscious reason for Mr. Palsover's selection.

"The flowers that bloom in the Spring, tra la," he trolled with all the strength of his lungs.

> *"The flowers that bloom in the Spring, tra la,*
> *Have nothing to do with the case.*
>
> *Not a damn thing,"*

he added, improvising relevant words when memory failed.

> *"Not a damn thing to do with the case."*

Senhor Pereira died quietly, as a gentleman should, any feeble sounds which he may have emitted being completely drowned, like mewling kittens, beneath the uproarious rushing spate of Mr. Palsover's song.

After a while, Mr. Palsover rose to his feet as with that sudden burst of energy of one who has dallied and wasted time too long.

Again noiselessly crossing the room as he took a bunch of keys from his pocket, he opened the cabin-trunk, and with the key on the watch-chain unlocked the flat steel box.

Yes, by Cripes. As he had seen. All of them good old honest-to-God British Treasury one-pound notes. A good two inches thick. About four hundred of the best.

Well, well, well! What a lad he was. What a nose he had got for the money! Chucking a good job on the *St. Paul de Loanda* to follow that nice wad.

Slipping the elastic-banded packet into his capacious pocket, Mr. Palsover again considered the foreign paper-money. Rum-looking stuff, but it might be worth a lot. He'd take that home and pay it into his Bank and see what happened. Real bit of luck that the English money was in one-pound notes and not those nasty fivers that suspicious-minded people keep the numbers of.

Now what should he do with the scribble? Looked as though the Senior had been writing a young book.

And these papers put together looked as though he had been making a book. Been to the Derby, perhaps.

Might be as well to keep 'em. You never know. Might be helpful when it came to forming the Company and getting the Rayjum Concession. . . . And all these letters and these papers in big envelopes? Better scoop the lot, perhaps.

On the other hand, if old Diego did think he had better bring the Police in, to save trouble in the long run, it might be as well for there to be something in the box. Otherwise some evil-minded blackguard might start them thinking it had been looted.

But surely he could square Diego.

Might be risky again if this Arab perisher turned up in the middle of it all. According to the old Senior, he might come any minute or any month. No telling how much he knew, or how much of a dust he might kick up if all were not above-board. If he was the only one who knew where this St. Tommy was, and the way to get there, the one and only go-between, the only what you might call lines-of-communication, between Santa Cruz and this St. Tommy, and came here a-purpose to pick up the Senior, well, he'd want to know what had become of everything, and how about it.

And if he was the white-headed boy at St. Tommy and an important man here too, there might be lots of trouble if he arrived before Mr. Palsover had departed.

And that Mr. Palsover couldn't do until the next Anglo-British put in.

The Arab would soon find out that the Senior had come to Santa Cruz, and had come ashore with another European. Anybody'd tell him; the Customs people, Police, longshore loafers, not to mention Felice Diego. No knowin' how much he and the Arab were hand-in-glove. No tellin' how many people, of his own, the Arab might not keep planted here, or that might roll up about the time of year he was expected.

No, Honesty is the best Policy. Keep the party pure, and your hands clean. Everything above board, ship-shape, and army fashion. And even if he got away on an Anglo-Portuguese before the Arab came, he might have endless difficulty in getting the Senior's stuff back on board ship and clearing out with it. Quite possibly the Police wouldn't let him take it on board when the ship came; not with Pereira's name painted all over it, him having come ashore as Pereira's servant, and Pereira dead on his hands, so to speak.

They'd want to hang on to it. They'd talk about next-of-kin—hoping to pinch it themselves in the end.

And he mustn't do anything that looked like a bolt. They'd be capable of saying he had done the old Senior in, for the sake of his dunnage and the coppers in his trousers' pockets!

And, besides, it might be unsaleable stuff or very difficult to dispose of. There wouldn't be much profit on the books, drugs and doctors' junk that the Senior was taking to this Norhona, for example; and Samuel Palsover would be a damn sight better without the automatics and rifles that Pereira was taking for the Armed Police or Civil Guards or whatever it was he had called 'em. Get himself into trouble, with that sort of stuff in his baggage.

No, let it all alone. Be content with the four hundred quid and whatever the foreign money was worth, and call it a day—until he could get his share of the rayjum and the other what-d'you-call-it.

Very nice work when you could get it—at fifteen thousand jimmy-o'-goblins a pinch. . . .

Closing and re-locking the box and trunk, Mr. Pereira returned to the bed, placed the watch on the rickety bed-side table, and regarded the face of Senhor Pereira.

The poor gentleman certainly did look very queer indeed. Very nice and tidy though. What about crossing his hands on his breast? No. Not yet. Wouldn't look quite natural, perhaps. Still, with the nice clean sheet smoothed out and drawn up to his neck, he looked a fair treat.

As nice a stiff as you could wish to see.

Well, he'd take a stroll down to the harbour for a bit, and see if there was any news of a big *dhow*. That Arab blighter could come any time he liked now.

Strolling round the derelict and almost deserted purlieus of the port of Santa Cruz, Mr. Palsover could see no signs of any new arrivals. *Dhows* could, of course, creep in and out, silently and unobtrusively as grey cats in the twilight; and of those that came and went in the night no record would remain. But so few were the ships, even *dhows* and bunder-boats, tied up in the harbour, that the presence or absence of only one would be noted by the accustomed eye.

No, there was no change. He didn't know a Lamu *m'tepe* from a Zanzibar *betela*, nor a Muscat *baggala* from a Bombay bunder-boat, but he knew that there was no new craft, and from what he had gathered from the Senior, the Arab's *dhow* was noticeable among the rest of the native ships, being bigger, smarter and better kept.

No, it wasn't there.

Well, he'd mooch round, have a chin with the ragged Port Officer and Customs men, in bazaar Hindustani, of which they understood not a word, listen to their foolish gabble in Portuguese, of which he understood not a word, and all laugh heartily together at the excellent jokes. Then perhaps a snifter at Sousa's American Bar, so called because there really was some American liquid in the place —the oil in the lamps.

And so back to the *Casa Real*.

Nothing had happened.

Senhor Pereira had not moved—and would never move again.

Descending the stairs in apparent haste, Mr. Palsover burst into the empty bar-room, the wind of his coming and the roar of his voice rousing from slumber the very large and dusky man who, dressed in a long night-shirt and embroidered skull-cap, was lying on the dirty floor behind the bar.

"*Boy!* Diego! Diego!" called Mr. Palsover. "Hi! Here, quick. *Ither ao! Jaldi*[20]! You boss-eyed bat-eared beggar. Hi! Come here, will you—and jump to it, you minnacher pimp."

"Sah?" enquired little Mr. Felice Diego, hurrying from the back premises in which he lurked, and pulling on a pyjama coat over his naked torso as he did so.

Staring, somewhat alarmed, he perceived that Mr. Palsover's usually bland and benevolent face was now dark, suffused and swollen. Obviously he was labouring under the influence of some violent emotion. Almost certainly this would be rage. These second-class Sahibs were men of wrath, and spoke loudly in their haste. Generally unkind things.

"Here! You Snuff-and-Butter bastard!" shouted Mr. Pals-

---

[20] Come here! Quick!

over. "What you been doing to Senior Pereira while I was out?"

"I doing, Sah? Nutting. I am not going up to his room. I have not seen."

"Well, up you go and see now! *Chello*[21]! *Jaldi!* 'Op to it, you flat-footed sunnuvabitch. Go on."

Raising the flap of the bar, the proprietor emerged and, not without propulsion from behind, hurried to the stairs, bounded up them and entered the room of the late Senhor Pereira.

Going over to the bed, he peered, drew back, turned a rapidly yellowing face to the minatory and accusing countenance of Mr. Palsover, and whispered something in Hindustani.

"Yes, yes! Mr. Schloots, he iss dead!" he whispered. . . . "*Murgya*[22]."

"Mur*der*ed too, if you ask me," replied Mr. Palsover. "Done-in while I was out. He was all right when I left him. Merry as a cricket. Chirping like a bloomin' canary. And now look at him!"

"But no one has been to the room. No one has entered in."

"And you mean to say he didn't let a shout?"

"No, Sah. Nutting. He has died without mentioning."

"You tell that to the Marines," advised Mr. Palsover. " 'Ere I leave him singing like a dicky-bird, and comes back and find 'im corpsed, and you pretend that no one has been up here! And never a squeak out of him, you say. Who's going to believe that? I *ask* you? What are you going to do about it?"

"Sah, he was very ill. Last night you are telling me. Very bad fever. Heart not working much."

"Well, yerss. That's true enough. I'll say that for you, Diego. I'll help you's far's I can. No doubt you'll wish to make it worth my while. I don't want to make trouble for you. God knows you'll have trouble enough. . . . I better see what's missing."

---

[21] Go on!

[22] He has died.

"Well, *thatt* is nott missing, Mr. Schloots, Sah," observed Felice Diego, pointing to the valuable watch and chain lying on the aged bed-side table.

"No? . . . No. That's there all right," agreed Mr. Palsover. "I better take charge of that, perhaps. . . . Well, what you going to do about it?"

"Send for Police, Sah," replied Mr. Diego bravely, though with a gulp suggesting pain, fear and horror. A dreadful thing, God wot, and an expensive, to send for the Police.

"Well, perhaps you're right. So long as you've got a clear conscience. But I got to obey my own, you know, Diego. I got to say he was all present and correct, merry and bright, when I went out 'smorning."

"Yes, yes. Man, you must speak the truth. Then you cannot be caught in lies."

At this simple proposition an almost cynical smile appeared on the benevolent face of Mr. Palsover.

"Butt, Sah, you will say how ill he was?" begged Diego. "You will say that he was at last gasps yesterday evening, and that you called me up into this veree room to see them?"

"Ar! But that was last night. He was right enough this morning. Yes, he was talking about going on a gin-crawl with me to-night. And, why, almost the last thing he said to me was, '*What's the girls like here, Mr. Schultz?*' he says, and I replied, '*Like they are everywhere else, Senior. Snares and delusions; and same value at any price you like.*' . . . That don't look as though he was thinking of his latter end and preparing to meet his Maker, do it?"

"Sah, I t'ink he had a stroke," said Mr. Diego brightly, as one who has probably solved a difficult problem.

"Wasn't a stroke o' luck, anyway, was it?" observed Mr. Palsover.

No, it was he who had had that, he told himself with an inward smile.

"Last night he was very ill, Senhor Schloots. Sir, he was veree sick. Sahib, you will give witness that he was dying man last night and therefore dead man this morning? You will tell that to the Police? Or, better still, saying nutting and helping me and Toto give gentlyman nice burial to-night?" begged Mr. Felice Diego, as he stood with bowed head and hands placed together as in prayer—to Mr. Palsover.

"M-m-m-m! What's it worth, Diego?"

Rapidly the proprietor of the *Casa Real* made calculation and submitted an estimate.

Mr. Palsover acknowledged its adequacy.

And, soon after midnight, all that was corruptible of Senhor Pereira received reasonably Christian burial in the mangrove-swamp that stretched its oily blackness from the lagoon to Mr. Diego's back premises.

PART IV

I

General Sir Reginald Jason, K.C.B., was suffering from the insidious and horrible, but not incurable, disease of boredom.

Like many another man of his type who has retired or been forced from a very active life, he bitterly regretted the step that had led him from the narrow path of work, activity, adventure, stress, strain and strife. He wanted to return to it and have them all before him again.

At the time, it had seemed the only thing to do, when his father, the oldest retired General on the Army list, had suddenly and most unexpectedly been cut off in the prime of his early nineties, leaving an extremely encumbered estate for his son to clear from debt, to save from the hammer and keep solvent, if he could. Apparently he could not. Taxation grew heavier, the times grew harder and harder, money became tighter and ever tighter. Things could hardly have been worse if he had remained in India, pursuing the straight course of his brilliant career. However, the dying wish of his revered father, expressed in what were almost his last words, and his own temporary but strong inclination for English country-life, had turned the balance. He had retired, come home, worked valiantly at straightening the desperately involved affairs of the estate, and had come to the conclusion that filial he must have been, bold he might have been, and a fool he had been.

To do the estate well, keep the house up properly, live as he and Antoinette liked to live, both in the country and in London, he needed about five thousand a year more than he had got.

And revolving these thoughts in his mind as he turned to enter his Club, he was aware of a bulky, upright and still soldierly figure, saluting him with vigour and the well-simulated guardsman-quiver of the raised right arm.

And who the devil was this ex-service-man in mufti standing before him with the back of the still quivering hand to the brim of a bowler hat? One of the Royal Wessex Fusiliers? God bless his soul, if it wasn't that old scoundrel Mess-Sergeant Palsover, whom he had always rather liked, and of whom Henry Carthew had taken so jaundiced a view. Called him the damnedest scoundrel unhung.

Lord! Why, the fellow looked as though, labouring under almost uncontrollable emotion, he were going to burst into tears of affection and joy. Not the emotions that General Jason had usually inspired in "Other Ranks," or in any other ranks.

"Sir . . . Colonel . . . General Sir Reginald, I mean," stuttered the worthy fellow. "You don't remember me, Sir, I . . ."

"Oh, yes, I remember you, Palsover. How are you?" replied General Jason, extending his hand, which Mr. Palsover wrung warmly.

"How are you?" he asked again, kindly.

"All the better for seeing you, Sir," Mr. Palsover assured him, his large face shining with happiness, veneration and a respectful benevolence.

"All the better for seeing you, Sir," he repeated. "And I been looking for you for a long time."

"Looking for me, Palsover?"

"Ar, Sir! And you can lay to that. I've walked up and down Pall Mall, and hung about this Club, Sir, since . . ."

"And what did you want to see me for? Want me to help you into a job?"

It would probably be something in the Club-servant line that he'd be looking out for; and an excellent one he'd make. First-class head waiter. But jobs like that weren't easy to get.

"No, Sir. No, Sir. Almost the other way about, Sir, though you wouldn't believe it. Putting it respectful like, I mean."

"And what the devil *do* you mean?"

"Could we have a talk somewhere, Sir, very private? I'm on to a thing, Sir, in which there's hundreds of thousands of pounds. Millions. And I'm afraid of losin' the lot through going to the wrong parties. I haven't said a word to a living soul, Sir. I waited till I could see you. I want to tell you all about it, because you are a gentleman and would never do a man down. And I want to let you in on the ground floor, Sir. There's big money in it; and if, when you've heard all about it, you don't want to come in, well, no harm done, and perhaps you'd be so good as to give me advice, Sir. It's *my* thing. I'm sole proprietor. And it's *the* chance of a life-time —a dozen life-times. The chance of a century. And I'll lose it, Sir. I'll lose the whole lot, if I get among sharks. If you'd go into it with me, Sir, there'd be more money for both of us than we could ever spend."

General Jason's cold and expressionless face almost thawed into a smile of amusement.

"Really, Palsover? You always were a bit of a financier, I understand."

"Ar! Financier is the word, Sir. What we want is a financier to help us to handle this—and it's ten thousand per cent per annum profit for us, if only things could be kept honest and straight and above-board. Fair play for the man that discovered it. But you see, Sir, the moment they know, they've *got* me! And it's

'*Thank you, Mr. Palsover. And good morning to you.*'

"They get the secret, they find the money, and they—carry on. Make millions."

The man was obviously sincere, patently genuine and speaking with the deepest conviction. If General Jason knew anything of men at all, here was an honest man labouring under the stress of an unshakable faith and belief in something big, something far too big for him to handle, but of the truth of which he was absolutely certain.

"And what kind of thing is it, Palsover?" he asked, half banteringly, in the style which Mr. Palsover knew only too well, the Orderly Room mockery that was apt to turn cold and savage before pronouncing a sharp sentence. "Infallible turf-system? If so, I'll tell you a profound truth. You can win a bet—but you cannot win at betting. Or are you setting up as a bookie?"

"No, Sir. No, Sir. Nothing of that sort."

"Don't say it's an infallible system for me to take to Monte Carlo to break the Bank. That's only done by arrangement with the Bank. . . . They are there to break *you*."

"No, no, Sir. No. This is honest-to-God real business. It is . . ."

"Not a gold mine, Palsover? Don't say it's a gold mine. I had the prospectus of one this morning. 'The Summit Flat.' Thought I was a *consummate* flat, I suppose."

"No, Sir, no."

"Well, tell me in a word. I must be getting along," and the General glanced at his wrist-watch.

"In confidence, Sir?"

"Absolutely," replied General Jason, eyeing the large earnest face with its moist yearning eyes which watched his own so beseechingly.

"*Rayjum!*" whispered Mr. Palsover.

"Radium?"

"Yes, Sir. D'you know the market price of it?"

"No. Pretty expensive article, I believe."

"Fifteen thousand pounds a gram, Sir. Fifteen thousand golden sovereigns for as much as you could put in a thimble."

General Jason eyed Mr. Palsover speculatively.

Thimble? Wasn't there a game known as Thimble-rigging? . . . The pea and the thimble. . . . Like 'Find the Lady.' . . . Yet perhaps he was hardly the person to whom ex-Mess-Sergeant Palsover would come with three thimbles and a pea, hoping to turn an honest penny.

"Fifteen thousand, Sir, for as much as you could put in your hollow tooth."

"Shouldn't care to do that, Palsover. But assuming one did want to, well what about it?"

"I got it, Sir. I got it."

"What? . . . A hollow tooth?"

"No, Sir. No, Sir. The rayjum. Unlimited supply, Sir. I know where there's a rayjum mine. I know where you could get it like getting coal in sacks. And at fifteen thousand pounds a gram!"

"Well, it wouldn't stay at that price long if you produced it in sacks."

"No, Sir. But even suppose the price fell until it was only a thousandth part of what it was, how would you like to sell rayjum at fifteen pounds a gram? Why, Sir, if you brought the price down to a fifteen-thousandth part of what it is, just work out what a quid per gram would be. And I believe that even coal-owners are pretty rich men, aren't they?"

"Well, I'd change with the Duke of Northumberland—financially speaking," replied General Jason. "Look here, Palsover, we must have a talk about it, as you say. Very interesting. Now, when and where . . . ?"

"Well, Sir, no time like the present, if you could spare it. And I know a nice little bar, near here, where we'd be quite to ourselves at this time of the morning, and I could give you a rough outline, if you wouldn't be too proud to . . .

"Lead on, Palsover. I'm not too proud to make kind enquiries after a line of goods selling at fifteen thousand pounds a gram. Tell me some more about it as we go along."

§2

General Jason had a friend who knew quite well a man whose brother was In the City. Up to his neck in the City. A live wire; a company promoter; a man who had tremendous financial interests and dealings, the interests being his own, the dealings being with other people's money. And the friend, being a fellow-member of one of the General's Clubs, was delighted to give him a letter of introduction to the gentleman who was up to his neck in the City. A little telephoning led to an arrangement whereby General Jason should meet the financier at his office at eleven o'clock on a certain morning.

The office proved to be luxuriously comfortable, its occupant charmingly agreeable—at any rate, to such people as General Sir Reginald Jason who came to him with Sound Propositions.

"Radium?" he said, after the pleasant preliminaries, as

he leant back in the well-sprung deeply-padded swivelling arm-chair behind his vast and magnificently-appointed desk. "I suppose the man who could corner radium would be just about ten times as rich as the ten richest men who ever lived—all put together. But you'd want a United Multi-Millionaires' Trust Company to start cornering radium."

"Suppose one discovered a new and enormous source of supply—and got control of it?" asked General Jason.

"Nearly as good," replied Mr. Scott-Marx, eyeing his visitor. What an extraordinarily handsome and distinguished-looking chap. What a figure-head Chairman for a Company. Nice useful-sounding name for a prospectus too.

"Very nearly as good," he continued. "I don't know much about radium, except that there are only seventy-five grammes of it in Britain, and that it is, I should say, by far the most valuable thing in the world. But I am under the impression that you don't dig it up quite in the same way that you do diamonds. I believe there is a process. . . . But I can go into that. I rather fancy you've got to have a uranium mine or quarry or what not, and then set up some sort of chemical smelting-works and treat your uranium as ore."

"Like smelting gold, for example," said General Jason, who knew much less about radium than did even Mr. Scott-Marx.

"Yes. Perfectly simple matter. They are getting various chemicals out of the waters of the Dead Sea at the present moment, for example. Well, this would be just as easy to do, and about exactly one million times as profitable. Where is this uranium deposit—if that's what it is?"

"Well . . . that I'm not at liberty to say, at the moment," replied the General.

"Quite so, quite so," agreed Mr. Scott-Marx, tapping his blotter with his pencil. He had heard very similar words before. They were almost routine with regard to this sort of thing.

"Well, now," continued General Jason, "suppose you found out all about the process and went into figures, I expect you could put up a proposition that would, well . . . that, while being attractive to yourself, would be—what shall we say, entirely fair to myself and my—er—principal."

"You can take my word for that, General," smiled Mr. Scott-Marx.

By Gad, he could! Supposing this chap really could deliver the goods. Suppose he, or rather his principal, some mining-engineer presumably, *had* discovered a real radium-bearing deposit. Made one's mouth water to think of it, in these hard times. He'd go into this to the uttermost farthing, but in point of fact he didn't believe that a very big capital would be required.

He flattered himself that he'd got a pretty cool brain. *But!* By the Seal of Solomon; by all Golconda; by the gold of Ophir and El Dorado—*and* a hatful of Koh-i-Noors! . . .

It didn't bear thinking about. Not in cold blood. Nobody could think of such a thing coolly. He had got to behave as though he could, nevertheless.

And as Mr. Scott-Marx smiled, the General smiled in apparent sympathy. In point of fact, what rather tickled his fancy was the idea of ex-Mess-Sergeant Palsover as General Sir Reginald Jason's "principal."

"Of course I appreciate that, at this stage, you don't want to blurt out details, General, such as where this deposit is, but it would facilitate figuring if I knew within a few hundred thousand miles. I don't want you to give anything away at all, but I'd like you to provide me with some idea if you could, roughly, as to what Continent it is in and what part of it, so that one could do a little costing, so to speak. The amount of capital required would be tremendously influenced, of course, by such questions as supply of local labour, transport; building, and other, materials; probable attitude of the Government of the country; accessibility; proximity to ports and rail-roads, and all that sort of thing."

"Yes," replied General Jason non-committally, "yes. All those are important factors."

"Might I ask whether you yourself know exactly where it is?"

"Well, I couldn't stick a pin in it, on a very large-scale map of the World, but I know within a little. I know the—er—

jumping-off place for it, for example. My principal, at the present stage, prefers to be the only living person who knows the exact spot."

"Quite so, quite so. Naturally," agreed Mr. Scott-Marx. "Quite. Quite," he murmured, thoughtfully tapping his desk. "Oh, quite. Now, look here, Sir. You've come and put this proposition up to me. . . ."

"In theory," observed General Jason. "To ask your advice on a more or less supposititious case; but with a sort of a kind of a proviso that if the thing became at all con-crete, we'd consider taking you into our confidence—very strictest confidence, of course—on the subject of how to set to work; how to go about floating a Company to develop this property, this deposit; and of how far you'd care to go into the matter with us yourself . . . financially and—so on.

"But meanwhile," he added, "secrecy is of the essence of the, at present, non-existent, contract. Absolute secrecy. A gentlemen's agreement to do something or nothing. And if nothing—to say nothing."

"Quite! Quite! Quite!" agreed Mr. Scott-Marx, slowly nodding his head. "What you've told me . . . not that it is much"—he laughed a little wryly—"doesn't go outside this office, except in my head. At the same time, we want to go a step further. I'm taking it for granted that you know what you are talking about, and are not wasting my time and your own; and I suggest two things.

"First of all, I find out all I can—and that will be pretty well everything—about radium. How, when and where you get it; what the process is, and what are the factors in production that make it cost—what did you say—fifteen thousand pounds a gram? And there again there are two things to bear in mind: first, that even if we can produce it no more cheaply than the few other concerns that market it, there should still be colossal profits; secondly, that we must know what sort of a proposition it is, from the point of view of estimated productivity and costs of mining, production, and marketing and so forth. Does it go an ounce to the ton of ore, or a hundredweight? That sort of thing.

"And the other thing is—what you yourself can do. Well,

now, the moment you send somebody to look into the matter on the spot—there's somebody else right into the very heart of the secret, isn't there?"

"I'm going myself," said General Jason.

"Splendid! *That*'s what I was hoping. Then we've got those two steps to take. Mine short and yours long. I learn all I can about radium production and marketing. I work out, as near as is possible in the circumstances, the general figures, going on probables and averages as to every class of costs. You carry on with the practical part, visit the actual spot, and bring back all the details on which the right sort of expert, mining-engineering-actuary or what not, could work. You could tell him absolutely everything except the place. As I said before; distance from railways and ports, conditions of local labour-market, if any; attitude of Government or competent authority, if any.

"And then I could get to work. With your name and guarantee, there will be no difficulty about floating a Company. . . . Without giving away the essential secret—not that I could do that if I wanted to—I could get hold of Aaronson and let him know how much we wanted, and he and his bunch would find the money and come in with us. No need to go to the public at all, I should think."

"Won't do to talk about it too much," demurred the General.

Mr. Scott-Marx laughed.

"My dear Sir! Talk about it! No. I'm not a fool. Deaf, dumb, blind and silly I may be, perhaps, but *dumb* I am certainly. I say nothing, 'and the rest is silence.' But I'll find out everything at the market-end of the business, while you study the production part on the spot. . . . How long do you suppose you'll be away?"

"Don't know, I'm sure. Take me about a fortnight to three weeks to get to the jumping-off point. Give me three months at the place itself. Back in six months, say."

"Splendid. Lunching anywhere this morning?"

"Er—no."

"Come with me, and we'll talk over details afterwards."

"Thanks very much. But before we go a step further, I

want to make it clear once again, at the risk of being tedious, that my principal must be absolutely on velvet. Up to now it is a one-man show, and he is the one man. He has got it in his pocket and all he needs is capital for its development."

"Quite! Quite!" agreed Mr. Scott-Marx once again. "Not but what there's a little more to it than that. 'Development' covers a lot. There's raising the capital; expert knowledge for production; expert knowledge for marketing. Your principal's concession isn't worth twopence to him until all that is found. He has got a cast-iron concession, by the way, I suppose?"

"There again I can't tell you at the moment, but . . ."

"Quite! Quite! Quite!" agreed once again Mr. Scott-Marx, who had heard something like this also, many a time and oft. "What's his idea, roughly?"

"Well, he talked about halves."

Mr. Scott-Marx smiled.

"What sort of a chap is he? Any brains or experience? Prospector? Expert? Mining engineer? Could we buy him right out and out-right?"

"I don't know. I don't think so. We must go into that. As I say, he talked about halves. I have guaranteed nothing at all except that he will not be swindled, and that I shall put his interests first—and protect them absolutely."

And again Mr. Scott-Marx fired off a gentle burst of "Quites!"

Very interesting indeed. *Very.* This innocent would require both gentle and careful handling. . . . *Interesting?* Oh, God of Golden Opportunities and Great Crimson Clean-ups! . . .

A gentlemen's agreement!

A radium-producing concession!

And a retired General straying with it into the City. Radium at fifteen thousand pounds a gram.

Be still, fond heart. . . .

Oh, *boy!* . . .

II

One evening, General Jason casually broke to Lady Jason the news that he was going away for six months or so. Lady Jason bore the blow with exemplary fortitude.

"Going alone, Reginald?" she asked, knowing quite well that, technically speaking, he was going "alone."

"Well, yes. Except for the man with whom I am going, and perhaps a score or two of porters and such."

"And who's the man?"

"I don't think you've met him. A very tall thin Scot with sandy moustache, freckled face, piercing blue eyes . . ."

"And piercing pink eyelashes, no doubt," interrupted Lady Jason who knew when her lord was romancing.

"Haven't noticed them. He speaks with a very broad Glasgow Highland accent and answers to the name of McClochity Angus Maclan," and the unsmiling General almost smiled wintrily as he compared Mr. Palsover with this inaccurate description.

Lady Jason was never inquisitive and rarely curious, but always pleasantly interested.

"Porters," she mused. "Waterloo Station kind—or for African safari?"

"Oh, both, my dear. Both, if I should ever get as far as Africa. I wonder what they'd call them in Tierra del Fuego. Doubtless porters by any other name would smell as sweet."

"Where is Tierra del Fuego?"

"Don't say you are as ignorant as all that, Tony. Have you never heard of Sinkiangkuankylung?"

"No, Reginald."

"Well, it's the capital of that parish."

"And is it to be a voyage or a journey? I mean, expedition or exploration?"

"Yes, I think so, Tony," replied the General gravely.

"And the object? Exploration? Scientific? Discovery?

Pleasure?"

"Yes, like that. Largely. Have you ever heard of that queer animal that . . ."

"Yes, Reginald. Are you going to get one? Will it be house-trained, or live in the park?"

"The Zoo, I expect."

With apparent irrelevance Lady Jason began to sing quietly to herself. Had the General listened—and considered the foolish words of her song—he would not have been interested.

> *"Gaily bedight a gallant knight*
> *In sunshine and in shadow*
> *Journeyed along singing a song*
> *In search of Eldor-a-do*
> *Over the Mountains of the Moon*
> *Down the Valley of the Sha-a-a-dow. . . ."*

She stopped abruptly and shivered slightly. The evening was getting colder.

"The Valley of the Shadow . . ."

No, on the whole it could not be said that General Jason was communicative on the subject of where he was going and for what purpose he was going there.

There was not, in the whole country, a single person who knew his destination, and only two who knew his purpose. He himself did not know his final destination, nor, for the matter of that, did Mr. Palsover.

This did not trouble General Jason in the least, and he counted it to the worthy fellow for righteousness, that he either could not or would not tell him more than that they changed for their terminus at Santa Cruz Junction, so to speak.

He might, of course, have hinted to Lady Jason that he had the highest hopes of making a truly enormous sum of money by this expedition, but for two reasons he judged it better not.

In the first place, it was *just* possible (so far along the primrose path of romantic hope had Mr. Palsover led him) that the expedition might fail to discover the source of fabulous wealth; and in the second, it was just possible again that Antoinette might talk. Not likely but possible.

For is it not well known that women are not only weaker vessels but leaky vessels; and that they have, practically speaking, nothing else to do but talk?

Nor, as General Jason was well aware, can they keep anything for long—their heads, their secrets, or their . . . No, no. Mustn't think like that about Antoinette. But still, what she didn't know she couldn't tell.

And Lady Jason was quite content.

Poor Reginald, within a year after retirement, had been first, worried to death; secondly, chagrined and regretful to the point of desperation; and thirdly, bored to tears.

And now he was perfectly happy again.

He had come down from Town one day, positively radiant—for him, that is to say. He didn't whistle or sing in his bath or give any such wild and unseemly demonstrations of light-heartedness as that, but he almost smiled once a day, and the austere and handsome countenance was not masked in inspissate gloom.

Yes, he was happy. She could tell. And she was very glad. Poor Reginald. It must be terrible to be so austere, so rigid, so statuesquely proper and correct. He was a dear, if he'd only let himself be one; and one of the finest men who ever lived. She was quite unworthy of him. How she did wish he'd be unworthy of her, now and again, just for a change. So much more human. . . .

And one night, after a particularly busy day at his desk and at superintending his packing, he told her that he was going up to Town on the morrow and sailing the next day.

"Letters, Reginald?"

"Bank."

"Positively no fixed abode?"

"And no visible means of support, by the time I get there."

"Return ticket, of course."

"Oh, yes. Kept line of retreat open."

"And I'm to expect you in six months' time."

"Roughly."

"Drop in to tea, or shall I keep dinner back, or . . . ?"

"I'll send you a wire."

"And if anybody should make kind enquiries as to where you've gone?"

"Patagonia. Between Polonia and Begonia."

"And Moronia," murmured Lady Jason. "It's beyond Ruritania, isn't it?"

"That's the place, Tony. You've pinned me down," admitted General Jason. And Antoinette knew how riotously joyful he was feeling.

And herself? Well . . . six months. Of this. And that. She'd write to Henry Carthew and make him fix up something. She would like a glimpse of the Season . . . and the sea, somewhere in the direction of Cowes . . . and she'd like to walk across some moors again . . . and lie in a deck-chair on a yacht off a Scottish island. And generally come up to the surface to breathe for a while.

Two or three months out of the six, anyhow. And Henry to be useful—as only Henry could—and without thought of reward.

"Well, good-bye, my dear," said General Jason, the next morning, with a kindly kiss and a cordial handshake. "Take care of yourself."

"I'm going to, Reginald."

"Have a good time."

"I'm going to. I'm going to have a marvellous time. Pity Henry Carthew's not in England. I'll send him a cable and ask him to take a spot of privilege-leave."

"Splendid. My love to the old boy. I was going to write to him. Good-bye. I shall be seeing you again in about six months' time. Good hunting. . . . G'-bye. . . ."

III

It is indicative of the fundamental adventurousness and romanticism of his sternly repressed nature, of the terrific boredom to which inactivity had reduced him, and of Mr. Palsover's amazing persuasiveness, that so essentially methodical, rational and disciplined a man as General Sir Reginald Jason should ever have entered the Fenchurch Street Offices of the British Southern and General Royal Mail Company and purchased, through them, a first-class and a second-class ticket that would enable him and Mr. Palsover to travel by one of their ships to Belamu, whence by changing to an Anglo-Portuguese Steam Navigation and Trading Company's boat, they could proceed to Santa Cruz de Loango.

But this he did, for Mr. Palsover had completely convinced him. General Jason knew when a man was speaking the truth, and he knew as well as he knew his own name, and better than he knew his own wife, that his former Mess-Sergeant whom he had known for twenty years, was speaking the truth, the whole truth and nothing but the truth, when he told him the story of the dying Portuguese and the radium concession. It was too like a "whole-cloth" tale; too like a cheap film story; too like the confidence man's trick; too like the gold-brick swindle and the Spanish-prisoner ramp, to be anything but truth.

No man, especially Mess-Sergeant Palsover, could go to General Jason with a yarn like that, unless it were true.

Some clever people would have laughed it to scorn, scouted it utterly, and have bidden Mr. Palsover to go while the going was good. But General Jason was a little cleverer than that. Palsover was the wrong man to invent such a tale, and General Jason was the wrong man to whom to take it. You couldn't have both men in it. Not two such men.

Given a Palsover who could think up such a *banao*,[23] he'd look for a mug, as he would call him, a flat, a fool, a Jubilee Juggins.

Given a General Jason who could accept such a yarn, the man who came to him with it would have to be something very different from a fat old ex-Mess-Sergeant of his own former Regiment. It would take something more like a plausible City shark, to come to General Jason with any hope of getting away with a thing like that.

That the real Mess-Sergeant Palsover could come and tell it to the real General Jason and be at once believed, showed what sort of story it was—one that bore the stamp of truth and carried the conviction of its own genuineness.

There were moments of course, such as those around four o'clock in the morning, when General Jason, with a sinking feeling in the pit of his stomach, asked himself if it were really possible that he was putting every spare penny that he could raise, into a wild-goose chase whereon he was led by the nose to an unknown destination by a silly old fool who had got hold of a Boys' Story-paper yarn about an inexhaustible mine of immeasurable wealth. A wonder it wasn't a tale of buried treasure, a story of hidden gold, or some such moonshine as that.

§2

As, on the voyage to Belamu, he sat in his deck-chair, going over the story again and again, General Jason's faith grew, his faith in Sergeant Palsover, in Mr. Pereira, who had so opportunely died, and in the account of the radio-active quick-sand and the uranium deposit—the uranium mines, indeed, as he began to think of them.

With a hint of the *credo quia incredibile* attitude of mind, he again and again worked through to the conclusion that the tale was too fantastic to be untrue, and Palsover too fantastic a tale-bearer to bring anything but the truth. . . .

---

[23] Plot, swindle, frame-up (Hindustani).

The only weak spot in the story was provided by the un-known Arab. There imagination boggled, and cold practical common sense intervened. But whenever Realism con-quered Romanticism and said,

'You are behaving like a boy. You are being silly, over-suggestible and gullible,' Hope came to the rescue and told a flattering tale. Why shouldn't there be a pearl-merchant, or any other kind of merchant, who called at Santa Cruz de Loango twice a year? Nothing more probable, and few jobs more profitable in that line of business—for the man who could get it. The twice-a-year arrangement was probably decided by the two monsoons. They blew every six months almost to the day, first north-east and then south-west. The Arab would go up with one and down with the other. And why shouldn't he be met at this Santa Cruz place, on each journey? Probably he had appointments with several differ-ent people at this last port that he touched on the main-land.

And not only did Hope come to the assistance of Romance and romantic imagination, but the somewhat comforting knowledge of the fact that this was a thing that was going to be put to the test. When they reached this Santa Cruz place, Palsover would, according to his story, take him straight to a Goanese feller who kept a ram-shackle native hotel, at which this Arab was in the habit of calling every voyage to enquire whether there were any letters, messages, or a passenger for him. General Jason did not really doubt this part of the Palsover story any more than he doubted any other part—particularly as it was open to proof and shortly would be proved.

Well, if this Goanese told him that he expected the Arab pearl-merchant but that he had not yet arrived, it was pretty certain that he would come toward the end of the north-east monsoon. Palsover had worked out the feller's dates pretty carefully, from the information the Goanese had given him.

He'd only have to sit down and wait for him, sit down in that same hotel, and the Arab would roll up. Very interesting and very romantic, to think that he, General Sir Reginald

Jason, recently of Simla, London and Hardingley Park, should be bearing down upon a tiny obscure spot on the map of the Southern Hemisphere, a place so insignificant and small as almost to answer to the definition of a point— that which has neither parts nor magnitude but only position—and that an Arab pearl-merchant from Basra, Abadan, Mohammera, Bahrein and Muscat would, in his *dhow* with its single sail and crew of three or four men, be also bearing down upon the same spot to meet him, though unconscious of that fact. . . .

Some part of each day General Jason spent in the company of Mr. Palsover, talking over the endless subjects of interest connected with the expedition.

"What are we going to do if this Arab fellow doesn't turn up?" he said one evening, as they walked the deck together after dinner.

"He'll turn up all right, Sir, sooner or later," Mr. Palsover reassured him. "He has never failed yet, according to the landlord of the *Caser Reel*. . . . Oh, yerss, he knows him all right. Knows him well. One of his regulars, you might say."

"And you've got the letter of introduction to him all safe?"

"Ar! That's right, Sir; and you can lay to that. I'll hand that over to you as soon as we gets to Santa Cruz. I keeps it locked up in my trunk for fear of losing it."

"That's right. Trust you to keep it safe, Palsover. We should be in a bit of a fix if you hadn't got it."

"Ar! That's right, Sir. Fair up a gum-tree. But don't you worry about that. And when I hand it to you, Sir, I'm going to ask you to take charge altogether—and carry on. Work it off on the Arab yourself, I mean. Just take charge and go ahead."

"Very trusting of you, Palsover. I appreciate it."

Mr. Palsover smiled, partly with pleasure at the General's kind words, and partly at the thought that he would thus stand from under.

Mr. Palsover had for many long years been an expert in the art of standing from under, and an unerring judge of the right moment at which to come in out of the rain.

Whatever danger there might attach to this St. Tommy business, began at the moment the Senior's letter was handed over to the Arab, and the bearer of it set foot on the Arab's *dhow*. The Arab had got him then, and got him for keeps, good and proper. Got him right where he wanted him, if so be he did want him. And if he didn't, but was quite prepared to take him to this St. Tommy place, the next danger-point, if any, would be that at which the bearer of the letter to this bloke Norhona, handed it over, and Norhona read it.

For Norhona had got him then, good and proper, and just where he wanted him, and no going back about it. Not if what the old Senior had said was true—that there was no way of getting from Santa Cruz into St. Tommy and out again except by the Arab's *dhow*.

Of course, there might be no danger at all, but that was not Mr. Palsover's impression. The old Senior had talked too much about '*Them*' and what They'd do to yer if They felt like it. And if all the truth was known, the Senior himself was in a bit of a perishing blue funk of doing anything that They did not like. Not only this Norhona fellow—who seemed to be the Big Noise there, or one of them—but this Regent or whatever she was, Donah What's-her-name, and the old Dook who had the same name as the greengrocer in the very street in which Mr. Palsover had been born, and that was a queer come-uppance if you like. Braganza. He'd been a very nice old Jew and kept a greengrocer's shop.

And then this Council that the Senior used to babble about, when he was off his rocker with malaria. From the way he had talked, the Senior wouldn't like to take a running kick at the pants of any one of that lot. No. Not he; not at any price. Talked about them like a rookie might talk about the Regimental Sergeant-Major; or like Mr. Palsover himself might talk about a set of Officers sitting on him in Court Martial, yes, or about the Commander-in-Chief and the whole Army Council put together.

No doubt about it, the old Senior had certainly got the wind up when he thought about that lot. And he somehow gave you the impression that anybody who got into St. Tommy uninvited would get on about as fast and far as a small fly in a big spider's web, and come to about the same sort of an end.

Well, far from wishing the General any harm, he wished him all the good luck in the world, but—better him than Mr. Palsover, wandering about St. Tommy. He was a British General and They had ought to have a proper respect for such. He'd know some silly foreign lingo in which they'd all be able to talk together, friendly and comfortable, and—well, he'd know the right knives and forks; know better what to do. Probably one look and two words out of him would blast 'em out of his way.

Anyhow, Generals first, Sergeants afterwards. A long way afterwards—if at all. No. He'd keep out of St. Tommy.

"Thank you, Sir," he said. "I'm quite sure it will be best for all concerned if, as soon as we get to Santa Cruz, I hand over, stand aside, and leave the rest to you. Everything."

"Well, probably you are wise, Palsover. You can trust me to do my best and to look after your interests," replied the General.

"I can, Sir. I do. From the day we land at Santa Cruz, I'm an on-looker. I won't even come to the place, or, at any rate, I won't go ashore there. I'll just keep out of it, for fear I said or did the wrong thing. Queered your pitch like, Sir, and was a hindrance and a drag on you."

This rather touched General Jason, although he gave no sign of the fact.

"Then I'll simply give the Arabic letter to this pearl-merchant, if and when we meet him, and tell him I want him to give me passage to—Where-is-it. By the way, you've never yet told me the name of the place, Palsover."

"No, Sir. No, Sir. We can't be too careful; and I thought if I didn't so much as whisper it, not even to you, Sir, until we had found this Arab, there couldn't be no possible chance of its leaking out."

"Quite a sound idea. But you don't suppose I should tell anybody, do you?"

"No, Sir. No, Sir. Not for one moment. But as my old

mother used to say, when more than one has got a secret, it isn't a secret any longer. Of course, you wouldn't tell anybody, Sir; nobody at all, neither that shark—I mean that finnanceer gentleman—in London, nor anybody on the ship here. I didn't even think it would slip out in conversation when some gentleman said to you in the bar,

'And how far are you going, General?' or something like that. I didn't think such a thing, for one moment; but I did think that if I just kept it to myself, the same couldn't happen to you as happened to that poor old Senior Pereira what died."

"How do you mean?"

"Why, he told me in his sleep, Sir! Well, not to say sleep. Delirium trimmins. Fever. Kept on babbling nonsense—and some damn good sound sense among it, Sir, though he didn't know what he was saying."

"Delirious? Fever?"

"Ar! And you can lay to that, Sir. Delirious as you like. And through it he talked by the hower; and told me all about this Where-is-it place, and about the you-know-what mines and concessions, and how he had got to meet this Arab who would take him from Santa Cruz to the place. . . . And—well—gave the whole show away."

"Well, no doubt you are right, Palsover. Don't go and do it yourself, though."

"Do what, Sir?"

"Get delirious and—talk."

"Me, Sir? It's many a long year since I had malaria in India; and I keeps my cabin door locked and bolted, and my coat hanging over the key-hole. No, Sir, anybody as wants to listen to me doin' deliriums has got to come down over the side on a rope and shove his head in the port-hole.

"And then he'd hear something to his disadvantage, Sir," added Mr. Palsover, and his benevolent face looked, for the moment, quite unkind.

IV

And in the fullness of time and exactly up to that time, the British Southern and General Mail Company's liner *Gibraltar* reached Belamu, and along with one or two other unfortunates, General Jason and Mr. Palsover exchanged its innumerable and admirable amenities for the comparatively squalid discomfort of the *St. José de Coimbra* of the Anglo-Portuguese Steam Navigation and Trading Company.

Fate in sportive merry mood and in the guise of a Portuguese gentleman, who probably hailed from Goa, and performed the functions of Chief Steward, Head Waiter and Purser of the *St. José de Coimbra*, allotted to General Jason the cabin corresponding to that occupied by the late Senhor Pereira on the sister ship *St. Paul de Loanda*. This was not a very remarkable coincidence, in view of the fact that each was the best cabin on the ship, and that the best was what General Jason demanded.

It afforded Mr. Palsover considerable private amusement and it tickled his fancy enormously, to knock on the General's cabin door in the early morning, enter, and regard him lying in what appeared to be the very same cabin and on the very same berth that was formerly occupied by the late Senhor Pereira.

It seemed somehow to be a good omen.

Not that it would ever for one moment enter his head to do anything so disrespectful as to sit on the General's chest and place his hand over his mouth. But—well—there it was. Lying in that berth, the Senior had given him one of the most colossal tips ever given by one man to another. Lying in that very berth now was General Jason, the man who would turn that tip into the gold it promised.

And he absolutely insisted on being allowed to valet the General, to bring him his morning tea, to tidy his cabin and to shave him.

Quite like old times with the dear old Senior, God bless him.

§2

In spite of what Mr. Palsover had already told him, the *Casa Real* and its proprietor, Felice Diego, came as something of a shock to General Jason. He had not visualized anything quite so low in the scale of accommodation for man and beast, although he had travelled Home by the overland route from India, and was not unacquainted with *khans* and *caravanserais* that were never intended for the entertainment of Europeans.

However, it was a small matter, and his sojourn in the leading hotel of Santa Cruz might be brief. He earnestly hoped that it would.

Having introduced General Jason as an English Sahib of the highest and noblest class, and demanded for him all of the best that the *Casa Real* could supply in the way of dirty rice, skinny chickens, fried bananas, goats' milk and Best Bombay Spirits, and seen the General installed in not only the room but the very bed in which Senhor Pereira had died, he sought a private interview with the proprietor.

"Well, Boy, so the Police haven't got you yet, then?"

"Police, Senhor Schloots? Why Police getting me?"

"Why not? Over the murder of poor old Senior Pereira, I mean."

"*Sah!* Sh-h-h-h. Master must not talk like that! Murder! . . . Senhor Pereira died in his bed. Willingly. Freely."

"And you never heard any more from the Police at all?"

"Not officially, Sah. No. When there was Police question about something of Senhor Pereira's at Customs House, I say he go off one night in *dhow* very sudden, very quiet, paying his bill and saying he not coming back for a long time."

"And then you paid the policeman's bill, eh? And *he* didn't come back for a long time, eh?"

Mr. Felice Diego put his head on one side, waggled his hands deprecatingly and smiled copiously.

"So you was lucky, eh? Well out of a nasty mess. Now when that trouble crops up again . . ."

"Sah?"

"Crops up. Turns up. Comes back. Trouble. When there's trouble for you again about Senior Pereira, I can help you. I can get you out of it. *Listen!* I *saw* him last month. Place called Belamu. See?"

Mr. Felice Diego saw, thanked Mr. Schloots or Schultz (*né* Palsover) effusively, and poured him a drink of the Best Bombay Brandy, Volcano Brand. Guaranteed Pure. Manufactured by Messrs. Yusufali Alibhoy Rahimtoola.

"Yerss, I saw him all right. Had a long talk with him. And I'll tell the Police so, if they give you any more *dik*. . . . And now *I* want a talk with *you*. Look here. *Listen*. And get it straight, if you want to flourish like the green bay-rum tree."

"Sah?"

"The Hadji hasn't been yet, has he?"

"Not since last time, Sah."

"Strike me pink! Not since the last time, eh? You don't say! Fancy that! . . . You mean it's about six months since he come?"

"Yes, Sah. I am expecting."

"You look like it. What you want is exercise. Well, when he does come, you be careful what you say. About Senior Pereira, I mean, and the General upstairs. . . . How long after the old Senior—er—left, did the Hadji come?"

"Oh, some time, Sah. Some days. Some week. Some month."

"And he asked for the Senior, did he?"

"Yes, Sah. He asked if Senhor come yet."

"And what did you say?"

"I spoke truth, Sah. I say he gone."

"What did the Hadji say to that?"

"Nutting, Sah. He say 'So?', and wait here for a few days to see if he come. Then he give me note for Senhor Pereira. And then he go."

"Well, now he'll come. . . . And you got to be careful—if you want me to look after you. Directly he comes, you let me know, if I haven't seen him first. And you tell him there's a gent here that's got a letter for him, *a letter that was given to the gent by Senior Pereira*. Savvy? *Sumja[24]?*"

"I understand, Sah."

"Right! That's number one Great Thought for the Day. There's a gent here wants to see the Hadji *because he's got a letter for him from Senior Pereira*. . . . Now another Great Thought, if you can hold more than one at a time. Can you?"

Mr. Diego assured Mr. Schloots that he could.

"Well, then, here it is. *I never had any truck at all with Senior Pereira*."

"Truck, Sah?"

"Sure. You seen a railway-truck, haven't you? Well, it's nothing to do with that. Listen. *I never knew Senior Pereira; never spoke to him; never came here with him; never set eyes on him*. Never. . . . See?"

"Yes, Sah."

"It was the Inglez gent upstairs. The General. The Burra Sahib. Got it?"

"Yes, Sah."

"I don't suppose the Hadji will want any particular song-and-dance about it, out of you, but if he asks any questions, that's how it goes. Nothing to do with me, and I never been here before. But the gent upstairs is the very one as came here with Senior Pereira. And here he is, back again. Perhaps he's come on purpose to meet the Senior here, eh?"

Mr. Diego smiled and waggled hands in a gesture that signified appreciation, amusement and doubt. Most expressive hands.

"Oh, and another thing. Get this. Don't you call me Schultz any more. It's a sort of a rank, a title, if you know what that is, Boy; and now the General's here, *he's* the Schultz. See? And don't you forget it."

"Yes, Sah. You are not the Schloots Sahib any more, but the General Inglez is the Schloots Sahib."

"That's right. Now that's the three things, and I'll tell you them all over again to-morrow morning, because if you make a mistake over one of them, it might be awkward. For

---

[24] Understand?

you, Boy. See? Very awkward, it might be."

And Mr. Palsover ran the tip of his forefinger round his neck, jerked it upward and emitted a curious sound which might be expressed as *Tchkk!* It seemed to Mr. Diego to come from under his own right ear, where the knot of the rope would be.

"Well, now everything's straightforward, cut and dried, and clear as mud. If the Police or anybody bothers you about him, I can testify that Senior Pereira is alive and kicking; and if the Arab questions you, you can testify that I have never been here before, but that *General Schultz came here six months ago with Senior Pereira.* Hang on to that, Son, and you won't have to hang on to nothing else. Not on to the end of a rope, anyway."

And when valeting the General next morning, Mr. Palsover explained that he was improving the shining hour by making straight the General's path, making things as easy as possible, and preparing the way for his reception by the Hadji without any sort of suspicion or doubt arising in that sea-farer's mind.

But one had to be, well—diplomatic. One had to be careful in the matter of giving information. One had not only to withhold as much as possible, but one had to, well—colour—the rest.

For example, it would be of no service to their under-taking if it were known to the Hadji that Mr. Palsover had visited Santa Cruz before. Still less that he had been in the place in the actual company of Senhor Pereira.

What the Arab would naturally suppose, on reading Mr. Pereira's letter, would be that the latter had given it direct to General Jason in person. Nor would there be any point in disabusing him of this very natural supposition. It was, as Mr. Palsover unnecessarily pointed out, a matter of strategy and tattics. The great thing was to get to the Where-is-it place; and Mr. Pereira's letter was the ticket that would authorize and direct the Arab to take its holder there.

"Quite so, quite so. I understand," said the General. "I'm not really an Arabic scholar, and unless this Hadji speaks

English, which is extremely improbable, we shan't make speeches to each other, nor have heart-to-heart talks. I'll give him the letter, and if he is under the impression that this Pereira gave it to me direct, I shan't disillusion him."

"And the same with the other letter, Sir, if I might be so bold as to make the suggestion and give advice. When you get to the Where-is-it place, you produce Senior Pereira's letter of introduction; and when they take it for granted that Senior Pereira gave it to you, there's no need to undeceive them."

"Quite so, quite so," agreed the General. "If I started trying to make explanations, they might get the idea that I was an impostor, mightn't they? Bad for Business!" The General smiled bleakly.

"Particularly if I were talking a language which they didn't understand," he added.

"Yes, Sir. And Them answering in a language which *you* didn't. Plenty of room for misunderstanding," agreed Mr. Palsover.

"I'll just present it to this—Dr. Norhona, did you say?"

"Yes, Sir. If you just hand it to him, it will speak for itself, as the saying is. That's what Senior Pereira said to me.

'*My dear old friend,*' he says, '*these letters speak for themselves. Give this one to the Hadji and he'll take you straight to Where-is-it. When you get there, show this other one to anybody who questions you, and hand it over to Dr. Norhona, to whom it is addressed. It will prove that you come direct from me, and that he has to do everything he can for you. . . . And, by Gum, he will too. Just about everything.*' "

General Jason was yet further interested, enheartened and intrigued.

V

Rightly or wrongly, General Jason decided that there could not be, on the whole surface of the earth, a more miserable abiding-place for one who waited from hour to hour, from day to day, and from week to week, than Santa Cruz de Loango.

Although accustomed to hard living in tent, bivouac and trench, he found this accommodation the most distasteful he had ever known; and increasingly he desired conditions under which he could, as he expressed it, either really rough it or not rough it at all. This was not rough, but disgusting. It was not hard, but it was definitely beastly.

Not only was there something curiously repulsive about the frowsy bed in which he slept so badly, but the bedroom itself had an unpleasant and disturbing atmosphere.

One of the least fanciful, sensitive or psychic of mankind, the General was nevertheless unable to ignore this minatory and charnel-house aura and suggestion. Although he well knew the room to be empty, and himself to be a fool if he imagined otherwise, he was aware, notwithstanding, of a curious sense of company—invisible and undesirable. Without being in the least degree perturbed or alarmed, he found himself constantly turning round, under the impression that there was someone behind him; often someone or something that moved just on the edge of his vision.

This was very annoying, and it added more than a little to the foul frowsiness of the room, its air of damp decay and dissolution; it made him wish that there were some spot of clean dry earth on which, beneath a decent tree, he could spread his ground-sheet and valise and sleep in the open air. But the compound of the hotel consisted of sand and filthy dust; in front of it ran a road of similar consistency; behind it lay a mangrove swamp that imperceptibly merged into an open lagoon which appeared to consist neither of land nor water, but of a black and oily-looking silt that was not quite liquid nor nearly solid. On the far side of this lagoon a sluggish river made its secret way into the sea.

The heat was terrific by day and scarcely less by night; the exhalations from the swamp and lagoon making the atmosphere like that of a hot-house or a Turkish bath. The appearance of the inhabitants of the abominable place bore plain testimony to its extreme unhealthiness. Without exception they crawled feebly and listlessly about, and bore the stigmata of sufferers from malignant fever.

Once again the General was moved to wonder why people live where they live. In many parts of the world this question had presented itself to his mind. Passing through a remote and ugly village of England, Scotland or Wales, he had speculated on the probable reason why any particular person should live in that particular place. Similarly in various corners of Europe and in out-of-the-way places in India and elsewhere. When a man inherited land, a house, a business or what-not, the question was answered; but as such people obviously formed but a very small minority of the inhabitants of any given place, it remained a problem.

And of all places on this earth, why should people select Santa Cruz de Loango as their residence or, having been born there, why should they remain?

Inertia probably, he decided, and if inertia were excusable anywhere, it was in this place where everything was inert, the very air stagnant, the water thick and poisonous, the earth sad and unfertile.

And why to this skeleton—or rather decaying corpse—of a port should people come, people like this man Pereira and this Arab? Well, for that matter, why should he, General Sir Reginald Jason, and ex-Mess-Sergeant Palsover have come?

On business.

The business of meeting the Arab.

And that was the business on which Mr. Pereira had come—and might it not conceivably be that the place's utter lack of attraction was the attraction that had brought such people there?

Well, he had put his hand to this queer affair. He had come all this way from Home. Here he was in Santa Cruz de Loango. And here he would stay, at any rate until the monsoon broke; and if the Arab did not arrive before the south-west monsoon was unmistakably blowing, he would have to make up his mind whether he would try again some six months hence, or whether he would cut his losses, refrain from telling Palsover what he thought of him and his wild-goose chase, and go back.

After all, no one need know how much of a fool he had made of himself. He could inform Scott-Marx that he was going no further in the matter, and tell Antoinette that he had enjoyed his expedition very much and had some excellent sport. Deep-sea big-game fishing—for shrimps.

He must write to her, by the way; let her know that he was still alive. And inasmuch as he himself did not know where he was going from this infernal spot, there would be no harm in mentioning the name of the place. The post-mark would show it, anyway. It would be something to do; and having done it, he would once more walk down the wide road of dirty sand, through the corrugated-iron-and-sacking Indian bazaar where the inevitable but amazing farthing-profit traders appeared to thrive by the keeping of shops the entire contents of any one of which would be dear at a shilling. One would think that if daily, between sunrise and sunset, each sold all that he had, the weekly profit on the turnover would be less than sixpence. And yet they found their way here from the Malabar Coast of India.

But once again, why, in Heaven's name *here*, of all places in the world? If they could come here they could go to Jamaica, Mombasa, Trinidad, Colon, Cape Town, Aden, Nassau or Zanzibar. Why come here, to about the most malarious, moribund and horrible place in the world, to sit from morning till night behind a small pile of green mangoes which might be worth about three a penny in times of greatest demand?

§2

General Jason wrote his letter to his wife, described Santa Cruz as his jumping-off place and as a really magnificent spot from which to jump, provided you jumped far enough; and added that it was in no sense an address, inasmuch as he would have been gone, please God, for a long time before she got this letter, and was not likely to return there. He informed her that it possessed no sort or kind of British Consular Agent and very little else save one or two policemen who were badly in need of safety-pins, a minor Government official who was badly in need of cash, and some ragged Customs sharks badly in need of victims; and that he hoped she was, like himself, having a splendid time. Love to Henry Carthew when she saw him; and he'd send her a line again from the next place.

A knock came at the door of the room and Mr. Palsover entered.

"Ah!" said the General. "I was going to ask you about the postal arrangements, if any, in this charming spot. Does one take one's letters away with one or . . . ?"

"Oh, that'll be all right, Sir. If you'll give them to me, I'll see them properly stamped and posted. There's a boat goes . . . well . . ."

"Every so seldom," suggested the General. "Slow but not sure."

"Yes, Sir. But I'll see them into the right hands," Mr. Palsover asserted briskly.

"Well, I should think they will probably stay in those hands if they are already stamped. However—thank you very much. What did you want to speak to me about?"

"Why, Sir," replied Mr. Palsover, lowering his voice almost to a whisper, "them letters of introduction. It struck me it might be a good thing if you had the Arabic one with you in your pocket, in case you see the Arab come ashore, or ran into him somewheres between here and the quay. It would look more natural-like if you had them with you, instead of having to come and get them from me."

"Certainly the Arabic one, at any rate," agreed the General. "I don't know whether the other envelope would convey anything to him."

"Just as well to have 'em both, Sir, perhaps. Sort of double proof that it was all right. I expect he'd know what the other was, even if he didn't take your word for it that it was a letter of introduction to the people where he's going."

"You may as well give me both, then."

And Mr. Palsover produced from his pocket, and proceeded to open, a flat package fastened with tape and sealing-wax. From this he produced a sealed envelope of stout paper, and from this again two letters, one of which was addressed in what the General recognized to be Arabic, and the other, in European writing, to

His Excellency Dom Perez de Norhona,
   c/o His Highness Dom Miguel de Guzman de Braganza,
                                    Marquess de Estoril.

"And where's the place, Palsover?" asked the General. "Or are you still going to keep that up your sleeve?"

"Yes, Sir. Yes, Sir. No offence, I hope—until the Arab comes. Just business, you know, Sir."

"Quite so," agreed the General. "Can't be too careful. Though some people might think you can—and are."

"I hope this Arab will come soon," he added as Mr. Palsover turned to go, with the letter addressed to Lady Jason in his hand.

"Oh, well, Sir, Diego says he's bound to come any day now."

"I suppose 'any day' is an earlier date than 'some day,' Palsover?"

"Oo, yes, Sir. Much!" agreed Mr. Palsover confidently as he departed to give quiet thought to Lady Jason's letter, its handwriting, information, idioms, and particularly, its signature.

Also to the question of its posting or other disposal in the event of certain contingencies.

VI

The General yawned, rose from the rickety table at which he had been writing, took his sun-helmet, and descended to the street of dust and sand.

Well, any day, some day—this year, next year, some time, never. What a queer thing life was, and what funny situations one found oneself in.

One more stroll down to that wretched tidal creek they called the harbour. Beginning to feel as though he had been born in the place. Even the pathetic pot-bellied children ceased to follow him about, and the half-Latin, half-Oriental-looking women to glance shyly through the doorways of their adobe pink-washed huts.

What did the men, other than the alien East Indians, do all day—beyond yawn, spit, scratch and adjourn to one of the numerous corrugated-iron bars to drink coloured wood-alcohol, weird vermouth, synthetic wines, syrups and near-absinthe?

And who might this be?

The General's pulse may have quickened a little, but no look of eagerness disturbed the serene cast of his austere countenance.

By gad! This was a Man.

It was *the* man. A very tall, broad-shouldered, fine-looking fellow in clean cotton robes; and an Arab undoubtedly.

Well, it would be a pleasure to have dealings with a chap of this type. What a contrast between his open self-reliant face, frank, fearless, handsome, and those of the European, Indian and half-caste Santa Crucians. How a man's profession and way of life stamped him! Here were the eyes of a seaman, eyes accustomed to distance and to danger.

"*Salaam!*" said General Jason as he and the stranger

447

met face to face. "*Salaam, Hadji Sahib.*"

"*Salaam, Sidi,*" replied the Arab, eyeing the General with some surprise and considerable interest. Saluting courteously, he enquired whether the Roumi gentleman spoke Arabic.

"I'm afraid I don't know what you are saying," replied General Jason. "I suppose you don't speak English—or perhaps French?"

With a flash of white teeth the Arab smiled pleasantly and admitted that he knew some English and as it happened, a few words of French. He added as an afterthought that, as he traded to Bombay, he also knew enough Hindustani to make himself understood.

"Well, we shall get along splendidly then," said the General. "I used to know some Hindustani, and I speak French pretty well. Er—*Hamara nam Jason hai. Main General hoon. Hadji Sahib ka nam kya hai? Ap kiwaste chithi hamara-pas hai.*[25]"

And from the breast pocket of his tussore silk coat, he produced a couple of letters, one of which he gave to the Hadji.

"*Mera nam Abdulla hai,*[26]" replied the Arab. "*Hadji Abdulla,*" and he read the superscription on the envelope.

"Ah, ha! *Mera waste béshak,*[27]" he said.

Having studied the envelope for a few moments, the Arab read the letter with obvious interest and considerable surprise.

"*Ce Monsieur . . . le Senhor Pereira. Où est-il?*" he asked.

"*Je ne sais pas,*" replied the General truthfully. "*Il n'a pas attendu. Il est parti.*"

The Arab seemed puzzled, and after a few more attempts at conversation in Hindustani and French, tried English. This was an improvement, for in this language the General was reasonably fluent and the Arab quite compre-

---

[25] My name is Jason. I am a General. What is your name, Hadji Sahib? I have a letter for you.

[26] My name is Abdulla.

[27] For me, without doubt.

hensible.

"You wish then to go to São Thomé?" said the Hadji Abdulla.

"Do I?" replied General Jason, and was about to add, "I didn't know it. Never heard of the place," when he realized that this must be the Missing Word, the name that Palsover had so long and wisely concealed.

São Thomé? . . . And where the devil might that be?

"Yes," he said quickly. "I've been waiting for you here for this purpose. The letter, I believe, instructs you to take me to São Thomé."

"Without doubt," replied the Arab. "When do you wish to sail?"

"The sooner the better."

"What is that? Sooner? Better? Go soon?"

"Yes."

"I would wish to wait for Senhor Pereira if he will come."

"He will not come. I am here instead."

"Instead? In place? In place of Senhor Pereira?"

"Yes. Could we sail to-morrow?"

"To-morrow. Perhaps. I must get some things for my crew. Water, food, fruit. I need salt and oil too. And I have business."

"All right, Hadji Sahib. We'll go as soon as you can. I'll be ready to start at any moment. Get everything packed up."

"Packed . . . Up," murmured the Arab. "To-day is *aljuma*. . . ."

"Friday," said the General.

"We sail *alahad*. It is Sunday. I hope to."

"Good!"

"Where has the Sidi pitched his tent?"

"Beneath the roof of Felice Diego," smiled the General.

"Ah!" nodded the Arab. "*Casa Real*. The Royal Palace," and his grave eyes twinkled. "I have business with that man also."

"Well, I'm going back there. Shall we go together?"

"I am honoured. It is as the Sidi pleases," replied the Arab.

The General felt that, although the conversation had been in dubious Hindustani, French and English, interlarded with Arabic terms such as *ma, sukkar, samak, milh* (which he believed to be water, sugar, fish and salt) he and this admirable and attractive fellow understood each other completely. . . .

As they crossed the compound of the *Casa Real*, the enormous man who was bar-keeper and general factotum, and who was sitting listlessly on the doorstep, caught sight of the Arab, roared in obvious excitement that the Hadji Abdulla had arrived, and advanced salaaming humbly.

Quickly Felice Diego appeared, buttoning a coat over his naked body as usual, and welcomed the Hadji with every sign of respect, a regard apparently not untinged with fear. Possibly he had an uneasy conscience.

From an uncurtained window behind the balustrade of an untrustworthy verandah, Mr. Palsover appeared. As he edged forward, wisely clutching the door-post of that upper chamber, it might almost be said that literally he hung in doubt.

VII

Well, the Hadji had come at last, and, although to outward eye unchanged, the General felt a new man. It really began to look as though he was justified of his faith, and that what had, at times, appeared to be a wild-goose chase, was really the sober and sensible following of a star, the steady treading of a hazardous path leading to great undertakings and vast wealth.

Particularly was he pleased that this part of Palsover's story had proved to be true; for from the very first it had seemed to him to be the weak spot in it. Or to change the metaphor, the fact or fiction of a wandering Arab who would turn up at some obscure and distant place at some vague and unspecified time and act upon incomprehensible signs, tokens and hieroglyphics, scribbled by a mysterious Portuguese—had been the most difficult part to swallow. Even if one accepted the tale of a radium concession, of vast uranium deposits only waiting to be worked, of a delirious Portuguese, and all the rest of Palsover's story, as feasible, reasonable and probably true, one had boggled at the point where the Arab appeared. One felt that here improbability entered; that one had come to a weak link in the chain of the story.

And now—behold the Arab. Here he was in the flesh, behaving exactly as had been foretold and making every other part of the story seem not merely probable but almost completely proven.

And Palsover, now challenged on the subject, immediately and joyfully admitted that São Thomé was the place.

He, too, seemed enormously cheered by the Arab's arrival, and delighted at his spontaneous reference to São Thomé. Quite evidently there was such a place, and most certainly it must be the place of which Senhor Pereira had talked in delirium, and the existence of which he had

451

admitted when sane and coherent. And who but a fool would now doubt that his reference to the radium—the radium that ought to be produced in vast quantities for the benefit of Suffering Humanity—was an allusion to something real and actual?

Suffering Humanity! Suffering Moses. . . . And what price Suffering Samuel now?

Samuel Palsover the multi-millionaire.

The conversation that morning between General Jason and Mr. Palsover was more than cheerful, and was marked by an optimism that bordered on certainty. With a light-hearted hopefulness that almost suggested gaiety, the General, ably assisted by Mr. Palsover, set about the work of selecting and re-packing the outfit that he proposed to take with him to São Thomé, a task not rendered easier, if more interesting, by the knowledge that he would either be in São Thomé for a few days or some six months.

A matter that seemed greatly to exercise the mind of Mr. Palsover and which he discussed at length with the General, was the question of his own sojourn on the island. Anxiously he reflected once again. Should he go ashore at all? Hadn't he better remain on board the *dhow*? Trusting to the prestige of the General's name and his power to protect him, should he go up to this Capital place that the Senior had talked about, and then clear out again when the Hadji did? Should he stay there the whole six months and keep his eye on things? Against that he had already practically decided, but the fact remained that if you wanted a thing done well, you must do it yourself. If you have to trust somebody moreover, there's only one person you can really trust and that is yourself. Look after Number One for nobody else will. Very good proverbs, and guiding stars on Mr. Palsover's mental horizon.

On the other hand, why burn your own fingers if someone else will get your chestnuts out of the fire? Silly to let the General in on this business, and then not trust him. Of course the General was straight. He was a white man, and wouldn't double-cross anybody, let alone the man who had put him on to a thing like this. And as for ability in handling the matter, Mr. Palsover fully and freely admitted that the General was worth a hundred of himself. No good going up to the Capital with any idea of being useful, and no need to go with any idea of preventing the General from cheating him.

Better not go at all. From what the Senior had said, both sane and barmy, St. Tommy wasn't a healthy spot for visitors; and although the old Senior had been all right and had given him the chit as a sort of Free Pass to the Show, the others, whom he called Them, didn't know Samuel Palsover and might not give themselves time to get to like him and appreciate him properly.

No, there was something very queer about that place. Something wrong about it; and he wasn't going to run any foolish and unnecessary risks. He'd go and have a look at it and he might perhaps go ashore, but he wouldn't go up-country. No inland journeys for Samuel. If he didn't stay on board the *dhow* the whole time, he'd keep pretty near it.

A rum start. Puzzling. . . .

§2

The long-awaited sea-farer, known to some as The Arab, and to others as the Hadji Abdulla, was also puzzled.

Six months ago he had come to Santa Cruz expecting to pick up Senhor Manöel Pereira and take him to São Thomé. Apparently Pereira had arrived according to arrangement, but had not waited. According to Felice Diego, he had disembarked from one of the Anglo-Portuguese coasting tramps with this other European, and, after waiting a few days, both had gone again.

Nor had there been any message save a verbal one from Pereira to the effect that he could wait no longer as he had to go elsewhere. Quite possible, but in the circumstances, rather strange; and there had been nothing to do but take delivery of the boxes left with Felice Diego and consigned to himself for delivery elsewhere. The boxes and packages had, as usual, borne the name of Manöel Pereira in roman capitals, and the Hadji Abdulla's, as consignee, in

Arabic.

And now again, on this occasion, Pereira had failed to meet him, but a stranger had presented him with an incontestably genuine letter from Pereira directing him to give the bearer passage to São Thomé. Curious. Very curious indeed. And, what made it more so, was the fact that the bearer of the letter should be an obvious Englishman, and apparently an English Army Officer of high rank. Queer.

Still, there it was. Definite instructions in black and white, in Pereira's handwriting, and attested by what he could not doubt to be Pereira's signature. He had seen it too often to be deceived. And had he had the slightest suspicion about this document, there was the other letter, or rather envelope, of unknown contents. No one but an authorized official from São Thomé could have written what was on that envelope; and again, no one who knew it could doubt that the handwriting was Pereira's.

Well, São Thomé was a somewhat mysterious country and its Government had its own rather mysterious ways.

Most certainly he must, and would, give a passage to this stranger, as Pereira's letter directed, and he would also take his servant. That wasn't in the bond, nor was any mention made of a second person, but presumably one might accept the guarantee of the person guaranteed. Since Pereira could vouch for this General, presumably the General could vouch for his servant, especially as the man, far from being inquisitive and anxious to explore, appeared to have no particular wish to go ashore. Nor was it as though the fellow was a seaman. He might have been suspicious had the second man been an obvious sailor and navigator whose object might have been to learn the whereabouts of São Thomé. He was quite an obvious land-lubber and what he purported to be, the General's valet and servant.

Besides, Pereira would hardly have instructed him to give a passage to anybody who was either a spy or likely to bring a spy with him.

Yes, an interesting business, but no concern of the Hadji's. Perhaps Doña Guiomar was going to marry again?

The Hadji smiled at the thought.

Perhaps the Council wanted expert opinion and advice on some important technical matter or other. Hardly anything naval or military though. And in any case, it was definitely queer that Pereira, or one of the other official Messengers of the Council, should not be personally escorting the General.

The mere notion of anything of the sort was rather fanciful, but had they actually been bringing someone from Europe, they surely wouldn't have wished him to find his way to Santa Cruz by himself, nor left him provided with no better credentials than a note to the Hadji Abdulla?

However, there it was. On his instructions he must act.

And on Senhor Pereira's instructions he acted, setting sail again in his *dhow* toward midnight, on the third day after his arrival, and taking with him General Sir Reginald Jason, Mr. Palsover, and their respective and not inconsiderable impedimenta.

It was not his habit to be inquisitive, but there was an enormous number of questions which he would have liked to have put to his eminent passenger.

What on earth could a man of this type be doing in the Hadji's particular and peculiar galley? For what possible reason could he be proceeding to São Thomé? Who could have invited him to do so, and what could have been that person's object? It must have been a Member of the Council, which in a way meant that the invitation must have come with the knowledge and consent of the Government, the Council as a body. Surely no one, unless perhaps it were Norhona, who seemed to be something of a law unto himself, would have instructed Pereira to bring such a man as this General to São Thomé. It all seemed contrary to the centuries-old policy and custom of the rulers of that shy and exclusive country, so remote, both historically and geographically, from the thronged highways of land and sea and the busy marts of men.

It would have been puzzling enough had the General been some obscure person, a skilled mechanic of some particular kind, an artificer or engineer, somebody of such insignificance that his comings and goings would be entirely unchronicled and his failure to return home quite unnoticed, save, of course, by the members of his family, if he had one.

Had it been the other man, his servant, it would have been more understandable, as a person of that type, with some special technical skill or knowledge, might have been brought by Pereira on promise of a dazzling wage and a long-term contract, an agreement which would doubtless have been fully honoured by the Council of São Thomé, if never terminated. But even so, it would be a new departure, and one perhaps not unfraught with danger to São Thomé, in the case of an Englishman. But no, that was absurd, inasmuch as the man would know nothing beyond the fact that his engagement began at Santa Cruz; and inasmuch as he himself would not know his real destination, he would be unable to name it to anyone interested in his future movements.

Well, to mind one's own business was an excellent plan —and had Koranic support, moreover.

As the days passed, the Hadji came to like the General more and more. His manners were accordant with his appearance. He was as pleasant, courteous and agreeable as he was handsome and dignified, qualities which particularly appealed to the Hadji, himself notably courteous, handsome and dignified.

It was matter for regret that he could not give the General more information concerning São Thomé, but in the course of their long and numerous conversations on the subject, he did his best to enlighten him and at the same time to warn him against—he knew not what. That São Thomé was a place of danger to strangers and uninvited visitors, he told him repeatedly; but inasmuch as the General bore not only Pereira's *laisser passer* but actually a letter to a Member of the Council, this danger did not seem to threaten him. But the fact remained that it was no secret that more people entered São Thomé than left it, and that so far as the Hadji knew, only those left it who were its accredited representatives, messengers, emissaries; some of them something between agents and ambassadors, others corresponding to King's Messengers.

From the Hadji's answers to his questions and the items of information which occasionally he volunteered, the General, himself necessarily uncommunicative, being not only ignorant but a gate-crashing intruder, gathered that São Thomé was a considerable island and an independent self-governing State, the rulers of which fanatically worshipped the ideal of independence. To them, what is elsewhere known as Progress was anathema, and the standards of modern "civilization" an abomination. What they feared and hated most of all conceivable things was the poisoning of the blood of their body politic with the destructive, degenerative and fatal disease-germs that had brought most of the world to its present pass; that had turned *homo sapiens* into a murderous and suicidal savage whose highest scientific attainments, whose greatest national effort, whose knowledge, resources and wealth, were devoted to— *destruction!*

As the Hadji, in slow and careful English, explained to the General, the rulers of São Thomé wished to avoid pestilence, commercialism, industrialism, wealth, impoverishment, anxiety, slaughter, conquest and enslavement. In other words, they feared their fellow men, dreaded contact with the Christian nations of the earth; viewed, with horror and hatred, Civilization Uplift, Improvement and Progress. Let them stay as they were, peaceful, self-sufficing, self-supporting and happy. Let other peoples strive for wealth, for markets and for trade; let them avoid commerce abroad and industrialization at home, for so long as a merciful God would hear their prayers. And, God helping them, they'd help themselves with every atom of their strength and ingenuity. Peace—and São Thomé for the São Thoméans. . . .

Who were they? What were they? And where did they get those quaint ideas? enquired General Jason.

Well, so far as the Hadji could make out, São Thomé had originally been populated by a mild and peaceful Polynesian people, much like the Hawaiians and the

Tahitians, a simple and delightful race who were naturally gentle, amiable and unwarlike. They still formed the bulk of the lowland population. But at some far-distant time, there had been an Arab invasion, probably quite accidental, and the more virile Arabs had either conquered the island or assumed proprietorship. These had inter-married with the Polynesians, but their descendants were to this day quite distinguishable from the aborigines, being bigger, stronger, more active and enterprising. Then, some three or four centuries ago, two or three ships of the great "silk and silver" fleet of Portugal, returning from the Far East, and bringing with it the retiring Viceroy of the Indies, had been wrecked on São Thomé. Apparently, the whole fleet had been driven far from its course, scattered and sunk, and the few ships that had been driven ashore at São Thomé had been the only survivors. As it happened, the Viceroy and his family and suite had been on one of these ships, and all of them had been saved.

As a matter of fact, according to what one heard at São Thomé, everybody and everything had been saved, the storm abating just after the ships had gone ashore in what, at low tide and quiet weather, were very shallow waters shelving to a sandy beach.

Nobles and ladies of high rank; officers and officials; soldiers and sailors; merchants; artisans; men of the long robe as well as those of the long sword; priests, doctors, artists, architects, lawyers; all had been saved; and, before the ships broke up or were swallowed in the soft and shifting sands, their entire contents had been salvaged in the ships' boats, with the help of the friendly and welcoming natives.

They named the island São Thomé, the day of their reaching it being that of St. Thomas, the Viceroy's patron saint.

It was as though a completely equipped expedition had set forth to found a Colony, as was later attempted and achieved in the Americas and elsewhere, by England, France, Holland, Spain and Portugal.

But there were two great differences between this new

foundation in the Southern tropic seas and those systematically-established Colonies.

The first of these differences lay in the fact that these people knew not where they were, having been driven many hundreds and perhaps some thousands of miles from their course, by that terrible storm of phenomenally long duration, which had sunk the greater part of the fleet and cast up the survivors to live or die in this unknown strange uncharted land. Whatever theories their captains and navigators might have were incapable of proof without ships wherewith to put them to the test, and the one or two tiny bands of heroic stalwarts who had set forth in small boats had been heard of no more.

The second of these differences lay in the fact that His Serene Excellency the Viceroy, a sick and ageing man, weary to death of the pomps and vanities of this world, of the cares of high places and the responsibilities of rule, desired nothing but peace, rest and surcease from trouble and tribulation.

To him the island was as one of the Islands of the Blest, another Eden; and all he asked was to be allowed to end his days in the green shade of its lovely dells and beneath the cool shadow of its mighty trees.

Listening to the Arab's slow, careful and sonorous English, the General was reminded of a Poet who might have been a contemporary of this world-renouncing Viceroy, and who wrote of another disillusioned courtier, the melancholy Jacques who, to his "co-mates and brothers in exile," said: *"Are not these woods more free from peril than the envious Court?"*

Quite in the spirit of the melancholy Jacques must have been the address made to his compatriots and followers by this disillusioned Governor who may have known Albuquerque and indeed St. Francis Xavier himself.

General Jason had visited Goa, had seen the shrine of St. Francis and what remained of the works of those mighty men of old who preceded the British in India, as they had done in so many other parts of the world, and could visualize this curious group of Portuguese *cavaleiros fidalgos* starting, undismayed, to build a new life in a new home, at the bidding of their leaders.

A most interesting and truly romantic story.

And there they had remained, the Hadji continued, marrying, first of all, among themselves, for several of the high officers and officials were accompanied by their wives and families; later inter-marrying with the daughters of the leading Arab land-owners who were the aristocracy of the country.

Doubtless, at first, there were rebellious spirits, hearts filled with a deep sense of exile and bereavement, brave spirits almost crushed beneath this weight of woe, and broken by this sense of loss of all that had hitherto made life worth living—this knowledge of ruined ambitions, wrecked careers, lost homes, estates and loved ones. But as the years passed and the second and third generation took the place of the original fathers of the new community, the beautiful and productive island became Home.

Within a very few more generations it was not only a home in which to live and move and dwell, but one to guard, protect and keep private, to keep hidden and secret; a garden enclosed, set in a protecting sea.

Naturally the new-comers had quickly become the aristocracy of the island, the Viceroy its supreme ruler, his nobles its government, and the remainder his trustworthy representatives throughout the island, administrators, executives, judges, soldiers and police. And, as naturally as they breathed the air, the priests who, proselytizing from Goa, had been converting Indians by whole villages at a time, set about the work of Christianizing, teaching and disciplining the aboriginal inhabitants of São Thomé.

Apparently for many years, for several generations, for more than a century probably, it was, in Europe, assumed that the entire fleet had been lost and that the Viceroy had perished with the rest. It had happened before and would happen again, while caravels of a hundred tons set out to circumnavigate the world.

Had the Viceroy and his entourage been normally anxious to communicate with the mother country, make known their fate and appeal for help, it was improbable that any such communication would, in their own life-times, have been feasible. Circumstances were in any case against it. But in view of the earnest desire and careful precautions of The Viceroy, His Excellency Dom Sebastian Gonçalo de Braganza (who now took the title of Marquess de São Thomé) that—in order to ensure their being left in peace to found a newer, higher and nobler state of their own—nothing should be known of their fate, it is not remarkable that the remote island remained unheard of and unknown unto the third and fourth and probably the fifth and sixth generations of the descendants of these argonauts, these founders and architects of a New Model and a real Utopia.

It was not at one session, or in one day, that General Jason learned thus much of the history of the island State of São Thomé; and as he listened and the story was unfolded, a doubt grew in the General's mind as to whether the tale or the teller were the more remarkable. With practice, the Hadji's English had grown more fluent, his vocabulary more copious. Nor did his explanation that he had been sent to an English-speaking school in childhood and had actually served and sailed on an English ship, seem to account for his fluency.

A most attractive and intriguing man, and his *dhow* an uncommonly fine specimen of the craft that have sailed the Southern seas and traded from Basra to Bombay, from Mombasa to Ceylon for a thousand years, and, in the past, had not only frequently but regularly made their way east of Ceylon and west of the Cape of Good Hope.

This particular *dhow* was a much bigger vessel than most of its kind, better built, and far better kept and equipped. In its high-built poop, with its flat broad stern, glass-windowed and beautifully carved, there was evidence of the history of its descent. From the waist aft, a Portuguese galleon; from the waist forward, a native Oriental galley, its low pointed stem rising with a long slope from the water, its strong thick mast raking forward and supporting the enormous yard, far longer than itself, which carried the one great sail.

Even to the eye of the General, a landsman, it was clearly apparent that the *dhow* was extremely well-handled, and that its crew, Arabs of dark complexion and mixed blood, were fine seamen. Moreover, to his surprise, one of them was also an admirable cook in his own line, chiefly that of rice, fish and chupatties. As he told the Hadji, he had eaten worse curries in India and in places where the cook had everything he required for success.

In fact, he thoroughly enjoyed the novel voyage, and not the less because he had his suspicions about it. He was sure that the Hadji left Santa Cruz with some suddenness and secrecy that night; that he had been somewhat insistent that his passengers should retire at once to the berths allotted to them aft; and that the *dhow*'s course for its destination was a curiously indirect and circuitous one.

Although he saw neither chart nor compass, he knew from the position of the sun by day and of certain of the stars by night, that there was something as queer and unusual about the sailing-directions as about so many other details of the whole fantastic business.

What was the Hadji thinking as he eyed him with those long speculating looks? What made him so meditative, and why did he thus ponder and ruminate upon the matter of his passenger's position and business? Plainly he was greatly interested. Was he also doubtful, possibly a little anxious as to whether the General quite understood what he was doing?

The latter decided that, while fully accepting the genuineness of Pereira's letters, the Hadji was extremely puzzled by them and by the whole situation. Without actually asking the questions,

"Do you really know exactly what you are doing, and are you provided with adequate guarantees and credentials?" he gave the General clearly to understand that this was something entirely new in his experience, and that the General and his servant were the first passengers whom he had ever carried to São Thomé unaccompanied by a São Thoméan official.

"We shall reach São Thomé to-morrow," he told him one evening as they sat cross-legged on the poop-deck and ate rice and curried fish which reminded the General of Bombay 'duck.'

"Oh, good!" he replied. "Though I shall be quite sorry to leave the *dhow*. When shall we get our first sight of the coast?"

"We shan't," smiled the Hadji. "We shall approach after sunset and drop anchor before dawn."

"Quite so," thought the General. "All very secretive—and interesting."

He felt himself to be on the threshold of a great adventure. It was almost like going to the Front again, on the outbreak of a war.

VIII

From the first minute of catching a glimpse of São Thomé, the General was in a state of thrilled excitement, though no one would have imagined it. On waking in the morning and coming out on to the deck, he found the *dhow* was at anchor in what appeared to be a land-locked creek, the shores of which were fringed with mangrove, behind which rose a profusion of palms and other trees, tall, green and magnificent; obviously a place of great fertility and enjoying a very adequate rainfall.

In the distance rose a great forbidding ramp, a solid wall of mountains.

So far as he had visualized anything at all, he had imagined and expected a harbour and town of the Santa Cruz sort. Here, there appeared to be neither harbour nor town; merely an anchorage for the smallest type of sea-going boat, such as that on which he stood; and what appeared to be a fort, a barracks, a look-out station and a few other official-looking buildings, trim, neat and well-kept.

As he gazed, a boat smartly rowed by dark-skinned sailors in white uniform, put out from a small wooden jetty and approached the *dhow*. As it drew nearer, he noticed that the man who sat in the stern appeared to be a European, the type of official who might have sat in the stern-sheets of such a boat in any Mediterranean harbour.

"With much apology," said the voice of the Hadji behind him, "will you please go aft into the cabin, while I speak with the Port Officer?"

As the General reluctantly turned away to comply with his request, the Hadji added,

"He is also the Doctor, the Customs Authority, the Senior Naval Officer, the Chief of Police, the Officer Commanding Troops, and several other things."

When later he was asked to join the Hadji and the Port

Officer, it was to gain the impression that the Port Official was as surprised and as puzzled concerning him as the Hadji had been. What was said between the two he did not understand, but from time to time the Hadji enlightened him as to the drift of the Port Officer's observations, enquiries and objections; but in the end the position seemed to be summed up in the official's statement that he had received no instructions, had no authority, and did not intend to take any responsibility.

After reading Senhor Pereira's letter at least a dozen times, he had decided that it did not concern him. It was ad-dressed to the Hadji, and doubtless the Hadji had acted correctly in obeying its instructions. It bade him take the bearer to São Thomé—and he had done so.

And did the Senhor imagine that Senhor Pereira had been so anxious that the bearer of the letter should be safely conducted to São Thomé in order that he might be immediately taken away again?

The official intimated that he was not privileged to know the contents of Senhor Pereira's mind or to understand its workings. He repeated that he had no instructions.

And the letter addressed by Senhor Pereira to Dom Perez de Norhona?

That was another matter. No one had any objection to that being delivered. On the contrary.

And having said all that he had to say, and demonstrated his power to obstruct, the Port Officer informed the Hadji that he would communicate with the Capital and obtain instructions. Meantime, the bearer of the letters was not to leave the *dhow*, and a soldier would be left on board with very definite instructions to see that he did not do so. Also the Hadji would be held strictly responsible for his passenger's "safety." And the letter addressed to Dom Perez de Norhona had better be handed over to the Port Officer who would see that it reached him safely.

But to this General Jason flatly refused to agree. He quite understood that there might be some difficulty about his admission to São Thomé; but this was his passport, his credentials, his letter of introduction, and he intended to deliver it in person. Would the Hadji kindly inform this Officer that he was not a stowaway, a tripper, a beach-comber or a casual wanderer looking for a job, but a retired British Officer of high rank, a General in fact, and that he had not the slightest doubt that the official's superiors would greatly deplore any discourtesy that might be shown him. Meantime the Port Officer need have no anxiety about his leaving the *dhow*, for he had neither wish nor intention to do so. Whenever, hitherto, he had visited civilized parts of the world, he had met with a different kind of reception from this.

Which, being interpreted, caused the Port Officer to smile and request the Hadji to inform the General that it was the particular boast of São Thomé that it was not a civilized part of the world—as civilization was understood to-day. However, he would communicate with the Capital, and when he received instructions would inform the General immediately.

Meanwhile, he hoped he would enjoy excellent health and walk with God.

§2

Mr. Palsover was neither depressed nor despondent. On the other hand, he was fully confirmed in the opinion which he had already formed, that St. Tommy was no place for him. He had rather gathered from his conversation with the Senior, and especially from what the poor gentleman had said during his bouts of delirium, that St. Tommy was going to turn out to be something like this.

No, that Capital sounded to him like a very good place to keep away from. For Mr. Palsover to keep away from, that is; but a very good place for the General to visit.

All this secrecy showed there was a secret.

All this defensiveness showed there was something to defend.

Why such a lot of fuss and bother over letting the General even go ashore, if they hadn't got something to hide?

Yes, so far so good. What price Samuel now? Here he

was, right on the spot, right on the doorstep. What a nose he had for money! He had followed the scent straight from that cabin on the *St. Paul de Loanda*, where the poor old Senior started babbling about stuff at fifteen thousand pounds a gramme; followed it to where the Senior had gone to ground (or mud, rather); back to London where he could find the right man for the job; back again to Santa Cruz where they had found the Arab; and now to St. Tommy itself. What a nose he had for money, and *what* a smell of it there was here! Afraid to let you set foot on their golden island. . . .

He'd much sooner have gone up-country with the General and kept his eye on things. Not on the General, of course, but on things *in* general. It would have been interesting, and he might have learned a lot. And he'd have liked to have talked things over with the General, day by day, as they arose—and put his oar in, when there was any occasion. It might give him a bigger claim, too, when the sharing-out was done—the shares allotted, as they called it—and they were making out who was who and who got what. After all, it was his show, wasn't it? It was he who had discovered the stuff. But he didn't like the sound of 'Them' at all. There was what the Senior had said about Them.

Ar! And there was what he knew for himself about a poor chap who went ashore in a place once, and was never heard of again. Gun-running, he was—and the wrong lot got the guns and him too. Nothing of that sort for Samuel P.

> "*I'll stick to the ship, lads,*
> *You've children and wives,*"

he hummed, and smiled humorously as he sorted the General's kit again.

IX

Although General Jason had in his time travelled in most parts of the world and used most forms of transport, varying from the yak, elephant, mule and camel to the aeroplane, he considered his journey from the *dhow* to São Ildefonso, the capital of São Thomé, as the most interesting that he had ever made.

It fell into two widely differing parts, that across an intensively cultivated plain, from the harbour to the bridge across the quick-sand; and that up a hair-raising zigzag track that literally climbed the mountain-wall to the plateau on which the Capital with its citadel was built.

The first part of the journey was made by bullock-carts which reminded him of those used for regimental transport in India, but differed from them in that the bullocks trotted at a speed hitherto unimagined, while the wheels of the lightly-built carts were well-greased and silent. To his mind, the word bullock-cart had hitherto connoted a speed of two to three miles an hour; a vehicle clumsy as those that crossed the steppes of Europe behind the armies of Ghengiz Khan; and a creaking, groaning, shrieking and screaming noise of never-oiled wheels revolving on their crudely-rounded axle.

The country and its crops also reminded him of the more fertile plains of India; swamps of rice; fields of sugar-cane; vast areas of corn and millet which he called *bajri* and *jowri*; large patches of intensive cultivation of vegetables, such as might have been the work of Chinese market-gardeners. The villages were less suggestive of India, with their pink, pale-blue, yellow and cream adobe huts and houses, neat and well-built, some of them thatched with palm-leaf, others tiled with what appeared to be slabs of wood.

Obviously a country of great fertility, agricultural industry, peace and plenty.

The natives reminded him more of those of Malaya, Samoa and Tahiti than of those of India, a bright, cheerful and happy people whose demeanour was in marked contrast to that of the sad, over-serious, poverty-stricken and malaria-ridden people of the plains of India. He was also reminded of a verse of Gray's *Elegy* which he had learned by heart at Prep. School and, God forgive him, had recited at the last prize-distribution. How did it go? He had a splendidly tenacious memory. . . .

> "*. . . The threats of pain and ruin to despise,*
> *To scatter plenty o'er a smiling land*
> *And read their history in a nation's eyes.*"

The rulers of this country could read in this people's eyes, a very laudable and creditable history of their governing. A smiling land indeed, and endowed with plenty.

At the end of the first day's journey, part of which he made in the Arab's bullock-cart, part on foot, marching with him, the General was in no-wise surprised to find, in a big clearing, what might well have been a superior *dâk-*bungalow on the Grand Trunk Road that runs from Calcutta to Peshawar. In a very large and well-kept compound stood a good-sized one-storeyed bungalow, in which was a big central dining-room on either side of which were three very adequate bedrooms, all opening, back and front, on to wide verandahs. This rest-house for travelling officials was clean and quite well-furnished, with plain strong chairs, tables, and beds of a dark and heavy wood.

In one corner of the compound were stables for the oxen.

What did surprise him was the fact that the excellent servants did not understand his Hindustani. So like were they to the Goanese "boys" of his Indian experience, that it seemed unnatural that they should understand neither English nor Hindustani. In their plain white suits buttoning up to the neck, they might almost have been Officers' Mess servants, ship's stewards, or the domestic butlers to whom he had been accustomed for a quarter of a century, whose mother-tongue was Hindustani, and who understood and spoke English almost equally well.

After an evening meal of excellent soup, of fish unknown to him, of rather tough chicken, and a choice of papaia, melon, bananas and admirable yellow-and-red mangoes, he sat for an hour in the verandah talking with the Hadji Abdulla, who had dined, presumably, in his own room.

After conversation concerning the Island and its Government, about which the Arab appeared to be either ill-informed or uncommunicative, the latter uttered once again what General Jason could only regard as a warning.

"You will not think me inquisitive," he said, "a rash, foolish and impudent person who would pry into your affairs, if I ask you whether you are quite certain that the letter you carry for His Excellency Dom Perez de Norhona, guarantees you—what shall I say—safe conduct . . . safety . . . freedom to come and go? And by that I mean not only to come and go as you please about the Island. I mean more than that. You have come here. Are you sure you will be able to go away again, when you wish to do so?"

"Oh, but surely . . . damn it all. . . . There's no danger of my being arrested, is there?" growled the General.

"That depends on the contents of the letter you have for His Excellency Dom Perez de Norhona," replied the Arab gravely. "Are you sure that Senhor Pereira gave you full and ample guarantee?"

"Well . . . suppose he didn't?" replied the General, beginning to wish that he knew more about the contents of the unopened letter.

"Then I would most strongly advise you to go no farther. Once you cross the bridge to-morrow, there will be no turning back; but, although it will cause awkward inquiries—and difficult explanations on my part—I will take you back to the *dhow* and leave you on board while I conclude my business at the Capital."

"Thank you very much. That's very decent of you. But I haven't the faintest intention of turning back. Why should I do such a thing? I have a letter of introduction to this

Member of Council, or whatever he is, from his own representative and agent, Senhor Pereira, and I am going to present it. What should I have to fear? What is there dangerous about it?"

The Arab gravely shook his head, as though pondering his reply and choosing carefully his words.

"Come, come, Hadji Sahib! You can't arrest a British General for presenting a letter of introduction! Why, bless my soul, I come here in good faith with a view to doing mutually profitable business with this Government, and if they don't like it they can leave it. It would be wholly advantageous to them, but they are quite free to turn it down; and surely I should then be quite free to go? How could they detain me? I expect they've heard of British Consuls, not to mention the British Navy?"

The Arab smiled.

"To how many people is it known that you were to meet Senhor Pereira at Santa Cruz with the intention of going on to some place called São Thomé?" he asked.

"Well—er—nobody, I suppose. No, nobody."

"Ah!" observed the Arab non-committally.

"What exactly do you mean by that?"

"Nothing. Nothing, Sidi," replied Hadji Abdulla in a tone and manner that contradicted the statement.

"Well, then?"

"I was just wondering how these British Consuls and the British Navy are going to know anything about it, should you be—er—detained here."

"Has Britain no representative whatsoever in the capital of this São Thomé?"

"No country has any representative in the Island State of São Thomé," was the reply.

"But why should they wish to detain me?"

"By reason of their distrust, their hatred, indeed their fear and loathing—of visitors. They consider that the State of São Thomé has the Government that suits it best, the civilization that suits it best, and that peace which is of all things the best—and the greatest of all blessings bestowed upon ungrateful mankind by the wisdom and mercy of

471

Allah."

"But damn it all, Hadji, don't they want to improve their trade, to enrich and widen their industry and commerce, to enlighten and develop the lives of the people by getting from every part of the world the things they cannot get here? Don't they want to raise the standard of living? To add luxuries to their necessities? Don't they want to march in the front rank of Civilization? Have they never heard of Progress? Don't they want Wealth?"

"No," replied the Arab. "They don't. Nor do they want any trade or commerce whatsoever. They don't want to change the wants and ways of living of a perfectly content-ed and entirely prosperous people. And not only do they not wish to march in the front rank of Civilization, or in any other rank of what the world calls Civilization to-day, but they want to avoid it entirely. And as for desiring what is called Progress, it is their greatest object to escape it. To them Progress is another name for the Devil himself, and modern Civilization the Hell in which he works against mankind. . . . That is why they hate and fear visitors who come as emis-saries, agents, scouts and forerunners of that Civilization."

"Good Lord! A pretty stick-in-the-mud lot, aren't they?" snorted the General. "Don't they want railways, telegraphs, telephone, electricity, motor-cars, aeroplanes, wireless and all that?"

"They don't. There is not one yard of railway in this island. There is not a motor-car. No aeroplane has ever risen from its soil or landed on it. Electricity and wireless are as unwanted as they are unknown."

"So they prefer these bullock-carts to motor-cars, eh?"

"Infinitely."

"And why don't they want aeroplanes?"

"Because they think they have brought little but evil to mankind."

"On what grounds?"

"Well, they have an idea that the inhabitants of the great capitals of the mightiest nations turn pale and quiver with fright as they look up into the air, because the aeroplane has brought war to their very doors, and made their lives as hazardous as those of soldiers engaged in the most terrible battles. The Government of São Thomé has no wish to see their people digging holes in the earth and living like moles, rats and rabbits rather than as men—by reason of the blessings that aviation has brought to mankind."

"H'm. And wireless? What is their objection to that?"

"Its disturbance of the lives of peaceful simple and unspoilt people. Should you spend a day or two in one of the villages, watching the lives of these well-fed, well-clothed, well-housed happy agriculturists, you too will wonder as to what might be gained by providing them with jazz music, the voice of the crooner, the raucous cries of the advertiser, the vitiation of their simple tastes, and the provision for them of a thousand new and undesirable wants, needs, habits and vulgar luxuries. These people have their own music and their own legends and literature. They know nothing of alcohol, tobacco, patent medicines and the rest of the poisonous injurious trash that makes up quite a considerable part of this wonderful trade and commerce."

"You don't mean to tell me . . ." began the General.

"Pardon me, Sidi. I don't wish to tell you anything, except the views of the rulers of this country on the subject of what is good and what is bad for their people. And strange as it may seem, foolish and wrong as it may appear, they include among the things that are necessarily and wholly bad, visitors from the outside world."

Ah! smiled the General to himself, they'd have rather a different attitude toward a visitor who brought them a proposition like this. Why, was there any Government in the world that could or would refuse to have its revenues doubled, quadrupled? Good Lord, in a place like this, the royalties from a radium-concession would probably multiply the Government's annual income by ten. Talk about Balancing the Budget!

And apart from that, what about the individual members of the Government? Was there a single man, in any more-or-less coloured Government in the world, who'd vote against a scheme that was going to give him a noble personal and private rake-off, as would inevitably be the case here—quite apart from what accrued to the State Treasury by their action as a Governing Council? Each single member would naturally sit-in on it as a private individual.

If—and it was a colossal *if*—they were above flagrant bribery and corruption, would not each one of them expect to have a seat on the Board, a block of shares, and fine guinea-pig fees?

The Hadji was talking nonsense.

§2

Next day the bullock-carts were left behind at the rest-house. The General, the Hadji and a number of porters carrying boxes, crates and personal luggage, crossed the bridge on foot, and found riding-horses, pack-horses and mules awaiting them at a sort of rural livery-stables on the other side.

To the General, the crossing of the bridge was the most interesting part of the whole journey. This bridge spanned no river or other water, but what resembled the narrow sandy bed of an almost dried-up stream, for the sand looked wet, and, here and there, was a small pool of unattractive water.

"River ever flow here?" he asked the Hadji, as they crossed the bridge.

"Never. It is a quick-sand, and whatever goes into it disappears almost immediately, and is seen no more. It is the haunt and abode of *djinns*, *afrits*, devils—and their breath is poisonous. As you see, nothing green lives within a hundred yards of the banks of this unmoving 'river' of wet and quaking sand. Farther up, on either side, it opens out into a bog of sand which nothing can cross, neither man nor beast. In my country we have lakes of sand covered in salt— they are called *shotts*—but they can be crossed. Here there is no possibility of crossing, save at this spot by this bridge which, in the almost impossible event of invasion, could be destroyed in a few minutes."

The military aspect of the situation immediately interested the General.

"But an enemy force could march round, of course," he mused.

"Yes, and come face to face with a perpendicular cliff from two thousand to three thousand feet in height, which only lizards can climb."

"And suppose they marched all along the base of this cliff?" asked the General.

"They would, in time, come to the sea. In either direction."

"And if they re-embarked and sailed on?"

"In time they'd come back to the only harbour, such as it is; the spot where they had originally landed, and whence they had originally marched."

"They could make a landing somewhere else, surely?"

"Only into mangrove swamps through which one or two of the hardiest and luckiest *might* eventually penetrate, exhausted; though I doubt it."

"So no one could get up on to the main part of the Island, except across this quick-sand?"

"That is so. Possibly an individual here and there might contrive it, with the help of Allah. But not across the quick-sand."

"And does the breath of the *djinns* and *afrits* and devils destroy all vegetation round the other parts of the quick-sand too, as well as by this narrow crossing?"

"Everywhere. Not only is it death, by engulfing, to attempt to cross; but it is death for man and beast and vegetation to remain within a furlong of it."

"And nobody knows why this should be?"

"No."

Whereas I do, smiled General Jason to himself. It is radio-active. This quick-sand is just a few million tons of highly radio-active minerals blended with earth and sand. And probably worth nearly its weight in gold. Pitchblende. Helium. Uranium. Tungsten. Manganese. Zircon. Rutile. Phosphorus. And rare valuable chemicals and minerals used in bulb-filament-making and the hardening of special steel for armour-plating, guns and such. He didn't know much about these minerals, but he knew that this tremendously radio-active stuff must be enormously valuable, anyway. And it only needed carting away and shipping.

"When I say that nobody knows, I mean the simple people are ignorant as to why devils should occupy this place," observed the Arab.

And thinking the matter over the General decided that the phenomenon of radio-activity was caviar for the general of this island State, and probably understood only by the more enlightened members of its Government, such men as this Dr. Norhona. Anyway, Pereira had known. And he himself was going to know before he set foot on that *dhow*, or any other boat.

"This Dr. Norhona," he said, "he's a Member of Council, I understand. Pretty important man, eh?"

"His Excellency Dom Perez de Norhona is an extremely influential and important member of the Government," replied the Arab. "Also Secretary to the Cabinet."

And what sort of a Government would it be, wondered the General. Presumably a Dictatorship, either that of an individual or a clique.

"Who's the ruler of the country?" he asked.

"Doña Guiomar is the Regent during the childhood of the hereditary Governor."

"And can she do as she likes? A kind of Begum of Bhopal? A sort of female King Feisal, Ibn Saud, Sultan of Muscat or Zanzibar? Like a female Sheikh of an Arab tribe, if there were such a thing as a woman-Sheikh."

"Well, no. Not quite. She could do nothing against the will of the Council. On the other hand, no order or act that the Council passes becomes law unless she signs it."

"And who elects this Council?"

"They are not elected. They are hereditary, and elect the Cabinet. The Council consists of the heads of the families of the descendants of those who occupied the Island and named it São Thomé, hundreds of years ago."

"I see. Sort of House of Lords without the Commons," observed the General.

"Yes. But just as the Sheikh of a tribe discusses all measures with a *mejliss* of elders, so the Government every year calls a meeting of the heads of the big land-owning families. They can thus ventilate their grievances, if any; and put forward suggestions—generally agricultural. They are men of mixed Arab descent."

"Big men, eh? Wealthy?"

"Wealthy in everything but money. They have vast estates, flocks and herds."

"And the people who cultivate the estates—are they what one might call slaves?"

"Slaves! No. They are free men. In some cases they own their own land. In others, share with their employers."

"And it works well, eh?"

"For centuries there has been peace and plenty. There is no poverty. Crime is almost unknown, and there has never, since the Island became São Thomé, been anything in the nature of a revolt of the peasants."

"And they have no share in the Government?"

"No, nor do they want one. They ask only to be governed and lightly taxed, and they are governed and taxed with justice and wisdom."

"Huh! The wisdom of excluding Civilization and Progress, eh?" grunted General Jason.

"By exactly that wisdom, Sidi," replied the Arab, as he led the way to the gates of the horse-corral which surrounded the thatched house of its overseer, and by which stood two good hacks and a collection of pack-horses, ponies, mules and donkeys. "Will you choose which of these horses you would like to ride?"

§3

And after three days of easy riding and two nights in *dâk*-bungalows (rest-houses) the wayfarers reached São Ildefonso, the capital of São Thomé. To General Jason, who had travelled in Portugal and Spain, following, for his interest and instruction, the course of Wellington's Peninsular Campaign, Ildefonso was reminiscent of a smaller and walled Lisbon, if it were crowned and overshadowed by the citadel of Cintra. Faintly, too, it suggested Goa, by reason of the dark complexion of the general populace. A clean attractive town; its better-class houses, each in its own beflowered compound, of colours pleasing to the eye and suggestive of cool repose, in the green setting of the great trees that shadowed and protected them. The bazaars again reminded him of those of India and somewhat of the villages of Cyprus.

But the castle was a little grim, a little awe-inspiring, and as he and the Hadji rode into the great outer court-yard, and ere the sound of the horses' hooves ceased to clatter upon the old grey stones, the clang of closing gates struck an ominous note. He shivered slightly, and wondered whether it presaged an attack of malaria.

Soldiers, neither particularly smart nor noticeably slovenly, had emerged from a guard-house on the shout of a sentry with whom the Hadji Abdulla had held brief colloquy at the outer gate.

Scarcely had the new-comers dismounted than two of the soldiers came to lead their horses away, and an official dressed in white European tropical kit descended the flight of steps and approached them.

With him the Hadji conversed a while, and then, turning to the General, asked for the letter of introduction to His Excellency Dom Perez de Norhona.

But the General was still obstinate on the point.

"No," said he, "I'll give it to de Norhona himself."

"How do you know that this gentleman is not His Excellency?" smiled the Arab.

"Well, is he?"

"No."

"Then if he will be good enough to take me to Dr. Norhona, as quickly as possible, I will present my credentials and talk business with him as soon as he likes."

"I'm afraid it won't be quite as easy as all that," replied Hadji Abdulla. "And listen, Sidi. You have come to São Thomé of your own free will. You have insisted on going with me to the Capital. Now, I would most strongly and earnestly advise you to remember that you *are* in the Capital of an independent State. Also that His Excellency Dom Perez de Norhona is a powerful member of its Government. So far as you are concerned, he is the Government; and there is no appeal from him. You have placed yourself in his hands and you are absolutely in his power."

"Well?"

"Don't anger him, Sidi. Approach him rather as the English nobleman, Sir Thomas Roe, approached the Emperor Akbar."

The General smiled somewhat bleakly.

But the Arab shook his head.

"I am speaking words of wisdom to a wise man, Sidi," he said. "Do heed them. And another thing. Have you any idea as to when your business may be concluded? Because I shall be sailing again soon. Probably in a few days. It would give me the greatest pleasure to carry you back to Santa Cruz.

"*Safely*," he added.

The official coughed to draw attention to the fact that he was present and extremely correct. Also, waiting.

"One minute," said the Hadji in Arabic. "I am taking farewell of the Sidi and receiving his instructions."

The official smiled meaningly.

"And look, Sidi," the Hadji said, turning to the General. "Suppose you don't sail with me, and suppose I hear nothing of you for a long time, and possibly don't find you here when I return, half a year hence? Is there anyone with whom you would like me to communicate, if I can, and tell them where I last saw you?"

"Good Heavens, no!" ejaculated the General. "Absolutely not. I do most particularly beg of you not to tell a living soul that I came to São Thomé. It is the last thing in the world that I want anyone to know. Is that clear?"

"Perfectly, Sidi. No one knows you have come here, and you want no one to know that you are here, should you unfortunately be detained longer than you now expect."

"That's it. Not a word to a soul."

"And your servant, Sidi?"

"Oh, he won't tell anybody."

"And is he to return with me to Santa Cruz?"

"He can please himself about that. If you'd be good enough to take him, I expect he'd be very much obliged to you. What about his passage-money?"

"Nothing, Sidi. It is the affair of the Government of São Thomé. I now ask your permission to leave you. May Allah protect you, Sidi."

"Good-bye, Hadji Sahib, and thank you very much indeed. You have been most helpful and obliging. Best of good luck. Good-bye. Hope to see you again soon."

"*Wallahi!* I hope it too, Sidi. Farewell. Allah guard you."

And with a long look into the General's eyes, he bowed, turned and strode back in the direction of a door in the thick grey wall at the far side of the vast courtyard, the expression of his face grave and sad.

The official, saying something of which the General understood not a word, pointed toward the flight of steps and bowing, indicated that he should proceed in that direction.

At the top of the stairs the man opened a small but massive door and led the way along a dark corridor. This debouched into a great hall, medieval, raftered and stone-flagged. Crossing this, he led the way to another flight of stairs which climbed to a gallery. This they ascended, walked along the gallery to the entrance of another gloomy passage, and, at a door therein, halted.

The official unlocked the door, stepped back and bowed General Jason into a fair-sized lofty room lighted by a large but heavily-barred window. Glancing round the apartment, the General got the impression of the sort of room one sees in a very old English house or castle, furnished in what is known as "period" fashion.

Again, saying something of which the General understood nothing, the man turned to depart.

"Oh, by the way, will you have my kit sent up here when the pack-horses arrive?" said the General.

Probably the fellow understood English, though he

couldn't speak it.

The man stared uncomprehendingly. How like an Indian Eurasian head clerk or hotel-manager or police official or lawyer he was. Surely he must understand Hindustani?

The General repeated his request in that language. And again in French.

No gleam of comprehension lighted the sallow face of the São Thoméan.

Well, one more shot—in German; though there wasn't much hope of his knowing that, if he didn't know French. Like many other keen and ambitious British Officers, the General had learned German, and had spent a year of his leave in that country studying on the spot, and as far as possible, the theory and practice of its military methods.

He repeated his request in German, but without result. Again with expressionless face, the man bowed politely, turned and departed.

Not only did he close the door behind him but, to the General's slight consternation, most audibly locked it.

Well, he was an old campaigner. He'd make himself comfortable. Very good bed. Very good chairs and table. What he would have liked would have been an arm-chair such as that in his study at home. Be rather nice to be back there for a while, relaxed in that deep comfortable chair, with one of his cigars alight and the morning paper in front of his face.

But he'd be doing that, before long; and without any of the old financial anxiety gnawing at the back of his mind like a rat at a wainscot.

Well, he had had far worse accommodation than this. Many and many a worse room, during the War.

But he had never been locked in one. Never in his life, so far as he could remember. And it wasn't a pleasant sensation. Not exactly a "bed-sit. with running h. & c. bath" —but really very decent quarters. He'd have to explain that he washed occasionally, and that this was one of the occasions. Doubtless he could explain in pantomime what he wanted. Somebody would be bringing him some food before long, of course.

He sat down on the brown blanket folded at the foot of the heavy wooden bed and, with equal mind, pondered the situation.

Anyway, here he was, and—by good luck, good judgment, the fortune of Fate or the will of God—right in the very middle of things.

§4

The door opened and, preceded by the same official, who bowed low and retired, a short swarthy man with big head, extraordinarily brilliant eyes and the general air, appearance and manner of an important Portuguese gentleman, advanced toward him.

As he rose to his feet and extended his hand in greeting, the General was reminded of someone whom he had met and liked in India. Who was it and where? Yes, at the Bombay Yacht Club. The Portuguese Consul-General, a cultured, charming and aristocratic individual, taller than this man, his handsome face less remarkably interesting.

What was it about this face? The eyes, of course. Almost luminous. Uncanny.

"Good evening, Senhor. How do you do? I . . ." began General Jason, apparently even more than usually reserved, reticent and uncordial. "I wonder if you—er—speak English or understand it?"

"Yes," replied the visitor, to the General's great relief, "I understand English perfectly and speak it as well as . . . you hear. Will you kindly introduce yourself?"

From the breast pocket of his khaki shooting-jacket the General produced the letter with which Senhor Pereira had provided Mr. Palsover.

"My name is—er—Reginaldo—er . . ." he said. He hated boggling and equivocating but—he must be careful. There might perhaps be good reason, later, to be glad he hadn't blurted out his surname, at once. And Palsover's own name might be in the letter. But no—he said this Pereira feller never knew his real name, "General . . . British Army.

Retired. I have a letter here for Dr. de Norhona. A letter of introduction from Senhor Pereira."

"I am de Norhona," replied the other. "Thank you. Won't you be seated?"

And as the General sat down again upon the bed, the man walked across to the window, opened the letter and read it.

Having done so, he turned and favoured the General with a long appraising stare.

"Ah!" said he. "You are an Englishman? A British Officer? A General? Reginaldo, did you say? And this letter was given to you by my friend Pereira? Interesting. *Very interesting.*"

Again he studied the letter thoughtfully, his brows drawn together in a heavy frown.

The General felt a little uncomfortable, and devoutly wished he knew the precise contents of the letter of introduction. Possibly this feller Pereira hadn't admired the worthy Palsover as much as the latter thought he did?

Anyway, the letter had got him here. Got him to the one spot on earth where he wanted to be. And that was the great thing.

Dom Perez de Norhona folded the letter and returned it to the envelope.

"And where is Pereira himself at the present moment?" he asked. "I have rather been expecting him. Did so six months ago, in fact."

"I'm afraid I cannot tell you, Senhor. My information is that he left Santa Cruz . . . in a hurry. Rather suddenly."

"I don't doubt it, '*General*,' " was the reply. "I feel pretty certain that Pereira left Santa Cruz quite suddenly. And before he went, he certainly wrote this letter. Unquestionably it is a perfectly genuine letter of—er—introduction."

"Oh, yes, quite so," agreed General Jason. "Shall we talk business now, or would you rather postpone that until tomorrow or till—after dinner, say."

Dr. Perez de Norhona smiled pleasantly—or perhaps unpleasantly.

"I think we will postpone business until, as you say, after

dinner, or perhaps till to-morrow. Unless, of course, you'd like to tell me, in a few words, to what São Thomé owes the honour of your visit. What is your *real* object?"

"Well, to put it bluntly and briefly, a radium concession."

"*Ah? So?*" smiled the doctor.

"I want to make an extremely advantageous proposal to the Government of São Thomé. We want to pay them a lump sum and a handsome royalty in return for permission to—er—mine for uranium and produce radium. And also to purchase a few hundred or a few thousand tons of that queer quick-sand of yours."

"*Ah! So?*" was again de Norhona's only comment, but he showed most of his gleaming teeth in a pleasant or unpleasant smile. "I shall give myself the pleasure of coming to see you later to-night or to-morrow, when we will talk of . . . many things. Meanwhile, is there anything that you require?"

"Well, I've been riding all day and I don't deny that I should enjoy a bath, and after that, a spot of something to eat and drink."

"*Cela va sans dire.* You speak French—er—'General'?"

"Oh, yes. Pretty well. No one would mistake me for a Frenchman, but I read and speak it pretty well."

"And German?"

"Yes, yes. Rather better than French."

And suddenly the surprising Dr. Norhona inquired in fluent if faulty German as to whether Senhor Pereira had given him any particular verbal message; as to whether it was he who had introduced the General to Hadji Abdulla; and as to how long he had sojourned at Santa Cruz.

And to humour this excellent linguist, the General replied to the best of his ability and in his best German, which was indeed very good.

Whereafter the accomplished doctor, bidding the General a courteous good night, bowed, and, still smiling his peculiar and enigmatic smile, withdrew, locking the door behind him.

That was a queer cove, mused General Jason. He hadn't

spent his life in São Thomé—to speak English, French and German like that. Naturally he'd have to go abroad to qualify as a doctor, and he might, of course, have studied medicine in London, Paris and Vienna.

Well, an interesting little adventure. Quite amusing, being locked in his bedroom like a naughty boy.

Anyhow he had got hold of the right man, straight away, the man who could start things going as soon as he had been sufficiently interested and had seen, not only his personal profit, but how enormous it would be.

So far, so good, and, after a most refreshing bath which involved getting into a large jar—as did those whom he humorously thought of as "the other Forty Thieves"—and quite a good dinner, the General retired to rest in a fairly happy and hopeful frame of mind.

§5

That night there was a meeting of the Cabinet of the Grand Council of São Thomé. At the head of a long table in the centre of the great hall sat Doña Guiomar, in a kind of chair-throne, Dom Miguel de Braganza being on her right hand and His Excellency Dom Perez de Norhona on her left. Among the other members present were the soldier somewhat grandiloquently known as the Commander-in-Chief of the Armed Forces of São Thomé; the Minister of Justice; the Chancellor of the Exchequer; the Secretary of State for Agriculture, Fisheries and Health; the Minister of Transport, Roads, Bridges and Public Works; the Minister for Education; and other Members of the Cabinet who, with the consent of the Council, governed, under the Regent, the State of São Thomé. Each of them was a gentleman of aristocratic and almost pure, Portuguese, descent.

His Excellency Dom Perez de Norhona, other business concluded, addressed the Council. One passage in his speech would have been of painful interest to General Jason, could he have heard it.

". . . I'm afraid that it sheds no light on the fate of our

excellent servant and friend, our agent and representative, Manöel Pereira, of whom I have, alas, already begun to think in the past tense, so to speak. But this letter is, without the faintest shadow of doubt, from him, written in his own hand, on our own paper, and in our own private and particular official language, and using certain words and phrases which no one else could have used. He describes this man, who pretends to be a British General, as being not only a German, an emissary and agent of the German Government's Department of Commerce, but also as a scoundrel, a thief and assassin. Also he is desperately disturbed—and indeed it is a most disturbing thought—by the fact that this fellow has, in some unaccountable and incredible way, learned of the mineral resources of this country. As I discovered long ago, and duly informed this Council, we are blessed, or cursed, with the possession of certain substances which in Europe are regarded as being of enormous value. This Nazi German, whose name is Fritz Schultz, has come here to open negotiations with us for the exploitation and commercialization of these mineral deposits! He, of course, wants concessions and mining-rights. He desires—and to-morrow will propose—the industrial invasion of São Thomé. . . . Why he should pretend to be English I don't know. It may be because the English are the ancient allies and friends of Portugal, or because there is English financial backing to the Company which he doubtless proposes to form."

"It is certain that he is a German?" asked Doña Guiomar, Regent of São Thomé.

"Pereira so describes him, here, and as I said, gives his name as Fritz Schultz, which is most definitely a German name. Also the man himself speaks German perfectly."

"And he actually referred to these minerals and the granting of a concession to mine them?" asked the Regent.

"He did. Briefly and in outline, of course; but he proposes to lay the whole matter before me at length and in detail to-morrow."

"Then I venture to suggest," said His Excellency the Marquess Dom Miguel de Braganza, "that we welcome our visitor, bid him stay here just as long as he likes and per-haps a little longer, and start him to work personally at the quick-sand to-morrow."

"Quick-sand and slow death," he added, and smiled pensively.

There was a general movement and word of assent from each member of the Cabinet.

"He certainly must not leave São Thomé," observed the Regent.

"No. He certainly must not," agreed de Norhona. "But I would ask that the Marquess should reconsider the ques-tion of his being invited to fill his buckets from our remark-able quick-sand. It would be in the nature of waste."

"Oh, but we have plenty of sand. We can spare a little," smiled the Marquess de Braganza.

"Waste of a good visitor, I meant," replied de Norhona, flashing his gleaming teeth toward the speaker. "If the Council would kindly place him in my charge, I could make far better use of him."

"And not waste him, eh?" said Doña Guiomar, her ex-tremely beautiful face, strong and very intelligent, lighting up as she smiled quizzically at her favourite Member of the Council.

"Definitely not. Far from it. He would be extremely useful to me, and I beg your Serene Highness to—er—allot him to me, so to speak."

"Why, certainly. Certainly. I see no objection whatso-ever. You'd take care, of course, that he never left the Island."

"I can most certainly assure Your Highness that he will never leave the Island," replied de Norhona.

And after the Council had given its unanimous consent to Dr. de Norhona's dealing with this German business and with the German himself, the Council passed on to matters of graver import.

PART V

For Colonel Henry Carthew life was never again quite the same after the departure from Sitapur of his life-long friends, Reginald and Antoinette Jason. To gain command of the Regiment that he also loved was small compensation for the loss of the only two people whom in the whole wide world he loved.

At first, he was utterly wretched, lost, lonely and depolarized. Nor was he ever quite clear in his mind as to whether he missed Reginald or Antoinette the more. He loved his friend Reginald with the amazing, abiding and selfless love with which a man may love another man, with a love passing the love of woman: the love of David for Jonathan.

Antoinette he loved as the best sort of man does love a woman, with adoration and something of apotheosis, the love and dazzled yearning of the moth for the star. Had she not married Reginald, he would have done his utmost to be worthy to marry her, and would have dared to lay his life and career at her feet, while overwhelmed by a sense of his utter unworthiness. As it was, he loved her with a gentle and unselfish devotion which is not too common. She was the only woman in his life, the only woman whom he had ever loved.

And these two were gone, leaving him desolate, lonely and miserable. Almost daily he wrote to one or other of his two friends, and occasionally he received a reply.

Realizing that he might be boring them, he then wrote weekly; and finding that this produced a reply from Reginald or Antoinette about once a month, wrote to each in alternate weeks, so that each had a fortnight of peace from his pestering.

When at length these letters remained almost unanswered, he began to write long and intimate letters, such as a man may write to his wife, a woman to her beloved husband—and then destroyed them.

Finding this destruction distasteful and indeed painful, he changed the letter-writing to diary-keeping, and to this diary he confided his inmost thoughts.

While fond of Henry, both Reginald and Antoinette Jason had always, and quite rightly, considered him a queer chap.

When the day came that General Jason retired, Colonel Carthew decided that, after giving them a few months or perhaps a year in which to settle down at Home, he would send in his papers, retire to England, and try to find a small house as near Jason's place as possible. Of course, it would be nothing like his friends' fine old house and timbered estate, but he'd be able to afford a nice little cottage *de luxe*. Perhaps in a tiny orchard with an acre of garden. Keep a dog or two and possibly a horse. Then he'd be able to ride over and drop in just whenever he felt like it, or rather, as often as he thought they could stand it. If he didn't over-do it, he would always be welcome. Reginald would be delighted to see him and to talk over old times far into the night, and Antoinette would be glad to have him about the place, making himself useful. He'd potter in the garden with her. She loved gardening and he knew a bit about it himself. He'd get some books and learn some more.

§2

One day toward the end of the time that Carthew had allotted himself as his final period in India, he received a rare and tremendously welcome letter from his beloved Antoinette. For a time he forbore to open it, gloating upon her handwriting on the envelope. He would keep it till the evening, and after his return from Mess, would settle down in perfect peace and comfort to read and re-read her words, which always delighted him with their playful, kindly, friendly badinage and jests at the expense of the crusty old bachelor and misogynist.

Misogynist! If she only knew. Indeed it was surprising that she didn't. It was wonderful that he had never given himself away in all those years when he was seeing her daily. Rather clever of him, really.

But actually he did not read the letter in great mental peace or any degree of comfort. Antoinette was troubled, worried and anxious. And no wonder, by Gad! Reginald was what she called "more or less missing." He had never returned from that trip! Carthew knew that Reginald had suddenly been moved to rush off on some mysterious expedition to some unknown place, leaving her with no more information than that he would be back in six months' time.

And now, not only had the six months expired but another six months as well. And in all that while she had had no communication from him whatsoever, save a brief and flippant note from a place called Santa Cruz, saying that this was the *starting-point* of the expedition.

Had he written to his old friend Henry within the last twelve months and given him any idea of where he was and what he was up to, she asked.

No, indeed, he hadn't, mused Henry Carthew. The old beggar hadn't written him a line for well over a twelve-month. Getting damned lazy, that was the fact of it. Not that he had ever been a brilliant correspondent—from the point of regularity and punctuality, anyway. Really too bad of him, to push off into the blue like this, and leave Antoinette to worry. Too bad to go even for six months without her knowing where he was. And then to make it twelve. What on earth could be the game? Some Government job? Surely not. Not with all that secrecy. He would have told Antoinette something about it. And if he couldn't take her with him, he would write to her.

Queer! What could it mean? Could there be a woman in it?

No. Utter rubbish. Reginald had always been a model husband. Never dream of doing a thing like that.

Greatly puzzled and somewhat perturbed, Henry Carthew thought of little else than this strange disappearance of General Jason. And, after chewing the matter over by night and day, revolving it in his mind until his mind almost ceased to revolve, he answered Lady Jason's letter, and told her that he hadn't had a word from her husband, alas, for quite eighteen months. And that he hadn't the faintest idea as to what he was doing, nor where he could be. But would she please bear this in mind—that there was nothing, literally nothing, he would not do to help her. As she knew, Reginald was his oldest and best, indeed his only friend, except herself, and if she thought Reginald was in danger or trouble, if she thought he was really lost, she had only to say the word, and he would throw up everything and come home by the next boat.

But of course, the first thing to do was to find out where, approximately, he was, or was last heard of. And if she could learn nothing from the British Consul or appropriate authority in that part, he himself would go to this Santa Cruz place, or any other from which she had received later information.

It was almost a year before Colonel Carthew received another letter from Lady Jason. In this she told him that she was reduced to a state of hopelessness and despair. Such was her anxiety, and so difficult was her position, that she was now being selfish enough to accept her dear friend Henry's offer of a year ago, and to ask him to come and help her.

Freely she admitted that she had been unable to discover anything at all, and knew nothing whatsoever as to Reginald's whereabouts, save that he had reached this place, Santa Cruz, from which he had last written.

By appeal to the War Office, the Foreign Office and Scotland Yard; by advertising far and wide; by writing to the offices of the Shipping Companies, she had discovered nothing at all, save that Reginald had sailed by the S.S. *Gibraltar* of the British Southern and General Mail Company, and had left the ship at Belamu where he had transferred to the S.S. *São José de Coimba* of the Anglo-Portuguese Steam Navigation and Trading Company. This ship had stopped to land him at Santa Cruz, an almost harbourless place which was not one of their ports of call, inasmuch as it was not worth calling a port.

Letters to such people as the Governor, the Mayor, the Chief of Police, the principal hotel (under that name) had all remained unanswered. And in any case, she was afraid, if any representative of General Jason made his way to this Santa Cruz place, it was unlikely that he would learn anything as to the General's destination. Since he had kept that information from her, he would hardly impart it to casual acquaintances, if he made any, at Santa Cruz.

Having done everything of which she could think, moved Heaven and earth to get news of him, she now appealed to her oldest and best friend, her dear Henry, to do anything that he could and would.

Colonel Carthew replied by cable that he was sending in his papers at once, and would come to England immediately his affairs were wound up. He then wrote a letter telling Antoinette that he would henceforth devote his life and all his worldly goods to the search for his friend, her husband.

§3

Henry Carthew found Lady Jason in better case than he had expected. He had feared to find a haggard and broken woman, half-dead with anxiety, fear and worry. He found a lady in excellent health, good spirits and a state of glowing resentment, annoyance and, indeed, anger toward her husband—not because he was lost, of course, but because he had gone and got himself lost in such an exceedingly silly way. Why on earth couldn't he have told her where he was going and why he was going there?

Sneaking off with all that secrecy and mystery!

Going off without making proper arrangements for the future, should he by any chance be away for more than his anticipated six months.

Going off and leaving her stranded, neither wife nor widow, nor—what was more to the point—his accredited financial agent. Things were getting terribly difficult from that point of view. Extremely so.

No, it was not so much a case of "my poor lost darling with his romantic ideas" as "the silly old fool with his idiotic tricks."

It was of course all to the good that Antoinette should bear up so bravely and incline rather toward indignation than to sentimentalism and premature grief. Or so Henry Carthew told himself, as he stoutly denied and rejected the idea that he was just a little shocked at Antoinette's hardness. No doubt this apparent hardness covered real grief, a sense of terrible bereavement, great anxiety and immeasurable tenderness. It was a good thing that she should show so brave a front to the world, and talk rather of the idiotic way in which Reginald had let her down and given her all this worry, financial bother and general annoyance, than bemoan the fate of her beloved lost darling. Better a warmly indignant woman than a miserable weeping Niobe.

But of course she must be desperately unhappy and must go in perpetual fear. How could it be otherwise? She must love Reginald completely. What woman would not? Especially one who had lived with him so long and really knew his wonderful virtues. Why, he himself felt sick with anxiety when he realized that Reginald Jason, his hero, his beloved friend who had been the star of his boyish admiration and the object of his whole-hearted and single-hearted love, had been lost for a couple of years; Reginald whom he had always followed with a fidelity which was but just this side of blindness; Reginald whom he had literally reverenced, and who, from his childish Prep. School days, had been his guide, philosopher and friend.

Friend. That noble word.

And now it was the turn and the time for Henry Carthew to be a friend indeed to his friend in need, and to show what a friend could do.

§4

And thus it came to pass that, upon a day of sullen heat

when the white incandescent sky brooded low over a waveless oily sea, Henry Carthew was rowed ashore from the old *S.S. St. Paul de Loanda* and landed at the rotting quay of the rotting, sun-smitten, swamp-encircled, disease-infested town of Santa Cruz, made his way to the *Casa Real*, and received what was undoubtedly the very greatest surprise, not to say shock, of all his life.

For, entering that dismal and all-but-derelict hostelry, he came face to face with the man who had once, and for years, been his best *bête-noir*—Mess-Sergeant Samuel Palsover!

"Good Lord above us!" ejaculated Henry Carthew, blinking his eyes, almost rubbing them in his incredulous amazement.

"Blimey!" responded Mr. Palsover.

And the two men stared at each other in utter wonder.

Well! thought Henry Carthew, of all the amazing coincidences! It is a world's record. Last time I saw this beggar was in Sitapur, and *now*—to find him here in this hole at the back of beyond, the last place God made!

Ah, but is it exactly coincidence? Reginald Jason came here. Is this fellow Palsover in any way connected with that? Of course he is.

Lumme! thought Mr. Palsover. Well, well, well! Who'd have thought it? What's the old devil doing here? Cor! You'd have thought you was safe in Santa Cruz, wouldn't you? And here of all people on God's earth, the old Colonel rolls up and walks in as large as life. That's a rum go, if ever. But was it so much of a rum go, after all? He must be on the track of the General.

Yerss. . . . That letter the General wrote to his wife. Perhaps he himself had been a fool to post it, after all. But there, it gave nothing away, except the name of this Santa Cruz place. And that was what had brought the Colonel here. Depend on it! He was doing the blooming hero salvation act. And here was as far as he would get.

He couldn't know anything about St. Tommy now, could

he? A million to one against the General ever having said a word to him about it. Why no, damn it all, what was he thinking about? He himself had never told the General, even; not until they got here and met the Arab. Could the General have written from St. Tommy? Not according to the Arab. Could the General himself have escaped? Not according to the Arab. And he himself had never seen hide nor hair of him, nor heard a word of him, for nigh on a couple of years. No, that was it. The old Colonel was on the noble salvation stunt. "Dr.-Livingstone-I-presume" stuff. Well, he'd soon get it out of the little Stanley. Stanley the Explorer lost in Santa Cruz, and finding his old pal Palsover behind the bar of the *Caser Reel*. Laugh! . . . Enough to make a cat laugh!

But half a mo'! What if the General had gone and told his wife all about the rayjum business—and she had gone and told Carthew! . . . He'd shoot him as soon as look at him, the old fool, if there was going to be any hankey-pankey, any double-crossing. Nobody in this world wasn't going to do S. Palsover, Esquire, out of his rights, and get away with it. No, by Cripes! . . .

On the other hand—suppose the General was really scuppered, as it began to look like. Couldn't sit here waiting for him much longer. The Colonel was an old swine—but he was straight. He'd play the blooming game, fair and square, if he was let in on it. Perhaps the best thing, after all, would be to . . . ?

"And what the devil are you doing here, Palsover?" asked Henry Carthew, none too cordially.

"Me, Sir? Keeping this little pub. Been here the last, oh, couple of years, nearly. Always thought I'd keep a pub when I left the Army, but I never thought it would be in this God-forsaken country."

"Well, how does it come to be in this country? Did you, by any chance, come out here with General Jason?"

"That's right, Sir. That's right. Met the General in England. And almost as soon as he claps eyes on me he says,

'Coming with me, Palsover? I'm going out on a expedition.' And 'What do you think, General? Not 'arf,' says I. And here I am."

"And where's General Jason?"

"Ar! Where, Sir?"

"But you know where he went from here, don't you?"

"That's right, Sir."

"Well, presumably he is there."

"You're telling me. I can't find out that he's there."

"Haven't you been there? Haven't you tried to find out for yourself?"

"Ar! And you can lay to that."

"But he can't have absolutely disappeared."

"You're telling me again. It's just percisely what he has done."

"Why did he go there?"

"Now you're asking me, for a change. I expect you know as well as I do, don't you, Sir, what he went there for?"

"I do not. I haven't the very faintest idea as to why he went there."

"Cross your heart? Cut your throat if you tell a lie? Strike you blind?" Mr. Palsover had evidently had a morning eye-opener. Or possibly an eye-closer.

"When I say I don't know why General Jason went to this place, you may take it for granted that I *don't* know," replied Henry Carthew coldly.

"Well," replied Mr. Palsover, politely raising his hand to excuse, if not conceal, a gentle hiccup, "he went to this place with the idea of making a bit of money—or so he told me. Brought me as far as here and left me stranded. And here I am to this day."

"Faithful hever," he added pensively as he reached for a bottle.

"I wonder you didn't go home, Palsover."

"No, Sir. No. '*Wait here*,' said the General. And here I waits. That's me, Samuel Palsover."

And even Colonel Henry Carthew was almost moved to sympathy and admiration as he gazed on the yearning, trustful, faithful-hound-like countenance of Mr. Samuel

Palsover, now regarding him with those large, moist, and alas, somewhat yellowing eyes.

"And you positively have no information as to where General Jason is, what became of him, or whether he ever left this other place? . . . Where is it, by the way?"

"Well, Sir, in a manner of speaking, I don't know."

"But you've been there, you say."

"Regular. Once every six months for the last couple of years or so."

"Well then, what do you mean by saying you don't know where it is?"

"Well, Sir, you goes by sea in a bloomin' bunder-boat, and how are you to know whether you're going north, east, south or west? Boat clears out of here at night, and lands you at this place at night too. How are you to know which way you come? Bloomin' boat may keep on tacking all night, or sail round in a bloody great circle, just to confuse you. That's my belief what it does."

"How long does it take?"

"Oh, best part of a fortnight. Time slips away like, when you got nothing to do but eat, drink and sleep."

"Well, could we get a boat and set off at once, to-morrow?"

Mr. Palsover laughed long and loud, to the great annoyance of Henry Carthew, who found something in his laughter that he disliked intensely. Cynicism? Contempt? Patronage?

"What the devil are you laughing at?" he asked sharply.

"You, Sir, in a manner o' speaking. Also the idea of taking a bunder-boat and pushing off to-morrow. Why, nobody here don't know where the place is. Never even heard of it, let alone the way there. You only get the chance to go twice in the year."

"How's that?"

"Because every six months a native feller comes in a big bunder-boat, what they call a *dhow*, on his way there. Puts in for water and grub and perhaps to pick up a feller or drop him on his way back. Letters perhaps, or messages or somethink. *I* don't know."

"And he took General Jason to this place?"

"Ar, that's right. Me too."

"When is he due again?"

"Oh, in a month or two. Any old time between now and the change of the monsoon."

"I'll wait for him," announced Carthew.

"The devil you will, Sir?" replied Palsover. "How do you know he'll take you?"

"Why shouldn't he?"

"Visitors not invited. *Not at Home*, if they call. '*Keep away with both feet. This means you*' sort of hospitality."

"How could they stop my going?"

"Because you couldn't get anybody to take you there. And if you could, it would not be a case of stopping you from going, but from coming. Coming back. Damned difficult place to get to and a damned sight more difficult to get away from. That's what General Jason found out."

"You think he's still there then?"

"Yerss. That's right, Sir. Unless he grew bloomin' wings, he's still there. Course he might have grown 'em.

"*Angel's* wings," added Mr. Palsover mournfully.

"Look here. You say that this mysterious fellow in his mysterious boat takes you. Couldn't you get him to take me?"

"I could try, Sir. I could try. We might square him. But it would require considerable dough. . . . Perhaps if you could put up enough, I might be able to work it."

Yes, that'd be the thing, pondered Mr. Palsover. Next time the Arab came, tell him this gent, another British Officer, wanted to find out what had become of his old pal General Jason. Find out for himself. And they could tell the Arab that if he wanted to save the St. Tommy people trouble, he had better take Carthew, otherwise he'd go back home and raise hell, and the first thing they'd know would be that there was a British warship banging off at 'em.

Perhaps the Arab would grin and say how was the British warship going to find the Island, for a start; and, *if* they found it, how was they to know that General Jason hadn't pushed off long ago?

Anyway, it was worth trying. For, to tell the truth, he was getting sick, sorry and tired of being Felice Diego's partner in this blasted pot-house, and living in this God-forsaken one-eyed hole. Trading up-country wasn't too bad, but it was mouldy chicken-feed compared with what he had come out here for. And many a time he had been tempted to "cut his lucky"—his unlucky, rather. Cut his losses and clear out. But he couldn't bring himself to do it, not with all those millions waiting to be picked up on that island, and the General there himself.

He had never thought much of old Carthew. He had hated his guts. But he was a gentleman. He wouldn't double-cross anybody, and no harm could come from getting him on to the Island. And a damn lot of good might come of it if he found out all about the General. And if the poor old chap had got one of these nasty diseases, or died of malaria, then the thing to do would be to let Carthew in on the rayjum business, and let him take the General's place. He'd sooner work with the General; but Carthew was just as straight. He wouldn't double-cross anybody. And that was the real danger, when you were up against big concessions that were worth millions.

Yes, he'd get Carthew over to St. Tommy, next time the Arab rolled up.

II

For five weary weeks, each as long as an ordinary month, Henry Carthew endured the society of Samuel Palsover, the appalling climate of Santa Cruz, and the amenities of the *Casa Real*—in that order. And it was a pleasure to him to do so, for increasingly he felt sure that he was on the track of his dearly-loved friend.

Little by little, Mr. Palsover, whom he could not bring himself to like but forced himself to tolerate, raised his hopes and increased his tiny stock of knowledge as to the probable whereabouts of General Jason and his reason for going—wherever he had gone. But until the arrival of the Hadji Abdulla, the words *São Thomé* were never uttered by the garrulous master of the *Casa Real*. Half proprietor Mr. Palsover might be; but wholly in charge, command and possession he was; Senhor Felice Diego being occasionally seen but seldom heard. Henry Carthew gained the impression that Palsover had some hold over the little man, and the certainty that the latter went in fear and trembling of the burly and overbearing Palsover.

'All done by kindness,' as Mr. Palsover would say, but done very effectively.

By the time that Henry Carthew had begun to wonder whether Palsover had been telling him a pack of lies, and was keeping him kicking his heels at Santa Cruz in the interests of the profits of the *Casa Real*, the auspicious day dawned when Mr. Palsover, bringing him his morning tea, announced with great solemnity and evident joy, that He had come. Mr. Palsover spoke with the *empressement* and solemnity of one who announced the Second Coming.

After a hasty shave and sketchy breakfast, Henry Carthew, dripping with perspiration, hurried down to the quay of the almost silted-up harbour, and there beheld, among the coasting bunder-boats and *dhows*, a remarkably fine *baggala*.

Seating himself on a bollard, he watched and waited until a large *toni* was paddled ashore from the big *dhow*. In its stern sat a big bearded man whose face, size, white robes and green turban marked him as the individual so often described by Palsover as "the Arab," the Hadji Abdulla.

Carthew, long a student of Arabic, and holder of the Indian Government's Honours standard certificate for proficiency in that language, correctly greeted the man who ascended the rickety ladder and stepped on to the quay. He announced himself as an Englishman, a soldier, retired Colonel of a British Regiment and the friend of one General Jason, who was now definitely regarded as missing, and whom, as he was informed, the Hadji Sahib had given passage in his *dhow* from Santa Cruz.

While studying the speaker gravely and with deep interest, the Arab replied that his information concerning the British General was correct, and that on one of his visits to Santa Cruz he had taken that Sidi to São Thomé.

"São Thomé!" repeated Carthew. "Where's that?"

"Well," replied the Arab, "it's a long way from here. Quite a little voyage."

"You are going there from here, are you?"

"I'm going to many places from here, Sidi."

"São Thomé among them?"

"I shouldn't be surprised."

"Look here. I want you to take me, and I am prepared to make it worth your while."

"To take you to São Thomé, Sidi? I couldn't do that. I never take strangers to São Thomé."

"But you took my friend, General Jason."

"Oh, but that was different. He had a letter of introduction—a letter which proved to be perfectly genuine—given him by a Government official, and addressed to a member of the São Thomé Government."

"But you took another man with him?"

"Yes, his servant, Sidi. I took him too, because the Sidi who had the letter guaranteed him."

"Well, now let him in turn guarantee me."

"That's hardly the same thing, is it?" replied the Arab. "The British Officer had a letter for me as well as the other letter, and said,

'*This is my passport to São Thomé and I wish to take my servant.*' You have no letter of introduction, have you? No? Well, I don't think I can take anyone to São Thomé because this servant guarantees him."

"Why, what harm could I do to the State of São Thomé?"

"I don't know, Sidi. But there's another question. What harm could the State of São Thomé do to you?"

"Well, I am ready to risk that."

"So was General Jason. And he has not been heard of since he reached the Capital. I am the last person outside São Thomé who saw him, and that was two years ago; and I have been entirely unable to learn anything whatever about him on my subsequent visits."

"That's why I want to come."

"Do you think, Sidi, that you could find out what is entirely hidden from me who am accepted and recognized by the São Thoméan Government, and who visit the Island twice a year, not only with their knowledge and consent, but at their request? I take goods, letters, messages and so forth, up to the Capital. I sojourn there for days at a time. I go about the *suqs* and bazaars, talking with all manner of men. In the cafes and bazaars I hear all the rumours and the gossip of the town. Could you, an uninvited stranger, do more, even if you had the opportunity—which you would not have? The Sidi General interested me. I liked him, and each time that I have returned, I have tried to find out where he is or what has happened to him. If I took you with me, without credentials, safe conduct, or letter of introduction, you'd be arrested instantly, and I should be summoned before the Council for examination—as to whether I had gone mad or whether I could give any other reason for having brought a stranger to São Thomé."

"Well, suppose you said that I told you that I had most important business with the Government of São Thomé? And suppose I paid you a considerable sum of money to take me there? And suppose you decided that you had no right to use your own discretion as to the importance of the matter? It might be something of the most vital urgency, something on which the very safety of the State depended. Who are you to decide whether . . ."

The Hadji smiled and shook his head.

"Sidi," said he, "suppose that, when you were commanding a Regiment, you gave a certain subordinate the very strictest orders that never, under any circumstances whatsoever, should he do a certain thing. And suppose he did it, and for no reason except that he thought he would? . . . No, it is probably more than my life is worth, certainly more than my trade is worth, for me to break the first and greatest of all the commands laid upon me by the Government of São Thomé. Let us come along to the *Casa Real*, and there give me the pleasure and the honour of hearing anything more that you would like to say. The Roumi named Palsover can join in our conversation, should you wish. But let me repeat, once and for all, that I have no authority to take you to São Thomé, and cannot possibly take the heavy and dangerous responsibility."

"Oh, come, Hadji Sahib. Dangerous? A man like you to use such a word?" smiled Carthew.

"I have no hesitation in using the word 'dangerous' in connection with São Thomé," was the grave reply. "Danger? It would be certain death for you, probably death for me; certain loss of my valuable trade, and probably confiscation of my *dhow*."

Henry Carthew's heart sank, but his courage remained high and his determination unshaken.

Where there's a will there's a way, and God knew he had the will. There are other methods of killing a cat than by choking it with melted butter. (How was it that Reginald used to paraphrase that? "There are other ways of making an elephant laugh than by tickling it with a feather.") And he'd find some way of persuading this Hadji chap. But damn it all—it began to look a bit grim for Reginald. God grant that they hadn't done more than detain him there. If they had, it would be up to him to help him to escape. A prisoner's chances are quadrupled by having a friend outside, and surely, between them, they could put up enough to bribe the Hadji to take a risk.

What a nice fellow he seemed. Sort of man one took to, at once.

§2

As, talking amiably, the Hadji and Colonel Carthew entered the gate of the sand-covered compound of the *Casa Real* they heard a shrill scream and saw a young girl, almost a child, run headlong from the front door of the hotel.

As they looked in her direction, the huge negro, whom Mr. Palsover had whimsically gazetted as Giant Pander of Santa Cruz, appeared in the doorway, his ugly face convulsed with rage, a bottle in his right hand.

In a language which the Hadji understood, he roared filthy abuse at the child and, with all his might, flung the bottle as she fled a few yards in advance of him. The big heavy bottle struck her squarely on the back of the head and was shattered in pieces by the violence of the blow which sent the girl sprawling, face downward, on the ground, where she lay still and apparently dead.

It had all been so sudden and swift that the child was down and the negro seizing her by the hair, before Carthew and the Hadji had time to intervene.

With a shout, Henry Carthew sprang forward and rushed toward the negro. But quickly as he moved, the Hadji, though bigger and heavier, moved more quickly.

With a shout of "*Hi!*" he rushed at the negro, and drove a crashing straight-left at his face, knocking him down. Springing up, the powerful brute in turn leapt at the Hadji with extended hands, attacking him as might a gorilla. Closing in, the Hadji most scientifically hooked with his left, upper-cut with his right, and, as the man staggered back, drove a terrific left at the point of his jaw.

Tottering backward, the negro collapsed and fell, and the subsequent proceedings ceased to interest him for several minutes.

Tenderly lifting the child from the ground, the Hadji carried her into the house, shouted for Diego, handed her to him, and bade him fetch Almeida who, at any rate, called himself a doctor, and see that the women-folk looked after the child properly.

"And you had better keep that brute of a *hubshi* out of my way, for a time. For if I set eyes on him I'll beat him insensible."

"What about handing him over to the Police?" suggested Henry Carthew.

"Oh, a lot of trouble for nothing. Merely stirring up bribery and corruption and blackmail for both of us. I can deal with him better than the Police would."

"Right. Now may I ask you a question, or rather, make a statement?"

"Certainly," replied the Arab with raised eyebrows.

"Well, look here. You're an Englishman and a remarkably fine boxer."

"An Englishman?" replied the Hadji.

"Yes, of course you are. Do you mean to say that an Arab cries '*Hi!*' in an emergency, and drives the straightest left I ever saw, and hooks, upper-cuts, and goes for the point like a champion heavy-weight?"

"Wonderful are the works of Allah," replied the Hadji somewhat evasively, as he regarded a skinned knuckle.

"Oh, quite," laughed Henry Carthew, "and I rise to remark that you are one of them. You really must forgive me for butting in, but I spoke hastily in my excitement at my own cleverness. In point of fact, it was a bit obvious, wasn't it?"

"We'll have a talk later on," replied the Hadji in the ordinary words and accent of an educated Briton. "I've got to fix up one or two things with the—er—management here, and then I must go down to my ship again. I'll give myself the pleasure of calling on you after dinner to-night."

"Oh, but won't you dine with me?" smiled Henry Carthew.

"Thanks, very much. I'd love to, but it would be unwise. I don't want to cause comment. A Hadji I am, and a Hadji I must remain; so I don't want any scandal concerning my holy name. If you'll excuse me, I won't eat and drink with Unbelievers, infidel consumers of alcohol, and those who smoke the Forbidden."

"I say, are you really a Hadji?" asked Carthew as the Arab turned away.

"Just now it was *'Are you an Englishman?'* " smiled the Hadji. "Yes, I am a Hadji. If I am not, there isn't one in this world, and never was. Yes, I've made the Pilgrimage all right. May I look you up at about eight this evening?"

"Splendid."

And that evening, as Henry Carthew sat in his bedroom at the french-window that opened on to the untrustworthy verandah, he received the promised visit from the man known as the Hadji Abdulla.

"Come along. What about a whiskey-and-soda and a cigarette?" suggested Carthew hospitably.

"I'd love to," replied the Hadji in English. "But I don't think I will. I expect Palsover will be coming up presently, and I don't want him to get suspicious. . . . Do you know, this is only about the second or third time I have given myself away, in half a lifetime."

"Well, I'm awfully sorry if I have . . ." began Carthew.

"Not at all, for I'm quite sure I can trust you never to say a single word to a living soul, that . . ."

"Good Lord, no! Sooner cut my tongue out," Carthew assured him. "And look here, I won't ask you any questions at all with regard to yourself, but I'm awfully glad to find that you are English, and that I can really talk to you as man to man, about my friend's disappearance."

"Right. We will. I'll introduce myself first," replied the Hadji. "Name's Dysart. Brodie Dysart. My father was Rear-Admiral Sir Sinclair Brodie Dysart. I've been both a sailor and a soldier, and served my five years in the French Foreign Legion—in the Indo-China campaign. Lived in Moroccan Africa for years, and in Arabia. Did the Pilgrimage to Mecca. Got to like Arab life nearly as much as I do sea life, so went Arab again and combined the two. Bought a *dhow* and learnt the business, and then had that *baggala* built under my own eye. Finest craft of its kind afloat. And I live the finest life on earth—only it's on water. All the joys of a Cowes yachtsman and a deep-sea sailor as well. And those of a keen trader too—and they are many."

"Sounds simply wonderful," said Henry Carthew as the Hadji paused.

"Pearls, coffee, hides, silk and what not, up North, and a special cargo twice a year for São Thomé. Handle anything that's good value in small bulk, except hasheesh, guns and slaves. No trouble with the Police in any port, or with the British Navy in any sea."

"Gad, how interesting. Marvellous," murmured Carthew. "I said I wouldn't ask any questions, but I really must ask one or two. Only please don't answer me, if you'd rather not. I shan't be in the least offended, of course. No earthly reason why I should be. I've no right to cross-question you. But I have come down here to find out what has happened to my oldest and dearest friend, General Sir Reginald Jason. I'm going to track him down, find him and rescue him, if he is alive; and I want you to help me."

"Wish I could," murmured the Hadji. "Not only for the sake of helping you, but because I myself liked him very much indeed. Very fine specimen of a very fine type. I warned him. I begged him not to go to São Thomé, although he had a letter of introduction."

"Well now—the question that I am going to ask you and that you are going to answer or not, as you think fit. This mysterious São Thomé place. How is it that *you* can come and go safely?"

"Oh, it's a long story. To cut it short—a good many years ago I was able to save a man who was in bad trouble in a certain port that has a very bad and very well-deserved reputation. He was up against the local Governor and in the hands of a pretty bad police-gang, and was undoubtedly for it. I thought he was a Portuguese and a fellow-European. Anyway, I got him away on my *dhow*, and he was more than grateful, because apparently something very much more important than his life was at stake.

"Well, in short, he paid me very handsomely to take him home—having made me swear on the Koran, the Beard of the Prophet, the head and the life of my first-born and all else that I might hold sacred, that I would not publish anything I might learn about his destination.

"We got very friendly on the voyage, and, having aroused my curiosity and horrible cupidity, he did, after long and deep cogitation and terrific mental struggle, make up his mind to take me ashore at São Thomé, and actually to the capital of the State. His intention and object was to bring me before the Regent and Council and, more particularly, the Secretary to the Cabinet, with the view to my being appointed official business-agent, special messenger, bearer of a sort of private and confidential secret post-bag and what-not. There's no harm in my telling you all this, because you haven't the faintest notion as to where São Thomé is, and are not likely to visit the place.

"To them I am a trusted, and I think I may say, honoured and respected, servant, agent, employee; an Arab *dhow*-master, to whose interest it is to keep a closed mouth, and who neither knows nor cares anything about São Thomé save its position on his secret chart. If they don't trust wholly to my integrity, they most certainly do so to my cupidity—to behave with the strictest honesty and discretion, inasmuch as I have nothing to gain and everything to lose by treachery."

"Now you know the position pretty clearly," he concluded.

"Thank you very much indeed," replied Henry Carthew. "I am honoured by your confidence and you can be perfectly sure that nothing on earth would tempt me to abuse it. Now some more questions, if I may? Do you know why General Jason went to São Thomé?"

"I haven't the faintest idea."

"Do you know how he came to hear of so unknown and remote a place?"

"I have not the slightest idea."

"Do you believe he is still at São Thomé?"

"I have every reason to do so, and none to believe otherwise. I don't want to depress you unnecessarily, but I am bound to say that, although I have heard of people contriving to get there, I have never heard of any unauthorized intruder getting away again."

"But even if it is as lonely as Pitcairn Island, St. Helena or Ascension, surely ships must sight it sometimes."

"Well, it's hundreds of miles from any steamer-route, and there is no reason why any sailing-ship should be in its vicinity."

"Suppose one were blown off its course and driven there by a storm?"

"Well, that would be a case in point, I should say—of those who come but don't go."

"What—massacred?"

"Good Lord, no. Nothing of the sort. They are a most enlightened peaceful and friendly people. If sailors and travellers were driven ashore there—genuine castaways— they'd receive every kindness."

"And continue to receive it, eh, until they died?"

"Exactly. Until they died of old age. But that would hardly apply to people who deliberately and intentionally made their way there. It is conceivable that they would not die of old age."

"And if General Jason is still on the Island, do you think he's . . . well-treated . . . and unlikely to die any but a natural death . . . disease . . . old age?"

"Depends on his object in going there; on the opinion they formed of him and his intentions. The Government has a short way with undesirable intruders, and I am bound to confess that I am quite certain he is not at large, if he is still there. As I told you, I liked him very much, was interested in him and tried to prevent his going; and for those reasons I have always done my best to find out what happened to him. I have failed entirely. I have ventured to ask a member of the Government who is by way of being a friend of mine, and have been reminded that those who ask no questions will be told no stories. One or two people whom I trust and who have no reason for telling me any lies, have assured me that there is not now, and there never has been, an

English General on the Island. Inasmuch as I took him there, I can hardly accept their statement—though from their point of view they may be speaking the truth . . . because they have never heard of any such person. Which seems to indicate that he wasn't at liberty, even for a short time, and probably never went outside the Citadel—to which I took him."

"He might be alive inside the Citadel, though."

"Oh, yes. Quite possibly he is."

"An honoured guest, eh?"

"Yes. Honoured and beloved. So beloved that they couldn't possibly part with him."

"Well now, look here, Mr. Brodie Dysart. . . ."

"Hadji Abdulla while in fancy dress, if you don't mind."

"Right. What I was going to say was, doubtless you've heard of Richard I and his faithful Blondel."

"Yes. Richard was caught on his way home from Palestine, wasn't he, by his enemy the Duke of Austria and imprisoned in his castle of Durenstein? And Blondel having some sort of a rough idea as to where he was, went round calling at all the castles."

"Or singing rather than calling, perhaps," contributed Henry Carthew. "Sang the Old Home Tunes under likely windows. Well, sounds a bit old-fashioned, but suppose you took me to São Thomé and I tried to get a look round this castle. Not that I'm anything of a singer."

The Hadji laughed.

"I could take you there, and if I did, you'd certainly be invited up to the Capital, and you'd see the inside of the Citadel all right. Whether you'd ever see the outside again is another matter."

"I'll risk that."

"I won't, though," replied the Hadji. "If you've got no valid pass, letter, safe-guard or guarantee, it would be unfortunate for both of us, especially for you. I don't think they'd detain me because they trust me and I'm pretty useful, but I might lose what is at present almost my only visible means of support."

"Why should you?"

"Simply for breaking the first and most important rule of my contract with the Government of São Thomé. I don't think you quite realize the extent to which they don't want visitors."

"Well, I should hate to be the cause of any trouble or anything unpleasant happening to you—but I'm going to get to São Thomé."

"How?"

"I don't know, but I expect I'm going there with you. You see, my friend General Jason undoubtedly came here with this fellow Palsover. He undoubtedly went with you to São Thomé. That's where he was last heard of. And that is where I am going."

"To certain death, or imprisonment in São Thomé for life? That won't help your friend, will it?"

"I don't know, but I'm going to spend the rest of my life and the rest of my money in finding him; or I'll 'perish in the attempt,' as the noble stories say."

"Well, you'll perish, if only of old age, if you go to São Thomé, and I'm not going to have any hand in your death."

"Now look here, Dysart—I mean Hadji Sahib—you are an Englishman."

"I'm not. I'm a Scot."

"All right. Better still, no doubt. And you're an honest man; by which I mean to say you are not to be bought and sold, and your word is as good as your bond and all that."

"How do you know?"

"I don't know how I know it, but I do; and I realize that you are not going to betray—I mean, let down—your friends or principals in São Thomé. I'm not going to ask you to do them the slightest harm whatever. That clears the ground so far."

"Aye? Well?"

"On the other hand, there's a fellow-countryman of ours, a fellow Briton, who, if he is alive, is imprisoned in São Thomé."

"You don't know that."

"You believe it though. You think it, don't you?"

"Aye. Well?"

"Suppose you could save him, rescue him, get him away, without doing the slightest harm to São Thomé, wouldn't you do it?"

"I advised him, I warned him, I begged him—not to go. And he wouldn't listen to me."

"Yes, so you see what comes of not listening to people. Now you listen to me, Dysart. Supposing I guaranteed you against any financial loss—if the Government of São Thomé, in effect, cancelled their contract with you and forbade you to return there any more."

"It would cost you a good deal, and I should be very sorry indeed. It is a most interesting business, and I have the greatest admiration for the São Thoméans, from the Council to the peasants. It is a unique place, and they've evolved an almost ideal way of life. It would be a damned shame to . . ."

"I know, I know; and I'm not going to ask you to," interrupted Henry Carthew. "Don't forget that one proviso was that not the slightest harm of any sort or kind should come to São Thomé. Well now, suppose I guaranteed you against financial loss and took no step whatsoever of which you did not approve. Wouldn't you—to save a fellow-country-man, one of the finest men who ever stepped—take the risk of their being annoyed with you and telling you not to come there again?"

"Suppose I would take the risk of upsetting a way and a habit of life to which I am very much attached. Suppose I took your word for it that you could and would reimburse me for the loss of my lucrative business as agent, *entrepreneur* and merchant. How would you propose to set about finding out whether General Jason is at the Capital or elsewhere, on São Thomé; and, secondly, if you discovered him, alive and fit to travel, how would you propose to get him away?"

"I haven't thought it all out in detail. Obviously impossible until I get there. Have to improvise. But the first step in finding out whether he is at São Thomé, is to go there."

"Well, I am the only person who can take you there," asserted the Hadji. "And suppose I did so, what would you

515

propose to do? If I, who am well known, trusted and respected, have been entirely unable to find any trace of him, what could you do, a stranger inevitably under suspicion? Besides, you'd be more than under suspicion—you'd be under arrest," added the Hadji with a smile.

"I don't know. But I do know this. That I am going to spend the rest of my life in trying to get to São Thomé. Now look here, Dysart. General Jason is most happily married. Think of the appalling position of his wife, the constant terrible anxiety, hope and fear; hope deferred. Look here, I hate to talk like this," continued Henry Carthew shamefacedly. "I don't know whether you have a wife yourself, Dysart, but surely you've loved a woman, and a woman has loved you. Well, think how she'd be feeling if you disappeared. . . . Lost. . . . Not a word from you for years and . . ."

The Hadji sighed involuntarily and thought of a woman whom he had loved indeed and who had loved him as dearly. Lost.

He broke the silence.

"I'll think it over," he said. "But bear in mind that if I did take you to São Thomé, you'd probably never be seen again. I might or might not share your fate, and if I were lucky, should only be ruined. . . . Excuse me now. I must go to the *dhow*."

Henry Carthew rose.

"You'll do it, Dysart. You'll do it. As your father would have done."

"My father? Did you know him?"

"No. But you told me he was an officer in the King's Navy. A British Admiral."

A little ashamed and alarmed at such a flight of eloquence, he changed the subject abruptly.

"By the way, what do you make of this chap Palsover?"

"Haven't seen much of him, but speaking with purely unwarrantable prejudice and unwarranted bias, I feel he's much too good to be true. In point of fact, I detest him."

"Good. So do I. And not wholly intuitively. I've known the gentleman for many a long year. Longer than I care to think about. What I cannot understand is Jason bringing him on an expedition like this. And I cannot help feeling that he knows a lot more than he says. Knows a deal more than he tells us. And what on earth has kept him here for a couple of years? In a hole like this!"

"Fidelity. Deep love for his master. Anxiety as to his master's fate. '*Ever faithful ever true*'—I don't think."

"No, nor do I," agreed Henry Carthew. "The man is the most pernicious money-grubber I have ever met; and as for interest in General Jason's fate—the only interest Palsover ever took in anything was the interest on his capital. I wish we could make the brute talk. He knows why the General came here, and whatever it was that brought Jason here, is what keeps Palsover here."

"I'll see what I can do with him," replied the Hadji. "If we were Wicked Men, I have some lads on my *dhow* who'd make the dumb talk."

He sighed whimsically.

"Does he drink? We must consider the problem. . . . As to taking you to São Thomé. I'll think the matter over, and come round and tell you my decision in the morning. And do please understand that whatever my decision may be, it will be unalterable. It would be absolutely useless for you to try to change it."

"I'm going to São Thomé, Hadji Sahib," smiled Henry Carthew.

"Ah, we may meet there then—though I doubt it," replied the Hadji as he closed the door. "Good night."

III

Henry Carthew did not sleep that night. Hope, fear, doubt and excitement kept his mind too active.

What he could do if this amazing Hadji Abdulla or Brodie Dysart flatly and finally refused to take him, he did not know. But in the simple faith of his simple mind, he felt that Fate had not intended him to come all this way; and to find here, in Santa Cruz, Palsover, who had travelled with the General; and then the Hadji Abdulla, who had actually taken him to São Thomé—unless it were intended that something more should come of it. And when Henry Carthew said Fate he meant God; for in a personal and merciful and loving God, Henry Carthew, queer fellow, most firmly believed.

As he sat at his breakfast of curried eggs; tea, with buffalo milk; soggy toast and buffalo butter, papaia and mangoes, served in his horrible bedroom because it was less horrible than the one public eating-room below, he heard the sound of feet upon the bare wooden stairs.

With a perfunctory knock at the door, Mr. Samuel Palsover entered and stood aside to make way for the Hadji Abdulla.

"Morning, Sir. Finished breakfast? Hope you found everything all correct? Here's the Hadji wants a word with you. Any objections if I join you? Just stand by, like, in case I could be of help, me having come here with the General and having gone with him to—where he went."

"I've no objection," said the Hadji to Carthew, in Arabic. "The man might be of some use; and it's just possible he might say something of interest, something which would give us an idea of what General Jason was after."

"Yes," agreed Carthew in the same language. "He's a cunning brute, but he's not clever; astute and artful, without being particularly intelligent; and we might lead him to say something. For I am absolutely certain that he came here, and has also stayed here, for some very good reason —and it's the same reason that induced Jason to come here."

"Excusing me, gents," interrupted Mr. Palsover at this juncture, "but if I don't know a word of what you are saying, I can't very well give you my opinion on it. May be sense all right, but it don't make sense to me, yer see."

"No. I beg your pardon," replied the Arab. "I'll speak in your language to the best of my ability."

"Right. Let's all sit down then," was the sensible reply.

"Well, I've thought the matter over, back and forth, most of the night," said the Hadji Abdulla, "and I have decided . . ."

He paused, watching Carthew. How desperately anxious this poor chap was. How tightly clenched his fists and eager his gaze.

"Get on, man! Go on! Quick!" implored Carthew.

". . . that I will give you a passage on my *dhow*, provided you most clearly understand that the responsibility is yours, and that . . ."

Henry Carthew sprang to his feet, seized the Hadji's hand and wrung it.

"And I was about to add," smiled the latter, "you agree to follow the plan which I have evolved. . . . It is that or nothing."

"It's *that*, then, and God bless you," breathed Henry Carthew.

"Ah, but you haven't heard it yet. . . . I had a very bright thought and if you like to take the risk, I'll play my part."

"I'll take any risk," Carthew assured him.

"Well—provided you will agree to do nothing to injure the State of São Thomé, to give any publicity to its existence, or be the cause of anyone else going there, I will take you with me—in disguise."

"In *disguise*! Disguised as what?"

"As an Arab. My fellow pearl-merchant. They won't like my bringing you, even so, but they'll forgive me this once, because you've brought with you a pearl of great price, from which you refuse to be parted, and which you hope to sell to

Doña Guiomar. I have a parcel of pearls for her, and I shall make it known that, while collecting them as she requested, I came across one of the most magnificent pearls that I have ever seen (which is true), and that I had not sufficient ready cash with which to purchase it. But I felt that I ought not to let it go. And as its owner wouldn't part with it, the only way to bring it was to bring the owner with it!"

"By Gad!" whispered Henry Carthew.

"That's the stuff to give the troops," guffawed Mr. Palsover.

"It is risky but it is feasible," continued the Hadji. "You speak Arabic extremely well, a good deal better than the Arabic-speaking people there do, and I have got plenty of the right kit. I don't, for one moment, fear that you'll give yourself away, because the people with whom we shall be dealing speak Portuguese with a mixture of Arabic, and you'd not run the sort of risk that you would if I were to take you to Jiddah or any other such Red Sea or Persian Gulf port, in the guise of an Arab. The only risk is that the Council should take the view that, while not unappeasably angry with me for bringing you, they think that perhaps, on the whole, I had better not take you away again."

"Hardly do that with your fellow pearl-merchant, would they?" protested Carthew.

"Probably not. We'll hope not. We'll have to hope for the best, in fact. . . . Now—are you willing to run the risk of being permanently detained?" he asked, his eyes searching Carthew's face.

"That or anything else," was the reply. "Not that it looks to me as though it is much of a risk."

"Well, there I know better than you do, Colonel, and I assure you that there *is* a danger of the Secretary to the Cabinet or the Foreign Minister or the Commissioner of Police or some Member of the Council taking the view that it was very nice of you to come with the pearl—and that it would be even nicer for you to stay."

"But wouldn't the Regent, Doña Guiomar, protect me? If I am going to take her one of the finest pearls in the world, wouldn't she rather I went off again to look for a better one?"

"Probably. And if she expressed herself strongly on the subject, the Council might give way. On the other hand, they might take the view that after all, since it was I who had brought this pearl and its owner, I could bring more."

"But if you most strongly objected to my detention, and pointed out that you had acted in the Regent's interest and all that, wouldn't they listen to you? Especially if you insisted on the fact that you have given me safe-conduct. It would look as though you had deliberately led me into a trap. And wouldn't it look uncommonly like theft, if they 'bought' the pearl from me and then chucked me into prison?"

"Who said they'd do that? You'd have the freedom of São Thomé, no doubt. You'd be quite at liberty to build yourself a nice house and enjoy all the amenities of Utopia."

"Well, it's to get my friend out of Utopia that I'm going there, and I should certainly like to come away with him. Anyhow, more thanks than I can express. . . . I'm quite sure that I can say for General Jason as well as for myself, that if it cost us our last penny, we'd see that you lost nothing by your . . ."

"Well, we won't bother about that now," interrupted the Hadji. "Do you know anything about pearls?"

"Nothing whatever. Never bought one in my life."

"Well, I must tell you all about them. Teach you the selling-patter. By the way, what languages do you know beside Arabic?"

"The Latin ones. French, Spanish, Portuguese and Italian."

"*Wallahi!* Know them well?"

"Yes. I hold the army rank of Interpreter in all four."

"By Allah! That's good! And you understand Portuguese thoroughly, and can speak it well?"

"Yes."

"Well, the great thing at São Thomé will be the speaking. Don't speak it well. Not a word of it. Don't let anyone get the faintest idea that you know a single word of Portuguese, and that might be very useful. Stick to Arabic, as I do—and listen hard when they talk Portuguese to each other."

"And they'll understand my Arabic all right?"

"Yes. Though when it is a matter of doing business, or their giving me any instructions, they always have the Government Interpreter there, a chap who knows the three languages of the Island and a few from outside. I repeat it all to him in Arabic to show that I have understood.

"By the way, there's one man, a Dr. de Norhona, Secretary to the Cabinet and a Member of the Council, who speaks and understands English perfectly. Studied medicine in London and Edinburgh, not to mention Paris and Vienna. Quite a linguist. He's the man of whom we've got to be careful. Finest brain I've ever come across; and one of the most scholarly and widely-read men I know. He's a great genius in his own line. Tell you more about him later. . . . Well then, you think all that over and . . ."

"My dear chap, I've nothing to think over! I have only got to thank you, and I have no words with which to do it. I'll start growing a beard at once, and practise squatting cross-legged and so on. You'll have to put me through some of the drill when you teach me the pearl patter."

"And what about me?" enquired Mr. Palsover who with closed eyes had sat nodding silent approval as the scheme had been propounded. "Reckon I'll go along too, if it's all the same to you, Mister?" he added, turning to the Hadji.

"Well, if the Colonel Sahib agrees, and if you can give us a little more information about why General Jason came here in the first place, how he ever heard of São Thomé, and why he went there."

"Well now, it's like this, gents," said Mr. Palsover in his most confidential manner. "You see it's this way. I want to do anything that lies in my power to help you, but what I don't want to do is to betray the General's trust in me, or say anything that I ought not to say."

"And do you suppose it could do any harm to tell me anything, Palsover?" asked Carthew.

"Why, no, Sir. No, Sir. Course not. But, in a manner of speaking, well—two's company and three's none."

The Hadji rose, glanced meaningly at Carthew, and

again turned his sober regard upon the speaker.

"If that's the difficulty, I'll go away," he said. "Then you can tell the Colonel Sahib all you know, eh?"

And forthwith Mr. Palsover told Henry Carthew not exactly all he knew, but all that he thought was good for him. Practically all that he had told Colonel Jason. And when he had set forth the facts and the fictions and completed his golden story, it was with difficulty that he believed his own ears when Henry Carthew observed,

"Well, *I don't give a damn for your radium mines* or anything else. What I want to do is to find General Jason and get him safely out of the beastly place."

Mr. Palsover was so hurt, so offended, so utterly disgusted with this—*fool*, that he arose and departed without another word, lest it be a word too much.

Right! If the flaming B.F. didn't want a fortune, let him go without. Let him scratch along on his tuppenny pension, while Mr. Samuel Palsover, J.P., rolled along the highway of life in the biggest and finest motor-car that money could buy. Sir Samuel Palsover . . . Lord Palsover of Plaistow . . . Samuel, Earl of Palsover. . . .

Not care a damn about a concession worth a million, the pudding-headed, pie-faced . . . *Pah!* There were no words.

There was one thing, though. Carthew would keep his head shut, as he had given his promise; and he'd never play any tricks or do any double-crossing. Hadn't the sense, for one thing.

Yes, the best plan would be for Samuel Palsover to go over to São Thomé again, and once more try to get the low-down on what the General was up to. That's where Carthew would be some good, anyway. If the General was still on that perishin' island, Carthew'd find him. And if the old bird was shut up in the *calaboso*, or had passed out and passed over, then Mr. Samuel Palsover had better go Home and start afresh. Find somebody else, like the General, who'd be as straight as he was, and have more sense than to muck things up like this. Somebody who could have that São Thomé lot on a string. Josh 'em along. Fool 'em. Give and take, or promise and take—anyway. Promise a lot, so that they'd jump at it.

Still, it might be all right, even yet. No doubt it takes a long time to fix up these concessions and things, and the General might have been doing a whole lot of spade-work these last two years. He'd ask Carthew and this Hadji chap to get the General to come down to the port place, and meet his old pal and business partner, Palsover, on the *dhow*, and tell him how things were going.

And if there was no news at all this time, he'd go home. Might not be half a bad plan to go and look Lady Jason up. She'd be glad to hear some news of her old man and what he was up to. Pay for it too, handsomely, if he put the screw on properly.

Nothing for nothing in this world and damn little for sixpence, if you were dealing with Mr. Samuel Palsover, Esquire.

IV

A few nights later the Hadji Abdulla's big *dhow* again set sail for an unknown or, rather, unadvertized, destination.

During the voyage, the Hadji came to like Colonel Henry Carthew more and more, and by the time the *dhow* reached its devious journey's end, he felt as though he had known him for years, and that he had grown fonder of him than of any man he had ever known, save perhaps Dacre Blount and the man whom he had known both as Chandos and el Sidna el Sultan Mahommed el Kebir. He wrote him down as a gentleman, in that he was courteous, kindly and truthful; simple, unselfish and honourable; a man who thought of and for others before himself; one who, to his friend, would be a friend faithful unto death. A man perhaps difficult really to know, to understand and to appreciate, but worth any trouble taken to those ends.

At times his heart sank as he thought of Carthew pitting his brains against those of the rulers of São Thomé, if ever it came to that. What he hoped and expected was that Carthew would pass muster as a somewhat stupid and inarticulate Arab, who had come all that way to get the best price possible for his wonderful pearl; the type of man who would go round the world with it, rather than let it out of his possession, save to a satisfactory purchaser.

It might work. It ought to work. There was no real reason why anything should go wrong. He himself would do nine-tenths of the talking; and, inasmuch as it was really he himself who was selling the pearl, it would be easy enough to act as though he were the other pearl-merchant's representative and go-between, trying to effect a sale in which he himself would have, at any rate, a small financial interest.

Of course it ought to be all right; and this sense of anxiety and foreboding was foolish and unwarranted.

But at times, as he sat on the poop of his fine *baggala*, watching the helmsman, the great sail, the moonlit water and the stars, he thought of the last passenger whom he had carried to São Thomé. What had happened to him? He had vanished without sound or sign. He had last seen him in the outer court-yard of Ildefonso Castle, the citadel of the Capital, when he had said farewell.

Looking back at the gate he had cried *"Ma-es-Salaam."* That had been the last word he had said to him, the last sight he had had of him, and the rest was silence.

When he returned six months later and ventured to ask His Excellency Dom Perez de Norhona if he, Hadji Abdulla, would be taking the General Inglez back with him this time, Norhona had stared at him coldly and uncomprehendingly.

"General Inglez? What do you mean? We have no foreign General here, English or otherwise, that I have heard of. What do you mean?"

"The man I brought with me on my last voyage, Your Excellency."

"Oh, that rascal! A scoundrelly Nazi German. No, he won't be going back with you this time, Hadji."

"German!" said the Hadji, "but I thought . . ."

"Well, suppose we cease to think, shall we? And begin to remember. Let us also practise the great art of forgetting, eh?"

Queer—and sinister.

One day, six months later, finding de Norhona in high good humour and delighted with his share of the cargo and the way in which the Hadji had executed his personal commissions, he had again plucked up courage to ask about the man who had, at any rate, called himself a British General.

At first de Norhona had either failed, or pretended to fail, to remember the man. But on the Hadji's endeavouring to refresh his memory, he had said,

"Oh, I remember the chap; the German whom poor Pereira sent me. Yes, he masqueraded as a British Colonel or General or something. Dead? No. Not so far as I know. He wasn't the other day. Saw him myself last week."

"I expect he'll be wanting to take a return-ticket soon, won't he, Your Excellency?" the Hadji had said politely, with a smile that showed he was merely talking for the sake of conversation.

"No, I don't think so. I don't fancy he has the slightest wish to leave São Thomé."

"Doesn't want to go back to his home, even yet?"

"Apparently not. But if he should ask you to give him a lift back to Santa Cruz, do so by all means."

"Without referring to you again, Your Excellency? Without the written permit?"

"Yes, yes. Certainly, certainly. Pereira asked you to bring him, and I give you full permission to take him back, if he asks to go."

But the Hadji knew his Norhona, as he knew all the members of the Government of São Thomé, and was not deceived. His Excellency Dom Perez de Norhona was an honourable man. So were they all, all honourable men. But the great doctor liked his little joke. They were apt to be grim little jokes, and the Hadji felt in his bones that this was one of them.

It was a favourite jest of de Norhona's to speak perfect truth when telling an absolute lie. Inasmuch as he said that the General was alive, he probably was alive.

Since de Norhona said that he had probably no wish to leave São Thomé, no doubt that was, for some reason or other, the case.

But—when he said that, should the General ask him to take him back, he was quite at liberty to do so—there the snag showed its ugly head. If the General were quite at liberty to make the request, then for some reason or other, he was not in a position to do so. He concluded that doubtless he was in gaol.

But when, on his last visit, he had casually inquired of de Norhona whether he wanted him to give anyone passage to Santa Cruz, and de Norhona had said 'No. No one this time,' he had (apparently jokingly) asked,

"Not the wicked German? Isn't he ready to go yet?"

"Apparently not," de Norhona had replied. "He has said nothing about it to me."

And when the Hadji had laughed again and said,

"Perhaps he hasn't had the chance, Senhor?"

De Norhona quizzically, and with simulated indignation, had replied,

"Every chance! Every opportunity! Comes and goes as free as air. I see him almost every day of my life, and I assure you he has never broached the subject of his departure."

True again, no doubt. Absolutely true as far as the words went, but covering something false as hell.

Had he done rightly in bringing this Colonel Carthew to face the same dangers?

Well, he was a soldier and danger-facing was his trade. Moreover, had he left him at Santa Cruz, he'd have been there for the rest of his life, rotting in that foul hole, living in that appalling hotel, eating his heart out that he could find no one who knew where São Thomé was, or who would take him there if he did.

That would have been a bigger tragedy. If he read the man aright, as he felt sure he did, nothing would turn him aside from his purpose of finding and rescuing his friend. And this would be the better fate, even if it meant brief action and sudden death; and if it meant detention on São Thomé, a thousand times better that than self-imposed detention in Santa Cruz.

He would have found his friend and that alone would make him happy.

At other times the Hadji realized that this last was the sheerest optimism. São Thomé was medieval, its Government four hundred years behind the times; and the Middle Ages which still prevailed in São Thomé was a cruel time, an age when people were burnt alive; when devilish torture, for the extortion of evidence or confession, was an integral part of the judicial system; when inconvenient or offending people—such as the Prisoner of Chillon—were cast into underground dungeons and left there for a lifetime.

The São Thoméans were a happy, kindly and peaceful people, ruled by men of good-will, good heart and very considerable wisdom; but undoubtedly they were centuries behind in the march of progress, and knew nothing of such refinements and improvements upon the medieval system as free, open and impartial Courts of Law, where the strictest justice was administered; Parliamentary government by the elected representatives of the people; vote by secret ballot; equality of all men before the Law; compulsory free education; wireless; or aerial navigation. They knew nothing of such improvements and advantages as bombs that in a few minutes could lay towns in smoking ruins and reduce such places as Westminster Abbey, Canterbury Cathedral and York Minster to dust; or of magnificently up-to-date engines of war that can slaughter the maximum number of human beings in the minimum period of time.

So São Thomé, being as backward as all that, it was quite possible that something very unpleasant had happened to the intruder, that charming gentleman who, according to his own account, was a British General but to that of His Excellency Dom Perez de Norhona, was a Nazi German, an assassin, a fraud—and a menace.

Occasionally, after long long thoughts on these lines, the Hadji Abdulla would make another attempt to dissuade Carthew from going ashore when the *dhow* reached São Thomé.

Let the Hadji, he begged, go up to the Capital alone and see how the land lay, do his utmost in the *suqs*, bazaars, arcades and cafes, to discover any news of General Jason; do his best to find out, by the right, proper and judicious treatment of soldiers and policemen, as to whether there were any foreigners in the Ildefonso Gaol at which, from time to time, they did duty; ask de Norhona once again, as though in idle and uninterested curiosity, whether his former passenger were returning this time, and try to learn from him something about the mysterious Anglo-German. And if he could learn nothing whatever about the missing 'General,' let him then make formal request to bring up to the Capital a pearl-dealing colleague whom, bemused, bewildered and practically blindfolded, he had brought with him, in order that he might offer for sale to Her Highness the Regent a very marvellous great pearl.

But against this scheme Carthew protested, raising the undeniably valid objection that, in the event of de Norhona's replying with a flat and final refusal, it would make things a hundred times more difficult than they were already. No, the Hadji must let him accompany him to the Capital in the hope that de Norhona would accept the *fait accompli* and raise no objection to his remaining there.

And when the Hadji had to set sail again?

Why, then Carthew would decide and act according to circumstances. If he had discovered General Jason, and it were at all possible to do so, he'd somehow get him down to the coast and on board the *dhow*, with the Hadji's permission, and help—for which they could never be sufficiently grateful or offer adequate reward.

If, on the other hand, they completely failed to learn anything concerning the General, why then Carthew would of course stay behind.

"And what do you propose to do?" asked the Hadji.

Well, go into hiding at first, and act as seems wisest. Remain in disguise of course. Probably as a São Thoméan. Do his best to get himself up like one of the middle-class Arab-Portuguese agriculturists of whom the Hadji had told him; or perhaps as one of the aboriginal islanders, and keep to the uninhabited jungle country, the smallest villages, fishing communities; go into market with the others, bearing baskets of fruit or fish, like a coolie—and sit about in the market-place.

The Hadji smiled as he wondered equally at the man's courage, fidelity and ignorance.

V

As General Jason had done, Henry Carthew gazed about him in amazement while he journeyed from the landing-stage in the creek up to São Ildefonso, the Capital of the Island. As the General had been reminded of the Gray's *Elegy* of his school days and its reference to that obvious peace, contentment and prosperity which were written on the faces of the people, making them an open book on which the observer could read the virtues of their rulers, so Henry Carthew, in his turn, was reminded of his favourite poem *King Robert of Sicily*, and could not forbear to quote aloud,

> *"Days came and went;*
> *And now returned again to Sicily the old*
> *Saturnian reign;*
> *Under the Angel's governance benign*
> *The happy island danced with corn and wine."*

Happy indeed for the islanders, although the Government did not appear to consist entirely of angels. Happy islanders—but what of his friend?

He thanked God literally and actually, night and morning, that he had reached this place; and although, at times, depressed by the Hadji's complete lack of optimism, he kept a stout heart and a hopeful mind by telling himself that God had brought him on yet another stage of his journey so that he might be the instrument of His Will and fulfil His purpose. And what else could that purpose be but the salvation of his friend and his restoration to his wife and home and country?

As for this nonsense of Palsover's about radium concessions, money was the only thing the fellow thought about; but if Reginald Jason had come here with a view to opening commercial negotiations with the Government of São

Thomé, surely there was no harm in that? And if these queer people did see harm in it, and were detaining him, surely there wasn't the slightest doubt but that Reginald would be perfectly willing to give the matter up and come home with him at once? Of course it would be all right.

"By the way," he said to the Hadji one night, as they sat on the verandah of a rest-house, "just supposing, for the sake of argument, that a foreign war-ship did by some strange chance happen to come this way, did sight São Thomé, dropped anchor, and sent a boat ashore, what would happen?"

"Well, they'd find the flag of Portugal flying, down at that landing-place."

"Does the Island belong to Portugal, then?"

"Oh, no! It is absolutely independent. It is Portugal's pet protégé, and they are very proud of its history. But it is absolutely an article of faith with the Portuguese Government that they should never in any way interfere here or allow anybody else to do so. If any wandering war-ship, if there were such a thing in these waters, came along, and thought of annexing it, they'd find they had caused an international incident of grave importance, and that the sooner they cleared out and apologized, the less likely would they be to find themselves at war with Portugal, backed by Great Britain, her oldest ally and guarantor."

"I suppose, though, that if such a war-ship came and paid a perfectly friendly visit, without any sort of *arrière pensée*, the São Thoméans would be friendly and hospitable?"

"Oh, yes, absolutely. No doubt about that. But it is extremely unlikely to happen. Coal costs money, and what would a war-ship be doing in this part of the world?"

"There has never been any kind of British war-ship here, I suppose?"

"No, never. Nor likely to be."

"Don't the Portuguese ever send one?"

"No. Why should they? They know that the constant prayer of São Thomé is 'Leave us alone, for we are perfectly happy and wish to remain so.' "

"But is there no communication whatsoever between

São Thomé and the outside world?"

"Oh, yes. Certain hand-picked Thoméans of the original Portuguese families go to Europe when young, to specialize in something useful to the State, as de Norhona did, for his medical training. Then at least one of the Members of the Council goes over every year to Portugal and other European countries—the Commander-in-Chief, the Foreign Minister, the Chief of Police, and other specialists. De Norhona went over about three years ago to see Freud, Jung, Adler and the other great neurologists and psychologists, as well as the Vienna surgeons and physicians. By all accounts, he's a wizard at medicine, surgery and this latest stuff—psycho-therapy, don't they call it? Hypnotism is his special line, if you can mention any one thing that is more special than the rest, with him."

"Fancy a man like that being content to live in a place like this."

"Well, why not? It's his home, his country, and to him the most desirable spot on earth, apart from its actual physical attractions. Even by the time a São Thoméan is seven years old, he knows, better than he knows anything else, that São Thomé is the Garden of Eden, the finest spot on earth, and the only place in which a sensible man can possibly live. They go on the Jesuit principle—'Give us a boy for seven years and you can do what you like with him afterwards.' No São Thoméan has ever left the Island and intentionally failed to return. Nothing but death would prevent him; and if ever a messenger fails to return, as a São Thoméan named Pereira did, a couple of years ago, they know that he's either in his grave or a prison."

"No wonder so little is known of the place," mused Henry Carthew. "Personally I had never heard of it."

"No, in view of the facts, it would be a queer thing if you had," replied the Hadji. "To the outside world it is merely a Portuguese island of neither interest nor importance, which is self-supporting and has no productions and therefore no commerce. Not that the rest of the world, outside a Government office in Lisbon, has ever heard of it, anyway. . . ."

§2

At first glimpse, São Ildefonso, the capital of São Thomé, reminded Henry Carthew of Funchal and Madeira. Having passed the police guard and entered the gates, he likened the tree-embowered town to a miniature Adelaide, to a castellated Indian hill-station, to a town in Crete, and to Carcassonne.

Nevertheless, he realized that it was unique, and like his friend a couple of years earlier, thought of the combination of the castled crag of Cintra and an extremely clean green and colourful Mediterranean town upon which it looked down, as mightily it dominated it.

In point of fact, he was too excited and anxious, to take very careful note of his surroundings, as he and the Hadji rode through the town in the direction of the Citadel.

At any moment he might come face to face with his friend!

Within the hour he might hear news of him; might learn that he was dead and buried; that he had lain in gaol all this while, perhaps in some noisome dungeon; and he might hear that he was alive and well and free.

What a wonderful thing if he could promptly return to Santa Cruz and send a cable to Antoinette,

"Reginald safe and well. Returning immediately."

If he could do that, he'd really feel that he hadn't altogether lived in vain. He'd be able to feel that he had done something in return for all their kindness to him; something to make himself worthy to be Antoinette's friend, Reginald's friend.

Lord, how he hoped they'd let him share Dysart's quarters when they got to the end of this amazing journey. He'd be comparatively safe for his search-work, then; could go everywhere with him, and use his eyes and brain to the utmost. What a mercy of Providence that he knew Portuguese so well! But then, everything was an act of

Providence and, in the long run, a mercy. More and more he felt that he had not been brought all this way to fail in the end.

Once again, the Hadji was permitted to cross the drawbridge and enter the great outer court-yard of the Castle. A perfunctory glance at him was sufficient for the Sergeant of the Guard, who took it for granted that the other Arab, in white robe and turban, being in the Hadji's company, must be guaranteed by him, have a permit, and be allowed to enter.

In the centre of the court-yard, the Hadji dismounted, and Carthew followed his example.

As usual, soldiers came and led away the horses, and within a few minutes, a sallow man in a sort of civilian uniform, approached and conversed in fluent and faulty Arabic with the Hadji.

"Salaam, Hadji Abdulla the Merchant," said he. "And whom might this be? And by whose permission have you brought a stranger into the Citadel of São Ildefonso?"

"Oh, that's all right. No permission and none needed," laughed the Hadji. "Wait till Her Excellency Doña Guiomar hears about him, and why I brought him."

"Wait till His Excellency Dom Perez de Norhona hears," sneered the secretary-clerk or flunkey, his unpleasant tallowy face assuming a threatening look not untinged with contempt.

"Any need to wait?" growled the Hadji. "I didn't really come here for the purpose of a long conversation with you. Tell His Excellency that I have come and await his pleasure."

As the man, with an ugly clearing of the throat, as though about to spit, turned away, the Hadji remarked to Carthew,

"I'm no Sir Richard Burton, but I know exactly how he felt when an English subaltern gave him a sharp kick in the rear, called him a black beast, and bade him get out of the way.

"*Cave!*" he added. "That's Norhona."

And looking up to where a man stood at the head of the flight of stairs which, as he knew, led up to the Great Hall of the Castle, the Hadji saluted by raising both hands to his forehead, touching his heart and bowing respectfully.

As he nudged him, Carthew did the same.

"Salaam, Senhor Hadji Abdulla," called the man. "Come up.

"Both of you," he added, staring hard at Carthew who, with his month-old beard, was not looking his best, and was indeed far from prepossessing.

Entering a room of noble proportions, on the walls of which were pictures that had been painted by masters in Portugal, taken to Goa and brought by the survivors of the ill-fated silk-and-silver fleet to São Thomé, de Norhona seated himself behind a great desk, and with a wave of his hand, indicated a rug upon which his visitors might sit in their favourite cross-legged attitude.

"Well, what's the meaning of this?" he asked with a cold glance at Carthew, as soon as polite salutations and mutual inquiries as to health and prosperity had been exchanged.

"Oh, that!" smiled the Hadji, glancing at his companion. "That's what Your Excellency might call a parcel or a package."

Norhona raised his heavy eyebrows.

"It contains the very finest pearl I have ever seen, and I couldn't get it out of the parcel or package, so I brought the whole bundle along. Doubtless Her Excellency Doña Guiomar will find a way to open it."

"Full of parables to-day, Hadji. I'll open him fast enough, if . . ."

"No, no, Your Excellency. It really is an amazing and incredible pearl. The Biblical Pearl of Great Price. But as I hadn't the cash to pay for it, and the fool wouldn't trust me, I was on the horns of a dilemma, and for long I halted between two opinions. Should I let it go, lose the chance of a lifetime, a chance of giving Her Excellency great happiness and of marvellously enriching the jewel-hoard in the State treasure-house—or should I do as the fellow asked?"

"And what did 'the fellow' ask?"

" '*If you have a market, take me to it, though it be a thousand miles away,*' says he.

" '*It's all that,*' says I, and made up my mind to encourage such an enterprising merchant."

"You know the Law," replied de Norhona. "You know the very first order and charge that was laid upon you when . . ."

"Ah, but look, Your Excellency! The man has not the faintest idea as to where he is, and hasn't the least notion as to how he got here. I shall take him back to his home at Bahrein, and if he sits and *faddhls*[28] with his cronies for the rest of his life, he can only say he went to a far country and . . ."

"Is he a *dhow*-master himself?"

"Hardly ever been on a *dhow* in his life, Your Excellency. He's just a pearl-broker. He bought this pearl within a few hours of its being taken out of the oyster; and I saw it, and was dickering with him about it the next day. We can get it from him at a price that will make him quite happy, and that will be about half what it would be worth—in Paris, say. Not that it will ever go out of São Thomé, of course, but the bargain will be as wonderful as the pearl."

"Let me have a look at it," ordered de Norhona.

The Hadji bade Carthew produce the pearl, and from some place of concealment beneath his voluminous sash, the latter brought out a little leather bag, tied at the mouth with a thong.

Opening the bag, he produced a pearl of almost the size of a pigeon's egg, a breath-taking marvel of beauty.

"*Madre de Dios!*" whispered de Norhona, "I don't wonder you brought the man. Her Excellency the Regent will certainly approve! But listen, Hadji. Are your ears wide open? Then hear my words and do not, on your life, forget what I say now, or disobey the order. Never again, under any conceivable circumstances whatsoever, bring anyone from your *dhow* up to Ildefonso. We trust to your discretion as to whom you take on board your *dhow* at Santa Cruz, but don't you ever again assume you've got any discretion as to

---

[28] Gossips. Arabic.

whom you bring ashore at São Thomé. Do you hear?"

"I hear, Your Excellency. And to hear is to obey."

"Well, we'll overlook it this time, in consideration of this pearl and the pleasure it will give Her Highness. But never again, my good Hadji. Never again. Meantime, you'll be responsible for your friend, and when you sail, you will take him with you, unless anything happens to give me the impression that it might be more desirable for him to remain here. And if he goes with you this time, you'll take him back to Bahrein yourself. And don't let him go ashore at Santa Cruz."

"While he's here, I had better have him with me in my quarters, Your Excellency," suggested the Hadji.

"Yes. And you had better keep him under your own eye, the whole time. . . . You have my permission to go. But not to leave the Castle precincts until I have had another talk with you."

The two rose from the rug, and Carthew, cool as steel, acted his part well.

"And the pearl?" he grunted uncouthly, looking from de Norhona to the Hadji. "I want my pearl."

"May Mohammed bin Yussuf take his pearl, Your Excellency? I'm afraid he'll get no sleep otherwise."

"Let him remain awake then," was the cold reply. "I will take care of the pearl. Mohammed bin Yussuf has given hostages to Fortune! Worth a King's ransom and a little more than a pearl-broker's ransom, eh? . . . As I mentioned before, you have my permission to go."

"Come on, you fool," urged the Hadji in a loud stage-whisper, and took Carthew's arm.

"I wouldn't have left it in the hands of the Sheik of Mohammara," growled Carthew.

"*Imshi, ibn kelb*[29]!" growled the Hadji, and hustled the foolish fellow from the Presence.

---

[29] Get out, you son of a dog.

VI

For the next two or three days the two Britons enjoyed each other's company, talking all day and far into the night, Brodie Dysart telling of his experiences on the ship called *Valkyrie* which made one of the most tragically amazing voyages in the checkered history of the Merchant Service, a voyage on which murder and mutiny disposed of so many of the personnel that the ship, that started out with a Captain and full complement of officers, was brought home by the Apprentices.[30]

At another time, he told Carthew of his later experiences as a slave in Southern Morocco; as an instructor to the native troops of a Sultan; and of his experiences as a Pilgrim to Mecca[31]; at another, of his life as a member of the French Foreign Legion on active service on the Indo-Chinese frontier[32]; and again of further experiences in different parts of the world, ashore and afloat, experiences which led to his decision to buy a *dhow* and see life.

In return, Henry Carthew told him tales of soldiering and sport in India, of adventuring on the Pamirs when, by way of spending a year's furlough, he journeyed to Kabul and thence to Bokhara, Khiva and Samarcand and back by way of Kashmir to India.

And the more that Brodie Dysart saw and heard of Henry Carthew, the more he liked and admired him.

But no news could either get concerning the fate of General Jason. Time after time, Carthew was tempted to forget that he was a Gulf Arab, and to question soldiers and the minor personnel of the Citadel, in Portuguese. To talk to any but the bucolic and less educated people in pure Arabic was to be uncertain as to whether he was completely understood. The use of pure or diluted Portuguese would, he felt,

---

[30] *Action and Passion.*
[31] *Sinbad the Soldier.*
[32] *Fort in the Jungle.*

have been much more helpful in the town.

One day a messenger arrived at the ground floor room which opened off the outer court-yard—and which was allotted to the Hadji's use when he was visiting Ildefonso—and bade the two Arabs follow him.

This man led them up to the main floor of the Castle, across the Great Hall, up a flight of stairs, along a gallery, down a corridor into another corridor, and so to a room in which sat the Doña Guiomar, the Regent of São Thomé.

Carthew, forgetting to salaam in the correct manner until nudged by the Hadji, stared in admiration at the extremely beautiful and intellectual face of the woman who, with the help of the Council of Notabilities, ruled the country in which, as he hoped and believed, his friend still lived.

She looked curiously attractive—but attractively curious also. Why was that? . . . Because she was in a sort of Fancy Dress—as though going to a party, or as though this were an act in a film play.

Of course—she was dressed much as the women one saw in Spanish pictures of the seventeenth century. Old-fashioned. And with a high comb and mantilla. The men, too, looked old-fashioned in their "tropical" silk suits—like the pictures of wealthy American planters of the slave-owning period, in their Old Colonial style houses.

With a gracious wave of the hand, Doña Guiomar indicated that the two Arabs might seat themselves on the floor before her.

"Well, Hadji," she smiled, "I trust that your health and the health of your house is good."

"By the favour of Your Majesty," murmured the Hadji, bowing low.

"And what is this I hear about you bringing a man all the way from the Persian Gulf to show me a pearl?"

"This is the man, Your Majesty," replied the Hadji. "A poor thick-headed nit-wit of Bazra—(the home town of Sinbad the Sailor, Your Majesty may remember)—who refused to be parted from his Pearl of Great Price. But as I was determined at all costs that Your Majesty should have the pearl, I got over the non-separation difficulty by bringing the pearl with the worthy half-wit attached to it. He was actually babbling of taking it up to Bagdad and showing it in the pearl-market there; and, if he did not get his price, of taking it to show such people as the Sheikh of Mohammara and the Sultan of Muscat."

"However, I told him we could do better than that," he added.

"At a price, doubtless, Hadji. A nice little commission for you, eh?"

"*Wallahi!* Your Highness. Is it not written in your Book that the labourer is worthy of his hire?"

"Easy labour, Hadji, if a little dangerous—for you—in view of the Law. However, we'll say no more of that, as the pearl is indeed wonderful. Let me see it again."

Dom Perez de Norhona, from no more secret place than the trousers pocket of his light silk suit, produced the bag and the pearl.

"Yes. Wonderful. Truly wonderful. I must have it," said the Regent as she fondled the lovely thing.

"If we can come to terms with the merchant," observed de Norhona. "How much is the fellow asking for it?"

And with a strange cry of eagerness and of anguish, the alleged pearl-merchant of Bahrein and Bazra broke into a torrent of impassioned Arabic. . . . *The pearl was to all other pearls as the Moon to the stars. It was perfect in shape and colour, incredible in size. Behold its flawless skin. Behold*
. . .

"Yes, we are beholding, thank you," interrupted de Norhona. "It is a good-enough pearl. What have you the effrontery to ask for it?"

And the haggling began, the hot combat of wits and words in which the Hadji joined and quickly took the lead. Thankfully Carthew dropped out and gazed about him at the furniture, hangings and pictures which must be of priceless value and great age.

Some distance behind the Regent's chair a magnificent bird of the parrot or macaw family sat and, with a look of cynical wisdom, eyed the proceedings, from time to time contributing a cryptic remark.

At the base of the stand on which it perched, a beautiful little monkey sat and ate of the crumbs of fruit and sweet-meats that fell from the rich bird's table. From time to time each cursed the other with vindictive if perfunctory virulence. They appeared to understand each other perfectly.

Behind them, in the dark corner, lay what Carthew took to be a huge ape, and he wondered that so big a creature—something between a chimpanzee and a gorilla—should be found in those latitudes. And idly regarding it as it slept, with the top of its shaggy head toward him, he felt a little surprise that such an animal should find a place in a lady's boudoir. He decided that it was quite possible that the creature was in the nature of a bodyguard, more powerful and intelligent than a dog.

Rather a bright idea, having a great ape of enormous strength, as a watch-dog, guard and companion. Not that he'd care about it much himself. He remembered the occasion on which he had visited a friend, a planter in Sumatra, and a huge brute of an orang-outan had come in, toward the end of dinner, and been given a chair at table and a plate of fruit.

His friend had bidden him shake hands with the 'Man of the Forest,' and he had done so. But he had never forgotten the inexpressibly unpleasant feeling of having his hand in a steel trap, a vice, and his realization of what would be the feeble worthlessness of his strength, had he to pit it against that of the orang-outan. The great brute had held him for a couple of minutes, and he had never forgotten it or quite forgiven his friend for the humiliation. And ever since, he had loathed meeting the gaze of any kind of ape or monkey and looking into its shallow soulless eyes.

What was that they were saying?

"You have my permission to go."

That was good news.

"I'll think it over and give you my answer in a day or two, Hadji Abdulla."

And rising and bowing low, the two pearl-merchants departed from the Presence.

Later in the day, an orderly brought the Arabs written

permission to leave the precincts of the Castle and go where they pleased within the bounds of the town of São Ildefonso.

§2

Meanwhile, Mr. Palsover . . .

Existence upon a small ship, without employment, recreation or society, is apt to be boring, especially to one not blessed with particularly extensive mental resources.

Certainly Mr. Palsover found it so.

At first, it was well enough, this sitting and thinking, and then just sitting, but even to the most contemplative of Europeans, the attractions of mere sitting must, in time, begin to pall. And Mr. Palsover was no *faquir*, endowed and fortified with the blessings of an understanding of Yoga.

Within a few days of the departure of the Hadji and Colonel Carthew he got bored, got fever, and got drunk.

It must be said in his defence and indeed in mere justice, that only in such unusual and untoward circumstances could he have been defeated by those tropical enemies of white mankind, boredom and alcohol. Mr. Palsover was no drinker, but when he did drink he undoubtedly drank.

It is probably to this and this alone that his moral downfall and his abandonment of his own high standards of discretion, if not of loyalty, can be ascribed.

Thus, when young Ensign Fernandez Machado, who also had nothing to do, was rowed out to visit the *dhow*, Mr. Palsover was not himself. He was depressed to the lowest depths of mind, body and soul; he was maudlin; he was genuinely and unwontedly friendly and affectionate, nay, loving; he was the soul of hospitality; he was filled with joy and gladness, and merry, merry laughter alternated with lugubrious tears and fits of abandonment to despair; he was forthcoming and communicative.

But he was not Mr. Samuel Palsover.

The mere fact that he was communicative proves it; for,

when sober—and for every hour of every day of at least fifty-one weeks of the year he was sober—there was no man alive less communicative than Mr. Palsover.

It was bad luck, bad luck for Henry Carthew especially, that Ensign Fernandez Machado should have found Mr. Palsover in one of his rarest hours, his defences down, his inhibitions relaxed, his noble mind o'erthrown, his benevolent and ultra-respectable self defeated; should have found Mr. Palsover, in short, noisy, garrulous and—very drunk.

It was again unfortunate, for all save himself, that the Ensign was a boy of some intelligence, great ambition, and considerable education, his 'special' foreign language being English. Marked out for promotion by his friend and patron the Commander-in-Chief, he was likely to be one of those meticulously-selected few who were sent occasionally to Europe; and, besides studying, in Lisbon, Paris and London, the Arts of Love and War, would further study the English language. Were not the English the *chèrs alliés* of Portugal the Mother; and was it not a passport to the very valuable favour of His Excellency Dom Perez de Norhona that one should be able to talk to him in English, his favourite foreign tongue?

And so having cast a seemingly idle and casual eye over the *dhow*, its crew—big black tough-looking men who fished, disported themselves in the water, or did nothing with all their might—Ensign Machado mounted the poop and with punctilious courtesy answered Mr. Palsover's greeting.

Hullo, this was interesting. Who was this quaint bird in khaki shirt and shorts? Spoke English, did he? Most certainly he had said, among other things, '*Good evening.*' But perhaps that was all the English he knew. Anyway, he'd soon find out.

But this there was no need for him to do, as Mr. Palsover, apologetically suppressing a noble if deplorable hiccup, asked him if he had seen anything of the Hadji—and that other silly old bastard who didn't know a good thing when it was shoved under his fat nose. . . . Hadn't the sense to go out in the rain when it was snowing five-pound notes.

He was a fool, that's what he was. And the Hadji was a fool to have any truck with him. Carthew was his name, and he'd always had a down on Mr. Palsover. Was always picking on him, from the time he was a rookie and Carthew a one-pip wart.

Still, one thing he'd say for him. He was straight. He wouldn't double-cross anybody. And Mr. Palsover didn't regret having let him in on the ground floor. Not that he'd be any good, mark you, for N.B.G. was his initials. But he might find out something about the General. Had the gentleman come across him, by the way? And wouldn't he have a drink?

The gentleman would certainly sit down and have a talk with the Senhor.

"Thass right! Come and sit down and have a drink."

And Mr. Palsover hospitably wiped the neck of the bottle on his shirt.

Ensign Machado, as fanatical a teetotaller as a Wahabi mullah, courteously declined, and in fairly good English, begged Mr. Palsover to continue his most interesting remarks.

He was an Englishman, wasn't he?

Course he was! What a silly question! Couldn't any benighted foreigner see he was an Englishman? What else would he be?

Yes, yes. True indeed. Of course. And the man who had gone up to Ildefonso with the Hadji? What was his name, by the way? Kar . . . Kar . . .

"Wha'? Colonel Carthew? Course he's an Englishman. Wha' cher think? Think he was Dutch?" jeered Mr. Palsover. No doubt about him being English all right. Never said he wasn't. All he said was that he was a B.F. and too fond of picking on people. And that Mr. Palsover had always hated his guts, right from the very first. Awful old swine, he was, when he was commanding the Regiment. And he didn't know enough to pick up a packet of fivers when he saw them lying at his feet.

Fivers? Yes? Well, it wasn't very likely he'd see any lying at his feet in Ildefonso, was it? No? opined the Ensign.

Now that's just where the young gentleman was wrong. In a manner of speaking. If old Carthew had had his wits about him, he could have picked up a sackful of fivers. A cart-load of fivers. More than he could bloomin' well spend with both hands and all his pals helping him. And who had shown him how? Why, Mr. Palsover. It was awful. 'Orrible.

And Mr. Palsover wept.

Now the General—*there* was a man. He was on to it in half once. But the trouble was—where was he? And what was he up to? Perhaps the young gentleman had run across him, had he, up at that Capital place? General Sir Reginald Jason. Used to be Carthew's Commanding Officer. Mr. Palsover's too.

No, the Ensign hadn't had the pleasure of meeting the General. He hoped to have the honour of meeting several famous Generals in Europe, but he had not met the one Mr. Palsover mentioned. What was his name again? Ah, yes. And what was the name of the other one—the one who had just gone to Ildefonso with the Hadji Abdulla?

Carthew. Colonel Carthew.

Ah, yes? And it was his humour to go about in the dress of an Arab at times, was it? Yes? No?

Ar! Silly trick. Didn't catch General Jason acting the goat like that. Where was the sense in it?

True. And did the Hadji Abdulla know all about this man . . . this British Officer . . . Colonel Kardieu, was it? And that he was an Englishman in disguise?

Hiccuping with an explosive violence that made the welkin ring, Mr. Palsover apologized as one who knew his manners, took a drink for his stomach's sake, and, returning to the matter in hand, affirmed that the Hadji Abdulla did not know anything of the business at all. He was just a blooming old boatman, a bargee-bumboat-woman, long skirts and all. A bloomin' native, and little better than a nigger. The gentleman—Mr. Palsover hadn't the pleasure of knowing his name. Oh, Machado? Ensign Fernandez Machado. He'd heard a name like that before. Place called Sitapur. Bloke kept a nice little soldiers' canteen. Miggy Machado. Done a lot o' good business with him. But what was he saying. The Hadji? No, the Hadji Abdulla wasn't in on the business at all. Didn't know anything about rayjum nor the concessions nor nothing.

No. No, exactly. The Hadji Abdulla was a very ignorant man of course. A what was it? A bum-barge-boatman? Exactly. But the man with him was Colonel Kardieu of the British Army. No? Yes?

"Late retired," murmured Mr. Palsover and settled himself to sleep.

Wouldn't Mr.—what was his name? He didn't think he'd had the pleasure of hearing his name—have another drink, suggested Ensign Machado.

Well, perhaps he would. For was it not written—and an accepted fact—that another little drink wouldn't do us any harm? Bloth-frower. Yes. Broth-flower. Wot? Yes. Floth-browers. Of course he'd have another. Here's to Down with old Carthew and up with the General. . . . And God bless ole Senior Pereira.

The eyes of Ensign Machado narrowed, and his brows drew together in a frown of concentration.

Yes. Yes-s-s. Senhor Pereira! We must not forget him. Where was he now, by the way?

The ole Senior? Where was he? . . . Well . . . *One* place or the other! And Mr. Palsover chuckled at some amusing memory.

Through the gathering clouds of alcoholism Mr. Palsover suddenly saw a light. Momentarily brilliant, shining its warning from the blessed light-house of sober sense and sanity.

Mustn't say too much. Had he said too much? No, he'd only said old Carthew was a fool. So he was.

"Senior Pereira?" he murmured. "He's . . . he's . . . where the birds won't bite him. Good old Senior."

"I suppose it was he who told you and this General and this Senhor Colonel Kardieu all about São Thomé and the—what did you say—radium?"

"Thass right. Thass right. Poor ole Senior."

And Mr. Palsover burst into a flood of bitter tears.

"Here's to 'um," he said, took a long drink at the bottle

and went to sleep. Nor could any amount of the application of the toe of Ensign Fernandez Machado's boot awaken him.

Within the hour, one of the State's swift messengers set forth from the port, bearing a cipher message which informed His Excellency Dom Perez de Norhona that the Hadji Abdulla's companion was an Englishman in disguise, a Colonel Kardieu.

There is a providence that watches over drunks and other good men, as well as over babes and sucklings. The young Ensign could not refrain from being self-important, mysterious and portentous, nor from acting omniscience. He failed to describe the nature of the accident that had provided him with such important news, and entirely omitted mention of the humble loquacious individual, lurking on the *dhow*.

Alone he had done it! Ever watchful, ever brilliant, he had performed this fine peace of Intelligence-work, single-handed. (Why admit that he had merely happened to hear a drunkard babbling?)

Thus for a time was Mr. Palsover spared the consequences of his indiscretion.

§3

And the Hadji Abdulla with the merchant Mohammed bin Yussuf, wandering about the town, entered into converse with all sorts and conditions of men; in cafes; in music halls (where Henry Carthew was enchanted by the reed bands that discoursed marvellous music); in the market-places; in the public gardens; and wherever São Thoméans were wont to congregate. Persistently they sought information as to a General Inglez who was said to have visited the country some two years previously; but never a word of information could they glean.

Evidently General Jason had come, seen, and disappeared.

"I'm afraid it means that if he's in São Thomé he's in the

Citadel—or under it," said the Hadji one night, as the two sat upon the floor of their room, on either side of a vast platter of rice and mutton flavoured and enriched with onions, chillies, pimento and strange, appetizing herbs.

"What's to be done?" sighed Henry Carthew. "I suppose you'll be sailing soon? Personally, I'm not going until I have found out what has happened to him. . . .

"If I learn nothing, and nothing else happens, sooner or later I shall tackle de Norhona," he added.

But in the event, it was de Norhona who tackled him—and much sooner.

VII

Next morning, early, there came a heavy knock at the door and, followed by a couple of soldiers, a Corporal entered and peremptorily bade the man calling himself Mohammed bin Yussuf to follow him at once.

As he rose slowly to his feet, Henry Carthew whispered to the Hadji, in English,

"You know nothing about my being a European—if there's trouble. I have deceived you. Stick to that. We must tell the same story."

And turning to the Corporal he bade him lead on, for he was ready. He also thanked him courteously for having so kindly waited until he had broken his fast.

"Good morning, Colonel Kardieu," smiled His Excellency Dom Perez de Norhona. "Won't you take a chair? Cigarette? I hope I am not being troublesome and intrusive, but I did so want a little chat with you."

Henry Carthew thought quickly. Obviously the game was up. His disguise was penetrated, and not only did this man know that he was a European, but he actually knew his rank and name. Treachery somewhere. Was it possible that the Hadji . . . ? No. He thrust the thought from his mind. Quite impossible. If the Hadji were a treacherous liar, there was not an honest and decent man on the face of the earth. That Brodie Dysart had betrayed him was out of the question, unthinkable.

Jason! Jason? Could Reginald have seen him here, and told this feller . . . that . . . ?

No, that was just plain silly. Why should Reginald do anything but rush up to him and shake his hand if he caught sight of him?

Because Reginald was under restraint? Saw him from a window? But surely the last thing in the world that Reginald would do would be to give him away?

But it might have been unintentional. He might have called his name. Nonsense. He'd have called out "Henry" if, in his amazement, he had called out anything at all. He certainly would not have shouted out "Colonel Carthew."

It was utterly amazing, astonishing.

But the question of the "how" of it could wait. The immediate problem was that of what line he himself should take. He must say something and say it quickly.

Well, the truth, the whole truth and nothing but the truth had, all his life, been his general policy, and it had been a good one. What about telling the plain and simple truth now? If you tell the truth you cannot be caught out in a lie; and wasn't it an undeniable fact that the most subtle diplomacy, the line best calculated to puzzle and confuse an artful opponent, was that of the plain and simple truth?

"Charmed, Your Excellency," he said. "Thank you," and taking a cigarette from the big silver box upon the desk, looked round for a match.

"Allow me," said de Norhona, and lit the cigarette for him.

"Well, so you do talk English, and no doubt will admit that you are Colonel Kardieu, late of the British Army."

"Certainly," was the cool reply. " '*But yesterday the word of Cæsar might have stood against the world*' and so forth. . . ."

"But yesterday you were a thick-headed bazaar-Arab from Bazra, anxious to sell us what I must really admit is a most beautiful pearl. Well, well! '*All the world's a stage*' and—er—*some men in their time play many parts*. Arab to-day; Englishman to-morrow. *Here* to-day, but . . ." and his suave voice changed from light and pleasant banter, ". . . I doubt it you will be *gone* to-morrow, Colonel."

Suddenly with a deep and angry frown, he dropped his voice to a menacing growl.

"What do you want in São Thomé? Why have you come here, eh? Answer me! *Instantly!*"

"Certainly, Your Excellency. I came to São Thomé for the sole and simple reason that I want to find my friend General Sir Reginald Jason, who undoubtedly came here from Santa

Cruz. If you will be so exceedingly kind as to tell me what has become of him, I shall be infinitely grateful. I mean—what really *has* become of him? . . . I had no other object whatsoever in coming here, and all I want to do is to depart, when I have either found him or got authentic news of him. I have come at the request of his wife. Or widow—perhaps?"

"Really! And who the devil might General Sir Reginald Basin be? I've never heard of him in my life."

"No, nor I," replied Henry Carthew coldly. "I said Jason. A distinguished British General. Sir Reginald Jason."

"Well, I'm afraid you've come to the wrong place. This isn't Colchis, you know."

"General Jason came here about two years ago."

"I venture to doubt it, Colonel. I don't think many people come to São Thomé without my knowledge, or land here without my consent."

"Look here, Your Excellency. Whatever may be the ultimate upshot of this affair . . . to put it plainly—whatever you may do to me . . . would you kindly tell me just this, plainly and truthfully, as a gentleman and a 'man of honour' as you'd call it. Have you ever seen or heard anything concerning General Sir Reginald Jason?"

"I have never, to my knowledge, set eyes on any such person, and I most certainly have never heard any such name," was the reply. "But it was rather to talk about yourself that I asked for the pleasure of your company, Colonel. If, as you say, you came here in search of what I'm afraid I must view as a mythical Mason or Basin or Jason, or what you please—why exactly did you come in fancy dress, as an Arab pearl-merchant?"

"Simply and solely as a means of gaining admission here," replied Henry Carthew, looking his inquisitor squarely in the eyes.

"Now, just supposing for one moment that that were the truth, how did you ever come to hear of São Thomé, and what gave you the idea that your friend, this famous British General, had also heard of São Thomé and had, in fact, come here?"

"Well, he wrote home to England from this place Santa

Cruz, and said that that was his starting-point or jumping-off place for his ultimate destination."

"And did he name that destination as being São Thomé?"

"No, he didn't. He simply said he was at Santa Cruz, and was going somewhere else from there."

"And did you discover from our friend the Hadji Abdulla the name of the place to which this General went?"

"No, Your Excellency. That I most certainly did not. And that is the plain and simple truth."

"Ah! I don't want to sound medieval or melodramatic or just funny, but, among the other ways in which we São Thoméans are a little behind the times—or rather, perhaps, ahead of them, like the Nazi Germans—we have our own ways of making people speak the truth. If we don't think they are doing so, that is."

"Torture? It doesn't sound very civilized; but believe me or not, I am telling you the truth, and no amount of torture would enable me to improve on it. It was not the Hadji Abdulla who told me about São Thomé."

"Then who was it?"

"It was the man who told General Jason."

"General Jason, General Mason, General Basin! I'm getting a little tired of this figment of your imagination. *Suppose we talk about one—Schultz. Fritz Schultz!* Are you sure that *he* wasn't the man who told you about São Thomé? Are you quite certain that you haven't followed him up, in the hope of getting what he failed to get?"

"Quite certain, Your Excellency. I never, to my knowledge, heard the name Fritz Schultz in my life. It conveys nothing to me whatsoever."

"Do you speak German yourself, as you do Portuguese and English and Arabic?" growled de Norhona.

"No. Not to say speak it. I could just make myself understood in a German hotel, or roughly make out the sense of a simple advertisement in a German newspaper, but I certainly couldn't say that I know German."

"Ah! Did you ever meet a man named Pereira?"

"Pereira? . . . Pereira? . . . It isn't an uncommon name in

India. The Indian Goanese all took Portuguese names, as no doubt you know, when they were converted. I have known da Silvas, da Costas, da Sousas, and no doubt Pereiras, but I cannot call one to mind at the moment."

"Not a São Thoméan gentleman, cultured, travelled, middle-aged, English-speaking? . . . Manöel Pereira?"

"No. No, I cannot remember ever meeting a Mr. Manöel Pereira. Would it be in India?"

"No, it wouldn't. It would be in Santa Cruz, and it would be a little over two years ago when our friend, Rasin, Mason, Basin or Jason—or shall we call him Fritz Schultz—honoured us with a visit and certain fantastic get-rich-quick proposals. It was he and his gang who were to get rich—and São Thomé was to be turned from a Garden of Eden to a Ruhr Basin, Donetz; a British 'Black Country.' São Ildefonso another Newcastle or Pittsburg!"

"No, I certainly haven't met a Mr. Manöel Pereira within the last three years or so," replied Henry Carthew patiently. "In point of fact, I don't think I ever, in India or anywhere else, met a Manöel Pereira, and I'm quite certain I never knew a Fritz Schultz. Might have had a German prisoner of that name through my hands during the Great War, but . . ."

"But you didn't know he came here, eh?"

"No, I certainly didn't."

"Well, as you weren't told anything about São Thomé by anyone named Pereira or anyone named Schultz, who is the mystery man who *did* tell you, since it was not the Hadji Abdulla?"

"In point of fact, it was General Jason's servant who told me."

"Really, Colonel Kardieu, or whoever you are! Don't you think you are being a little unnecessarily aggravating? And do you think it is entirely wise in the circumstances?"

"I am extremely sorry if you find me aggravating," replied Carthew. "I haven't the slightest wish to be anything of the sort. I am merely trying to tell you the truth, and also to find out what has become of my friend."

"Well, look here. Let's make a bargain. You admit that your friend was named Fritz Schultz, and I will tell you what became of him, fast enough."

"I'm afraid I cannot admit it, Your Excellency. I doubt if I have ever heard of a Fritz Schultz in my life."

"Ah, well; that's that, then! We'll have a talk later on, when you may have thought better of it. I believe one's memory improves when the mind has no distractions."

De Norhona rang a heavy bell that stood beside his chair.

The door opened and a secretary entered.

"Take this man along to the room that Schultz occupied," he said, "and tell the Officer of the Day to put a sentry over the door, and that I shall hold the Officer personally responsible for the prisoner's safety.

"Sorry, Colonel," he added, turning to Carthew with a somewhat sneering smile and a slightly sarcastic note in his voice, "I'll come and see you this evening. Meantime, it would be a good plan if you'd try to stimulate your memory."

"Especially good for yourself," he added coldly.

"And send me Fonseca," he said, as the secretary turned to go.

A few minutes later a small insignificant man, yellow, rat-faced and unprepossessing, glided into the room.

"Anything fresh?" asked de Norhona.

"Nothing important, Your Excellency. They still talk together and to the people they meet—shopkeepers in the bazaar, policemen off duty, soldiers, men sitting idle on the seats in the gardens."

"Ever any reference to the German, Schultz?"

"No. I haven't been able to trace that."

"Puzzling. Very puzzling," mused de Norhona. "Very interesting too. I wonder whether Schultz—who certainly got the better of Pereira in some way—actually passed himself off on the Hadji and this man as an English Officer . . . 'General Jason.' It's possible. But then Kardieu really seems to be looking for an actual General Jason. *Corpo de Dios!* That's an idea. There may actually be a British General of the name of Jason who is really missing. And Schultz may have impersonated him to Kardieu. I wonder. Possible, but not very probable. Really puzzling, but I somehow think that our Colonel Kardieu will have to stay with us. Since he has followed Schultz so far, we might see that he follows him a little farther; follows him to the end. Schultz's end. . . ."

"Go and tell the Hadji Abdulla I want to see him," he ordered, turning to his spy.

§2

"*Salaam aleikum*, Hadji Abdulla bin Ibrahim," smiled de Norhona, as the Hadji, escorted by the spy and an orderly, entered the room. "Sit down. I want to talk with you."

The Hadji, salaaming profoundly and calling the blessing of Allah upon his kind patron's head, seated himself cross-legged beside the desk.

De Norhona regarded him long and thoughtfully, the Hadji returning his searching stare with a look of meek humility and simple innocence.

"Where did you pick up this Colonel Kardieu?"

"Your Excellency? Colonel Kah-duh?"

"Yes. You introduced him as the merchant Mohammed bin Yussuf."

"Pick him up, Sidi?"

"Yes, come on. Who is he? What's the game?"

"He's a fool, Sidi, but stubborn. And I think his price is a fair one. We shall have to pay it. But even so . . ."

"That's enough! . . . Where did you first see him?"

"At Basra, Sidi. He had just come from Bahrein, where he buys pearls."

"Sure you didn't meet him first in Santa Cruz?"

"What would a pearl-merchant be doing there and with such a pearl as that? It would more probably be in Cairo."

"Do you mean that you met him in Cairo?"

"No, no, Sidi. I meant that that is the sort of place where one might meet a man with a big pearl to sell. But I don't think he'd been farther than Baghdad in his life."

"How did he ever come to hear about São Thomé?"

"He didn't. How should he, Sidi? I simply told him that I knew where he could get the best and biggest price, and that I would take him there and help him to sell it; the commission to include his passage money."

"Well, if you are speaking the truth, Hadji, you've been a fool, and somehow I have never taken you for a fool."

"The pearl is not real, Sidi?"

"It's the man who isn't real. Does he know any language but Arabic?"

"How should he, Sidi?"

"Has he ever spoken to you of the man you brought here about two years ago? Let's see, what was his name? Jason, wasn't it?"

"The name, Sidi? Was it Yasoon? Yes, that must have been it; Yasoon. No, this man has never uttered the name Yasoon. Why should he?"

"Did he ever speak of a man named Schultz?"

"Schools? No, Sidi, he is an ignorant man."

De Norhona studied the Hadji's face long and thoughtfully. Was he as simple as he looked, and as truthful as he sounded? He hoped so. Almost passionately he hoped so, for the Hadji was invaluable. It would be really a shock to find that he had been bought. It would be one of the most painful things he had ever had to do, if he were compelled to . . . to detain him. To deal with him.

"Well, looks to me as though you have been fooled—as I nearly was. I'll talk to you again later, Hadji. But let me say once more now what I have said before. Bring *no one* to São Thomé unless actually accompanied by an authorized person whom you know. A São Thoméan like Senhor Pereira.

"Where is he, by the way?" he added sharply.

"Sidi, who am I that I should know all things? The last I ever saw of the Senhor Pereira was his handwriting—on the letters he had given to the General Inglez—Yasoon, who is— 'Schools,' did you say?"

The following day was a busy one for the Hadji. Almost every member of the Council sent for him and gave him commissions of a private and personal nature. In the evening he was bidden to appear before the Council in session, to receive instructions, to be reprimanded for bringing an unauthorized stranger to São Ildefonso. Also to be informed that, while the parcel of pearls that he had brought was acceptable at the price he asked, and would now be paid for, the big pearl would be retained until more was known about the man who had apparently deceived him.

This last piece of information seemed to be something in the nature of a severe blow to the Hadji, who humbly and respectfully protested.

Had he not acted in good faith? Was he not responsible for Mohammed bin Yussuf? Would not the name and the face of the Hadji Abdulla be blackened among pearl-dealers from Basra to Bombay, from Zanzibar to Ceylon?

No member of the Council appeared to worry excessively over this contingency, and the Regent, Doña Guiomar, bade him hold his peace even as she would hold the pearl, until more was known as to its ownership.

"If, as I am inclined to suspect, it is your own pearl, Hadji," observed de Norhona, "it is, as you know, in good hands and safe keeping. If it belongs to the man whom you brought here, why the anxiety?

"Should we retain it, you shall have your commission," he added with a cynical smile.

The business of the Hadji being concluded, he was bidden by the Regent and Council of the State of São Thomé to start on the morrow for the coast, to sail forthwith to Santa Cruz, again make the fullest enquiries as to the fate of Senhor Manöel Pereira, and to return as usual six months later.

Arrived at the *dhow* he found Mr. Palsover in good health and spirits and particularly interested in the fact that Colonel Carthew was, for the time being, remaining at the Capital.

And had the Hadji seen anything of General Jason?

He had not.

Mr. Palsover, after considerable cogitation, decided that he would continue his hotel-keeping and trading pursuits for another six months, and if, on the Hadji's next visit to

Santa Cruz and São Thomé, there was still no news of General Jason, he would write him off.

He would return to England and find such another—unless of course, Colonel B. F. Carthew learned sense during the next six months and saw no fatal objection to picking up a bloody great fortune. Otherwise, he'd go home, start afresh, and incidentally find out how much the news about the General was worth—to his sorrowing widow.

VIII

His Excellency Dom Perez de Norhona, Secretary to the Cabinet, and considerable power behind the throne, found himself more and more inclined to like his 'honoured guest,' and to enjoy his conversation.

It was becoming a real and great pleasure to have long talks with this man of great experience, high intelligence and admirable character. Really a most likeable fellow and a gifted listener. The only thing he regretted was that this Colonel Kardieu was not a scientist. But one can't have everything, and he was undoubtedly a widely-read and an extremely thoughtful man; and, if unable to argue and dispute on the higher psychology, he could at any rate understand one's discourse and grasp what was said to him, provided one's language was not too technical and erudite. It clarified one's mind to put one's ideas before a man of this type and to listen to oneself as one expounded and expanded one's theories.

He hoped that, later on, the good fellow would lend him his mind for experiment. Nothing injurious. Nothing lasting, of course. He had thought, at one time, of using him for another permanent-hypnosis experiment, but he had come to believe in him—almost; to accept him at his face-value, and to feel that whatever he said was the simple truth.

That was what he was—simple and truthful.

And these were traits that were not too common with the educated, the "upper" class, the sophisticated, especially the European of that type. And if he were, as really seemed to be the case, quite truthful and honest, he could not be a Nazi German follower of this Fritz Schultz; for he still stoutly and solemnly swore that he was not a German and had never heard of Fritz Schultz.

And yet it was an amazing business, really puzzling; and whatever puzzled Perez de Norhona was something pretty deep and intricate.

Not a German. Never heard of Schultz. He was looking for a Jason. And who was Jason but the leader of the Argonauts? And of what were the Argonauts in pursuit but the Golden Fleece? The Golden Fleece of Colchis.

Could it be that he, Perez de Norhona, was the simple one, and that this Kardieu was the second of the Argonauts in pursuit of the golden treasure, nay, the far more than golden, treasure of São Thomé? It was possible. . . .

Corpo de Dios! If he were German and he could catch him out! He'd *use* him. He'd teach him to try to fool Perez de Norhona. He'd make such an example of him that if ever word of it got abroad, there would not be another of these Argonauts visiting this particular Colchis, for a century.

As Henry Carthew sat in his room, drinking his excellent coffee after dinner that night, there came a punctilious knock at the door and de Norhona entered.

"Not finished yet? I'm sorry. I'll come in later, and . . ."

"No, no," replied Henry Carthew, rising. "Please do sit down, Senhor. Will you take coffee?"

"No, thanks," replied de Norhona, seating himself. "I want to make you a proposal."

Henry Carthew smiled pleasantly, perhaps a little sceptically.

"I wonder whether you'd accept my given word, my solemn word of honour?" asked de Norhona.

Carthew stared at his pleasant gaoler.

A difficult question. On the whole he would—with some reservations, some uncertainty. Undoubtedly he was—well—a trifle medieval in outlook, and perhaps a little cruel, but one really had no reason to think him treacherous.

"Yes, Your Excellency," he said, and then, with a rush of truth to the head, qualified the statement. "Up to a point."

"Ah! And to what point?"

"Well, in the first place, the point of probability. Naturally I couldn't take your word for it if you told me you were going to do something that I didn't believe possible. And of course I know that a man in your position has to use the language of diplomacy which is not always that of plain unvarnished truth . . . and all that."

"Well now, see whether you consider this improbable, or the language of diplomacy. . . . On one condition, I will let you do anything you like about this mythical, or at any rate, mysterious, General Jason. I will do my utmost to help you in your search for him, and when you have at last decided—what you will discover to be the obvious fact—that he is not in São Thomé, the Hadji shall take you back to Santa Cruz next time he comes. Or anywhere else—provided you give me your word of honour that you will supply no information to anybody concerning São Thomé, or endeavour to find your way back here. . . . You see, I trust you, even if you don't trust me."

"And what is the condition, Senhor?"

"That you write me, in German, a brief and simple account of yourself and your friend, and of your tracing him here to Ildefonso."

Henry Carthew laughed a little bitterly.

"I thought there was a snag somewhere," he said. "I tell you I don't know any German. I don't know a word of German. Well, that's an exaggeration. But I could tell you all the German I know, now, in one minute, and any educated European knows as much. *Hier Man sprecht Deutsch*, and *Schlafen Sie wohl*, and *Guten Tag, gnadige Fraulein*, and *Kommen Sie hier*. That's just about all the German I know, and I picked those scraps up accidentally and unintentionally. I don't even know whether *bitte* means *please* or *thank you*. I just don't know German any more than you know Chinese. Possibly less," he smiled.

"Well, the offer remains open, should you remember a little more German than that. Enough to write me a letter for my archives."

Henry Carthew sighed and shook his head. Wasn't this chap honest enough to know when he met an honest man? Truthful enough to know when he was up against the truth?

"By the way," said de Norhona, rising as though about to go, "didn't you say that your elusive friend had a loving wife now weeping and forlorn, heart-broken and distraught?"

"Lady Jason naturally is in the lowest depths of grief and

anxiety," replied Carthew coldly.

"And you'd like to—I won't say 'put her out of her misery,' for I keep that phrase for more unpleasant contingencies— you'd like to set her mind at rest?"

"I'd give anything to do so."

"Well now, you write a letter to her, telling her that all's well, a letter that will relieve her mind and make her happy."

"Why! Senhor de Norhona . . ." cried Carthew, taking a step toward him, "if it were only true, and I could write to her and . . ."

"Very well, you write it to her—in German—and we'll send an exact translation—and what you say in it shall come true."

Henry Carthew's hands clenched.

"I tell you I cannot write a letter in German. I tell you I know no German."

"H'm! I wonder! You know, Schultz wasn't so anxious to disguise the fact that he spoke German."

"*Damn* Schultz! I know nothing of any Schultz, I tell you— and I am not concerned with what he did or did not do."

"No? Well, I'm sorry we've got at cross purposes to-night, Colonel. I had hoped we were going to have a talk. A nice long chat. I am in a talkative mood this evening and I wanted to ask you to help me, if you would. The fact of your being a foreigner and a stranger—and an Englishman, if that's what you are . . . but never mind. Ah, well . . . a pity."

As he reached the door, de Norhona turned.

"Look, Kardieu," he said, "I'll make you an offer that will test your sincerity and give you a chance to test mine. You want to find your friend more than anything on earth."

"Yes, literally."

"More than a signed radium-concession, eh?"

"I neither know nor care anything about radium or radium-concessions, and I would rather find my friend than a million tons of radium—all my own."

"Well, then. You shall see the man *to-night*. To-night you shall see the very man who came here with the Hadji two years ago; Fritz Schultz, the man who talked to me in English, and who said he was a British General. *Now then?*"

Henry Carthew stared at the speaker incredulous, bemused, as in a dream, a stupor of hopeless hope. Was the man still mocking him? Was he as devilishly cruel as all that?

"You *could*?" he whispered.

"I could. I can. I will. If you'll ask me now, in German, I'll do it—and I'll not demand it in German writing. Just ask me in your own tongue to bring you face to face with that man and I will do it now."

"Your Excellency, I am doing so. If you have any mercy, decency, honesty, believe me that I am now asking you, in my own tongue, to bring me face to face with my friend."

"And that is your last word, is it?"

"No, my last word is 'Go'—before I . . ."

De Norhona eyed his prisoner, sighed and went, locking the door behind him.

An hour later he returned.

"Now don't scowl at me like that, my dear chap. I have come to say that I believe you, that I am prepared to take your word that you are not a German, and to offer you an opportunity of finally removing the last vestiges of doubt from my mind. You'd like to prove that you are telling the truth, wouldn't you?"

"Of course."

"Right. You shall. And when you've proved it, I shall offer you your absolute freedom and put you on parole to undertake no sort or kind of investigations of a commercial or industrial nature. I mean that you will promise not to use your freedom to look into possibilities of future exploitation of any of this island's resources. What do you say?"

"Well, I don't wish to sound ungrateful, but what I say on the spur of the moment is—Snags! There has been one in each of your offers to-night. Excuse me if I sound ungrateful or discourteous, but what is the snag in this?"

"Oh, I don't think it is to be regarded as a snag. I want you to let me hypnotize you. I'll attempt to find out whether you know German or not. There you are, my friend, there's the final test—and your opportunity. If you accept, I will undertake to believe you innocent if I cannot prove you guilty—of being a Nazi German, and therefore a liar and a public danger to the free and independent State of São Thomé. On the other hand, refuse, and I shall know what to think."

"Why should I refuse? I have nothing to hide," replied Carthew. "If you wanted to injure me, you could do so without hypnotism, I suppose. All right, I agree."

"Good. Sit down in that arm-chair, lean back and relax. Now then, look me straight in the eyes. Relax. Relax. No resistance now. Relax. . . ."

"Ah! . . ."

And Dr. de Norhona got to work.

§2

"He is not German, Your Highness," said Perez de Norhona that night when interviewing the Regent as usual, before she retired to her own suite in the "Royal" wing of the Castle.

"You are certain?" replied Doña Guiomar. "How do you know?"

"I'm as certain of it as one can be of anything in this world. If I don't read that man aright, as a simple and straight-forward Englishman of a common British Army type, then I'm no psychologist. First, I offered him all he wants and the only thing he wants, in return for a few words of German. He knows none. To make assurance doubly sure, I hypnotized him, talked to him in German, told him he was a German and dug up all the German he knows. You could write it on a postage stamp. He's no German. He's English all right."

"I'm glad, very glad, for several reasons. It was rather a dreadful thought that the new Germany had learned about us and our mineral possibilities, or rather certainties, at last. . . . If this had been another German looking for the first one, I should have felt that your Argonaut theory was right. It has been a nightmare. I've been expecting every day to hear that a German warship had anchored off the creek, and that a large and heavily armed deputation had landed to 'protect' us—and turn us into a submarine base, a naval and military base, an airport, and one vast coal-field, mineral-workings, and industrial mining and smelting area. Three hundred years of peace shattered, our independence gone, and our civilization reverted to modern barbarism. . . . I am glad, too, for his own sake, for I have grown to like him."

"Yes, he's a lovable sort of chap, isn't he?" agreed de Norhona.

"Yes, that's exactly what he is," mused the Regent.

"What's the position with regard to him now?" she continued. "You haven't done him any harm, of course. Not one of your terrible experiments?"

"No, no. Not the slightest harm. He found it 'very interesting'! As to his position, I think we will give him the Freedom of São Thomé, on a platter."

"And eventually?"

"Well. . . . See how he shapes. See if he drops this Jason obsession. If we came to trust him completely, he could be extremely useful to us."

"Yes, he could."

"Both here and abroad," he added.

"You'd trust him to that extent, would you?" asked Doña Guiomar.

"Not in a hurry. Not till I had satisfied myself as to what is in his mind. But, sooner or later—if he continues willing to submit to hypnosis—the day will come when I can say, with absolute certainty and finality, whether it would or would not be wise to use him abroad. I think he's going to turn out to be one of those perfectly simple characters with one-way one-track minds whose word literally is their bond, and who are absolutely trustworthy."

"Yes, a man whose word is worth a thousand stamped and witnessed contracts," agreed Doña Guiomar. "That's what I think you will find him to be," and she sighed deeply—perhaps over the rarity of such phenomena.

"Suppose he simply wants to go. Just say good-bye and . . . leave us," she continued.

"Well, I don't know. I pretended to offer him that freedom in return for the confession that he was a German—but I don't think we'll take any unnecessary risks. He knows too much. I don't for one moment suppose he could ever find his way here again, or direct anyone else, but if one takes no risks, one does nothing—risky."

"Quite so," agreed Doña Guiomar. "We'll keep him on the Island."

And she fixed the smouldering gaze of her heavy-lidded lustrous eyes upon those of de Norhona.

Faintly she smiled, and there was an answering smile on de Norhona's face, as he bowed deeply, took her hand and touched it with his lips. Between these two people who understood each other perfectly, enough had been said.

Next day, Colonel Henry Carthew was given the freedom of the City of São Ildefonso and of the State of São Thomé.

§3

As the days passed by, Henry Carthew discovered to his great surprise, if not pleasure, that he was not only a free man but a genuinely honoured guest, and although he realized that that phrase is apt to bear a sinister connotation, there was apparently nothing of the sort in this instance. Not only was he treated kindly, but his society was actually sought and cultivated by certain of the Members of Council.

True, these were at first the Commissioner of Police, the Commander-in-Chief and the Secretary for Foreign Affairs; their conversations were tendentious, their questions sudden and artful, as though he were still an object of suspicion. But after a while he began to feel that he was accepted for what he professed to be, and both regarded and treated as a very interesting English traveller of rank and position, whose intentions were completely innocent and harmless. It was realized that he really was looking for a missing friend, and that he had cleverly deceived the Hadji in pursuit of that object, and whether he ever left São

Thomé again or not, was an acquisition and an ornament to the society of the Capital in general and the Citadel in particular.

And among the high Government officials and leading members of society, Henry Carthew was quickly accepted as an English aristocrat and representative of Portugal's oldest ally, and a personage who could give them all sorts of useful information about great and admired England and the rest of the outside world.

What surprised and puzzled Carthew more than anything was the attitude of Doña Guiomar, who seemed quickly—almost too quickly—to change, from a cold and offended attitude of hostility, to one of approval and friendliness that rapidly warmed. In point of fact, she too accepted him as precisely what he was, an English army-officer who, in some utterly incomprehensible manner, had heard that the lost friend for whom he was searching had made his way here to São Thomé. How this had come about was a complete mystery—one which could only be solved by Manöel Pereira.

Quite possibly, as de Norhona surmised, the evil Fritz Schultz was at the bottom of it.

All very puzzling indeed. But of one thing she was certain. This Senhor Kardieu was a *fildalgo*, an aristocrat and an Englishman, and had not the faintest interest in any commercial or industrial concerns whatsoever. . . .

Thus, at a series of strangely medieval social functions, formal, mannered, and of rigid Court etiquette, Henry Carthew found himself treated with signal favour by Doña Guiomar, seated on her right hand at State dinners, and occasionally given the somewhat embarrassing privilege of being promoted to partnership with her in a Court dance of formal stateliness.

Yes, not only was Colonel Henry Carthew a free man, but one who, were he anything of a careerist, might well think he saw a strange and brilliant future opening before him.

But Carthew was not a careerist. He was a simple-minded man of single purpose. Enough that he was free to pursue that purpose.

IX

It was almost too good to be true, and he scarcely believed it, even yet. To think that that damned door was really unlocked for good, and that he could, at any hour of the day or night, open it and walk out.

After dinner, one evening, Henry Carthew rose from his straight-backed uncomfortable chair of high old-fashioned shape, went to the door, opened it, looked out into the dim stone passage, and closed it again.

Yes, it was still true. He was still free.

Well now, what should he do—this evening and for the rest of his life? As to the former, he'd just wander about for an hour or two for the sheer joy of the feeling that he still could do so; could come and go as he liked. As to the latter, he would continue his search for Reginald, with the utmost of his energy and ability and resources, for as long as he lived.

He would now stroll about this floor of the Castle, for the ever-fresh pleasure of sampling his freedom, and in the hope of learning something from somebody—anybody.

Wandering along corridors, through galleries, across great empty stone-flagged rooms, seeing no one but an occasional belated servant, secretary or other functionary—for this non-residential part of the Castle was almost untenanted at night—he at length came out on to the broad inner balcony or gallery which looked down into the Great Hall. The light of the full moon streaming through the high windows that gave on to the court-yard, lent the huge audience-chamber a somewhat ghostly and unearthly appearance, very attractive to the artistic eye.

To Henry Carthew it was like looking from this world into another, from this point of time into an earlier one, especially when a door opened and a woman of quite medieval appearance crossed a corner of the hall, passing as she did so, through a pool of moonlight, and looking, in her somewhat old-fashioned, somewhat Spanish dress, like a visitant from that earlier time.

Doña Guiomar.

A further note of eeriness and fantasy was added by the silent and shadow-like appearance of the great animal that followed her. A beast which, but for its somewhat clumsy movements, heavy and awkward gait, might have been a bear or a great ape; except for its lack of grace and of ease of movement, a huge dog.

As the woman paused to produce a key and unlock the door through which she was about to pass, the great ungainly creature squatted down, raised its head, and gazed upward toward the window through which the moonlight shone.

As Henry Carthew, conscious of a queer discomfort and distaste, not to say fear, gazed at the animal, it threw back its head and bayed deeply.

So it *was* a dog! A huge bloodhound, baying the moon.

Well, it was the strangest dog that he had ever seen. But São Thomé was a strange place, and might well contain animals that he had never heard of. How the kangaroo must have astounded the first Europeans who landed in Australia! Well, if the world could still produce animals, till recently unknown—creatures like the okapi in Western Africa and the giant panda in Mongolia, there was no reason why São Thomé should not produce a new breed of dog. As far as one could tell in this dim light and at that distance, it was the biggest dog that ever barked, and the least dog-like in shape.

But a dog apparently it was.

"*Quiet! Lie down!*" cried the woman sharply as she opened the door, and the animal instantly fell silent, crouching low with its head upon its paws. As she opened the door and the dog rose to follow, she spoke to it again.

"*No! Stay there! Wait!*" and she cracked the whip she carried.

Withdrawing the key from the door, she passed through, closed it behind her, and ascended a secret flight of stairs.

Carthew's enquiring mind was filled with curiosity.

What kind of beast could it be?

Neither bears nor apes bark. On the other hand, dogs do not walk as this animal did; nor is the slope of a dog's back downward from tail to head.

A dog of the size and shape of a large bear!

Why shouldn't he go down and have a look at it? He had been told he could go where he liked, and that he was as free as de Norhona himself. Naturally, he wasn't going to construe this complete relaxation of all bonds into a licence to peep and pry, but there could surely be no harm in his going down into the hall and satisfying a normal and healthy curiosity as to what kind of a dog this was.

Evidently it was Doña Guiomar's body-guard and watch-dog, whatever else it was.

Of course! It was the creature that he had imagined to be a great ape when he saw it lying asleep in the corner, behind her chair, on the occasion when he had been brought before her in the guise of Mohammed bin Yussuf the pearl-merchant. The top of its shaggy head had been toward him then, and he had noticed that it had a hairy or furry body, or else wore some sort of covering or clothing of fur or hairy skins.

He'd go and have a closer look at it.

Suppose it attacked him. It might be an enormously powerful beast; and, even if he had been armed, it would be a poor way of celebrating his release and acknowledging his gratitude, to kill what was evidently the Regent's pet and body-guard.

But come! This wouldn't do. He must have been getting soft in his easy captivity. Getting nervy and cautious. He'd go down and have a look at the beast. Why should it attack him? Being a real dog-lover, he had always got on splendidly with dogs. The thing had been quiet enough when he had seen it before, that day in Doña Guiomar's room. He'd take a risk. What was life without them?

As he went along the gallery toward the stairs that led down into the hall, he kept an eye on the dog. Hearing him move, it looked up, and he saw that it was evidently watching him through the shaggy hair that hung down over its face, as does that of an old-fashioned English sheep-dog. Pausing, he called to it, as he would have done to an ordinary English dog in like circumstances.

"Hullo, old chap!" he shouted, and then whistled.

The dog instantly sprang up, alert, propping its body on its fore-legs, but without raising its heavy hindquarters from the ground.

"Hi! Here! Come here, boy! Come on. Here!" he called again, as he descended the stairs.

Suddenly the dog raised its head and uttered a curious cry; to Carthew a strangely moving sound, heart-rending almost, a sound between a banshee howl and a whimpering wail, as though the creature were in agony. It was somewhat like the noise his own dog made when, welcoming his return, its emotion was too powerful for any utterance but a whimpering—as though it wept aloud for joy.

But there was no joy in this dreadful sound. He found himself using a banal but useful cliché—'the despairing cry of a lost soul, a soul in agony.'

"Come on, old chap," cried Carthew. "Come on. What's up?"

And the great heavy animal, rising to its feet, lumbered toward him.

Was this its mode of attack? There had been no baring of teeth, no sign of snarl or growl.

"There, there, there! Well, well, well!" he said, and leaned forward confidently to pat its head as the dog reached him.

Sitting back on its haunches it rose, shook its head with an awkward toss, that threw back the overhanging hair, and gazed into Carthew's face.

Absolutely friendly!

But what an amazing creature!

What was it?

It wasn't a dog.

A barking ape?

No. No ape had square shoulders, a pale face, a moustache and beard, a high-bridged nose. . . .

Damn this dim light.

It was . . . it was . . . *human.*

It was a man.

"Here! Turn your head this way!" and he wrenched the head toward the moonlight as he swept the face clear of overhanging hair.

It was a man! . . . It was . . . *Oh God!*

No! No! Oh, God—no!

For a moment he closed his eyes and leant back against the great newel-post of the stairs.

It was not until he again opened his eyes and stared, sick, shaken and horrified to the depths of his soul, that his mind accepted the truth.

His search was ended.

§2

As he sat at the bottom of the stairs, trembling from head to foot, he looked into Reginald Jason's eyes and, recoiling, shuddered.

As the creature, the-man-that-thought-he-was-a-dog, his friend, raised its paw, its hand, and laid it on his knee, Henry Carthew's strong self-control broke down entirely, and burying his face in his hands, he actually wept, cried like a child, cried as he had not done since boyhood, his body shaken by hard, rending sobs. . . .

From an agony of grief, pain and dreadful despair, his mind turned to blind and terrible rage; and then again to grief and pity inexpressible.

This had been Reginald Jason, his friend, this man-that-behaved-as-a-dog, that thought itself to be a dog, that, but for its skeletal form and structure *was* a dog, with the mind of a dog.

For how long he wrestled with it mentally he knew not. He did his utmost, using every device of which he could think, to strike a spark of human response.

But completely without success.

This, that was a man, was mentally a dog, a friendly

good-natured dog that was devoid of anything but canine understanding and power of response.

Did it understand English better than Portuguese? No—not so far as he could tell.

Did it respond, in the slightest degree, to his attempts to awaken memories? Memories of the days when it knew it was a human being?

Not in the slightest.

At times, he found himself patting and stroking the long-haired shaggy head, and talking to it as to a dog.

At others, he would seize the creature's hand and beg, implore, *pray* that he would recognize him as Henry, Henry Carthew, his friend; remember Antoinette, Toinette, Tony, his wife.

Mastering himself with a great effort, he contrived to whistle the Regimental march of the Wessex Fusiliers, which Reginald Jason had heard ten thousand times. The effect was neither more nor less than it would have been if he had whistled it to his own dog in England.

This must be a nightmare. This was something happening in Hell, in the most horrible of all conceivable hells.

He was mad.

This dog was a *man*! . . . This man was a *dog*! This *dog* was General Sir Reginald Jason, one of the most dignified and distinguished-looking men that ever lived.

They must make him, Henry Carthew, a dog too. The good Dr. de Norhona would do it with pleasure. Then she would have two dogs. And Reginald Jason and Henry Carthew would keep each other company as her bodyguard. They could be her double bodyguard, pad about behind her, come to heel, and lie one each side of her chair. And he could live with Reginald in whatever cell was his kennel. Did he eat from a trough or use his hands? No. He would think he was a dog, and dogs don't have hands.

And would they not one day spring upon her and kill her? Would they not tear Norhona in pieces?

No. Both would have first been hypnotized into thinking

themselves good obedient dogs, faithful and devoted to their masters. And his brain would be maimed and injured as Reginald's had been, and he would remain a dog for ever. *Her* dog. . . .

And she might come back here now, at any moment; and in his present state of mind, he would certainly kill her.

He, Henry Carthew, was thinking about killing a woman. Then he must be mad.

She would not have left it, him, the dog, lying there, having told it to wait, had she not intended to return. He must go before she came.

Would the dog follow him?

He released the hand, the paw, that he was holding and patted the creature's head.

"Come," he said, and began to ascend the stairs.

The dog followed him.

That was curious. Was it something in his voice? Was some elusive chord of memory touched by the voice of Henry Carthew in what had been the mind of Reginald Jason?

Along passage and corridor, across gallery and room, the human being that thought himself a dog followed him to his door.

"Come in, old chap," he said, as he opened it, scarcely knowing whether he spoke as to a man or as to a dog.

Having locked the door he flung himself down upon his bed, and was again shaken by uncontrollable grief.

Deeply ashamed of his surrender to emotion, he at length, by a great effort of will, contrived to conquer it, or, rather, to curb its expression.

When sufficiently calm and self-controlled, he again set to work to establish communication, if not communion, with the human soul of the creature who had been a man and his friend, and was now a dog and a living horror, the thought of which would haunt him to the last day of his life.

Can a human soul be killed? Had this dog the soul of a man? Had this man the soul of a dog? Do dogs have souls?

. . .

He must not think, he must work.

And throughout the night he worked to awaken a memory, a response, a sign of humanity in what had been Reginald Jason.

Several times during the night, the man-who-thought-himself-a-dog lay down upon the floor to sleep, lying not as a man does, but at times unnaturally curled, at others, on its side, with arms and legs stretched out at right angles to the body. He could not induce it to take his bed.

And in its sleep it whimpered piteously.

For hours Henry Carthew endeavoured to establish contact with the dormant mind, quietly speaking the name Reginald! . . . Reginald! . . . Reginald! . . . into the apparently unreceptive ear. He would then repeat Lady Jason's christian name; then his own; and, in a desperate hope of penetrating to the inner consciousness, the name of any mutual acquaintance of whom he could think. He talked of places and events known to them both, all with the vague idea and faint hope that some sort of connection might be established with the sleeping creature's subconscious mind, since he had been unable to reach its conscious mind when it was awake.

Occasionally the dog stirred in its slumber, opened its eyes, raised the upper part of its body and shook its head, yawned and lay down to sleep again. When this happened Henry Carthew would cry aloud "*Reginald! . . . Reginald!*" in the hope that, in the act of waking, the subconscious mind might be receptive.

By morning he had come to the conclusion that what lay sleeping at his feet was a human being with the mind of a dog, a creature with no human soul and with only such soul as a dog may have.

The man-who-thought-himself-a-dog. . . .

In the morning, the usual servant, looking so like a Goanese "boy," brought breakfast, glanced with some surprise at the dog lying in the corner, but made no comment.

With a sick feeling of utter horror and heart-aching grief,

Carthew went to the corner where lay what had been his friend Reginald Jason, and put food and drink on the floor. The dog, propped on rigid fore-legs, looked up through its shaggy hair, a gleam of interest and pleasure in its eyes.

With a shudder of pain, Carthew turned away as the dog put its head down and drank from the bowl of milk, sucking and lapping until the bowl was empty.

At the egg dish it smelt dubiously, ignored the fruit, and hungrily devoured a fillet of fish, eating as a dog does. When the servant returned to remove the breakfast tray, the dog, rising to its feet, looked at him, looked at Carthew, and approaching, rubbed its head affectionately against his leg.

"Oh, God!" he cried, stepping back. "Oh, *don't*! Oh, *please . . .* !"

Feeling blindly for his chair, he sat down before his trembling limbs failed him, and covered his face with his hands. The man-who-thought-himself-a-dog went out with the servant.

It is probable that had there been eye-witnesses present, from his first realization of this tragic horror, Carthew would have maintained for himself the reputation of being a cold phlegmatic Englishman, unemotional and imperturbable. Alone, he had not the strength of will and purpose, nor the incentive of fearing to show emotion; and, within limits, he gave way to it. Had the great and famous man who once cried,

"These English! Bah! A nation that knows not how to weep!" been present, he would have seen one weeping, seen a usually calm reticent and inscrutable-faced Englishman sitting at a table with his head upon his arms; abandoned to grief, horror and despair, a picture of a broken and broken-hearted man.

When at length, worn out, he threw himself down upon his bed, it was to try to think, to make a plan, to decide what would be the best thing to do.

In the first place, matters that were beyond doubt must be accepted and set aside.

To begin with, this creature, in its present state, could

not be taken back to England, even if there were no obstacle to such a course. Judging by its effect upon himself, the sight would drive Antoinette stark staring mad. She must never see him . . . it. . . . She must never *know*, even. The very thought of such almost unimaginable tragedy would be enough to cloud her mind for the rest of her life.

That was the first decision—and quite final.

Secondly, this animal must either die, as a dog, or live— as Reginald Jason. And what could be done must be done quickly. It was an offence in the sight of God, an offence against Nature, and against the profoundest feelings of the human mind.

Yes, that was the second indisputable fact. This Thing must cease to exist.

Thirdly, he must find out, in such a way as to leave no shadow of doubt in his own mind, as to whether de Norhona could undo what de Norhona had done. That he must somehow discover. And if he felt certain that de Norhona's sentence of living death was irrevocable, the lost soul of Reginald Jason irretrievable, and this dreadful act final and complete for ever—then the dog must die.

On the other hand, should there be the faintest glimmer of hope, then de Norhona must, in some way, be compelled to do his utmost to undo what he had done.

He must think of some way of compelling or inducing de Norhona to achieve this.

How could he compel him? How could he induce him?

He was in no position to utter threats. He was in no position to make offers. Could he play on de Norhona's vanity as a scientist? Could he hide his own feelings sufficiently to be able to talk to de Norhona naturally and quietly? Could he pretend to be filled with wonder and admiration of what de Norhona had done in this hellish triumph of Permanent Hypnosis, and then say to him,

"Ah! But you are not clever enough to render permanence impermanent. You are neither sufficiently great a neurologist nor surgeon to restore this brain to its natural condition, to make it function normally, as it did before your experiment!"

Yes, with Reginald's life at stake, he could dissemble sufficiently to pretend that he had not recognized this creature as his friend Reginald Jason, and was merely interested in the scientific aspect of this experiment in mind fixation, destruction, metamorphosis, or whatever it was.

He rose from his bed, and for hours walked to and fro, to and fro, thinking, scheming, deciding. Action of mind and body kept grief at bay, that horrific beast of grief and horror which, sooner or later, would spring upon him, and overwhelm him.

When the servant brought his mid-day meal, he told the man that he wanted nothing, but would be glad if he would inform Dom Perez de Norhona's private secretary that Colonel Henry Carthew would be grateful if he might have a few words with His Excellency, at some time that day.

The man returned later with the information that His Excellency Dom Perez de Norhona would give himself the pleasure of visiting Colonel Henry Kardieu that evening, after dinner. Until then, he would be very busy.

Throughout the long afternoon and evening, Henry Carthew fought like the soldier he was; fought to retain sanity, normality; fought against the devils of fear and despair; tried to conquer grief and horror to the extent of keeping his mind sufficiently clear to be able to think. From time to time, nevertheless, grief, rage and horror had their way, and he was seized with a rigor of sheer agony. He was suffering unbearably, and utterly unable to think . . . to believe . . . to pray.

When evening came and a servant brought dinner, he had so far won his battle as to be able to force himself to eat and drink, that his strength might be maintained; to force himself to appear calm and normal; to speak naturally: and when, after dinner, de Norhona knocked and entered, his hands scarcely trembled as he placed a chair for him.

Now to be strong, to be wise, to be calm and cool, and to fight warily, to fight for the life, the mind, the soul of the man who, all his days, had been his admired and beloved friend, his more than friend, his brother—Jonathan: the man whom he had loved more than any other human being. And he was able to talk idly, as it were, with de Norhona until the latter said,

"Now what was it you wanted to see me about?"

"Why," he said, gripping the arms of his chair and holding taut every muscle of his body, "I've been examining that extraordinary animal . . . creature . . . man-dog or whatever it is, that I caught a glimpse of some time ago in Doña Guiomar's room. . . ."

"Yes? My prize exhibit. The most wonderful piece of psychology and surgery ever yet done in this world—though I say it who shouldn't. There you have a human being with the mind and attributes of a dog. I think I once told you how deeply interested I have been, for many years, in the phenomenon of Hypnotism. We are only on the threshold of it. As an applied science, Hypnosis is in its infancy. Personally, I think it's going to take the place of medicine altogether. . . . And when I had come to the end of my studies of what you might call normal hypnosis, talked with all the big men and read all the big books, I began to dally with the idea of inducing a condition of Permanent Hypnosis; in other words, to hypnotize a person into a certain state of mind, and then make that state of mind unchangeable, fixed, permanent, and unalterable. I realized, of course, that it involved interference with the grey matter, damage to the cortex of the brain, and I determined to experiment. I thought about it so much that at length it became an obsession."

His Excellency paused to light another cigarette.

"I fail to see the scientific value of the experiment," observed Henry Carthew coolly, his mind a cold hell of inexpressible and almost uncontrollable hatred of this inhuman devil who talked so lightly of the minds, souls and bodies of other men.

"Well. Art for Art's sake. Art should not be prostituted to base commercial ends, nor used for propaganda. Science for Science's sake. Doubtless some other scientist would find some very valuable use and practical application for

the scientific triumph of Permanent Hypnosis. I cannot say I
have gone very deeply into the subject, but at first glance
one can see uses, such as—operation on the criminal mind,
say. Take a murderous thug of the gunman type, hypnotize
him into the belief that he's a saintly clergyman, and then—
nail him there."

De Norhona laughed loudly.

"I'd love to have one or two gentlemen who are troubling
Europe at the present time, and see what I could do for
them and the unfortunate nations who suffer from the
workings of their minds. Supposing that by Permanent
Hypnosis I could turn them into modest, retiring and peace-
loving philanthropists! *And* mind you, I could do it. If anyone
submitted himself to me, I could hypnotize him into thinking
himself to be whatever I wanted him to think himself to be.
And I could then submit him to a somewhat difficult piece of
brain-surgery, including trepanning, and then perform a
delicate operation on the cortex of the brain. *And* I can
guarantee that, on recovery from the operation, his mind
would be permanently in the state in which it was when I
operated.

"Would you consider that a useful piece of scientific
work, Colonel Kardieu?"

"It opens terrific vistas," replied Carthew, and drank a
little water to moisten his leathern-seeming tongue and
lips.

How long, oh Lord, how long? . . . God give him strength
and self-control.

"Well now, here's the point that interests me and what I
really want to ask you," Carthew said. "To leave the hypo-
thetical Dictator or what-not, and to return to the actual
case in point—could you undo the marvellous work that you
have done? Could you restore this dog to manhood?
Operate again, hypnotize him again, and make him think he
is what he used to be, *make* him what he used to be, a
human being, a man of the highest type?"

"No," replied de Norhona without hesitation. "Utterly
impossible. No! That would be a real miracle! It would be a
miracle as great as Christ's raising Lazarus from the dead

. . . Jairus's daughter . . . or the widow's son of Nain. No, I have done what no man has ever done yet, but I cannot undo it. God alone could do that."

"If you could hypnotize him so that he thought he was a dog, why cannot you de-hypnotize him, so to speak?" asked Carthew.

"I've told you. Because of the little surgical operation on the cortex of the brain. I cannot restore what I have removed from his brain, any more than I could restore your appendix if I removed it. The hypnosis is nothing. Any fool with the gift and knowledge could hypnotize anybody who is willing to be hypnotized. But the whole point of my discovery, my successful experiment, is the cerebral operation, the actual elision of a tiny portion of the brain. As a well-educated man, although not a scientist, you must realize that a portion of the brain, once removed, cannot be replaced a couple of years later—or a couple of seconds later, surely."

"So the case is completely and utterly hopeless? What you have done cannot possibly be undone, and that man will always be a dog?"

"Yes, because he will always *think* he's a dog. The first example of Permanent Hypnosis and the last—until I, Perez de Norhona, choose to perform the experiment again. Not even Harvey Williams Cushing could do it, I believe."

"And *do* you propose to perform the experiment again?" asked Carthew.

"I should like to. Yes, if I ever give an account of my successful attempt at establishing the possibility of Permanent Hypnosis, those fellows in Vienna and Paris will say that, if I really did it, it was an accident. Not that that matters much; but for my own satisfaction I'd like to be quite certain that it wasn't a fluke, that I actually did what I set out to do—induced a state of mind and rendered that state of mind unalterable."

"You don't regard it as a form of murder? The most terrible form of all—*soul*-murder."

"No. Why should I? Where's the murder? The whole point is that I did not kill the patient in attempting to perform the experiment. You cannot have a murder without a corpse, can you? And as to murdering souls, I am not scientifically interested in souls. I'm only concerned with minds and bodies."

"I see. And this dog-man or man-dog is merely an object of interest to you."

"Of the deepest interest, as I said before. My prize exhibit. What else should it be but an object of the most intense interest?"

"Not one of regret or remorse? Not an object of pity?"

"My dear Colonel, you've fought in many battles, no doubt. You've led your Regiment and sustained heavy losses. Are you filled with remorse, regret and pity? Or is the battle a matter of the deepest professional interest to you?"

"I pity the wounded and the dead."

"And lead the rest to fight again another day, eh?"

"I've no doubt you will get the better of me in argument, every time, Your Excellency, so I won't pursue that particular train of thought, though I might remark that there is not the slightest similarity between the cases. I am not responsible for the death or mutilation of the men I command."

De Norhona smiled tolerantly, and, with an airy wave of the hand in which he held his cigarette, dismissed that aspect of the subject.

"Yes, I should like to do the experiment three times, given two more suitable subjects," he said, breaking the heavy silence of the room.

With a great effort, Henry Carthew contrived to ask, in his ordinary voice,

"What do you call suitable subjects?"

"Oh, in the first place, criminals who ought to be executed, enemies of the State; and in the second place, people of a certain standard of intelligence, high or low, according to my hypnotic intentions and object. I have, psychologically speaking, turned a man into a dog, faithful to its master, affectionate, responsive to kindness, abso-lutely reliable as a guardian and protector. Putting it crudely, I had, for my dog-experiment, a man with the best of the dog-attributes that are possessed by a human being, if you understand. One wouldn't expect to make a really admirable house-dog, watch-dog, out of some base, cowardly sneaking criminal. It would, on the other hand, be interesting to hypnotize such a human reptile into the belief that he was a high-minded virtuous man with a noble mission in life; and, while he was filled with that belief, render the hypnosis permanent.

"But that wouldn't be quite as interesting. Critics would say afterwards,

'*He was a man and he is still a man. You say he was a criminal and now you say he is a reformer. Nothing much in that. There have been plenty of such conversions, without any talk of hypnosis or cerebral operation.*'

"No, I think if I had a man of that type for a subject, I'd hypnotize him into the belief that he was a snake and I'd say to him, '*On thy belly shalt thou go all the days of thy life,*' and he'd damn well do it, after I had performed the De Norhona Cerebral Operation on him."

Words . . . words . . . words. . . .

How the man talked. . . . What a joy it would be to take an automatic out of one's pocket and shoot him dead, the smug cold-hearted devil.

But not yet.

No, nor ever. Colonel Henry Carthew, late of the Wessex Fusiliers, was not a murderer.

What was the fellow saying?

Damn what he was saying! He himself had something to say, when he got a chance to speak.

"Who was this man upon whom you so successfully operated? I mean, how did he come to be a 'suitable subject' for experiment?" he asked, in a pause of the monologue that was in fact an infinitely erudite and interesting scientific exposition.

"Well, I'll tell you, Colonel. He's a German. One Fritz Schultz, who came here with the most evil intentions. . . . An Enemy of the State, if ever there was one, a secret and deadly dangerous Public Enemy Number One."

"How do you know?"

"Because the clever fellow brought a letter of introduction from my own friend, one of the very best of our
emissaries whom, almost certainly, he had murdered. And
the letter introduced him as a Nazi German, a treacherous
scoundrel, one of those loathsome villains who are sent
into a country to foment trouble and cause unrest, the first
of the vanguard of invasion. In this case, it may have been
commercial and industrial invasion *which we will never
allow*. But if it were, what is *that* but the preliminary to
military invasion, of annexation, absorption and—
destruction?"

The hitherto cold and unemotional scientist began to
warm, to glow with the heat of anger, and rapidly to turn
from the detached man of science into the hot-blooded
patriot and statesman.

"The indisputably genuine letter that he gave me was
his death-warrant. Self-condemned he stood, lies in his
mouth, the truth in his hand. The truth that he could not
read.

" *'You dog!'* said I to myself, as I smiled at him. *'You
damnable dog. You shall go on all fours. A dog you are and
as a dog you shall live henceforth. On all fours you shall
crawl and your food you shall eat from the ground.'*

"That's why he became the subject of my first
experiment. He had been a faithful dog to his employer,
even to the extent of risking his life. His master's trusted
hound. . . . Blood-hound. . . . And I turned him into . . ."

But Henry Carthew ceased to hear what de Norhona
was saying.

What could have happened? What could be the truth
behind this horrible tragedy? Reginald calling himself Fritz
Schultz, and bringing a letter that described him as a
German *agent provocateur*? Impossible. What was the real
truth? For de Norhona was obviously telling the truth as he
saw it. He had done a terrible thing in the pursuit of
scientific knowledge, but he had done it to a man whom he
honestly regarded as an appalling danger to his country. A

living danger—to be destroyed.

Why could not de Norhona be quiet for a moment—hold his tongue and give him a chance to think . . . to think. . . ?

Words . . . words . . . words. . . .

If the man wouldn't be silent, he'd lose control . . . and seize him by the throat . . . and . . .

Henry Carthew buried his face in his hands. Covered his eyes with his hands.

Reginald could never come back. Reginald must live his life out—like this.

De Norhona had not done this thing to Reginald, but to some German named Fritz Schultz. How could Reginald have been Fritz Schultz?

How? . . . How? . . . How?

Why? . . . Why? . . . Why?

What must he do?

Suddenly he rose to his feet. He must make one final effort, cost what it might.

"Your Excellency," he said.

"*Corpo de Dios!* But you look ill! What's the matter?" exclaimed de Norhona.

"Nothing, Your Excellency! I would ask you a favour. Might my friend . . . Might it . . . the dog . . . be brought here now?"

"Certainly. Why not? Do you want to see the scar, or . . . put him through his tricks, or what?"

Rising and going to the open window, de Norhona whistled high and shrill.

"If he's loose, he'll come," he said.

Sick, faint and trembling, Henry Carthew leant against the stone mullion. A door was opened in a corner of the courtyard. A man appeared and stood aside as a great grotesque form bounded forth and crossed the court-yard in a clumsy gallop.

"There you are! . . . I'll send someone down to open the door at the head of the steps below, there. See how he keeps to his hands and feet. Never stood upright since the operation. I suppose one could train him to do it as one trains a dog to sit up and beg. Extraordinarily interesting. He does as a dog all those things that his human structure permits—such as eating from the floor without use of hands. Other things that he must do, but cannot do in dog-fashion, he does as a man. Very interesting. Reflex muscular action—or purely subconscious memory? He'll provide me with interesting study for years, apart from being my . . ."

Henry Carthew went from the room—in haste, before he committed murder.

A minute or two later, the man-who-thought-he-was-a-dog came panting toward him, sniffed at him in a friendly way, licked his hand and went into the room where de Norhona stood.

Henry Carthew followed, closing the door, locking it and putting the key in his pocket.

"Well, old chap," said de Norhona kindly, and patted the shaggy head.

The dog peered up through the overhanging mat of hair.

"Here! . . . We are going to do some tricks. . . ."

"We are," said a quiet voice behind him.

And turning he saw Carthew about to attack him—holding, high above his right shoulder, a heavy chair.

"De Norhona," he said, "I'm going to kill you unless you restore this creature to manhood. I feel I should kill you, in any case. For that thing lying there was General Sir Reginald Jason, my friend! You've done worse than kill him. . . . Why should I not kill you?"

His voice broke on a kind of scream, a cry of cruel pain.

De Norhona did not flinch. Coolly he replied,

"Don't talk nonsense, man. That"—and he pointed contemptuously with his foot—"came here with . . . But why should I go all over it again? He was Fritz Schultz and he murdered Pereira. You've talked a lot about your friend. What about *my* friend whom this dog killed?"

Carthew moistened his lips.

"You talk too much, de Norhona," he said. "This is . . . this was . . . Sir Reginald Jason. Now—before I kill you—can you save him? If not, save yourself from me, if you can.

Quick, or I'll brain you!"

And Carthew swung the heavy chair back.

Dr Norhona smiled and shook his head.

"I can't. Can't be done, Kardieu. Sorry. Nothing on earth can . . ."

"*Then I'll . . .*"

There was a sudden low growl and a heavy body flung itself against Carthew, sending him staggering sideways, and knocking him down.

The dog had saved its master.

It stood growling, its weight pressing heavily on Carthew's chest.

Carthew lay still.

Dr Norhona laughed quietly.

"My experiment was quite successful, Colonel, wasn't it? *Good* dog!"

X

Henry Carthew never knew how long the next period of his life lasted—the period between his attempted attack upon de Norhona and the day when he was arrested and told of the fate to which he had been sentenced.

What he did know was that, during that time, he was barely sane; that certain things happened to him; that he himself committed certain acts and deeds; and that his reason or excuse for having done them was that he was really of unsound mind.

The only person to whom he afterwards spoke of those days or weeks or months was his friend Brodie Dysart, and to him he tried, later, to give a coherent account.

At the beginning of that utterly dreadful period, his memory of which was, to some extent, mercifully obliterated, two things surprised him.

One was that the incalculable and unpredictable de Norhona apparently bore him not the slightest ill-will for what he might well have regarded as a murderous attack upon himself.

The other was that it was a perceptible addition of sorrow to his almost unbearable burden of grief, that the dog should have turned against him; should have defended against Henry Carthew, his best and oldest friend, the man de Norhona, who had done him this appalling wrong. But realizing how foolish, nay childish, it was in the circumstances to feel like this, he told himself that it was, alas, only one more proof of the completeness of the success of de Norhona's experiment. Had there been one trace left of the original mind and soul of Reginald Jason, it could not have happened.

Night and day, eating little and sleeping scarcely at all, he wrestled with the problem of what he must do; now deciding that he must wait and hope, now that he must accept facts and, abandoning childish optimism and wholly unwarranted optimism, accept realities and act accordingly.

He must not act precipitately.

But, on the other hand, how much longer could he bear it? How much longer could he continue to see Reginald like this, knowing in his heart that the state was permanent. It would be a terrible thing if he himself were to die, to go mad, to be imprisoned, to be deported, before he had done what he knew he must do.

He must cease to ask himself how long he could bear it. He *must* bear it. He must bear it until the hour came that he felt was the appointed one, the hour of his destiny.

Another addition to his misery was the fact that de Norhona seemed increasingly to like him and to seek his company. He spent his life upon a rack of pain and grief, but an extra turn was given to the instrument of torture whenever de Norhona entered his room and talked; bade him come out and walk, for his health's sake; insisted on his riding abroad with him into the lovely semi-tropical country of the plateau; or demanded his attendance at a State dinner or other function.

It seemed to Carthew that de Norhona was a living intelligence, an intelligence almost freed from the hampering restriction and misguidance of emotion; a man whose mind was neither cruel nor kind, but almost purely scientific.

And yet he was human enough in his fanatical patriotism.

Carthew entertained for him curious and contradictory feelings of murderous hatred, fear, considerable respect and a most unwilling liking. So inevitably fair and just himself, Carthew had to admit that de Norhona had done nothing to Jason as Jason, an honest and honourable gentleman who had come to make certain right and proper proposals and suggestions of a commercial nature. Quite obviously de Norhona had used for his great experiment a man whom he believed to be a deadly enemy of his country, inasmuch as he was the first of an invading army, insupportable, detestable and loathsome in the eyes of people to whom independence was the very breath of life and the very religion of their soul.

And he fully admitted that de Norhona was as puzzled as himself at the inexplicable chain of events whereby Carthew's Jason had become de Norhona's Schultz.

And so, exercising great constraint and self-control, he talked with de Norhona as and when de Norhona wished, and restrained himself from precipitate action.

§2

Was it on that same dreadful day upon which the dog had attacked him, or on the next, that he had begged de Norhona to let him see as much of the dog as possible?

De Norhona had had no objection. It was loose at night. Doña Guiomar liked to have it about her in the daytime.

How could she? How could she bear it? One would have thought it would have made her ill . . . driven her mad.

Oh, nonsense. Carthew must remember that, here in São Thomé, they were still in the age when the Court had its jesters, dwarfs, freaks, monsters and such. Of course the Regent wasn't a cruel woman. She was deeply interested in de Norhona's amazing experiment, and there was no doubt that she derived a certain feminine and real satisfaction from seeing, crouching at her feet, one who had been the enemy of her people, seeing him reduced literally to the level of a dumb animal.

Was he for ever dumb?

For ever. Absolutely. Inevitably. To the extent that a dog was dumb. He could growl and bark, of course. . . .

Was it that same night, after the dog had attacked him, that he saw it in the court-yard and whistled to it as de Norhona had done, had attracted its attention, found it friendly, and induced it to follow him up to his room?

That night or the next, no doubt. And he had been curiously thankful to find that the dog was perfectly friendly again. But though he again spent the night in trying to effect more of a *rapprochement* between himself and the dog than is possible between a human being and any ordinary animal, he had failed entirely. It was just as friendly and responsive as a dog, in that it liked to have its head stroked, liked to be patted and talked to—but it would, on the whole, rather go to sleep.

Henry Carthew, all his life until now, a man of very sane and well-balanced mind, calm, undemonstrative, the tenor of whose way was even, knew that he was approaching the end of his tether, that he was losing grip, that such nights were dangerous.

He was in despair.

A man in despair is like a drowning swimmer who frenziedly clutches at straws.

Carthew could think of nothing but Reginald Jason, wherever he might be or whatever he might be doing, even if seated, incredulous and amazed, beside Her Highness Doña Guiomar at a dinner-party.

One day a thought suddenly came to him.

Might it not be possible that the power of suggestion could have some effect upon what was left of the mind of the creature that had been Reginald Jason? He did not know much about psychology, though he had learned a lot from listening to de Norhona's eternal monologues on the subject. But like any other educated person who keeps abreast of current ideas, he knew that suggestion was now known to be a powerful weapon in the armoury of the mental physician.

Was it conceivable that some possible good might accrue from the dog being treated as though it were a human being?

Suppose he could induce de Norhona to try the experiment of having it treated as decent and kindly people would treat a wild-man-of-the-woods whom they had captured and wished to reclaim? Suppose the hair of its head were cut and the moustache and beard removed. Suppose the dress of shaggy skins, like that worn by a pantomime "animal" on the stage, were removed.

Suppose what had been Reginald were dressed as though it were Reginald?

Might not that awaken a memory, strike a chord?

Surely if he were bathed; if his nails were cut and cleaned; if he were shaved, valeted and treated exactly as though he were a man, he might respond? Surely if an attractive meal were properly served at a table, he could be induced to sit on a chair and use a knife and fork?

It was an idea. It was—one could hardly say a hope—but . . . he'd try it, if de Norhona would consent, and help by giving the necessary orders. . . .

De Norhona had not the slightest objection—nor the slightest expectation of any result.

"My dear chap," he said, "when I can amputate a man's leg and replace it so that he can walk perfectly, *then* what I have done to that man's brain can be undone."

And of course he was right.

The only result of the complete and careful carrying out of de Norhona's orders was to make things even worse for Carthew; and, if such a thing were possible, to increase the pain that he suffered.

To see Reginald Jason, the most dignified man whom he had ever beheld, acting like a dog—or like a king playing at being a dog—was worse, far worse.

It had been as a knife in his heart to see Reginald Jason dirty and degraded, dressed in a suit of skins, his face hidden with matted tangled hair. It was as though the knife turned in his heart, cutting it to pieces, to see General Sir Reginald Jason, dressed, as he should be, in the tropical kit of an Englishman, behaving like the dog he now thought himself to be.

The very next night, Henry Carthew, with hands that trembled slightly, poured his after-dinner coffee into a bowl, added milk and sugar, and placed it in the dark old heavy cupboard which was used as a kind of side-board. This *café au lait* the dog was known particularly to like, de Norhona having discovered the fact by giving it small quantities in his saucer after dinner, his reason being that he was interested in the question of how far the dog retained any human tastes and likings.

And in Carthew's inner pocket was a little phial which he

had almost constantly carried, ever since he first went on active service on the North West Frontier, where "the women come out to cut up what remains"... When going to the front or on what might be a dangerous journey, he always took it with him. No lingering death for Henry Carthew.

XI

Henry Carthew spent in prayer the greater part of what he intended to be Reginald Jason's last night on earth.

Properly valeted and dressed in his own clothes, the tragic creature now looked like Reginald Jason. He *was* Reginald Jason—physically. Had Carthew come upon him suddenly, as he lay there now, he would have had no feelings in his heart save those of greatest joy and thankfulness, and a little wonder as to why Reginald should be lying on the ground.

Before dawn, he made the longest and greatest endeavour that he had yet made to find a mind, a soul, in the body of this his friend, and to communicate with it.

At dawn, the living effigy of Reginald Jason sat up, yawned as a dog does, shook itself and looked at Henry Carthew.

The time had come.

Going to the cupboard Carthew took out the bowl of sweetened *café au lait* and put it on the table. The creature looked pleased and expectant.

Then, kneeling before it, he implored it to speak to him, almost prayed to it to do so.

Foolishly, childishly, he thanked God that it was friendly and responsive, much more responsive than usual.

What he had to do, he must do quickly or he could never do it. . . . Never. . . . If he failed Reginald now . . . Never.

Rising, he took the bowl from the table, put it on the ground, and dropped the contents of his phial of cyanide tablets into it. Turning away, he sat upon his bed, his face almost touching his knees, his hands clamped hard upon his ears.

Thus he sat and prayed.

A few minutes later he looked up.
His friend was dead.

Putting forth all his strength, he placed his arms about him, raised him from the floor and laid him upon the bed, straightening the limbs and crossing the hands upon the breast.

His friend Reginald Jason lay there exactly as in life.

But, thank God, there was no longer any life in him.

XII

He sat by the body of his friend, in a stupor of grief and of horror at himself and what he had done. The arguments of the night seemed treacherously feeble, inadequate and weak in the light of day.

He had killed his friend. He had murdered his friend.

He had done it for the best.

It was the only thing to do.

Who was he to say it was the only thing to do? How did he know that de Norhona was right, and that the experiment was absolutely final and complete, a *fait accompli* which nothing could ever change?

But his sturdy common-sense, his singleness of purpose and the discipline of mind and body to which he had submitted all his life, stood him in good stead. Before the sun shone into the room he had attained a calmer and serener frame of mind. Whether de Norhona's act were final and irrevocable or not, his own was. He had done what he had done, and he would be a fool and a weakling if he now regretted it and permitted the intrusion of remorse.

Repressing emotion, thrusting it, for the moment, to the back of his mind, he sent a letter to de Norhona telling him of what he had done.

De Norhona came immediately, incredulous. His reaction to the realization of what had happened was anger almost uncontrollable. He seethed with a cold but furious rage, and uttered abominable threats, one of the least of which was that Carthew should become himself something lower in the scale of animal creation than any dog.

His savage contempt almost equalled his consuming wrath.

The fool! The lout! The wretched, interfering, clodhopping half-wit! To dare to wreck and ruin and spoil and destroy and end the greatest and most successful experiment ever made by a psychologist-surgeon.

It was always the way! A sluttish serving-wench could burn a manuscript worth ten thousand times its weight in gold—or her own weight either. The lowest gutter-scum of the filthiest slum could set fire to a building housing pictures that were the world's masterpieces. And as for this accursed *louse*—he'd . . .

Colonel Kardieu! Let his infamous name be known as that of a man who destroyed an experiment that would have taught the greatest scientists facts that would have revolutionized their ideas on . . .

God grant him patience—to think out a fitting punishment. . . .

When again would he get such a subject for experiment as this Fritz Schultz? A man highly intelligent, but deserving of death and worse; a man willing, in his ignorance, to submit to hypnotism.

When de Norhona's tirade was ended, it seemed but to anger him the more that, with a quiet dignity and no sign of being in the least intimidated, Henry Carthew replied,

"He was my friend, a noble and upright man—no *agent provocateur* of Germany and no more German than yourself. It is only because I believe you to have been honestly mistaken, that I have not killed you, that I don't kill you now, de Norhona."

His Excellency Dom Perez de Norhona spat. His savage anger and contempt were rising fast again. As he turned to go, he eyed Carthew malevolently.

"And if you are thinking that you will resist hypnotism and prevent me from using *you* as a subject for experiment —don't build on it. . . . Believe me, I will deal with you . . . adequately."

As he flung open the door, Henry Carthew spoke.

"Your Excellency," he said, "look," and he pointed toward the bed. "Is that the face of a swindler and a rogue and a murderer? You know that there has been some amazing mistake. He has done you no wrong. You did him the most terrible wrong that one human being ever did to another. Admit it, and give him proper Christian burial."

"I'll give you burial—*alive*," snarled de Norhona, ere he slammed the door behind him—and locked it.

§2

When de Norhona returned, toward evening, he was again the philosopher-scientist. His wrath had evaporated, leaving a cold and bitter sediment.

"You've bothered and pestered me intolerably for weeks past about your accursed friend. You say this is your friend and you beg that he may be given Christian burial. Well, of course he will. He was a man. Whether he was a Christian or not, I do not know. But he served a far more useful purpose than you ever will. If he was your friend and an Englishman, I am sorry that it was he who was fated to be the subject of my experiment. If he was what I think he was, I am glad. But whoever he was, the operation had been performed, and you had no right to interfere . . . to kill him . . . to cut short my experiment from which I still had so much to learn. . . . A lifetime's study. You have done me and Science a greater injury than any man ever did before, and I will punish you for it.

"Oh, I'll punish you. A case for the quick-sand, I think—if it's not too good a death for you . . . too easy."

§3

The body of General Sir Reginald Jason was removed with reverent care and gentleness, and his funeral obsequies, by direction of His Excellency Dom Pedro de Norhona, were like those of a São Thoméan gentleman of position.

Henry Carthew formally thanked de Norhona, who coldly replied to the effect that he had given the man the benefit of what doubt there was as to his identity; that he had no quarrel with the dead.

It was against the living that his anger again burned.

XIII

"I don't care," stormed Doña Guiomar. "You and your scientific rubbish! . . . And suppose it was the greatest successful experiment ever made in the history of surgery and psychology, as you're so fond of telling us! . . . Can't you repeat it? If it were not a mere accident, you can do it again. Do it a hundred times. There are plenty of subjects for experiments, aren't there?"

"Your Highness, I . . ." began de Norhona.

"Don't talk to me. Don't interrupt. This man is of more importance to me than a thousand of your silly experiments. Suppose that poor sickly boy dies. No one knows better than you what a weakling he is, in-bred and in-bred for ten generations. Twenty generations. I am the last of the family, the last of the line, and if my nephew dies, who is to follow me?"

"Your Highness, you . . ."

"Be quiet. I will not marry a São Thomén."

Her hard proud face melted into a charming and delightful smile.

"Or I'd have married you, Perez, long ago—for the sake of your brain. Not your beauty, so don't strut. I had thought to remain content to be the Regent and the real ruler, even when the boy was a man, and if he died, to be Ruler myself, and appoint my successor. You perhaps, Perez. But now I won't. I have changed my mind. Say I've fallen in love if you like. I am going to marry this English nobleman."

"Your Highness, he's not a nobleman. He is only . . ."

"Have I told you not to interrupt? Will you be quiet? . . . Not a nobleman? You will not be Perez de Norhona much longer, if you thwart me. Now then. You can just go back to Colonel Kardieu, and in spite of what you may have said to him about your beastly Schultz, you can eat humble pie, apologize, and tell him the gist of what I have just said to you."

601

"That Your Highness is graciously pleased to ask him to make you an offer of marriage?"

Doña Guiomar rose to her feet.

"Listen, Perez," she said quietly. "A truly clever man is never too clever. May I offer you, in spite of your wonderful cleverness, a word of advice? Don't go too far. We are old friends, but if you presume upon my friendship . . ."

"Your Highness, I was only doing my poor best to see that I have your message correctly, and that you wished . . ."

"Silence! Don't talk to me. Do as I tell you. And if you're as clever as you think you are, you'll do your utmost to obtain the forgiveness and the favour of the future co-Regent. . . . What? Of course he will be co-Regent. And should my poor little nephew die—in spite of your marvellous skill—my son will be the next ruler of São Thomé. And he'll be strong and vigorous, hardy, brave, not a puny hot-house plant of no stamina."

"But Your Highness, we know nothing of this man except . . ."

"You will interrupt me, will you? Suppose now I interrupt you, and venture to contradict you. We know one thing about him. And that is that he is going to be my husband.

"You may go," she added coldly.

Dom Perez de Norhona went.

So she would kick over the traces, would she? She would fight the most powerful man in the State. Defy and abuse and threaten Perez de Norhona. Amusing creatures, women. And His Excellency laughed aloud. She'd do this and that. Not only without consulting her best, ablest and most faithful counsellor, but in absolute defiance of his wishes and advice.

She would, would she?

She'd marry this wandering mystery-monger who had destroyed the proof of the success of the most marvellous example of applied psychology and surgery that the whole history of medical science had ever known.

She would, would she?

Well, she wouldn't. She'd marry Perez de Norhona. And

she'd do it in his own good time. And if she produced a son, the child would be the heir to the throne. He'd succeed too.

Guiomar! Guiomar! Foolish woman. Haven't you yet learnt that Perez de Norhona has his way? Has always had it, and will always have it?

Colonel Kardieu! Huh! *Colonel Kardieu!*

§2

A few hours later, His Excellency Dom Perez de Norhona paid a visit to his prisoner, in spite of the fact that the mere sight of that abominable man disturbed his scientific calm, caused his blood to boil, and made him a mere human creature of like passions with other men.

It was by no means an amiable side of his character that he now displayed to the unhappy Carthew. And after telling him that he would have submitted him to a remarkable surgical operation, save for the fact that it would render him ignorant of how grotesque and despicable a creature he would be. . . .

On the other hand, no. He would not say that. He would wait a year or two perhaps, and at the end of that time would inflict some such punishment—and during that period the good Kardieu could spend his time in visualizing himself in his metamorphosis. Perhaps. Perhaps.

Or again, there was that Bridge of Sighs that spanned the Quick-sand of Death. That could be either a reasonably quick or an unreasonably slow business. Just engulfment, or a slow rotting of the flesh from the bones.

And when de Norhona had finished his monologue on crime and punishment, Henry Carthew replied briefly,

"Really, de Norhona! I thought this was a more or less civilized State, and you one of its enlightened Rulers. If you are as upset as all that by what I did, and are out for my blood, why not shoot me and have done with it? I assure you I shall raise no objection."

De Norhona laughed unpleasantly.

"I thought I'd made it pretty clear that, whatever else we are in São Thomé, we are not civilized by your standards, and with the help and favour of our Eternal Father, we never will be. But don't make the mistake of thinking that because we loathe and abhor and despise your Civilization we are in the slightest degree barbarous, savage, or . . . cruel. No, no. But we believe in punishment for wrong-doing and in making the punishment fit the crime."

"Well, I killed my friend, your victim. Kill me—as humanely, and don't be barbarous, savage and cruel."

"Oh, come now. You're hardly putting it fairly," replied de Norhona, as one who expostulates in a just and reasonable manner. "That's not making the punishment fit the crime. You did not merely kill my victim. You spoilt my experiment. Wouldn't it be much more fitting if you offered to take his place? Agreed to submit to hypnosis, and left me to do the rest. But not a dog. Not a dog this time, Kardieu. Not a dog."

Carthew repressed a shudder.

"Or there is another idea. How would you like, while retaining such wits as you have, to take the place of your alleged friend? Remain a man and become the body-guard and pet of Her Highness the Regent?"

Carthew stared at de Norhona in silence. What was the fellow driving at?

"I don't suppose she'd thrash you, Kardieu, like she did Schultz. She trained him with the whip, you know. It was only after many a flogging that . . ."

Henry Carthew rose to his feet, his fists clenched, his eyes blazing.

"You damned Dago cur!" he cried, "I'll . . ."

"Sit down!" ordered de Norhona. "If you're going to behave like a wild beast, I'll chain you up like a wild beast. How would it suit you to wait in the late Schultz's kennel—until I have decided what I'll do with you? . . . That's better. . . . Now then, listen to me, for I have something amusing to say to you. It's this.

"Her Serene Highness, the Regent, Doña Guiomar, offers you a fair, free and full opportunity of escape. No—*not* from São Thomé, but from your present unpleasant position. She proposes to raise you up. High up—out of the rather awkward hole into which you have fallen; or foolishly leapt head-long. She proposes—to propose, Kardieu. Thinks she'd like an English husband. I am not joking, Kardieu. She has always refused to marry in her circle of relations here. How would you like to be Vice-Regent, Viceroy-Consort, Doña Guiomar's tame . . . ?"

"I'd sooner be shot. Much sooner," replied Henry Carthew without waiting for de Norhona's sneer to finish.

"Sooner be shot than marry Guiomar, eh? And why?"

"For several reasons. Chiefly because she kept my friend as . . . But why should I answer such a question? And why should I take you seriously?"

"She'll take you seriously—if I tell her that, with reference to her kind suggestion, you say you'd sooner be shot."

"If Doña Guiomar said anything of the kind, which I don't for one moment believe, my answer is that I do not wish to marry."

"Ah! And you'll repeat that to Her Highness if she refuses to believe my report, and sends for you?"

"Certainly," replied Henry Carthew.

"Ah! . . ." smiled Perez de Norhona.

§3

When de Norhona went as usual, that night, for the final report-making and instruction-receiving interview with the Regent, he appeared worried, anxious and diffident.

When his mistress enquired as to how His Excellency the Colonel Henri Kardieu had received the news that she proposed to offer him a seat beside her in the Regent's place of power and honour, de Norhona appeared to be too confused to reply.

"Do not ask me," he said at length. "The man is mad."

"I suppose it turned his head, rather," smiled Doña Guiomar. "At first he would think it was a joke of yours. He would not realize that no one may propose marriage to the Regent, and that it is for her to choose. . . . What exactly did he say?"

"That he would far sooner be shot than be married to

Your Highness," replied de Norhona in a painful whisper, his eyes lowered, his expressive hands outspread, his whole body registering pain, horror, apology, shocked grief.

Blood tells, and Doña Guiomar's genuine dignity and breeding stood her in good stead.

With a shrug of her beautiful shoulders and a thin pale smile,

"His own choice," she said.

After a full minute's silence.

"I leave him to you, Perez," she added.

XIV

The waiting, the uncertainty, the suspense were bad, very bad indeed, for, from time to time, de Norhona visited him and made unpleasant suggestions, dropped very disturbing hints, or made contradictory promises—sometimes that his case would be dealt with that night, sometimes that ten years rigorous detention would precede a painful and remarkable punishment.

Definitely, decided Carthew, the man in whose hands his fate lay, was a person of vindictive and cruel nature when his enmity and vengeful feelings were aroused.

Suppose this half-caste Portuguese-Arab, or Goanese or whatever he was, kept up this cat-and-mouse game for the rest of his life?

Well—he could shorten it himself, by his own act, when he had had enough. He hoped that he would never be driven to suicide though, for he had a duty to perform. Antoinette was still waiting, and he must not fail her if it were humanly possible to avoid it. He must live and hope—hope to escape and in some way communicate with her. While there is life there is hope, and he was still alive. So was the Hadji Abdulla—Brodie Dysart. It was quite possible that somehow, some day, he might have speech with him, tell him of Reginald's fate, and ask him to let Antoinette know that her husband was really and indubitably dead. No need to give her any of the dreadful details. . . .

Meanwhile existence was only just bearable.

§2

But Henry Carthew's patience and fortitude were not tried for long.

One night he was aroused from sleep by a Sergeant of Police, bidden to dress quickly, to prepare for a journey. . . .

"The Bridge of Death, as they call it," thought Carthew, and was filled with regret, grief and impotent anger that he should be killed thus without opportunity of sending a word to Antoinette—waiting, watching, fearing, heart-sick with hope deferred.

Of de Norhona or anyone else in authority he saw nothing. In silence, his cavalcade of the Sergeant and six men rode out of the Citadel and through the sleeping town. . . . As they halted while the city gates were opened at the Sergeant's order, the latter reminded Carthew that, inasmuch as escape was entirely impossible, he would not be shot if he attempted it, but would make the rest of the journey on foot, at the end of a cord, and with his hands bound behind his back. . . .

As the day wore on and he recognized various landmarks, Carthew could not forbear comparison of this miserable descent with the free and relatively happy journey up from the coast, in the company of the Hadji Abdulla.

At night, in the rest-house, a soldier with a loaded carbine kept watch, while others were posted as sentries at the window and door of his room. The Sergeant, in spite of his statement that escape from São Thomé was impossible, was evidently taking no risks. At dusk of a rather dreadful day, the little troop came in sight of the Bridge of Death, and Carthew's mind became painfully active with plans, fears and speculations as to the manner of his swiftly approaching end.

Would the seven men close suddenly in upon him, tear him from his horse, and fling him over the parapet? Should he put up a fight? Of course he would. It would be entirely useless, naturally, one unarmed man against seven, with carbines, revolvers and ugly machete-like swords. Nor could he put spurs to his horse and make a dash for it, inasmuch as he had no spurs, a stout leather rein buckled the bridoon of his horse's bit to that of a trooper's horse, and on one side of the road rose a cliff, while on the other, a precipice fell away to the plains below. Still, fight he would, in the hope of dying fighting. Far better that than a hideous death by slow engulfment in the quick-sand—or a long-drawn lingering agony if, as de Norhona had hinted, he was so suspended from the Bridge that he would not completely sink.

What should he do?

He decided to wait on circumstance, and fight like a tiger when seized by the escort.

Nearer and nearer to the Bridge.

Now it was but a few hundred yards to where the descending road levelled out toward the horse-corral and the Bridge head. A few more minutes. Past the *hacienda*. . . .

On . . . On . . . On to the Bridge of Death. . . .

On . . .

On to the centre.

He thanked God that his hands were free, as the escort closed in. The Sergeant and two men in front of him. Two men knee to knee with him. Two men close at his back.

Perhaps they would shoot him before throwing him over. The Sergeant seemed a decent fellow and had been quite correct in his attitude and manner. And no one would know if a merciful bullet had been put through his brain. Should he appeal to the Sergeant to do this? No. . . . No appeals. . . . He'd fight.

Suddenly the Sergeant turned his head and shouted an order.

The troop broke into a trot, crossed the Bridge, and a few minutes later reached the rest-house.

That night, Henry Carthew slept well, his mind relieved of the hideous nightmare of the quick-sand that had haunted him.

But what did it mean? Could it be possible that de Norhona's bark was worse than his bite? That he was not as savagely vindictive as he seemed, and that, far from condemning Carthew to a horrible death, he was merely deporting him—setting him free, in fact, having decided that he had punished him sufficiently?

Or had he Doña Guiomar to thank for this release? That seemed more probable. Women were kind and gentle creatures, fundamentally. Or so he had always thought. On the other hand, there was the unpleasant theory about a woman scorned; and it was quite possible that the Regent, failing to understand the utter impossibility of his living in luxury where his friend had crouched in a kennel and cringed under her whip, might consider his refusal scornful and insulting.

But his mind was running ahead too fast. The fact that he had crossed that terrible Bridge was no proof that he was going to be deported to Santa Cruz. De Norhona doubtless had other ways of disposing of an enemy than throwing him alive into a quick-sand.

Next morning, soon after sunrise and an adequate meal, the cavalcade resumed its journey, and in a few hours reached the tiny embowered group of little Government buildings that sweltered beside the shallow creek and constituted the entire port of São Thomé. How terrific the heat seemed after the cool uplands of the great plateau, at the edge of which stood the town and Citadel of São Ildefonso.

Well! Thank God. He had misjudged de Norhona. Or else Doña Guiomar had ordered his deportation.

And there was the ocean. The blue sea that he had scarcely hoped ever to cross again. He could have cried aloud, "*Thalassa! Thalassa!*" but he was not given to crying aloud. And should his eyes, at the turn of the road, behold the Hadji's *dhow* lying at anchor, a few cables from the landing-stage, hope would become certainty, and a ray of positive happiness would lighten the darkness of the grief and horror through which he passed.

Arrived at Santa Cruz, he could feel that his mission and task were successfully accomplished. He had done what Antoinette had asked him to do. From Santa Cruz he could communicate with her, and tragic as his news would be, it would end suspense. A cable telling her that Reginald was dead would be a shock and a blow, but from these she would recover. It is uncertainty, anxiety and suspense that kill.

No. No sign of the *dhow*. But instead, a tiny armed steamer flying the flag of Portugal.

What was this?

In his eagerness, he turned for information to the Sergeant now riding beside him.

"That?" replied the worthy fellow. "That's our *dhow-chaser*. You're going for a trip on her."

"To Santa Cruz?"

"No. To our Leper Island."

XV

It was Ensign Machado's not too painful duty to take delivery of the prisoner and of a letter addressed to him by His Excellency Dom Perez de Norhona in his own handwriting. A *lettre de cachet*, in which the Secretary to the Council charged Ensign Machado, as he valued his life, to see that the prisoner was delivered safely and without delay at the Island of Todos los Santos. The use of the word "safely" in this connection struck the young officer as being a pleasing euphemism, and he wondered why His Excellency had not referred to the leper island by its popular name of the Health Resort.

Well, it's an ill wind and so forth, and though he could find it in his heart to be sorry for this fine fellow, it was indeed a fair wind that should blow a bored young officer far from these hot and malarious plains out on to the health-giving ocean. Unlucky prisoner. Lucky Ensign Machado. And perhaps on the voyage he'd be able to obtain information wherewith later to impress his superiors.

Thus it was that Carthew found himself pestered, bored and annoyed by the undesired company and conversation of a pleasant, olive-skinned, oily-haired youth who appeared anxious to practise his English.

As the young man was friendly and disposed to be sympathetic, Carthew bore with him until his inquisition became wearyingly persistent. If, thought Carthew, he had been condemned, and was on his way to receive his punishment, why should he be troubled by this gad-fly? He had quite enough to bear.

So it came about that when Ensign Machado entered the bare and cell-like cabin allotted to Carthew, and after enquiring naively as to his health and happiness, began another unofficial examination of his prisoner, Carthew replied briefly, sarcastically and without his usual strict regard for truth.

"Now what really brought you to São Thomé?" asked the intelligent and ambitious young officer.

"A *dhow*," growled Carthew.

"Yes, but why did you come?"

"To see you."

This statement gave Ensign Machado pause. He realized that it was evasive, and tried to imitate the tone of the older man.

"Quite so," he agreed. "Now what else did you expect to see?"

"My friend."

"His Excellency Dom Perez de Norhona?" enquired the youth, smiling ironically.

"No. General Sir Reginald Jason."

Hullo! What was this? Mr. Machado literally sat up and took particular notice. He was learning something. Thus do keen young officers gain promotion. Intelligence Department. Staff.

"Yes?" he said smoothly. "And did you see him?"

"I did."

"Met him? Held communication with him?"

"Yes."

"And having come all the way to São Thomé, and having actually found your friend here, what then?"

"I murdered him."

Not so good. The man was endeavouring to deceive and mislead him. But stay. Might not this be a deeply interesting case of vendetta?

The alleged friend had wronged him, had somehow heard of São Thomé as the remotest and most secret hiding-place in the world, and had fled thither; this Kardieu, his enemy, had tracked him down, even to São Thomé, and had taken his revenge at last. Poisoned him, according to citadel gossip.

Rather nice.

But a disturbing thought that these two men should both have found their way to the hidden Island of the Blest.

"A woman in the case, of course," murmured Ensign

Machado.

"Of course," agreed Carthew gravely, eyeing his persistent and irritating tormentor in a manner that the latter did not wholly like.

"Ah! *Cherchez la femme!*" breathed the wise young man, exhibiting not only his knowledge of life but of three words of the French language.

Henry Carthew did nothing to break the ensuing period of silence, during which the amateur intelligence officer pondered the situation and the possibility of yet further enlightening, surprising and pleasing his superiors.

"It did, of course, come to my knowledge—in the course of my official investigations—that you also came to São Thomé to spy out the land, especially the mineral-bearing parts of the land."

"Did it really? It never came to mine," murmured Carthew as he lay back wearily upon his wooden bunk.

"Strange," sneered the youth. "It was also reported to me that you hoped to obtain an incalculably valuable concession."

"No one reported it to me," whispered Carthew, closing his eyes.

"And I'll tell you for *what*," said Ensign Machado sharply.

"Do," sighed Carthew.

"Radium."

"What's that?" asked Carthew, smothering a yawn.

Ah! Contumacious. And silently the Lieutenant's lips moved as, in imagination, he wrote that part of his report. "*On being suddenly accused of being a concession-hunting radium-seeker, the prisoner showed signs of guilty confusion, even pretending not to know what radium is. . . .*"

§2

Just before dawn, Carthew was awakened from uneasy, nightmare-broken slumber, by the stopping of the noisy engines of the little wood-burning steamer. A few minutes later, a Corporal and a file of soldiers entered his cabin cell and bade him prepare at once to leave the ship.

Putting on what clothes he had removed, Carthew, escorted by the soldiers, went up on deck.

Saluting his prisoner, and speaking with kindly politeness, Machado expressed his regret that duty compelled him to disturb the Senhor so early. That he was about to abandon him for life on a tiny islet inhabited solely by lepers, did not appear an occasion for apology.

As the light increased, Carthew saw that they lay off the low sandy shore of an island as different from São Thomé as it was possible to be. A flat, lonely, gull-haunted pin-point on the face of the waters, that was probably unrecorded on any map and unknown to any man save the São Théan authorities and the wretched lepers whose dreadful home and grave-yard it was.

He was surprised to find how calm he was, how far from anything like terror. He decided that this state of quiet resignation to an appalling fate had little to do with courage, resolution or hope. Terror, horror, despair and madness would doubtless come later. At present he was stunned, from hope and fear set free. Too much had happened in too little time, and for the present he had ceased to feel.

"It is my painful duty, Senhor, to request you to descend into the boat. You will be rowed ashore," said Machado.

"Sharks abound in these waters," he added pensively.

Having thanked the Ensign for the courtesy and good treatment he had received, Carthew descended the short ladder and seated himself in the stern-sheets of the boat which was manned by four sailors and the boatswain. The Corporal and file of soldiers followed him, and the boat pushed off. A few minutes later, it grounded on the sandy beach, and the Corporal signed to him to get out.

"*Addios, Senhor,*" he smiled. "You are now free."

"You may be free yourself, some day perhaps," replied Carthew. "*Addios.*"

Hastily the man crossed himself and, with clenched fist and two extended fingers, made the sign which is well-known to be efficacious against the threat of evil.

Having waded ashore, Carthew seated himself on the sand and watched the boat as it was shoved off and rowed back to the ship. A few minutes later, the vessel raised anchor and began to move away. As she gathered speed, Carthew saw a puff of white steam beside her stumpy funnel, and a second or two later heard the sound of her siren.

How decent of Machado, or perhaps the Captain! They were saluting him. Rising to his feet he bowed.

"*Moriturus te saluto!*" he said, and smiling grimly, turned and saw someone approaching him—a strange weird figure of a man who had neither fingers nor toes nor anything that could honestly be called a face.

Ashamed, but impelled by uncontrollable horror, Carthew turned and hurried away.

But the leper, in spite of his deformity, could travel across the sand-dunes as fast as Carthew, long practice having perfected his curious technique.

On and on, across patches of soft white sand, fine as dust, through thin wind-blown bents, up and down the little hills and dales of the dunes, pursued by the living Horror, that squeaked and gibbered as it followed. . . .

This was absurd. Cowardly. He was behaving like a frightened child. This was but one of his companions. This place was his new home, his long home. Here, with such people as this, he would live—until he died.

Halting, he turned about and faced the creature, who poured forth a torrent of whistling, gasping speech.

What was he trying to say?

Something about priests? Something about lepers?

"What do you say?" said Carthew sharply, scarcely conquering his repugnance. "Speak slowly."

Medieval Portuguese interlarded with Arabic and a Kanaka dialect, spoken by a toothless and almost mouthless man, is not easy to follow. The leper tried again, articulating slowly and deliberately.

"Who are you?" he asked.

"I am a leper," replied Carthew.

"I see no signs."

"No, I'm a moral leper."

"What kind is that?"

"The worst kind."

"Then you had better come to the Holy Fathers."

"Right. Will you show me the way?"

As he strode along with the leper shambling beside him, Carthew questioned the man, and understood about half of what he said. He gathered that there was a small band of monastic Fathers who devoted their lives to endeavouring to ameliorate the lot of the living dead of this island grave-yard, doubtless strengthening and saving their souls if they could do but little for their bodies.

If Carthew rightly understood his informant, the Fathers were a tiny community no member of which was ever allowed to leave the Island. When a São Thoméan priest elected to go to Leper Island, he went for life. When he died, he was buried in the grave-yard with the lepers, and there was a vacancy, quickly filled, for another obscure and nameless hero of the highest and noblest class.

"Do any of the priests themselves ever become lepers?" Carthew enquired.

"Yes," replied the man. "Nearly all do, as they grow old, and then they leave the Priests' House and live as lepers in the leper village."

Carthew further understood that the Fathers taught the lepers to work, that they might not starve or go naked. They tilled the soil, cultivated fruit and reared goats. . . .

Had the Senhor's family refused to come with him? piped the leper.

The Senhor had no family.

Ah, there the leper had the advantage of him. He had a wife and daughter, and they had refused to be parted from him when he had been caught and deported.

"Caught?"

Yes. When it was certain that he had contracted leprosy, he had gone and lived in the jungle. His wife had looked after the estate as well as she could, with the help of the bailiff, a faithful fellow who asked no questions and kept his own counsel. But they had not let even him know of his master's hiding-place. It had been his daughter who had brought him food and other necessities. It had been a very dreadful time for his wife and daughter. A time of anxiety, fear and grief. And at first he had been desperate at finding himself a leper. However, one gets used to things.

Carthew regarded the man who had got used to things, and wondered how long he himself would take to follow his example.

"But then misfortune befell us," he continued quaintly. "The Leper Inspector, a big and very important official, visited my property and enquired about me. He remembered that he had not seen me on his last tour. My wife said that I had gone to São Ildefonso on business. He asked how long I had been away, and though he tried to bully and trap her, and made further enquiries he never discovered the truth. But he fell in love with Maria who was a very beautiful girl. Still is. . . . He is a bad man and evil-looking, and has a wife and family. Maria feared and hated him. He made a suggestion to her, and when she said she would sooner die and very much sooner cause him to die, what do you think he did? Denounced *her* as a leper, saying he would get her sent to Leper Island, if she did not give way. He did it too.

"She said she'd much sooner go to Leper Island than to his bed, so he said very well she should, and reported to the Ministry of Health that Maria Garcia, daughter of José and Caterina Garcia of the village of Goncalo, was a leper, and obtained the usual form of expulsion to be enforced by the Police. Of course, I at once came out of hiding, denounced myself and accompanied her. My wife came too, as she refused to be parted from us.

"That's how I came to be caught. Funny, wasn't it?"

"Very funny," agreed Carthew.

"That's the Priests' House," said the man as they topped another dune, and pointed to where a large hut, long and low, stood in the middle of well-tended gardens, and on the edge of a wide area of cultivated land.

XVI

Carthew's arrival was obviously a cause for perturbation among the good Fathers. Evidently this man, simply flung ashore as the lepers were, must be some kind of a criminal, and an enemy and a danger to the State. As a public enemy he must be treated, since such he was; on the other hand, he was a Christian, a man of culture and education, and a person of good-will. And moreover, he was a European of pure blood, and apparently what he professed to be, an Englishman.

Father Sebastien, who during his time in Europe had travelled widely and seen men and cities, said roundly that he was a *fidalgo caballero*, a gentleman. What else was a man who talked as he did, who behaved as he did, who knew English, French, Italian, Spanish and Portuguese—not to mention Arabic—as was quickly discovered by the five Fathers who, among them, professed these languages and two or three more.

Gentle and kindly questioning as to the cause of his summary and terrible punishment elicited only the statement that, having visited São Thomé in search of a friend, he had had the misfortune grievously to offend not only His Excellency Dom Perez de Norhona, but Her Highness, the Regent herself.

At this, the good Fathers left it. And on enquiry as to what Carthew wished to do, were delighted to learn that he wished to work in any way that might be helpful to them. He, of course, had to earn his living, and if he could do it under the Fathers' direction, he would be only too pleased.

Wise Father Simão, who, preparatory to devoting his life to the lepers, had been allowed a year in Lisbon where he had learned English, decided to appoint him fisherman, to supply the House and such of the lepers as could not work, with food.

§2

One day, fishing in deep water from a flat rock, Henry Carthew suddenly realized that he was accepting life on Leper Island exactly as one accepts life in a dream, its incredibilities, incongruities and stark horrors.

The horrors were here provided by the lepers themselves, all too real and concrete spectres of the waking nightmare.

For the attitude of São Thomé to Leper Island was, as in most other matters, medieval, in other words, barbarous. The leper was something to thrust from sight, to segregate, and to leave to perish miserably and horribly—and the sooner the better.

Thus it was that the Fathers, who devoted their lives to these grievously afflicted people, could devote little else, there being no official or other regular supplies from São Thomé, of medicines, surgical appliances, food, or anything whatsoever, wherewith to make and maintain the most elementary form of hospital. Occasionally the Government *dhow*-chaser, which was also the leper boat, dumped a case of gifts from the monkish community at São Thomé, some charitable private person, or relative of one of the lepers. But the boat came but seldom, and with complete irregularity, and only for the bringing of a new victim of disease or injustice, and even among the religious, the charitable and the relatives, the opinion prevailed that lepers, like past sins, were best forgotten. In fact, a leper was a living sin, a warning against sin, and a walking example of punishment through the wrath of God.

"Have any of them ever escaped?" Carthew enquired one day of gentle and innocent Father Simão.

"Escape?" had been the reply. "It would be a long swim back to São Thomé, my son. And no leper or . . . other person . . . would find a welcome when he arrived. . . . Boat? No. We monks are only allowed to come here on the clear understanding that we shall never build a boat or allow one to be made. Not so much as a raft. If we helped or willingly allowed anyone to leave the Island, we should be expelled, and the lepers would never have any friends or helpers again."

"And no one, leper or other, has *ever* escaped?"

"Never. It is utterly impossible."

"Has no foreign ship ever called here and sent a boat ashore—for water or fruit or something?"

"One did—some years ago. The men saw some of the lepers and rowed away even more quickly than they rowed ashore."

Carthew's heart sank, and he realized how much he had built on that foolish hope.

To live and to die on Leper Island!

To die a leper . . .

"And do any of the lepers ever recover?"

"No. How should they?"

"Has any non-leper escaped contagion?"

"Only one."

That was something anyhow! Perhaps Henry Carthew would be the second.

"He committed suicide, poor fellow," continued Father Simão, "thinking that he had become a leper. But he was mistaken. Pure imagination. . . . It does prey on one's mind if one is not watchful."

Carthew admitted that it did. Then studying the Father's gentle, kindly and happy face—yes, actually serene and happy—he realized, with a sense of shame, that he had been thinking only of himself. This truly good man whose religion was one of works as well as faith, was in as great, or even greater danger than himself, and nearer to his horrible and inevitable end.

With what immeasurable calm courage had these men deliberately made their rendezvous with Death, in one of his most awful manifestations.

He must do more for them than he had. Work harder. Pull more than his own weight in this Charon's boat.

Fishing! Sitting on a flat rock in the sun!

Impatiently he rose to his feet. Who was this coming across the dunes? Garcia's daughter. Maria Garcia.

Aye. And there was another quarter in which a man could learn something about courage, unselfishness and practical piety.

This slip of a girl had shown a sustained and unflinching bravery of a higher kind than that which is rewarded with acclaim and decoration. If a middle-aged soldier like himself shuddered at the sights he saw, and trembled at the thought that his own end must be such as that of those around him, what must be the feelings and fears of this girl, young, undeniably beautiful, and hitherto delicately nurtured in a home of gracious comfort?

She could laugh. Sometimes even, she could sing. To-day, he noticed, she had put a scarlet flower in her hair above each ear.

And to Henry Carthew that was one of the most pathetic things he had ever seen.

On Leper Island. Tending people whom even to approach was an act of courage. Waiting for—no, he could not bear to think of it. . . .

And in such circumstances, she could put a flower in her hair, and come to greet him with a smile.

§3

The days and weeks and months drifted slowly by. Carthew made a garden about the hut he had built with the help of the monks; worked as a field-labourer, a common carrier of burdens for the common good, a carpenter, cook, nurse, secretary, fuel-cutter and gatherer, washerman and general factotum to the Fathers—occupation his salvation.

In spite of restricted diet and the absence of almost everything that makes for mental and physical comfort and health, he kept well and, to his amazement, far from despair or chronic misery. He was not happy but he had happy hours—talking with Maria or the highly-educated priests, with some of whom conversation was a pleasure and a privilege.

Trying to copy them, however ineffectually, he sought the society of the lepers, came to know them all, to like many of them, and to find the majority admirable beyond words, for their courage and uncomplaining fortitude. . . . Political "criminals" who watched daily, hourly almost, for the dreaded spot which told them that their fate was sealed and that the death, which would take years to arrive, was now approaching. . . . Lepers who watched for this sign in wife and children who had accompanied them from their homes. . . . Women who watched and waited thus for the ineluctable signal to be shown by husband, son or daughter.

And His Excellency Dom Perez de Norhona, the Great Physician, sat over there in São Thomé and studied psychotherapy, hypnotism, brain surgery and the perfecting of experiments in Permanent Hypnosis!

Why could he not study the cause and cure of leprosy, and stamp it out in São Thomé, instead of stamping the lepers out, and acquiescing in the horrors of this grave-yard of the living?

Oh, to have him here! To make him work among the lepers as the monks did, and to tell him he should go when the last leper was cured!

What was it that Carthew had once read about the discovery of some vegetable oil that was thought likely to cure leprosy if used in time?

Since Norhona could get drugs and apparatus, surgical instruments and books from the best sources, could he not also get this oil? If name and fame were what he wanted, surely here was a field wherein such could be found. The Man who conquered Leprosy! Would not that be a finer title than The Man who achieved Permanent Hypnosis—at the cost of the destruction of human minds, bodies and souls? And Henry Carthew dreamed foolishly of kidnapping de Norhona, with the Hadji's help, and bringing him to Leper Island to work out his own salvation by fasting, prayer and study, until he could fight a successful battle against the disease, cure the lepers, and earn remission of his punishment. . . .

Idle day-dreams.

And, meanwhile, the beautiful and wholly admirable Maria was daily risking infection—and worse than risking it. She was inevitably and certainly being infected; and that lovely face and form would assuredly be, one day, as repulsive as those of any leper here.

XVII

So Henry Carthew worked and dreamed, fought with Beasts of Despair, Fear, Horror and Hatred; endured and endeavoured to imitate the Fathers, not only in their work and conduct, but in their serenity and peace of mind. At times his strength failed, horror overcame him as he thought of his inevitable end, and he remembered the man who was not a leper, and who "escaped." How had he done it? An easy way would be to swim out to sea. Swim until one could swim no longer and then peacefully and thankfully drown.

Sharks. . . .

Cowardice would forbid that sudden death.

Did any of the Fathers ever think of suicide? Did the girl Maria? No. Nor would Henry Carthew.

But there were moments. There were dreams.

And one night, lying on the warm sand outside the crude hutch that was his home, he dreamed of the Hadji Abdulla of whom he so often thought. He dreamed that the Hadji was calling to him; had seized his shoulder and was shaking him, and that suddenly he flashed a bright light into his face; that he was saying, with amazing reality,

"Come on, Carthew. Quick. . . ."

Rising to his feet, he followed the Hadji as he turned and strode swiftly toward the water.

But was this the Hadji Abdulla? He was different. But that had been his voice, most undoubtedly. Of course he was different. He was naked except for a loin-cloth, and bare-headed instead of wearing a turban.

Why? Had he swum ashore? No. There was the *toni* which was used as a dinghy for the *dhow*, drawn up at the edge of the water.

No. It must be because he did not wish to be recognized, if seen. That was it.

This was rescue!

The Hadji had heard of his fate, had sailed for Leper Island, had arrived under cover of darkness, had come ashore alone in the *toni*, and had sought until he found him. He would naturally expect to find a new hut somewhere near those of the Fathers. Dysart would not want to be seen and recognized, for if the news of what he had done ever reached His Excellency Dom Perez de Norhona, São Thomé would forthwith become a most unwholesome place for the Hadji Abdulla.

Yes, he was running a big risk. That of losing his valuable São Thomé business, and of finding, one day, that he was trapped in the Citadel to which smiling de Norhona had welcomed him once again.

What a wonderful fellow Brodie Dysart was. The perfect Hadji. The complete *dhow*-master. As genuine an Arab sailor as any *nakhuda* between Baghdad and Singapore, between Karachi and Cape Town. What a life he had led! And here he was, doing what. . . .

Suddenly a thought sharply struck Carthew's bemused and wandering mind. He couldn't go off like this—without a word to the Fathers. It seemed so ungrateful, so discourteous. It seemed like deserting comrades in distress.

And—*Maria!*

But he was dreaming of course.

His bare foot struck against a piece of stone and he swore mildly as he always did when he stubbed a toe.

No, he was not asleep and dreaming. . . . *Maria*. . . . He couldn't possibly . . .

"Dysart!" he called.

"Shut up!" was the peremptory reply. "We don't want to be seen off by a large crowd with a brass band. Come along, man."

"I must go back."

Poor fellow gone dotty already? wondered Brodie Dysart.

"You're going back. To England. Come *on*."

"Just a minute, Dysart," pleaded Carthew. "I really won't delay you for more than a few minutes. I can't go like this. Let me bring a friend."

"What? A leper? No, I can't do that. I've no . . ."

"She's not a leper," interrupted Carthew.

"Oh! Like that, is it? I see. H'm. I'll take your word, Carthew. And I'll give you ten minutes. I'll wait here, and if you're not back in that time, I *must* push off."

"Thank you, Dysart," said Carthew simply. As he turned and hurried away, Brodie Dysart stood in frowning thought.

Poor old chap!

Quite probably a leper himself by now, and had fallen in love with a leper girl. Well, the disease couldn't be sufficiently far advanced to be recognizable, or Carthew would not have given his word.

By the time that Dysart estimated a quarter of an hour had passed, Carthew came hurrying down to the water.

"Won't come," he said, and doubtless the queerness of his voice was due to the fact that he had been hurrying at top speed across loose sand.

"Won't come?"

"No. . . . Parents. . . ."

"Sticking to them, eh?"

"Yes."

"Are they bad?"

"Father three parts dead. Mother in early stages."

Dysart eyed Carthew's face, ghastly in the moonlight.

"Look here, Carthew," he said. "Feel bad about it?"

"I'd as soon stay as go, if . . ."

"Look then. I'll stretch a point. If she'll come away with the mother, I'll take them both, and for the love of Allah, hurry."

With a word of thanks, Carthew ran back toward the tiny settlement behind the little dune cliff.

He returned alone.

As Dysart looked up, Carthew shook his head.

"Come on, then."

Dysart pushed the *toni* well into the water, waded after it, and balancing carefully, got into it and took up the paddle.

Carthew followed him.

§2

On the long voyage from Leper Island to Santa Cruz, the seeds of a warm and strong friendship between Henry Carthew and Brodie Dysart, sown long before, put forth shoots, took root and grew. Instinctively they had liked each other from the first, and now Carthew's deep if mute gratitude, and Dysart's admiration of this simple, brave and honourable man quickly turned liking into a sentiment much stronger.

Seated side by side on the high poop of the big *dhow*, they talked for most of the day and much of the night, Dysart giving Carthew news of São Thomé, Santa Cruz, of mutual acquaintances, and of the great world from which Carthew had for so long been cut off.

"How did you come to know that I was on Leper Island?" asked Carthew one evening, as he watched the rising of the tropic moon.

"From the loquacious young gentleman who took you there," replied Dysart.

"Oh, yes. Of course. What's his name? Machado."

"That's the lad. Small head, full of big ambitions—and nothing else. I don't know whether they employ him to give away State secrets that they want given away. If so, they've got the right man there. I suspect him of having spotted you as a European, and given us away intentionally or unintentionally. But how the devil he found out, I can't imagine. How should he know that you were a European disguised as an Arab, when hundreds of cleverer men than he never dreamt of such a thing?

"Yes," continued Dysart, "he's one of the leakiest vessels that ever slopped all over everything, or else he's a very clever man—which I doubt."

"He didn't strike me as being a marvel of intelligence," agreed Carthew, "but I liked him. He treated me very decently. He mayn't be too bright, but he's a gentleman."

"Oh, quite," smiled Dysart. "I am sure that the worthy

Palsover thought so. He talked with him a lot, I knew. . . .
Nasty piece of work, Mr. Palsover. I've seen as much as I
want of him. Took him back to São Thomé twice. He didn't
go ashore, but I got very tired of him on the *dhow*. Shan't
take him again, whatever fare he offers to pay.

"By Allah!" he interrupted himself, "could *he* have
double-crossed us that time, and given you away?"

"Good Lord, no," laughed Carthew. "Mr. Palsover never
yet did anything against his own interest. He had absolutely
fantastic hopes of making a fortune in São Thomé. Radium,
I believe. Got hold of some wild story of the place being stiff
with it. I never paid much attention. All I wanted was to find
Jason. Besides, if he had told Machado that I was a European and that you were treasonably concealing the fact
from the Government, wouldn't Palsover have been afraid
of being arrested himself? If he talked to Machado, he must
have done so in English. Machado would have arrested him
at once, surely. . . . Besides—the motive. Why on earth
should he do a damn silly thing like that?"

"It's a mystery," mused Dysart. "Hallo, though. Here's a
point. Whether Palsover talked to Machado in English or
not, Machado talked to him in English all right, which must
have told even the brainy Machado that Palsover understood it."

"How d'you know?" asked Carthew.

"Why, the excellent Palsover came to me with a cock-
and-bull story that Machado had told him. Palsover said he
now knew all about the fate of his great hero, General
Jason. According to Machado, Jason had been imprisoned
in the Citadel, then another British officer, Colonel Carthew,
had gone there to do a deal with the Government, and,
finding that the General had got there first and was going to
get the concession, he just up and killed him. Palsover was
grinning like a dog. I daresay he did the same when
Machado told him the yarn, for obviously Machado 'proved'
the truth of what he had been saying, by asking Palsover
why else he supposed that the disguised Colonel Carthew
had been sentenced to a lingering death on Leper Island.
Which he had been, for had not he, the important Machado,

been given charge of the prisoner?"

Silence fell between the two men as Dysart stared toward the horizon and Henry Carthew sat with his hand across his eyes.

"Wonder whether Palsover invented the whole yarn for some excellent reason of his own?" said Dysart suddenly. "I certainly took Jason to São Thomé, and I've never heard a word of him since.

"What a farrago of nonsense," he laughed. "Colonel Carthew found General Jason doing a deal and so did him in. Oh, yes," he added, "and there was a lovely lady in it too."

"Carthew," he said, and laid a large strong hand on Carthew's knee, "you and Jason were also rivals for the hand of Doña Guiomar. So what did you do but murder him! All's fair in love and war, Carthew, but you shouldn't have poisoned him. For that's what you did do, according to either Palsover or Machado. One of those two lads has got a mind! . . . My God, what a yarn!"

Carthew raised his head.

"It's true," he said. "I did find Jason. I did poison him."

Dysart met the gaze of Carthew's tragic eyes, and made no reply.

§3

When the *dhow* reached Santa Cruz, and the two went to the *Casa Real*, they found that Mr. Palsover had departed. According to his unsorrowing partner, he had taken ship for Belamu and England, promising to return when he had "done a bit o' business."

A day or two later, the *dhow* sailed again, and once more Carthew and Dysart sat and talked the long drowsy hours away. To Henry Carthew, it had seemed impossible for him to let the *dhow* go without him while he remained behind in that appalling place to await, perhaps for months, a visit of the Anglo-Portuguese coasting steamer. As Dysart was going, in any case, to Belamu, where Carthew could get a ship for England, the latter felt that his need for haste was not so urgent that he must miss this opportunity of exchanging lonely misery in Santa Cruz for the peace of the *dhow* and the comfort of Dysart's society.

On the first night out from Santa Cruz, as the beautiful boat slipped ghost-like through the sparkling phosphorescent water, Henry Carthew unburdened his soul of its load of grief and suffering, told Dysart the whole story of Jason's dreadful fate, and felt the better for the other man's deep silent sympathy.

"I should rather enjoy killing de Norhona," said Dysart. "Try an experiment of my own, on him."

"I suppose he thought he was justified," said Carthew. "If he really thought Jason was a German, a public danger to the peace and safety of the State of São Thomé. And I suppose he'd think almost any man who was a suitable subject for his experiment, ought to be proud of the honour of contributing to the March of Science. . . . What's a life to a fanatical enthusiast like de Norhona?

"And Jason never suffered," he added. And again as though to convince himself, to comfort himself and assuage an almost unbearable pain,

"No. No. He never suffered at all. He never knew. . . ."

On the second night, as they talked, Carthew suddenly remembered a matter that had occurred to him many times on Leper Island, as he sat and pondered the chain of events that had followed his encountering Palsover in Santa Cruz.

"That marvellous pearl," he said. "Did they return It to you when you left São Thomé—or when you went back?"

"No," replied Dysart. "I never saw it again. Never shall, I imagine."

"Good Lord! And you were never paid for it?" exclaimed Carthew.

"Not a farthing."

"I *say*, Dysart. . . . Doesn't that mean a terrible financial blow. . . . I am sorry—and I feel that I . . ."

"I shall recover," smiled Dysart. "Blow not fatal."

"But, Dysart! The value of that pearl must have been . . ."

"No. Not as much as all that, Carthew. It wasn't genuine, you know!"

Carthew stared in amazement.

"Oh, no. When I've got something really good to sell, I don't let it go out of my hands until I've got the money. Once pearls go behind the purdah, for example, they are in no small danger of remaining there, and their substitutes coming forth—with polite regrets that the price is too high, or the pearl is not good enough. I've got some quite nice substitutes of substitutes," he smiled.

"Aren't you ever caught out?"

"No. And if I were, I've only to explain that I never do the preliminary dealing with the genuine article, and that these pretty models are samples. One wouldn't attempt to play that fool game with experts, of course. But experts don't steal.

"From one another, I mean," he added.

"Aren't you sometimes tempted to sell a dud—to a person who has tried to swindle you, I mean?"

"Sorely," laughed Dysart, "and I don't deny that I once sold a gentleman his very own substitutes at quite a good price—the price at which he himself had valued them as pearls, in point of fact. But I don't go about planting culture stuff on my honest clients, or on anyone who treats me fairly, when they want to buy a genuine pearl."

"No, I didn't suppose you did," replied Carthew.

"By the way," he asked, "what exactly would you do if Doña Guiomar or de Norhona offered to pay the price you asked for the big pearl?"

"Take it and change the pearl. But I don't anticipate that that will happen for some time. When de Norhona's suspicions are aroused, it's a devil of a job to allay them, and he definitely was suspicious that I knew more about you than I pretended. The tale was a bit thin, you know, and it was lucky for me that even de Norhona gets frightfully insular and provincial, not to say gullible. Out of touch with realities, and no wonder. As I daresay you noticed, he combines amazing scientific knowledge, wide and deep learning, and superhuman cleverness with what one might call curious patches of unexpected ignorance. . . . Wonder what kind of places he thinks Bahrein and Basra are, for example. Anyway, for all his science he does not know a pearl from a good fake."

"Another thing that occurs to me, Dysart," said Carthew, breaking a long meditative silence. "How long will it be before my escape from Leper Island is known. And won't you come under suspicion again?"

"How long would it be before your escape from a churchyard would become known, if I came and snatched your body and left no traces?"

"Never, I suppose," admitted Carthew.

"Same with that damned living grave-yard. Unless I or the *dhow* were seen and recognized by someone on the Island, why should I be suspected by the Fathers, or anyone on Leper Island? And there's practically no communication between there and São Thomé. Next time the Government boat goes to the Island, it'll be to dump some poor devil at the water's edge, as they dumped you, and clear off again at once. At the most, they might put one or two boxes of food, or medical comforts on the beach, and it's an understood thing that neither monk nor leper goes anywhere near the sailors while they do that."

"Suppose there were a letter for the monks from their Father Superior?"

"Oh, they just chuck it down and put a stone on it, or something."

"And if the monks wanted to write to him?"

"They'd have to want," was the answer. "Absolutely nothing is allowed to go from Leper Island to São Thomé."

"And will you ever go back to São Thomé?"

"Oh, yes. Rather. Most interesting place in the world. And my most lucrative place of call. I haven't missed a trip, you know, since someone gave you away and de Norhona blew up. I have to pretend to be very worried about the pearl, of course."

"Have you got the one of which he has the model?"

"No. Wish I had. But there's a poor ragged old millionaire up the butt end of the Persian Gulf who has. If de

Norhona thinks my services are worth retaining, he'll agree to the Regent buying the pearl."

Another silence.

"What made you take Palsover back again?"

"Greed. . . . Amusement. . . . The human comedy. . . . And I'm not sure that there isn't a small touch of a faint malicious hope of seeing something of the human tragedy if that rascally humbug screws up his courage to go ashore and get taken up to the Capital—so that he can lay an attractive business proposition before the dazzled eyes of de Norhona and the Council of State. Give them a chance to put São Thomé on the map, and boost home industries.

"Wonder where he is now," he added.

"Probably 'interesting' the financial magnates of the City of London," grinned Carthew.

In point of fact Mr. Palsover was at that moment seeking a good home for four hundred pounds, honourably forwarded to him by Lady Jason on receipt of Carthew's cablegram to the effect that he had found General Jason, and that he had since died.

XVIII

At Belamu, Carthew said farewell to Brodie Dysart and exchanged the grateful peace, if narrow comfort, of the *dhow* for the bustle and luxurious amenities of the liner *Somali*, sister ship of that which had brought him thither on a day which seemed like one of a former life, decades ago.

He was amazed at the extreme reluctance with which he left the *dhow*, and concluded that it was the parting with Brodie Dysart that was the real cause of his depression.

Rarely in his life had he met a man whom he had liked so much in so short a time, admired so greatly or so completely trusted. In fact, next to Reginald Jason, this Sinclair Noel Brodie Dysart, ex-sailor, ex-soldier, ex-legionnaire, ex-member of a desert tribe, who had made the pilgrimage to Mecca and had travelled far and wide, seeing and doing things most rarely seen and done by white men—appealed to him more as a friend, than any other man whom he had ever met.

As, leaning on the rail, he looked down from the ship's deck at the *dhow* moored at a few cables' distance, he felt a sense of loss and loneliness that surprised him. It reminded him of that day at Sitabad when he had said farewell to Reginald and Antoinette, and their train had steamed out of the station, leaving him feeling like a small boy abandoned by a beloved Mother to the lonely terrors of the first day at school.

Yes. It was surprising. Amazing.

Positively he'd miss this chap Dysart as he had never missed any man since Reginald left the Regiment.

XIX

Carthew's voyage from Belamu to England was not the happiest he had ever made.

On the contrary, it was probably the most miserable journey of his life. He thought constantly of the past horror and the future fear, the fear of his approaching interview with Antoinette. He could not and would not tell her the terrible and incredible truth, and he would tell her no lies. She would question him closely—she was that sort of woman—and before long she would have him tied in knots. At times, especially at about four o'clock in the mornings, as he lay awake thinking of Reginald, of the girl Maria, of the lepers, of the super-human men who voluntarily buried themselves alive with them, of Brodie Dysart, his courage would fail and he would decide to write to Antoinette.

Yes. He would go to his Club, sit himself down in the library, with reams of paper, and write a full and true account of it all, from the day he landed at Santa Cruz to the day on which he returned there. Then his mind would recoil from his own cowardice. How could he, for one moment, contemplate telling poor Antoinette the appalling truth about the man whom she adored, the man whom she had loved almost from childhood and with whom she had lived so many years. Reginald, her noble, dignified, stately husband, the finest figure of a man in the British Army, crawling about on all fours in a suit of shaggy skins, and behaving like the animal he thought himself to be.

No. That would be the ultimate cowardice. He must go straight to her, and just say that Reginald had died. . . .

And added to the terrors of the past and future was that of the present. The ever-present dread that he was, even now, himself—a leper.

Unclean! . . . Unclean! . . .

Had not Father Simão told him that not one of the monks had ever escaped, and that of the non-lepers who were sent to the Island, only one had ever done so, and that by committing suicide. Why should he not rise from his berth at once, make his way to the stern, dive overboard, and end his troubles in a few minutes?

Why?

An act of cowardice.

He had a duty to perform. He had promised Antoinette that he would do his utmost, and surely that included returning and telling her everything. . . . Nearly everything. Certainly he must *himself* give her his personal assurance that, of his own actual, indisputable, certain knowledge, Reginald was dead. He could assure her, on his word of honour, that he was dead, and buried in consecrated ground. Not only that, but in the precincts of a Cathedral.

Being a woman, that would in some curious way, comfort her.

Of course he must go home and face his painful duty. What was happening to him, that he should ever dream of shirking it? Besides, wasn't he longing to see her? What was there on earth that he desired more than to see Antoinette, whom he had always loved so deeply?

Now that poor Reginald was gone, she was the greatest friend he had. Almost the only friend. Of course he must go straight to her, directly he landed, without wasting an hour.

But it would be a dreadful and a difficult interview.

§2

It was.

Antoinette seemed changed.

She had always been a cool woman, inclined to irony and sarcasm, a trifle hard at times, and prone to say slightly bitter things, but he had never known her to be like this.

Even when she had first sent for him, told him all she could about Reginald, and begged him to go in search of the poor chap, she had not been like this. Distraught. . . . Off her balance. . . . And well . . . queer.

It was almost as though it was *his* fault that Reginald had wandered off. Got into trouble. Disappeared and never returned. Why did she take this line of knowing more than he told her? And why did she seem to take everything that he told her, as though with a grain of salt?

Could there have been some garbled account of the affair in the papers? Of course not.

Could the Hadji have written to . . . ? Of course not. What a hopelessly idiotic idea.

Good Lord! Could that fellow Palsover have . . . ? Even more utterly idiotic.

What he had been through must have affected his never too brilliant brain. Why should Palsover write to Lady Jason, or come here and . . . ? Lunatic moonshine. For, in the first place, Palsover knew nothing about what had really happened to Reginald. Did anybody in the world, except de Norhona, Dysart and himself know the truth about the death of General Jason? Of course not.

Why, de Norhona himself didn't. What he knew, or thought he knew, was that the vile Colonel Kardieu had wrecked his marvellous experiment by killing a hypnotized adventurer who had come to the Island, guaranteed by Pereira himself to be a German named Fritz Schultz. De Norhona was not the man to take a stranger's verbal assurance against his own agent's written word. True, he had given poor Reginald the 'benefit of the doubt' as he had said, and a Christian burial, but that in itself showed there was a doubt.

Anyhow, Palsover . . . No. Utterly impossible. . . . And yet . . . And yet . . . Who else could have betrayed them at São Thomé?

Who but Palsover could have told Antoinette anything at all? Palsover, according to his own story, had been associated with Reginald in the beginning, and up to the time the Hadji took him up to the Capital.

If it *were* Palsover . . .

"What did you say?" asked Lady Jason sharply.

Carthew gave a guilty start. He must have been thinking aloud.

"Er—Palsover . . ."

"What?"

"Excuse me, Antoinette. I'm even more stupid than usual to-day. Before we go any further, would you mind telling me whether you've had any sort or kind of communication from a man named Palsover."

"No. Never heard the name in my life," she answered somewhat curtly.

"Why?" she asked.

"Well—er—it's a bit difficult to—what I mean is . . ." faltered Carthew. "Why—look here, Antoinette, I wouldn't dream . . . You seem to . . . I mean, I wouldn't dream of suggesting that you doubt my word, but we do seem to be at cross purposes. It's as though you had earlier and—er—better, wider, information . . . and . . . When I got to Santa Cruz I found a man there, a fellow of the name of Palsover, who used to be in the Regiment, years ago. Recognized each other at once, and when I asked him what on earth he was doing there in Santa Cruz, he said that Reginald had brought him with him. And he was just sitting there waiting for him to return."

"Are you sure his name wasn't Jones?" Lady Jason asked coldly. "David Jones."

"Quite sure," replied Carthew quietly. "The man whom I saw at Santa Cruz, and who said he had come out from England with Reginald, was named Palsover."

"What sort of a man? To look at, I mean. Could you describe him?"

Carthew described Mr. Palsover in a manner that would have given that gentleman no satisfaction. It is doubtful whether he would have recognized the description as a picture that resembled him in the least. The last touches would have seemed ridiculous.

"And a plausible, lying, swindling rascal he is," concluded Carthew.

Lady Jason thought of her five hundred pounds, and seethed with rage. Normally a calm, even-tempered woman, when really angered she was apt to lose her admirable poise and self-control. She must hit out. Strike back. Punish someone.

"A man somewhat of that description, but of the name of Jones, did come to see me," she admitted.

"*Ah-h-h-h!* Now we're getting at it," said Carthew, and laughed a little drearily, perhaps a little unkindly.

"And what did he tell you?" he asked, a contemptuous note creeping into his voice.

Lady Jason rose to her feet—the better, perhaps, to strike.

"Among other things, Henry, about a woman and a concession, he told me *that you killed Reginald!*"

And as one who, with a terrific effort, throws off a crushing burden, Henry Carthew, too, stood up.

"I did," he said.

There it was. It was out. It was off his mind.

Since Palsover had told her—and God alone knew how that fellow, Machado, had come to know of it—it was far better to admit the truth.

But . . . God grant that the unspeakable Palsover (and let him wait until Henry Carthew found him) had not told her the reason.

He couldn't have done so. No. He couldn't have done so. How could he possibly have known? Poor, poor Antoinette. If Palsover . . .

She was speaking again.

"So he spoke the truth, did he? And *you* killed Reginald?"

"Yes."

"Why?"

Turning away, the picture of guilt, Carthew walked to the window and stood looking out, seeing nothing.

"Why?" came the inexorable question.

"I . . . I . . . He . . . he . . . he was better dead," he mumbled.

Henry Carthew heard a distant bell ring and the closing of the door, as Antoinette Jason walked out of the room.

XX

"Colonel Carthew in the Club?"

The hall-porter looked up from his desk and saw a remarkably sun-burned stranger, a very big man with piercing blue eyes, grim mouth and what the hall-porter was wont to term a sort of a kind of a *look* about him. Probably Admiral or Captain Somebody, R.N.

"Yes, Sir," replied the omniscient man promptly. "George, take this gentleman's card to Colonel Carthew in the library."

A minute or two later, Carthew entered the marble-flagged hall, beaming welcome.

"Good Lord, Dysart! You! I *am* glad to see you. What a surprise. Shock, in fact. The last man on this earth I should have expected to see here. You'll stay to lunch, of course. Come along."

And thus talking, for him, almost garrulously, and taking Dysart by the arm almost affectionately, he led the way to the vast and magnificent smoking-room in a deeply embayed window of which were two huge arm-chairs, a small table and complete privacy.

"Here we are. We can have a great *bukh* here, in peace. What will you have? Nothing? No one here watching to see if you break the laws of the Prophet, y'know. No? Well . . . neither will I then. Sun not over the yard-arm yet. Smoke? . . . Thought you weren't coming to England for years."

"So did I," replied Dysart, with a laugh. "But you never know, y'know, as those who know, say."

"Given up the sea?"

"No. And shan't—until it gives me up."

"When the sea gives up its living, eh?" smiled Carthew, briefly happy for the first time in a very long while.

"Or my living. No, it'll be the case of the sea giving up its dead before I quit it voluntarily. About the only clean and peaceful place left, nowadays.

641

"Not so peaceful either," he added. "Really what brings me home. I have found something I have been looking for. Been hunting it for a long time. Submarine base and depôt. Very neatly done. Just a poor little Arab fishing village. Reed huts. Stakes, nets and everything. Worthy of Wassmuss. So I've come home for a chat with a lad at the Admiralty who is deeply interested in that kind of thing."

He eyed Carthew narrowly as the latter stared gloomily at the thronged pedestrians and cars in busy Pall Mall.

Poor chap looked very ill. And most profoundly miserable. Was that ghastly Jason business preying on his mind? One wouldn't have supposed so, for he was a brave man with a strong will and character.

"And what are you doing?" he asked, breaking a silence that was growing over long.

"Nothing."

"It's not an amusing pursuit," hazarded Dysart.

"What isn't?"

"Doing nothing."

"No."

"I daresay you'll excuse me if I have the impudence to butt in, Carthew, but you look to me as though you are doing something. Something damn bad for you."

"What's that?"

"Brooding. Why don't you come back with me?" he continued. "Finest life on earth—or water. I'll teach you the tricks of the trade and make you as good a *naukhada—dhow*-captain—as ever sailed out of the Persian Gulf. Teach you the pearl business, too, if you like. And later on you could buy a *dhow* of your own and make a fortune. Give you something to do."

"Most kind of you, Dysart. I should love it."

"Nothing to keep me in England," he added sadly, and a little bitterly.

Oh, that was how the land lay, was it? Nothing to keep him in England. So he had been wrong in supposing Carthew was in love with this Lady Jason. As a rule, when a man refers to a woman as his best and dearest friend, he means something by it. And her husband had been as good

642

as dead for years before he died. Something pretty wrong. That would account for his glumness and general air of depression.

Would he be putting his foot in it and stirring up horribly painful memories if he referred to that subject?

No, quite obviously, by the look of him, the poor chap thought of nothing else. Absolutely getting him down. Do him a world of good to talk about it. Get it off his chest.

Carthew's next words gave Dysart the opportunity he desired.

"Heard no more of that infernal scoundrel, Palsover, I suppose?" he said.

"Why, yes. He was back in Santa Cruz the last time I was there. Large as life. And sitting at the receipt of custom again at the *Casa Real*. Wonderful feller. He's going to make me a millionaire, this time. All I've got to do is to interest de Norhona and the Council. They give me a concession. That's all I've got to do, to be let in on the ground floor. Mr. Palsover then goes to London, and approaches the necessary capitalists—once he's found a real gentleman to look after him and see he isn't swindled by the City sharks. I haven't the slightest doubt that that is the part poor Jason played; and that is how he came to find himself in São Thomé."

"Good Lord!" ejaculated Henry Carthew. "I never thought of that. Even when he approached me . . . The lying scoundrel."

"Palsover! Palsover!" he said under his breath. And Dysart saw his knuckles whiten.

"Yes," said Dysart. "The death of General Jason. Your sojourn on Leper Island. And I haven't a shadow of a doubt that he had a hand, both hands, in that Pereira business."

"And another little item. Haven't told you about it yet," said Carthew.

"Palsover?"

"Yes. He went to Lady Jason."

"What on earth for? Make a touch of some sort, I suppose. Some form of blackmail . . ."

"And told her that Jason was dead, and that I had

murdered him."

"Did he mention the reason?"

"Oh, yes. We quarrelled about a concession."

"Lady Jason didn't believe a word of it, of course."

Carthew regarded his foot, swinging nervously, to and fro.

"You know what Palsover is. The most plausible rogue unhung."

"Yes," agreed Dysart. "The whitest sepulchre that ever covered corruption. You'd be ashamed to doubt him when he's telling the tale. Until you know what he is.

"But Lady Jason knows you, even if she doesn't know Palsover," Dysart continued. "She could not possibly, for one second, take his word against yours."

"No. . . . Not really. . . . But it was unfortunate," replied Carthew. "How was I to tell her what Reginald . . . was . . . when I found him? How could I?"

Carthew fell silent.

Dysart regarded him from beneath the hand with which he shaded his eyes.

"Suddenly she said," continued Carthew,

" '*Is it true that you killed Reginald?*'

'Yes,' I answered, and although her question nearly stunned me, I was almost thankful to know that she knew, and to get the confession off my mind.

" '*Why?*' she asked. And there it was, Dysart. I felt dreadful . . . dreadful . . . for I could not and would not tell her the truth, and what was I to say? I knew I should bungle it. . . . Make a mess of the whole thing. And I felt terribly constricted about the throat. And that was another shock. For that's how leprosy often begins to show. And when I could find my voice, and while I could find it, I just blurted out,

" '*Because he was better dead.*' "

"And then, of course, you had to explain why he was better dead," observed Dysart.

"No, thank God. She just went out of the room.

"What on earth could Palsover have said to her?" he continued on a note of pain and protest.

"Lord knows," mused Dysart. "But I'll bet he had a wonderful water-tight story, and no doubt, completely convincing proofs. Wonder if our friend Palsover is a good forger? I should be very much surprised if he wasn't, and he must have had plenty of samples of Jason's hand-writing and signature.

"And by Allah! That reminds me," he said, sitting up suddenly. "Jason was frightfully upset when he was on my *dhow*, about a ring he had lost. He was certain he had put it down on his bunk when he was getting a smear of caulking-pitch off his hand. Quite likely Palsover pinched that, and one or two other things that helped to establish his *bona fides*."

"I think I'll take a trip to Santa Cruz on purpose to interview Mr. Palsover," said Carthew ominously. "I'd love a quiet talk with Samuel Palsover. . . .

"Was there any idea of his coming to Europe again, when you left?" he asked.

"No. Not at any early date, anyway. He was going up-country to see a chief with whom he has dealings. . . . Going to sell him a hundred-weight of lead razor-blades or dud electric-light bulbs, I expect."

"A pup of some sort, no doubt. Probably gas-pipe guns and wood-alcohol."

The two men smoked in silence for a while, each following his own train of thought.

"Where's the *dhow*?" asked Carthew suddenly.

"Belamu."

"When do you pick her up again?"

"I'm sailing in the New Year; probably first week in January."

"Shouldn't be surprised if we met at Liverpool Street."

"Why? Going to see me off?"

"See each other off, Dysart. I'm for Belamu too."

"What, coming *dhowing*?"

"Dunno. But I've got to go to Santa Cruz again. I must have a quiet word with our Mr. Palsover."

"Well, combine business with pleasure. Come with me to Belamu and I'll run you down to Santa Cruz in the *dhow*.

Bit slower than the Portuguese steamer, but you're in no hurry. More likelihood of Palsover being back by the time we arrive."

Silence again.

"What are you going to do with him?" asked Dysart, as he laid the ash of his cigar in the tray.

Personally he wouldn't care to be in Mr. Palsover's shoes if Henry Carthew were after him and feeling as he looked just at the moment.

"I don't know. Depends on what I can find out. . . . Whether he belied poor Jason to Machado, and so to Nor-hona. Whether it was he who betrayed us. Anyhow, I want a word with him about his visit to Lady Jason."

"Yes," agreed Dysart. "Personally I'd like to further his radium-concession scheme."

"You would? To make money, do you mean?" asked Carthew in great surprise.

"No. There's no money to be made in that direction. But I'd like to do exactly what he asks. Take him to de Norhona and let him tell his artless tale."

"Wonder what de Norhona would do to him?" mused Carthew.

"Wonder what de Norhona would do to me? That's more to the point," returned Dysart. "Do to him? . . . Do to him? . . . He'd either make him the subject of one of his Perma-nent Hypnotism experiments, or else dangle him up to the waist in the radium quick-sand, until his flesh rotted off his bones."

"Well—I don't want anything unpleasant to happen to him," said Carthew gravely, "but I feel I must see him once again.

"Once will be enough," he added.

§2

By the time he took his departure, Dysart was fully convinced that Carthew, whom more than ever he liked and admired, was in a thoroughly bad way. His morbid, hurt, unhappy mind grievously afflicted his body, and caused the insomnia, lack of appetite, and general feeling of indefinable illness of which he complained.

Also that the causes of his mental trouble were partly incurable and to be ameliorated only by the passage of time; partly curable and needing a cure which he, Brodie Dysart, could at any rate endeavour to perform.

In the first place, he was suffering from the loss, and still more from the manner of the loss, of his great and life-long friend, General Jason.

In the second place, he was naturally and inevitably suffering from a terrible fear of becoming a leper. Quite obviously, although he said nothing about it, he had handled them, tended them, worked with them and for them, as freely and fearlessly as the Fathers did.

And what made this even more cruel still, was the fact that he was in love with this woman, and now that he was at last free to hope that she might marry him, here was this new and insurmountable obstacle. He might be a leper.

Of course, he had admitted nothing of the sort, but from the way he spoke of her it was as clear as daylight that he was not only in love with her, but had been in love with her all his life.

His oldest and dearest friend. . . . His best and kindest friend. . . . The woman for whom he had undertaken this quest for her missing husband. Of course he was in love with her. And of course Carthew, being Carthew, had not spoken up for himself. Had not given her the faintest idea of the tremendous moral and physical courage that had been called for. . . . The devotion. . . .

Well, here was a chance to befriend Carthew. Fools rush in? Might be cases where the fool had more pluck than the angel. He hated butting in, and minding other people's business, but Carthew was a sick man, and this might be by far the biggest cause of the misery and unhappiness that were turning him so morbid.

Why, if she were worth her salt, she'd jump at the chance of making some amends, some return for all that he had done for her.

Once she knew the truth, surely she wouldn't be put off

by the fact that he might possibly have contracted leprosy. She ought to be given the chance, anyhow. And she should be. It was only fair to her as well as to Carthew.

Poor devil! Sitting there, day after day, in that gloomy Club library, writing letters to her and tearing them up—because he was unable to explain why he had killed Jason.

Well, things couldn't be worse, and he'd have a damn good shot at making them better: and if he failed to help him in that direction, he'd get him aboard the *dhow*—and keep him there.

Sunshine and salt sea air. Take him to Santa Cruz and let him have his "word" with Palsover, if that would make him feel better, and then he'd take him as far as a *dhow* could go. Show him some of the loveliest places in the whole wide world. Places to which this blight called Civilization, this curse called Progress, had even yet not penetrated.

And in all pure selfishness too, for the one thing he lacked in life was a man of his own kind with whom to talk.

XXI

Lady Jason was more than a little surprised, and read the card once again.

Sir Sinclair Brodie Dysart?

The name was absolutely unfamiliar to her.

Travellers' Club? Some friend of poor Reginald's? He had never mentioned the man so far as she could remember. . . . Some business acquaintance? Lady Jason inclined her head in assent, and the butler, returning to the hall, informed Dysart that Her Ladyship was at home.

"Sir Sinclair Dysart, my Lady," he announced, and softly closed the door.

Yes. A complete stranger, thought Lady Jason, and also noted that the stranger was a remarkably personable figure of a man. Looked like something from the bridge of a battle-ship.

"Good afternoon, Lady Jason," he said. "I would apologize for this intrusion, but for the fact that I hope and believe that you'll be glad that I came, when you've heard what I have to say."

"I'm sure I shall. Do sit down," smiled Lady Jason, quite prepared to forgive the intrusion, whatever this attractive visitor might have on his mind, provided it was neither silk stockings nor a vacuum-cleaner.

"It's about your late husband."

A mask seemed to settle over Lady Jason's face.

"And Colonel Carthew."

"Do you come from him?" she asked, in a cold and level voice.

"Most definitely I do not. Let us have that absolutely clear from the beginning. I am prepared to find him extremely angry and resentful when he hears that I have been to see you—about this tragic business."

Lady Jason leant back in her chair and, without reply, prepared to listen.

Then succinctly, clearly and convincingly, Brodie Dysart told Antoinette Jason the story of the disappearance of General Jason; of his evil genius, Palsover; of the still unexplained mystery of his being taken for a Nazi German emissary; and of his fate at the hands of a Government to whom such people were anathema.

Sparing her feelings as much as possible, he told her the plain unvarnished truth. Told her of the state in which Carthew found her husband, and endeavoured to make her realize that the only thing that Jason's truest friend could do, was what his friend did do.

Nor did Brodie Dysart fail to impress upon his hearer that he had done his utmost to prevent Carthew from venturing into the place where he believed General Jason to be, for his going there was inevitably fraught with the greatest danger.

"So I felt sure, Lady Jason," concluded Dysart, "that you would like me to come and tell you all I know about the matter, and particularly to tell you all that Carthew—being Carthew—was bound to leave unsaid."

For a few moments he eyed her in silence. "A man of marvellous moral courage as well as physical courage," he mused aloud.

Lady Jason appeared to have no comment to make on that subject.

"Not that you'd ever dream that he had run any particular risks, nor had had to make a decision of a kind which few men have ever been called upon to make."

"All he said to me was that he had killed my husband because he thought he was better dead," said Lady Jason.

"He would," observed Dysart. "Knowing Carthew, didn't you question him further?" he asked.

"No. He had come to tell me everything—and that was all he had to say."

It would be a bit difficult to say more after you had marched out of the room, thought Dysart.

"M-m-m. Yes," he said. "Well, that is why I came. He's a dumb fish, isn't he? Not much better with a pen. I believe he has made a few score efforts to write to you about it."

"Why didn't he, then?"

"Didn't want to give you unnecessary pain. More delicate-minded than I am, I'm afraid, Lady Jason. No doubt he thought you'd understand, and find it quite enough, when he said that it was the best thing to do—or he wouldn't have done it.

"Incidentally," he asked, as he rose to say farewell, "he didn't mention, I suppose, that in trying to serve you and General Jason, he has probably contracted leprosy."

"*What?*"

Ah! That penetrated. That was a genuine look of horror.

"Yes. He was arrested and imprisoned, and condemned to death. The slowest and one of the most dreadful deaths conceivable—confinement on a tiny leper-island, already over-crowded. He naturally thinks that he has contracted leprosy—as he may have done. And it hasn't done him any good, I assure you. He sits and broods, and watches for the first sign. What he needs, beyond anything, is company, friendship, sympathy."

Before Dysart's level gaze, Lady Jason's eyes fell.

"Poor Henry," she murmured. "Poor Henry. . . . I didn't dream . . . I'll write to him."

"I'm sure it would do him a lot of good," said Dysart crisply. "And I'm sure when you've thought it over and grasped the situation, you'll get him down here, and—er— look after him. Enough to drive him mad, sitting in a Club bedroom, expecting the worst, and waiting for it. And it's not only that, you know. He took a most frightful knock over General Jason, his life-long friend. Imagine what it was to a man like Carthew, to find him in that state, and then to do what he felt was his duty.

"Can't you understand how he sits and chews that over? While he waits to find that he is a leper."

"Oh, *don't!* Don't tell me any more. I'll write to him. I'll write . . ." said Lady Jason.

"Well, as I've said before, I hate butting in, but I do feel that it is up to you—to save him. And you can, you know," and, as he extended his hand, he added,

"I wish you could hear how he speaks of you."

Poor old Carthew, he thought as he left the house.
Still, I'm glad I've seen her, and so long as he thinks she is what she certainly isn't, well . . .

XXII

Carthew sat at the window of his Club bedroom and gazed, unseeing, across the tree-tops, visualizing as now he so often did, a lonely islet, a pin-point speck upon the face of the illimitable waters, the haunt only of sea-birds and lepers.

What he saw, as he sat staring, was not the London scene of blackening trees or reeking chimney-pots, but white sand and waving bents, and a blue sea that lapped gently with soft susurrus on a lonely beach, and coming across the dunes down to the water's edge, a girl. A girl who, living in the midst of horror, pain and privation, lacking almost everything that is dear to the heart of a girl, could still place a flower in her hair and sing as she walked.

That was a girl of courage. A fine spirit.

But what was this, her singing and her poor little effort at personal adornment, beside the splendour and nobility of her act of renunciation and self-denial—when he came to her in the early dawn and offered her escape, freedom?

If he lived to be a hundred he would never forget those painful minutes while he did his utmost to fight against her unselfishness, her sense of duty, her love for her father and mother. It had been truly dreadful. The girl longing, with all her heart and soul, to get away from that abominable prison and return to a way of life that was worth living.

But the teaching of the Fathers, the innate loyalty, sense of duty, and simple filial piety had conquered; and, as she cast herself down upon the sand, tears streaming from her eyes while she begged him to return, he himself had faltered, half tempted to stay.

But he had given his word to Antoinette that he would find Reginald or discover beyond shadow of a doubt what had happened to him, and that he would himself give her his personal assurance of the truth and certainty of what he had to tell.

Besides, what folly. What quixotry run mad. Dysart was waiting and running a risk on his behalf.

Curious how frequently that picture of the Island now occupied his mind. How constantly he thought of those wretched lepers, those noble Fathers, and of Maria—a heroine as deserving of a niche in the temple of fame as was any Joan of Arc or Florence Nightingale. . . .

He looked at his watch. Good Lord, he had been mooning here since breakfast, and had missed lunch. He must really take himself in hand and conquer this miserable morbid mooning, this day-dreaming . . . looking back at São Thomé with horror, the Leper Island with regret and to the future with fear.

The future! What should he do if the worst happened?

A leper!

Well, time he was getting along to the School of Tropical Diseases again.

Wonderful chaps those research men. And very comforting and reassuring. God grant they were right but . . .

§2

No. He could stand it no longer. No sign from Antoinette. It had been most exceedingly kind of Dysart to go and see her and tell her all that he himself had left untold. Had it been cowardice that had kept him from doing as Dysart had done? He didn't think so. He had honestly wished to spare her, and there had really not been the slightest reason why she should ever have known the real facts, but for that unspeakable hound, Palsover. She need never have known that Reginald had not died a natural death. . . . malaria . . . dysentery . . . cholera; or met with an accident, exploring, big-game shooting.

Still, as it was, she at any rate knew from Dysart's independent testimony that Reginald was dead, and that, however bizarre and dreadful his end, he had suffered nothing at all.

But it was strange that she had never written.

Suddenly Carthew, who was walking up and down his room, stopped.

Good Lord! Could it be—could it possibly be because Dysart had told her about Leper Island? Could *that* be the reason why . . . ?

It was the reason.

Lady Jason, like most other people, had a great horror of leprosy and lepers.

She had seen them in India.

§3

No. He neither could nor would stand it any longer. It was bad enough now, while Brodie Dysart was in England and they were able to meet quite frequently. What it would be like after the New Year he did not care to contemplate. There was not a soul in England with whom he could sit and talk about what filled his mind. Or better still, sit in companionable silence and refrain from talking about it. More and more, his mind dwelt on the thought of going with Dysart to Belamu, joining him on the *dhow*, and sailing once more for Santa Cruz.

What would happen there was on the knees of the gods, but his resolution as to what should happen when he reached that accursed place was crystallizing out, was hardening fast. Each time that he and Dysart met, he parted from him with increased determination, increased longing—*longing*, could that be possible?—to see Leper Island again.

No, it must be for the *dhow*, the sunny peaceful days and glorious tropic nights that he was longing. Surely not for a lost island over which the sea-birds screamed in thousands, where one of the noblest and bravest bands of men worked and waited, and Death brooded.

XXIII

Lady Jason sat at her desk, the one at which poor Reginald had worked so hard in those last days before he went away for ever.

A difficult letter to write.

Poor dear Henry. It was of course splendid news. She had always been under the impression that *that* was absolutely incurable. Was it possible that he could be mistaken? No. He wasn't the sort of man to make a mistake of that kind. And if he were, those oriental-disease specialists were not.

Poor darling, what a fright he had had! Now that it was all right again, she must try and make it up to him.

A pity he was so over-modest and diffident. She would positively have to make the running.

She had always been fond of Henry, from the time he was a scrubby untidy subaltern. Such a contrast to poor dear Reginald. Ordinary-looking, where Reginald was so amazingly handsome; insignificant, where Reginald had such a magnificent presence and such a dignity of bearing; rather stupid, as compared with Reginald's brilliance—and so dreadfully *dull*. *Dreadfully* dull.

But then again, he was a contrast to Reginald in other ways, she must remember.

Reginald had never really loved her, whereas Henry adored her. From the very beginning, Reginald had put his career first and his wife a bad second. With Henry, it would be Antoinette first and everything else nowhere . . . nowhere. So faithful, so unswervingly devoted to her all these years.

Yes, and she must remember the tale of the years if she were going to marry again, which she most certainly was. Dear Henry. Dear dull Henry. But so faithful. So unswervingly faithful. So obedient too. And a woman who had been married to Reginald Jason could appreciate that.

Lady Jason's eye wandered from the letter in her hand to the window and her beautiful garden beyond. Why were good obedient children always so boring?

Well, better a little peaceful boredom than the worry and anxiety of the last three or four years. Love (even with Henry) . . . Peace . . . Security after this damned mess that Reginald had gone off and left her in. Just like the man. . . .

Lady Jason, after one or two efforts that she found unsatisfactory, wrote Henry Carthew a letter that should surely have brought that humbly-devoted and single-hearted man hastening to her side.

That it did not do so must be considered as largely due to the fact that he never received it.

"Where do Colonel Carthew want his letters addressed to?" enquired the desk under-porter of the Hall Porter as he sorted the members' letters.

"Nowhere I shouldn't think," was the reply. "I asked him, and he just smiled sad and sarcastic and said,

'No fixed abode, John, and no visible means of support.'

"Better keep 'em all," he added, and Lady Jason's very beautifully worded letter was accordingly kept.

§2

"Well, well," smiled Brodie Dysart warmly, as he came face to face with Carthew on Liverpool Street platform, and wrung his hand. "Allah be praised."

This was good. This was splendid. It wasn't often that one could combine the purest selfishness with one's good deed for the day—or for the year. For many years, he hoped. It would make all the difference, having this good chap with him. One of the most lovable men he had ever come across. Just such another as Dacre Blount had been; such a deeply interesting mind, well-stored, judgmatical, and clever in the best sense of the word. A man with a fine and a high philosophy of life. Most attractive. Never a dull moment in his company, and yet a man with whom one could sit in absolute silence and enjoy the quiet communion as much as the long, long conversations about every interesting thing on earth. A man after one's own heart, of one's own sort and kind, with similar likes and dislikes, and who spoke the same language.

Well, there was one thing. Once aboard the lugger he'd not part with him lightly or easily. Thank God he had been mistaken about him and Lady Jason. Brittle as well as hard, that woman. Shallow as well as deep.

Still, he was glad he had done what he had conceived to be his duty in the matter. For he had most firmly believed that Carthew's future happiness was bound up in her—"the very best and dearest friend he had ever had."

And he wasn't sorry that he had let her know what sort of a chap Carthew really was, and what he had done and suffered for her and her Reginald. Though that was beyond her knowing. Nor could he suppose that Carthew, as soon as he knew for certain that he had escaped leprosy, had proposed and been rejected. He had none of the air of a rejected lover. On the contrary, his health and spirits had seemed to improve from the very day that he had rung him up and, with an unmistakable note of satisfaction and cheerfulness, if not joy, said,

"I have decided, Dysart. I am coming with you on the *Ceylon* to Belamu. Does your offer hold, to run me down to Santa Cruz?"

And when he had laughed and replied that nothing on earth would suit him better than to have Carthew as a passenger, the funny old chap had said,

"Ah, but I want to take a frightful lot of stuff. How much could you manage?"

And when he had replied,

"Oh, say a hundred tons or so," Carthew's laugh had been positively merry.

He had wondered why the devil he wanted to take a lot of stuff down that way. Not Bond Street creations for the belles of Belamu. And it wouldn't be "trade" either. Carthew wouldn't have the slightest idea as to what sort of goods would be profitable.

Besides, he'd leave that side of it to him, the owner of

the *dhow*, naturally.

§3

On the way to Belamu, as they walked the deck or reclined in long chairs, Brodie Dysart did his best to paint in radiant hues the picture of the life that he himself so loved. A life of the uttermost freedom known to civilized man. A life of simple joys, rude health, constant change and activity. A life of the deepest interest and one not closed to modest ambition and reasonable financial success.

To be one's own master. To be like the wind that bloweth whither it listeth, and to be constantly in a sufficiency of danger to give life that savour without which it must be dull, even if profitable.

Yes, he must convert Carthew from soldiering to sailoring, teach him all he himself knew, and sweeten his veins with the salt of the sea.

§4

At Belamu he was, in spite of what he had said, a little surprised at the number, weight and bulk of Carthew's packages, and deeply disappointed to learn of his plans.

He realized that this feeling was purely personal and wholly selfish, fought against it manfully, and strove entirely to conceal it.

For, as they stood in the heat and glare of the white stone quay, between the great ovens that were the corrugated-iron Customs sheds, Carthew asked him if the *dhow* could not only carry the lot to Santa Cruz, but on from there to Leper Island.

"O-oh, I see. Stuff for the Fathers. And medical comforts and so on, for the lepers, eh? Yes. I'll dump them there for you, Carthew. Of course I will. Only too delighted. You'll come too, naturally."

"Oh, rather. I want you to dump me likewise."

And it was then that Dysart's heart sank. He might have known it. The sort of thing this noble lunatic would do.

"Not for six months, surely," he said, conscious of a sense of shame in saying even so much in discouragement. Too well he knew that nothing that he could say would deter Carthew, but he might at least have the grace to refrain from the attempt. But no, it wasn't wholly selfish. One should, one must, do something to prevent such a man as this from such a fearful form of suicide. He was not a dedicated priest, a super-human being who had renounced Life and offered himself to Death that he might do a little doubtful good among men whom God had stricken.

No. But he was of the stuff of which such men are made.

Could it be that Jason woman, after all? Had he so loved her that he had now no further wish to live—with such memories?

"Yes, I'll take you, Carthew," he said. "And I shall come again for you at the end of six months."

Carthew smiled his thanks.

§5

At Santa Cruz, Carthew learnt with regret that Mr. Palsover had not yet returned from his up-country trek to the territory governed by the paramount Chief Poaha, a man who inclined to drastic measures, arbitrary methods and power politics.

Felice Diego, Mr. Palsover's partner, in the ownership of the *Casa Real* and other less obvious business ventures, was indeed of opinion that it would be quite a long while, a very very long while, before Mr. Palsover returned to Santa Cruz and the circle of friends who undoubtedly missed him.

"Why?" asked Carthew, seated in an uncertain long chair on the unsafe verandah, together with the Hadji Abdulla, who in turban, robes and cotton *silham*, sat cross-legged on an unworthy mattress, supported by what Senhor Diego described as cushions.

"It's that Poaha, Sah," explained the Goanese. "That man, Sah. Blaming Palsover Sahib about dem shields."

"What shields?"

"King Poaha's. All him warriors have big ox-hide shields, Sah. Brown for one *pultan*, brown and white for another, black for another, but best of all, King's own bodyguard must have black-and-white. Very few black-and-white cattles in King Poaha's country. So he send messengers to King Loratu offering to buy all black-and-white ox-skins he got, because King Loratu's people live by keeping cattles and drinking their milk. Got *lakhs* and *lakhs* of cattles.

"But King Loratu not liking King Poaha for always shooting him up and playing the other mischiefs, says,

'*You get to Hell outa this*,' and cuts off their heads.

"Just then Palsover Sahib goes up to Poaha's country with Best Bombay Spirits and things."

"Trade gin and gas-pipe guns," murmured Carthew. "Yes?"

"And he does big deal with Poaha for black-an-white hides to make shields for number one *pultan*. Very clever man," sniggered Senhor Diego. "He go to India *ek dum*, and buy all white ox-hides, black ox-hides and black-and-white ox-hides. Municipal Slaughter-house, Karachi, Bombay, Madras, Calcutta. All places. Also makes advertisements wanting black, white, and black-and-white hides. Then he ships whole lots to Santa Cruz and we sort them out."

"Smelt nice, didn't they?" enquired Carthew, visualizing vast stacks of raw hides in the sweltering heat of the *Casa Real* go-downs.

"Nossir," contradicted Mr. Felice Diego. "Not so very nice. Then Palsover Sahib takes up big waggon-load of black-and-white hides which pleases King Poaha very good. And while Palsover Sahib gone, I have to dye black patches on white hides, and have to paint white patches on black hides.

"Then Palsover Sahib comes back, and we send up the rest with Toto."

"Who's he?"

"Bar-man, Sah. Man Hadji Sahib beat up, for bumping

little *chokri*[33] with bottle."

"Oh, that swine."

"Yessah. Then Chief Poaha, very big *bahadur* now he got brown shield regiment, brown-and-white shield regiment and what he think very good best of all, real black-and-white King's Regiment. So he tells his regiments to sharpen their spears, because he go for make war on King Loratu.

"Then, after big barley-beer drinking and war-dance, he sends more messengers with rude words to King Loratu. He leads out his fine army to invade country. In front goes Royal Regiment with black-and-white shields. Very proud, pomptious and contemptious. But suddenly it becomes rain like Hell. And black dye on white shields runs over all shield, making it black and drips off.

"Then King Poaha shout, '*Oh, my goddam. Oh, my blast it all.*' His heart break and he go home. Royal Regiment coming last, not cockahooping, but all drooping and gone to damn, so that the women laugh. Then King Poaha sit down and think up something good for Palsover Sahib. But he can't think up nutting better than old country custom.

"So he send for Toto still waiting there for payment for the hides.

" '*Get you up, oh man,*' he say to Toto. '*Harness your oxen to your waggon and go you back.*'

'*Without payment?*'

'*Sure,*' says Chief Poaha, '*an' you go quick unless I alter my mind and pay you. Go before the sun sets, and go to your master an' tell him to come here to me, to King Poaha. And I will pay him for his hides and for something else.*'

"And from the way King Poaha speak, Toto don't think King Poaha like Palsover Sahib so much no more. Toto think King Poaha's country damn bad place for Palsover Sahib, so he come back quick an' tell Palsover Sahib that King Poaha very pleased, very glad. Want more hides same black-and-white. Pay more for nex' lot. And if Palsover Sahib come up now, he pay him for first lot and make agreement

---

[33] Girl.

about new lot."

"And he went, eh?" asked Carthew softly.

"Yes, Sah. Palsover Sahib go *ek dum*."

"I gather that—er—Toto was not very fond of Mr. Palsover?"

"No, Sah. Not so much. Palsover Sahib beating him up and cutting pay."

"And you've heard nothing more of Mr. Palsover?"

"No, Sah. Only his boots, and they all gnawed about."

§6

It was, as Mr. Felice Diego had said, an Old Country Custom of the dwellers in the Santa Cruz hinterland, and a very unpleasant one, final in its effects on those to whom it was applied, and deterrent to others contemplating similar malefaction.

Descending from his waggon, Mr. Palsover had thrown the reins to his giant factotum and strode across to the royal village, before the largest house of which sat King Poaha, who, long before, had been notified of the approach of the mule-drawn cart.

"Greeting," said King Poaha, rising from the royal stool.

"Greeting," replied Palsover, extending the right hand of honest friendship.

This the King did not grasp, but raised his spear aloft with a royally dramatic gesture.

But not to strike. The spear-blade pointed to the sky and, as though conjured from the earth, stalwart unarmed men stepped forth from within and behind the huts, and from the shelter of rock and bush and tree.

Mr. Palsover gazed about him in some anxiety as the great silent crowd closed in about him. This was not the manner in which he was accustomed to be received by Poaha or any other dirty native. This was something new and uncomfortable-like. Had the words 'sinister' and 'minatory' formed part of Mr. Palsover's vocabulary, he would have found appropriate use for them now.

The point of Chief Poaha's spear fell. His men crowded yet closer about Mr. Palsover and suddenly he was seized from behind. A stout thong of plaited leather was tied about his waist, and to this his right hand was firmly lashed behind him.

" 'Ere, wot's the game?" shouted Mr. Palsover in good honest English.

In his own deplorable tongue King Poaha offered apology. He greatly regretted that the funeral baked meat was not quite ready. The cook was doing his best.

From the Chief's brief and polite speech, Mr. Palsover garnered only the words, 'meat' and 'cook,' and failed to connect the cooking of meat with this unseemly fastening of the cord about his middle, and the firm attachment of his right hand thereto.

However, King Poaha continued to the effect that the provision of meat should be made forthwith, in order that his honoured guest should be in no danger of starving.

"No," pondered King Poaha aloud, as grimly he eyed the large and paling countenance of Mr. Palsover. He did not think there would be any danger of hunger.

Mr. Palsover understood the word 'hunger,' and was the less amazed when, from the King's own hut, emerged a fat perspiring man who bore in his greasy grasp what Mr. Palsover recognized as a nicely roasted goat. Done to a turn. Beautifully browned.

Rather reassuring, but undoubtedly a rum go. Meat. Cook. Hunger.

And here was a very nice bit of posho. But why had he got to eat it there and then, standing up, and with only his left hand to use?

Some blooming native custom, no doubt.

Puzzling. Very puzzling. And increasingly so when his other arm was seized and the savoury roast was not merely tied, but firmly lashed, to his hand and fore-arm.

What was the game? . . . What the Hell? . . . And 'ere, what was this? . . . This 'ere goat.

They were tethering a live goat to him. Actually. What did they think he was? A perishin' post in a bloody farmyard?

Native custom? Well, he had never ate a damn great joint tied on to his fist yet, and he wasn't going to start now, custom or no blasted custom. He'd bloomin' well . . .

Again King Poaha raised his hand, and the men crowding about him fell away, ran from him as though he were stricken with pestilence.

Then Mr. Palsover saw that some thirty paces in front of him, a line of young warriors, each bearing a white shield badly stained with an unstable black dye, held their throwing spears aloft.

As one, the sinewy arms went back behind the shoulders and,

"Run!" shouted Chief Poaha.

With a swift glance behind him, Mr. Palsover saw that the way was clear, for the crowd had formed a double line, a lane through which he could escape. . . . And scarcely had the Chief uttered his one word of good advice, than Mr. Palsover was running as he had never run since, as a young recruit, he had entered for the hundred yards event in the annual sports-meeting of the Wessex Fusiliers.

Behind him leapt and cavorted the goat, swiftly realizing that its immediate future was bound up with that of Mr. Palsover.

A great spear passed over his head and embedded itself in a tree-trunk just ahead of him. But he could not increase his speed. As he dashed past it, the haft still quivered and swung. Could be possibly reach the cart before a spear like that struck between his shoulder blades, impaling him as, when a boy, he had impaled flies upon a pin.

If he fell . . .

If he fell . . .

This cursed goat . . .

This weight upon his arm . . .

How could he run straight . . . keep his balance . . . one hand tied behind him?

The damned cowards! That swindling, lying swine of a Poaha! Let him wait till . . .

God! That was a near one. And he had nearly fallen.

When would he reach the cart?

Where in Hell? Why . . .

And with a terrible sense of defenceless nakedness, he realized that the cart was not there, that he must have passed, far back, the place where he had left it. That, had it been here, right in front of him, without the use of his hands it would have been utterly impossible to climb into it, snatch the reins and start the mules.

But Toto? He had left Toto there. The swine had deserted him . . . betrayed him. Or else Poaha's devils had killed him. He hoped they had.

His breath came in painful gasps and, from time to time, he stumbled, staggered and almost fell.

Were the sounds of pursuit growing fainter?

Yes. Thank God.

He had shaken them off. He had beaten them. Fooled them. Escaped from them.

He had—by reason of King Poaha's strict order to his young men that not a hair of Mr. Palsover's head should be hurt.

Soon he fell into a jog-trot. Into a shuffle. A walk. And, before long, sank exhausted to the ground. The goat, nothing loth, rose on its hind legs and began to sup upon the succulent young leaves of the bush beneath which Mr. Palsover lay and fought for breath.

When, at length, the sobbing of his labouring lungs grew quieter, the man sat up and took stock of his position.

Unhurt. Night coming on. A hundred miles from home. A damn good supper tied to his left arm and beginning to weigh like a half hundred-weight sack of potatoes.

A perfectly good goat tied to his backside.

What a B.F. he'd look, walking down the Avenida at Santa Cruz.

Got to get there first though. Take him four days, with luck.

He'd come back and drive Poaha over the same course with a rhinoceros-hide whip. Yes. Harness him beside the mules. He'd teach the tricky swine something about mule-skinning. Skin him alive, he would.

Ah! And take more than four days over it too.

But why had the beggar given him this roast meat? Just to make him last the longer? That was it. Wanted to spin out his sufferings, knowing it would be just about damn-all he'd find to eat between Poaha's country and Santa Cruz.

Dirty swine.

Yes. That was the only reason why he had given him the food. And he had tied it on to his fist so he shouldn't drop it when he bolted from those murderin' savages with the spears.

That was why he had tied this roasted meat on to him, but why the Hell had he sent the goat along?

Suddenly Mr. Palsover's question was answered in the wide deep silence of the night.

For, from either near or far, from either the east or the west, or perchance from the north or the south, came the terrible cry of the hungry, questing beast.

Mr. Palsover leapt to his feet.

Which way? Which way?

Could he climb a tree? Of course not.

Where could he hide? Where could he run?

The frightened goat uttered a loud and piteous bleat.

"Shut up, you — — —," hissed Mr. Palsover, fiercely yet ludicrously.

Again the terrible cry, as the great beast, on the strong scent of its prey, drew rapidly towards it.

Blindly, Mr. Palsover ran with all his ebbing strength. Dashed into dark shadows in search of safety. Dashed into a tree and fell to the ground, winded and half stunned.

Again the terrible cry that made his blood run cold.

Looking up, he gazed wildly about and saw, or thought he saw, the moonlight glinting upon two terrible eyes.

A great crouching form. . . .

And again, with a superhuman effort, he rose to his feet and fled.

The last sound ever uttered by the plausible and

persuasively garrulous Samuel Palsover was a long scream —suddenly cut off.

XXIV

So Henry Carthew failed to have his quiet "word" with Mr. Palsover, but bore with fortitude the news, brought by Toto, that he had been able, beyond peradventure of a doubt, to identify his late and deeply-lamented master by his boots—both of which had frequently kicked him.

And when his business in Santa Cruz was completed, his *dhow* provisioned and her cargo bestowed, the Hadji Abdulla informed his admired passenger that he would sail, an hour before dawn; would make land-fall at Leper Island; disembark him and his baggage on the beach at another dawn, and then weigh anchor for São Thomé and what might then befall.

"Why not land the stuff and leave it, Carthew?" he said, as they sat on the verandah. "*Do*. Be sensible. You've escaped once. The leprosy, I mean."

"The Fathers . . ." began Carthew.

"Think of the joyous amazement of the Fathers when they find the Island smothered in good things. They'll think it's direct answer to prayer—and you'll have founded or fathered another indisputable miracle. Everything they'd been praying for. Parcels from Heaven. Carriage paid. Why, they'll . . ."

"The Fathers, I was going to say," interrupted Carthew, "will be rather glad to see me. And to know that I'm going to carry on with the bit of work I was doing."

"They'll be damned sorry to see you—committing suicide by leprosy."

"It's what they are doing."

"Well—it's their job. I mean they've made it their job."

"Can't I?"

"They've renounced the world."

"Not sure that I haven't."

"Don't be a fool. Excuse me; I didn't mean to say that.

You've no right to do such a . . ."

"I promised. I ought to have told you."

"*Promised?* The Fathers?"

"She just sank down on the sand in such an agony of grief as I could not bear to see. It was like murdering a child that trusts you utterly. And when she sobbed '*Come back! Come back again!*' I stooped and stroked her hair and said '*Yes. I will . . . I'll come back, Maria.*' And she sprang up and threw her arms about my neck—and then thrust me from her. She wouldn't leave her father and mother, Dysart, and I am going back."

"Of course," said Brodie Dysart.

§2

On the voyage to Leper Island, Dysart did his utmost to dissuade Carthew from taking any irrevocable step, such as solemnly dedicating himself to the service of the Fathers as a lay-brother and helper in their life-work of succouring the lepers.

"I don't know," was the only reply that he could get. "It depends—to some extent."

Dysart could make an accurate guess at what it depended upon.

"But why not take her away from the Island?" he expostulated. "Now. This voyage. I'll take you both straight back to Santa Cruz. I'll take you to Belamu if you like—or anywhere else."

Carthew put his hand on Dysart's shoulder, for him a very rare gesture. Scarcely had he made it a dozen times to Reginald Jason, his life-long and only friend till now.

"Extraordinarily good of you, my dear chap," he said. "She wouldn't come while her parents are alive."

"Suppose they're dead?"

"Suppose she's a leper?"

"Suppose she's not," countered Dysart.

"Well, if her parents are both dead, and she has, so far, no sign of being a leper—and cannot of course return to her home—what should I do with her? Supposing she were willing to leave the Island."

" '*Willing*' to leave the Island!" repeated Dysart in tones of amazed incredulity.

"Yes . . . The Fathers, you know. They get a wonderful hold of you. They did of me. How much more so of an impressionable young girl. And she's of that type—the born devotee. Yes. They get a wonderful hold of you," mused Carthew.

"Not intentionally, of course," he continued. "But you can't live with them, watch them, know them, without—oh, you know what I mean. They radiate the sort of thing from which the hardest cases aren't immune. She'd want to stay with them."

Dysart eyed his friend, and smiled.

"She would, eh?"

"Yes. And if she wouldn't, what could I do with her at Santa Cruz, or Belamu, or even Portugal if I took her there?"

"Marry her," replied Dysart succinctly.

"My dear chap!" expostulated Carthew, and also smiled.

And Dysart found that, for all his quietness, gentleness and apparent meekness, his passenger was a man firm of purpose, immovable as a rock, when once his mind was made up, his goal before him, and his duty clear.

The utmost concession that Dysart could wring from him was the promise that he would "look out" for him, daily, at dawn, for a week or so, some six months hence; and that until he had pondered the matter for that period, he would give his promise to no one that he would remain permanently on the Island.

"And if you do tell me any nonsense of that sort when we meet, I'll bring every one of my crew ashore, armed to the teeth, and kidnap you, my son. I will. And then how will you find your way back again?" he asked.

A day or two later, just as the moon and stars began to pale, and a faint new light to tint the eastern horizon, Dysart roused Carthew from his mattress on the high poop deck.

A bad moment.

Bad as when he left the *Valkyrie*.

Bad as when he realized he had lost Dacre Blount.

Bad as when he knew that never again would he see his leader, Walter Manny Chandos.

Almost as bad as that day in Luong-Tam-Ky's tent.

This man whom he had come to love so well, was going to his death.

And what a death!

No. He shouldn't. He shouldn't, if Brodie Dysart could prevent him.

Six months hence he must . . .

Carthew sat up.

"Just over there," said Dysart, pointing to the bows. "A couple of cables."

"Thanks."

Carthew went forward to where the short bow-sprit pointed him his way.

Would she come running across the dunes, the sunlight of the fresh sweet morning gilding her lovely face?

Would she have a flower in her hair? A song on her lips?

A song in her heart, to answer his?

Yes. It would be like that.

He and she, alone by the kindly sea, between the golden sands and the azure sky.

And afterwards?

Available P. C. Wren Titles
from
Riner Publishing Company

The Collected Short Stories

Volume One: ISBN 9780985032609
Volume Two: ISBN 9780985032616
Volume Three: ISBN 9780985032623
Volume Four: ISBN 9780985032630
Volume Five: ISBN 9780985032647

The Collected Novels

Volume One: *The Geste Novels*
    Part A: ISBN 9780985032678
    Part B: ISBN 9780985032685
Volume Two: *The Sinbad Novels*
    Part A: ISBN 9780692639382
    Part B: ISBN 9780692639429
Volume Three: *The Foreign Legion Novels*
    Part A: ISBN 9780999074909
    Part B: ISBN 9780999074916
Volume Four: *The Earlier India Novels*
    Part A: ISBN 9780999074923
    Part B: ISBN 9780999074930
Volume Five: *The Later India Novels*
    Part A: ISBN 9780999074947
    Part B: ISBN 9780999074954
Volume Six: *The English Novels*
    Part A: ISBN 9780999074961
    Part B: ISBN 9780999074978
Volume Seven: *A Mixed Bag of Novels*
    Part A: ISBN 9780999074985
    Part B: ISBN 9780999074992

Further information can be found at
rinerpublishing.wordpress.com